CAUGHT U... ...G
TIDES O...
BOUND BY...
AND A SHAT... ...NY....

DORIAN TRÖZEN—Born the illegitimate son of a black slave and a white master; his long, perilous journey to freedom would lead him straight into the inferno of war and the adoring arms of a woman he would risk his life—and his darkest secret—to possess.

GRACE MacHUTCHEON—This treacherous backwoods beauty would stop at nothing and stoop to anything for revenge, including betraying her country and marrying her most despised enemy . . . the man she held responsible for her brother's murder.

WYATT CRAIG—A secessionist whose black powder fueled the lifeblood of the Southern cause, he was little more than a lethal weapon in the hands of powerful, sinister Northern cartel.

ALEXANDER WALLACE—The half-Greek son of Iphigenia Trözen and Lucas Wallace, his search for his half brother would take him back to his aristocratic Southern roots—and into a battle to wipe slavery off the face of the earth.

ORIENTA—The quintessential Southern loyalist, she was blindly devoted to the Confederacy and her love for Dorian—until a shocking disclosure sent her life spiraling into tragedy.

YULA—Undaunted, clever, and unconquerable, she defies her new master only to return to the Virginia tobacco plantation where she had once been a slave in search of her son—a search that would lead her through years of agonizing hardship and a life on the sharp edge of change.

BOOK TWO

★

DISTANT DRUMS

RISE DEFIANT

D. L. CAREY

★

BANTAM BOOKS
NEW YORK · TORONTO · LONDON · SYDNEY · AUCKLAND

RISE DEFIANT

A Bantam Domain Book / August 1992

*DOMAIN and the portrayal of a boxed "d" are trademarks of
Bantam Books, a division of
Bantam Doubleday Dell Publishing Group, Inc.*

*All rights reserved.
Copyright © 1992 by Diane Carey.
Cover art copyright © 1992 by Ken Laager.
No part of this book may be reproduced or transmitted in any form
or by any means, electronic or mechanical, including photocopying,
recording, or by any information storage and retrieval system,
without permission in writing from the publisher.
For information address: Bantam Books.*

ISBN 0-553-29366-4

Published simultaneously in the United States and Canada

Bantam Books are published by Bantam Books, a division of Bantam
Doubleday Dell Publishing Group, Inc. Its trademark, consisting of the
words "Bantam Books" and the portrayal of a rooster, is Registered in
U.S. Patent and Trademark Office and in other countries. Marca
Registrada. Bantam Books, 666 Fifth Avenue, New York, New York
10103.

PRINTED IN THE UNITED STATES OF AMERICA

RAD   0 9 8 7 6 5 4 3 2 1

TO DONALD EDWARD BRODEUR

Wherever you are,
we're sure you're merrily engaged
in showing them how to
run the place better.

We'll try to carry on here,
doing the same.

Thanks, Dad.

In the eyes of Europe in 1861–63,
the North was destined inevitably
to defeat. . . . The Federal Union
of the (founding) fathers was at
an end. Two republics at least
would occupy the area formerly
ruled by one; not improbably,
four, five, or even more independent
nations would rise on the ruins. . . .

—BURTON J. HENDRICK,
    Statesmen of the Lost Cause

PART ONE

———— ★ ————

1857

PROLOGUE

———— ★ ————

"Get her! Stop her!"

Everyone within earshot paused against the day's business to watch a scene resembling more than anything else a pack of fat dogs trying to chase down a chicken.

White and black hands alike snatched at the osnaburg skirt of a gangleshanked negro girl whose body was made of nothing but blades and corners. She sprinted from every grip, insecty legs spinning, and lay wrack to everything in her path. They tried to intercept her, and in fact did, but since no one had yet given a thought to how to hold on to her, she slipped away and streaked back and forth across the chandlery yard, setting it to pandemonium.

Wherever she ran, she pulled something down behind her—stacked shipping boxes that broke open like eggs and spilled the carefully packed tapers and votive candles all over the dirty ground for her pursuers to trip over. Suddenly the people trying to catch her were dodging tiptoe through mounds of spilled candles, skidding and falling, while the girl continued on her rampage. This time she yanked over a crate of bull's-eye lamps. Their eyelid shades winked at her as she left them behind.

Negro skin hid age well, but all who had worked with her knew she wasn't a girl, as her tiny frame suggested, but a woman who claimed to have at least one full-grown son. No one looking now would guess she was an adult, for she dashed and dodged and flew and ducked with the limberness of a teenager. The scene would have been mighty funny, had it not been for the rage of the chandlery owner, who had a reputation for taking out that rage on the workers.

"You'll all be punished if this goes another minute!" the

3

owner shouted, but the words were hollow today. The factory's slaves and the bulk of five families who had come here from Connemara for manual labor were all doing their best to catch her, but the negro woman's pickax feet gobbled up ground, and her hands went like spades in the air.

She was small because she was small, but she was quick because she was smart. She outthought and outguessed every person who tried to head her off, sent them twisting in the wrong directions, and led them all a merry plunge this way and that across the chandlery's shipping yard, between stacks of crates and piles of boxes, delivery tins, and loading platforms. For a few moments there was a dash of fun about the whole affair, a wrinkle in the fabric of the day's work.

That was how the workers and slaves reacted.

For the widowed owner trying to keep her business from suffering her husband's early fate, and for the overseers and foremen she employed, the sensation was as remote a thrill as could be. Instead there was a jolt familiar to every slaveholder whenever a slave acted up these days, much different from twenty years ago, or even ten. How much had this slave heard about the outside world? Outside of slavery? Such was always the question these days, when a new slave stepped off the wagon. What information would she bring? What rumors to contaminate discipline? What bad habits?

Ten years ago slaves had little recourse. Escape and go where? A few might make it through the South to the North, fewer still through the North's obligation to the Fugitive Slave Law and on to Canada, but even there they faced starvation because they didn't know how to motivate themselves, and competition for work if they did know was fierce. It would be a meager life for those few, and in most cases their hearts would forever linger in the South, for not many could bring their loved ones with them.

Not long ago freedom had meant separation, solitude, struggle, and longing.

But times had changed. Now there was support within the white community for those who wanted freedom. There were groups and agencies and whites working with the Underground Railroad, carrying slaves northward and teaching them the elusive arts of freedom . . . how to make a decision . . . how to make a living . . . how to make change for a dollar.

At moments like this, whenever a slave fought back, every slave owner remembered just how different things were.

The underweight slave woman hadn't appeared such a wild card at first, nor did she even now, really, dodging about the yard with her sickle arms crooked and her lips stuck out in determination.

Then her feet left the ground, and suddenly she was vaulting upward toward the sky, carried on a chariot of wooden crates.

The owner lifted her own heavy skirts and plunged forward, her small mouth opening so wide that her dry lips split. "Get her down from those crates! The globes!"

The precious glass globes, carefully wrapped and crated, newly arrived on the noon train and just delivered to the chandlery yard—globes for hurricane lamps, railroad lanterns, and carriage lanterns—were her hedge against competition from the advent of gaslighting in the cities.

Down they came.

The crates flipped backward from the negro woman's flashing feet, tumbled end on end over each other, and crashed to the dirt. First the crates themselves broke open, almost like stiff flowers whose petals were parting to the sun, then the tulip-shaped globes slid from squared packing cubbies, plunged forward, and one by one exploded into shining sapphire, amethyst, and opalescent splinters across the ground. *Pop! Pop! Pop!*

The owner clapped her hands flat against her cheeks and shrieked.

Those globes were meant to offset a shipment of blown globes to local hotels from the Boston and Sandwich Glass Company—her greatest competitor. If they broke, *she* was broke. She had tried desperately to move into the new age of illuminants, even to the point of hiring her own glassblowers—nothing had succeeded as yet in knocking over candles as the household mainstay, not yet . . . but "yet" could be a short time, as her husband's early demise had taught her, and she was determined never again to know that insecurity.

She would save these globes somehow—

All around her, slaves and workers scampered to avoid

shards of broken glass that glittered between them and the fleeing woman.

"Stop!" the owner shouted, her voice suddenly hoarse with a new imperative. She surged forward again, but this time she went for one of her overseers and snatched his pistol from his belt. Why hadn't he used it? Why wouldn't he shoot a slave who was wrecking her chandlery yard? What kind of man had she hired who would hesitate to blast the face off a rebellious nigger?

The slave woman paused at the top of the mountain of globe crates, planted her bare feet upon the scratchy wood, turned, hauled a crate into the air—where in those thready arms did she find the power?—and heaved.

The Connemarans scampered for distance. None was willing to take wood splinters in the face on behalf of an employer, nor end up cut to pieces by the glass of those shattered globes.

Into the suddenly empty patch of ground at the foot of the crate mountain, the chandler herself skidded to a halt, her hooped skirt twisting like a weather vane, round and round. The pistol came up at the end of her arm.

"Stop! You, stop!"

The negro woman, holding another crate high over her dirty yellow turban, paused.

The owner had a young face still, but one with many creases, the longest of which struck across her cheekbones when she talked. Now, as she squinted into the bright sunlit sky, her face became a fierce map, and her threat caused what she thought was a flicker in the negro woman's determination.

Yes . . . the crate wavered high above the yellow turban. Brown eyes and brown cheeks glistened in the sun.

The pistol barrel pointed straight at those eyes.

"Down gently with those," said the chandler, "or I'll do you this justice in my hand."

The Irish workers grumbled oaths and prayers, then a sudden silence fell.

With a hook of her thumb, the chandler cocked the pistol. *Clack.*

"Come down," she said, "or you'll be the deadest nigger in Norfolk."

For an instant scarce a heart beat across the chandlery. A

thrill ran up every spine. They would talk about this for weeks, maybe months, and how good a story it made . . . well, that would tell out in the next few seconds. Would it be a dead-nigger story or a day-she-almost story?

Slowly the negro woman began to lower the crate. Her thin arms quivered with the strain, but none showed in her face nor did her eyes ever leave the chandler's eyes.

There she stood, a bonded negro, fifteen feet in the air on top of a box mountain with a pistol trained on her. No one could guess what would happen. Threat of punishment meant nothing to this one. In trying to make her a functional worker, the chandler, overseers, and foremen had shunted her all over the chandlery, hoping to eventually stumble upon some work she *would* do. Slicing fat to toss into the rendering vats, stirring, skimming, cleanup, repair, candle dipping, wick weaving, cooking, chimney polishing, bottling burning fluid— nothing worked, because the problem was not in this chandlery, plain and simple.

She had come off the slave wagon primed, loaded, and cocked, and at a dear price for such low production value.

The chandler kept her pistol high and battled with her shuddering wrist to keep steady, or at least appear steady.

Overhead the negro woman put the crate down on top of the other crates and for a moment the diversion seemed to be nearing an end—until she forced the tie off the crate, flung the lid open, and began hurling the tulip globes one after another to the ground. Striking like lightning, the globes exploded as they hit the ground.

"Stop!" the chandler shouted again, still louder. But another and another glass globe blew up at her feet, embedding splinters in the fabric of her big skirt. "Stop or I'll shoot you! I swear I shall shoot you! I shall shoot you dead!"

Death, though, seemed not to be the thing this slave feared. To the naked eye, she was inviting it with every glass globe that broke against the splintered remains of the one before.

The foremen were driven back by shards of glass. The negro woman continued to hurl the globes, each one catching the sun as it streaked to the ground, hit, and broke into a thousand bits of light. The tinkle of splintered blue glass rang against a stack of wick-picks and snuffer boxes. The stack tilted, went over, and hit dozens of Betty lamps being stacked for shipping. The spadelike wrought-iron Bettys clanged as they hit the ground.

"All right! All right!" the chandler shouted.

The negro woman paused, one hand high in the air with a globe clutched in her brown fist. She glared downward and waited.

"All right!" the chandler shouted. This time there was a touch of resignation in her voice, a touch no one missed. "All right . . . I'll take you back where you came from."

And the negro woman paused, one arm high in the air. Now she put down the last globe in that crate, climbed down from the stacked crates, and she stood still as the foremen closed upon her with their chains and their collar.

★

CHAPTER ONE

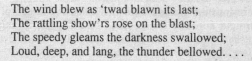

The wind blew as 'twad blawn its last;
The rattling show'rs rose on the blast;
The speedy gleams the darkness swallowed;
Loud, deep, and lang, the thunder bellowed. . . .

—Robert Burns

"If she jostles again, slice off her left hand and dash it to the mud."

"Yes'm."

The jangle of sleigh bells was an incongruous and pleasant surprise against a glowering night, but there was no sleigh, nor any snow. Rather, the night was iron-gray with torrential rain, and hot, hot enough to make men talk about hell as though they knew the how-hots and the how-far-downs. The ride had been a long one, and no one was in good humor. Rain had that power over travelers, to wear away the human heartiness as steadily as it wore away the very stone of the ages. Neither snow nor wind seemed to have such power.

In the front of the uncovered wagon was the owner of the chandlery, buried deep beneath her wide-brimmed hat and heavy mantle, and still she was soaked. Beside her, one of her foremen also hunched into the tall collar of his shabby overcoat and tipped the brim of his own hat westward against the needles of rain.

Behind them, in the bed of the wagon, the jingling of the sleigh bells prevented their having to look back there to make sure the slave woman hadn't slipped away, and that she had heard the warning muttered in front.

9

She sat still now, the rain hammering relentlessly on the burlap hood over her head. *Whappa, whappa, whappa.*

Many miles ago she had become immune to the stink of the burlap hood and managed to breathe the dank air that came through the coarse, dirty fibers. At first she hadn't trusted them when they said they were taking her back. Half the trip she had plotted and schemed another escape, lest this wagon be taking her farther south, farther away. Only now did she tense with a different emotion, because of what came through the burlap and touched her nostrils—the aroma of orinoko.

Even the weather couldn't completely rinse out the strong scent of thousands of orinoko tobacco leaves bending against the rain. Into the woman's mind flooded the image of what was around her. She blinked and blinked, but through the burlap she could see nothing but a gray blur. She knew what was there.

On either side of the welter of muddy ruts pretending to be a road, acres of tobacco leaves steamed and trembled. Strong, aromatic fields, acre after acre, in various stages of growth— orinoko, and beyond it a field of sweet-scent from the seed sown early in winter, soon to be taken out of the mold beds during these seasonal rains and transplanted to fields in the hills. Repetitive hoeing and plowing to loosen the soil . . . then the plants with eight or more leaves would be topped off and cease growing . . . suckers had to be plucked from the bases of the leaf stems . . . someone would have to check for hornworms. For years that had been her job.

The orinoko field had turned yellow . . . she could smell the color. It would have to be cut soon, close to the ground, to force the leaves to wilt before air curing. She knew the process as she knew the shape of her own hands. It carried a rush of sentiment, of rightful place, of her imprint on the world. Though she couldn't see, she could clearly *smell* how much time had passed. Harvest on a tobacco plantation wasn't like other plantation crops, wasn't so seasonal. Rather than one crop a year, there would be several. She ticked it out in her head—how the smell was when she left, how it was now. So, a year and a month. Maybe a year and two.

The road had narrowed to a barely passable river of mud banked by the fields. She felt it in her induced blindness . . . felt every rut and counted every bend in the road. Yes . . . this was right. The next bend would bring the wagon around to the plantation's great circular carriage drive.

From here—if she could see—she could have glimpsed the tobacco houses, where the stalks were pegged at specific distances from each other and left alone to cure to six weeks or more while other fields were being put in. On a moist day, not as moist as today, but maybe tomorrow, the leaves would be stripped, made into hands and put into hogsheads.

Her fingers quivered with the wish to do the work they were accustomed to. There was tremendous security for her in knowing she was an expert at something. She was a hornworm expert. That to which she had been accustomed for more than twenty years suddenly rushed back into her fingertips and set them twitching.

On the wet wind came a whiff of decorative hedges, then of subsidiary crops, young corn, beets, peanuts, produce with which the plantation fed itself, and close upon those came the overwhelming aroma of the brewery and the blacksmith's forge where all the plantation's nails and hinges and horseshoes were made, and she knew they had come around the bend.

Her flesh pimpled with anticipation. Every fiber of her being said *home*.

The wagon shuddered beneath her as the horse slowed. The chandler and the foreman muttered a few words to each other, then there was a snap of the reins and the horse jolted forward.

Why? Why were they passing by the main carriageway?

Flooding? Flooding must be the reason. They would find another way in. There had been talk every year about filling and grading the mouth of the carriage drive, but inevitably the season dried up and the grading was forgotten. Guests rarely came out this far during the rainy season, and no one else minded using the yard entrances.

The slave woman's heart jumped and pummeled against her breastbone. The only other way in from this direction would take them right through the slave quarters. Yes—she could smell the lingering stink of warm rosin and lard. Someone had been making or repairing shoes.

And fireplaces . . . the smell of woodfires through the rain! Smoke rolling up through wooden chimneys . . . black smoke against the black night, yes. Yes!

A virtual community unto itself, the slaves' little red-brick dormitories gathered themselves in her imagination as the wagon clunked around the end of the fence and one wheel grated against the butt of the boardwalk.

She smiled under the burlap hood, knowing that now the chandler would witness those controversial brick slave shanties, tiny imitations of the big three-story mansion—*brick!* With plank floors and pins for hanging clothes upon. The master had been forward-looking when he built those cabins and had been criticized by the local gentry for it. There was always fighting among the blue-blooders—how comfortable should they allow their slaves to be? Should the breeze be kept from blowing upon sleeping negroes because the better the sleep, the better the work? Or was that a slip in control? Fight, always fight among the whites. Argument about the workers' condition going back and forth above the bobbing black heads of the workers themselves. Argument in which they were not welcome to participate.

If this tobacco plantation's yearly yield increase was any monitor, its master was no fool to tend his slaves as he did. There had always been general contentment here, slaves who did their jobs steadily, and thus were left alone after hours, to feed themselves as cleverly as they could manage, to keep their own tiny households and families, to sing their songs and have their own lives as best as they could manage. The white folks stayed up at the house, and the negroes were allowed their privacy. Generally it worked.

In fact, she herself represented the only burr on an otherwise glistening hide.

There were voices. A chant. For a moment the woman was confused. This plantation had no chanting negroes.

"Pull! Pull! Pull!"

Oh, it was work. Men at work, pooling their strength, and not a chant at all.

"Over there," the chandler said, raising her eyes. "Those men working in that barn. Perhaps they can direct us to the main house."

"Yes'm."

The foreman clucked to the horse and drew on the left rein. The wagon surged in that direction, then pulled to a halt in the mud. It had hardly been worth turning.

The chandler peered into the wide-open door of an enormous barn, where three men were putting their combined weight into hauling a rope that came down from the ceiling. The rope was on a tackle and gave them leverage to raise a piece of farm machinery that the chandler did not recognize. Perhaps it was a hoeing machine or a tiller or a gin of some kind, but to the untrained eye it appeared to be nothing more than a mess of iron blades and handles. Two more men were pushing upward on the machine, and another was shoving brick blocks underneath.

"Pull!"

The machine inched upward. Torchlight glistened across rounded muscles, bare arms, and hard backs. The men were calf-deep in mud even inside the barn as the rain sheeted inward and soaked the floor for a good twelve feet beyond the doors.

"Hold'er there! Hold'er! One more second! That does it— let'r down. Easy! Slow! Little more . . . that's it, she's down. Good job, boys, good job. Yessir . . . a good job."

The man talking straightened and surveyed what they had done so far, then bent once again to inspect the underside of the hiked-up machine. His backside and legs were soaked completely through with brownish-black mud, no doubt with some manure involved. His hair was nothing more than a headpiece of muddy strings, though clearly he was not a black man, but a white plantation hand, or perhaps a foreman.

When all the other workers fell silent at noticing the wagon outside the barn doors, this man also paused and turned. After a moment of wordless digestion that what he saw was not a trick of the driving rain, he rubbed a palette of new mud—his hand—over his already sopping whiskers, retrieved a wide-brimmed hat from a peg on the barn wall, and strode out into the rain toward the wagon and the two people in the driving seat.

"Something we can do for you on this perditious night, sir? Ma'am?"

The woman answered, and immediately the chain of command became clear. At least now he would know whom to address.

"My name is Opal Bouchard," she said. "I am owner and proprietress of the Bouchard and Smith Chandlery in Norfolk.

I have business with the master of this plantation, but the main drive is flooded over and we cannot see clearly the way from here. Can you direct us to the main house?"

"Oh . . . yes'm, I can take you up to the house myself."

"And put that mud all over my wagon seat? Better not, I should think."

"Then, if it please you, ma'am, I'll walk in front."

"Do so."

He nodded once, then waved briefly to the negroes in the barn. "Boys, you keep right on working. See that axle's mended and replaced secure by morning, and you'll all get half the day's rest tomorrow."

"Rest?" Opal Bouchard blurted over his head. "On a weekday? Does your master know you initiate such luxuries upon your man-slaves?"

The filthy worker turned to her again, his mustache dripping rainwater and causing streaks of wetness on his mud-caked beard. "Oh, yes'm, I reckon he knows whatever I do."

He slipped his hand under the horse's cheekpiece and clucked. The wagon jolted, dug into the mud, and yanked forward.

The big brick mansion's third story was cradled in an arm of fog, making the house seem almost an illusion. Dwarf box-wood trees lined the wide porch, over which several neoclassical columns had been added. In better weather the picture would have been worthy of artwork. Presently rain reduced visibility to a few yards and beat down the gaze of anyone who dared glance upward.

A few moments later having left their cargo in the wagon, the woman and her foreman stood dripping on the woven floorcloths of the main foyer, their outerwear being peeled away by several house slaves who flurried around them.

"Right in here, ma'am," the muddy field hand gestured, waving them through a pair of elaborate double doors into a particularly beautiful room. One wall was nothing but books, backdrop to the huge rectangular grand piano that crawled across one full quarter of the room's space on legs thick as dinner plates. The mustard-yellow facing wall was offset by a sprawling red Persian rug, a walnut stepback cupboard, and a butternut and tiger-maple writing desk. There were wing chairs and drop-leaf tables, which the chandler thought she recognized as Chippendale, and there were tapers on sconces, which comforted her, and one modern gaslamp, which didn't.

Several house slaves and two of the swarthy servants followed them into the room, and right behind them were three rather frightening Mediterranean types. Turks, perhaps. Or Spaniards, or were those cheekbones Egyptian?

Mrs. Bouchard backed into her foreman's shoulder, and her eyes went wide, but she managed to clamp her lips on a squawk at the sight of these big swarthy men with their big hanging mustaches and cylindrical red hats. What kind of household was this, to keep heathen servants?

The mud-covered field hand gestured again. "This is the library. We're mightily proud of it here on Plentiful. The bondswomen'll dry your coats over the wood stoves in back, and the servants'll turn out some hot tea and refreshments. There's no lady in the house to offer you a comfort, ma'am, but we'll do our best for you in spite. In spite of there being no lady here, I mean."

"I'm not surprised," Mrs. Bouchard muttered, trying to imagine what kind of proper housewife would allow these Arabian Turkish Egyptians to live beneath her roof. Swept up by her own curiosity, she pointed at a small hand-painted portrait beside a Bible on one of the drop leafs and said, "I had no idea Presbyterians espoused the Bible."

"Where'd you get the idea the household is Presbyterian?" her foreman asked.

"It's implied," she said. "There is no crucifix in the hallway, or anywhere, so what else could they be? You haven't seen one, have you, Mr. Ringman?"

"No, ma'am, guess I hadn't looked," her foreman replied.

"I had no idea," she grumbled again, gazing at the picture of Christ and wondering if the Bible had the same books in it as hers did. "I'm glad I noticed. I wouldn't want to insult the master when he arrives."

"No, ma'am, he won't be insulted," the field hand said, twisting his sopping hat, seemingly indifferent to the fact that he was dripping muddy water onto the expensive Persian rug. "If you'll wait here in the library just a minute, I'll see you're tended proper. You'll be wanting a good hot meal, and likely you'll best be put up here overnight, as it's a mite dangerous ride into Norfolk in rainy season."

"Are you suggesting we were unwise to come?"

"Oh, no, ma'am. Just making a hospitality."

"I think the hospitality of the house is best left to your employer, sir."

"Anything you say, ma'am." Caked mud on the man's cheeks cracked beneath his eyes—a smirk? Sarcasm?

Then, in a move that caused Mrs. Bouchard to gasp outright, the field hand dropped his wrung-out hat right on the tapestried arm of a Louis XIII chair.

"Sir!" she blurted, snatching the hat between her thumb and forefinger. "Have some consideration for your master's furnishings."

"Oh," he said, "right," and took the hat.

And tossed it onto the glistening piano bench.

"Uch," Mrs. Bouchard gushed. "If this isn't the . . . if I wasn't fatigued . . . if I hadn't just come all the way from . . ."

Her voice tapered off as she stood up from retrieving the hat a second time.

As she rose, she became aware of a stirring presence, or perhaps the eyes of a ghost, dark eyes, set in an olive complexion, eyes that never blinked, never flinched. A portrait . . . as tall as its subject, and painted right on the wall over the massive piano just inside the library doors.

A full-length portrait, nothing so mundane as a head-and-shoulders picture, but a surprising trompe l'oeil that blended so well with the wall, it seemed the subject was simply walking down a set of hidden stairs into the room.

The chandler stepped back and forced herself to breathe, but she couldn't draw her attention from the mural.

A woman, her hair like Dresden, her wrists thickened by gold bangle bracelets, a rosette over each ear, with a cluster of ribbons framing her face and a headdress with a semicircular plume—and braidwork, tons of braidwork, and gold coins on chains around her waist, layered over still more layers of embroidered linen aprons joined at her tight waist in proper style for a ball gown. Yes, the enormous skirt was tier after tier of the finest pure ivories and blush satin crackling in an illusion of Virginia sunlight, tipped sideways just enough to show a glint of lace petticoat trim, each tier decorated with gold tassels, and she wore an ivory shawl-bodice caressing her shoulders and cradling her breasts, and a diadem of coins on her forehead. Her hair rested in a roll over one shoulder, her painted lips turned up just a thought at the corners, and one hand lay upon the foliated curves of her ball gown in such a way that made the gown seem like an afterthought.

How foreign! How shocking! How wonderful to be that woman!

The chandler remained enthralled with the mural, and in fact came gradually to notice the background so carefully added behind the painted woman. There were statues standing in a garden, their postures relaxed, and still somehow heroic, life observed and copied with great deliberation. Beyond there were buildings with pillars, on an imaginary horizon, with an imaginary dawn casting light on all.

Instantly she was thinking of how to ask tactfully for the artist's name, and how she might contact him to paint such a mural on her own wall . . . and at how dear a price.

The thought of money brought her limping back to reality, and she turned with several ideas on her lips.

She found herself staring out the library's double doors at the mud-covered field hand. He was now out in the hallway, standing before several house slaves who were just plunking a half barrel of water onto a bench—right in the middle of the hall. Immediately the field hand stepped into it, plunged his entire head into the water, and set to bubbling and thrashing until the water sheeted over the brim and splashed the floorboards.

At the same time, the slaves peeled away the man's mudsoaked shirt, showing shoulders the color of tallow and a tuft of peppery chest hair. The servants were ready with cotton towels when he pulled his dripping head out of the water, gave a shake just like a big hunting dog, and mopped himself about the head and neck, then clutched the excess water from his beard, which looked more neatly trimmed now that it was clean. One of the Bolivian Eskimo Turks came up behind him with a comb and raked the cinder-gray hair back, then pushed waves into it with his fingertips. While this was going on, another swarthy creature arrived with a plump quilted smoking jacket in the brightest burgundy and trimmed in silver velvet, and on it went.

"Oh, don't tell me," the chandler muttered on a grieving sigh.

What turned on her and her foreman then, as she feared, was hardly a field hand anymore, but a broad-shouldered, trim-bearded, ruddy-cheeked man of the Southern gentry. He strode in, tying the belt of his smoker.

"How do, ma'am," he said. "I'm Luke Wallace, master of Plentiful. I'm your servant."

Opal Bouchard tightened her lips, unsure whether she should be embarrassed or disgusted.

"Sir . . . you might have made your identity known to us."

"Sorry, ma'am," Wallace said, grinning beneath the whiskers, "I declare it felt a bit nostalgic to be treated like a common worker just for once again. I came out of the docks, you know."

"No, sir, I didn't."

He rubbed his nose and made a rude noise that she assumed had something to do with having had his head under water a minute ago. Then he snorted and gestured her deeper into the room. A snap of his fingers sent most of the slaves and servants hopping, and judging from the purposefulness of their strides, they knew exactly what he wanted just from the look in his eyes.

At least half of Mrs. Bouchard wanted to get down to business, as was her habit, but she couldn't resist gesturing to the magnificent mural.

"Is this your daughter, Mr. Wallace?" she asked, trying not to seem too eager, or too jealous.

Wallace's salt-and-pepper brows flinched. He looked at the mural also.

"My wife," he said, "in her wedding gown."

"Your wife is . . . Spanish?"

"Macedonian." At her perplexed look, he added, "Greek."

"Ah . . . are you a widower, sir?"

Wallace caught a legible glint in her eye and put a bit of extra space between them.

"Presently she and my son and daughters are on a voyage to her homeland and have been there for the past year and some."

Disappointment flickered but momentarily in the widow's face. "An extended voyage, then."

"Well, my son is attending university there. My wife desired to stay with him, and with her parents, and to steep my daughters in Greekitude. Well, Europe. Well, mostly Greece."

"How interesting." That chance guttered, the chandler remembered her business and got back to it. She turned to her foreman and said, "Bring in the negro, Mr. Ringman."

"Yes'm, I'll fetch her."

"What's the trouble here, Mrs. Bouchard?" Wallace asked, tightening the belt of his smoking jacket and taking his usual direct angle to business matters—and some inner sense told him this was indeed business and no aristocratic whim, of which the South possessed plenty, despite the woman's upper-crust accent and manner.

"I purchased a negro woman off the auction block nigh onto a year ago, and paid a dear enough price for her, considering her age, because she came with credentials from a successful plantation. She's turned out to be incorrigible."

"Incorrigible?"

"She refuses to work, and martyrs herself to any punishment. What good is it to whip a slave until she cannot stand, only to have her take the time of other slaves to make her well again, so she can go on with her refusals?"

"Yes, I understand."

"She's downright destructive, Mr. Wallace. Turned my shipping area into a shivaree and ruined a month's work. I came that close to killing her, but my investment turned before my eyes. She has escaped four times. Four. And each time we find her somewhere on the road right back to Plentiful. I bring her back to you in hopes of assuaging her curiosity about this place, and perhaps then she'll become a decent worker. Ah, Mr. Ringman—"

There was a jangle of bells.

The foreman reappeared at the library door, this time leading the hooded slave woman, and Luke Wallace sneered briefly behind Opal Bouchard's back. The negro's head was completely covered, and around the neck was an iron collar with four long prongs that kept her from lying down or even leaning, and from each of the prongs dangled a sizable sleigh bell. It was a gruesome device, but common enough that he made no mention about it. Until now he couldn't recall that any of his slaves had ever experienced such a contraption.

Cold awareness penetrated him.

"Her chemise, Mr. Ringman," Mrs. Bouchard said.

The foreman maneuvered the colored woman to a three-quarter position, then yanked the osnaburg chemise down. Pointy brown shoulders poked over the frayed collar. Pale creases of whip marks, fresh pink ones over shriveled older ones, glittered in the lamplight.

Mrs. Bouchard looked at Wallace, raised her eyebrows, and said, "Nothing I do makes her work."

The sentence blistered its way between them with a hundred references. For an instant the stink of coercive burns, of withheld food, the whine of the whip and snap of the paddle, seemed here and real.

"Remove the hood," Mrs. Bouchard instructed.

The foreman yanked upward on the burlap hood now, which caught for an awful moment on the iron collar.

Mrs. Bouchard held out her hand and turned to Wallace. "You know this drumhead woman, sir?"

The past can be as frightening as a looming and unreadable future, and Luke Wallace was staring into the abyss no matter which way he turned—forward or back. He thought the matter was at least partly finished, that his remedial measure had erased the physical evidence of his life's greatest mistake, but here stood a part of it, and he began to worry about the other parts. Would they, too, reappear?

Apprehension jarred him.

"Mmmm," he groaned, his mouth pursing. "I know her."

All too well he knew the downcast glare burrowing into his rug. He knew the little twist of turban and the knots of raisin-brown fist. He knew also that the docility was a sham, a mask. He knew that while across the nation slaves had begun to awaken to their own potential, a great slumbering creature suddenly becoming aware of itself, this little cuffee woman had long been a mantis on his leaf, a mantis to which even the spider gives a wide berth.

"There is something about this plantation, Mr. Wallace," the chandler said bluntly, "that this drumhead cannot or refuses to forget. She's played havoc with my whole operation for the sake of it. She's corrupting my slaves with her rebellions, and slaves can go bad like any crop if there's one bit of rot among them, do you agree?"

"Oh," Wallace said by rote, "I agree."

He more than agreed. He too well knew.

"A negro with a memory is a canker," Mrs. Bouchard went on. "Memory is a worse poison than their heretical religions can be, sir, and I only hope you can offer some assuagement to this negro."

Luke Wallace cleared his throat, but he said nothing. He wiped a dollop of water from the corner of his mustache, thrust his hands into the pockets of his smoker, and took a wide path across the rug to the narrow slave woman.

They stood a mere yard apart, remembering things about each other's bodies the memories of which were well over twenty years old, yet etched by the crude encounter that had burned itself so indelibly into each of their very divergent fates.

He waited until the skinny colored woman raised her eyes to meet his. She wasn't afraid. He had never for a moment expected her to be.

Bluntly he asked, "What do you want?"

She never flinched. Though her lips were raw from rubbing against the burlap hood, and her turban was soaked through from the rain, and her elbows quivered slightly from fatigue, she gave him no signal of his superiority. Rather, her face was doused with arsenic for him.

She parted those raw lips.

"I want see my boy," she said.

In her toneless words was hidden the stamina of spirit that Wallace found suddenly so familiar. He knew there was nothing he could do at this point. Nothing against the tides she would move out of her way in order to get what she wanted. If she would fight with such termerity and move so firmly against the stream in order to see her son, he knew there would be nothing that would belay her endurance now.

Nor had he any such intention.

Offering at least a feint of indecision, he wandered to his writing desk and plucked a thick cigar from a gold-leafed canister, rummaged for a match, and puffed a few seconds away. Home grown. A good crop. Plenty of body, substance.

Then he turned to those who waited and shrugged.

"All right," he said.

★

Ten minutes later the scrawny colored woman was standing beneath a thundering sky. Around her were the hills of her teenaged years, hills to which she had been sold, and where her feet had impregnated the dirt with the salt of her body for more than two decades. She knew what a decade was because her son had taught her. Her brilliant son, for whom she had risked her life once, and lately subjected the black skin of her back to the whip and anything else a slaveholder's mind might conjure.

Within the cradle of those gentle hills, deep in the creases of field after field of docile tobacco leaves, she stood now in the rain, oblivious to the drizzle pouring down her face and back.

Around her, here in this negro cemetery, were two dozen or so bolts of thick wood in the shapes of crosses. These were the only crop in this humble little field, and the tiny hip-high picket fence kept dogs out, usually.

When the lightning flashed, she could recognize the letters and numbers carved into the only stone marker in the cemetery and regret that she had let him teach her to read, even a little. Even this much.

And though she felt it on her face, even the lightning couldn't move her.

DORIAN

1833 to 1856

★

CHAPTER TWO

———— ★ ————

LATE SUMMER 1832
A TOBACCO FIELD, STATE OF VIRGINIA

Wallace's hand closed around the girl's corded wrist. He spun her around and dragged her toward the nearest cabin, yanking her along like a rag doll. As he mounted the porch steps, he pulled his shirttail out and yanked his trousers open in front, pausing only to push the girl into the cabin. He didn't bother to shut the door.

Outside, the slaves of Plentiful looked back and forth at each other, each wondering if any of them had the nerve to stand up for the new girl, but none of them cared enough about her yet to put her before himself . . . the children among them watched the dark doorway unashamedly and craned their necks to listen.

There was no sound. None but the jangle of the fire and the crinkle of pigskin curling in the flames. That and crickets . . . and the sound of the bed scraping against the wood floor.

They all flinched visibly, every last one, when the bed sounded a final thud. A moment later Wallace staggered out. His face was a mean crumple.

He stuffed his shirt back into his breeches, but it didn't stay. Exasperated that the cuffees were all standing exactly where they had been when he went in, Wallace bullied his way through them, shoving any aside who were in his way, and threw the whip onto the floor of the carriage.

The wheels cut ruts into Plentiful's moist grass.

From the shadow beneath the cabin awning, Yula reappeared.

Sheathed in firelight, she watched him leave. She pushed her apron back down over her skirt. In her other hand she held her turban, now just a twist of red cotton. . . .

SPRING 1833
NORFOLK SHIPYARD

Down the sagging gangplank the men came. Some led live goats and lambs. Others hauled carpets slung over their shoulders in big rolls. They carried vases, urns, and jugs . . . not the plain clay vases of primitive lands, these were glazed, and intricately decorated with geometric designs and detailed drawings . . . borders of meanders and zigzags, chariots and charioteers driving across the fired-clay receptacles that smelled of rare spices. . . .

Once again the gangplank moaned. This time, though, there were no men carrying heavy crates or jugs.

Exotic women. Four, six, nine, they filed from the ship. Women from some other world. Older ones guided younger ones as though to shield them from the new world's contaminations. . . . Women in black clothing so unlike the dome-shaped gowns of the South's belles . . . fabric offset with bright embroidered zigzags and pyramids, floral designs, stripes, all in defiance of the female form. Quilted aprons, all heavily embroidered, layered the stiff clothing. There were coins dangling from the clothing itself. . . . Some of the women had coins across their foreheads on thin chains. . . . What business could Lucas Wallace have with such elemental beings?

SPRING 1833
THE SLAVE VILLAGE OF PLENTIFUL

The cabin was dark and warm. A fire crackled in the stone hearth. Three iron Bettys cast their dim, eerie glow as they clung by swivels to iron bars sticking out from the walls, and provided an underlying scent of burning lard. Over the smoky aroma of firewood, there was the strong smell of blood, of sweat. . . .

"Light a lamp," Wallace snapped. "Haven't you got a whale-oil lamp with a glass globe? Didn't I give them to you cuffees? Why don't you use them?"

"Glass be fo' de white folks, Boss," Moses grumbled from behind him.

One of the women, an elderly cuffee who had worked for him since the beginning, swiftly obeyed the order and brought him a small chamber lamp with a glass chimney. He took it without looking at her, dug for a match, lit the wick impatiently, and lowered the chamber lamp. Its soft buttery light washed over the cradle.

"Lawsy . . . ," Samson murmured as he too leaned over. "Dat ain' no mulat' baby," he said. "Dat baby white!"

A white baby. But white in a parenthetical way . . . hair thick and silky . . . made of obsidian curls rather than the soft wool of negro hair . . . skin like watered sepia . . . not exactly white, but clearly Wallace's.

Dulled images told him of a little poontang one drunken night . . . and he didn't like being made the ass in front of the cuffees.

He looked back into the cradle, folded his arm, and covered his mouth. He tried to imagine taking the child for a cuffee, and couldn't. The little nose already had a strong line. The infant's jawline was a gentle curve, not the jutting feature he would have expected, and the rose-petal lips nothing at all like a slave's. Even as the hedge-born boy lay with miniature fists curled beside his tiny scrunched-up face, Wallace recognized the bone structure of his own family. This was a vest-pocket version of himself.

"I can't have this here . . . not now . . . keep that baby hidden. As soon as it can be weaned . . . it'll have to be sold off."

And the words rang and rang around the cemetery as though the markers were bells and the trees harps. Rang and rang, until the negro woman's ears pounded and the name on the marker blurred.

Dorian . . . Dorian . . . Dorian . . .

Memories piled one over the other, each a cul-de-sac which trapped her for an instant. She'd carried that baby his nine-month cookin' time, and from three sides she'd looked like a wire with a knot in it. Boss hadn't been an absentee planter, like so many who hadn't the physical background of a former dockworker, and she had seen plenty of him in that nine-months. She had learned to read his face, and to some extent, his mind. Now that the baby was born, she had guessed his intent to slap a bearing rein on the problem by selling the mustard baby.

But scrawny Yula was tough as a pine knot and absolutely fearless.

She stared at the hump of dirt until grief sucked her dry and the storm galvanized her.

And the bells of grief in her head became music, the spangled music of mandolins and drums and clarinets, twisting, writhing music, as intriguing and alien as a serpent coiling in her heart, and she remembered again, as though yesterday had her by the throat.

1833
PLENTIFUL

Southern women in immense ball gowns drifted like dogwood petals turning on a green river. They clung to the arms of gentlemen in ascots and tails . . . all seemed amazed and disturbed . . . their murmur was almost a constant hum behind the music.

There was a decided difference about this wedding . . . an undertone. Women spoke in subdued voices, not the gay babble that would ordinarily dominate, and they clung to their husbands. . . .

There was a flash of bright white silk, a glint of gold, a rustle of crinoline and a jingle of coins, and Iphigenia Trözene bloomed onto the lawn.

The crowd's eyes were blistered by gleaming ivory silk, brighter than the marble statues towering around them. . . . Her symbolic dowry was draped on chains at her waist, a dia-

dem with small gold coins winked on her forehead. . . . The guests collectively gasped, "Ohhh!"

This was no European misfit! This was no foreigner. . . . He wasn't marrying a barbarian at all!

Somehow the Greeks had done it. Somehow they had taken their vastly different cultures and blended them like fruit and cream. Iphigenia didn't look Greek, and yet . . . she did. But more than the Macedonian female with her eyes turned downward, this was a cosmopolitan society bride. She was the dream of every girl on every plantation, everywhere. She was a Southern *woman*.

Iphigenia smiled at her husband again with perfect Olympian serenity, as if to tell the guests they would never see the likes of this again . . . and they should look carefully. . . .

Yula pulled the bride toward the shadows. On a spring day like today shadows were spare, and it was a tight fit between the topiaries. Yula drew apart the rags she'd used to cover herself, and thus doing she revealed the real treasure.

Iphigenia's lips parted and she gasped.

A baby no bigger than a kitten wiggled at the slave girl's breast. His two-day-old skin was like eggnog and his hair was soft ebony curls. He turned his head as daylight struck him, and looked for the light. His eyes were lumps of coals, so dark that the pupils were invisible within them. . . .

Iphigenia automatically reached for the child. She was captured by a sensation beyond instinct, utterly caught by primal memories and the beauty of something so pure, something that needed to be held and comforted, to cling to an adult's body and to be guarded by an adult's arms. . . . If only she could hold him, just for a moment. He lay against her throat as though ordained to fit there.

She gazed past the shaded veranda to the banquet grounds, through the milling guests to the bridal table, past her parents, finally to her husband.

She looked at Yula and understood.

The baby wiggled briefly, then rested his tiny face like a cameo against her warm throat and enjoyed the moment with his whole tiny being, as only the innocent can.

"Dorian," she whispered.

Dorian, the twigs whispered, picking at Yula's turban as they dipped with the rain. *Dorian,* they scratched.

The baby had stayed, on the proviso that he be shared, the beloved possession of two mothers, of two worlds—of the bonded slaves, of the Greek aristocracy.

A boy for the century.

She had shared him in order to keep him, shared him with the lovely foreign bride, the angel woman, and the two of them had been his mothers. Yula still a teenager, Iphigenia barely a woman herself, they had walked together into the quiet recesses of motherhood, black hand clasping a Greek hand, guided by the beautiful baby boy, and together they had protected him from the hatred of his father. Even in the light of the children born of Iphigenia's own body as the years passed, there had been no more beloved nor more brilliant light for the two women.

Yula's heart twisted. Had they told Iphigenia? Had they written to her in the far-away country and told her they were putting him in the ground?

The lightning slithered across his ivory skin. The dark of night recoiled in shame from the obsidian of his eyes and the keenness that lurked behind them even in his silence. He stood before her again, on the other side of the grave marker, and she held out her narrow black hand as though he were really there. He was dry and untouched by the rain, as any spirit should be, untainted by the big world from which he had been cloistered, a dark-haired, prideful boy with a sizzling intellect and callused hands. For a moment, in the lull between lightning, his linsey suit made a ragged silhouette along the shoulder seams, for his muscles were beginning to cause a strain there. She would have to dismantle the suit, put in gussets to allow for his growth. After all, he was nearly fourteen. . . .

Lightning flashed. He laid his hand upon the grave marker, and he was shimmering. The linsey suit was gone. In its place rippled a gentleman's linen shirt and the flutter of a silver cravat. His shoulders and waist were wedged into a high-collared gray waistcoat of quilted satin, and he was suddenly a boy poet, a controversial spider in love with the dangerous web he trod upon.

His black brows arched like sickles. Even after all these

years of labor beneath the sun and the threat of a bullwhip, his skin was still light and carried that tint of saffron, his eyes still inkdrops on manila, set deep like an elf's or a demon's, and he could play both roles. His lips were somewhat full—not like a negro's lips, but like a statue's, as if drawn with a sharp pencil. He was forever a chameleon . . . none looked as Greek as the boy who was not Greek at all.

He was a boy conceived by the devil as done by Shelley, or a pearl by Poe.

Again the lightning gashed a bonded woman's negro features and mutilated the slave cemetery with its bolts. The trees recoiled. The wind crashed through them. It was a night for the devil, a night for Dorian, and somehow he *was* here.

And there was someone with him now. His alter ego—blond, rangy—

No . . . the ranginess was disappearing. The grace of a gentleman came as the bones grew and the muscles lengthened to fit them. Another boy, nearly white blond, point for point the opposite of Dorian, yet they carried the same silhouette, brothers in all but coloring. And temperament—no, they were not brothers in temperament. For every spark of the demonaic in Dorian, there fluttered the angelic in Alexander Wallace. Where Dorian saw danger, Alex saw hope.

Alex saw hope in Dorian, better even than the two mothers.

Rain collected on her spiky eyelashes, and Yula blinked. The rain sheeted her cheeks. She blinked again.

A moment, and they were men. Young men, standing together, dwarfing the grave marker, standing with their arms folded and their shoulders touching, smiling their very different smiles down upon "little Mama."

And the clothes . . . it was as though the clothes knew.

While Alex wore a gentleman's blue daycoat, a vest, a white cravat and riding boots, Dorian's fine upper-cruster clothing suddenly dissolved, fell away, to the plain cotton field shirt, perpetually crusted with sweat, most of the buttons missing, the sleeves rolled.

He looked down at the rolled sleeves, he saw his bare arms, and she too saw them, and Alex saw them.

Dorian reached up along his own body with his left hand and touched the meaty part of his right forearm, where the skin was branded . . . branded with the mark of a slave, leaving a puckered mess where his skin had once been perfect. He dared to touch the boiled ugliness of the burn, daring to bring attention to it. The mark sizzled and smoked. In Yula's reverie his face crumpled briefly as he felt the pain again. He was branded. Branded with the *S* which no one else on Plentiful was made to bear, *S* for *slave*. Only Dorian, because he had been Boss's singular bane—

The symbol of the only crack in Wallace's foundation.

Stepping around the gravestone, Alex reached for his half-brother, his face limned with sympathy, but Dorian turned away, covering the *S*, forcing the pain to leave his face. He would have none of the pity; he knew what he was. Pity was a ridiculous waste of brainwork.

Now it seemed to Yula that the grave marker began suddenly to grow, two, three, ten times its own size, until it drowned out the image of the young men and stood as big as a tree, reaching upward after the lightning as though to beg a strike. When it spoke, it had Dorian's voice.

Strike me, God. I put the dare upon you.

The rain continued. Thunder in the distance took its lightning with it and no longer filled the sky above the slave cemetery. Now there was only the rain.

Yula's lips parted, and her slave voice made a word on the wind.

"Dohrian . . ."

And the wind took the name and whisked it away.

Gone, just as he was gone.

Gone into the ground.

Ten minutes later she was standing like a soaked twig, dripping on Wallace's Persian carpet with impunity.

Something in her face brought sudden silence to the room. Neither Wallace nor Mrs. Bouchard nor the foreman spoke, though Yula could tell they had been talking, talking about her, about Dorian, and she wondered passingly what kind of subject Dorian made in Boss Wallace's parlor. Surely most of the truth would remain untold if Wallace could keep his druthers.

No matter how much or how little Mrs. Bouchard or anyone else knew, all that mattered was that Yula knew, and Boss knew.

She never took her eyes from him.

Pat, pat, pat went the drops of water from her sopping form, slapping into the patterned fibers of the imported carpet.

He couldn't manage to look away from her. For once, for the first time, they were equals.

After this had gone on long enough to make anyone itch, Yula broke the stupor and padded around Boss as though she owned the room instead of him. She went around to the business side of the tiger-maple desk, yanked open the drawers until she found stationery, then appropriated the quill pen and dipped it into the inkwell. It dribbled black ink across the fine, glistening wood of the desktop, for she had never before held a pen and had no idea how to make it not drip. And the drops of ink were Dorian's eyes upon the desktop, gazing up at her, and they gave her power. She swore one even winked.

She slapped the piece of stationery onto the blotter, and straightened.

She looked squarely at Boss, indignant toward the other two people in the room, and held up the pen.

"Now you write de words to make me free," she said.

Luke Wallace stood with his hands crushed into the pockets of his smoking jacket.

The pen dripped black ink onto the blotter, and the cuffee woman was still glaring at him. She never so much as flinched.

Rare that a cuffee would look at her master with that face.

But it was a rare day, brought upon him by a rare day from the past, which now plunged forward to haunt him.

There was nothing he could do. Between his shoulder blades he felt the stare of Opal Bouchard, to whom he owed an obligation for having sold her an incorrigible slave. A step behind her was the foreman, who would spread word of business practices unbecoming to a successful plantation owner.

Before him, the rattle-boned cuffee woman who had borne his nigger child and conspired with his mail-order bride to keep that child on the grounds.

There was nothing else to do.

He stepped to the desk. He sat down. The cuffee woman

didn't move aside. She watched over his shoulder, as though she could read the words he scrawled with the overburdened quill. Word after word scratched onto the white parchment. Word after word, to make her free.

I, owner of the establishment of Plentiful, Norfolk, Virginia, do hereby testify and make appropriate that the bondswoman Yula shall heretoforever be known as a free person, having bought her freedom at a price duly noted by the undersigned. L. Wallace, proprietor, Plentiful.

And he stood up.

While the ink dried, he dug in a drawer for a box. Out of the box he pulled several hundred Dixie notes and counted out the price of a slave of Yula's age, sex, and experience, then added another two hundred for the trouble. For two hundred dollars he would buy away the dent in his reputation.

He strode to Opal Bouchard without looking up. He counted the money into her hand. One hundred, two hundred . . . four . . . five. Five hundred for a woman slave and for silence.

Then he glanced into the hallway. "Samson!"

A thin, aging negro butler appeared almost as if in a puff of voodoo.

"Boss?"

"Pack up a week's worth of traveling grub, deploy a blanket and a coat, give them to this cuffee woman, then take her out to the front drive and see that she starts walking. Stand there until you don't see her anymore. Got it?"

"I got it, Boss."

With that, Wallace turned to Yula. He no longer owned her, just in that one instant. Suddenly she was free to go.

Where?

Wallace glared at her from within the silver livery of his drying hair and his trimmed gunmetal beard, and his hands went back into the smoking jacket's pockets.

"Get on the move," he said with faint suggestion. "And if I ever see your face on Plentiful again, I'll do what I shoulda done twenty years ago."

Plain enough.

Yula nodded. She had always admired Boss for his plain talk.

★ ★ ★

THE BURNING FUSE

APRIL 1858

A proslavery constitution for Kansas Territory is drafted by the territorial legislature and is almost immediately rejected by the population of Kansas. Kansas becomes a powder keg, a microcosm of the struggle engulfing the entire nation.

★

CHAPTER THREE

————— ★ —————

1858
PLENTIFUL
TIDEWATER, VIRGINIA

"There it is, Uncle. There's home."

The hired coach protested the country road, in spite of the fact that an extra team had been added to pull it over the ruts. Rarely did a city cab venture beyond the paved or cobbled streets of Norfolk. But the gentleman had wanted a big coach, to handle all their luggage, and this was the biggest on the wharf. Big enough for eight people, but there were only two inside. Two people, and two large trunks, and more trunks on top, and crates of books and bits of antiquity making way like so much flotsam to the New World.

Alexander Wallace blinked into the bright Virginia sunlight and defied it in order to see his plantation home. They'd waddled several miles beside the wooden fence that flanked the endless tobacco fields, and he was impatient to finally see the house. Not that anything was waiting there that would give him comfort. Even if he ultimately went back to Europe, he had finally had to come home, if only to see for himself. He opened his mouth to speak, and what came out came in Greek. Odd how natural the other language had become—he had almost stumbled over English when the ship pulled in and he had to use it, really *use* it again.

"I've never felt about Plentiful as I feel now," he commented, brushing his blond bangs aside as the wind blew them into his eyes.

"And how is that?" his uncle asked.

"I'm without words."

The swarthy man on the seat across from him didn't turn much, but only leered at him from the corner of one pitch-black eye. "The last time I saw you without words, you were gawking up at the Parthenon. A good two years ago."

"Well, it's appropriate, then," Alex said. "I was thinking of him then, too."

And he looked out the coach window again, through the trees, to the mansion.

"Look at it," he murmured. "Like myself . . . only pretending to be Greek. Look at it. Statues in the garden . . . revival columns . . . it never appeared so artificial to me before. Pretending to be something and somewhere else. Hmm . . . looks rather new and garish, doesn't it? After we've been all these months basking in antiquity . . . doesn't it?"

Nick Varvaresos furrowed his black brows and didn't look. "I grew up in the fetid mud and stinking crowds of that antiquity. Streets not big enough to fit a goat cart. The smell of humans everywhere, with no place to put our sewage but outside our own doors. Even our children smelled." When Alex gave him a placating smile, he snapped, "Why do you think I was so quick to promote your grandfather's plan to infiltrate America? I was happy to leave Europe behind."

"Like so many others," Alex said appeasingly. "Everything here is new. . . . The grass seems young, the trees are bigger, the land itself has a muscle beneath it. Everything in Europe is so settled. Women attach their clotheslines to thousand-year-old ruins." He laughed suddenly and added, "I traveled to Europe and discovered what it is to be an American. Strange . . . I had so little identity before. The appearance of Alexander the Great, and the personality of a sea sponge. I wasn't really Greek. I wasn't anything but a shadow of my exceptional half brother." He touched the fabric of the carriage door with two fingers. "The only real Greek among us," he added quietly, "was Dorian."

Shocking that feelings could be so mixed . . . what he saw when he looked out the carriage window, and what he had seen when he left it two years ago. Two years in Europe, saturated by things continental, swallowed by streets ten times older than his country.

"Suppose it's only nostalgia working on me?" he wondered aloud.

"I don't know." The swarthy man's eyes turned away completely.

Alexander watched the fence go by, the broad tobacco leaves shimmering in the breeze off the hillside. Beyond the row of planted trees that created a barrier between the tobacco field and the mansion's wide lawn, he could clearly see the house now, the beautiful brick walls, the wide shutters, and the sprawling veranda with the Greek columns added the year of his parents' wedding. Scarcely older than he was.

"Imagine being nostalgic about the spanking-new United States. Lord in heaven, how I'd have snickered once. To the Europeans, *I* looked new and garish, didn't I?"

"You did. You always will."

"Look at it, Uncle Nick. . . ."

"I cannot look."

Nor did he. From the first glimpse of Plentiful's miles of wooden fence, Nick had turned his eyes inward, put his shoulder to the black quilted seat back, set his wide mouth in a line, and refused to look out the window. His normally straight spine now sagged into the curve of the carriage door, and there he huddled. His distinctive Greek profile, with the black mustache and ring of black eye lashes, and the pocks in his cheeks, all fitted flatly against the dark sheen of the quilting like a bas relief, and just as timeless. He could not look out upon Plentiful—the goal of their four-thousand-mile journey across Europe and over the sea. He settled into an irrational resentment of place and house, brick, pillar, and earth, as though these things had somehow failed to step between death and Dorian.

He would never forgive them. Hate comes cheap to a man in mourning.

And the carriage turned to the right, rumbled between the two Naxian lions that stood in endless vigil at the plantation's entrance, and started up the driveway.

A terribleness awaited them up that long curved driveway. Nick's body went stiff. Nothing in this new land or the old one could make this moment easier.

He knew, even without looking, that the welcoming party was lined up on the veranda . . . a dozen negro faces, dark spots set in clothing, and another half-dozen Greeks in their servant's gear, the foremen with their wide-brimmed hats held politely before them at about belt level, and before them all, standing a little apart, would be Lucas. The gunmetal beard and wavy hair, perhaps a bit whiter than the last time they'd seen him . . . a man who in fact had taken on character as the years took hold of him. Other than his proximity a few paces in front of the foremen and servants, he would be indistinguishable from them. He usually wore the same clothing and always the same calluses.

Nick didn't have to look. He knew by the change in Alexander's posture that the scene was exactly as he imagined it. Alex was gazing out the carriage window with a look of baffling regret upon his young face—hungry for home, sad to have come home under these circumstances. The arrival would be painful at best, for even if all of Norfolk had flocked here to stand on the veranda and greet them, it would still be an empty place.

The negroes were waving at the upcoming carriage from behind Luke Wallace's back. Alex smiled as he saw them, and he was careful not to return the wave. As the carriage drew closer, he could see some of the negroes' eyes welling up, their sad smiles puckering, and he was warmed that they thought so well of him. Oh, they looked so beautiful to him . . . there was an honesty here which he had found nowhere else in the world. The openheartedness of these people simply had no match in the world. Once loyal, they were fiercely so. Their greatest flaw was also their greatest virtue—single-mindedness. These were uncomplicated beings by nature, and that was their appeal, uncomplicated and yet Dorian had loved them, prince though he had been, and they had loved him. Had Alex grown up without Dorian's link to the slaves, he might see them today as some other members of the white landed gentry did, as tools that cleaned themselves.

They were glad to see him, to have even one of the children back. He saw that in their eyes, their expressions, yes, but they were crestfallen too, because his return meant enduring the tragedy again—perhaps even more a tragedy for the field cuffees than for the family. To them, Dorian was a reminder that perhaps it wasn't their color that kept them enslaved, for Dorian was white, or their illiteracy, for Dorian was a scholar, but instead just a trick of fate. If Dorian could be enslaved legally, then perhaps it wasn't skin or stupidity at work, but a habit of generations.

Alex began to wish the driveway could swallow the carriage before they reached the house.

The carriage shuddered as the coachman drew it up, wheels biting then settling into the crusted mud from last night's rain, and then rolled back half a foot before stopping. The impatient horses jostled and protested, having settled into their rhythm. Stopping hurt. It made them aware of their aches.

Alex stepped first from the footboard as the footman drew open the door, and a waft of sweaty hot breeze with horse smell upon it hit him full in the face. He coughed and waved as though it were a cloud of flies—but it smelled better than Europe.

The negroes were twitching. The Greek servants who had been his nurses and mentors and cooked and served his fare for the first twenty-odd years of his life were a little more controlled, but it had been a long two years with no young folk about the plantation, and likely a dark two years. Were they disappointed when only Uncle Nick stepped from the carriage behind Alex? Were they expecting the lovely face of Lydia Wallace and the plain expressions of Rose Dimitra, whose simpleheartedness matched the slaves'?

Lucas Wallace clattered down the wooden steps of the veranda and put out a hand properly to Nick Varvaresos, his wife's uncle and his own best man, his mentor and guide through the intricacies of Greekitude, and if he had to admit to owning one, his oldest friend. Then he turned to his blond-headed son, who now stood half a head taller than Luke. There was a thought behind Alex's eyes, an unspoken issue, something he didn't want to mention and probably wouldn't.

"Welcome. Welcome back to America, both of you," Luke said. "Welcome home."

All morning Alex paid polite attention to his father before he slipped away and stole down to the cabins. The negroes had apparently been waiting and keeping a watch out for him, for they were lined up at the end of the slave village just as prim and proper as any Sunday barbecue, all the women in their white turbans, and all the men in their hats and coats, just as if Alex were somebody special come a-visiting. Evidently they now thought he was.

Oh, their faces! Their eyes, mouths, cheekbones, broad brows, and pitch-black hair; skin a hundred different shades of brown, some tinted with ocher, some with rose; and dark eyes flashing at the sight of him, curly black lashes rimming a hundred gazes, and finally, finally he was able to hold out his arms and let them flood around him, grasping and hugging each one of them. The men pumped his hands and patted his back, and they babbled their joy at having him back on the farm. The women patted him and commented on how his shoulders were a little wider and his waist a little more slender. All the men smelled like tobacco or soot—wonderful!— and the women of corn and flour and chickens, and he breathed and breathed until he thought he would burst.

He was laughing with joy when something got hold of his hand and began to crush the bones and twist his arm right out of his shoulder.

"Ah—who's that?" he bellowed, the pain drawing him out of character, and he twisted with the force until he came face-to-face with it.

An enormous black man, with frost on his temples and innocence in his eye gaped at him from an inch away. Alex was suddenly crushed against a broad chest, smothered in two thick arms.

"Jeff!" he gasped, laughing. "Why, you're like to squash me!"

"Mr. Alexander . . . Lawd save me for this day, Mr. Alex. . . . We missed you, suh, sure dint have a sunny day the whole two year!"

"Oh, Jeff, don't be silly." Alex held the man at arm's length, though his hands could barely grip the huge biceps, and tried to get his breath back.

"Git back!" Jeff swatted at the crowd of slaves. "Let the mister get some air! Acting like swarmin' bees, yawl."

"That's all right," Alex drawled, winking at the rotund woman named Rowsie, who promptly winked back and giggled until her entire bulk shook.

"You women get off," Jeff insisted. "Off to fix a fine table for Mr. Alex, now. Go on!"

That cut the crowd by half, but it guaranteed that Alex would go to bed so stuffed with peach cobbler and quail that he probably would find sleep rather elusive.

Well, he thought, who wanted to sleep? Who *could* sleep?

"You boys!" Jeff called to the remaining men. "Yawl git on down to the pit and git that fire started. Gonna be dark soon, and you don't speck Mr. Alex to sit in a musty cabin and eat his cobbler, do you? Git that fire goin'."

The men laughed, threw a few pats and slaps at Alex, then rushed off to prepare their part of what would probably turn out to be a down-home evening of rhythm and boot slapping and fine fare. Alex smiled, thinking of the dark night, the dark faces, the stirring music, and his silly white face and yellow hair standing out like a firefly.

In a minute he and Jeff were standing alone, and he was waving perfunctory hellos and good-byes to the slaves and slave children who dashed this way and that, preparing the evening's feast.

Then he turned to Jeff, and the two began to walk slowly along the path behind one row of cabins.

A familiar sight all of Alex's life, Jeff was a well-spoken slave whose loyalty to the Wallace household was legendary across Tidewater. They could send Jeff out with a wagon all the way to Norfolk and depend upon him to come back, and even fight to come back if necessary. And he was big, oh, was he big.

"Has it been all right?" Alex asked by way of transition. "Is everyone all right?"

"Oh, well, suh, that old cuffee Mablene, she finally up'n died lass spring," Jeff told him. He said it softly, more so even than his usual tone of voice, which was soft for his size. He was touched by Alex's asking, for some day this young man would own them all.

Alex nodded regretfully. "Yes, we received a letter."

"And they been four new babies born in that time."

"Babies! And four of them. . . . Well, I shall have to look at those beautiful faces and pass a good judgment. You know, Jeff, I've looked at children the world over, and I've come to think there's no child so lovely at birth as a negro infant."

"Funny, but I think that too, suh. One of them is my own fust granbaby."

"Little Martha? That *Little* Martha of yours? Married?"

"Not so little anymore. She married a whole year now, nigh seventeen year old, and done had a baby tipped the scale at ten full pound, suh."

"Ten pounds! Dare I say he'll be the size of you someday, Jeff."

"I hope not, suh. She be a funny-lookin' lady at my size!" the big man laughed. "Named her Ginny after your fine mother, Mr. Alex," he added.

Alex cast him a look that he hoped gave off the gratitude and flattery of such a gesture, and made a mental note to mention the new baby in his letter to his mother in Greece.

"Who'd your daughter marry?"

"She caught eye with Mr. Tuggle's footman when he come visiting. After a while, Boss up'n bought him, and put the two of 'em to work as house slaves so they could be together. You know, suh, your daddy, he a hard man sometimes, but sometimes he can be right good-hearted."

With a roll of his eye at the irony of it, Alex fought against the grumbling in his heart and managed to say, "I suppose."

But the subject wouldn't go away; it had been aching and pushing at his chest since he set foot on the boat in Athens. He didn't look up, but fixed his gaze on the ground before them as they trod along behind the cabins.

"How did it happen, Jeff? And was there . . . much suffering for him?"

Jeff wobbled his big head from side to side and involved himself with the ground as they strode along. "Happened at night, suh. Dint none of us know about it till clean into the next day. You know how Dohrian used to . . . he called it "declined" . . . to go out after the day's work was done and before the sun all the way set, and he'd sit and read?"

"*In*clined."

"Oh, yeah, that was it. Mr. McCrocklin found him out there . . . just a couple foot from where a cottonmouth snuck up and took him by the back of the leg. We figured maybe he took a step onto its tail and it come up on him."

Jeff hesitated, feeling Alex stiffen, but there was no real

new information here, and nothing Alex wasn't expecting. He took a deep breath and forced out the rest.

"Them black snakes, them'll come after you, suh. I see'm chase a person before. Mr. McCrocklin, he said Dohrian killt that snake, killt it good. Broke its neck—if a snake got a neck. And they brought back the snake, hangin' from a big stick, to prove it to Boss."

"You saw it?"

"Oh, yeah . . . yeah, it was big, suh. Big round as my wrist. Big snake. Dohrian and that snake . . . they died together out there, Mr. Alex. . . . He killt it with his own bare hands." He turned to Alex and added, "Don't that sound like Dohrian?"

Alex managed a weak grin.

"Boss, he put Dohrian right in the parlor, and he shut the door and wunt let nobody come in," Jeff said. "Mr. Alex, I swear it were like he all of a sudden accepted Dohrian as one of the family. Like he all of a sudden knowed what Dohrian meant to yawl and all of us. He put up two big candles on the outside of the door, and he lit them candles hisself, and he kept 'em lit for a whole day and a whole night while the coffin was bein' builded. And you know, suh . . . he called in the minister from Norfolk."

Alex looked up. "He did? The white minister?"

Jeff returned an exaggerated nod. "The white minister, and it was a fine, fine service. Good as any. And Boss called off work for the next two days. Why, it was like he up'n accepted Dorian for his own son, just like he shoulda twenty years past."

"Yes," Alex said, though his voice failed him. "He should have."

"Well, suh . . . sometime we don't know what we got till it fall through a hole and we can't have it no more. How's your mama, suh? She take it bad?"

"Oh, yes. Yes. She took it very poorly, Jeff. It struck her down to her bed for days on end. Such a blow—she may never return to America. If she ever does come back, it'll only be because of her sense of duty as mistress of this plantation."

"That be a sad thing, suh, if she don't. We all love that lady, Mr. Alex. Any ten of us walk over coals for that lady."

"I know you would. Sometimes I'm baffled that a man like

my father managed to gather such a loving and loyal family of cuffees to serve him and his own."

"Partly because he let us do our job, suh. He trust us. We 'preciate that. Good half of us know what it like to work on a worse plantation. Or, Lawd help 'em, in them factories in the cities. Believe me, Mr. Alex, we teach our children how good they live compared to the common nigger. On Plentiful we won't starve, and won't die too young."

"Jeff," Alex began, lowering his voice, "has there been any sign of Yula?"

"She disappear, you know, after Dohrian went to his reward," Jeff said, "but then, 'bout a year ago, she got brought back here by a white woman and a white man one rainy night. You know, we was all afraid she'd come on some hard white man in some awful place, but there's no stopping a slave who just don't wanna live in a place anymore . . . not really, suh." Jeff lowered his voice too and gave Alex a sidelong glance. "Anyway, when these whites brung Yula back, Boss bought her freedom and sent her north."

"Then Yula didn't run off," Alex said. "Father lied to us. I had a feeling!"

"Now, Mr. Alex, we don't know the story of the white folks who brung her back here. Maybe that white woman was a slaver, you know, one of them who catch niggers no matter what papers they got, and just sell 'em again."

"She wouldn't have brought Yula back here, Jeff, if she was one of those."

"No, I s'pose not. . . . Sure are plenty of them types around these days, though. I'm skeered to go off Plentiful hunting or fishing, case somebody grab me and sell me off someplace else."

"No sign of Burlie from these people?"

"Not a peep about the little boy."

"And none of you managed to talk to Yula before she left? Not even one of the house slaves?"

"Nary a one of us. What I think is Yula just didn't wanna live here after that night . . . when we put Dohrian in the ground. That was a hell night for us all. Still nary a Sabbath Day go by that Dohrian doesn't get mentioned in the traveling preacher's sermon, 'cuz he know how we feel."

"Did you . . . see Dorian?"

"Oh, no, suh, Boss didn't feel right putting him on the slab for us to walk by. He said Dohrian . . . dint look too good, and better we remember the strappin' man. . . . But I think there was something else."

"What else? What do you mean?"

"I think he felt bad that yawl couldn't see Dohrian laid out, you and your mama and your sisters and Mr. Nick. I think he dint feel it was right for the cuffees to see him when the family couldn't, you know? I think he felt right guilty about the whole thing, suh. He just sat in that room with . . . well, he sat in there all alone, thinkin' and thinkin' for the longest time."

"He did?" Alex skewered his brow and tried to imagine that. "Perhaps I've misjudged him. . . . "

Jeff's big eyes rolled.

"Oh, yes, suh. I've seen your daddy come round on things before. Like he come round on me. You remember, he bothered to buy my whole family so I wouldn't have to walk twelve mile every Sunday."

"Yes, I recall that day very well. But Jeff, we're discussing a man who branded the arm of his own offspring."

"Oh, sure, but that were in a different time, Mr. Alex. Boss, he's more settled now. Took Boss twenty year longer to grow up than most folks, is all. He fretted and smoked over writing a letter to you and your mama over in Greekland, a good two weeks before he got one he wanted to send off. I know, 'cuz I drove that letter to the ship my very own self. Had to stand waiting twenty minutes before he'd actually turn loose of it and let me get going. I think he was plum good and sorry about what he did to Dohrian. Anyway, that's what I *think*."

"And you know Boss rather well, don't you, Jeff?"

"Since a year and a half before the Greeks come."

"Yes."

They strolled together down the ragged path behind the cabins, pausing now and then for Alex to greet one of the other slaves—everyone seemed so happy. He had trouble associating himself with that happiness, considering his mood as Plentiful had drawn closer and closer. What did they see in his face? Paleness, probably. Compared to them, even with the sunburn that had come upon his fair cheeks at sea. His father was a stiff man, but not a cruel slave owner by any definition. That his own presence should bring such joy to them, Alex couldn't fathom. And yet, their presence brought a joy to his heart—and an actual physical relief in being among them once again.

He and Jeff walked in relative silence now, as they crested the top of the incline and looked down into the . . . well, no one had ever called it anything more than "the down-there."

Down there was the slave cemetery.

Alex paused—but not for himself. Nick was down there.

"Oh, dear father in heaven, I should have guessed," Alex murmured as he saw his uncle's form, kneeling at the side of a grave that looked painfully old and weathered. Why wasn't it a new grave? Could rain and wind make the earth forget? But Dorian had died, it seemed, only last week, the letter had come only yesterday. . . . It was all new to Alex and to Nick, who had been deprived the emotional bridges of seeing Dorian's body and standing through the funeral, and throwing their handfuls of dirt upon the coffin. Dorian had been dead for months before the letter even got to Macedon. So he hadn't seemed fully gone until now.

And there was Nick, his back to Alex, his shoulders shaking, his body weaving slightly from side to side as the agony surged through his muscles and veins. They had mourned in Greece, and now they would mourn in Tidewater.

Alex started down the incline, and only after ten steps or so did he notice that Jeff hadn't come down with him. He paused, turned, and looked back up at the enormous negro. Jeff's handsome squarish features were mild with sympathy.

"We had our time, Mr. Alex," Jeff said. "You go on ahead."

Alex felt an inappropriate smile tugging at the side of his mouth, and hoped it didn't look too flippant. Softly he said, "Thank you, Jeff."

The hill was wet from dew even now, for it was in the shade of a matched set of giant magnolias and a holly. The sun might not touch it until nearly sunset.

As he thought of that, he also felt the sunlight leave his blond curls as he shuffled down the hill into the shade. Yes, he felt it leave—he felt himself walk out of it. It was all he could do to ignore the symbolism, which would have given Dorian an afternoon's worth of philosophy, and concentrate on Nick.

Nick was on his knees, his dark head bent forward, his

pocked face reddened, his body bowed with sobbing. Alex recognized the demonstrative habit immediately; he'd seen it at the funeral of a cousin in Greece. The louder the wailing, the more crippling the sobs, the deeper the apparent love for the deceased. Sometimes it was genuine, even if the mourner hadn't spoken to the dead for years. But even though he had been raised among the emotional Greeks, this kind of demonstration had always seemed a little embarrassing.

Dorian, Dorian, everything was Dorian. Everything was the impassive, logical philosopher to whom all things were worth studying, the young man pulsing with sense and sensibilities, who never had one emotion at a time.

Alex moved quietly behind Nick, but when he slid his hand onto Nick's quivering shoulder, there was no jolt of surprise. Nick had either expected him, heard him coming, or *felt* him coming.

They had both known this moment would arrive. Both feared it.

Nick remained on his knees, a mourning European, and Alex stood there beside him, a stoically mourning American. Nick's hands wrung and twisted between his knees. Alex battled with the grief welling in his chest, determined that it would not show itself. It pushed at his throat from below like a tangible thing, and pushed at his eyes from behind. For a moment, as he fixed his gaze on the headstone, he thought he might burst.

D O R I A N. 1833 to 1856.

Oh, God, God.

A snake.

A little-brained reptile, sneaking in the dirt.

He felt it, writhing in his stomach, and wanted to stab himself. God! The sensation was overpowering! Self-recrimination knotted itself inside him. Perhaps if he hadn't gone to Greece, Dorian might have been playing a game of Mansions with him and not reading in a field, where a snake lay in wait.

Now I shall have to kill every snake on Plentiful, just to be fair.

Later the real grief hit him.

When he was alone and his daycoat was off, and his shirtsleeves were uncovered, the candles were dimming and the household was quiet, the grief came. His throat tightened up so that he couldn't have responded to the slightest greeting. Not even so much as a nod.

He sat alone at the kitchen table, his legs chilled as the cold from the stone floor filtered through his boots and into his bones. He wasn't inclined to drinking, but the bottle in front of him was half-empty now, and he hadn't precisely enjoyed the bitter, pungent taste, and it was only wine. He couldn't stomach brandy, never had been able to, or whiskey.

That's what he had wanted when he got the bottle from the cellar. Not to enjoy it.

The kitchen was a comfort. Cool. Low-slung, low-ceilinged stone. It was negro. It was Greek.

It was Dorian.

It was Yula.

Yula was gone, Burlie was gone, all traces of Dorian, gone.

For a while, Alex shuffled his feet on the stone floor. Cold feet, cold stone. Gradually this slowed down and stopped, and his legs began to grow numb from lack of movement. He had for a while tilted the bottle back and forth, his eyes fixed on the colorless liquid shifting inside this way, that way, and he played a game with the wine to see how far he could tip the bottle without actually spilling any.

Poor Nick, poor Uncle Nick. The first night home would be the worst.

Alex was pretty sure Nick was someplace in the house in no better condition, though with Nick it would take a bottle and a half instead of half a bottle.

Another hour passed, and the tilting of the bottle stopped. Alex just sat there with his entire right arm spread on the tabletop and the edge of the table pressed into his armpit, and felt his eyes get hollow.

Misery gripped and paralyzed him, chopping most thoughts in half. He had seen a wrong and let Dorian talk him out of righting it. Any gentleman of true honor would never have yielded to leaving things as they were, when those things were obviously a mistake. Alex knew his honor must not be true, then, and he must strive to make it true. Somehow or another.

That's what had finally dragged him back to America before his college education was complete.

As he gazed through grief-fogged eyes at the wide stone fireplace and the hanging iron pots and utensils, he gathered a series of memories that made him believe Dorian had engineered the trip to Greece.

Yes, it must be. In the whirl of those days, Alex hadn't put that together, though now he decided that plain coincidence wasn't enough to spur Iphigenia's sudden decision to go to Europe on the very same day Alex had voiced an abolitionist intent to Dorian.

Coincidence. Alex sniffed bitterly. Nothing was coincidence where Dorian was concerned. Why hadn't he realized that?

Dorian had been the seed and had thus sealed his own fate by making sure that Alex wasn't in the United States when the snake came.

Must be getting late. His brain was going numb.

It was in this unmoving, bone-soldering quietude that something came into his eyes when the lamplight flickered . . . something that hadn't been there thirty seconds before. A thought brought on only by the unique condition of grief . . . only the void of pure misery could allow such a flicker in a civilized man's eye. Only grief could make a son think something like this.

Something ugly and inconceivable.

Something . . . about his father and Dorian.

Terrible rain slashed at Plentiful. Thunder growled overhead. The tobacco fields moved like ocean waves in a hurricane, the wide silver undersides of the leaves flashing in unison. Next few days, they'd be topped off, a prelude to harvesting, drying, and smokehousing. He knew the pattern as he knew his own breathing.

All the slaves were asleep in their beds as the seasonal rains fell around them.

In the library Luke Wallace was just finishing a late-night glance at the Norfolk newspaper. Not much worth reading. Trouble with a miners' strike somewhere. More talk of war, always. Who wanted it, who didn't, why it was inevitable, why it wasn't. Same story, for a good thirty years. Ever since he'd started thinking about changing jobs.

The double doors crashed open. *Bam! Bam!*

Wallace jumped, and nearly fell backward from shock. He looked up just in time to see a muddy shovel thump onto the expensive Oriental carpet. Bits of wet dirt flew all over the piano.

An instant later the heavy, rotting carcass of a goat landed on top of the shovel. The *whump* shook the whole room.

Wallace sucked in his breath and drew his hands to his chest in shock.

Hardly more than a skeleton, the big carcass was eaten through by insects, some of which still clung to the undersides of the rib cage and the holes in the skull. The legs clung to the rest of it only by dry strings of sinew. Only the horns and hooves were undecayed, no sign of having lain in the cold ground for better than a year.

Wallace held that breath. His first thought was he hadn't expected to see that goat again. And what would the slaves think of him when they found the grave dug up and the coffin empty? Funny, he thought he'd covered all the possibilities.

A figure stood solidly in the doorway of his library, silhouetted against the foyer candlelight—had the form been less lean and slightly shorter, it could have been Dorian. Just for an instant he thought it was. Haunting him.

Alex's linen sleeves were rolled up. His legs were muddy well past the top of his boots, and his chest heaved. His face glistened with rain and sweat. Rain had taken most of the curl out of his sopping hair, the lines of effort made his soft face more like a native mask.

"You miscalculating fiend," he began.

Wallace said and did nothing as his heir stumbled into the room, past the grotesque carcass, and plunged to the desk.

Alex leaned forward, both hands planted on the desk, shoulders hunched. His words roared out.

"What have you done with my brother?"

CHAPTER FOUR

───────── ★ ─────────

14 May 1858

Dearest Mother,

> *I write to you from America with some very disturbing news regarding your adopted son, my half brother Dorian, and I hope with all my heart that you are sitting down . . .*

Dorian.

His name, his face, the flash of his cordovan eyes haunted her all the way to Greece, and all these enduring months. The journey was intended only to be an extended visit, a few months in Macedon. But she hadn't possessed the courage or will to return to Tidewater, where her adopted son was buried, and now she had been here nearly two years.

Adopted . . . in name only. In all other ways, he had always been more hers than her own children, than the children she bore from her body, for he was the true child of her *heart*.

Iphigenia Trözene Wallace sat in the garden of her father's ancient gabled house outside Salonika, with all the smells of Macedon around her, the smells of antiquity. Fresh-baked *koulouria* cooling on a bench, goats, sheep, turkeys fussing nearby, barrels smelling of the live fish stored in them.

She raised her own dark eyes from Alex's handwriting and waited for them to clear. What a strange sequence of events had brought her to this juncture. She had been part of her father's plan to pay off an old score in Greek currency, to rebuild the Greek culture after throwing off Turkish oppression. Dimitrios Trözene and his peers had been proud that the Turks

50

had failed to crush their culture, but other than the classical trappings, there was little left in the bankrupt economy of Greece. They'd even had to import a royal family.

So there was this connection . . . this deal . . . with the American tobacconist Lucas Wallace of Tidewater, Virginia. Wallace had turned his fifth profit crop in a row and still garnered criticism from other planters because he ran Plentiful as a business and not a prison camp. None of his slaves bore the mark of the whip. None from Plentiful, anyway. The Wallace colored were forbidden from visiting other plantations for risk they'd spread tales of treatment so decent it was considered indecent. Tales of slaves raising their own crops for food and profit, of new clothing twice a year, of families kept together, of a little slave community with its own contained society, and of brick slave cabins with wood floors. Wallace set a bad example, so said his Tidewater peers . . . but his yield said otherwise.

Still, they wouldn't let their daughters marry him. He was middle-aged at the time, and he was a former dockworker. He wasn't of the Virginia bluebloods.

So the scheme was launched. Through Nick Varvaresos, to Luke Wallace, to Dimitrios Trözene, heedless of the ocean in between. Dimitrios knew he had stumbled upon God's plan for Greece—a Greek renaissance in the New World, where it would flourish.

"Greek civilization has existed since the beginning of recorded time," her father had said to her on the night he told her of his plot. "It will exist always. We shall see to that, you and I."

And so his eldest daughter Iphigenia was to become a mail-order bride.

They made her a wedding dress of blinding ivory flounces, a headdress of flowers and veils, and a dowery of golden coins to wear on her aprons; they painted a tiny blue cross on her forehead, and off she and her entourage went, on a ship to America. They were going to become immigrants and have American children.

She'd met Lucas Wallace and married him in the course of three short days. A grand affair, that wedding. Met him, married him . . . and gotten his child.

Yula's child. The child of a slave raped by Iphigenia's husband, born just before her wedding day.

Dorian.

Her capricious, brilliant boy. Hers and Yula's. Yula had spent her days in the tobacco fields and every morning brought the baby to Iphigenia. While the other slave children were being tended by elder slaves, Dorian was being raised by the Greek wife and her people. Every sunset Yula would cart him back to the cabins, where he would become a negro child again, never mind his beautiful olive-rose complexion, which took no tan even under the Virginia sun. No matter that his cheeks were like rose petals dusted with maple sugar and stood out brightly against Yula's raisin-brown breast.

Iphigenia sighed warmly, and even smiled. Dorian had thrived on this chameleon life. What a child he had been. . . .

A child so quick to figure things out that he was nearly impossible to entertain. A child who had taken his first step during a line dance, and at the same time began turning his hands in the air to the rhythm of the mandolin. It was Iphigenia whose loving eyes had gazed at him in the bright of day, she who had nuzzled the wriggling baby. He was her confection, his skin her sugar, his hair her twists of licorice, and it was she to whom he had given his first kisses. His first word had been *bird*—but it came out in Greek. *Pouli.* His second had been *glyko,* to get a sip of Iphigenia's sweetened coffee.

His third had been *nigga,* because Yula was his mother too.

But that was years ago, decades. Years during which Iphigenia had never stood up to her husband's rule that the bitchborn boy never be allowed off the plantation grounds. She had been a perfect Southern wife for him, and a perfect Greek daughter for her father, and said nothing about it, in return for keeping the boy in spite of Lucas's hatred of the child.

Her only solace had been in Dorian himself, who was so very Greek, and so passionate about it.

And without a drop of Greek blood in his body. She had poured her homesickness into him. Even after the birth of her own son, a blond boy, Dorian was her only truly Greek child. Four more pregnancies had followed in six years. The one after Alex ended in a miscarriage that had nearly killed Iphigenia. The second and third resulted in healthy daughters. The fourth was another disaster, and ruined her ability to bear any more children. Never for a moment did her love for Dorian flag, even in light of her own children.

If anything, her devotion to him had been enhanced by the situation. Her miscarriages had frightened her. What would become of him if she died?

Years and years, living like that.

Dorian had been a young man when he died, not her baby any longer.

She blinked her eyes hard, and they began to clear, though slowly.

Ultimately she looked down at Alexander's letter and continued reading.

> *We find ourselves at a turning point. I am ashamed to tell you that my father, your husband, conspired to murder Dorian on that night so long ago when you and I departed for Macedon. There are no human remains in the grave that bears Dorian's headstone. In great joy and anticipation, I am telling you that Dorian apparently did not die of snake venom, and that there exists a good possibility that Dorian is not dead, but alive.*
>
> *Mother, I cannot perceive your thoughts, nor shall I presume to judge your husband in your stead. Rather I shall attempt to seek out my brother, no matter the time or price, and amend my father's injustice to him.*
>
> *At every turn, I shall keep you informed of my progress or failure.*
>
> *Your loving and obedient son,*
> *Alexander Wallace, Esquire*

The sun glowed hungrily over Macedon's alabaster towns just before it set.

It was in that angled sunlight that Dimitrios Trözene found his eldest daughter collapsed senseless in the garden where she had been reading her mail.

He found her, and as she moaned and touched her brow, he read the letter crumpled in her hand.

Dimitrios Trözene set his dazed daughter on the marble bench in his garden and waved a lilac stalk beneath her nose until she roused.

As she blinked her eyes, he was sitting beside her, crying. Tears dripped onto his silver beard. His face was flushed with joy.

"Dorian . . . ," he murmured, "alive . . . " He vaulted to his feet and shook the letter into the sunset. "We should know he would live through anything, that boy! Anything!" He shook the letter at Iphigenia and brought his thick brows together. "I was right to send you to America! I was *right*. No power can hold Americans by force. America was the last open land on earth—other Europeans were idiots to try to conquer America! Ridiculous—any dog with an army can conquer. But to build—people must be held by the heart, by their passions! The Spanish were kicked out, the English, the French, the Portuguese, no one can leash the young stag! And now America has thrown death out! I was right, by the God and gods, I sent you to marry an American and begin a new Greece. From Hudson's Bay to the Oregon Trail, it was that get-it-done spirit I wanted for my grandchildren, and now it is coming true. Dorian is still *alive*!"

Iphigenia drew a deep, steadying breath, wiped her moist palms on her linen skirt, and blinked. "Papa," she said calmly, "you are ranting again."

"Ranting," he huffed. "This is how you speak to your father."

But he flopped his arms to his sides and lumbered to sit beside her on the cool marble.

"Do you understand what this means?" she asked him.

He shrugged. "Means Dorian is not dead after all. What else should it mean?"

"It means," she began slowly, "that Lucas tried to . . . murder my boy . . . my Dorian." Her eyes welled up. A tiny sob escaped her lips. "Oh, Papa, why couldn't Lucas be proud of his son? In spite of everything, Dorian's spirit was indomitable. His stamina was bottomless . . . why couldn't Lucas be proud? Our own children are industrious, yes, but none of them were as inventive as Dorian . . . among the four of them, his leadership came to the surface so quickly when they were little . . . and he *looked* like us—"

Another short sob cut her off.

Dimitrios gazed at his daughter. For the first time he noticed the threads of gray among the sable of her hair. When she talked of "children," it was Iphigenia and her sisters Dimitrios thought about.

He saw little Dorian in his mind, a boy of rugged mythological handsomeness, a mixture of a white father and slave mother. Iphigenia's natural children were good-looking replicas of her, though fairer-haired, but none looked as Greek as the boy who was not Greek at all. Iphigenia had told Dimitrios how the slave woman Yula always made sure Dorian did more than his share of slave work, to make sure he was valuable in the yard, but somehow everyone knew Dorian couldn't be kept a slave forever. They knew he would look outward.

But no one had any idea he would be pushed out by his own father's attempt to have him killed, pushed into the big world by Luke Wallace's insecure fears.

"Lucas isn't a bad man," Dimitrios said thoughtfully. "He does extreme things to get what he wants."

Iphigenia shook her head. "How can I go back to him now? Be a wife to him now?"

Dimitrios took her hand in his big one and shifted his large body sideways on the bench.

"Listen to me," he said. "You'll go back to him. You'll go back, because you are Macedonian. You are strong, and you never forget. We never forget, we Macedonians. Our suffering is underneath our survival as a race, but we always remember first that we survived, not that we suffered. When we were fighting for our independence from the Turks, we set siege to a group of them who were hiding in the Acropolis. I myself shot bullets between the stone columns. *I* shot into the Acropolis! You see, I took the risk for the stone. When my bullets struck the stone, it was my heart being struck." He put his hands on his chest and thumped his heart. "I was shooting at myself. The Turks shot back, of course, and it went like that for a while . . . until the Turks ran out of bullets."

Iphigenia pressed her dry lips together.

"A tragedy," Dimitrios went on. He gazed outward, looked back over the years to a land streaked by lava and pumice, a place scorched by the Mediterranean sun. "These Turks began dismantling the great columns stone by stone. They were taking out the metal skeleton. They were going to make bullets. We saw what was happening, and this horrified us . . . for one battle, down was coming the majesty of Greece. The Acropolis. It had stood for ages, and now they were picking it down." He turned to her again and looked squarely into her eyes. "We sent a letter up the mountain to the Turks and their unrespectful brains." He knocked his own head with a knuckle. "'If you need lead,' we told them, 'we, your enemies, will send you some.' And we did."

He squeezed her hand and looked at her.

"That," he went on, "is what it means to be Greek, Iphigenia, my child. You will be your husband's wife, no matter his crime, because you owe it to the stone. We all do. We owe everything to what has been built before us, to make sure it doesn't get pulled down. You . . . me . . . even Dorian, who is Greek in his heart . . . we are in the stone. Macedon, Thessaly, Cyprus, Crete, Thrace, Epirus . . ."

His eyes turned upward to the pantheon of history, and his voice dropped away.

Thinner than the mist, he whispered, "We are in the stone."

She stood up slowly. Her legs were still weak from the shock of that letter, and the fear of more letters to come. She moved a few steps away and did not turn to face her father as she spoke.

"War is coming in America, Papa," she said. "Your plan might have worked once . . . this idea of a new Greece . . . but my children will not be Greek. They are American. You see it in Alex, don't you? In Lydia, in Rose Dimitra? When Greek people travel to America, they don't stay Greek. The same with Irish . . . German . . . Slavics . . . they don't stay. They turn into something new. Americans. When war comes, it will stir the pot. War in America won't be like war anywhere else, where Greeks fight Turks, or Spaniards fight English, or Muslims fight Christians. Americans don't fight by bloodlines. They don't fight to put some above others. They fight by philosophy. You don't tell one army from another by the color of their mustaches, Papa—not in America. America is new and strong and . . . very dangerous. Nobody knows what will happen or what it will cost, or where it will scatter my children. . . ."

She bit her lip, but there was no covering the anticipation, the fear in her mind that came from knowing her adopted culture so well.

"When Americans rise," she said, "they rise defiant."

PART TWO

--- ★ ---

1858–1859
THE RICE
COAST

O, Sinner Man, where you gonna run to?

—Traditional Slave Song

★★★

THE BURNING FUSE

AUGUST 1858

A little-known one-term representative challenges the nationally known incumbent Senator Stephen Douglas. Debates between the incumbent and the challenger emphasize issues currently dividing the nation. Douglas wins the election, but challenger Abraham Lincoln emerges as a powerful spokesman on the subjects of antislavery and unity of national identity and philosophy.

★

CHAPTER FIVE

————— ★ —————

22 August 1858

My dear Mother,
Father was quite surprised at our discovery of his secret regarding Dorian. However, he exhibited no outward remorse, and apparently he believes his actions were justifiable. Considering his mind, I elected not to pursue the ethics of his action. He has given us the name of the slave broker to whom Dorian was given, a man named O'Roy out of Murfree's Boro.

Father informed us that O'Roy's orders were to dispatch of Dorian. I suppose that translates into killing him.

I regret raising your hopes, on the assumption that this man fulfilled his bargain with Father. Rest assured we shall find him and wring the truth out of him. Should anything befall us, you at least will have that name to use as a lead.

Uncle Nick and I are off to track this man O'Roy to the utmost and find out the fate of my brother.

Rest easy if you do not hear from us for a few weeks.

> *Your humble servant and son,*
> *Alexander*

13 September 1858

   Dearest Mother,

   I apologize for my late communication, but we discovered that O'Roy is a vagabond slave broker and there was little sign of him in Murfree's Boro. After many days of fruitless questions, it occurred to Uncle Nick that we employ the universal language of notes and coins, which immediately drew the attention of O'Roy's breed.

   It would never have occurred to me to place a bribe, and therefore I am gratified that Nick returned to America with me. Without him I would be flopping this way and that like a grounded fish, I think.

   Did I mention Roanoke?

   Our clues suggest that we deviate northwest to that town. Thus I shall write to you when I arrive, considering whether they have heard of mail in Roanoke.

   Nick sends his regards to all there.

                             Your son in heart and mind,
                             Alex

8 December 1858

   My dearest Mother,

   It is my great joy to tell you that good news is following.

   Of course, I have no idea how promptly these many letters will find their way to Greece, or even in what order. Thus I shall hope for the best. At any rate, we found O'Roy.

   You always warned me to stay away from such men, and I always have, but I must confess a certain morbid curiosity about people who never change their underclothes. It strikes me that such poor personal habits must bring on itching after a time, and act as rather a buffer against intimate relationships.

   In any case, the man had information. Luckily Dorian is hard to forget.

   I should have known that Dorian would never submit

to death by brokerage. He is a tougher nut to crack than that. I predict that he is still alive and well. If he survived Father's scheme, certainly he can survive other unforeseen hardships. Indeed, the hardships probably never saw him coming. Dorian has a bit of the snake in him, you know.

Thus Nick and I are embarking on the extended journey southeastward to South Carolina, to a plantation on the Great Pee Dee River, where this man apparently sold Dorian.

This plantation, should you have need of the name, is called Chapel Hill or Chapel Crown. There O'Roy's memory crippled.

Mother, I am plagued nightly with thoughts of Dorian in chains. Though legally a bonded man on Plentiful, never in his life had he felt gyves upon his ankles or wrists. Such thoughts torture me. As I imagine irons upon my brother's wrists, I cannot help shivering. How can we as civilized men place irons on limbs so like our own? Though in my rational mind I know we Americans did not start slavery, that indeed we are the tail of a long line of slave owners from the most primitive of times, I am coming to believe we may have carried on the wrong tradition.

I pray Dorian and all bondsmen and their issue will someday come to forgive us.

With luck and the will of the Almighty, this mystery shall end and I shall have my brother beside me once again.

In the meantime, something drives me to change underclothes before we set off in the morning.

Then, on to South Carolina.

> Our deepest regards and hopes,
> Alexander

CHAPTER SIX

——— ★ ———

Two and a half years earlier . . . 1856 . . .

It was hot here—damned hot. At first he thought the heat came from fever in his beaten body, but no. Now that he felt the breeze, he could tell the heat was in the air itself as it moved past him. Scorching, damp heat, even this early in May.

And the air smelled different! Where was the constant smoky aroma of tobacco leaves? He'd never smelled air that wasn't permeated with it—how strange and how perfumed! The jessamine and lilac fragrances were pure here! He hadn't realized the outside world would actually smell new!

It was a thoroughly different world. For Dorian the differences were intoxicating, because they weren't confined within the pages of a book or the past-tense tales of other slaves. They were here, within easy reach of his own eyes. Everything smelled damp instead of smoky. The trees were different, deep-swinging willows and oaks dripping with Spanish moss. There were no open fields of broad green leaves, no sense of the tropical here. He heard the gabble-gabble of wild turkeys, and even caught a glimpse of deer once. The fields were different . . . the sky a different blue . . . and a wide blue-green river on whose waters swam big white swans and geese—which river?

——— ★ ———

"Your name is Sutton now. It is a proud and historic establishment to which you now belong. Forget wherever you've been before. You will never see it again. Life outside these grounds is over for you. Empty your minds completely. There is only

one thing you need to keep in your mind at all times, and that is this: we kill rebellious slaves here by roasting them on a spit over an open flame."

CHAPEL MOUNT RICE PLANTATION
FEBRUARY 1859

"Afternoon, sirs. Ain't usual we get travelers come by this way. Might I be of some help?"

Alex and Nick looked down from their horses at a scruffy white man who was dressed like a farmhand, except that he wore a bow tie. Probably a foreman or headman. He looked like an angel to two fellows who had been traveling for nineteen hours straight and gotten lost twice at the cost of almost ten miles. Saddle sore and stiff, Alex lumbered off his tired horse and hit the ground one foot at a time. Behind him Nick gave a grunt as he too struggled to remember how to walk.

Alex winced and put out a hand to the white man, deliberately not looking beyond to the enormous two-fronted stone mansion. The least he could do, tired or not, was look the man in the eyes.

"My name is Alexander Wallace. This gentleman is my uncle, Mr. Varvaresos."

"Oh, my pleasure, Mr. Wallace . . . Mr.—uh . . ."

"Varvaresos," Nick supplied with an unsurprised grin. He took the man's hand. Gritty.

"I'm Jasper. Welcome to Chapel Mount."

Alex choked back a remark and managed a stiff, "Thank you." Emotions shook through him. Dorian was here somewhere. Dorian was here somewhere, being abused. Or Dorian *wasn't* here. Maybe Dorian had never been here. Or Dorian was here, but hidden . . . or Dorian had been sold . . . Dorian had been killed.

And every thought, no matter which one, gave him a shudder. He hoped only Nick could see that.

No reason to wait. Amenities seemed annoying right now.

Alex stepped toward the man.

"Sir, we're searching for—"

He stopped. Because he was being interrupted.

A horse walked past them. No rider, no bridle, just a horse walking by. All three men paused, for the little mare passed them as though she were a gentle caretaker of the plantation.

The mare was all feminine, round eyes, round haunches, the lovely lines of her body offering no mistake about her sex. She was plainly a girl, a lady. Long gray lashes batted over her chestnut-sized eyes as she turned her head to look at them. What a pretty mare she was, and intelligent of face and of manner. She hadn't a skittish twitch in her whole body.

"Bombay, you git on back to your paddock," Jasper said, just as though talking to a child.

If only children would be so well behaved. The round-eyed mare glanced at them, blinked her long lashes, almost nodded, and moseyed on her way.

"Sorry," Jasper said. "That's Bombay. She's kinda special hereabouts, and she gets the run of the place. You were saying?"

"Hm?" Alex inhaled to clear his tired mind. "Oh yes . . . we're looking for a man. A wrongfully bonded man who came to you as a slave, brokered by Seamus O'Roy out of Norfolk."

He drove down a shiver, and waited.

Jasper rubbed his chin. "Sir, we ain't had a new slave in some time on Chapel Mount."

"This would've been some two years past."

"Two years?"

"Yes. A slave named . . . Dorian."

"Dorian, Dorian." Jasper contemplated the grass, then shook his head. "Nope."

Alex pursed his lips. This was taking too long. "All right," he said. "We're discussing a half-breed man with skin the color of mine and eyes the color of coffee and black hair, a man with the ability to melt into negroes as though one of them, yet speak like a king at will."

Jasper's face suddenly lost color. His eyes changed.

In a funny low voice, he said, "Oh. Oh . . . oh. Hmm . . . Did you say your name was Wallace?"

"Yes, I did."

"Uh-huh . . . yeah. Hm."

His face regained its color, then plunged fully into a flush of discomfort as he added two and two. Wallace . . .

"Noah!"

All three men turned toward the call. It came from the wide front porch.

There was a face there . . . a man's narrow face, unshaven, high-browed, with a fierce edge. The voice carried a practiced pitch. The man, thin as dried herb, brown-haired, and rather knightly, sat in a tall rocking chair and knew how to speak over distances. He glared at them from the porch.

Jasper waved immediately. "Yessir, Reverend. Be right there," he called. "Pardon me, gentlemen."

He left them and strode to the porch, and spoke momentarily to the gaunt old man.

Alex glanced at Nick. They were on the edge of getting their answer, and were not about to be set back, so they paused only a moment before following Jasper to the porch.

"No, sir, they're just passing by," Jasper was telling the thin man in the chair.

The reverend's eyes snapped from him to Alex and Nick. Only then did Jasper realize they had followed him.

"Oh . . . gentlemen . . . may I name the Reverend Sutton to you . . . Reverend, over yar is Mr. Wallace and Mr. Var— uh—"

"Varvaresos," Nick supplied again patiently.

The old man's eyes—flaming blue eyes that glared unsettlingly—rolled to them, focused with some effort, and blinked a few times.

The Reverend said, "You are welcome to dine with us. However, I must give you the news that my daughter is no longer accepting gentleman callers. I have the pleasure of announcing that she will be joined in holy wedlock to a young man from the next farm. I shall not be able to join you for dinner, as I must deliver a sermon this evening at the revival." He turned those ambulatory eyes to Jasper. "However, my son Noah here, he does a fine job of operating the plantation and shall of course one day be its master. He shall serve as your host in good order, I am quite certain."

Jasper shifted to one side of the rocking chair, out of the reverend's view, looked squarely at Alex and Nick, and warned them with a roll of his eyes.

Alex managed not to nod at Jasper, but spoke to the old man instead. "Thank you, Reverend. My congratulations on your daughter's engagement."

"Praise the Lord."

"Yes, of course."

Jasper nodded and waved them off the porch. Behind them the old man's eyes settled again on Chapel Mount's open lawn and the river bank beyond, and he began waving and nodding at the grass.

At a safe distance, Alex murmured, "Goodness."

Jasper sighed. "Sorry about that, sirs. Now you see why we don't incline to take guests hereabouts. The reverend . . . he's not right in the head. Been that way for some time. Lost his congregation a few years back 'cuz of it."

"Senility? Is it his age?" Alex asked.

"Well, I ain't no doctor. Won't you come round the other front, and I'll . . . fill you in. Reckon we owe you that."

Alex drew up short, stopped altogether. Both Jasper and Nick had to turn.

"Then he *was* here," he murmured. "Dorian was here."

Jasper shifted uncomfortably.

"Uh, yes, sir, he was," he said. "We called him Hinny."

Alex felt as though he'd been punched.

"You called him . . ."

"Hinny." Jasper urged them to start walking again, and talked as they went. "The master's son—that's Noah—give 'im a new name. That were common. Plan was to give 'em the idea that they was starting a whole new life when they come here, better forget everything else."

"A great deal to demand," Nick mentioned.

"Well, your average nigger slave, he generally's got no sense of family like you and me. They don't really think like us, most of 'em. You know what I mean."

Alex clenched his teeth. "I know exactly what you mean."

Jasper led them onto another porch, exactly like the other one, set in a facade also exactly like the other, but which faced the road. This plantation, like many, had a front front and a back front—the river front. Jasper bade them sit on a set of iron chairs.

He leaned back on the porch rail and folded his arms.

"As plantations go," he began, "Chapel Mount were one of the bad ones. We turned out a high yield of rice every year, but this was on account of our slaves working the way they done. They didn't have nothing like they got nowadays. We didn't have but a couple women, and uh . . . anyway, I'd be ashamed to describe."

Alex settled into the iron chair, unable to find a comfortable position. "Go ahead. Describe it."

Jasper knew by looking at them that they understood what he was not saying, what a plantation could be. How ugly, how isolated, sovereign, sanctioned by a master whose sadism had free and legal reign. Here the term *chattel slave* found its fullest meaning.

"Mr. Noah was the reverend's boy," Jasper continued, growing more uneasy. "Well, I mean, he still is. His son, I mean. He had what you might call a tough time. Couldn't make it through schooling and like, on account of he didn't like taking orders nor toeing nobody else's line. Had hell in his eyes." Everybody on the farm learned real early not to cross him."

"And . . . Hinny," Alex said, nearly choking, "crossed him, I'll bet."

Jasper dragged his hat from his head and twisted the brim.

Alex stole a look at Nick. "Wouldn't you know it?"

"Was he injured?" Nick asked Jasper.

"Your man? No, sir. In fact, when Hinny left, Mr. Noah was on the ground with manure smeared on his face."

Nick couldn't keep a satisfied grin from spreading on his lips. Alex covered his own mouth and tried not to enjoy the picture too much.

Jasper shrugged and went on. "When he walked off Chapel Mount, he done took Mr. Noah's influence away with him. After that, we all pretty much quit listening. I don't know why." He paused and blinked at the sky. "We just got a look at something we had all forgot, I guess."

"Go on."

"Used to be, this was a horrible place for slaves, plain and simple."

"Used to be?"

"Right, but it ain't like that no more. Now some slaves even live in the big house. Sir . . . you could make trouble for us, but I feel like you got a right to know, seeing as your friend got it all started."

"What you say here," Nick promised, "will remain here."

Jasper nodded. "Right gentlemanly. Well, you seen the reverend. He's living in the past. His Noah . . . that was a brutal, mean-hearted son of a—preacher. But he went away, and we figured things couldn't get no worse, so me and some of the other hands started making things better. The slaves built themselves some real cabins instead of the big dormitory that used to be down yonder. Burned that dormitory to the ground, they did. Certain niggers took over certain jobs and took a share of the profits, and we all just keep the place going, and we take care of the family."

Alex leaned forward. "Are you telling us the slaves run this plantation?"

"Yes, sir, that's what I'm telling you."

"Why don't they run away?"

Without apology Jasper simply asked, "Where they gonna go?"

His statement, and the shrug that accompanied it, carried a certain logic.

Nick nodded his agreement, if only to be polite and get the man on with his story. Luckily Jasper sensed their priorities and carried on.

"Well, anyhow . . . later that same night that Hinny left here—"

The foreman hesitated, worrying that poor hat brim like dough between his fists. Whatever he had to say, he didn't like it and wanted neither to recall nor repeat it.

Alex sat resolute, with his posture insisting upon hearing the whole story. Dorian wasn't here. He knew that by now. He admitted it to himself. But there was a story to tell, and he resolved to hear it all, to commit its every detail to his memory, so that he might find his brother.

"Please, Mr. Jasper," Nick said. "Go on."

"Just Jasper, sir."

"As you wish. Go on."

"Well, ain't no nice way to say it."

"Say it."

Jasper looked at Nick Varvaresos for a moment. The stocky dark man was robust, foreign, and fierce, obviously controlling a lifetime of experiences, which Jasper preferred not to knock up against. He stiffened his spine and said what he had to say.

"The reverend's daughter had her room broke into. She was tied up to the bedpost and . . . uh, they said your man doubled back and took revenge on the lady for what Mr. Noah done to him."

Alex cracked a heel against the foot of the iron chair. "Good God, sir!"

"But they said there were proof," Jasper desperately added.

"What proof!"

"He said his name while he was in there with her. Hinny."

"His name is *not* Hinny, sir! He would never refer to himself by such a word."

"And he tied her up with his sash."

This cut the blond man off short. He clamped his lips.

"Yes, sir," Jasper said to the other men's expressions, "a fancy satin one with stitching and designs. You know. Emb'oidry."

Nick watched Alex and the storm forming in the younger man's eyes, the regret and confusion pulling at his mouth.

Without a word Jasper pushed himself up from the porch rail and strode into the house, leaving the two of them alone for a long moment of silence, but directly he came back out and handed Alex the very sash left behind that night by Dorian. Left behind in the act.

The sash lay in Alex's hands, draped across his lap.

"I gave him this sash," he groaned. "I gave it to him the day I returned from the university."

Color flooded Jasper's pale face. "Any rate, sirs, you can see that the reverend is fooling himself about his daughter. Ain't no respectable man in the state would have her after . . . that. Next night, the barn burned to the ground. Took some fine horses with it. Mr. Noah lived for horses. Like that little mare you seen over there. We all knew it was the slaves that done it. They weren't gonna live like pigs no longer. They weren't intending to run off, but they just weren't gonna live like they'd been living. We whites—we'd about had enough too, I gotta tell you."

"I should think," Alex spat with unshielded contempt.

Nick scolded him with a click of his tongue, then gestured for the foreman to continue, in hopes the tale might get any better.

Jasper knew what they were hoping for and felt all the smaller for his inability to provide it. "Mr. Noah set off that very night after Hin—after your friend. He sweared he'd find him and bring him back in chains . . . and . . . "

"And," Nick prodded.

"Punish him in a style accustomed to Chapel Mount. I'd ruther not go into no detail."

Fondling the old Cyprian sash, Alex breathed, "Please don't."

"For a while," Jasper went on, "we was skeered Mr. Noah might come back and find out about this place, and try to change it all back like it was. I hope he don't come back, because these niggers'll just kill him. I reckon he ain't found your friend yet, on account of he ain't come back. But he keeps drawing money on his daddy's bank, so we know he ain't dead. That little gray mare come back on a train about six or seven months ago, and she been living the high life ever since, except that she pines for him sometimes."

Alex looked up. "He sent his horse back on a train?"

"Yup. The mare, anyways. He's still got her foal. Well, I supposed it ain't a foal no more. If he sent the mare back, stands to reason the colt is big enough to train and ride. Although I can't hardly imagine training that crazy-mad colt of his. Of course, Mr. Noah could ride a thundercloud bareback. You never saw nobody ride like him. He had this colt special bred out of that little sweetheart mare by a big—*big* snarly-lookin' black Percheron son of a bitch he shuttled over from Ireland. What a butcherblock of a stallion! They hadda hitch him to a heavy wagon with a full load and just let him pull it all the way from the depot to here, just to tucker him out enough so as they could control him. I felt mighty bad for that pretty little angel when they put her in the paddock with that devil. Hell, he was twice her size. The foal nurly killed the mother. The foal was pitch-black and looked just like the father. Big, black, crazy, out of control, all legs . . . and just like the mama horse, that colt just loved Mr. Noah. Hateful as that young man was, I can't help thinking there has to be some good in a person who a little animal loves that much. Animals, they got a sixth sense, you know."

He pulled his hand from behind his back—only now did they realize he'd been hiding it there—and with a crackle and snap.

Nick and Alex found themselves staring at a warrant poster.

REWARD! WANTED REWARD!

Jasper cleared his throat. "Think you should know about this. The law's after him too."

For Assault and Ravagement on a White Virgin Woman The Mulatto Slave Formerly Called DORIAN WALLACE also known as HINNY . . .

Ravagement, ravagement. White virgin woman.

Bears an "S" Brand on Right Arm, Speaks Good English . . .

"Oh, Dorian, Dorian," Alex murmured. His throat twisted. "He didn't do this."

Jasper refused to let the slightest bias show in his face. "Ain't for me to say, Mr. Wallace. I only—"

He stopped abruptly, and for a few seconds they didn't know why. He had heard something, or some extra sense came into play, and he suddenly dropped to silence and looked at the front door of the mansion, down a few planks on the porch from where they were sitting.

Alex looked at the door too, and so did Nick, but they saw nothing unusual, and even when a flash of white tulle and lace appeared in the door, it really wasn't worth getting silent over.

A girl. She floated across the threshold until the sunlight crossed her white skirt in a wedge so bright it made the men blink. Even under the awning, the sun reached for and danced upon a fiesta of rather messy caramel-colored ringlets in which her tiny white face was set, a pinched face, like a witch living inside a doll and making the arms and eyes move. Someone had bothered to do her hair, but apparently she had been pulling and twisting the whole time, for there was no order whatsoever to the tumbling mass. Her eyes were bright, dark green, but ringed with a brownish shadow of discolor, and only this destroyed the image of a perfect, pampered young woman hedging twenty, her body so narrow and frail a man could crush her between two fingers.

The young woman.

Alex's insides shriveled as he looked at her and understood. Perhaps this was part of the reason Dorian hadn't contacted them. Would he think they would be ashamed? Think he had really done this thing of which he was accused? Perhaps Dorian hadn't wanted to leave a paper trail that would lead Noah Sutton's vengeance back to an innocent family at Plentiful. Who could be sure of Dorian's thoughts?

With the faintest rustle he managed to hide the *WANTED* poster behind his thigh.

The girl blinked at the grounds, then blinked at the porch—and saw them.

The lady's notice brought Alex and Nick to their feet with astonished silence. Rarely does a man see a ghost during the daylight.

She wore what appeared to be a dressing gown of snow white, which floated in the breeze off the river, tiny breasts bundled tightly into a corset, her childlike waist banded with a plain pink sash. Her hands moved constantly, without purpose, picking and pulling at the lace and the ends of the sash.

"Ophelia," Alex murmured. Behind him Nick uttered only a little groan.

The girl's tiny pink lips parted, and a shrill voice sounded.

"Oh . . . company?"

"Yes'm," Jasper said simply. "Afternoon, Miss Rachel."

"Well, it's a good day," the girl said, and it seemed she instantly dismissed the presence of Alex and Nick, never mind that any other young Southern miss would have instantly given special attention to gentlemen's company. "A very white day," she said, and blinked tightly into the sunlight—*right* into the sunlight, until her eyes watered. "Aristocratic sky. You must tell Papa it's a good day. He should go hunting today. Perhaps he can kill an antelope. Mammy Dagny should have antelope meat for supper today. It helps her knees."

"Yes'm," Jasper said again.

Alex leaned sideways toward Nick and whispered, "Non compos mentis."

With a tilt of his head, Nick silently agreed.

Under his breath Jasper cautioned, "Just don't say nothin'."

Rachel Sutton's long thin arms drifted up, down, her wrists bent delicately and long fingers spread like seaweed as she drifted down the porch steps and down the path. "I'm going to Florida," her tiny voice twittered back, "to pick palms."

Taking very small steps with her slippered feet, she went down the path between the magnolias, to wander there like a bit of foam drifting upon waves of green.

So that was her. The girl supposedly raped by the mulatto slave, with no chance of marrying in the white community now. But this added element—this dementia—

Alex sank back against Nick. "Dear God . . . my dear God."

He lowered himself onto the iron chair, his eyes glazing.

Nick drew his brows together.

"Alex?"

"Don't you realize what this means?"

"What does it mean?"

Alex motioned to the floating figure in the trees. "The reverend . . . it's not his age at all, Uncle Nick. It's the family. Hereditary insanity. They're completely brainsick!"

As the sun sparkled coldly between them, Jasper sighed and folded his arms. "That's dead right."

Nick pressed a hand to Alex's shoulder, but there was cold comfort for either of them.

Alex gazed out over the expanse of lawn, past it to the road, and in his mind he saw the vastness of the nation, and a thousand dried-up trails.

"Somewhere in the South there's a madman hunting my brother down like a dog," he said. "I must reach one of them before they find each other."

★

THE BURNING FUSE

MARCH 1859

The United States Supreme Court reverses a decision by a Wisconsin State Supreme Court, thereby ruling that state courts shall not release Federal prisoners. The prisoner in question had rescued a fugitive slave. By this decision the U.S. Supreme Court simultaneously confirms constitutionality of the strict Fugitive Slave Act of 1850. The act says that the North is compelled by law to cooperate in capture and return of runaway slaves, and that harboring of runaways is a national criminal offense.

★

CHAPTER SEVEN

———— ★ ————

"Well, that was a disappointment."

"That," Alex Wallace amended dryly, "is a lesson for us. Never travel five hundred twenty miles to follow a rumor in a railroad station."

He winced and shifted his aching backside in the saddle's hard seat.

"We're searching for a missing man who doesn't want to be found," Nick Varvaresos pointed out. "We have no choice but to follow rumors."

"I should have guessed," Alex said. "What on earth did we imagine Dorian would be doing in a small-scale Indiana logging camp? What was I thinking?"

"Whatever he was doing," Nick said, "he did it over a year ago. That camp has been abandoned who knows how long. At least a year."

Alex nodded, scolded himself with a frown, and shifted again. This was a western saddle, enormous and somewhat unpleasant after the English saddles he was used to. Instead of a slim fold of leather, which let him put his legs forward around his roan's narrow withers, this saddle put his legs where it wanted them instead of where *he* wanted them. Wide, and off to the sides, around the roan's barrel. Not as nice. Not as comfortable.

Not . . . worth worrying about right now.

He sighed.

Around them autumn had tarnished the land. Ordinarily Alexander enjoyed and relished autumn as the most invigorat-

77

ing time of the year—fresh, crisp air, without the lank wilting heat of summer, brilliant colors in the mountains, no bugs . . .

"Two years," he grumbled. "Two empty years. False lead after wrong turn after bad judgment. . . . How do we know some bounty hunter hasn't responded to that 'wanted' poster and murdered Dorian for the money?"

"Because," Nick said patiently—for the fourth time this week—"the last telegram from Jasper at Chapel Mount told us that no one has done that, Alex. Dorian is alive, frustrating the hair out of someone's head . . . somewhere."

"Uncle Nick, it's a big continent," Alex mourned. "You and I are going to have a very good idea just how big before all this is over." He drew the reins toward his chest, and the roan jumped back toward the road. "We better get back to that boardinghouse before midnight. We'll have to be rested to catch the train again in the morning."

Nick's dark eyes met his in the waning afternoon sunlight. "And go where?"

Alex paused and looked at him longer than was comfortable. He didn't want to say he didn't know. That they'd run out of leads. Dorian had disappeared like a leaf on a fast-moving river.

Nick knew all that; Alex just didn't want to *say* it.

Their horses plodded beneath them. For a good half mile they were silent on the old road. An old road that Dorian may or may not ever had trodden upon . . . there was no way to know or even to guess.

"Where is he, Nick?" Alex murmured into the sun as it slipped behind the hills. "Where in all these states could he be? Or did he leave the states and go to the territories? Perhaps he tried to get to us in Greece and was waylaid somehow . . . or in a shipwreck . . . or caught an illness. How can we know? When do we give up?"

Over the twenty-odd years between their ages, Nick eyed his nephew cannily.

"Do you want to give up?" he asked.

Alex almost came out of that enormous saddle. "No!" he shouted.

Then, quite abruptly, he realized what Nick was doing and shook his head.

"I'm sorry. I'm very sorry."

He drew his roan to a stop. The horse craned around to get one big blue-ringed eye on his rider, but the young blond man was gazing thoughtfully at the territorial horizon.

His uncle pulled up beside him and drew rein. "Alexander?"

Alex only stared at the distance, and beyond it to where he could not see. His shoulders drooped inside his daycoat. He felt his uncle's eyes on him. And he felt the blood rush up behind his own eyes and cheeks. Had the months of empty searching made him soul-blind?

With a crack in his voice, he asked, "How far must I go?"

Nick's stomach contracted. There were lines in Alex's young face that hadn't been there two years ago. Growing up on an American plantation, Alex had been overshadowed by the spirit and intellect of Dorian, yet he hadn't been resentful. Dorian was brilliant, arrogant, perceptive, obviously the favored son of Iphigenia—though not really her son at all. Alex had never learned to resent that favor, because Dorian had been deprived in so many ways. Alex had always perceived the deprivation. Rather than resent Dorian, he had unfailingly defended and protected him, done all he could to make Dorian feel valued and wise, treated him in every way like a brother and done all he could to make Dorian *feel* like the eldest, the wisest.

More than treating Dorian kindly out of sympathy, Alex had possessed an unshakable faith in him. That faith had not diminished at Chapel Mount when Jasper handed them that notice. Nick knew, and realized Alex knew, that Dorian had done no such thing to any woman. Had the accusation been murder—oh, yes, Dorian would be capable of murder. But this—no.

Dorian had been raised by women. Yula, Iphigenia, the Greek aunts and serving women . . . if he had nothing, he had a phenomenal respect and adoration for womankind. He had always spoken of the classical women of Greece, of the goddesses of myth, and of women as though they were goddesses. Alex had learned how to look at women through Dorian's eyes. They had dreamed of going to Greece together and standing in the Temple of Artemis.

Then Iphigenia had taken Alex and the sisters to Greece— and Dorian had stayed in America, forced by Luke Wallace to stay because he was a possession, not a son. Held to a bride's promise, the boy who was most Greek had not been allowed to go to Greece.

So Alex had gone to Greece as a rich American's son, and for the first time as the eldest. In Richmond he had been American. In Greece he became *the American*! Suddenly cut from under Dorian's shadow, Alex had found himself in the limelight. A fair man was rare in northern Greece, especially one who spoke fluent unaccented Greek *and* perfect English. When Alex talked, the Greeks listened, almost frantically— and he saw in their eyes the wonder of what was happening in America. They truly wanted his opinion.

What did the Americans think of this or that? What was happening in America? Did he hunt raccoons?

The world was a sprawling underpopulated place, made of cloistered bundles of humanity, each man descended from the same pack as the next man in his cloister. People were used to seeing others who looked like them and spoke with the same accent. While no one was totally out of place in the great stew of America, Macedon was an altogether different kind of stage.

Alex had made a discovery in Greece. He realized he had something he'd never noticed before. A personality.

And a sense of humor, a sense of spontaneity, a tendency to push for change—a tendency that Europeans scarcely comprehended, never mind acted upon. Europeans were used to things remaining the same for hundreds of years. Sons, grandsons had the same skills as their great-grandfathers. There were whole dynasties of fishermen, farmers, sheepherders.

In America, if no change came, change would be *forced* to come. Alex's father was a dockworker who had become a wealthy tobacconist. Luke Wallace had *forced* change to happen. No Southern aristocrat's daughter would marry him, so he had forced change. He had imported a wife of high standing and long bloodlines.

What Alex would someday be . . . only America could tell.

Nick watched his nephew and remembered the many long months in Greece after the letter came—the letter that lied, that said Dorian was dead of snakebite. Iphigenia hadn't been able to bear the idea of coming home to Plentiful. Her daughters were continuing their education in Macedon. Alex had stayed at the University of Athens . . . or had tried to.

But finally the responsibility of being American had played too loudly in his mind. He was safe in Europe while his nation was tearing itself apart. A young man couldn't bear such a pull without tearing also. He was a rich young man who resented the way the world had treated his adored brother. Alex still felt guilty about his money, second-generation wealth that he knew he had not earned. Nick knew Alex could not then, and still didn't, perceive how Lucas Wallace had worked for every dime and therefore felt no guilt. All Alex saw was that his father lived in splendor because Dorian was a slave.

And Alex had always considered Dorian his better.

Some things never did add up.

"I'm going farther away from Dorian with every step," Alex murmured. "I can feel it . . . like a log in my stomach floating the wrong way in a stream. . . . "

Nick eyed him, but stayed quiet. Alex wasn't really talking to him.

"I'm doing something wrong," Alex said. "Somehow I'm not handling this as well as I should be able to. I'm wasting my time, yours. I'm failing Dorian horribly. I have to think again about all this, about what I'm doing and why, and how to . . . I don't know—do it better . . . more efficiently. I have to screw my reasoning on straight, then get my methods in order—"

"Alex . . ." Nick grumbled.

"The door swings both ways," Alex went on. "By law a slave is chattel. Property. But he's legally accountable for his crimes. That crazy family at Chapel Mount . . . they think Dorian committed a crime for which they'll happily hunt and hang him. He'll be tried as a man, not as chattel. He has no legal rights, but he must abide by the rights of others."

Nick smiled roughly. "Alexander the Egalitarian."

Alex suddenly turned and looked at him with a terrible crease in his brow. "Someone who is legally a negro shouldn't be tried by laws that otherwise don't protect him . . . should he?"

"That is not a question," Nick responded. "You already have your answer in your head. I can see it from here, sitting in there under that yellow hair."

"Perhaps you do. You know, Dorian always talked horribly and uncharitably about God, and I'm beginning to think he was right. If God's hand is in all this, it's a dirty hand indeed."

Nick laughed. "You and Dorian and that way he talks! And me a good Eastern Orthodox, and I have to listen to the two of you. It's worse than being around Roman Catholics."

Alex relaxed somewhat and drew a deep, steadying breath. With a poke of his heel he coaxed the roan forward, and Nick kept up on his bay mare. "At least no one's suggesting you follow the Constantinople church anymore."

With a huff Nick said, "I'd talk the way Dorian talks first. Even an angel who asks a Greek to follow a Turk is looking for trouble."

"Mmm," Alex mumbled and nodded. Then his brow creased and he asked, "Who *is* heading the Eastern Orthodox Church now?"

Nick pursed his lips. "I suppose the closest authority would be the metropolitan of Moscow."

They looked at each other, and both laughed, and all that other talk slipped away. Again. The conversation would come back; it always did.

Alex's horse suddenly shuddered and sidestepped. He drew the reins, checked in front of the horse, and sat up straight—as straight as he could in this boat of a saddle. "What was that?"

"What was what?"

"I thought I heard something."

"Out here?" Nick huffed. "I think we intrepid Greek explorers have proved there's nothing here but burrs and back trails. Even the trees weren't worth logging anymore."

"Say it again, without the accent. Maybe I'll—"

Then, without the slightest warning, Alex's horse snorted and reared up under him like the rising bow of a ship. All he saw for three long seconds was a flopping white mane and two ears pointing back at him.

In an equestrian saddle he could have stayed aboard, but

unused to the western saddle, Alex lost his balance and landed hard, flat on his back.

Nick dropped off his prancing bay, swatting Alex's roan out of his way. "Alex!"

"I'm all right . . . I think." Alex stiffly levered himself to a sitting position just as Nick dropped to his side.

"What spooked my horse?"

"I don't know—these brainless rented beasts," Nick swore. He cast a scowl at the horses.

The bay mare was wandering a hundred feet down the trail, waiting for the two-leggers to catch up, but the roan stood only a dozen feet away. Fetlock-deep in gorse and weeds, he hung his head and blinked apologetically through his white forelock at the two men.

Didn't they realize he heard something in the woods?

The slave catcher dragged his prey through the wilderness just as he had dragged them across the fields, over the hills, through the creeks, and under the rocks. Every few hundred yards he uttered one of ten or so set threats. Something about killing or maiming or leaving behind. He was so used to the phrases he never even thought about them anymore. Each new set of runaway slaves thought he was making them up fresh.

The Fugitive Slave Law was his bread and butter, and he was in a hurry. Who knew how much longer the law would be in effect, with all this war talk? With all this free-the-slaves mumbo jumbo? He would hurry to deliver these runaways back to their master, get his money, then hurry back and do it again. And again, if there was time.

Beside him the slaver dragged the eight-year-old slave boy by one skinny wrist. He picked the boy because he was old enough to walk and young enough to threaten. The catcher knew one of the babies would make a better threat to keep the parents and the other young'uns moving, but he hadn't wanted to carry no baby across no two and a half states.

The nigger grown-ups hauled their other children over the knotty land behind him. He didn't turn back to look very often. If they wanted their boy, they'd just have to come along. He'd discovered long ago that hauling nigger families back to their rightful owners was not only more profitable than hauling one at a time, but it was easier. They were fiercely devoted to their family structure and wouldn't leave their boy just to go live in the North. The North was no playland for runaways with children to feed. Hell, he was doing 'em a favor.

In a week, maybe less, he'd deliver them, get his money, and go back north and do another favor.

All at once the boy he was hauling along pulled backward—resisted for the first time.

The slave catcher twisted around and looked—then looked back at the other slaves. He screwed up his face under the mustache and frowned. What was going on?

The wiry black man was gathering his other children behind him in a kind of panic, calling at them and waving his hands like a flapping rooster, and the woman was herding them toward the man, glancing with fright in her eyes at the little boy the slaver held by the wrist. What were they doing? Had they seen a badger? A snake?

Now they were staring up into the setting sunlight—up to the higher ground where the trees were thinner, over the carpet of tangled overgrowth—

The slave catcher looked up there too, and squinted.

And found himself staring up the barrels of a matched set of revolvers.

Even if he hadn't been able to see the guns in the setting sun, the posture of the two men on that hillock, and the silhouette of their fine clothes, made it clear to the slave catcher that he was being aimed at by right well-off folks.

He would have to move fast.

A knife blade scored the skin of the scrawny negro boy and made a thin red mark on the boy's shoulder. His mother screamed and stumbled toward him, but the negro male, possibly the boy's father, hauled her back before she got their son killed for sure.

The filthy white man leading them suddenly dragged his hostage backward, shielding his own body with the boy's body, and shouted, "You gents haul off, or I'll knife this pug—I'll slice him so he be no good to nobody. Haul off on your way. You—" He wagged his head at the mother. "Git behind me. You man, git over in front of me. Go on!"

Without lowering his Colt Dragoon, Nick leaned toward Alex and commented, "Kentucky."

"Yes, I think so," Alex muttered.

The two adult negroes did as they were told . . . one behind him, one in front, their little boy caught in the center. The man dragged the boy backward toward a grotto underneath two fallen trees. Where the trees crossed and lay against each other, there was a pit of black shadow.

Alex didn't lower his gun either. He took a deep breath and shouted, "What are you doing with those people?"

The man didn't answer.

"What's the matter with him?" Alex muttered.

"No gun," Nick pointed out.

"How do you know that?"

"He would have used it if he had one."

"How do you know?"

"I saw it in his eyes."

"Well, he'll use that knife on the child," Alex pointed out. Another deep breath. "You! Answer me! What are you doing to those people?"

"I can't hear you," the Kentucky man shouted.

"What . . . are you doing . . . to . . . those—"

"I'm deaf."

Nick clapped a palm to his forehead.

Beside him Alex groaned. "He's deaf. . . . "

"Can't hear you!" the man repeated. "I can read your mouth if I'm close, but I ain't getting close. Just turn around and haul off. I got my business and you got yourn. You mind it."

"No," Alex said, more to himself and Nick. "That's not good enough."

"How can we talk to him?"

"I don't know, but look at those people's faces. They're terrified."

"He is their master. What can we do?"

"He's not their master, Uncle Nick. His clothes are more

tattered than theirs are. He doesn't own one slave, much less a whole family. Look at them. He's got three, four . . . six of them down there."

"Do you think he kidnapped them to sell them in the South?"

"He couldn't kidnap an entire family as large as that. I think he must be one of those lowlifes who makes a living recapturing runaways. More likely he's been holding those children hostage for hundreds of miles and forcing the parents to follow him south. Uncivilized pig of a—"

From the grotto the Kentucky accent flew again. "Come up close and I'll look at your mouth! Just one of you!"

Alex glanced at Nick with a *How did we get into this?* expression and took a step forward.

"Not you! Send the other one over. I'll talk."

Alex paused. Perhaps the slave hunter didn't like the looks of him—or perhaps he just didn't want Alex and Nick to make the choice. But send Nick down there into the darkness alone?

"I refuse," he called, making his mouth move as big as possible, never mind that the whole idea was silly from here to way over there. He exaggerated a shake of his head, just to make sure his message traveled.

Beside him Nick put out a hand.

"Alex," he said, "I'll go."

"Too dangerous," Alex insisted. "I can't condone it."

Nick's black brows came down into a hard set of angles. Over his pocked cheeks and black eyes, this made a formidable picture indeed.

"Nobody's asking you to condone. In the war against the Turks, I was a colonel with seven hundred men following me. So what do you want me to tell this man, Alex, or should I make it up myself?"

Taken aback, Alex hesitated. What was war really like, that Nick had never mentioned this before? He put his uncle's experience into the perspective it deserved and concentrated on the man in the grotto.

After a moment he cleared his throat. "He could be lying about being deaf, just to get you to come up close."

"If he's lying, what can we do but play it out? So what do you want me to tell him?"

"Tell him . . . if he gets out of that grotto immediately, leaves those people behind, and starts walking south," Alex said thoughtfully, "I will allow him to keep every bone in his body."

Nick's harsh expression dissolved into an appreciative grin.

"Oh, that's very good," he said. "I like that."

He shifted his Dragoon revolver to his other hand, wiped the palm of his gun hand on his thigh, then switched back again. He stepped off the path toward the grotto.

Nick made his way into the thick overgrowth and rocks, his pistol nudging branches and ferns aside while always pointing forward.

On the hillock Alex raised both elbows, leveled his own Dragoon's barrel on his left wrist, tilted his head, adopted a stance, and steadied himself to kill a man if he had to.

The barrel wavered slightly; Alex kept aim just to the side of Nick's head as his uncle struggled through the almost untraversable growth and stubbly little trees. The ground had been chewed out by the ages and now was a spongehead of bumps and pits to confound any human foot. Not one was the right size, or even sunk at a cooperative angle.

It was all Alex could do to keep his own footing and his aim at the same time, but he was determined not to let his uncle die for whatever was about to happen.

Halfway to the grotto Nick paused. He didn't turn, nor take his eyes off the man and the little negro boy, but he called back to Alex.

"What if he can prove he owns them?"

A twinge of commitment ran like blood blisters up Alex's arms. He had never before tampered with another man's property. . . .

But these were changing times. And he had come back to America to help change them.

His blue eyes ached in the angled sun.

"Then he doesn't own them anymore."

The wind whistled in the trees as though it understood.

Without turning, without changing his posture, without commenting on the rite of passage for Alex and himself, those slaves and that man, Nick simply continued walking toward the grotto. His dark head bobbed as he scouted for footing.

Alex tried to keep aim on the Kentucky man, hoping that if he should fire, he would hit the man and not the boy or the woman behind.

Nick disappeared as the lowering sun put a crease of shadow two feet higher on the wilderness.

Something moved in the grotto. Forms, shadows, a scuffle—or was it only branches rustling in wind?

Suddenly Alex felt absurd, standing here on this hillock with the rapidly dying sun casting a single weak spotlight on the mauve wool of his overcoat, on his raised arm, on the pistol, and the side of his face. He couldn't see anything but dark blurs down there anymore. He was standing in the only patch of light left in Indiana.

His arms began to tingle, but he didn't lower the revolver. The creases in the heavy wool of his coat hurt like blood blisters up and down his arms.

Instead, he gritted his teeth until his jaws ached.

Should he fire a warning shot? Should he plunge off this hillock and hope that the deaf man couldn't hear where he was in the dark, couldn't pinpoint the panicked scramble of the negro family as they flew for cover?

If he fired blind, he might hit Nick, or the little boy, or the mother.

Mother . . . we never expected this to be our destiny when he planned the journey to Greece, did we? When we packed the carriages . . . when Dorian—

More movements. Heads bobbing in the shadows. Forms coming toward him like a cold breeze moving along the ground.

"Nick?"

"Yes, it's me. It's all right, Alex. He's gone."

Alex straightened his head. "Pardon?"

"The man is gone."

"What?"

"Stop talking like that. He was afraid of you."

"Just like that? That was all it took?"

"Not every man has stomach to fight, Alex."

"How do you know he's not doubling around? Did you take his knife, at least?"

"If I took his knife, he would have no way to skin his

catches and he would starve in this wilderness. I checked for a gun, and I watched him go." He turned and motioned toward the seven dark forms that had tagged behind him.

The negro man was holding the sobbing boy who had moments ago been hostage. The woman held a toddler on one hip and a girl of about four on the other. Three more children of various ages peeked from behind the adults.

So there weren't six. There were eight.

"Marvelous," Alex drawled. He looked at the slave woman. Sobbing. The undernourished man, trembling. Their six sag-eyed, swollen-bellied children, cowering, starving.

They were waiting for the white man of authority to make a decision. To feed them, to protect them, to find them decent shoes, to salve their scratches and bandage their cuts, and to find them shelter for the night.

"It's all right," Alex said, for lack of anything better. "You'll be all right. . . . You're not going to go wherever— well, wherever that man was taking you. I'll . . . I'll do something."

He sighed and let his arms drop. Then he groaned and shook his head at Nick.

"Now what?" he complained. "What in hellation am I supposed to do with those?"

He waved a feeble hand at the negroes, but suddenly turned and paced away through the underbrush to stand alone in the onset of darkness.

Above them the stars were beginning to focus, every bit as near as their chances of finding Dorian. When Nick came up behind him, there was something markedly changed about Alex's demeanor, and a twist in his voice that pulled at Nick's heart.

"Why hasn't he written to Mother?" Alex choked. "In all these months . . . why is he silent?"

There was even more silence from behind him, and that was a kind of shock. Nick not knowing an answer? Not having a ready wisdom to fill the hole? The adults always knew . . . but now Alex realized he was one of the adults himself, and he felt unsureness in Nick's presence over his shoulder.

"It's because of me," he struggled. "Because of them." He

tossed a self-scolding glance toward the negroes. "Because I've failed to do anything in my life to change all this."

"No, Alex, no," Nick feebly attempted.

"Dorian must hate us," Alex murmured. "For letting him live in slavery . . . for leaving him behind when we went to Greece . . . for not standing up to Father—I should've done that a decade ago. It was my duty to change things. I was the heir! I had the power in my hands! Why didn't I use it?"

"That is your guilt talking," Nick said. "Dorian is not that way. He loves his family."

"Then why hasn't he contacted us?" He turned suddenly, and the force of his question pushed Nick backward. "Do you have an explanation?" he demanded. "What could keep him mute all these years, if he has been free since 1856?"

But Nick had nothing to say. Perhaps he hadn't let himself think about the time passing, and the questions that Alex apparently was finding the courage in himself to ask. With nothing to offer, Nick took another step back, and thereby gave the future to his nephew.

Seeing that, and feeling it, Alex's throat knotted. He stared up at the stars without really seeing them.

"I have to go back," he said.

Nick asked, "To Greece?"

"To Plentiful. I have to go back and do work Dorian can be proud of, so he'll come back to us."

He turned to face his uncle, though they could barely make out each other's features in the waxing moonlight.

"If he wants to be found . . . he'll find us."

Dear mother,

I regret to say that Nick and I have stumbled head over heels, at respectable inconvenience and expense, into yet another dead end. If Dorian was ever in Indiana, he left no signs of his visit.

You must not lose heart. While I was stumbling over Nick, I was stricken with a revelation. I discovered a flaw in my plan of action. We are chasing with great enthusi-

asm a thoroughly intelligent man who does not wish to be found. We are chasing him across an enormous nation and hoping to stumble into him instead of each other.

I have come to the conclusion that in order to find a needle in a haystack, all one really needs is a magnet.

Therefore, we have decided to return to Plentiful. We shall write you upon arrival.

By the way, while concluding Indiana travels, we happened upon a negro family who had temporarily lost their master. We gave them some money and a letter of protection and recommended that they look for him up north. If they have not found him by the time they reach Canada, I suggested they give up looking.

Nicholas sends fondest regards, as do I.

> *Your faithful son,*
> *Alexander*

★

PART THREE

———— ★ ————

DEVIL'S DANCE

Satan said, "Sinner Man, walk right in."

—Traditional Slave Song

CHAPTER EIGHT

———— ★ ————

"My wife, Irene, and I are couturiers. That is, we are in the industry of clothing for women and girls, accoutrements such as handbags, drawstring bags, ribbons, lace collars, beaded scarves and shawls, sachets, brocades, taffetas, hair bows, gloves, mouchoirs, vanity covers, and infants' clothing."

Yula stood with her hands clasped behind her back and nodded at her new employer's list as though she knew what half those things were.

The big round man before her stuck his thumbs in his waistcoat and rocked on his heels. He didn't look at her, but stared at the heavy floral carpeting under them, and spoke through a mustache and beard that looked like nothing more than a perfectly round yellow scrub sponge stuck over his mouth.

He must love to hear himself talk, because surely he knew she had no need to know all these details of his career.

"Currently we're developing a business as couturiers for several theatrical and ballet companies in Maryland and in Pennsylvania. We design and manufacture satin bodices, tulle and tutus, satin flowers, silk fruits, covered buttons, and so on . . . the business is booming. We've taken on six new seamstresses this month alone, to accommodate several recent contracts. This requires quite a bit of travel for both of us. You'll go days, weeks, sometimes months at a time without seeing either of us, and therefore you must be trustworthy and a strong presence for our children."

He paused to clear his throat, but didn't meet her eyes.

"You will tend the children and only the children," he continued. "We have slaves to tend the house, the stables, the dogs, and do meals, and I certainly have no intention of paying a freed woman such as yourself to do such easy tasks. It's the children you'll be paid to care for, and they shall garner your every attention. Since I am finding it difficult to buy slaves in this state anymore, I'm accepting you in my employ, but the conditions are absolute."

"I understand, boss."

"You'll address me as Colonel Richard."

"Yes, Colonel."

"Colonel Richard."

"Yes, Colonel Richard."

"I understand you've worked as a cook on a cotton farm, yes?"

"That right, Colonel Richard."

"And as a domestic in two places in Maryland and Virginia?"

"Yes, Colonel Richard."

"Anything else?"

"I take odd jobs anywhere I could," Yula told him, "just work my way up to here."

"What can you say to make me believe you won't simply move on?" the Colonel asked her. "That you're not just a black vagrant trying to reach Canada at my children's expense?"

Yula tried to appear as cow-eyed and homey as possible, including a little pouching of her lower lip. "Oh, Colonel . . . I loves little ones. I had two little ones mahself. . . . I just loves 'em . . . and if only I can be a nanny to your babies for the whole rest of my life, sure ain't no cause for me to go up to that cold place of Canada."

"Excellent point. Why anyone would want to live in that wilderness is beyond me. Understand, now, that I would not ordinarily hire a former field slave, but trained nannies are hard to find these days, and you do have adequate household experience. It is critical that my wife and I give full attention to our business now. Therefore, we must leave it to you to attend to our household. Come with me now. I will present you to my children."

Yula followed the bulky man up a carpeted stairway and along a narrow hall to a nursery—a playroom, not a sleeping chamber. Inside, when Colonel Richard entered, seven curly heads ranging from bright auburn to lemon blond popped up and came to attention.

Every child carried a tumbling mass of sunlit natural curls, even the boys, and the curls bounded as the children suddenly scrambled, a flurry of organza and linen—until they stood in a line, in order by height, and apparently by age. They were all barefooted, wearing pretty pale-colored play clothes, and looked like seven figurines in an Easter basket. Every last one had eyes of ice blue, and a face of polished bisque porcelain.

And every one of them, from the eldest to the youngest, looked at Yula with *perfect* indifference.

She pursed her mouth, looked right back at them, wide-eyed, and tried not to shiver.

Colonel Richard held his hand out toward the tallest child, but didn't actually make contact.

"This is my eldest, Florence. Next is Charlotte. Then the twins, Ernest and Abigail. The three young ones are Malcolm, David, and Darby, in that order. Florence is fourteen, Darby is three. Their former nanny grew too old to care for them and got bursitis in her hands, and therefore I recently sold her down to Barnesville. They are all your responsibility now. They rise at six in the morning, breakfast at seven, and the five older ones attend school beginning at eight. The two younger ones remain here, but have a preparatory schedule to maintain."

He pivoted his bulk toward his offspring.

"This is Miss Wallace. She is your new nanny. She is a paid woman, not a slave. You will treat her accordingly. Do you understand?"

"Yes, Papa," the children—all seven—chimed.

Yula screwed her eyebrows into a knot and openly scowled at their choral response. Were they children, or music-box dolls?

"I will leave you to become acquainted."

"Good afternoon, Papa," the children—all seven—chimed again. Other than the littlest boy coming in a bit late, perfect chorus again.

Yula frowned again, but said nothing.

James Clempson Richard left the nursery.

The children remained standing in a line. The sounds of their father's footsteps thunking down the stairway was the only noise.

Yula cleared her throat.

"Hello, there," she said. "Yawl can call me Yula. We gon' be good friends, hm?"

The children made no response. The three-year-old stuck a finger in his mouth and twisted a leg impatiently, but stayed in place.

Yula just let them stare at her. She'd been a slave, and that was just like being a trained soldier at the drill. She could stand here all night if necessary.

Seconds ticked by.

Finally the eldest child, Florence, stepped forward and licked her pink lips, and raised her chin to Yula.

"We will have nothing to do with you," she said.

Orders were to take care of the children. However, that instruction assumed the children would allow her within two rooms of them. So far—and it had been thirteen days—they hadn't.

All Yula had managed to do so far was lay out clothing, draw baths, turn down beds, and sit within earshot during family meals.

Otherwise the older children took care of the younger ones with bitter efficiency. No matter what their parents believed, the children would have no association with Yula at all. Since the parents were seldom home, the performance was simple to maintain. Only while the older five were at school was she able to touch the two younger ones at all. She dressed them and played with them, and gradually succeeded in winning them over. A four-year-old and three-year-old couldn't be trusted to keep up whatever bitterness was driving the five eldest to shun her.

Having had two babies of her own, she knew how to play her way into their little hearts. It became her secret and theirs that the three of them were beginning to like each other.

Otherwise, the Richard family and their servants were

proper, polite, practiced, beautiful, elite, and by all standards
the coldest group of people Yula had ever encountered. She'd
met more compassionate slave traders and mule drivers. At
least paddling a slave took working up some kind of enthusiasm. The parents evidently had no enthusiasm for anything except their business, and the children's natural enthusiasm had
been warned, scolded, and shamed out of them.

As the days passed, Yula paid close attention to the household and determined to learn as much as she could about cul-
tured life. In her years as Dorian's mother Yula had paid
attention to her brilliant son, and she had learned *how to learn*.
As she dressed the Richard children, she paid attention to how
they spoke to each other, and she endeavored to speak that
way. Never before had she been so close to well-spoken people, and even Dorian had spoken like a slave when among
slaves.

Yula wasn't a field slave anymore, and she determined not
to talk like one. She was a free woman, and some day she
would make her own living as something other than a servant.
These seven cherubs would be her unwitting educators. She
began listening very carefully to their diction. She began
putting the ends on her words with such determination that it
sounded as if she were working at it—which she was, of
course, but her employers misread her reasons. The adult
Richards found her effort annoying, because they assumed she
was mocking them. They reprimanded her for speaking better.

She continued anyway. If they wanted to fire her, they
would fire a better-spoken woman that the one they had hired.
And something of Dorian—his constant quest for personal bet-
terment—would live on in his little brown mother.

She paid attention to the adults' conversations and learned
the difference between the Roman chair rail in the dining room
and the scalloped corner moldings in the foyer, and that the
foyer runner was French tapestry. She found out that the mail
was delivered to a freestanding iron box on the sidewalk outside, that the squarish front-door gas lantern was called a
Franklin light, and that the heavily patterned and bordered carpeting throughout the lower level was Brussels, which had
something to do with the way the complex patterns were loop
piled to make it look like needlepoint. The drawing room's
bright red, yellow, green, and teal carpet was done entirely in

patterns of strange-looking birds. Eventually Yula learned they were called peacocks.

This arm's-length life-style went on for nearly a month before Yula discovered why the children were so cold to her.

It was revenge.

Revenge against their parents.

Yula made her discovery when she realized the cause of a very curious behavior in the Richard household—the children cried themselves to sleep. Every night they went to sleep sobbing.

This mystery disturbed Yula for many days. She had never witnessed children, even hungry ones, even poor ones, crying themselves to sleep *every night*. In spite of the wealth, the opulence, the warmth, the spectacular meals, the mountains of toys—these were sad children.

After a month of this, Yula had a long chitchat with little Darby, and squeezed out the final clues to the mystery.

The next day, just after school, she ordered the seven curly heads to huddle around her in the nursery. Three huddled. The two little ones sat on her lap. The two elder ones folded their arms coolly and leaned against the farthest wall.

"You all sit and listen to me. I tell yawl a story," she began. Her animated face changed with every phrase. "I had a baby once. A boy. His father was the boss of the plantation. That's right. Then I had another boy. His father was a breeding nigger going round the countryside, giving babies for money. A white boy and a black boy, that's what I had, and I loved both my babies, and they loved me. And they loved each other, 'cuz that's the way brothers's supposed to be. My white boy . . . he was smart! He spoke Greek . . . spoke French . . . could read anything in the whole library. You never saw such a boy. Could use a pistol jus' like a gentleman. My other boy, my black boy . . . he was gettin' *big*. He was a sweet, but he was *big*. Well . . . you know that happened?"

She paused and made sure she had every face riveted to her story. All but Florence were looking right at her.

So she went on.

"The white folks killed my first boy. He was too white for 'em. They couldn't live in a world where a boy with black blood look so white and be so smart. They killed him. And they sold me off so I couldn't tell. And they sold my black boy in another direction, so he'd forget. They took my babies from me."

She paused. A field of blue eyes and curls spread before her, and for the first time—she saw sympathy. She saw tears.

She lowered her voice and gazed at them each, one by one.

"Just like they sold off your nanny from you . . . just like selling off your real mama. Wasn't it?"

Abigail broke into open sobbing. An instant later David started to cry too.

Yula cuddled the boy.

On her other knee, Darby asked in his high, squeaky voice, "Can you bring my nanny back?"

"Not right now, sweetmeat," Yula cooed, gazing deeply into the baby's blue, blue eyes. "But the future change anything. And till then . . . there's one thing I *can* do."

"What?"

She traced his chubby pink cheeks with her brown finger, narrowed her eyes, and pushed forward all she felt about her own sons, and what children deserved. Rich children, poor children, slave children.

Lonely children.

"I can *love* you," she said. "An' I'm gonna."

Little Darby flung his chubby self into her arms. David piled on top of them. Malcolm and Abigail buried themselves in her skirts.

Yula hugged them all as best her two skinny arms could engulf. As she looked up, she was most profoundly moved by the sight at the far wall.

Across the room, Florence Richard's hard shell had broken. The girl was openly weeping.

Soon she too fell into Yula's arms.

Yula stroked head after head of tumbling pale curls, and as she looked up at the oldest boy, who still stood against the far wall but whose face was now a mat of grateful emotion, she simply said, "It don't matter what color love come in, do it?"

CHAPTER NINE

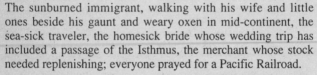

The sunburned immigrant, walking with his wife and little ones beside his gaunt and weary oxen in mid-continent, the sea-sick traveler, the homesick bride whose wedding trip has included a passage of the Isthmus, the merchant whose stock needed replenishing; everyone prayed for a Pacific Railroad.

—Hubert Howe Bancroft

1859
COUNCIL BLUFFS, IOWA

"Good evening, sir. Welcome to Council Bluffs," the young ethnic-looking foreman said. He did not extend his hand. "If you continue in this direction, you shall find Mr. Dodge waiting for you in the gray house where the road ends. He knows more about land west of this place than most men ever will."

"Thank you, sir. May I ask your name?"

"My name is only a jumble of letters," the foreman said. "It's the Dodges and the Judahs you must remember from now on. Go forth, Mr. Lincoln," he added, "and make rail."

Abe Lincoln's rawboned jaw broke into a smile. He regarded the foreman warmly, decided the young man must be Arabic or Turkish, with that black hair, those eyes, and that cream skin. He chuckled another thank you. The foreman had something more than a welcome behind his eyes, and Lincoln understood the occasional need for a mystery.

The young man wanted anonymity, so Lincoln didn't push for conversation, didn't even comment on the extra-long silver watch chain hanging from three of the young man's belt loops. It was the man's only decoration. There were no rings or pendants, as those of the dark classical races often wore.

Lincoln concluded he might be wrong about the man's heritage and opted to leave that alone too. It was getting dark. Better get on with the matter at hand.

The pony didn't jolt as the reins snapped. Lincoln had a lightish touch, sympathetic of the beast. Off they went.

Leaning on the creaking doorway, the foreman watched the carriage rattle past, poetically heading west, toward a vision that moved like a slumbering creature beneath the winter earth.

Vibrations . . . the shudder of industry, of rails. The iron veins of expansion.

Even the blood in a snake's cold heart bubbled at the sensation, the concept. . . .

Dorian knew. His own blood was on the damned cold side.

He folded his arms, fingered the gritty cotton of his shirt, which in its dreams had been white, and stood on the porch of his tiny pine-plank office shed. He watched the wagon go away with Mr. Lincoln aboard, going to meet with Grenville Dodge. That would be a meeting plus three. Dorian momentarily fancied seeping into the woodwork and eavesdropping. He could. Wouldn't be the first time. Wouldn't be the tenth. A smile creased his dirt-smudged cheeks. He licked the dust off his upper lip and thought of Grenville Dodge and the life he must have led up to this point. Dorian allowed himself a twinge of envy.

Here they called Dorian "Mr. B." They thought his name was Burns or Barnes. But they weren't *exactly* sure. He made no friends. Only workers. Railmen. Germans and Chinese, Irish and Italians, gypsies, free or escaped blacks. Engineers, switchmen, brakemen, coal handlers. He rarely introduced himself, having never been brought up with that habit. He stayed in his cabin, reading books borrowed from people on passing trains and wagon trains. Books in French and Italian from the immigrants. He was born speaking Greek, but there were no books in Greek coming west.

Books were . . . beginning not to be enough for him. They only made him hurt for home, for the one-roomed slave cabin where he had slept the only peaceful nights of his life. He didn't want to see things in print anymore. He wanted to see things for himself.

Thus the envy for Dodge and explorers like him.

Signed by Rock Island power man Thomas Durant to survey the great Platte River Valley, Dodge had just returned after five years of charting, adventuring, trail hacking, Indian dealing, and general surviving. He'd come back with a good map of the Emigrant Trail, and lawyer Lincoln was here to inspect land that would be security for a loan, and to hear about the possibilities of a railroad out to the Rockies. Out, and beyond. All the way to salt water. Men like Dodge and Durant and the young Connecticut civil engineer Theodore Judah looked west and saw railroads doing the jobs of rivers, main arteries with a thousand feeders, towns springing up along them just as towns had traditionally sprung up beside water, rattling with pioneers and immigrants, roaring smithies and brimming shops, shouting children, each town with a church and a doctor, all part of a magical word that was completely new . . .

Transcontinental!

Dorian ached to go. To forget his personal quests. He gazed after the skinny, trouble-tossed lawyer who today was representing the Rock Island Railroad. A fundamental man, this lawyer who had inspired such acrimonious headlines, a pleasant man in spite of that drawstring appearance that made him game for newspaper caricatures.

So it was to boil to a froth, finally. All the scrabbling for the past decade over whether or not, and where, to put a transcontinental railroad. Twenty million acres of government land grants had bent to railroading. In 1853—or was it fifty-five—Secretary of War Jefferson Davis had received Congressional instruction to conduct a year-long survey of possible routes to the Pacific. Davis was a Mississippi plantation man, and he wanted a southern route. Lincoln, a possible presidential nominee, wasn't and didn't.

Dorian remembered hearing about Davis back on Plentiful—hearing through Alex how the Mississippi man had been given little choice by Congress, which ordered immediate surveys of other routes than just the Southern. Survey parties struck off from a half-dozen points, led by the Army Corps of Engineers.

But there was more . . . something that killed Dorian's grin as he remembered it. Something in the lawyer's fast eyes. Lincoln was here to view the railroad situation for himself. Dorian had seen a daguerreotype of the man once, but now knew no picture or drawing could capture the speed of those eyes, or the ripple of underlying layers. Looking at Abe Lincoln in the flesh was like looking at the ocean—there were plenty of fish going unseen under the surface.

So Dorian had simply done one of his best tricks: keep the mouth shut and point. Lead one man to another.

After flying headlong into the outside world at the age of twenty-one, he'd found himself an immigrant in his own land. He hadn't really *been* to America before . . . he'd only heard of it. He had lived his life on the tobacco plantation, trapped by his father's pact with his Greek bride. *He shall never leave the grounds.*

The world of Plentiful had been all fable. All myth. *The World,* by Thomas Malory. By Sophocles. Bulwer-Lytton. Robert Burns. Alex . . .

Always through the eyes of someone else.

Once he realized there was no Greek play going on out there, no poetic justice and damned little plain justice, he started about the business of surviving. He had discovered in himself a natural talent for intermediating, and how lucrative butting in could be. His name never appeared in a newspaper. No one remembered him when the deals were done. Other people got credit. Blame rolled off his anonymous shoulders. It was perfect.

Dorian had introduced Judah to Dodge. But nobody remembered. And he made sure nobody wrote it down. He had followed the railroad promoters, canvassed investors, accepted communication with the ambitious Judah, written lawyerlike letters, arranged surveyal maps, judged the grades, supervised the excavations, built embankments, hired the workers who poured masonry for foundation of crossings and bridges—all pieces of the corridor to the western mecca. He had done these things and signed a false name to many documents.

History wouldn't care, as long as the trains went. Whose name had he signed? Even he didn't remember. That was the unkind, indifferent past.

The Pacific Railroad would get built now. Lincoln was that

kind of man, and Dodge certainly was. Rails would soon
stretch past here, across the border to Omaha in the tall
Nebraska Territory, on from there to the fork of the Platte
rivers, to spear right through the Rockies to the Sacramento
trail.

Perhaps it was time to move along.

That wise, wary, even conspiratorial grin on Lincoln's face
made Dorian nervous today. It said, *I know you aren't telling
something.*

Time to move on?

He fingered his twenty-inch watch chain and allowed himself a little sigh of relief when the carriage stopped down the
road and the elongated man made his way up the rough steps
to the front door of the gray house. Dorian caught a glimpse of
Grenville Dodge as Dodge opened the door and gestured
Lincoln inside with obvious excitement and anticipation. His
every gesture was twice as quick as it needed to be, and in his
posture there was a hint of a thousand spark-killer smoke-
stacks and wood-fed boilers and howling 4-4-0's. If Dodge
had his way, "remote" would soon be a word applying only to
Canada—

His nerves jumped at the crash of the window in the back
of his storeroom. He swung around but he was alone here—
alone for miles in the direction of that window.

Glass tinkled to the floor inside. The shack had only two
areas, the office and the storeroom.

A man with a price on his head hears everything. Dorian
heard a very expensive footstep. Someone was in the storeroom.

Dorian raised one hand to his waistcoat. Drew out the
heavy watch . . . unhooked the chain at the other end and drew
it through the three belt loops. He took one step into the office,
filled with maps and river charts and engineering plans, which
for some reason he cared to defend. The chain was warm and
oiled in his hand. The finest case-hardened Damascus steel,
handmade interlocking links made from a set of throwing
knives given to him by a grateful Italian traveler whose life
Dorian had saved in a railroad accident. The wealthy gave
wealthy gifts. At the end of it, a rock that kept time. It dangled
to his knee. He judged the weight and balance, just like last
time and the time before.

A piece of shadow blew at him out of the dark corner. Dorian's arm went numb. He had to think rationally to realize that he had been struck, but he knew the choreography of an assault and responded without thinking. Experience and all his senses clicked into place. No one here had cause to attack him—and he could sense a hired hand when he felt one strike him. He knew the difference between a passionate blow and a paid one. Even in the darkness he isolated the attacker by height and heaviness—height showed where to retaliate, and weight told him the speed of the man's next move. All he really needed was the height.

Dorian lashed out with his right hand—the watch flew and took its chain with it. The chain hit the man's neck and coiled around his throat. The watch whipped in a short arch, looped over the chain and into Dorian's hand—

He drew it sharply toward his chest. His attacker came with it, a great slumping mass of sweat and muscle.

Dorian twisted his hand. The chain came with it, tighter, until the man was choking and on his knees, virtually hanging himself so Dorian didn't have to work hard. Moonlight came in the tiny window as the clouds moved, and Dorian felt it on his face. Now his attacker looked up and saw Dorian's face, his eyes.

The fight flooded out of the black man when he saw that face. It wasn't like most other white folks' faces.

The man dragged down on the chain and gagged.

"Hurry up," Dorian murmured. "Quietly . . . go . . . sweetly done."

The chain grated against itself. The intruder slumped, convulsed, and the moment ended.

Dorian straightened, his arms throbbing. He tugged his foot from under the shivering body.

Clumsy attack on his life. Unprofessional murder. Such a shame, all for lack of a plan. Why couldn't people think about what they were setting out to do, and do it efficiently? Murder and everything else should have a plan, and a method of execution.

Dorian paused. His bat-wing brows flared a little.

"Murder by execution," he chuckled. "I like that. . . . " He tilted his head at his fallen assailant. "You've entertained me. Doesn't happen every day. Good work."

Dead as mutton. Half as appetizing. The look of death never ceased to intrigue him, especially in these first few moments. He watched to see if there was any hint of a fleeing soul.

So far he had never caught one sneaking out.

"*Pax vobiscum*," he murmured.

Why had this man tried to kill him? Was the negro a runaway, protecting himself, trying to hide? No, Council Bluffs wasn't on any Underground Railroad track. Most of Iowa wasn't. There was nowhere to escape from or to around here. End of analysis.

He stooped and patted at the man's clothing. One pocket was stiff, and in it was a folded piece of paper. As he unfolded it, Dorian knew this wasn't the paper of a freed slave, but the paper to capture an unfree one.

The poster. WANTED . . . RUNAWAY HALF-BREED . . . DORIAN WALLACE . . . 'S' BRAND ON RIGHT ARM . . . $5000 REWARD.

Suddenly his right arm was aching. The information was old, but the paper was worn only around the edges. Not sun faded. It hadn't sat pinned to a wall in some town or settlement. It had been carried in a valise all these months, probably, and distributed.

Now Dorian knew what he had to do. He must look for a giant four-legged creature that once had been a spindly four-legged colt on a Carolina rice farm.

He must look for the thundering black horse carrying a man with shellac eyes and a razor temper.

A flash of silver . . . a tug . . . and he was choking.

Noah Sutton didn't need to see the features of the man who was attacking him from behind. He sensed in the skill of the attack that this was no common thief or maniac. There was a chain around his throat. One of his fingers was caught in it. He struggled, but he was thin and had always hired his muscle from other sources than his own arms. That's why horses liked him on their backs.

He was off balance. He dug his heels into the dust outside the mangy little hotel where he'd been foolish enough to be caught, and knew perfectly well who held the chain around his neck. Damn that dead nigger for giving them away—now the half-breed knew Noah was here and had caught him—

These flashing thoughts all came together at once, in that first instant when he heard the shuffle behind him and felt the chain cuff his throat and its first yanks.

His mind remembered the classical features in which all corners of humanity were hidden, the moonstone skin, and the voice—trained to speak clearly, softly, the pronunciation of an aristocrat.

"Still one of the handful, aren't you, Mr. Sutton?" that elegant voice said into his ear.

"Mongrel," Noah choked.

"The handful of men who make the world stink for all the rest of us," Dorian murmured thoughtfully. "I always thought you needed a good garroting. I should have dispatched you the day I left Chapel Mount, I see that now. Ah, the inspiration of hindsight—then, God should have dispatched you in the womb. It may be the only thing He and I have in common."

"God is watching you, dirt," Noah coughed.

"As long as he doesn't interfere. What do you want me to do with your stallion when you're dead? I may give it to a slave or a Chinese and let him sell it. He'll be a wealthy man with a horse like that."

"No man can bridle Pledge but me—try it. He'll kick you dead, half-breed."

"Your life is ill spent hunting for me, sir," Dorian said, keeping the chain just tight enough. "My death meliorates nothing for you."

"It will when I throw your hide on a bonfire in front of my slaves and make them cook their dinner over your burning corpse!" Noah rasped, clawing at Dorian's arm. "Then they'll see who runs Chapel Mount!"

His spit hit the wall.

Dorian said, "Is one rice plantation still the scope of your little world? Most children grow up after leaving the homestead. Perhaps that's why your world is so foul, and why you seek my death to absolve you of your own smell. What have I done to you that I should merit your obsession?"

"You humiliated me."

"In front of whom? A handful of slaves? A headman or two?"

"God. You humiliated be before God!"

"Oh, him."

"I'll have respect when I bring you back, breed. My father, my sister—"

"*Memento mori,* sir. Your sister and father are insane."

Wrong thing to say.

Noah Sutton's razor temper sparked to life. He thrashed with both feet, and his shoulders wrenched from side to side, and he hissed and screamed. "Don't you say that! Don't you *say that*! I'll screw you into the earth, you nigra-blooded insult to humanity! How dare you say that about my father!"

The pitch of his voice hit a high note. He twisted, kicked, and nearly hanged himself on Dorian's relentless watch chain before finally settling down to a ragged series of gasps.

"You hate the harebrained bastard more than I do," Dorian reminded. "Unfortunate you haven't admitted that to yourself and gone on with your life. You were as much his slave as I was. More, for I left him behind."

"Why don't you kill me then," Noah said, "or I'll just keep finding you."

Moments ticked. Neither man breathed.

Finally Dorian said, "All right." He caught the wagging steel watch in his left hand while holding the chain tight in his right. A miner's-style watch—with a cover. His thumb flipped the cover open. He held the watch out at the end of his arm, where Noah could see it. They could both see it. Ten forty-five at night.

"Tell God what time you died," Dorian said.

And he began to tighten the chain in earnest.

Noah thrashed like live fish on a griddle. The sense of death crept up from his numbing legs. Panic set in—he struggled, yanked—but tremors of experience ran through Dorian's arms, and there was no contest. Noah began to sink toward the ground. Dorian ushered him down, keeping the chain mercifully tight, never teasing his victim with an instant of slack. The chain bit into his hand, his wrist, corded his flesh—

Sudden impact struck the tip of his left shoulder and drove him backward into the wall. Dorian had been struck by every mentionable projectile mankind could muster, with one exception. This was his first time to be hit with a bullet.

For an instant it confused him. There was no pain—only pressure, thrust, then numbness racing up his shoulder and into his neck. He lost his grip on Noah's throat, and the watch flew wild at the end of the chain. Only habit kept the end of the chain in Dorian's fist as he dropped backward.

Noah's onionskin face drew taught. He sucked in a breath and shrieked.

"Kill him! Kill him!"

Another black face filled the air—for an instant Dorian thought the dead slave had come back to life to defend his master, but no, this was a second slave, bigger, uglier, smellier, and angrier.

Without waiting for proprieties, Dorian lashed out with a leg. The arch caught the negro's hand and sent the pistol flying—it smashed into the nearby horse trough and hit the ground with a thump.

Tethered to the trough, a giant black stallion with a two-foot mane and a five-foot tail thrashed like a tied-up tornado.

Clearly the negro wasn't accustomed to holding a gun and keeping it. In an instant Dorian analyzed that tidbit and used it.

He kicked again, connecting with the negro's midriff. Because he was off balance, there was only half-enough impact in the blow. The man staggered, but didn't go down.

Dorian swung the heavy steel watch. It turned into a compacted steel projectile at the end of its chain and caught the negro on the side of his face, in front of the ear. The man howled, clapped both hands to the side of his jaw, and stumbled to one knee.

On his own knees a few feet away, Noah choked, "Get the gun, you black ass! Kill him!"

But it was too late.

His half-breed quarry slipped into the night with a pocket full of warning, and disappeared. The giant black horse was still yanking at his tether, whistling furiously at the disturbance.

Noah staggered to his feet, wobbling, furious.

"Damn you, damn you!" he squealed, whipping the man over and over with his bare hands.

The slave cowered and held up an arm to ward off the sharp fingers.

"You'll go to hell for failing, damn you!" his master howled. "I'll kill you for failing!"

Noah snatched up the discarded pistol, and when he turned, his face was brittle and his heart parchment. His lips peeled back from small square teeth. The pistol barrel was the only part of him that wasn't shaking.

"But I save yoh life!" the slave bellowed, trembling, holding his arm against his face.

Noah trembled and aimed. "Then you'll go to heaven instead."

He pulled the trigger.

Blood splattered back on the gun, Noah's hand, his sleeve. The slave's arm was blown through, and his black hand dangled from the gushing mess, but the man was already dead. Terror-stricken eyes bugged at Noah from beneath a perfect reddish-blue hole in his forehead. The crushed iron bullet, slowed by passage through that arm, protruded from the hole just enough to be seen. The rest of it was in the man's brain.

A few seconds, and the body collapsed like a puppet. Convulsed. Heaved. Fell still.

"Do your assignment better in heaven," Noah grumbled.

He stood over the body of his slave and with morbid satisfaction watched the dead man's eyes go blank. That's what the man had been bought for—to die for him if need be.

He rubbed his shredded neck. With an audible growl, he sank his kerchief into a fire bucket and held it to the scored flesh under his chin.

"I need a professional," he told himself. "I'll hire one."

Dorian pressed a discarded rag to his bloody shoulder and allowed himself a wince. He selected a boxcar and climbed aboard. This train would leave before dawn. Instincts had struggled to serve, and Dorian had failed to heed them soon enough. *Move along, move along.*

He would go east and spend some time not being found there for a while. Then he would go somewhere else and not be found. Interesting hobby. Of course, he would have to be better at it than of late. Somehow he *had* been found. Perhaps he had lingered too long. He hadn't quite squeezed all the secrets out of this trick of persona incognita.

Not one to put his money in the four clapboard walls and a tin box they called a bank out here, his salary and any gambling revenues were tucked safely in an eastern bank. He would go and visit it for a while.

"Our lives shall be tangent until one of us is dead, Mr. Sutton," he murmured to the empty night.

The arms of shadows embraced him, and the scent of rail-truck grease became his bedmate.

At least now he could say he had done railroads.

★★★

THE BURNING FUSE

NOVEMBER 1860

Abraham Lincoln is elected President of the United States with a majority of electoral votes, but a questionable showing of popular votes.

DECEMBER 1860

South Carolina secedes from the United States. Federal Fort Sumter, in Charleston Harbor, is one of several Federal installments now behind "foreign" lines.

JANUARY–FEBRUARY 1861

Mississippi, Florida, Alabama, Georgia, Texas, and Louisiana secede. Kansas joins the Union with a nonslavery constitution. The merchant ship Star of the West *is pressed into Union service and dispatched with provisions and reinforcements for Fort Sumter.*

As the ship approaches Charleston Harbor, it is fired upon. These are the first, though unofficial, shots of the Civil War.

The ship is undamaged, but turns away. The Federal troops at Sumter remain unreinforced. Major Robert Anderson refuses return of fire, unwilling to be the man who commits the Union to war with the South. Stalemate.

Later several Federal installations including the Federal Arsenal at Appalachiacola, forts Barrancas, Marion, Pickens, McCree, Pike, Jackson, Massachusetts in the Mississippi Gulf, Oglethorpe Barracks in Savannah, the U.S. Hospital in New

Orleans, and the naval yard at Pensacola are occupied by Confederate troops.

Fort Sumter remains stalemated.

MARCH 1861

Arizona secedes.

Revolution had left Mexico debt ridden and unable to pay. A combined British-French-Spanish flotilla employs a common practice of seizing a port and its customs house to collect.

Being involved in its own war, Washington officially recognizes this as not in violation of the Monroe Doctrine, the doctrine which stipulates that the United States will tolerate no further establishment of European colonies in the Western Hemisphere.

France intends to colonize Mexico. Britain and Spain abandon the effort, and France puts the puppet Maximilian, in-law of King Louis Napoleon, in control of Mexico.

The War between the States now threatens not just the North and South, but the entire Western Hemisphere.

APRIL 12

Confederate-held Fort Johnson begins rotation fire on Fort Sumter. Four thousand shells later, no one is dead and few are wounded, but the unreinforced, unprovisioned commander of Fort Sumter surrenders his hungry, exhausted, valiant men into Confederate hands.

APRIL 17

The state of Virginia, philosophical bastion of the New World, finally accepts secession. Because Virginia has waited so long to secede, few Confederate leaders come from this state, even though it is a precolonial seat of foundation, wealth, education, and intellect, and even the birthplace of the Constitution.

The Confederacy, therefore, is led not by bluebloods, but by the nouveau riche—men who have come up from the com-

mon soil, rather than from the bloodlines of the Founding
Fathers.

It is this new generation who must deal with what makes a
nation, how the South will fight, and how far the Confederacy
will go to ensure its survival. The ringing question of Mexico,
and the licking of European chops over the shaky continent,
are nearly audible to the naked ear.

CHAPTER TEN

————— ★ —————

"Belligerent rights, my Aunt Polly's skinny blue ass!"

Secretary of State William Seward plunged back and forth like a swarm of bees in front of the clawfoot sofa on which both of his assistants sat. Neither of the two aides said anything as he steamed out his reaction to the latest communiqué from the United States' emissary in England.

A hawk-faced man with an enormous hooking nose, bushy brows, a small round-tipped chin, and almost no lips, Seward seemed ready to be launched from a cannon. He shook his fist and the shag of silver hair on his head at the same time.

"Damn the Queen and her declaration of neutrality! England should make up its mind whether she speaks for them or not! If this doesn't construe recognition of the Confederacy by Britain, I'd like to know what does!"

His senior aide, Lloyd Copeman, sat holding the communiqué from Charles Adams, their minister to London. He remained calm as usual and simply spelled out the implications.

"Belligerent rights on the high seas," he said slowly, "simply acknowledged the Confederacy's status as a temporarily separate entity from any other nation—"

"I'll temporary them, by God!"

"Under international maritime law, the Confederacy can now flag its own ships, search and seize vessels under suspicion—without being called pirates—and buy arms in neutral nations without implicating those nations in conspira—"

"I pity the nation that sells those rebels arms!" Seward roared. "They'll swallow their neutrality whole!"

"England is just waiting to see which way the wind blows," the other aide, Smith, offered. He watched in fascination as Secretary of State Seward rammed this way and that across the room.

"I'll show them the wind, damn them all," Seward growled. He stuffed his hands in his trouser pockets to keep from shaking them. "This is very liable to be construed as recognition. Spineless English title kissers . . . 'neutrality' . . . no wonder we broke off from them."

"If the South were just a lump of land," Copeman continued patiently, "with a thousand or so citizens, it wouldn't be recognized as a belligerent. But the Confederacy is three quarters of a million square miles of territory, with a third of this nation's voters. If they claim belligerent rights, they have them for practical purposes, Great Britain or not. Parliament might as well recognize them as a legitimate belligerent, and make good on doing business with them."

Smith took the chance to add, "The English textile workers are dependent upon Southern cotton, Mr. Secretary."

William Seward stopped dead in his tracks and turned so sharply that he made a mark in the carpet. He boomed down at the young aide.

"I know that! How do you think a man gets to the top of his government! By ignoring economic realities?"

Smith turned pink under the flaming glare of his superior. "I . . . I'm . . ."

Instantly Seward twisted into his pattern again, leaving a little pool of melted Smith behind on the leather sofa.

"And now I'm supposed to accept their entertaining those three Confederate envoys, what's their names, Yancey and the other two—"

Copeman looked up.

"Those would be Rost and Mann, Mr. Secr—"

Seward whirled again. "I know their names, Copeman! Don't fill in every pointless detail, suck your eyes!" Instantly he whirled again and paced away. "God damn them, I'll give them hell."

Copeman glanced at Smith, to let the younger assistant see he wasn't alone in the fumes of Mount Seward.

"The South'll take this belligerent-rights business as a step toward full recognition. I daren't ignore that shadow. Copeman, take this down—"

Copeman scrambled for his quill and inkwell on a side table. "Yes, sir."

"—and send it to Charles Adams and tell him to serve notice on the Court of St. James. As follows: if any European power provokes war, we shall not shrink from it."

"Yes, Mr. Secretary."

"Foreign intervention would oblige us to treat those nations as allies of the insurrectionary party, and to carry on the war against them as enemies. The President and the people of the United States deem the Union damned well worth all the cost and sacrifices of a contest with the world."

Copeman would have responded, but by now his tongue was poking out the corner of his mouth as he feverishly scratched upon his note book, dipped for more ink, and scratched again. He was gratified when Smith had the brains to reach for the inkwell and quill on the secretary's desk and start taking notes as well, while Seward blustered from the window to the sofa and back.

"And send the same message to Dayton in Paris and tell him to tell the French and tell 'em *good*."

Copeman was writing feverishly, but the Secretary was getting ahead of the ink. "Yes, sir—"

Beside him Smith also battled with the eccentricities of the quill. Between them they should get most of the words, in that general order.

"You move the words around until it sounds right," Seward said, waving his hand at them both.

"Yes, Mr. Secretary," Copeman croaked, preoccupied.

"And I want to see Lord Lyons face-to-face. And that French ambassador, Mercier. France has backed us in two wars—they'd better keep their allies straight."

"Yes, sir. I shall arrange meetings immediately."

"Better arrange smelling salts, because I'm going to have 'em both on the floor."

"Yes, sir."

"Dependent on Southern cotton, my foot . . ."

His volume tapered off, but not his intensity. He swung about twice more, then slammed into his office chair and grabbed at his cigar box. A moment later the secretary of state was lounging back in the tall chair like a Kodiak bear scratching his back against a tree. He blew gray smoke into the air and watched it twist toward the molded plaster medallion in the ceiling.

Many seconds passed in silence. While his two aides watched in renewed awe, the savage man metamorphosed into a calculating, thoughtful manipulator.

They could see him thinking. The ranting was over for now, and he was looking for a subtle trap to spring upon Europe and the Confederacy if they so much as whispered *alliance*. They watched his changing face and ambivalent eyes, eyes that flamed even while narrowed in calculation.

Finally he drew in a long breath and spoke in a tone of pure conspiracy.

"I'll make 'em dependent on Northern *money*, that's what I'll do," he said. "Copeman . . ."

"Sir?"

"I want to talk to someone in the powder business. Explosive powder. Not from Maryland or Kentucky . . . too risky. They have to be located in a decidedly Union state. Maybe the people we contracted for blasting powder for the Union Pacific Railroad. That Delaware family."

"The Du Ponts, Mr. Secretary," Copeman said. "Of Wilmington, Delaware."

"That's right. I want to talk to one of them."

Seward leaned back and lit his cigar, inhaled deeply, and let the smoke draw a design over his head.

"If I have to, by God, I'll go to war with the world."

★

CHAPTER ELEVEN

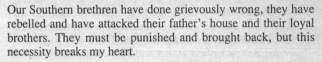

Our Southern brethren have done grievously wrong, they have rebelled and have attacked their father's house and their loyal brothers. They must be punished and brought back, but this necessity breaks my heart.

— Major Robert Anderson, Commander
Fort Sumter, after the surrender

May 15, 1861

My dearest Mother and Grandfather Dimitrios,
It is now nearly summer of this new and unsteady year. Uncle Nick and I have missed the entire winter and spring seasons, owing to an outbreak of typhoid, which we both contracted while passing through an infected town in lower Ohio. We were both in makeshift beds at the mercy of local women acting as nurses. Nick was incapacitated for nearly four months. I was down for nearly five, though in my case it was as usual difficult to tell sleep from conversation.
I awakened from my delirium to discover that the entire nation has caught a fever. A little something happened at Fort Sumter that has changed the picture. When Rip Van Alex roused, more than four thousand shells had been exchanged over Charleston Harbor. A wonder Nick and I weren't shaken from our slumber by the sound of it. We fell asleep in our own country and wakened in enemy territory.
While we lay recovering, the Virginia Convention fi-

nally voted to secede, but too late to supply the Confederate cabinet with the blood of the Founding Fathers. As a Southerner I am trepidatious. As an American I am grief stricken. As a brother I wonder how I can find our dark-haired Dorian through battle's black cloud. He will blend too well in all that thunder, I fear.

I have discovered that Norfolk Navy Yard has been evacuated by the Federals and is now in the hands of the Confederacy. I wonder if that means the South will now have a navy. Do you think we can make a navy from the old Frigate United States *and refloating the half-dozen ships the Federals burned before they abandoned the yard? Remember when Father took Lydia and Rose and me to see the* United States *and the* Constitution *on my twelfth birthday, and told us about the Revolutionary War?*

The Federals towed the Constitution *out into the Chesapeake to keep her out of Confederate hands. Makes me consider putting a grappling hook on Plentiful and towing the plantation out a bit. Perhaps we can anchor beside Old Ironsides for the duration and sell Tidewater cheroots to both sides.*

We shall contact you again once we safely reach home.

Honor and hopes,
Your devoted son Alexander Wallace

LATE MAY 1861
PLENTIFUL

"There they are, Uncle . . . the Naxian Lions and the dogwood trees at the gates of home."

"Alex—wait."

They drew up their horses not ten feet from the stone lions. The past months—years—suddenly fell away to dust, and it was as though they had been out only on a short ride. Yes, years. Since 1858 they had been searching for Dorian, only to conclude that Dorian didn't want to be found. Alex looked at Nick with foreboding silence. For miles now he had sensed something.

"I'm not going in," Nick said.

Alex slumped in the saddle, his wrists crossed over the horse's withers. "Oh, my savior in heaven . . . I was afraid of this."

Nick Varvaresos's dark eyes and pocked face were resolute in the bright daylight. The silver in his hair only made him seem more decisive. His fist was closed on the reins, lifted against his chest, and prevented his horse from moving forward.

"I cannot go back to someone else's life," he said. "The epidemic came too close to killing both of us, Alex, and I lay thinking for many days in my bed. My legs and arms were useless to me. All I had was my brain, my heart, my heritage." He looked at Alex squarely. "You are not Greek anymore. You have different dreams. Society doesn't intimidate you as it did us in those days when I first came here with Dimitrios's plans for the South. . . . I know what you're going to do with Plentiful when you go inside those gates," he finished, "and I cannot be part of it."

"What can't you be part of?" Alex shot back. The question had been waiting five hundred miles to pop out. "Am I the only man in our family with a conscience? Even Dorian refused to help. What a blow he might have struck against slavery! Behold, a half-negro man with the mind of an Aristotle! But he refused . . . and I know why. The negroes will need help to become free—the help of white men. It will take white hands to break those chains."

He paused, tried to see through the determination on his uncle's face. Nick's sudden silence implied that his decision was weeks old and unbreakable.

The idealist inside Alex Wallace pushed up and out, and he tried one more time.

"Whatever I do here, it won't bring Dorian back," he said, "or make my father understand that of all of us, Dorian was least at fault. Father's bargain with my mother, to keep Dorian a secret, was spawned of the status quo twenty-eight years ago. Slavery has poisoned the South, that such deals should be made, and that my father should have been ashamed of a son like Dorian. My brilliant brother is missing, possibly even dead. My family is fragmented. My mother is in Macedon with a shattered heart, and the man who caused it all is in that house, living in comfort and splendor, tended by human beings whom he owns like goats!"

He pointed through the dogwoods, past the vine-carpeted, orange-treed garden with its Greek statues and its memories.

With a heavy voice he challenged, "How can you go fight for the system that would enslave Dorian?"

Nick shook his head and huffed impatiently at the idealism of youth. "Alex, the Greeks had slaves for thousands of years. The Egyptians before that, the Assyrians before that. I cannot throw away a whole culture for one ancient habit. I will join the Confederate Army, and fight to save the South for the sake of Dimitrios's dream of a new Greece . . . but this war will take all the men, South and North. There will be no way to keep the slaves from walking away, even if the Confederacy is victorious. Either way . . . slavery will be finished. As for the South, we must save it now," he added. "We can change it later."

They watched each other. A generation apart, the gap widening.

"The cost of saving it is too high," Alex said, his throat tight.

Nick merely nodded. This is why they had both silently evaded the conversation for so many months. They were both right, in their ways.

Like the North and the South. A war not to throw off tyranny, nor to strike against an aggressor, not a war to gain land or wealth, but a war between two "rights" that could not mingle.

Nick reached out a hand and cupped Alex's blond head as though his nephew were once again the little boy he had helped to raise. Little Alexander the Great . . . a blond among the swarthy, a dreamer among soldiers.

"*Andeeo*," he whispered, "my son."

★

CHAPTER TWELVE

———— ★ ————

"Revenge."

"Is that a good idea, madam?"

"It's the best idea of all, Mr. Pinkerton. This man doesn't seem like what he is, and that's the worst kind of man."

"I see. Can you tolerate this man's company?"

"Anyone can tolerate his company."

Grace MacHutcheon tightened her mouth as she remembered the deceptively affable nature of her nemesis. The man she would ruin by joining the Union cause.

Wyatt Craig. He put everyone and everything at ease with a word and a pat of his hand. To know him is to trust him. *I hate him*.

"So tell me. How shall I become a spy in the Secret Service for the Union?"

The compact Scotsman in front of her leaned back in his banker's chair and studied the twenty-something-year-old woman who had relentlessly refused to leave his office until he talked spying with her. Despite her proper clothes, she was blunt and unladylike. While he might not prefer such a direct manner in a luncheon guest, he did respect it, especially in a woman, and in a culture where women were "taught" to behave a certain way. She said she was from Richmond, but she wasn't. A man needn't be a detective to know that at first glance, or even to feel it in the tough way her feet struck the floor when she walked. This was no belle.

Pinkerton rubbed his beard absently and gave her a long

125

look, without blinking. He openly poured over her dark auburn hair, and noted the winks of red between the filaments of the net holding it, decided the color was real, noted the length of it—probably to the waist unnetted, noted her square jaw and narrow lips, the rather severe grass-green eyes—and got what he wanted. She didn't flinch, didn't fidget, and didn't care how long he stared at her. She plain didn't care. She knew what she wanted. He liked that.

It was a special effort to keep approval from showing in his own eyes. "You're a Northern woman, Miss MacHutcheon?"

"Born and raised in Kansas. Germans. Immigrants. They called my folks white trash," she said unashamedly, and surprisingly without bitterness. "We *were* white, and we certainly were trash. We had it bad in those days. Plenty bad, but we survived. My little brother could shoot a mouse on the moon with that rifle of his. He barked squirrels for our pot, and I worked as a house girl for a woman of the same nationality as you. It's her name I've taken, and even a few of her manners. Just as well. My parents' manners weren't worth taking anywhere."

"But you are lately of Richmond, you say."

"I followed my brother to Richmond when his job moved—now this is where all these things begin to play, so you listen to me," she insisted, her eyes narrowing.

"I always listen," Pinkerton said. His accent punctuated the claim just right to her American ears.

Grace MacHutcheon scooted forward on her bustle, took a deep breath, and said, "My brother Patrick had been working for the Craig Tannery, but they were proslavers and we were Free-Soilers. Those proslavers killed my parents, so I burned their factory down."

Pinkerton blinked. Was she joking? Testing him? Dead parents? Burned a factory? Of hides and tanning chemicals?

He wrinkled his nose, imagining the stink of it. The countryside had probably smelled for months.

"So," she went on, "the Craig got a deal to make gunpowder for the Confederacy, and he took it, and my stupid brother saw fit to move to Richmond with him. What could I do but go?"

The Craig, Pinkerton noted. As though he were royalty. The Duke. The Marquis. The Laird. The Craig.

Pinkerton waved a finger. "Your brother . . . he didn't burn the factory?"

"He was lying in a bed, half-crippled from a factory accident. Both legs broken. Took him the better part of a year to get up and walk with canes."

"I see. And he didn't know you burned the factory?"

"Hardly. He had the sensibility of a puppy. Beside," she added, "he'd have tried to stop me. So I couldn't tell him. So what could I do but go with the puppy when he followed the Craig to Richmond? What could I do? You tell me what."

"And this puts you in Richmond and in position to take work at this powder mill as a schoolmistress?"

"It did, and I took the job." She leaned forward even a little farther, and her green eyes widened. "It's a powder mill, Mr. Pinkerton. Gunpowder. Blasting powder, and he's selling it to the Confederacy. Lately he even accepted a commission and mustered his workers together into a what's-it-called."

"A brigade?"

"No, the other one."

"A company."

"Suddenly mill workers were turned into soldiers overnight, and the Craig was Major Craig. Just like that! No soldiering, no military training, no time served, and he's a major! Land sake!"

"And . . . ," Pinkerton began, "you can use this man . . . your position in his powder mill, for the Union cause—"

"Yes, yes." She sat back in the straight chair and huffed, "What've I been saying? The Craig killed my brother in front of my eyes, and I want revenge. It's simple, and I like simple."

Pinkerton rocked in the chair. Sudden silence fell in the office. Only the creak of the chair disturbed it. Grace began that look again, the look that said she didn't care how long he made her wait.

Revenge, she had said. And he had yet to ask the one pertinent question. He knew now who she was, roughly how old she was, and a sketch of her background, enough to add up the evidence of her sensibilities. There had been a brother she had followed to the South, and that's why she had been there. The brother was murdered. Or killed, and murder was this woman's chosen word. He'd seen that before—the redesigning of words to fit a perception. Murder can easily be accidental, given the right circumstances.

"How do you know," Pinkerton began again slowly, "that this Craig killed your brother?"

"Because I *saw* him! He put a pistol to Patrick's chest and shot him! These two eyes saw it!"

Pinkerton touched his beard. "Oh—well," he said, "that would seem solid evidence."

The woman stood up and shouted, "I saw him shoot my brother dead! What more do you want!"

"Yes, Miss MacHutcheon, yes, yes. I did hear you. I do understand. I accept your case."

"It's not a case! I want to be a spy for you! I want to hurt him and hurt his cause!"

"Do you want the Union to win?"

Grace drew back suddenly, her jaw stiff. It was a test.

She sat down, rather firmly, and the fury went out of her voice, realizing she was on the brink of a mistake.

"Yes," she tightly said. "Of course."

"Of course," Pinkerton echoed.

He may or may not have believed her, she decided.

"You'll have to learn to control that temper," Pinkerton said, "if you're to work as a counterspy."

"I'll worry about that. Your only concern will be to tell me what to do. I'll worry about doing it. I can keep working as a schoolmistress at this powder mill and funnel information out to you. Deliveries . . . military positions . . . sizes of shipments. Isn't that the kind of thing the Union Army might just like to know about the Confederates?"

Pinkerton tapped the tips of his fingers together thoughtfully.

They understood each other completely. Within moments of their first glimpse of each other, Pinkerton and Grace MacHutcheon had each other sized clean up. He was the ambitious, quick-eyed agent who had gotten Lincoln safely to Washington despite death threats, and she was a German immigrant's daughter—he had heard the remnants of German inflection on one or two of her words long before she had volunteered the information. In his business one didn't wait for information to be handed over. He had learned long ago to skim the surface of anything or anyone he encountered and instantly break that surface down into a roster of facts. Her vocal inflections were nothing an American should be able to catch, but he was Scottish and used to the idea of accents changing every five miles down the road. He'd made a practice of pinning people's origins from their accents, or even their lack thereof. The Northern accent was different in Michigan than in southern Ohio, different in Ohio than in Indiana. He picked up on the German touch, but might have been tempted to place her from Pennsylvania rather than Kansas. Luckily she'd provided the information before he guessed wrong.

He didn't mind guessing, but he wanted his guesses to be right.

"Very well, Miss MacHutcheon," he said. "We shall try you out."

"What do you want me to do first?"

"A bit anxious, aren't you, miss?"

"Am I? The soldiers here are living a little too fine a life here in these camps, Mr. Pinkerton. I want to act soon and know my information is being used. I want to get this war over with and get on with my life. The South will be destroyed one man at a time, and I know where to start."

Tempted to tell her anything that would keep the wrath in those eyes down, Pinkerton hesitated. He saw in her face that she had been witness to a dark recess of the man's soul, that some part of her was bitter, and he suspected she intended to take revenge on the whole South.

Grace took his silence as some kind of answer, and started putting her gloves back on. "You like cigars, don't you, Mr. Pinkerton?"

"Cigars? Yes . . . why?"

"I'll send you some." Her brows shot up to punctuate her meaning. "You understand? Confirmation. One cigar for a piece of good interest, two cigars for something very important, and three cigars for critical information. Then you'll know it's from me."

"Ah," he said. "I understand."

His own professionalism gnawed at him, and he just couldn't let her get out without asking one more question.

In a much depressed tone, he asked, "How is this major's information any more accurate than that of my more trusted sources?"

"Because I *am* one of your trusted sources!" Grace shot back. "This major runs a powder mill in Richmond for the Confederate Army. Gunpowder, cannon shot, so on. I'll get him to tell me how much powder he's sending. And anything else you want. They won't send more than they need, will they?"

"Well—"

"If we know how much powder, we'll know how many men, yes?"

"Well, yes . . . theoretically. But he's an officer and all due credit to you, Miss MacHutcheon, you're no Rose Greenhow. How will you get information out of this major and destroy him at the same time . . . without his suspecting?"

Grace stood up and plopped her bonnet back on her head, its brim casting a shadow on her eyes.

"Simple," she said. "I'll marry him."

★

THE BURNING FUSE

21 JULY 1861

MANASSAS JUNCTION, VIRGINIA,
NEAR A CREEK CALLED BULL RUN

The Union and Confederate armies, throbbing with anticipation after a series of skirmishes, prepare for the first clash of army-sized numbers as they come together near Bull Run. Names begin to appear that will not fade. Beauregard. Johnston. Sherman. Burnside. McDowell. Early. Jackson. It is the beginning of a long series of legends, some deserved, some distorted.

One legend sparks when Fourth Alabama's Brigadier General Barnard Bee begs Thirty-third Virginia's Thomas Jackson for support. Jackson promises to advance, but does not. Bee's regiment continues fighting, expecting help from Jackson, which never comes. The Fourth Alabama is slaughtered. In reaction to Jackson's refusal to move, Bee cries, "Look at him! Standing there like a stone wall!"

The nickname Stonewall sticks to Jackson henceforth. Bee's outcry was bitter, not congratulatory, but the Confederate population and press prefer the image of stout defense under fire rather than a recrimination of stubborn refusal, and tilt the debate their own way until half of it disappears.

Stonewall Jackson's brigade is not under fire at the moment he acquires that nickname. Since General Bee dies later in the battle, clarification dies with him.

Manassas, the first full-scale battle of the Civil War, is a

Confederate victory, and the Union army retreats across Bull Run. The Union searches for a new military leader. It eventually turns to the general who led Union troops to control of western Virginia, a portion of Virginia that has broken away in order to stay with the North—George McClellan.

McClellan will soon be recognized as the best candidate to assume control of the Union's Army of the Potomac.

---- ★ ----

CHAPTER THIRTEEN

———————— ★ ————————

19 July 1861
Twenty miles north of Sheboygan, Wisconsin,
on Lake Michigan

The place had been hard to get to. The travel alone had taken two months. Half-built railroads didn't even connect with each other. Scrawny, overused, hired horses. Hitching rides on farmer's wagons. Canoe like a goddamn savage up from Milwaukee. Just try canoeing north on that choppy lake. Arms were still aching even after three days walking. Take a hell of a lot of days to get where he was headed, all the way up to Oshkosh settlement, near where the Wolf and Fox rivers came together. If anybody was still alive up there in this steamy forest.

Trekking boots made an elephant out of a man. Ferns everywhere, and more on top of that. A crust of moss on top of every rock, beaches bare as a dead man's ass and twice as ugly. Man'd have to be a fuckin' seal to get along in this off-lake wasteland. Funny how spoiled a man could get down in that Virginia territory. . . .

Lake. Big goddamn waste of water. Nobody here to use it except them Winnebago Injuns, and they didn't know how to use it.

Orville Quist was following a trail of solid leads up from Richmond, where he'd found, caught, and arrested the man he had been hired to find. Dorian Wallace, called Trözen, half-breed runaway slave, looked white, spoke good, dangerous. Quist had accepted his contract from that squeaky mama's boy Noah Sutton, taken the advance funds, searched his prey, baited his lines, and found the runaway hiding among the white aristocracy. Quist had caught the mulatto, paraded him before the morning crowd of white people among whom he had lived and cloaked himself. Slapped him in the jailhouse, assuming the iron bars would protect the slave from those who wanted to hang him.

Gone for a drink—and lost him. Escaped.

The man was good at escaping. And he had help, probably from his boss, Wyatt Craig. Gone like a blowed-out candle.

Five thousand dollars as good as in his pocket, and out of it again just like that. Not prone to tantrums, Quist had simply spat into the empty cell and started over. For a bounty hunter worth his gristle, failure was only a setback. His contract was binding and without deadline. He was hunting again.

Quist had haunted Richmond and that powder factory for nine weeks without showing himself, but there was no further sign of the runaway. Dorian Wallace Trözen had been in Richmond, and unlike a year ago, Quist now knew the runaway's personality, demeanor, and preferences. A mulatto runaway had so few friends—sooner or later he would come back to Wyatt Craig. Quist had kept an eye on the powder factory, on all the banks, all the whorehouses, sniffed around, bought extra eyes here and there, but . . . nothing. The runaway was gone. Maybe too smart to act predictable.

So Quist thumbed through what was left of his retainer and started searching a cold trail before it got any colder. If the money ran out and he couldn't find Noah Sutton to get more, that'd be it. He'd be done with this contract. The half-breed would lose a shadow.

Quist hadn't seen Sutton since the scrawny, shrill aristocrat hired him back at Hannah Dishman's Emporium in St. Louis way-hell back in fifty-nine. Two years, almost. But he'd kept in touch through letters and on the wires. Noah Sutton was in the Confederate Cavalry, Seventh South Carolina, Gary's Brigade, prancing around on that giant black monster of his, the stallion no other human could even walk past without getting kicked or bit. Bought himself a lieutenancy. Plenty of money, that pompous boy had. Acted like it too. The *Elite*. That's what the Reb cavalry thought about themselves.

Being a man without a state, Quist didn't much care who won the war, or how, or when.

Struggling through a dense wall of tangled growth, Quist

yanked his boots up, down with a crunch, up, down, worse than going through mud. Every step took him down to the knees. The heavy, steamy forest growth sucked at him, wanted to eat him. The bugs wanted his skin. The bluejays and tawny owls wanted his eyes. The stoats and beavers wanted his bones. Critters would eat anything. Didn't care if God would say, "Hey, you ate a man. Git to hell."

He took a broad step, trying to clear the weeds—and went down to his thigh in it. His backpack slid violently to the side and took his considerable bulk with it. *Crunch*—his big body made a perfect image of itself in the low-growing vines. His left arm was caught under the weight of him. His left leg was immobile, completely buried. His fur hat plopped off onto the greenery.

He growled, cranked up with just his rib cage and got the arm free. Pushing it against a tree, teeth grinding, he bellowed like a bear and yanked his leg out of the tangle. Lying on his side across the mound, he panted.

Just like a fuckin' bear. The layers of leather he wore for protection, much of which still bore the tails of the animals that had grown them and still stained with their blood, bunched forward around Quist's wide brown beard. In frustration he batted them down—

A whining sound made him bat at his ear as though swatting off a mosquito.

Pop-boom!

The echo rang through the bare, spindly woodlands. Gunfire!

Quist rolled across the ground and dropped his enormous bulk into a bank of leftover stalks from last year's wildflowers. They cracked under him.

He squirmed out of his backpack, tin pan jangling against his little iron coffeepot. Couldn't have them ringing like bells and giving away his position. Under skimpy cover of the trees and the lay of the land, he followed that gunshot back to its point of origin—the bank of Lake Michigan.

Beyond the banks there was only gunmetal-gray water, chopping in no particular direction as the wind kicked it around.

Quist scrambled along this collar of scruffy bank, his boots scraping half the time, catching the other half. He sneaked, slipped, clawed, and dug his way along the lake bank until he saw what he wanted to see at the angle he wanted to see it.

Then he came up the bank and through the woods, howling like a wounded moose, both hands striking out before him in two claws.

The claws closed around a gritty neck.

Quist dragged the smaller man down. Instantly he assessed what he had in his hands—the smell of blood, raw meat, a dangling beaver carcass—a trapper.

The man twisted around, yellow teeth gritted in the center of a filthy face and black stubble. He looked like a misplaced chimney sweep.

Quist didn't wait. He flung down upon the man until they were both lengthwise in the weeds and the other man was gasping for breath. With nearly three hundred pounds of Quist on top of him, there was no such thing as air.

A yank, a grunt, and Quist pulled out his twelve-inch bowie knife. A jolt—a pop—

The man beneath him choked, eyes bulging, mouth suddenly wide open without making a sound—except maybe for the squeaking of complete astonishment . . . agony . . . and the sensation of his own blood draining out, his guts following . . . somewhere under the layers of rags.

The man vomited onto Quist's hands.

"Fuck you," Quist gagged, and wiped his hands one by one in the vines. He dragged out his bowie knife and showed the man his own blood. "What're you shootin' at me for? Who hired you?"

His spit made tiny brown puddles on the man's filthy face. He shook the groaning lump of humanity and glared into the terrorized eyes.

"Who *hired* you?"

"Nuh . . . nuh . . . nobody . . ."

Quist shook the trapper harder. "Who hired you? I bin a hired man thirty years, and I know a contract killin' when I see one. There's a look in the eye ain't there for no other kind of killin'. Other kinds of hate ain't got the right look. You got the look. Who put money in your pocket to cut my gullet?"

"I—don't know—"

Another brain-rattling shake made the man's blood gush

out the open wound. Quist twisted his fingers into the man's collar until he felt a pulse.

"Where, then? Give me the name of the place you got hired!"

The man glared up at him, and Quist saw a refusal there that he didn't like. He growled, hauled back and swatted the man in the face with the back of his hand, then shook him again. Blood spurted from the man's mouth, coloring what were left of his teeth. Odds were this man had been hired about fourth down a line, but if Quist worked it right, he could follow right back up that line to the third, the second, and finally the person who had seen Dorian Wallace Trözen in person.

"Who hired you!" Quist bellowed. "Talk—oh, shit . . . shit!"

Suddenly the whole picture changed. Quist got a flashing insight into the mind of Dorian Trözen.

Trözen had taken a contract out on *him*!

"Shit—shit!"

Everything was different now. From now on Quist *couldn't* drop the contract, retainer or not. He couldn't do anything else to make a living other than hunt Trözen down. Couldn't do anything but kill or be killed.

From now on he would have to go underground, live off the land. Couldn't tell anybody what he was doing or why. Couldn't use his right name. From now on he was the prey of his prey. Suddenly he knew what he had done to people all these years—knew what it was like to be hunted, to have to hide, to have to strike first like a goddamned snake before it gets stepped on.

He squeezed the trapper's throat until the man's face turned white, then gray.

"I'll tell you who hired you, you stupid gullible son of a bitch," Quist spat. "A nigger half-breed runaway slave passin' for white! He raped a plantation woman! That's who!"

The trapper stopped gasping. His eyes widened until the whites turned red . . . shuddered a death throe—but there was abject horror in his eyes that came from something other than the hole in his guts. He was a nigger's tool. Took money without checking where it came from.

He had his mind on hell. He was looking right inside.

His blood found its way through the clothing and poured onto both their boots. Quist pulled him forward, got both feet planted firmly on level ground, stood up, still holding the man in front of him, and lowered his voice the way his daddy used to.

"I bin hired to bring the half-breed in," Quist growled. "He hired you to get to *me* first. Start talkin'. 'Cuz you're dyin', man, and you don't wanna take this with you. Unless you plan t'burn, you better shed your sin right here and now. Think about it . . . think . . . got it? See it? Feel that grim reaper coming up your spine? Yeah . . . that's right. Now . . . where is he?"

★

CHAPTER FOURTEEN

―――――― ★ ――――――

29 August 1861
Craig Powderworks, Richmond, Virginia

"Henry!"

"Yo, Chief?"

"Wanna come in the office for a minute?"

"Be right in."

The broad, snowy-headed man sidled between rows of two-hundred-pound powder kegs, past the chief's window, and into the brick office building's tiled foyer. He stomped in without heed to his dirty boots, and in a minute his dusty backside was sitting in the office on a tufted leather chair.

In front of him, between the desk and the same window he'd called from, the owner was pacing again. Back and forth, back and forth. His taupe-brown hair fell forward in two soft wings from a not-quite middle part, and he was worrying a piece of paper over and over. Henry Brecker sat and watched.

The tall young man before him didn't look like a businessman. There was nothing pressed or pleated about him. His manner was unartificial in every way. His white shirtsleeves were rolled up to the middle of his forearms. His navy-blue bow tie was knotted crooked. His brown vest hung open, and the hand-tailored Confederate officer's uniform he was supposed to be wearing was hanging over there on the coat rack, untouched in nigh onto two months.

Untouched, except for last week, when the powder mill women took it to replace the royal-blue collar, cuffs, and trim with deep scarlet. This was a slow-starting war, and there was hardly any standardization in uniforming the South's untried armed forces yet, especially in the infantry, but there were some efforts to make units look like units whenever possible. Months ago they'd been the First Richmond Light Guards, but that didn't work out. The Confederate Ordnance Department had decided that Craig Powderworks should be the Craig's Richmond Artillery Supply. For their own protection, the mill workers were now in the Confederate Army. Sabotage of a civilian factory was much easier than infiltration and sabotage of a military installation. Now they had guards at the entrances, with rifles. Now they were soldiers.

That meant standard branch-of-service colors instead of the royal blue, which one of the mill wives had thought was pretty when the women were making the uniform. Everything was still so confusing . . . hardly anybody had the same uniform as the next man, even in his own unit. The Confederate command was desperately attempting to standardize, if for no other reason than to have its men not firing on each other, mistaking each other as enemies. Blue facings would be medical corps, and a powder mill didn't qualify. Off came the blue. White would be the Corps of Engineers. Cavalry would wear yellow. Artillery would be red, scarlet or crimson facings, and a commissioned powdermill was considered a unit of the Confederate artillery, no matter how much its owner—commander—wanted to stay civilian.

Wyatt Craig was the most civilian officer the Confederate Army would ever have. The red facing bothered him. He saw the poetry in it. Sure enough, he was totin' a load.

"Have a cigar, Henry," Wyatt offered finally, not looking up from the paper.

The foreman eagerly plucked a Norfolk belvedere out of the canister on the desk. He didn't light it up, because he knew the chief wasn't partial to smoke and only kept the stogies on his desk for visitors, or moments like this when he wanted somebody on his side.

"Thanks a bundle, chief," Henry said, and slipped the cigar into his vest pocket. "Smoke it later. Off the grounds."

The young owner and manager of Craig Powderworks paused, faced the older man, and dropped any veneer he might have put up for someone else. The old man knew him very well.

Right now it felt good to be known well.

He hooked a thumb in the pocket of his open vest and murmured, "Thanks, Henry."

"Somethin' up, son? Got trouble with the niter again?"

"Hm? Oh . . . now that you mention it, yes," Wyatt admitted, and tried to change his thoughts from what was really on his mind. "The British are talking about freezing their niter. I've arranged to get some from limestone caves in Tennessee, Kentucky, Georgia, and Virginia. It's crude and hard to get at, though, and it'll cost a damn sight more than English saltpeter. Don't know if we can make it work. I'm also looking into getting Chilean saltpeter directly. Have it brought up in ships."

"Round the horn?" Henry asked. "Cost a mint."

"Can't be helped. Well, we can talk about that later. I do have one new thing for you." Wyatt rustled through the papers, seeming distracted. He was worried about something other than whatever he was looking for.

Henry could tell. He'd been looking at this young man for a long time, and he knew the moods. Wyatt had business on his hands, but something else on his mind.

The business, though, came up in the form of a piece of paper with bent corners. Apparently it had been read several times.

"Want you to take this new process on over to the mills, Henry," Wyatt said. "Comes from a man by the name of George Rains. Maybe you've heard of him."

"Yep, sure. Prospected most of the limestone caves for niter in the South. Just what we was talkin' about. He figgered most of the process for refining and processing."

"That's right. Well, he's got something new for us. He's been using a microscope to look at carbon particles in his powder. He found pores even in finely ground carbon. You know . . . pits. Little ones. He figures the saltpeter ought to fill the pits and make the powder that much finer. He's developed a formula to distill the powder into mush. The saltpeter crystallizes in the charred carbon. What do you think?"

Henry pursed his lips and bobbed his head. "Think it'll take down the rolling time. Be a good thing."

"That's what I figured."

Wyatt nodded, somewhat relieved that Henry had picked up on another chance for improvement. The industry was changing so quickly! He always relied on Henry's down-to-the-dirt workman's knowledge of these things to counterbalance his own college chemistry.

"Rains says it does," he said. "I think we'll have to do it."

The old man snorted. " 'Kay. What's the process?"

"Wet the mixture, then steam it until it turns to mush, then cool it into a wheelcake after that."

"Mmm. That adds time. Ah, never mind son. We'll give a whistle and see if it barks. Hand it on over."

Wyatt passed him the paper. "Any questions?"

"Just one," Henry said. He looked up. "What the blue heck's a 'mikerscrope'?"

He hoped it would loosen up the boss, but Wyatt didn't even hear the joke. He knew he hadn't been called here to be given a new process. Wyatt would've walked down to the mills if that had been the purpose of the visit, not called Henry up to the prim office building and made him sit inside four walls with paisley paper on them. So there had to be something more.

Henry swung one leg over the other and slouched back in the plush chair. "Blockade trouble, son?"

"Some," Wyatt sighed, "but this is something different." He wagged the paper. "Got a telegram."

"From?"

"Well . . . that's the odd part. I need advice, real bad."

"I got all the bad advice a man can use, son. Let's have a look see."

Wyatt came around the desk rather than reaching over it and handed over the telegram.

"What do you make of this, Henry?"

Henry squinted until the telegram came into focus.

" 'Your presence . . . is requested in the office of the Honorable Alexander H. Stephens, Vice President of the Confederate States of America . . . at three o'clock in the afternoon, on the twenty-ninth August in the Year of Our Lord eighteen hundred sixty one . . . humble servant . . . Captain D. X. Parthens.' " Henry looked up and refocused on Wyatt's decipherable blue eyes. "Who's 'at?"

"The Vice President?"

"No, this D. X. fella."

Wyatt straightened up and frowned.

"I've never known anybody with an X in his name . . . not

to recall, any case. You don't, do you, Henry? Somebody I'm forgetting?"

"Can't say as I do." Henry read the telegram again. "Knew a fella named Dixon while back. . . ."

"What do they want *me* for?" Wyatt started pacing again.

He thrust both hands into his trouser pockets and hunched his shoulders.

"Mebbe they want to place a powder order," Henry suggested.

"They wouldn't call me over there in person for that . . . besides, the Ordnance Department already has a half-dozen standing orders for shipments of cannon shot and gunpowder. You had to walk through the kegs yourself just now to get in here." He paused and gestured outside. "What've I done?"

He paced away, then back, and stopped again and looked at Henry with a boyish expression of worry.

"Have we done anything wrong? Made a mistake? Are we sure who we've been selling our industrial blasting powder to? The Vice President doesn't just up'n send for folks."

"Reckon not."

Wyatt flopped down into his desk chair and rocked back. Suddenly he looked exhausted.

"You know, Henry," he said, "I'm getting a little worn with being contacted by people I don't know. I just wanted to run a business, and look what's happened. Along comes a war, and all of a sudden my business is accessed by an army. Here I am with men calling me Major, and Vice Presidents sending me telegrams. All this activity, generals and captains and who-all . . . powder orders coming in on army-requisition forms—oh, I don't know. All we got is skirmishes all of a sudden. Harper's Ferry, Rich Mountain, Hoke's Run . . . Blackburn's Ford . . . that awful fight at Manassas Junction . . . four hundred sixty Union men dead—how many of 'em went down because of black powder from that yard right out there? We can't figure we're playing a big game anymore." He paused, and his thoughts made a hard ball in the middle of his chest. "I wanted to build railroad tunnels and dams and clear ground for houses, and open up industry . . . not blow up men with a Northern accent like my own. Know what I mean, Henry?"

"Sure do."

Wyatt sighed. "Guess I'm just not used to this business of two nations."

They sat in silence, listening through the open window to the doings of the powder mill, which dominated the countryside around them. Wagons coming and going, the rolling mills grinding, the creek running softly behind the office building, powder men shouting back and forth between the tin shop and the keg factory while they walked toward the creekside with their lunch pails, children playing outside the workers' houses—a small town unto itself.

Wyatt threaded his fingers together and looked sidelong at the older man.

"So, Henry," he began, "what do you think?"

Henry tossed the telegram onto the desk between them, sniffed deeply, and craned his neck toward the coatrack.

"I think I'm gonna fetch your dress grays."

Wyatt tugged at his uniform coat's stand-up collar and vowed to get somebody to make him a frock coat that could pass for a uniform, with a nice set of flat lapels. Wasn't too much for a man to ask, was it? Flat lapels?

He sat in his carriage like that, thinking about his neck and feeling overmastered by the Confederate White House towering in front him. If he thought about getting out of the carriage, anticipation would come along and jar him. His horse twisted her head around to look at him, then just shifted her feet and waited for a decision. At the door two nervous corporals guarding the entrance watched him making his decision.

Why was he being called to audience with the Confederate government? He hadn't done anything—that he could think of. He couldn't even tell the Vice President or anybody that he was owner of Craig Powderworks in name only, that he only ran the place. That all the money and much clandestine management was put up by a Massachusetts dynasty . . .

The Du Ponts.

He was coming to realize he'd unwittingly attached himself to a family so strong, they could subvert governments, play both ends of the table—a shadowy force, not in total accord with itself . . . very dangerous at the wrong moments. The

Du Ponts had seen his vulnerability, given him money to start up a powder mill in Richmond and rein to either pay off or hire all his former workers from his deceased father's Kansas tannery. After fire destroyed the tannery, of course. Now there was nothing there but dust and confused memories, and he was here in Richmond. A very well-to-do pawn.

Who knew . . . maybe the Du Ponts had burned the damned thing down, just to get him to move. He'd thought of that, but it had all seemed on the crazy side back then.

Who really spoke for the Du Ponts? Wyatt didn't know. It was a divided family . . . more or less. The head of the family was loyal only to his company, because the company was on its way to being bigger than either government. But there were branches of the Du Ponts all over the continent, known and unknown. A hundred radiations . . . were they for what they said they were for? Federal? Confederate? Was there a schism in the powerful family or not? And to what lengths would they go to cover it up?

He had always depended on their emissary to be his barometer of Du Pont thunder.

He had always depended on Dorian.

But Dorian was gone now. The bank account Wyatt set up for him had gone untouched. Had the bounty hunter caught up with him? Had his wry humor struck the wrong man just wrong enough? Had he simply died in one of the myriad skirmishes that had broken out all over the South? Or in the big one . . . at Manassas? The one that convinced everybody from the spectators to the reporters that maybe this was going to be a real war and not just an object lesson?

Whatever happened to Dorian, Wyatt was alone.

Alone with the Du Pont secret. Not even his workers knew. Du Pont money, Northern money, had bought this uniform and the star on the collar, and the papers to prove commission.

A lot of question marks. No answers. The only way to get answers would be to shake his boots off the running board of this carriage and march on into that big white building, announce his arrival and pretend to belong in such company.

The Vice President! The Vice anything . . .

Wyatt had heard about Alexander Stephens. An intellect to shame most scholars. A man of such mental stature as had seldom been seen since the Founding Fathers. A Georgia man, if the newspapers could be trusted to get a thing right.

Beyond that Wyatt knew nothing. He wasn't a news-hungry fellow, as long as his business ran all right. Gossip among the workers kept him up on secession, skirmishes, and whatever else affected them in whatever way. The nation's equilibrium was up on its side . . . there were two nations now, but not really. Could the North survive without the South's agrarian staple, and could the South survive without the North's industry? Hardly a plantation was left that could be self-sustaining, like the farms thirty years ago. Few plantations grew subsidiary crops anymore and fed themselves. The world was opening up. What a time for a war of division . . . and here, on the world's continent of hope.

It put a chill to anyone who thought twice. Wyatt was plenty chilly these days. Sometimes enough to make him look away from the headlines.

But he'd heard of Alexander Stephens.

"This way, sir," the Vice President's aide motioned, and Wyatt realized he'd made it to the door, past the butler, and into the corridor without even being aware that he was introducing himself. And here he was, walking behind a skinny red-haired negro in his forties, obviously a mulatto, through a set of double doors with blue velvet curtains, into what appeared to be a receiving parlor.

"The Vice President will be with you in short order, Mr. Craig," the mulatto said.

"Thanks . . . thank you." Wyatt waved his hat, then realized he shouldn't be holding his hat when the Vice President walked in.

"I'll take that for you, sir," the aide offered, plucked the hat smoothly, and left, just like that.

"Thanks—here you go." He dug in a vest pocket and pulled out a coin and gave it to the mulatto.

"Thanks to you, sir," the man said with a little bow, and left him alone.

Fine, except that Wyatt found himself suddenly waving two empty hands. In the pockets? No, not a good idea. This wasn't a mill yard. Thumbs in the waistcoat—probably no better. Too pompous.

So he started feeling the furniture.

The draperies were heavy velvet, the camelbacked chesterfield was imported lemon-yellow damask, and two mahogany wing chairs covered in hideous green brocade flanked a burled-walnut grandmother clock. In the corner there was a drop-leaf table with a hurricane lamp, a vase of white rose-buds, and a steaming tea service. Near an open window, there was a small spinet piano. Beyond that there wasn't much in the parlor. Not even a bookshelf or desk.

He stepped to the wall and touched what looked like carved borders—and discovered it was gaudy trompe l'oeil wallpaper. There were three borders of swags and Roman blocks, and under those, seraphs and Roman statues of women danced across the tops of urns, twisting painted garlands. He reached to touch one of the women, then suddenly flinched, not used to the flash of red cuff every time he moved his hands.

Wyatt wrinkled his nose, moved back toward the middle of the room, and stopped touching things.

The parlor was warm from almost direct sunlight through two very tall windows, glittering on a white marble mantel carved with cherubs. In fact, it was *damned* warm in here. Wyatt tugged at his collar again.

Suddenly the double doors swung open. Wyatt spun around.

A scrawny houseboy entered, carrying what Wyatt guessed was the Vice President's cloak. The boy threw the cloak over a wing chair with shameful abandon, then started throwing off shawl after shawl. Wyatt came within a breath of advising that the garments be properly put in a closet or on a rack. He didn't like to see domestics get into trouble.

But even worse—being chastised by the master's guests.

Clamping his lips shut, Wyatt plotted to drape his own jacket over another chair so the Vice President wouldn't feel right scolding the boy.

The brown-haired boy was pouring tea now at a table across the parlor and hadn't even noticed Wyatt. What a day this was turning out to be. Wasn't anything going to go smoothly?

As if in answer, Wyatt accidentally backed up against an end table and set the lamp to rattling.

The houseboy spun around—and hit Wyatt with a pair of fierce, dark, burning brown eyes set in a face of gaunt cold marble.

Wyatt sucked a sharp breath.

There stood not a boy at all, but a frail-looking particle of a man in a corroded little body that barely scratched five foot six, and only generously guessed at over a hundred pounds. It was a *man*—an adult of nearly fifty years, who looked as if he'd been struck by a snake and never treated. The hair that was brown in back was laced with silver across the brow. He resembled more a puppet than a fully grown man, someone who should be bedridden, not prancing about at the top of a rebellious government.

Except for those eyes.

Wyatt almost shriveled. Venomous eyes burned over him with all the ferocity the body lacked, twice the power.

The dapperling pointed a bony finger and said, "So! *You're* Craig!"

Wyatt tried to figure out a way to deny it, except for one little detail—he *was* Craig.

He cleared his throat and stammered, "Well, I . . . was told to . . ."

The whippet came toward him, waving that thin white hand. His voice was high and girly. "I've a bone to pick with you, sir! I'm Alexander Stephens."

"*You* are? I mean, you *are*?"

The white hand batted the air again. Wyatt almost instinctively caught the little man, but stopped himself at the last second. Stephens wasn't fainting; he just looked on the edge of it. Wyatt wasn't an oversized man, but he suddenly felt like one.

Stephens wasn't intimidated. He glared up at Wyatt with fearlessness and scalding acrimony.

"I just arrived in Richmond myself," the Vice President said. "I'm a Georgian man and shrink if I'm long from my native homestead. There I shall live and there I shall certainly die. The sooner done with you and back home, the better to breathe and feel my Georgia wind, and it's *you,* sir, who have caused me to come here."

"Me?"

"You've got things to answer for." The Vice President flew like a fly back to the tea cart and poured the two most vicious cups of brew Wyatt had ever witnessed. "Where are you from, sir?"

It sounded like a trick question. The kind a lawyer asks the witness he wants to discredit.

Wyatt stumbled over the answer. "Oh—I'm from Massachusetts originally, Mr. Vice President."

"A Northerner," Stephens huffed, and pivoted with two cups of steaming tea in his girlish little hands.

He motioned Wyatt to the chesterfield. "Sit down, sir."

Wyatt was perfectly happy to sit down, because it diminished the difference in height between the two of them. He kept telling himself Stephens was probably used to looking up at people, but he was still glad to sit.

"You're a reconstructionist aren't you?" Stephen accused in his broad Georgia accent. "You want the South and North back together?"

Wyatt blinked. He'd never heard that word before. He took a deep breath. "I don't believe the North and South can be strong as two separate nations in this industrial world. Most of my raw materials come from the North or overseas—"

"Hmm," Stephens uttered as he sipped his tea. He swallowed quickly, coughed, and nearly shouted. "The South is finally and forever a separate nation, don't you see that?"

Wyatt held his breath, but didn't look away.

The Vice President lowered spindly eyebrows. "What about slavery? Where do you stand?"

If this was a trial, it was a strange one. Wyatt felt trapped.

"Our negroes have never had to compete, sir," he said. "What'll they do to eat and live if they suddenly find themselves free? They'd be fighting the Irish, Germans, Italians, and Chinese for jobs."

Stephens struggled to his feet, and his tiny body towered over Wyatt with sheer power of will. He aimed a bony finger and bellowed.

"Sir! You defend the Southern ways while conspiring with a Northern dynasty! They moved you and your workers to Richmond, set you up with your powder mill, and they secretly own it! While the Wilmington mills supply the North with gunpowder, you supply the South. The Du Pont hand is in both corners, making both profits. The Du Ponts are completely manipulating you! You're allowing it to happen so you can gain financial and political power and push the South back into the Union! Tell me one reason I shouldn't have you arrested for treason, here and now!"

Wyatt nearly fell off his cushion. The Du Ponts!

He bolted to his feet and stood there like an idiot, gaping, stepping backward. His chest filled up with apprehension, and suddenly he couldn't breathe. Was this more testing of his character? An attempt to get information? How much should he admit? If Stephens was testing him to confirm a suspicion, Wyatt knew he had already damned himself with his expression.

Dorian had warned him about the danger if anyone found out—that the Du Ponts would do whatever was necessary to protect their anonymity . . . those ominous words, the silence from Wilmington since war broke out, the divisiveness between Northern and Southern factions of the widespread dynasty—loyalties just as scattered, just as combustible . . .

Stephens was watching his reaction with a touch of devious purpose in those flashing eyes.

Shifting in his self-conscious puddle, Wyatt couldn't talk. His tongue was locked between his teeth. He was careful not to even nod his head by accident. Stephens wouldn't miss that. Wyatt just stood still and wished to be back in his powder yard. Was this a trick, to get him to implicate the Du Ponts? To cause economic trouble for the North?

But there were Southern-sympathizing Du Ponts. Their influence could easily reach to the top of government . . . was he seeing it now?

He stood in his cage and stared at the Vice President and gave himself away with his bad poker face.

The Vice President was straightening his minnowish little body when the red-headed negro aide appeared at the double doors and bailed Wyatt out for a minute.

"Mr. Vice President?"

"What on earth do you want, Gustav?" Stephens barked.

The aide came in with an envelope. "The letter you were expecting from Mr. Toombs," he said, "and also, Captain Parthens has arrived."

"Well, show him in, man!"

"Sir."

There was that name again. Parthens. Again Wyatt scoured his memory for some receipt or letter with that name on it—

"Well?" Stephens roared at him when Gustav was gone. How did that little chest get such a big sound out of it? "Shall I have you arrested?"

Wyatt licked his lips and ended up biting his tongue. He flinched.

There was a shuffle of activity outside the double doors, the corner of a blue-gray garment swirling in the corridor, but Stephens forced Wyatt to ignore it by glaring at him and demanded answer. Wyatt knew he was standing stiffer than a pipe, but it wouldn't fix.

"Mr. Vice President," he began softly, too softly, "sir . . . we still have habeas corpus in our law . . . even the Vice President must show cause to justify an arrest."

"They've suspended the writ of habeas corpus," Stephens said, and instantly there seemed no way to beat this man on the intricacies of law. "You're a traitor, Mr. Craig."

Wyatt felt his brows knit. His fear suddenly flushed away. Anger flushed in. He bristled. Something about that phrase, having it said right out like that . . .

"Sir," he said, "Vice President or not, you shouldn't be talking to me that way. We broke away from the Union to get away from the tyranny of core government who would suspend law arbitrarily. I turned my back on one country because of my principles, and I'll do it again if the Confederacy is made of the same kind of men. I won't give up my principles for a little thing like winning a war."

He put down his teacup and straightened.

"And I won't give up my freedom just to avoid going to jail," he added. "So arrest me."

He clamped his lips tightly and let his silence represent him.

Stephens didn't move. Didn't call for guards or shout at him anymore. Merely stared at him with smoldering eyes.

Wyatt didn't move either. But he no longer flinched or fidgeted.

There was a shuffle at the door. And a voice—

"Didn't I tell you, Aleck?"

At the sound Wyatt turned.

A startling and dangerous presence strode as boldly into the parlor as any devil into a tomb. Captain D. X. Parthens took a pose that favored a ruffled ivory neck cloth, zinc-gray daycoat, and waistcoat of Pompeiian red damask. Black sideburns and collar-length curly hair offset a provocative pair of black eyes, sharp black brows, and a mouth chiseled from the peach complexion as though from stone.

There was a *London Times* tucked under one arm.

"Wyatt Craig, the second most principled man on earth," the Captain said, "meet Aleck Stephens, the *first* most principled man on earth. After all . . . someone had to make up for the likes of *me*."

Immobilized by the newcomer, Wyatt stood gaping.

The man strode in and stopped a few steps into the room, bounced a brief nod off Wyatt, then addressed the Vice President with Olympian stateliness and an extended hand.

"Aleck, *kalisperah. Ti ora arkheze toh programa?*"

Stephens laughed and took the man's hand. *"Kalisperah,* my friend. *Ti kaneth?"*

"Kahla, pollee kahla. Sinithos o keros ene toso zestos opos tora?"

"Come in, come in," Stephens said. He took his guest's arm and asked another question in Greek.

The two men were like two opposites on a mural, prattling at each other in Greek, pausing only to laugh. Apparently they were both very funny, or at least enjoyed each other's company.

Wyatt just stood there, pop-eyed. His thousand questions suddenly clicked into place.

Parthens looked at him in a remotely amused way. *"Mila kanes anglika endo?* Ah, yes. Sit down, Mr. Craig. You've seen a chair before."

While Wyatt hovered wide-eyed and thunderstruck, and the dark-haired man gazed back at him with a benign grin on his face, Stephens poked out the double doors and called, "Gustav! Bring the wagon of cakes in, if you will."

"Right away, Mr. Vice President," the aide called from several rooms down.

"You were quite right," Stephens said to Parthens. "I forced him to defend his rights, and he stood up to me." He warmed his frail hands on his teacup. "You're a sensible young man, Mr. Craig. I like you very much."

Wyatt felt himself sweat around the collar. He wasn't used to being grilled. He bottled any attempt to speak to Parthens . . . because he didn't know the rules today . . . yet.

Stephens watched him like a bird off its feed. "I've been bluffing you, Mr. Craig. You're in favor of going back with the Union . . . and so am I."

Wyatt squinted. "You are?"

"Yes. I'm a reconstructionist too," Stephens said, then had to pause to clear his throat.

"Some people call you an *ob*structionist," Parthens said with a wicked grin.

Stephens laughed at that teasing face, but he nodded.

"I disagree with secession, but I support the *right* to secede. I resisted leaving the Union to the very last moment. Until Georgia seceded. Then, being a states'-rights man, I went with my state. Once the majority had voted, I felt I had no choice. I agreed to be Vice President of the Confederacy only because I now have the power to be a fulcrum in dissolving it, but with states' rights firmly in place. The same majority will come to its senses once the North is slapped down. You see, I am a true worshiper of the Constitution of the United States. It's my passion in life. That document is unimpeachable. Under it each *state* is sovereign. The nation must not be a tyranny. It should be a coalition of independent nations, each with a Constitutional right to secede. Like the right to property. Or breathing. It's so endemic to humanhood that it needs not be mentioned in a list of rights. Do you know that the original draft of the Constitution said, 'life, liberty, and property'? They changed it to 'pursuit of happiness.' I think they should have left it 'property.' Then we wouldn't have any doubts."

Stephens sat down, leaned his consumptive body back on the cushions, and rooted those blazing eyes into the past.

"I begged the Georgia legislature not to secede, gentlemen," he said. "Begged them to grab the Constitution, to use it as an anchor of states' sovereignty. Abe Lincoln assured me in writing that his Republicans will *not* interfere with slavery. He knows the real issue isn't slavery, but its extension into the new territories." Stephens paused, gazed into his tea, and sighed. "Seven little weeks after he wrote that letter to me, I found myself Vice President of the Confederate States of America."

Wyatt empathized with the frail man, but said nothing.

The Vice President looked at Parthens. "Now that you're here, my friend, we can get down to the business at hand. Britain."

"Ah, yes," Parthens said. "That earth, that realm, that England."

Wyatt slowly lowered himself onto the chesterfield again and kept his mouth shut.

Stephens shuddered, sipped his tea, and held his knees close together as though he'd just come in from an ice storm instead of a warm Virginia August. He leaned back on the tufted cushions and stared at an empty chair. "My grandfather was an English Jacobite who went with Charles Edward Stuart in the attempt to take the British crown. There's still a bit of the rebel in my own soul. Britain's important to me for a very new reason. I was just about to tell Mr. Craig our problem."

Parthens plunked onto a piano bench, dropped the *Times* on the bench beside his leg. "By all means . . . tell."

He didn't look at Wyatt, but fixed his gaze on Stephens. No matter how Wyatt eyed him, he didn't shift.

Wyatt remained silent, acutely aware of Parthens sitting there watching Stephens kithlessly, perfectly happy to play second fiddle.

"England and France have been at war since time started ticking," Stephens said. "They're still very jealous rivals. Neither wants the other to gain footholds on this continent." He leaned forward with a conspiratorial glint in his eye. "We can *use* that."

He looked at Wyatt, but waved his hand toward Parthens.

"My excellent friend here assures me that you can be trusted, Mr. Craig. You've kept the Du Ponts' secret . . . I think I can trust you to keep mine."

Wyatt glanced at Parthens, then said, "I won't compromise your trust, Mr. Vice President."

Stephens smacked the cushions beside his bony knee. Then he struck Parthens with a look and said, "You were so right about him!"

Parthens crossed his legs and flipped casually through his *Times*. "Lucky guess."

"You have slaves at your establishment, don't you, Mr. Craig?" Stephens asked.

"Yes, sir. Most of them came with me from my father's tannery after it burned down. That was in Kansas."

"I know," the Vice President said offhandedly, and Wyatt was suddenly on edge again. "You remember the Kansas-Nebraska Act? Eighteen fifty-four?"

"Remember it?" Wyatt blurted. "New territories deciding for themselves about slavery before they joined the Union."

"The act was supposed to quiet legal storm," Stephens said.

"Didn't work," Wyatt said. "I lost my factory to that dispute. Burned right to the ground."

"Mmm," Stephens murmured, and huddled around his steaming teacup as though ice fishing, elbows tucked in and his knees and ankles flush together. "It was mine."

Wyatt stopped in the middle of a sip. "The Kansas-Nebraska Act?"

"Was mine."

As his teacup clinked onto the saucer, Wyatt tried not to groan.

"I was raised on my father's little farm," Stephens said. He raised his hands and waggled his fingers. "These pathetic members swatted the sheep and kerneled the furrows behind my father's plow. I was a corn dropper. Do you know what that is?"

"No, sir."

"It means you do the work a slave would be doing, *if* you owned one. It left me with a life that is one unending illness, and a place among the nouveau riche . . . the rich who know what it is to be poor." Stephens paused a moment. "Most Southern businessmen aren't like you. They don't understand how dangerous it is for the South to remain broken off from the Union any longer than it takes to make our point. The European jackals are salivating to break this continent apart and count how many bites of it they can each get. Monarchies and dictatorships are watching us right now, hoping the great experiment in democracy will crumble like a hollow monument. Demands for democracy are being heard all over their empires. If democracy collapses in the United States, despots will be able to crush it all over the world without guilt.

"I'm a great admirer of Abraham Lincoln," the Vice President said, "but even this fine man is being corrupted by the dictatorial sense of power. He suspended habeas corpus, like any monarch would. The South isn't obeying the rules, so Lincoln is changing the rules. The Northern way is destroying their finest citizen." He shook his bony head. "I despise monarchies . . . ridiculous, to be 'born' to power, where blood, not ability, determines the future. Imagine! The British House of Lords is still handed down through bloodlines. But for the time being, we'll have to depend on monarchies to save the South. And after chastising the North, the Confederacy must get back into the Union damned quickly, under a properly interpreted Constitution. We'd better fight a good war, Mr. Craig, and we'd better win it. The Union should *not* break up," Stephens added, "but must always have the *right* to. Otherwise, how can we keep any dominant areas of the nation from breaking the constitutional contract?"

"Yes!" Wyatt vaulted to his feet. "Yes! The right or wrong of slavery isn't the issue! When the nation was formed, slavery was permitted and understood—it was part of the agreement. That's what everyone agreed upon, right or wrong, so if the Northern states decide on their own to break the contract, how can they hold the Southern states *to* the contract!"

"Yes!" Stephens laughed, rocking in his seat. "Yes!"

"Oh, grumble," Parthens uttered, just loud enough. "Now I've got *two* of them . . ."

"Somehow we must engineer European support for the Confederacy!" the Vice President shouted.

Wyatt paused in the middle of their excitement. "That won't be easy, sir. The rulers of England and France are pretty sensitive to how their working classes feel about slavery. They don't like it."

"So we have to get them on our side about everything else," Stephens said. "We have an advantage. Lincoln doesn't dare antagonize Europe, but he doesn't dare make this a war against slavery either. Otherwise Missouri, Maryland, and Kentucky will go with the South. If the South will only have the brains to keep its mouth shut—"

"The South's blighted by its own insularity," Parthens commented.

"Yes," Stephens said. "The Confederacy is on the verge of making huge mistakes." The frail little Vice President's eyes were dark and luminous on both men. "And I want you gentlemen to help me head off those mistakes. The French want to take over Mexico and put the Austrian emperor's brother in power as emperor—"

"Maximilian," Parthens provided.

"Yes. He's married to Carlotta, who's the sister of—"

"Eugenie."

"Yes, who's married to Louis Napoleon of France. They want to put Maximilian and Carlotta in Mexico to solidify the Hapsburgs in this hemisphere. They have the same idea about the Baltics. The Roman Catholic Church likes the idea because the Hapsburgs want to extend Church influence because Rome preaches the Divine Right of Kings."

"And the Hapsburgs are Catholic kings," Parthens said.

"One happy family all over Europe!" Stephens said "And they want to be all over us as well!"

Wyatt's groan interrupted them. "You lost me back there with the emperor's brother."

Impatient that Wyatt wasn't grasping it, Stephens said, "To ensure a Southern victory, we need Europe's support. I'm willing to suspend the Monroe Doctrine and tell them they can *have* Mexico if they support us, and England can take California and the Territories."

Wyatt gasped. "Mr. Stephens, my God!"

"Well, this is war, Mr. Craig! War!"

"And here's my left one," Parthens muttered, " and you can keep it in your saddlebag."

Wyatt turned to him, his hand outward imploringly, but nothing came out of his mouth.

Parthens let him suffer, then said, "The South will win the war, then rejoin the North under a proper interpretation of the Constitution . . . then we'll kick the Europeans' butts off our continent. What can they do from over there?"

"You mean lie to Europe?" Wyatt asked. He turned to Stephens. "You'd betray your word?"

"To monarchs and despots? Who cares?" Stephens said. "Promises made under duress don't count."

Parthens shrugged. "Divide and preserve."

"Yes."

Wyatt shuddered. "Good grief . . ."

"Oh, Mr. Craig, please!" The Vice President jumped up and whirled toward Wyatt like a wraith. "If the Federals win, the South will be destroyed. If the South wins with the government in the hands of separatists like Jeff Davis, the continent will never be what it *can* be! They're so anxious for an independent nation that they forget we already have one! Our leaders forget in their righteous anger that the North is our country too! No matter who wins, we'll spend years at each other's throats! There's a better way! A *third* alternative."

The little man pressed both hands on Wyatt's wrists as though to hold his attention just one crucial moment longer.

"Reconstructionists like us will subvert the Jefferson Davis government—prevent it from making any political accomplishments with Europe, and then we'll make those strides ourselves. Then, later, *we'll* be the ones who have say over what kind of peace happens between the South and North!"

"The Davis government is sending delegates to Cuba, where they will board a ship for Britain," Parthens said very steadily. "These delegates must not be allowed to succeed in getting Britain's ear. Davis can't be allowed to get credit for getting Europe to support the South."

"How do you plan to head them off?" Wyatt asked.

"Oh, we'll find a way," Parthens canted.

Wyatt broke away from the Vice President and put half the room between himself and the other two men. His back was to them, and he stared at the carpet. Without turning he swallowed several times before he could make himself speak.

Finally he said, "You're asking me to sign on to treason."

The word rang through the room. No one spoke for a long time. Tension lay on them like glue. From behind Wyatt, the Vice President's voice held a tone of calm reality.

"I'm asking you," Stephens said, "to take a further stand on your principles. Principles are no good if we fail to act upon them, sir."

His stomach twisting, Wyatt grasped the mantelpiece with both hands and stared down into the hearth.

Somewhere inside the burning tannery's main building, a floor gave in. Thunder—the boom of machines crashing through from floor to floor, all the way to the basement, of supports and joists cracking like bones—the god-killing noise of it all—rang against the hillsides. . . . it was as though his own bones were cracking, his innards falling through his body . . .

Gustav reappeared, pushing a tea cart overflowing with marzipans, candies, and finger sandwiches.

"Mr. Vice President," the slave said, "You asked me to remind you about the visit to the infirmary."

"Is it that late already?" Stephens began wrapping himself in the half-dozen shawls and mufflers buried in the cloak he'd cast over the chair when he first came in. His blazing eyes flicked from Wyatt to the newcomer and back. "I must hasten to the hospital for a brief appearance," he said. "I mustn't let the patients down."

Wyatt turned back to the land of the living in time to see Parthens stand up and gesture at the tea cart. *"Boro na ekhse peretetho monass?"*

"Of course," Stephens said. "I had it brought in for you, both of you. The finger sandwiches are pheasant." He paused, looked at Wyatt, and waved his bony hand. "We'll see each other again soon. I shall arrange a meeting, at the right time, at the right place, with appropriate people. Certainly it will happen within a few weeks. If you have second thoughts, Major Craig . . . please have third ones."

He buttoned his overcoat all the way up to the nest of scarves.

"Kheretesmata," he added.

"Good afternoon, Aleck," Parthens said. *"Diaskedasa pollee."*

Taking a step forward, Wyatt waved awkwardly. "Thank you, Mr. Vice President."

Stephens's parchmenty face made one more acknowledging flash, then disappeared. Gustav went out with him and pulled the double doors behind them.

Wyatt swung around to Parthens.

"Dorian!"

★

A few seconds of awkward eye contact—and they took each other by the arms and swung together like dancers between the furniture.

"Lord how I've missed that double-barreled tongue of yours!" Wyatt cried out. "I've sat here getting grilled by the Vice President, wondering what in tarnation I was doing sitting here! Now I know! *You* did this to me!"

"Intuition serves you again." Parthens said, smiling.

"Where've you been? It's been almost three months! Did you even leave Richmond? The bank account I left for you went untouched—"

"You know I'm nothing but a shadow in the sepia," the composed man said, but he smiled and held on to Wyatt longer than he had to. "An anonymous magistrate, a silent suffete—which is Punic, I think, or Carthaginian . . . that's a dialect of Phoenician, if anyone asks."

"Who *cares*?"

"Not a soul. That's why I can say it out loud."

Wyatt tried to snap a response, but ended up just laughing again, his joy venting itself.

The other man tried to stay remote, but the laughter was contagious, and soon both men were smiling at each other.

"Did you change your name because of Quist?" Wyatt asked.

"Wouldn't you, if a bounty hunter had you by the delicate tissues? God rest his soul . . . soon. Have you had tea and cakes? Bless me, I'm starving."

Parthens squeezed Wyatt's elbow, then aimed for the tea cart. "Maneuvering under the rubric D. X. Parthens has proved both convenient and prudent," he said.

"What's the *X*?"

The sharp black brows went up. "A pretty letter."

Wyatt laughed again out of sheer relief and dropped a hand on the newcomer's shoulder. "What do you tell people those letters are for, Dorian?"

"Oh, Duane Xenophon, David Xavier, Dumbstruck Xylophone, whatever the fancy conjures." He chuckled at his own joke, and the firewall finally came down. He sighed. "Quist is a very competent tracker, Wyatt. I haven't shaken him yet. Of course . . . he hasn't cornered me again either."

"And where's that nice Captain's uniform I had made for you?

"I still have it, never fear."

"I was *sure* you'd left Richmond for good."

"Because of a bounty hunter?" Dorian said incombustibly. He loaded several marzipans on a small plate and topped them off with a chocolate drop.

Wyatt moved a little closer. Close felt good.

"Stephens had me spinning! I couldn't figure how he knew all about the Du Ponts and me. . . . Why didn't you just contact me at the yard? I'd have met you anywhere—you know that."

"Because I wanted you to get acquainted with His Littleness," Dorian said. "Wyatt, open the portcullis. You two have a great deal in common. You're the most self-effacing, large-hearted Saxon in this realm, and Stephens wants to be philosopher-king."

"I think he could do it."

"Yes, he could."

"How did you get—you know."

Dorian shrugged. "He likes me. I can speak Greek to him. And I like his cross-disciplinary intellect. We give each other new things to think about."

"How long's he been ill?"

"He's not ill. He always looks that way. His young years were hard years and made him frail. He was a poor farmer's son. His health was troweled into the soil very early. Now he suffers a chronic absence of any general fitness. But that ectomorph's as full of wit and piss as anyone I know. He's rarely in Richmond. He rushes back to his estate in Crawfordville because he's determined to die there, and he's been expecting to die all his life. He's the most honest soul I've ever encountered, other than you . . . that's why so many politicians dislike him. And why Abe Lincoln *does* like him. Both Lincoln and Mr. Flyspeck opposed the Mexican-American War. Aleck has never forgotten Lincoln's support." Dorian raised his teacup in a toast to the closed door where Stephens had gone out. "His lack of rosy-cheeked health is compensated by a brainpower I actually envy."

The black eyes flickered. They gazed at each other through a personal exchange of trust. Wyatt realized he should have seen Dorian's hand in all this. He had underestimated Dorian, expected him to behave like an escaped convict, or a runaway slave, or any of the hundred things he was. He should have known Dorian would move on the least-trodden paths—right to the precipice of power.

Shaking his head, he said, "It's hard to think of you by this new name, when I'm used to the other one."

"Why?" Dorian Parthens tossed back. "The other wasn't real either."

Wyatt gripped Dorian's forearm and squeezed it, as though to see if his friend was real. "You had me worried."

"About this meeting today?"

"No!" he laughed. "About you!"

"Needn't waste worry on me, Wyatt."

"You're not a waste. Quit that kind of talk."

He gazed at the mystery that surrounded Dorian like smoke, and always had.

"Look at me," Wyatt said. "Why don't you tell me the truth? Why are you involved in the Confederate government— you, who doesn't care about any government or any flag? You've even got the Vice President to help you. What are you up to, Dorian?"

Staring at him penetratingly, Dorian murmured, "God's back teeth, you give me pause with your disarming ways. . . ."

The he shook his head and sighed.

"My dear friend, I'm going to talk to you about the nature of this war," he said, "and what you and I are going to turn it into."

He coiled his arm around Wyatt's shoulders and walked him toward the chesterfield.

"I admire Aleck Stephens. I admire his philosophical buoyancy. As you saw, he has no respect for monarchy, and to him the South is beginning to look like just another monarchy. He intends to overthrow President Davis . . . and you and I are going to help him do it."

Wyatt stumbled back a pace. "Holy rolling God—you agreed to this?"

"Yes, I gave him the end of my arm on it." Dorian said. "And you'll help me too. We all believe in the same things.

Toi, moi, and Aleck Stephens. Jefferson Davis will get all the blame, Abe Lincoln will get all the credit, but the three of us shall be the nameless touch upon history."

"History?" Wyatt choked. "Stephens is talking about not defending the Monroe Doctrine! He's going to promise to let Europe back into the continent! The South is betraying the principles that caused it to secede in the first place! Dorian," he pleaded, "I want an honest answer . . . why are you doing this?"

"Don't rule out senility."

"Come on! None of this is you. I know you don't care who wins this war or how, you're not driven by loyalty to a state . . . and you're . . . well, you're—"

He interrupted himself, unable to say what he was thinking.

Sympathy softened Dorian's face, and the cockiness left his eyes. He realized he owed Wyatt one straight answer.

"Because I must keep the Confederacy alive at any cost," he admitted. "If it means maneuvering European support of the Confederacy, then I must move Europe. The Southern status quo must be held in place."

Wyatt held on to him as he tried to turn, and buttered the tension with his voice. *"Why?"*

"To keep slavery going, that's why!"

"How can you say that? You're . . . legally . . ."

Dorian wrenched away from him suddenly.

"I know what I am! Even more, I know what I'm *not.* I'm not black, I'm not white, I've been owned most of my life, and I'm a hunted man. But I'm not a slave anymore. I'm an expellee. An exile. I'm nothing. No one. I can derive great power from that anonymity, and I intend to use it."

He drew a deep breath, faced his friend squarely, and poked Wyatt's uniform with his forefinger.

"Wyatt, you are looking at the castaway who will hold the South together. With my own lily white hands, I must keep the plantation system from falling apart."

Sympathy clawed at Wyatt like sorrow. His eyes asked the one last *why?* that he could make himself speak aloud.

"If the Union wins," Dorian said, "all slaves will be freed. The slave system will dissolve into a gaggle of displaced people, scattered all over creation, no homes, no papers, no surnames, no traces. . . . Did you know there's talk of creating a nation of former slaves, or sending them all back to Africa? Or down to South America? My God . . . what do I know about South America?"

He forced himself to the tall window and gazed out, past the garden of white roses, into the world in which he was so solitary.

"I will do anything, Wyatt . . . even if it means keeping generations more in bondage. I will make a war, I will stop a war, I will give the west away and cut a thousand throats to steal it back. I will rearrange the hemisphere, redress the globe, and manipulate nations. I will sacrifice the freedom of every negro on this continent. I will hold all of history at bay if necessary. I will do whatever the devil demands . . . to find my mother."

★

CHAPTER FIFTEEN

———— ★ ————

"Are the daylight streets of Richmond safe for you?"

"My idea of hiding from the law is to sit on its back. No one expects a wanted man to show his face, so no one looks at my face. I count on human nature as my camouflage. Anything to bank the boredom, you know."

They pulled up before Wyatt's 1809 Flemish bond manor house at the top of Governor Street. With its gateposts and skirt of brick fence and marble-framed upper windows, the three-story brick was an appropriate home for the owner of a major industry in Richmond—except that Wyatt was less comfortable here than rolling onto one of the company cots in the powder yard dormitory with the other unmarried workmen. The house was a front, insisted upon by the secretive Southern Du Ponts, who wanted to be sure Wyatt looked like the real owner of Craig Powderworks.

They climbed out of Wyatt's carriage, also supplied discreetly by the Du Ponts, and were instantly met by Wyatt's black coachman, *also* supplied . . . and so on.

As Dorian climbed down and his sleeve inched up from his right hand, Wyatt pointed and asked, "What happened to your hand?"

A pattern of scars in crisscrossed rows formed a diagonal pink mesh from between his thumb and forefinger down to the inside of his wrist.

"Did you get caught in barbed wire?"

"No," Dorian said. "Just got caught." Then he saw the coachman approaching them and simply added, "I'll tell you later."

"Afternoon, Major Craig," the coachman greeted, bowing

his head, then skewering Dorian with a look and adding rather cannily, "and Mr. Trözen."

Wyatt winced at the sound of that other name, the criminal name. No one had seen Dorian since he supposedly escaped from prison and disappeared. Most people went about their business and forgot about him in the tumult of current events. War could make folks forget a lot.

War was here, and so was Dorian.

Bold as ever, at Mr. Craig's side, same as always.

Dorian smiled and said, "Not anymore, Reemond. From now on, I'm Captain Parthens. Can you remember that?"

Reemond glanced at Wyatt with an "Are you crazy, sir?" on his face, but he only said, "I remember it, sir."

"Good," Dorian said, and patted Reemond's shoulder. "I should hate to think of what ills may befall you if you should forget."

He smiled when he said it, but Reemond caught the message. Dorian was a gentleman on the skin, but he wasn't beyond a threat now and then, just for safety's sake.

Reemond busied himself with the carriage and its sweating horse. He made himself think about the hot weather and other things that were his business. The rest of the world could take care of itself. One of the advantages of not being allowed in the white man's world was not having to participate in its risks.

Wyatt covered Dorian's shoulders with his arm as though it were a cloak, and pulled him along toward the steps to the wide front door. He had to get Dorian out of the daylight and poor Reemond off the hook of those black iron eyes.

"I don't think he'll say anything," Wyatt murmured as they slipped side by side into the foyer. "They're all a little bit scared of you."

"That's all right," Dorian said magnanimously. "I'm a little bit scared of myself."

The butler, Edmund, met them at the door, and had the same reaction as Reemond, including the same expressions— not so odd, since the two slaves were brothers. That bridge crossed, the first thing Wyatt did was shed his uniform tunic into Edmund's waiting hands and steer Dorian through the archway to the music room and toward the cut-glass double doors of the parlor. Dorian stopped briefly to run his fingers over the full-sized concert harp that stood beside the spinet. Suddenly the music room's gilded oxblood walls were ringing with the chromatic scale.

The two men paused and listened as the sound shimmered away.

"Pretty," Dorian commented.

"Sure is," Wyatt said. "Makes me wish I could play the darn thing."

Dorian tossed over his shoulder, "Why don't you learn?"

"Me? I can't play a game of checkers and you know it."

"Just as well. If you did learn, the government would probably find a way to tax the music."

"Pardon me?"

"Hadn't you heard? The Federal government has instituted a tax on people's income this month. To fund their war effort."

"Tax on wages?"

"Yes," Dorian said. "But you and I needn't pay up, because we're not in that country anymore."

"Doesn't seem right . . . did it get voted on?"

"What difference? The big danger with the privilege of voting is that it gives people the idea that anything the majority wants must be morally correct. The majority thinks it can vote away the rights of an individual if those rights are unpopular. It's the only flaw I've found in our democracy."

Wyatt frowned. "Sounds funny when you say it that way."

"Because nobody ever thinks of majority vote in those terms."

"You just did."

"I'm not anybody."

In the parlor they caught one of the housemaids, Almeda, and her great-grandfather shoveling ashes out of the fireplace.

The girl was doing the scooping while the shriveled old man held a bucket half-full of cold ashes. The difference in their ages, the condition of their skin, and even its color jumped to life immediately. Almeda's youthful skin was brown and smooth as polished maple, while the old man's skin was almost dark as chestnut and a pattern of lines and creases. Her hair was still black, his pure white. The two slaves swiveled their heads up at the unexpected return of the master and his shadowy friend. They looked as if they'd just been caught stealing.

"Don't mind us," Wyatt anticipated to them. He peeled off his uncomfortable Confederate tunic and dropped it onto a standing coatrack. "You keep right on with your work."

"Oh, no, suh," the old man said. He tucked the bucket under his arm and gestured to Almeda to gather up the sheets they'd put over the nearest two rosewood chairs to keep ashes from floating onto the satin seats. "We come back when yawl done wi' de room."

"At least leave the sheets," Wyatt said. "No point you're having to drag them back and forth."

The old man bowed slightly. "Right kind of you, suh."

He waved Almeda out, then followed, without ever really straightening up. At the double doors he paused and looked back at Dorian.

"Good seein' you agin, suh," he said, but his eyes twinkled with a wisdom much cannier than his words. "Good you dint chicken out when dem pugs tell dem lies about you."

Dorian smirked and thanked the old man with a silent nod.

Wyatt looked from one to the other and asked, "Lies?"

"Shh," Dorian uttered.

The elderly slave nodded cagily. "Musta been some other man they mistooken for Mr. Dorian when they t'row him in the jailhouse. Dat's what I think."

Wyatt blushed. "Oh . . ."

"A very generous assumption, Wang'ombe," Dorian said. "Thank you."

The old man bobbed a silent response, grinned around a good set of teeth for a man of his age, and wobbled out through the servants' entrance to the kitchen.

Sunlight poured through the tall atrium windows, simmering through lace curtains and making the entire room and its impeccable furniture shine. Wyatt always felt as though he were visiting here. When he first moved here, the house had been already furnished and decorated for him. Beautiful, but patently impersonal. Like one gigantic receiving room. When he left, it was kept clean for him. His real home was that little office over at the powderworks.

Dorian, though, chameleon that he was, could be instantly comfortable anywhere, in any splendor or any squalor. He collapsed lengthwise on the long tapestry sofa and unashamedly put his feet up on the marble-topped tea table. Then he pulled off a long—very long—chain with a silver watch, a small apothecary's bottle, a handkerchief, which he draped over one thigh, and went about placidly polishing the watch and chain, link by link.

"Ah," he sighed, "home sweet hideaway . . . how old is Wang'ombe now?"

Wyatt unbuttoned his shirt cuffs and sat down in a wing chair.

"He's not sure. Between eighty-three and eighty-seven."

"Getting a bit crotchety finally."

"Yes, but it took the whole eight decades to crotchety him up," Wyatt said. "His age changes, depending on his memory day to day. The only consistent bit of information is that he really was one of the last boatload of Africans brought to the States just before Congress abolished the international slave trade."

"The year 1818."

Wyatt raised his brows, then suddenly remembered that Dorian, of all people, *would* know.

"That's right," he said. "That story never changes when Wang'ombe tells it, so I figure it's true. You know, I was thinking just today how awful it would be if the South lost the war and all the slaves were freed, and what would happen to Wang'ombe. He can't even read. He barely works anymore, but I just love him."

Dorian grinned and gazed with open affection at his friend. There weren't many white men who would admit that about a slave.

Wyatt just continued rolling his sleeves, not realizing he was being appreciated.

Dorian allowed himself a twinge of homesickness. He thought about Plentiful and how different his life had become since then, and since he walked away from Chapel Mount, branded a renegade and a rapist. He had mapped his life out slowly and carefully, covered his trail at every turn, judged men as coldly as they could be judged, and taken great care in his accuracy, yet today he once again stood beside the only man who had held his loyalty for better than five years. Not since Nick and Alex . . . not since Yula.

He owed his intellect to Iphigenia and the Greeks, yet his loyalty was to Yula, the tiny girl who rowed upstream on his behalf and never asked anything in return. Nothing she had done was for herself. She had even shared her child rather than let him be taken away. Shared him with the boss's Greek wife.

Deep down Dorian considered himself more Greek than black or white. He even possessed a lingering devotion to his grandfather's dream of a new Greek aristocracy in the South. If the plantation system failed, Dimitrios Trözene's plan would fail. There would be a new society, and there would be no place for negroes in that society.

He had his life and his purposes all arranged. He would survive first. Second, he would look for his slave mother and her other son. He would not go to Greece until he found Yula and his little half brother, Burlie. He would never care for anyone. He would be a coffin for devotion. It would be dead inside him.

And he had promised himself he would never stay in any one place for long. . . .

Yet here he still was.

Because a wild card named Wyatt had come along and coaxed that deep devotion to rise.

Dorian pressed back into the cushions. "I really should slap you."

Wyatt looked up. "Why?"

"Oh, just to keep you in line."

Wyatt puzzled over this for a moment, then dismissed it with his usual attitude. "Okay, if it makes you happy." He squinted at Dorian's watch and chain. "Is that silver polish you're putting on there?"

"Oil. Sperm-whale oil. The purest lubricant in the world."

"Oil on silver?"

"No, oil on steel."

Being a student of chemistry and a good man of ores and minerals, Wyatt glowered and got up. "You're not making sense. Have I ever seen this before?"

"No. I used to wear it during my past travels, but I put it away when I settled in Richmond. I took it out again after . . . Quist came here."

"Why? What's a watch got to do with a bounty hunter?"

He leaned over the chain. Looked like silver. He fingered the end of the chain and noticed that it carried a gray-bluish tint instead of a whitish tint.

"It's Damascene steel," Dorian said. When Wyatt picked up more of the chain, Dorian grabbed him by the wrist and added, "Be careful. Every third link in the middle of the chain has a razor edge."

Wyatt gasped and dropped the chain. "Why!"

"Because steel will take an edge and silver will not."

"That's not what I mean! Why is there a knife edge on your watch chain?"

"You asked what happened to my hand, didn't you?"

Dorian stood up, casually glanced around the room as though to pick a target, and went to the coatrack where Wyatt's tunic hung. With a flick of his arm, he let fly the steel watch and chain. The chain hit the rack at throat level, and dug into the collar of Wyatt's coat—and Wyatt didn't miss that it was theoretically his throat.

The chain whipped, and the watch came back around with a cold grating *crunch* to its master's waiting hand. It looped perfectly into the fleshy web between Dorian's thumb and finger, and there it cut in. The links into the scar, the blades into the collar of Wyatt's tunic. The coat wrinkled into the noose, twisted, and died.

Blood began to trickle.

"Dorian, your hand!" Wyatt was across the office before the words were out. He fumbled for his handkerchief, but too late to save Dorian's cuff from the red trickle.

"Unfortunately, the coatrack isn't as thick as a man's neck," Dorian commented, dabbing at his lacerated hand. "In actual practice, I have it rather well measured out."

Wyatt dipped his handkerchief into a vase of cut flowers.

"Here. This is a terrible weapon you've got!"

"Precisely. I put the edge on after it failed to serve with brute strength. Mighty *sharp* of me, eh?"

"You haven't actually used this on human beings, have you?"

It was a sharp question, more accusation than interest, and it put a curtain of ice between them suddenly.

Stepping back a pace, Dorian gave him a glare. "Grow up, Wyatt."

Animosity crawled over Wyatt's shoulders as he straightened. "You put that thing away right now."

Edmund appeared at the double doors and said, "Major? Miss MacHutcheon's here to see—"

He was bumped aside as Grace MacHutcheon swung past him, brushing the furniture on three sides with her big skirt. Suddenly the room was lit with personality.

"Thanks, Edmund," Wyatt said, waving the butler out and thanking him again with a pat on the back.

As the butler gratefully escaped, Grace aimed her volatile eyes at Wyatt and started to say something—

The she spotted Dorian.

She paused and stared at him. "I thought they hanged you by the neck."

"Snakes have no neck," Dorian popped back without a beat, still staunching his cuts.

"What did you do?" she asked, nodding at his hand. "Scratch yourself on your reputation?"

"On a woman's tongue."

She cocked a hip beneath the layers of overskirt, underskirt, petticoat, and crinoline and made a disapproving sound in her throat. He was hard to push off balance, this one.

She had tried. Damn right, she had tried. She had figured out his secret, and she had notified the bounty hunter Orville Quist in her fit of rage, intending to get her revenge on Wyatt Craig by hurting his friend—but here they both were, still untouched. Dorian had ended up in jail, Wyatt had ended up with a bullet under his ribs, and somehow they'd both bounced back with hardly a scratch. And *here they both were,* happy as clams!

Dorian was watching her from the corner of his eye. She felt the glare, and the layers under it. She had plenty in common with him, and they both knew that somehow. Always had, since the first of these glares they gave each other.

Maybe he was a spook or something. Maybe he was one of those people who was protected by the moon or something.

It had been a mistake, talking to Orville Quist, putting him on Dorian's trail three months ago. She'd done that in a flash of anger, hadn't thought her plan through, but had only given in to the rage of hurting Craig somehow. Dorian had gone away, and now he was back, once again pretending to be what he wasn't—as was Grace—and he would be protecting Wyatt again.

That changed the rules.

She knew now that a bird couldn't be cooked without putting the spit right over the fire. She'd have to come up with some alternative plan. Get to Wyatt Craig *around* Dorian instead of through him.

So she dismissed him and swung to Wyatt.

"Mr. Craig," she said, "you wanted to see me?"

Wyatt blinked, bounced a glance off Dorian, then realized how dazed the day's events had left him. "Oh! Oh—yes. I'm so sorry—slipped my mind. Won't you sit down?"

"I don't know if I will," she said. "How much trouble am I in this time?"

Wyatt hesitated. "Uh . . . what do you mean?"

"Only that the last time you called me in to speak to you, it was because some of the dour old biddy wives of your powder workers decided I hadn't shown up enough to church that month, and they questioned my worthiness as a schoolteacher. Is this the same conversation?"

Color flushed Wyatt's cheeks, and he glanced again at Dorian, his personal lifeline, but Dorian only sat down, unconcerned that Miss MacHutcheon hadn't sat down yet. He lounged back and watched the show.

"Uh . . ." Wyatt uttered again.

"Oh, gadamighty," Grace blustered. She swirled around again, threw her shawl across the back of a chair, and puffed into it like a giant mushroom. "Say it."

Wyatt turned a little redder. "It's only that . . . some of the, uh . . . one of the . . ."

"Saw me where, doing what?" Grace prodded impatiently.

Dorian chuckled, melting with enjoyment of Wyatt's discomfort.

"Saw you, uh . . ."

Grace suddenly turned to Dorian and snapped, "Do you know? Whatever it is, I'm sure *you'll* say it."

Wyatt made a placating gesture toward Dorian and said, "No—he doesn't know. I should be the one to say it . . . it's my responsibility."

"Well?"

Her dark green eyes glared up at him, set in her squareish face and crown of rolled and netted russet hair, and she resembled more than anything a store of raw copper shavings and rare earths ready to be processed—into explosives.

He gathered himself and figured that if she could face it, the least he could do was say it.

"Some of the ladies saw you coming out of . . ."

Nope, maybe he *couldn't* say it.

Grace blinked at him. "Oh," she said suddenly. "Evee Mapes's Emporium. That's got to be it."

The relief in Wyatt's face took away some of the pink, and he licked his lips and nodded.

"Is *that* all?" Dorian blustered. And he laughed.

Grace studied him briefly, not really sure whether to be grateful for his support or annoyed at his sarcasm. Both were present in his tone.

After a moment she ignored him and looked at Wyatt.

"You tell them I'll teach their children to spell and add, but I'm no marm," Grace said. "They can't tell me what to do or say or who to see when I'm outside that schoolhouse."

"Sorry, Miss MacHutcheon, but they think they can. Actually, they can. They do pay your wage, and that means they can call your behavior."

"Mr. Craig," she said, "if they want to find another school-teacher while a war's going on, they're welcome to it. I wasn't 'behaving' in Evee Mapes's establishment. All I was doing was trading buttons with her."

Wyatt leaned forward a little. "Beg pardon?"

"Buttons," Grace insisted, "buttons. I collect rare and interesting buttons. See?"

She held up her drawstring bag for him to look at. He stepped closer.

The drawstring bag turned like a jewel on its little ropes before him. Green silk winked between a patternless meeting of buttons stitched all over it. No two were the same.

There was a spider encased in a drop of glass. There was a portrait of Queen Elizabeth I on a tiny oblong node of porcelain. And a damned detailed hunt scene painted on enamel. Some buttons were gilt or silver, wood or pewter, with heavy engravings of animals, flowers, cherubs. Some were etched, some printed, and some fitted with paste jewels, some were foil, bone, and even clay. There was at least one papier-mâché, and another glass button encasing a very tiny flower arrangement. They sparkled and flickered in the broad sunlight from the windows.

"Well, I'll be darned," Wyatt murmured.

"Evee Mapes, in her . . . business dealings," Grace went on, "has occasion to collect odd buttons from far and wide. I'll never be so much a sniveling snob that I make her meet me in some neutral place, skittering around in some back alley as though I was ashamed. Apparently your 'ladies' didn't have stiff enough corsets to face me in person, but went through you and made you do their dirty asking for them. I ask, who's ashamed here?"

He straightened and shook off his fascination with the drawstring bag.

"I know. I had the same thought. It's just that they're used to a certain code of conduct for schoolmistresses, and they feel that we should stick to it. She has to be unmarried, attend church every Sunday, no going out after dark, no keeping the company of men—"

"No associating with the local whorehouse," Grace filled in for him, since he probably would never get to it.

Dorian snickered and shook his head in bald admiration. He stuck both hands into his pockets and stood to one side as if watching a play.

Wyatt glared at him, annoyed.

"Well . . . I'll forward your objection to their objections," he said to Grace, "and I reckon we'll just have to wait and see what happens."

"That's fine," Grace said. She snatched her shawl. "You tell them I'll step down the minute they find a qualified unmarried woman who's not rolling bandages, sewing uniforms, taking over her soldiering brother's trade, or setting up a field hospital. Good afternoon, Mr. Craig . . . Mr.—"

"Captain," Dorian said quickly. He raised those black brows as if making a point she would understand. "Parthens."

"Mmm," Grace acknowledged. "I like that one better than the other one."

Wyatt stared at her. Could nothing knock this woman off balance? She was completely unsurprisable. Almost as bad as Dorian.

"Well, good-bye," she said.

She whirled out of the room, stalking through the dining room, hauling that big skirt indelicately.

When she got out to the main entrance of the house, Grace paused at the door to slap her hat back on her head and ended up growling to herself.

"Goddamn motherflaking son of a lowlander," she grumbled. "*Ich glaube gar!* What's *he* doing back here. . . . He's going to wreck it all . . . damn it, damn it, damn it. . . . *Nun ist es aber zappenduster. . . . Um den ist es niche shade. . . .* He's going to get in my way if I try to lasso—"

She cut herself off and looked back down the hall to make sure neither of the men or any servants were lurking around, hearing her. There was no one there—except that she had inadvertently paused in front of a gilt-framed mirror. She paused and saw the bitter-eyed girl staring back at her, with lines on either side of her mouth that hadn't been there a year ago.

With an ugly sigh, she muttered, "I'll just have to get rid of him, *again*."

Wyatt let out a gasp, wiped his mouth, and flopped into a chair as though he'd run a mile.

"Judas," he sighed.

Smiling, Dorian poured water for both of them. As he handed Wyatt one, he said, "She's an unconventional bit of flash, isn't she?"

"She catches me off guard even more than you do."

"Maybe you should marry her and raise a batch of little warlocks."

Wyatt looked up. "What?"

"Well, she's strong and not much of a scratch on the eyeballs, and she's got a frontier background—"

"How do you know that?"

"I just know it. She's prime wife material. Hard work and a good head, and you wouldn't have to worry about her when you go away to the war. . . . She can take care of herself, and she can take care of you. Marry her, Wyatt, and be done with the tamperings of society."

Wyatt's blue eyes blinked several times, and he shook his head. "I think you're crazy sometimes."

"Most of the time," Dorian said, crossing the room from the table with the water carafe.

"Why don't *you* marry her, then?"

"Me?" Dorian jolted. "I shall never marry."

"Now, that's one I've never heard before," Wyatt said. "Why not?"

"No colored woman will have me, and no white woman dares take me. I wouldn't curse myself with dragging a colored wife through the parts of society I intend to map, and . . ." He paused and his tone changed. "And I would wish no white woman the thunder and rain of . . . me."

He hesitated again, and suddenly the more teasing tone returned.

"Besides, anytime a man is rendered to stammering in the presence of a woman, he is better off marrying her."

"But . . . she . . . I . . ."

"Precisely." Sitting once again, Dorian touched the cool glass to his cut-up wrist rather than drinking the water. Lowering his voice, he said, "She does that to you, and she knows it. The art of diversion. It is the sign of a person with a past, Wyatt."

"You mean—she might be going to Evee Mapes's place for something . . . other than what she said?"

"No, not at all. I know she really does collect buttons. And, my friend," he said, tilting his head toward the double doors, "that kind of woman doesn't go through intermediaries like Evee Mapes. Or anyone."

Wyatt paused at the mention of intermediaries. He sat forward on his chair and clasped his hands, resting his elbows on his knees, and stared into the red-and-black Oriental rug.

"Dorian, I have some leads about your mother. I wasn't sure how to tell you."

Dorian sat up and all expression dropped. His throat was tight. "What . . . what—"

Wyatt held up a hand. "She worked as a cook in Virginia during the latter part of 1859, I know that much for sure, and a few months after that, there's word of a free darkie woman of her description working as a seamstress in Maryland. I'm not a hundred percent sure it's her, but the description is close. It's real close." He paused to thumb through a small pile of papers and notes he'd made to himself about this. "Some is hearsay—

some folks'll say anything to get part of a reward. But there's one tip I'm sure of. A woman named Yula Wallace was arrested for vagrancy and held for investigation about a train robbery, but while they were checking to make sure she wasn't still a slave, they caught the real train robber. In the meantime this Yula Wallace slipped away from them. They didn't bother looking for her when she got away. Didn't seem much point, I guess . . . that was in March of this year—"

He looked up and paused.

"Dorian?"

The black eyes were suddenly staring at nothing. The air of elegance had collapsed like an autumn flower. Suddenly the man in the chair was vulnerable, caught in his own reverie and hopes like any other human being who dared wish for something he may never have again.

He felt Wyatt's eyes, but couldn't meet them. In his mind he was staring at a candle that had suddenly been lit in the darkness of his life. His dry lips cracked open.

He whispered, "She's alive. . . ."

Sympathy cut through Wyatt's heart. He drew his brows and sighed at his friend's expression.

"Oh . . . sure she is," he murmured. "Sure she's alive."

Dorian slumped back in his chair and suddenly looked much older than twenty-eight. His arms were limp, and his hands trembled. "He didn't kill her. . . . All this time I thought . . . I might be fooling myself. . . ."

"I'm sorry," Wyatt said. "I wanted better news for you."

Suddenly Dorian's eyes reawakened and struck him.

"Nonsense," he said. "No one knows more than I what a titanic effort it is to find one little colored woman in a sea of colors."

Wyatt frowned sadly, but could only watch and regret he had so little of comfort to offer. He was deeply saddened that Dorian should be heartened by such mediocre progress.

Dorian stood up without quite finishing the sentence and paced to the fireplace, then back again, gazing at the floor.

Shrugging like a little boy, Wyatt stood up too and said, "It's just a matter of time."

"Yes, time." Dorian sighed.

He paused now at one of the windows, in a shaft of sunlight which he normally avoided like a vampire.

"Time, my enemy of enemies. This war is clacking along so fast I sometimes think it'll be over before I wake up tomorrow. The North is talking about scattering the slave population all over the world, or starving them right here. I have to stop them, Wyatt. I have to be sure that neither side can prevail too soon—now that I *know* she's alive and out there! He put both hands to his head as though to hold his intentions inside. "If the North is funding its war effort with income tax, then I must make sure the Southern army is funded too. I've got to keep it all held together, just for a few more weeks!"

He stepped forward, his fingertips lying against the window glass, and he stared for a long time through that clear barrier to the garden and the bright light of day.

"I must redress the world events," he said. "I must move continents aside and do whatever I have to do . . . until I find the woman who risked everything for me. Then . . . let them all kill each other."

The sun lay against his face as though upon a marble statue. Birds chattered outside the window in frivolous punctuation.

Wyatt came to stand beside him in the sunlight and leaned on the sill.

"I hope you're ready to live by those words, Dorian," he said, "because the Vice President is dragging us into treason."

★

CHAPTER SIXTEEN

———— ★ ————

Ah, the joy.

Back in Richmond, in Virginia where his heart lingered, the only place in the New World that made him think spontaneously of Greece. Back here, with his finger once again on the pulse of the changing nation. After wandering the dirty frontier, gathering his bits of wealth, only to spend it all again on bribes, tips, candy for the slave children who might have seen a woman of Yula's description, then following those leads both good and bad . . . back here finally, close to the place he had once called home. From Richmond he could almost smell the salt grass of Tidewater, the tobacco fields of Plentiful.

It was morning. Dorian drew in a lungful of riverside air and imagined smelling the tobacco drying in the smokehouses. Perhaps it was only the linger of some passerby's cigar, but he thought he caught that scent on the passing breeze. Spending yesterday with Wyatt had reinvigorated him after these months of travel, of glancing back at his own trail day after day. He was a hunted man, and he was hunting. Hunting Yula in front of him, and Quist behind him. No word either way.

Wyatt was the only one who had made any progress. That was because Wyatt was methodical and thought the world was a requisition form printed on white paper with a clear watermark.

Dorian, on the other hand, knew the world was a pot of stew spilled from the top of some universal harvest table.

He looked up at the sky and tried to see past the spackled blue firmament to a glimpse of heaven, but there was nothing. Just clouds, sky, a bird. Humanity was alone, except for the rest of humanity.

When he looked down again, he nearly choked.

There, like the scary corner of a nightmare, his worst fear walked out of the crowd. Orville Quist!

Dorian twisted off the seat and struck the ground in a crouch, glad that he had stopped the carriage before seeing Quist walking along the street. He pulled his opera hat forward over his eyes and stood behind the pony, pretending to fuss with the harness, and he listened to the dreaded boot steps.

A snort, a cough, more boot steps—the gravelly crunch of big wooden-soled frontier boots. A wad of chaw tobacco struck the pony's front hoof.

The pony shifted her weight and turned her head to watch the massive stranger until his bulky, layered form disappeared past her blinder. She returned his snort, then turned in the other direction and looked for her master.

Dorian noticed the pony's bewilderment, but he was concentrating on something else. On not moving, mostly. On listening to the location of those boot steps.

Quist!—alive and in Richmond again, in spite of Dorian's efforts to draw him away. The man was a shark, a barracuda! Alive, in spite of Dorian's counter contracts. That meant the killers Dorian had hired were probably dead too, or had been bribed. Yes, that was it. They must have told Quist to come back to Richmond, that the half-breed was hiding there again.

The sound of boot soles crunched past the carriage and on down the street toward the wharves. Dorian barely heard it over the slam of his heart and the pounding in his head and the whine of his internal bells.

Well, that was it. No going back to the powdermill. No respite from the hunt. No quiet suppers with Wyatt at the pub. No warm company, no friendly understanding. Alone again. Playing the dangerous game again. Draw the bounty hunter off and live to tell it.

He pressed his hand against his breast pocket, where he kept the miniature volume of poetry from which he drew his strength. *Poems Chiefly in the Scottish Dialect,* by Robert Burns. It was the only thing he wouldn't leave behind, thus he never put it down. He might leave it on a dresser in a room he would never go back to, or he might leave it in a satchel that he would abandon. No—it stayed in his waistcoat pocket, along with the earthy large-heartedness, which helped him ignore mankind's gnatlike behavior. He couldn't remember the poems he needed now, the lines that would give him strength. He couldn't take the time to dig through the pages of his Bible, disregarding title after title because the words didn't fit what he was feeling right now—

He didn't want to read Burns now. It would only remind him of Wyatt, and he must stop thinking of Wyatt. He must find the strength to go away again, for Wyatt's safety and his own.

When his legs stopped shaking, Dorian made his way to the mare's bridle. She pushed her flat face against him in greeting, and he passed her a carrot from his pocket.

"That's it, Shockoe," he said quietly, looking down the street through the dockside bustle of sailors, shoppers, dockworkers and deliverymen. He sighed, and there was a quiver in his voice. "Let's go . . . while the shadows are still long. I wonder where Aleck Stephens would like to send us this time."

Trouble in the doorway.

"Mr. Craig?"

At the sound of his name, Wyatt looked up from the order for duckshooting powder he was working on.

"Miss MacHutcheon," he said, "come right in."

Grace came in less forcefully than usual, on purpose, and she could tell he was waiting for one of her usual combustions. She gazed with feigned interest at the piles upon piles of papers on his desk.

"My," she said softly, "such a lot here. What is all this?"

"Oh . . . orders, mostly," Wyatt sighed. Thoughtfully he flipped through the unevenly sized papers of stationery and order forms and letters. "I'm getting more every day."

She turned her green eyes to him and actually batted them once or twice on purpose.

"That's good, isn't it?"

Wyatt's blue eyes fixed on a bundle of military orders. "It's good. . . . When I came here from Kansas, I hoped to make soda powder and pellet powder, and here I find myself putting on a whole new shift of men to make prismatic powder and grade P. and T.P.—"

"Cannon powder," Grace supplied. "Gunshot."

He looked up. "Yes . . . how'd you know?"

"I teach it in my classroom. What do you think the sons and daughters of powdermen want to learn?"

"And you teach them that?"

"Of course. Why not?"

"What about mathematics . . . writing?"

"They want to write and add up things they see every day. I give them what they're interested in. They learn better." When she saw the disturbance this gave Wyatt, Grace added, "And I sneak in the odd geography and history when I can, never fear."

He paced away from his desk and tossed another log into the fireplace. "Bothers me to have our kids wanting to know about gunpowder. Don't imagine they'll be so anxious when they find out their fathers and brothers are being killed by this kind of ordnance. . . ."

"I thought you favored the war, Mr. Craig," Grace said, softly but firmly.

He looked up again, straightened up, cleared his throat, and asked, "Can I help you with something, Miss MacHutcheon?"

The fire had brought out the color in his cheeks and made the pupils of his eyes contract beneath a shingle of soft taupe hair. A gaze deceptively blue and innocent, boyish in its way.

Grace lowered her chin a little and took a very small step backward to keep—or make—a facade of innocence for herself, for her own purposes. If she was careful, he *might* believe it just long enough.

She looked at Wyatt Craig and pondered how deeply evil could be buried in a man, and how well disguised.

A hell of a defense, this appearance of no defense . . .

The rocks crumbled under her feet, and Grace fell forward, and the wind coughed out of her, costing precious seconds. She was on the dark side of the hill, picking her way up . . . the top of the crest was teasing her. It moved farther up with each inch she won with her toes and her fingernails. But no—here it was! She was up!

Her back wailed as she tried to straighten, and she staggered against a fallen tree.

The sun cracked between two distant hills and washed the gully with chalk-yellow light. There was the bridge . . . a metal bridge covered now with soot and splattered with wreckage.

And the human wreckage . . . men dead and dying. Over a dozen of them, a litter of gore. Grace could too easily tell which had been killed by explosion and which by weapons more personal.

Her gaze stopped on a vague movement below. Two pastel forms huddled together, both moving.

She stood breathless at the top of the crest, unable to scream. From that vantage point she was forced to watch in utter shock as Wyatt Craig drew his pistol and shot her innocent brother Patrick through the heart.

Wyatt had never seen her like this. Grace MacHutcheon, tornadic, hard-edged, eruptive, blunt . . . pausing, doubtful, silent? A deep pain pulling at her lips . . .

He didn't know much about women's undergarments, but he'd heard a few gentlemen's guesses about how some things made some women's circulation go bad and jaundiced their faces and made them faint. Maybe that was all. Maybe she had something on too tight.

They were uneasy together. Always had been. As though there were something between them, and she knew about it, but *he* couldn't for the life of him figure out what it was. They'd always been on a Miss and Mr. level—as though he were one of her students. He didn't know much about women. He'd spent time in college, studying, apprenticing, time in Kansas running a tannery that smelled too bad to attract feminine company, time building a powdermill in Richmond . . . didn't leave much time for socializing.

Only at times like this did Wyatt realize what a recluse he was becoming.

Sweat. In this collar. All the way around. The way she was

looking at him . . . the way she looked away now. The way sunlight glossed her moist lips.

He leaned forward and dipped his head slightly.

"Ma'am, you all right? Would you like to sit down? May I offer you some . . ." He glanced at the humidor of cigars he kept on his desk for guests. "Uh . . . tea?"

Russet lashes flopped once over her eyes, and the cloud left her face.

"No . . . thank you."

"Let me help you sit down."

Grace almost shook him off—in fact she almost hit him. What should she do to a man who had killed her whole family?

She let him help her sit down in one of the brushed-leather wing chairs.

Instead of kicking him in the pisser.

Christ, what a feeling! Grace loathed help. She never had been helped before. An unending form of teenage entertainment for her had been trying to figure out how her parents had survived in the Kansas wilderness before she was born and could do for them.

"Mr. Craig," she began, "I'm not fancy, and I'm not prim . . . I come from pioneer stock. I don't fit in very well here in the South, and certainly not among Southern women. I can't knit, I can't spin or do tatting or bobbin lace or crochet. My mother and I used to sew old rags into bed quilts and make new clothes out of old ones, and sewing has always been too much like toil to me. Since coming here, I've found Southern women naturally suspicious of a female who doesn't push a needle."

Wyatt pulled his office chair out from behind the desk and drew it around to the wing chair where Grace was sitting, slowly sat down in it as she talked, and leaned forward with his elbows on his knees in his best listening position. His eyes never left hers.

"I've been pondering your . . . what you said about how the ladies think of me," she said, averting her eyes briefly.

Deliberately being vague, he said, "I'm glad you have."

She looked up. "I don't want to lose my position. I may or may not be a very good teacher, but I *am* trying—"

He cupped his hand over hers quickly. "Oh, I'm sure you are!"

"They're good children, and I learn from them too—"

Wyatt insisted, "You've done a fine job, a fine job—"

"I'd like to amend my image," she said, almost with a gasp.

"Well, that's—"

"And to do it, I need your help."

Wyatt blinked. "My help?"

Grace leaned toward him—just a touch. Beneath his palm her hand turned over, and her fingers folded into his until they were holding on to each other.

"Drive me about," she began, "be my escort, go to chapel with me, be seen with me, and let me be seen with you. They respect you—if they saw us together, some of that respect would rub off," she added, "onto me."

"Oh," Wyatt murmured, "I'm sure they respect you, Miss MacHutcheon."

Her dark green eyes, normally so harsh when they touched him, today were soft and vulnerable, even sorrowful. "They don't. I'm just trash to them. . . ."

Wyatt caught her hand in both of his. "Oh, no, no!"

Her gentle breath wreathed his face. Her lips were glossed with olive oil. "Will you help me?" she asked, very softly. "Will you court me?"

His spine melting as she drew closer, Wyatt cracked out a feeble noise. "I . . . don't know about this, Miss Mac-Hutcheon. . . ."

She closed her eyes once, then opened them.

"Grace," she whispered.

In two days they went to three picnics, a social, church, and a summer soiree. Grace let him escort her out of her little house on the mill grounds, up to his carriage, and let him hold her elbow while she climbed aboard. This, never mind that in reality she could climb a scorched rock cliff in bare feet if she had to. She let him carry the picnic basket and open all the doors for her. In two days she had him treating her like a one-eyed cripple. She nearly quit talking altogether, and was careful to murmur what she did want to say. "Yes, please," "Oh, you're

ever so kind," and "I don't think I can do it by myself," came
up more than once.

She hated him for being so attentive. Was he an opposite?
Treat women one way, treat men the other? He always acted
so chivalrous in front of her, and it was confusing her. This
was the man who had killed her brother in cold blood.

Grace just kept telling herself that over and over again, no
matter where Wyatt took her during the next few days. It
didn't make any difference how well he treated her as long as
they were seen together a hell of a lot for just long enough.

Then, the right moment arrived.

It was a state function, held at a social hall near the
Confederate White House. Wyatt had been invited as an offi-
cer in the Confederate Army and a main supplier to the Army.
Everybody wanted him on their side.

Grace kept her arm looped in his, swung her skirt, and pretended to be demure. All the while she kept filling his brandy
snifter. Wyatt was so busy trying to converse with the fancy-
pantsers who wanted his attention that he didn't notice how
much he was drinking—

Until he tried to get into the carriage after helping Grace
aboard and suddenly reeled.

"Oh—what happened?" he blurted. "Did the horse move?
Oh!"

Grace reached down from the passenger seat and grabbed
his sleeve just in time to keep him from falling on his backside
in front of all the other departing dignitaries and guests.

"Yes," she said, "the horse moved. Climb aboard. One foot,
then the other . . . that's it. You just sit here and watch the
stars. I'll drive."

She picked up the reins.

Wyatt slumped back and slouched deep into the tufted
leather. Above them the surrey top shimmered in the starlight,
and beyond the fringe the night sky was turning faster than
usual.

"Oh . . . I don't feel very well. . . ."

"You'll be fine," Grace said. "Just keep your eyes on those
stars."

She snapped the reins, and the pony jumped.

The stars were whirling. Wyatt tried to watch them, but
they wouldn't hold still. He tried to blink, but his eyes stayed

closed too long. Another blink . . . the stars spun in the other direction. The surrey fringe wagged and shimmered. Buildings crisscrossed over each other. He tried to pull the reins to keep from crashing, but the reins weren't in his hands. He'd better find them—

"I dropped the . . . the rrr—"

"No, you didn't. You're doing fine," she told him. She easily held him down with one hand while driving with the other. "I'll have you in bed before you know it."

Another spin of the stars, and Wyatt rolled onto the unfamiliar puff of a goose down mattress. But he didn't *own* a goose down—his boots were falling off.

No, somebody was pulling them off.

His shirt was splitting at the seams. His jacket was gone. Had somebody stolen his jacket while he was groggy in the carriage? Had he remembered to say good-bye and thanks to the host of that party? Whoever's party it had been? He'd better go back and tell them thanks.

Intending to search for the floor, he moved his legs. The night air from the open window brushed over his knees. They were bare! Bare knees! But he wasn't home yet!

He went reaching for his trousers, to pull them up. Couldn't go saying thanks with no trousers on . . .

"Looking for something?"

"Hmm? I'm . . . gotta pull up my drawers . . ."

"They're gone. Forget about them. I have something better to cover your legs."

"Oh . . . that's . . . what it is?"

The juicy warmth of sweat and the velvet of skin flowed over his lower half. Moonlight dappled a dream folding over him—he saw it through the hair that brushed across his eyes. Not his hair—a curtain of rippled red . . . she was soft, and he was supposed to be touching her. Suddenly it had been a long, long time, and he remembered things from his earliest youth . . . the women who taught him things.

It was all right, his cousin had told him. *"All right, because you've got no wife. It's not a sin if you're not sinning against anybody. You got no wife, Wyatt. And you've got to learn to stretch your leather somehow, don't you?"*

His eyes were watering. There was a pungent aroma in the room. There was only the moonlight from the window, and one bare candle lit near a mirror. At first he thought it was two candles.

Feeling like a cow in church, Wyatt twisted to one side.

"No," a voice told him. "Not yet . . ."

He flopped back.

There was an airy form over him. The tips of breasts showed through a white gown, and the edges of hips shaped the cotton like two plow blades. The gown was watery white gauze that left one shoulder showing above his face. The breasts—

Her breasts—were crisscrossed with ribbon that went around her back and around her waist into a small bow. It was just plain ribbon, but drove him hungry. Her hair was partly rolled up and pinned, but a few long twists fell across his lips.

"It's all right," she murmured to him. Her mouth was partly open as she laid her lips upon his cheek. "I'll do it all."

Wyatt lay quivering, his hands and feet numb, and the rest of him beginning to boil.

You've got to learn somehow. . . .

Someone was crying.

He heard it through his pounding head.

It was still dark, but dawn was pulling at the horizon.

Wyatt rolled over and staggered to his feet, only to fall sideways into a dresser. His head stayed back there in the bed. He almost went back after it.

But somebody was crying.

The cabin was still dark. *Whose* cabin?

He found his trousers and hauled them on, relieved to at least get them on frontward. While buttoning them up he stumbled into a bed leg and rammed his little toe. That was plenty to wake him up. He bent over the bed, dug both hands into the rumpled coverlet, grimaced, and waited for the pain to subside. When he could walk again, he limped toward what he hoped was the shape of a doorway.

There was a parlor . . . very simple, very frontierish. An old dough trough holding apples, a couple of ladder-back chairs, a pair of German clogs, some rosemaled boxes, some painted mugs, and a topsy-turvy doll with a white head on top and a black head on the bottom and acorn eyes. That was about it.

Not until he spotted the rough-carved swan he'd bought for Grace at a church bazaar did Wyatt realize where he must be. *Her* cabin. He must be on the mill grounds.

Seeing the swan brought him back to reality, and he forced himself to think. He could do that all right, but he couldn't *remember*.

He heard a creak of wood and looked up. A porch. He forced himself forward and bumped the door open. The sound of sobbing flooded at him. He turned toward it.

Grace was sitting huddled on a porch swing, a shabby crazy quilt draped over her shoulders, covering the top of a white cotton . . . underneath thing. One of those woman underthings.

Wyatt moved toward her.

Her face was pink in the fading moonlight, her hair a clutch of twisted russet and pulled-apart ringlets.

He had never seen her cry. He moved toward her.

"Grace?"

"No, please!" she gasped. She pressed against the swing's armrest, away from him. The whole porch swing cranked sideways and squeaked. "Please . . . not again . . ."

Astonishment poured over Wyatt. His whole body went cold. He stared at her. She pressed farther away from him as the porch swing resisted.

All at once he remembered.

★

CHAPTER SEVENTEEN

——— ★ ———

The Craig Powderworks had its own little village, its own school, and its own chapel. Two Sundays later Grace left the school for the last time and went into the chapel. Surrounded by the delighted ladies of the mill, the wives of the workers, and the teenaged girls who had to learn anyway, she kept her arms in the air while they fussed and feathered over her dress.

It wasn't white, exactly. It was more like eggshell. More like faded linen. Three of the mill ladies had made it from scratch. Nothing store-bought for the bride of their boss, no sir. This was one wedding dress that would be made in the old-fashioned way—by the people who cared for the couple.

They didn't actually know the bride very well, but they adored the groom, and that was good enough. Grace kept her mouth shut and tolerated the attention. It was like being tended by all thirty mothers of the man she agreed to marry.

She kept away from Wyatt Craig during those two weeks and kept her fingers crossed that his memory of that night didn't improve. When she caught a glimpse of him on the grounds, she made sure he caught a glimpse of her too, then she would quickly nail the coffin shut by averting her eyes and pretending shame. It worked very well. He was going crazy. He'd wanted to get married the next morning, but she pretended not to want him around for a few days. Of course, she'd agreed to marry him that very night, right when he'd asked her.

Right there on the porch, with both of them half-dressed and the sun not even up. *"Please . . . allow me to marry you now."*

What a good boy he was.

Grace clamped her lips shut and kept her arms in the air as

the women stitched the long sashes into place on her gown.
The skirt was big and fat, resting on three petticoats, and each
sash was draped sideways and tacked with a linen flower. The
flowers looked more like knots to Grace, but if these women
wanted them, fine. She didn't care. As long as she was Mrs.
Major Wyatt Craig by the end of the day.

Wyatt hooked the stand-up collar of his frock coat and grimaced. The three bands of rank glimpsed back at him from the
mirror. He didn't look like a groom. Didn't feel like one.

Noise outside his office window drew his attention. People,
all dressed in their uniforms or their Sundays, coming across
the grounds for the wedding. He peeked out in time to see the
only wagon that came from Richmond. It carried his slaves
from the Governor Street house.

And were they proud! The mulatto brothers Reemond and
Edmund, the old Wang'ombe and his granddaughter—they
were dressed like royalty today. They put their chins in the air
and strutted through the mill workers without bowing to anybody, white or black.

Wyatt didn't have many friends off the grounds. He didn't
really want any.

That was it. Time to get married.

The marriage itself was tolerable. He hadn't ever really
given much thought to getting married, or love or anything
like that. His whole life had been tied up in his education, his
father's business, then his own . . . and Grace was a nice girl.

Until he'd gotten hold of her.

What had come over him? What college insanity had come
back on him in that brandy?

With a sigh he plucked his uniform hat from its peg at the
doorway of the office building. Outside, the bride was being
escorted across the grounds by the powdermill ladies, all
dressed in their finest. There was a veil over her face, but
Wyatt could tell her eyes were down.

Ashamed.

Getting married didn't bother him. Wrecking a nice girl
sure did. He owed her.

Even in the summer heat, even in a wool uniform, he shivered. Why was he standing here alone? Why was Henry Brecker waiting over at the chapel to be his best man?

Why wasn't Dorian here to do that? Disappeared for weeks now . . . again.

He gazed at the bridge that linked the powderworks to the rest of the world and indulged in a silly wish to see Dorian's carriage come rattling over that arch at the last moment. Dorian must know what was going on. Somehow he must be keeping tabs on Wyatt, on the mill. . . . Where had he gone so suddenly, after being back only one day?

Wyatt sighed and shook himself.

Time to get married.

He stepped out onto the front walk of his office building and pivoted toward the chapel. When they saw him, the little brass-and-drum band started playing. He didn't recognize the tune.

On a day when a man should feel the center of his world, Wyatt felt more alone than he ever had before.

★

———— ★ ————

PART FOUR

WRAP THE WORLD IN FIRE

★★★

THE BURNING FUSE

25 SEPTEMBER 1861

Charles Francis Adams, the American foreign minister, writes to Lords Russell and Palmerston, saying that Britain's resistance to the North's blockade can only be construed as hostile to the naval security of the United States. He says that any aid rendered by British ships to Confederate merchant vessels or of the South's claim to belligerent rights on the high seas "will be viewed as an act of war."

Secretary of State William Seward regards those belligerent rights as pliable . . . perhaps even applying to the North in this case of war. Secretary of the Navy Gideon Welles is bitter that England's merchant marine is supplying the Confederacy.

Pressure to break this building relationship between the Confederacy and Britain starts to make the North's ears ring.

8 NOVEMBER 1861
HAVANA, CUBA

The U.S.S. San Jacinto *pulls into Havana. Self-important and volatile Captain Charles Wilkes discovers that two Confederate commissioners, James Murray Mason and John Slidell, are about to set sail for England on the British merchanteer* Trent.

As the Trent *sails into international waters, the* San Jacinto *meets her and fires across her bow.*

Mason and Slidell are seized by Captain Wilkes and taken into Union custody under no particular authority whatsoever.

NOVEMBER 15

With his two prisoners, Captain Wilkes sails north to Union waters, and ultimately Mason and Slidell are put in prison at Fort Warren in Boston Harbor and held there indefinitely.

The United States government vascillates on the wisdom of this act, and becomes less enthusiastic as the temperature of British regard for the North turns chilly. Britain is indignant at the seizure of diplomatic personnel from a British vessel in open waters.

The Confederacy, however, is delighted and sits back to watch.

CHAPTER EIGHTEEN

———— ★ ————

It was obvious to everyone that the steamer was an American ship. It flew the Stars and Stripes, for one thing. For another, it had that dash about its men and its movement that somehow bespoke of Yankeeness. They were loud and laughing, spoke out freely, and they looked at London's skyline and harborline as though everything here was old, but not venerated. It skimmed the bridges dangerously. It dared more than British ships liked to dare in narrow waters. Or perhaps it simply lacked experience . . . but it was American, to be certain.

Anything American that came into the harbor these days was news, to those both high- and lowborn, and other than being news itself, any American ship inevitably *carried* news also.

But this ship carried something more than news. It carried fire.

The fire sparked the instant a tall and bony man in a black suit, with a black beard and a Northern accent, wearing a black stovepipe hat, stepped off that American ship. He came with a cluster of assistants and porters, copious luggage, and much interest in the shipping and dockwork going on around him. He spoke with great enthusiasm about the Merchant Marine and who was buying what from whom under which international agreement.

Within minutes couriers were racing through London, try-

ing to substantiate or refute the cry that came from a cockney
boy apprenticing to his father on the docks.

"Look! Abraham Lincoln has come to London!"

Nine days later

The venerable offices of Barings, Brown, Shipley &
Company received the young Lincoln lookalike with a touch
of suspicion. Especially when he claimed he was one of the
Delaware Du Ponts, whose British interests the company represented. He claimed to have been going about London,
Greenock, and Liverpool, privately purchasing almost all of
Britain's saltpeter supply. Prices had flashed upward because
of all this buying, he told the agents, and his creditors were
pressuring him for early payment.

Thus he would require a loan on the Du Pont account.

They gave him tea and conversation, but when he stipu-
lated the amount of the loan, the English bankers cleared their
knotted throats and escorted the young American to the street
without commenting on his impertinence. Then they locked
the door.

Lammot Du Pont squared the stovepipe hat on top of his
head, brushed at the whiskers he had hoped would make him
look older, and walked away from Barings, Brown, Shipley &
Company in a huff that practically left a cloud.

Within a matter of days, he was visiting the agents' competitor, Peabody & Company.

Peabody granted the loan . . . based upon the cargo of another American steamship which had just that day pulled into
London.

A steamship full to the rails with a half-million American
dollars worth of gold bullion.

Lammot Du Pont began to supervise the loading of saltpeter.

★

3 DECEMBER 1861
10 DOWNING STREET, LONDON

"I shall never trust nor hold any feeling better than ardent disdain for anything French. If Napoleon the Third wishes Britain to participate in the American states' war, that alone is sufficient impetus to refrain. Respectfully . . . et cetera. Do you have that?

"I have it, m'lord."

The last scratches of the quill pen nearly echoed in the quiet office. The large old man behind the desk was made to appear small by the enormity and height of the paneled wall behind him and the tall-backed, heavily carved rosewood chair in which he rocked. Nearly half a century had come and gone to make the chair comfortable, to wear the arms down to fit his resting hands perfectly, and the seat to fit his ego, and when Thorsby, his chargé d'affaires, once suggested the chair be replaced, Lord Palmerston had mentioned better to replace himself as prime minister than that trusted old chair. Palmerston took that many years to come around to trusting a thing.

He needed that chair. A gorilla of a man, he was highbrowed and small-eyed, with white muttonchop whiskers flanking a protruding lower lip, and stooped over as though carrying the weight of British world influence upon his shoulders.

Actually, that's exactly what he was doing.

Before him, seated in a stiff new tapestried armchair, Thorsby blew on the new ink to dry it.

"That is for Lord Russell's eyes only, of course," the prime minister said.

"I understand, your lordship," the assistant said. He folded the paper, placed it in an envelope, dripped wax on the flap, and stamped it with Lord Palmerston's personal seal. Then he dipped the pen again and wrote *Lord John Russell* on the front. "I shall deliver it myself."

Palmerston coughed briefly, then pondered aloud. "You know, Thorsby, my earliest memories allow me nothing but contempt for usurpers by the name of Napoleon," he said.

The assistant stopped tending the notes, crossed his wrists

while the ink dried, and looked up to pay attention to the prime minister's ruminations.

"Or any branch that sprouts from that dynasty," Palmerston went on, not looking, but quite aware of his assistant's small change of attention. "If Napoleon wishes to put Mexico under puppetship of his brother-in-law, let him do it without England's help."

"Very prudent, m'lord."

Thorsby turned to leave, but stopped when he saw that the door was already open.

At the doorway stood the British Empire's secretary of the Foreign Office. A small man with deep, dark eyes, very short wispy white hair that once had also been dark, and a completely clean-shaven face except for a thin frame of whiskers that ran down in front of his ears, then under his jaw and throat—none on his cheeks or chin at all—Lord John Russell commanded a magnetic presence in spite of his diminutive size.

Thorsby always noticed the odd excuse for a beard, but after a relationship spanning more than a quarter century, Palmerston was well used to Lord Russell's eccentricities.

"John," Palmerston greeted in a subdued manner, reading Russell's posture and therefore expecting news of some impact. "Something's amiss?"

Lord Russell was holding a *London Times* in both his small hands. He looked squarely at Palmerston and raised his brows.

"Pam," he said, "the Americans are misbehaving again."

★

CHAPTER NINETEEN

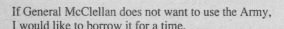

If General McClellan does not want to use the Army,
I would like to borrow it for a time.

—President Abraham Lincoln,
December 1861

3 DECEMBER 1861
ONE OF THE RING OF CAMPS, ARMY OF THE POTOMAC,
OUTSIDE WASHINGTON, D.C.

"Present . . . *arms*! . . . Shoulder . . . *arms*! . . . Right shoulder . . . *shift*! . . . Forward . . . *march*!"

Three companies of the Nineteenth Indiana, over four hundred men, marched in a startling blue, brass, and silver review past a single spectator.

The lone woman had to hike her mud-soaked skirt and step back as the flanking military band swung too closely by her. As she caught the eye of a tuba player and a rank of drummers, she got a clear feeling that the thirty-some musicians were playing just for her and were glad of her audience. Glad somebody was there to see the results of day after day of practice and drill, drill, drill.

Bayonets flickered in the Virginia sunlight, and the Regular Army blues made a sea of dark wool before her as the rifle company made a sharp spin-right turn. White gloves on officer's hands made a flash from time to time. In the background whole companies sat vigorously polishing their Enfield muzzle loaders. Beyond them were rows of big Sibley tents poking into the chilly morning air, with a constant smoke hovering around their conical tops. The camp possessed a gigantic singular stink—cooking smells, cigar smoke, sulfer.

The martial spectacle was stirring, but the woman pressed her lips tight behind her bonnet's veil. Only the veil obscured the annoyance in her eyes, and it was poor concealment for such a scowl. She was tempted to hike the skirt again, wade through the mud, and go on into camp, but she knew she'd be stopped and checked for passes she didn't have. She also knew that if she just stood here long enough—

"Miss?"

A young first sergeant stepped to her. Ah, the dependability of chivalry.

"Oh . . . Colonel," she gasped.

She'd had her eyes on him for ten minutes now and had been sending little mental cries for help, which eventually almost any man would answer if a woman knew just how to cast them. Here he came.

"Ma'am, may I help you? Are you lost?"

"Oh, Colonel, I've had such a day," she said, breathing heavily and touching her hat and her blouse in a frazzled fashion. "My carriage broke a wheel a few miles down that road, and I had to tramp my way here in the mud. I'm so pleased to be in the company of our fine troops and know I'm safe."

The man's little mustache twitched. "Ma'am, your carriage tossed a wheel and you didn't use the horse?"

She paused and gave him one of *those* looks. "Ride a horse without a proper sidesaddle? Ride bareback like a savage? Oh, Colonel—"

He shifted uneasily and hooked a thumb nervously in his belt. "It's Sergeant, ma'am . . . and, uh, I'm sorry for the presumption. If you would wait a few minutes, I'll finish my business in camp and see that you're provided means and escort back to the city."

"That's kind of you," she said, letting her voice twitter. "Where shall I wait?"

"Why . . . right here, ma'am."

"Here? In the road? I see . . . thank you, Major, for your kindness."

She clasped her gloved hands, rested them on the dirt-flecked front of her bell skirt, tilted her chin downward, and did her best to look small.

The sergeant started to step away toward camp, but now paused and watched her standing there. She looked like a daisy about to be trampled in the road, with her little hat, its veil, the little inadequate crocheted cape about her shoulders, the skirt too heavy for such an ordeal as she had described.

He tried to walk away. But he couldn't.

"Ma'am?"

"Colonel?"

"Perhaps you'd do me the honor of taking my arm as I conduct by business about camp?"

The woman gasped so convincingly that the sergeant puffed up right before her eyes. He felt especially gallant as she rushed to him and hooked his elbow with her hand. Only then did he notice she was almost as tall as he was, and he stood up real straight to hide that.

With a swirl of her muddy skirt, she all but pushed him onward into the camp, between the marching ranks.

Flanked on both sides by the Sibley tents, the company street unfolded before the unlikely couple. On one side a group of new inductees was being taught how to put up dog tents. They stumbled over themselves to give her a tip of their hats as she and the sergeant walked by.

The woman and her escort turned under an arch decorated with regimental banners and headed down another company street, when the woman suddenly stopped walking.

"This'll do fine, Sergeant," she said. Her voice suddenly dropped its quiver. She let go of his arm too.

He wheeled around. "Ma'am? You've got to proceed on with me."

"No, this tent is where I'm going."

"Here?"

"Yes. Isn't this Major Allen's tent?"

The sergeant caught his breath and realized his daisy was poison ivy after all, and that he'd been taken.

He gawked and stammered, "But you—but I—"

"Sergeant," a sharp voice interrupted.

They both turned to see a wiry, cold-eyed man in civilian

clothes and a plug hat glaring at them from the tent's opening.
He was holding a thick handwritten report.

The sergeant snapped straight. "Major . . . sir, this
woman—I thought—she claims—"

"Are you in the habit of escorting women about the
camps?" the man asked in a sharp Lowland Scottish tang.

The sergeant's mouth dropped open, but nothing came out.

The woman shouldered her way past him. "Don't look so
hangdog, Sergeant," she said. "You're not a bad soldier.
You're just too good a gentleman."

"But—"

The wiry Scot held up a hand and admitted, "She works for
me, Sergeant Roby."

"Then why didn't she show her camp pass!"

The woman turned to him and said, "Wouldn't it be
chicken-yard stupid for a Richmond spy to carry a Union pass,
Sergeant?"

She stepped past them both and went into the tent.

The two men stood through a brief silence. Then the
Scotsman said, "Wait right here, Sergeant."

Grace MacHutcheon Craig, spy for the Army of the Potomac,
pulled her bonnet off as she stepped inside Major Allen's tent
and stopped short. She found herself staring at another officer,
a young one, in a sashed and tasseled captain's uniform. He
stood up when she came in, his hand naturally poised on his
long saber.

"So, I've interrupted one of your tactical meetings, Major
Allen?" she commented, turning as the man in civilian clothing dipped back into the tent.

"In fact, you have," he said.

Discomfort needled at all three of them. Spies had a way of
never being completely trusted by men who put on uniforms
and boldly proclaimed who and what they were, and clearly
the young captain over there didn't know what to make of
Grace at all. But the Scotsman ran a deliberate middle ground
by making a gesture between them.

"Mrs. Craig, may I present Captain Parry," he said, then

looked pointedly at the captain and added, "The young lady is one of our Richmond informants."

The two men exchanged a look Grace couldn't interpret. Either they were communicating that it was all right to talk in front of her or that it *wasn't,* and she couldn't tell which.

The young captain motioned for her to sit on one of the velvet-covered stools near a small table. She plunked down, then both the captain and the major sat around the the table.

Grace fixed her eyes on the major. "I saw some of the Iron Brigade drilling out there."

"Ah," he said. "How did they look to you?"

"Well, all the elbows were touching, if that means anything."

"Ah . . . it does. Good, very good."

Both men watched as she bowed her head and fussed with her skirt. Motes of dust floated in what little sunlight came through the top of the Sibley tent to flicker on her russet ringlets and play on the freckles of her ruddy cheeks. Despite her complexion, her hair color, and her maiden name, the major knew she wasn't Scottish, but German. Her name was pretend. There was no Grace MacHutcheon in Richmond, but only a woman who used that name for her own purposes, and married the name Craig for the same reasons.

He also knew her purpose didn't involve Union victory quite so much as they involved Southern defeat.

"You have something for us, Mrs. Craig?" he asked.

By way of an answer, she boldly pulled her skirt up, then the underskirt, then the hoop. Secured with two hat pins to the inside of the hoop was a large folded piece of paper. The major averted his eyes, but the young captain didn't have any problem appreciating Grace's stockings. She felt his eyes, but ignored him. A little fight got the pins loose and the paper free, then she pushed her skirts down again and straightened up.

"Here you are," she said, "a hand-drawn map of the lower Rappahannock."

"Oh!" the Scotsman leaned eagerly forward, and his cold stare turned to a glitter of delight. He loved maps. He put his twenty-odd pages of report on the table and took the paper she handed him. "Anything's better than those store-bought rags we've had to use." He unfolded the map and gleefully examined the handmade sketch.

"Glad you like it," she said.

While the major looked at the new map, the captain reached for a bottle and a set of tin cups. "May I offer you a champagne?"

Grace sat up straight and twisted toward him. She'd *known* there was something different about this one!

"You're European," she blurted. "Are you French?"

He smiled. "Yes," he said, "but I have been living in England for some time, with members of my family."

His English was flawless, she noted, very educated, but the Frenchness was still there but good. He had a somewhat high-pitched voice, but it might have been his youth. His brows were low and sharp over a pair of blue eyes, and he tried to circumvent his youth with a full brown mustache and beard.

"Are you here as a foreign observer sir?" she prodded. "But you're wearing the uniform of a Union Soldier."

He smiled with a little coyness. "I *am* observing, and making a diary, yes. But I am also here to participate in the cause célèbre . . . the preservation of the United States of America."

"From what I hear lately, your France and England don't know if they share that sentiment yet," she said. "There's talk of them coming in for the South. Trouble over some diplomats on a boat or something."

The young captain's brows raised, but with a purse of his lips he showed her he wasn't going to offer an opinion.

Grace's expression clearly showed, as she intended it to, that she knew he was telling her only part of some story.

Both men saw that, and the Scottish major spoke up. "It's Captain Parry's job as a volunteer aide-de-camp to outline and abridge reports from this office to General McClellan."

"Mmm," Grace muttered, dissatisfied. "In any case, you needn't offer me champagne. I'd rather you offer me an explanation."

The major's flinty eyes came up from the map again. "Sorry?"

She faced him. "Thanksgiving is passed."

Suddenly he understood.

"Oh . . . yes."

"Well? What happened?" she asked. "Why didn't the Army move?"

He cleared his throat. "Armies don't move at the whim of civilians."

"Civilians my eye. I risked my life to bring you information that would get this Army on the road. What happened to General McClellan's plan to thrust through the Confederate outposts at Manassas Junction and Centreville by Thanksgiving? Did his aide-de-camp here fail to turn the general's calendar, Mr. Pinkerton?"

An awkward pause fell. To her left, Captain Parry's bemusement dropped like a rock.

Behind the table the Scots major's eyes went hard again. "Grace MacHutcheon Craig, I've always used your nom de guerre, and I prefer to use mine. E. J. Allen."

"That'd be fine, Mr. Pinkerton, if we had a guerre to use our fake noms in. It's been more than a month since I brought you information about the Confederates dug in at Centreville. What's the stall? Wasn't General McClellan going to make a thrust?"

Allan Pinkerton put the map down on the table beside his report. He knew she and the other spies in Richmond wanted the same answer. He could see that in her expression and weighed the prospects of not giving her one against his need for effective informants.

Captain Parry spoke up again in his precise English. "General McClellan is a very hard worker, Mrs. Craig," he said. "You are wrong to think he shirks any duty. I must follow him on horseback sometimes twelve hours a day, amassing men and materiel, and his men drill eight or ten hours and study weaponry and tactics—"

"And march round and round to nowhere day after day," she finished, shaking her head at him. "You're talking about duties of routine and ordnance, not command. The commanding general of the entire Union Army is troubling himself with administrative claptrap, while enemy outposts sit practically over that hill, Captain Parry. Johnston's Confederates are hardly fifteen miles from here. Why doesn't General McClellan do what everyone wants and get on with this war?"

"You don't understand," Pinkerton placated, "the general's

considering a . . . different plan of action than when you and I last communicated."

"Different?" she asked.

The two men looked at each other in one of those deciding-whether-to-tell ways again.

Then Parry made a decision, or part of one. "Even as we speak, his topographical engineers are analyzing the coastline east of Richmond—"

"The *coastline*?" Grace interrupted. "What's the coastline got to do with anything? What happened to President Lincoln's idea to snap the Confederate deadlock by going up the Occoquan and cutting Johnston's supply line?"

Pinkerton interrupted, "How did you find out about that?"

"You told me!"

He frowned. He didn't like being caught in front of Parry at having violated his legendary prudence by telling a plan to one of his shirttail informants.

But Parry was affected only by Grace's disapproval of the plan and said, "The Occoquan plan would put us up against superior forces."

"Hogwash," she said back. "I think McClellan's afraid of a fight."

Both men shifted uncomfortably, but for different reasons.

"Please," Pinkerton said, "keep your voices down. General McClellan wants to go in only when he can win." He lowered his own voice, and a note of sadness came into it. "We want no more ugly shocks like Shiloh and Ball's Bluff."

Grace rolled her eyes and barked, "He's just scared to be blamed for any losses. He's all dash and glamor, is what he is. And *you*—" She aimed a finger at him. "You can't judge the difference between good information and plain dumb gossip."

Beneath Pinkerton's expression was a certain message that he was tolerating her, and her insults, that he knew something she didn't know. More than anything Grace hated that under-current as she waited for a response.

Slowly he said, "Both the general and I have the whole future to consider, not just a month, come and go. Someday I hope to make the words *secret service* more than just any covert activity. I hope to build a national network."

"Assuming there *is* a nation," she snapped.

"There will be," Captain Parry said.

Grace twisted to him again. "Well?" She glared at him a moment, her cold green eyes giving him no quarter. Then she looked back at Pinkerton and hammered, "Well?" Are you going to let him tell me?"

If she gave Parry time, his enthusiasm would get the better of him. He was sitting on the edge of his velvet stool, itching to defend General McClellan. All she had to do was push.

She didn't want to appear frantic. She clamped her lips shut and determined to keep quiet until Parry couldn't stand it.

Parry looked at Pinkerton, his eyes wide and his youth playing against him, and after several seconds he got the nod he wanted from the other man. He leaned forward on his stool and proudly told Grace, "The general plans to bypass the Confederate groundholds at Manassas and Centreville by boating the Army into Chesapeake Bay, then up the Rappahannock River to Urbanna, Virginia."

Grace felt her eyes bug out, but she bit her lip and kept quiet. She stared at Parry, then looked at the man behind the table.

Pinkerton wasn't looking at her, but was gazing pensively at Parry.

Now he looked at Grace and seemed to be waiting.

Grace cleared her throat to see how loud her voice would come out. "Does the President know about his new plan?"

"Oh, well," Pinkerton said, "the President's not a warrior. He's incapable of comprehending these massive and critical operations."

"He's the President!" she shot back. "Good God, Mr. Pinkerton, at least have the stones to admit that General McClellan won't tell about the Urbanna plan because he knows Lincoln won't like it. I've half a mind to tell him about this myself. Damned if I don't."

Horror struck Parry's face, but Pinkerton remained calm.

"You understand," Pinkerton said carefully to Grace, "it's critical the Urbanna plan not leak out. General Johnston must not catch a whiff of what we're intending."

"Information leaks to me, not out of me," she said contemptuously. "Hell, this camp'll leak itself clean from bored desertion before Little Mac advances this Army. Your general is nothing but cold sunlight."

Her words threw a pall over them.

A touch of color came again to Pinkerton's stubbly cheeks. He bounced a glance off Parry, then shifted in his chair.

Captain Parry was practically shaking on his stool. "Madame—you—you—"

"Well?" Grace pounded.

"General McClellan is a model soldier! He is the tool of God!"

"According to him or God?"

"There is a divine reason in his appointment," Parry insisted. "He feels God has chosen him to save the nation. Not even the President must circumvent God."

"How convenient for God's tool," Grace countered.

Pinkerton remained typically tight-lipped as Grace and Parry smoldered before him. As Grace looked at him, it was impossible to tell whether Pinkerton doubted God or doubted McClellan. But he was obviously embarrassed that Parry had spouted McClellan's claim about the divine.

With two quick gestures Grace yanked off her gloves and threw them onto the table. She stood up and paced back and forth in front of Captain Parry, whose acrimony followed her with uncloaked suspicion. Her big skirt made swirl marks across the dirt in the whole front half of the tent. Suddenly she faced him.

"Why don't you be honest with yourself, Captain Parry?" she demanded bluntly. "You know it'll take weeks to assemble enough steamers to float a hundred thousand men and gear up the Rappahannock, and so does General Messiah. He wants what he always wants. Time! More time. He wants more time for more drilling and polishing. Meanwhile, the Confederates are sitting practically right *there*!"

She pointed at the hills west of the camp.

"Madame!" Captain Parry gasped. "The Urbanna plan is strategic! It takes fifty miles off the march to Richmond and avoids battle. Our troops will take Richmond fresh, not battle weary. The Rebels will be shocked. Confused. And Richmond . . . will belong to George McClellan!" He nodded a little punctuation. "Patience is his greatest virtue."

"Patience isn't what a general is hired for," she told him. "Cowardice is another word for all this."

Steel and brass clinked as Parry stood up sharply and glared. His face took on a terrible flush. With a fist clenching his saber's hilt, he spat, "Excuse me!" He dropped a stiff bow at Pinkerton and repeated, "Excuse me, Major."

And he walked out, stirring the motes of dust.

Grace didn't even bat an eye. She turned back to Pinkerton.

He was studying her with a buried wisdom and finally sighed. "Mrs. Craig, now that we're alone, why don't you tell me what you're really thinking?"

Almost disbelieving that he'd asked, she skewered him with a look.

"Very well," she said. "I think you're half-wrong."

"You mean, you think I'm wrong half the time?"

"No! I think you're off Johnston's Confederate numbers by half!"

Pinkerton rocked back in his chair and laughed. "Mrs. Craig."

"Confederate forces at Centreville and Manassas are seventy thousand all together, if not less."

"My dear young woman, please!" he chortled. "Interrogations of deserters and two runaway slaves say there are not less than one hundred fifty thousand Rebels waiting in those hills."

"Are there? I didn't want to embarrass you in front of the captain," she said, "but in October I gave you an estimate of Confederate numbers. You thanked me and said you would reduce the figures I gave you by fifteen percent to account for any troops too sickly to fight." When he started to blush before her, she knew she was on to something and leaned forward. "What you did was reduce the number by *one fifteenth*. There's a little difference between those figures."

A crease appeared across his brow. "It was a mathematical error. Both the general and I strive for caution."

"Caution!" she shouted. Suddenly she vaulted to her feet, snatched up his twenty-page report, and violently flung the papers at him. They struck him full in the face with a terrible crackle and spun like snowflakes. "The future chokes on caution!"

At the tent entrance, Sergeant Roby plunged inside, his hands on his sidearm's holster.

Pinkerton jumped to his feet. "No! No, Sergeant, it's all right! It's all right!"

Roby hesitated, his gaze flicking back and forth between Pinkerton and Grace. The pistol stayed in the holster, but the hand also stayed on the gun.

Grace didn't care. Pinkerton was the one who cared whether they were overheard, not she. She never even glanced at the sergeant, though she heard him shuffle behind her and felt the tension of his hand on that gun.

"The defeat at Ball's Bluff took the air out of the public's confidence in a Federal victory, and we've got to have one!" she said. "A hundred eighty thousand soldiers are parading around Washington like turkeys with bow ties on! McClellan's nothing but a drillmaster! I don't know when I've seen a man so constructed for greatness yet so inclined to let greatness sit and sour!"

Her invective made both men stiffen.

The young woman stood, snatched up her gloves, took great handfuls of her big skirt, and twisted it out of her way as she moved toward the tent opening.

"I'm risking my reputation and sometimes my life to give you information, Mr. Pinkerton, and I'm going to be sending you more," she said. "Just make sure you start using it."

As the woman stepped out of Pinkerton's tent with Sergeant Roby at her side, escorting her out of the camp as fast as he possibly could, Captain Parry strode anxiously back toward the tent. Just then Allan Pinkerton stepped out into the sunlight to meet him.

Pinkerton stifled a dreary grin that pulled at his lips. The hot-blooded French aide-de-camp beside him was still twitching after being so thoroughly scaled. There was something bluntly American about stripping the shine off a blooded aristocrat, and a down-to-earth man like Pinkerton couldn't help but appreciate the woman who had done it. The two men stood together, watching the woman go.

"My apologies," Captain Parry said then. "Pride took my tongue. I should have been more discreet and kept the Urbanna plan from her."

Pinkerton sighed. "I'd have told her myself. She needs to know what kind of information to get for us, and why. That's how the best spies work." He squinted in the bright daylight and turned to the younger man without letting that grin out. "Besides . . . it's very hard to be discreet in the company of that woman, Your Royal Highness."

CHAPTER TWENTY

★

"Shameful." Lord Palmerston threw down the latest *London Times* with Secretary of State Seward's latest saber still rattling among the pages. "The Cabinet may stand for this, but I do not intend to take this *Trent* atrocity lying down."

"It may be a blessing in disguise, Pam," Lord Russell said as he sat in the tapestried chair opposite Palmerston and twitched as though sitting on thorns. "Secretary of State Seward is bullying us in the North, the cotton barons are blackmailing us in the South, and now this insult on the high seas—a war with the Americans is England's only chance to maintain world supremacy, and now we can do it and save our dignity as well. The Americans have played beautifully into our hands."

"John, John, John . . . ," Palmerston said admonishingly. "Don't be so cold-blooded. War is a last resort in a diplomatic tangle, after all."

"Don't you be so innocent," Russell retaliated. "Think how many times you yourself have been driven to your last resort. The future of the empire demands that America's progress be checked. If we don't break up the Americas now, the focus of world power could eventually shift. The Americans could become preeminent in the world."

"John, really. The European powers are now, and forever will be, the world. The United States are finished as a nation. Soon the Americas will be taken by European powers and become permanent colonies, like India."

"Will they?" Russell insisted. "You've seen for yourself that we've lost influence in Central America because of the United States' domination of the continent. I've heard you say it.

"Yes, and I've heard *you* say it would be ignominious beyond measure to involve ourselves because the South threatens to hold back cotton . . . that Parliament will not stoop to cooperation under duress."

"Exactly," Russell said. "We would seem like an international dog on the Americans' leash."

For a moment Palmerston seemed confused.

Russell let him stew.

Then he said, "That's why *this* opportunity should not go unavailed. A deliberate rupture of maritime law and freedom of the seas exonerates us of any complicity in their moral struggle. If we take this chance, carve up that continent now, they'll become like Europe—a herd of independent countries forced to keep an eye on each other so no one becomes too powerful. But only if we act on this marvelous opportunity! This *Trent* business is a godsend, Pam. Use it! Distract the North or support the South on this pretext, but send a fleet *somewhere*! Keep that continent broken in half, or Great Britain could become second-most great."

A bell-like silence fell between them. Russell's words rang in the old halls for a long, long time. They were longtime political rivals, but they came together with the ferocity of lions when their pride was threatened . . . the empire. Russell counted on Palmerston's distrust of President Lincoln during those ticking moments and hoped that distrust would work on his longtime colleague. And neither of them trusted Russell's American counterpart, Secretary of State Seward.

"Ordinarily I might be disposed to just that action," Lord Palmerston said finally. "However . . . the Channel is not the moat of protection it once was. I'm reticent to commit dispatch of a large fleet to the United States. British soil would be open to aggression."

"Oh, rubbish," the Foreign Secretary huffed, squeezing and unsqueezing his hands. "The Atlantic Ocean isn't the moat it once was. There are no moats anymore. The future of England requires that America's progress be checked. And you well know it."

Palmerston wasn't unaffected by Russell's arguments, nor was he, after all these years, deaf to the Foreign Secretary's own brand of insight. Neither of them had ever trusted England's poor relations in America, and he knew the experiment in mob rule would ultimately cause the United States to collapse, as it seemed to be doing.

Question was . . . how much should England be seen plucking out the bricks of the foundation?

He picked up a letter, just received this morning, from the Queen's beloved consort, and let it drift across the desk to land on the edge, in front of Russell.

"The Prince Consort is not feeling well of late, but his attitude regarding the *Trent* crisis remains clearheaded and benign. He influences both myself and Her Majesty to restraint, John. The Prince does not believe the United States government intended an offense in capturing those two Southern men. Rather, that it was simple bad judgment on the part of the bombastic commodore of the *San Jacinto*, what the devil's his name—"

Russell raised his brows. "Charles Wilkes."

"Quite. An inappropriate man, I've heard, who did not carry with him the authority of President Lincoln."

"But he did carry the authority of the blockade of Southern ports."

"In a rather loose definition, considering it was a British ship going out of a Cuban port, not a Southern port." He paused and added, "I wonder how he even knew the Southern men were aboard the *Trent*. It's a British ship."

"No idea," Russell said. "If the United States meant no offense, why don't they release the diplomats?"

"That," Palmerston said, "is the question of the day. But I have the international prestige and honor of the empire to consider. Thus I agree there must be a strong British reaction to this seizure of passengers aboard a ship of the empire. . . ."

"The only problem is," Russell supplied, "*how* strong?"

"Precisely." Palmerston rocked back in his old chair, gazed unseeing at the molded plaster medallion in the ceiling. They knew each other very well.

After a moment he called, "Thorsby!"

The door swished open. The chargé d'affaires was careful to only half enter the office.

"M'lord?"

"Come in. Bring your notebook."

"I have it, Your Lordship." Thorsby came in and sat on a bench beside the prime minister's desk, close enough to use the pen and well on Palmerston's desk.

"Issue a note of protest regarding the *Trent* seizure. Charge violation of freedom on international waters upon a vessel flying the British flag. Demand an apology about what is obviously a misunderstanding during a difficult time, and the release of the two Southern gentlemen to continue on their visit to Britain. Be sure to use that kind of language. Find a way to subtly suggest possible recall of our emissary, Lord Lyons, from Washington. Also, refuse to send any more arms shipments to President Lincoln. Until the two passengers are free, the United States will not see one ounce of the niter young Mr. Du Pont is sitting on down at the docks."

Russell leaned forward. "Put a few redcoats on that dock, Thorsby . . . just to be sure Mr. Du Pont doesn't slip away in the fog."

Thorsby repressed only part of a nasty grin. "Very good, Your Lordship." He now looked at Palmerston. "May I also suggest a copy of this be sent to Prince Albert—"

The office door burst open suddenly.

There was Briggs, panting like a run hare, clutching the knob with two hands, both so white they glared against the wooden door.

"Briggs, what's the cause of this behavior?" Thorsby demanded.

"My Lords," Briggs gasped. Then he looked at Palmerston, "My Lord . . ."

"Yes, Briggs, what is it?" Palmerston encouraged.

Briggs licked his dry, colorless lips. He nearly choked on his words.

"His Royal Highness Prince Albert . . . the Prince—"

Palmerston, Russell, and Thorsby waited for the rest of the sentence. It never came.

Pure human perception took over.

Then Lord Russell dropped back in his chair, uttering a silent prayer. He closed both eyes.

Thorsby put a hand to his own lips in sudden reaction. He began to shake. "But he's only forty-two. . . ."

In that moment the entire British Empire heaved up and shivered.

Behind the carved desk Lord Palmerston's big body seemed to sink in place. His gaze lost focus.

His simple whisper filled the room and made the fire crackle.

"God save the poor Queen. . . ."

A pall fell over Britain. One of the strongest monarchs in history, Victoria, dropped from public activity and virtually disappeared into a shell of devastation. Likewise, England's soul turned inward upon itself.

Lord John Russell appeared at the door of his office and motioned his secretary into the room. Then he sat down in light of Prince Albert's death and the seizing of the *Trent,* and began to dictate a new policy.

"From now on we shall send advance notes to any Southern legates who attempt audience here. We'll begin by saying that Earl Russell—and you must refer to me that way, as a private citizen, not a Foreign Secretary—presents compliments to the gentlemen and would be obliged if they would send in writing any communications they wish to make."

"Yes, my lord."

"And do not date anything from the British Foreign Ministry. Date them from my residence."

"Pembroke Lodge."

"Yes." Russell leaned forward nervously and stared at the engraved leather desk cover. "And send an eyes-only note to Lord Lyons in Washington. Tell him this . . . if it can possibly be helped, Mr. Seward must not be allowed to get us into a quarrel. I shall see the Southerners when they come . . . but unofficially, and keep them at a proper distance."

★

CHAPTER TWENTY-ONE

———— ★ ————

Requisitions . . . orders . . . receipts . . . powder quality reports . . . accounting ledgers . . . employee records . . . a newspaper . . . an order for a new anvil for the cooper . . . livestock feed . . . excavation blasting . . .

Papers were piled in no particular order on Wyatt's big black-oak desk.

Grace sifted through them with mounting frustration. All these weeks she had maneuvered closer and closer to her husband's office and was finally in it with nobody giving her a second look. She had cleaned and mended her way across the powder refinery's grounds, made new curtains for every room in this building, never mind that the curtains were a little crooked here and there or didn't hang quite right because she couldn't sew worth a spit, and finally she was in Wyatt's office when he wasn't here.

She lit a single lamp against the weakening sun setting behind the building. The room was nearly dark. The little lamp struggled valiantly.

All she had to do now was figure out which of these papers came from Army sources and which from civilian sources. Which was just an order for blasting powder to put in a cellar and which was meant for the Confederate Engineers to clear a path for a brigade? There didn't seem to be any officiality to any of these papers, no "state" or "national" stationery, no watermarks to speak of . . . no sense whatsoever to the Confederate manner of doing business yet. Some of these were

220

orders for new uniforms, and none of them even specified the same kind of fabric twice in a row. Or even the same color. No sense at all. This "army" was going to look like a school yard full of immigrant children if they didn't get some standardization. At Manassas the armies hadn't even been able to tell each other apart. What was it about men that they couldn't keep one thing simple?

"Christ and crust," she grumbled. "Pinkerton, you're wishing down a dry hole, I swear. . . ."

Impatience nipped at her. She wasn't hurting Wyatt Craig enough. He was still living well, his business plucking along, supplying the war effort, and he still had her in his bed. She sent Pinkerton information about times of deliveries and made fair guesses about the sizes of those shipments. Occasionally she could wheedle out of some worker the grade of powder in the barrels being shipped. Pinkerton always thanked her and said she was doing well, but General McClellan had yet to make a move based on the information, and nothing had changed for Wyatt Craig—

Suddenly she flinched and looked up. She held her breath. Had she heard something?

Outside, behind the building, the constant *kssshhh* of the waterwheels at the mills made her nervous. They could hide the footsteps of someone coming into the building. She could be caught digging through this pile instead of hanging poorly made curtains.

Nothing happened. No one came in. There was just the waterwheels and the crackling ripple of the ice-rimmed James River.

But the floor was still creaking.

Grace looked down. The floorboards whimpered again, then were still. And she hadn't moved.

She followed the lay of the floorboards along the center of the office—to the closet.

With a yank that hurt her fingers, she wrenched the bottom drawer of the desk open and scooped up the pistol Wyatt kept there. In an instant she checked to see it was at least partly loaded, then she thundered across the office and kicked the closet door.

Before the rattle stopped, she shouted. "Get out of there! Step out! Now!'

For a moment there was only silence, during which Grace began to feel stilly for threatening an empty closet.

Then—a muffled voice from inside: "I ain't armed."

"Well, I am," Grace said. "Step out."

The closet door opened slowly.

A man in uniform came out of its shadow. He wore one of the yard's gray-and-red Confederate uniforms. He stood with one shoulder turned toward her as though to catch the bullet, and his eyes were insidious as a cornered cat's.

He would have been a nice enough looking fellow, except for the underlying veins of suspicion and doubt racing beneath the ruddy skin of his face, making thick red whiskers flicker in the lamplight. He twitched constantly around the mouth and nose the way a squirrel does, and his hair was so flaming red it made Grace's russet mane look the color of plums. Two horseshoes of red whiskers went down the sides of his face in the old seafaring style, the kind that keeps ocean winds from razing a sailor's jawline. His eyes were big and round and light-colored, but ringed with nearly invisible blond lashes that gave him a patently British anemia. Grace recognized it from the withered leftovers of youth in the Scotswoman who had raised her.

"I've seen you around," she said. "You're a powderman. What are you doing in my husband's office? What are you in here stealing?"

He hunched his shoulders and stammered, "The foreman sent me in for . . ."

"For what!"

"A work order."

"Halfway into the night?" She pressed nearer until the pistol nearly touched his nose. "You're stealing from my husband! Nobody steals from *my* husband but me!"

He was sizing her up; she could see that and sense it even in the near dimness. He crossed his eyes to look down the bore of the pistol. His hands clenched, and a piece of paper crackled.

A piece of paper?

He had it in his hand!

"Give that here!" she growled. She grabbed the paper.

Ordnance Requisition by Quartermaster Sergeant, authorization Colonel Nathan Bedford Forrest . . . I've heard of that one. . . . *refined black powder for U.S. M1835 flintlocks . . . infantry . . . double-barreled shotguns . . . cavalry . . .*

"I've been looking for this! What are you doing with it? What's your business with my husband's requisitions? You're in here looking for numbers to send outside! You're a spy!" She cocked the pistol. *Crack.* "Last chance."

The barrel of the pistol never wavered. She would shoot him. A slumbering old bear could have smelled her determination through a dream about fish.

"Some man in town give me money to come in here," the powderman admitted.

The powderman contemplated a half-dozen answers, but Grace knew he could see that she certainly would shoot him and that he better come up with an answer she liked, or at least believed.

"The man in town—"

"Gave you money?" she demanded.

"For any piece of information, ten dollars."

"Ten dollars?" Grace huffed. "And a coward enough to tell me about it just because I waved a gun in your face? What kind of simpering excuse for underground activity are you? You've got friends in this mill, and you'd betray them for money?"

So angry she was trembling, Grace lashed out with the pistol and smacked the man in the front of the face. He staggered against the edge of the closet door, bounced off, and hit a wall, holding his face with both hands. Enraged, she watched him and squeezed the pistol tighter and tighter in her hand, until the trigger actually shifted. She was a woman of decision, and she had decided to take revenge, but she had also decided to marry Wyatt Craig and had promised to honor and defend. Now her two decisions were in a clash. All thoughts of protecting herself went up the fireplace, replaced by fury of violation—the idea that someone would be in her husband's private office! Private!

Sounds of shock and pain choked from the burglar, and he spat blood on the floor. He stared down at it.

There was a tooth in the spittle.

"My 'ooth!" he managed. "You 'ocked out my 'ooth—"

"I ought to knock out more than that! I ought to slay you here and now! There's not a soul in the city or a law on the books that'd convict me for it! Coming in my husband's private office when he's not here!"

He bristled, holding his jaw. "What do you care?" he asked. "Word around the mill is you married the major for money—"

The pistol pressed into his nose. Grace grew abruptly calm, like the eye of a hurricane.

"You calling me a whore?" she snarled. He backed off and didn't offer any further comment. She was going to kill him. People like him had no purpose in the world as Grace saw the world, and she was about to pull the trigger. "You pitiful puppet of a man, I ought to shoot you in the leg so you can be nursed back to health and put in front of a firing squad!"

Even as she saw in her mind's eye the guns going off and slaughtering this man, an unlikely alternative, an opportunity, took form. A possibility to get her purpose off the shelf and moving. If Pinkerton could hire this man . . .

She demanded. "Who are you?"

"I work here," he said.

"What's your name?"

"Clyman."

"Clyman what?"

His mouth puckered as he bit at the torn inside of his lip. Finally he said, "Clyde Clyman."

Grace paused and snickered. "Your mother have a headache the day you were hatched?"

The man stiffened. He tilted his head downward until the whites showed at the bottoms of his eyes. His voice turned gravelly. "Don't fun with my name. I don't cotton to it."

"Oh!" Grace responded, not giving in to the attempt to threaten her with that glare. "You cotton to prison? Or worse?" She sidled to a window and with her free hand opened it. "What happens if I call to those men over there beside the loading dock? You're a man in uniform, and that makes you a traitor. I caught you red-handed, spying for the Union in our powder yard. They'll put you up against a wall and blow you open with your own powder. Or if you're lucky, they'll only hang you."

Her point was driven home by the shuffling and muffled conversation of men down the hill near the big loading gates.

All Clyman knew was that for some reason she wasn't

turning him in. He pulled out a dirty handkerchief and dabbed at the empty place in his lower row of teeth.

With more intuitiveness than his face belied, he asked, "What do you want out of me?"

"It's Pinkerton you're working for, isn't it?"

Clyman shrugged the one shoulder. "His name come up, but they didn't make no promises. They just said they'd pay me."

"When did 'they' approach you?"

"Been a couple months now."

"That boil on a pig's butt," Grace spat. "He didn't trust me! And all he does with my information is send it to that slug McClellan, who sits on it and frets like my great-aunt's dying dog. Of all the damn stupid waste—"

She drew a breath through her nostrils, scowled at the requisition, then at Clyman.

"Well, seems your fate's in my hands, Clyde," she said. "This is the new story. You're not working for Pinkerton anymore. You're working for me."

His eyes narrowed. "For you? What're you talking about?"

"You're a man, more or less," she said. "You can get information from the yard that I can't get. The other workers will talk to you."

"You mean . . . you—?"

"Yes. And keep your mouth shut about all this, or I'll hunt you down and shut it the hard way."

Keeping one eye and the gun on him and one eye on the floor, she stooped over and picked up the bloody tooth. With the hem of her skirt she rubbed out the bit of blood on the floor. Then she held the tooth up and showed it to him.

"Now I've got proof that this happened. You're missing a tooth and I've got it. You have to do what I say."

To illustrate the point, she put the tooth into the bodice of her dress, inside the collar and a little deeper.

Clyman digested the odd new information and licked his lips several times, thinking it all through.

Grace let him go ahead and think as long as he wanted to. She meant for him to soak it all in and distill it. No second thoughts later.

After a long pause, he narrowed his eyes at her suspiciously. "You gonna pay me? Bid higher than that other man?"

This time Grace hesitated.

Hiring a mercenary could be a costly and draining advantage to maintain. She also knew that she had no choice. He had seen her now, as much as she had seen him. Her fate to some extent was in his hands too. If she kept him a little afraid of her, he might not notice.

Besides, she was the major's wife. Who were people going to believe?

"You'll get paid," she said finally. "And you'll get something extra too."

Clyman's tongue moved inside his bruised cheek while he contemplated what she was saying—if she meant what he thought she meant.

Her expression said she did. Said she had that extra something that Pinkerton could not offer and was willing to give it to him. A little light came on in Clyman's pale eyes.

"Is it a deal?" Grace persisted.

He chewed his lip, then said, "Yeah. Yeah, deal."

Stepping away from the open window, Grace wagged the pistol toward it.

"Get out this window. I'll contact you tomorrow about what we're going to do and how we're going to do it."

Clyman moved carefully past her, still not ready to trust that gun in her fist, and lowered himself out the window.

Grace leaned out after him, grabbed his collar before he could step away from the sill, and reminded him what the gun looked like. "And don't come back in my husband's office unless I tell you to. He might be a son of a bitch," she added, "but he's *my* son of a bitch."

Grace pulled herself back into the room, shut the window, and flipped the latch to lock it.

"Too close," she sighed, shuddering, carefully replacing the gun in the drawer.

She raised the requisition and skimmed it. Farther down the scribbled page were amounts and how the powder and cartridges should be divided up and delivered. That, with careful analysis, could tell Pinkerton how many men were in that brigade, and whether that number had gone up or down from the last time somebody looked. *If* Pinkerton had people on his staff bright enough to add, subtract, and multiply and figure out at twenty cartridges per man . . .

"Grace?"

She flinched at the sound of her name. She swung around—

Wyatt stood in the doorway. His uniform frock coat was unbuttoned, his boots muddy and coated with flecks of black powder from the mill floors. He pulled off his broad-brimmed hat.

"Evening," he said in a strange tone. "What are you doing here so late? I thought you'd gone back to town."

Grace didn't move. The requisition was still in her hand. She could still hear Clyman's footsteps crunching even through the closed window.

She cleared her throat and covered the noise by asking, "Don't you have a system of order for these papers?"

Wyatt came toward her. "Beg pardon?"

"These papers," she repeated. She put down the requisition and picked up two of something else. "There's no sense here. How do you keep track of what you've done and what you've yet to do?"

Gazing now at the piles of papers, Wyatt looked a little guilty. "Well . . . those over there are mostly the requisitions from military companies . . . at least I think they are. . . . This is for a mining company to blast out a tunnel . . . and over here are the orders for blasting powder for the Army Corps of Engineers. . . . Oh, no, that's a railroad order—"

"Crackers," Grace huffed. She waved a hand over the pile. "It's a wonder you don't send duck-shooting powder to the Northern Navy, the way you've got this done. It needs fixing as much as anything I've ever seen. I'll set all this into order for you this week. And I'll make a system and label some files. I'll use that cabinet over there."

Wyatt stopped looking at the papers and now was only looking at her. At his wife.

It was almost as if she were still just working for him, for the mill. She had simply moved from the schoolroom to the bedroom. She even still kept up her little cabin on the grounds, and they used it for a house when they didn't want to go all the way back to Richmond. Sometimes she would go back to

Richmond, and Wyatt would stay the night in the mill yard. Sometimes she would go back to her little cabin, and Wyatt would go back to Richmond alone. He tried to be a good husband, but he could never quite make it past politeness with her. There was never any relaxed honesty between them as he always imagined there should be between a husband and wife.

Maybe he was wrong to hope for it. Maybe his parents' tense, distant marriage was the way marriages were, and his fantasy about affection in marriage only a fairy tale. Perhaps there was function and propriety and little else. Wyatt knew he was no expert, and now realized that he couldn't forge a marriage the way he forged a business. Not with a frontier woman who didn't really need him.

That was it. She didn't *need* him. She didn't care one way or the other if she lived in the Governor Street mansion or slept in his bed or on a cot somewhere. She hadn't even moved her things over there, and she was still teaching because they hadn't been able to find an unmarried woman in the midst of a war, so she didn't need his money. If business wasn't finished at the mill, she was just as likely to stay at her cabin there as to come back into Richmond to the big house. She didn't say much, so she didn't need his company, and she could even chop her own wood and mend her own door hinges.

"I'm sorry I've been gone so much the past few weeks," he began. "All these military deliveries . . . I know it's difficult for you."

"Not at all," she said. "It's fine. I'm used to doing for myself. Been doing it a long time."

Her tone was completely indifferent.

With his hat still literally in his hands, Wyatt hesitated, realizing that he didn't even know where his wife had been born or raised, nor had she ever asked where he had been born. They hadn't even shared that much. She didn't care if they were together or not. If they were married or not.

Why did she sit and eat a meal with him? Why did she listen to his babbling about the mill and even ask questions to keep him talking? Why did she come to his bed? Was it all just her perception of wifely duty?

Wyatt sighed briefly and tried to find the cores of those dark green eyes of hers.

"I worry about you sometimes," he said.

She went on tidying the desktop. "About me? Why ever do that?"

"I worry if I did the right thing, marrying you and all—I mean, if it was right for *you*. I thought it was, back then, but sometimes I just worry."

"'Bout what, exactly?"

"If you're . . . happy."

"Oh, I'm happy enough," she said. "Certainly had harder times in my life. You had to marry me, and I had to marry you back. That was our circumstance. What if there'd been a baby? I'd have to leave, and I'm not ready to leave. Some folks draw a certain lot, and I drew mine like everybody else. I could have it worse, you know. Could've married a man without that nice big house and without a dime to his name and without a nice head of hair."

Wyatt puzzled. Did she mean all that as a joke? He tried to smile a little, just in case she did.

"I guess, when you put it that way . . ."

"What's your point?"

"I kinda feel bad when you take care of me the way you do," he said, "knowing you got pretty much railroaded into all this."

"Why should you feel bad?" she asked. "I take care of all my men. Always have."

He hesitated, cut down a slice. She was lumping him in with all the other men she'd cared for in her pioneer life. He knew that every time he thought she might be warming up to him, she was just tending him in a fashion she thought dutiful.

So he grabbed for the only light in their odd little tunnel and stepped toward her.

"Am I . . . your man?"

He thought the question was profound, but soon found out otherwise.

Without so much as a pause for effect or even looking up, Grace lopped off her answer.

"Married you, didn't I?" she said, bending deeply into the fireplace. "Promised to honor and cherish and tend all your worldly needs, didn't I? The words came out of my mouth, didn't they? Vow's a vow. Can't break a vow without good reason. If I did that, broke my word without seeing it through, well, there'd be retribution from the forces of the world. I'm bound to you for now, and that's enough for me. Don't fret, though. You're not much bother, and I'm just naturally custodial."

As though to illustrate her point, she grabbed a hearth broom and began sweeping ashes into a pile on the brick skirt of the fireplace.

Clumsily Wyatt followed her halfway across the office, which seemed very small today, then ended up standing in the middle of the rug while she swept up ashes. Suddenly he felt like an ash himself.

"Is everything all right with you?" he asked. "Anything you need?"

Grace straightened, shifted, and looked at him. She couldn't figure him out. She had known a traveling doctor once who treated folks for almost nothing and seemed the kindest man that side of the Northwest Passage, but turned out to be stealing from the folks' houses, and sometimes even from the covered wagons.

Wyatt Craig must be something like that. Her brother had thought he was Wyatt's friend, but when Patrick went over to the other side, Wyatt had killed him flat out. Shot him through the heart.

Probably easy, because Patrick's heart had been such a big, innocent, tender target.

Grace could go to any man's bed, love or hate. And she had done that, plenty of times, to survive or see her own ends through. She didn't care who slept beside her, and there was no privacy left in her life. What disturbed her, though, was this *attitude* of Wyatt's, this damnable civility he kept on top, when she damned well knew he was hiding a ruthlessness to match her own.

She'd *seen* him do it! *Seen* it herself.

He worried about her. What a joke. He was concerned that she was unhappy.

Well, there was nothing she could do to assuage his worry that the front of marriage wasn't being kept up well enough. She couldn't be around him more than she was already. The distance had to be maintained. She wasn't repulsed by him, and that in itself was dangerous. She had learned to avoid him because he was the kind of man she could warm up to.

Dangerous warmth.

She had to stay cold. Cold and ready.

She knew that if he found out what she was really doing in his office, Wyatt Craig would put a pistol to her breast and kill her too. She had *seen* it.

Stepping back away from him, she said, "No, thank you. I don't need a thing."

She walked out of the bricked entranceway of her husband's handsome office building. She'd left him a little confused, and that was good. Just as prey should be.

The smell of refined sulfur and saltpeter from the press house and rolling mills and the charcoaly scent of powder from the graining mills pressed around her instantly as the sunlight hit her, creating an illusion that the sun stank. Then it continued on the light breeze, heading for the company town.

How about that? A mercenary of her very own. If she had to buy off the whole powder yard, she'd get Pinkerton's respect and spur some action out of that bump McClellan.

At the small white picket fence that circled Wyatt's office building, she was met by one of the errand boys, a rangy little immigrant with a cleft chin and nervous habits. One of her best sixth-graders. Would be an apprentice in the pack house by Christmas.

"Miss HacHutcheon? I mean, Mrs. Craig?"

"Cormac?"

"Message for you, delivered to the yard gate. I brung it down."

"Brought it, Cormac."

"Yes'm." He dug in his torn pocket, tearing it even more, and pulled out a travel-worn envelope.

"Thank you. Wait just a moment." She started to open the envelope, then said, "Oh, Cormac, would you be kind enough to step into the major's office and ask him for a cigar to bring out here?"

"You . . . want a cigar, ma'am?"

"Tell him it's for your father."

The boy shrugged and slouched his way past her.

Grace waited until he was inside and the clatter of his clogs faded, then glanced around to make sure she was completely alone. She pulled out the note. For want of a code, it was written in German. That Pinkerton. Always thinking.

Mrs. C. Plan to attend Yuletide
soiree, 20 Dec in W. D. C. at
residence Mr. and Mrs. A. L.
Await reply.

The note was unsigned. And now Cormac was returning with the cigar.

"Thank you," Grace said. She took the cigar from him, wrapped it securely over and over in the note, and stuffed both back into the envelope. "Take this and leave it on the fence post at the edge of the powdertown. Can I trust you to do that?"

"Oh, yes'm," the boy said, and she could tell by his face that he took her trust seriously. He looked at her with a funny curiosity.

She contemplated telling him to be silent, but that would arouse even more curiosity, of a more dangerous brand. Making a bet with herself that a boy his age would forget this if she didn't give him reason not to.

"It's a present for a friend," she said. "Just a joke."

"Oh," he said, grinning. "I get it."

"Move along, Cormac. Then get home and do that arithmetic I assigned you, hear?"

"Yes'm, I hear. Evening, ma'am!"

★

CHAPTER TWENTY-TWO

———— ★ ————

"Now, pay attention," Allan Pinkerton whispered, leaning to the woman at his elbow.

Pushing aside one of the annoying ringlets that kept falling forward onto her left cheekbone, Grace MacHutcheon Craig leaned toward President Lincoln's favorite detective, chewed and swallowed most of the spinach-cheese tart in her mouth, and garbled out, "What am I paying attention to? A puffy soiree of off-shoulder ladies mewling over Mrs. Lincoln's new French porcelain. So what? They're all dead in the head."

She held up her empty confection plate and wiggled it. The white plate, its wide burgundy band, and the gold fluted edge caught the candlelight. So did the wings of the fanned American bald eagle in the center.

She craned briefly to see what was going on in the northeast corner. A flock of women were pressing their skirts to crowd around a long table piled with what appeared to be lengths of ribbon, sewing boxes, silk tassels, and small squares of every kind of fabric from velvet to moiré.

"What's happening there?" Grace asked.

"Funding the war effort," Pinkerton responded.

"With ribbons?"

"Yes." His beard bobbed when he talked. "The women are paying for the privilege of making a Christmas ornament to take home from this soiree. Or they may simply purchase one that another women makes. Look around, Mrs. Craig. Be observant for details. If you pay attention, you'll notice many women at this party already wearing finished Christmas ornaments pinned to their bodices."

Grace scanned the crowd, and sure enough dozens of women's dress fronts, including Mrs. Lincoln's, rolled with velvet, satin, or moiré ornaments decorated with brocade or velvet ribbons, dried flowers, tiny strings of pearls or gold beads or silk braided trim, and each was wagging a long silk tassel.

"Well, I'll be crammed," she muttered. "Funding the war effort. Next year they'll likely be braiding the hair of dead Confederates, wrapping it around their ornaments and selling those too. What the hell . . . *I* would. I can think of one or two men whose hair I'd pin on my bodice."

"Speaking of men, how did you explain your absence to your husband?"

"I never explain," she said. "I keep a distance between us, so he never asks. It comes in mighty handy to have a man on your hook and never quite reel him in. I'm married, not welded."

Pinkerton glowered with annoyance at his newest spy. She hadn't the looks of a spy, but she had the manner of one. Under the blood-russet ringlets gathered to one side was a quick mind, afraid of almost nothing. Under the pretty pale-green flounce and blue sashes and ribbons was a frontier woman's body, tall, fit, filled out, willing to work, willing to get dirty. Her wide mouth and square cheekbones spoke of her German stock, the immigrant white-trash parents she had told him about, and the strength of a tough, bitter upbringing in the Kansas wilderness.

That was why she looked at these society women as she did. Intolerantly.

"Not the women," Pinkerton said. "The *men*. Watch the men's faces. Look how they communicate without speaking." The wiry detective screwed up his rosy Scottish face and quietly added, "Look over there, near the juniper garland. It's the English ambassador. His name is Lord Lyons."

"So?" Grace repeated, and bothered to brush pastry crumbs from the front of her mint-green gown. Some went down the low front into her cleavage, but she stopped herself before going digging in there. She wanted to keep the gown clean—after all, she had borrowed it from Evee Mapes. It had a bit of the trashy about it, but Grace knew perfectly well that she did too.

"He's pretending not to listen to the secretary of state," Pinkerton was saying to her. "There he is. William Seward."

She looked up. "The who? Where?"

"Over there. I told you about him. Right *there*. Mrs. Craig, can't you be more observant? He's the loudest man in the room. He's talking about Great Britain."

"Oh," she muttered. "That one."

She went back to brushing her gown.

"Yes," Pinkerton said. "William Seward. See the fire in his eyes? He's got his hackles all up tonight, but there's purpose in his face. Pay attention. I want you to know what's happening in the world. Why things happen. Who makes them happen."

"What do I care about Britain? For that matter, what do *you* care? You left Scotland to come and live here, didn't you?"

"Your government," he said, "or both of them, I should say, will care a great deal about Britain, and about France too, come the next year or so. And so you should. Being an undercover agent, you'll need to learn which information is current, and which is important. Which conversations to pay attention to. How to read the newspapers." Pinkerton raised one of his straight eyebrows and added, "You say England and France don't matter—do you know that your own name has already reached the court of France?"

Grace snapped him a round-eyed look of disbelief.

Pinkerton nodded. "You remember Captain Parry? The young officer you met in my tent at the training camp?"

"Of course. What about him?"

"His real title is Le Compte de Paris. He and the Duc de Chartres are in my camp with their uncle, Admiral Prince de Joinville, third son of King Louis Philippe of France."

Grace stared at him. Seconds ticked by, filled only by the rustle of crinoline and the buzz of conversation and the secretary of state's trumpeting.

After a second Grace swatted Pinkerton's arm, almost upturning the teacup in his hand. "Oh, you're shucking nuts."

His small alert eyes never wavered. He paced out the moments, not blinking, gazing at her in such a way that even Grace MacHutcheon Craig couldn't break away.

"You're shucking," she said again, "aren't you?"

"They are Parisian royalty," he said, "and you hadn't the experience to notice that you were being lied to, even though he obviously had a French accent. You never asked what interest a Frenchman has in wearing a Union Army uniform. Things like this should ring bells in your head. You must be on your guard for all things European these days, Mrs. Craig."

Annoyed at having been so easily caught, Grace argued, "I still don't know why England or France should care what goes on here."

"You'll find out by listening."

"To you?"

He took her elbow and moved her a few steps deeper into the reception area. "To the Secretary of State. Watch him . . . and listen."

They fell silent and stood together, pricking their ears over the constant buzz of conversation in the big room. Sure enough, the voice of the hawk-nosed man at the far end of the main buffet table was the loudest of all.

"The Union is fighting for the existence and integrity of all of America," he said to a crowd of White House guests. "Europe is salivating at the chance to surge back in and establish dynasties all over the continent. I'll be crucified if I let those packs of puss come back over here with their monarchies. This is a war for the entire hemisphere!"

Blinking, Grace shook her head. She leaned to Pinkerton and said, "He's going to make the eagle on Mrs. Lincoln's dishes pee all over the purple edge."

"But look at the apprehension on Lord Lyons's face," Pinkerton said. Then he pinched her wrist and made her look in another direction. "Ah—speaking of French porcelain . . . in that corner on the other side of the room is Mercier, the French ambassador. He's hiding from Seward. You can tell it in his posture."

Grace followed the little flicks of Pinkerton's thumb as he pointed without really pointing. Bewhiskered men in fancy suits maneuvered this way and that with bell-gowned women on their arms, mingling with their peers, and some their superiors. The French minister and other foreign dignitaries wore ambassadorial sashes over their severe black suits. Black suits stood out tonight, because so many gentlemen at Mrs.

Lincoln's yuletide reception were now wearing the blue-and-brass tunic, breeches, and sabers of the Union Army.

Some women were wearing black, their gowns like great buoys on a forgetful sea. Some were in half-black—only a black silk shawl or a black apron and bustle over bright pastels. Very few wore only little black ribbons, the last vestiges of a year of mourning. But there were far more women in full black.

Not many women had yet seen a full year of mourning. This year there had been too many fresh losses. Usually so much funereal black garb was rarely seen at a social event, but skirmishes had claimed the lives of sons, brothers, husbands, and there had been Bull Run and Ball's Bluff, and finally the realization that this was going to be a true war, and not merely a test of wills. Rather than avoiding social events, women in mourning were being encouraged to let themselves be seen, to keep the human heart in this war of high talk and long threats.

All that seemed lost on the dominant Mr. Seward tonight, though.

Guests mingled and paused around a lengthy holiday table crisscrossed by a great X of firethorn, decorated with prickly pears, nuts, berries, apples, and cherries. Aroma of sweetmeats, roast turkey, savory ham, rum eggnog, and a white wine, milk, sugar, and ginger concoction called posset made the air heady. Waiters in white tunics with gold tassels circulated with trays and carafes. On opposite ends of the room were two tall skinny Yule trees, draped with garlands of gold braid and studded with white lace ornaments and small United States flags.

The room was lit not by lamps or even the enormous chandelier, but only by forests of foot-long red or white tapers clustered on tables, set in silver Georgian candlesticks that resembled the White House mansion pillars. In the center of the room, on a small raised stage, a string quartet played continuous Christmas music and soft versions of Union patriotic songs.

A black waiter smiled at her, met her eyes more boldly than any Southern black man would, and offered, "Meats and cheeses, miss?"

"Mmm—yes!" Grace gasped, making a dive for the tray. "I don't even remember how folks live on such little bits of food at a time. When I was back in Kansas, my ma and pa and my brother would have to split a squirrel for our supper when my brother barked one off a tree . . . you know, these are better, though—"

"Look—look at Lord Lyons," Pinkerton interrupted, suddenly excited.

The colored waiter stepped past them, and Grace maneuvered to see where Pinkerton was pointing.

"He's walking across the room toward the coffee table," Pinkerton said, "but he's deliberately avoiding Mercier. There! See that glance? They don't want to be seen conversing with each other, else Secretary Seward might construe it as a hint of cooperation between England and France against the United States."

"I've caught them casting looks at each other," Grace commented.

"That's fearful caution," Pinkerton quipped. A grin of approval for Seward touched his expression in a way he knew was naughty.

They watched as Lord Lyons and his lady strode right past Mercier. Mercier suddenly became very interested in puff pastries and epergnes on a nearby serving table.

A moment later Lord Lyons was rescued by the President's wife, who floated to him and hooked his elbow. A stout, severe woman whose shoulders were round as snowballs over the drop-sleeved bodice of her gown, Mrs. Lincoln exuded a constant air of social pretense without the weight of sincerity, and she seemed to do that on purpose. Every gesture was right on top, every smile paper thin, and she looked at other women with a jealous tightening of her expression.

Grace wrinkled her nose. "I don't like her."

"No one likes her," Pinkerton said.

"Why do they come to her parties, then?"

"Power," he said. "And . . . they all like the President. He makes up for his wife." Pinkerton sipped at his tea, now cool. "They say she's why he's so thin."

"Oh, that's just a joke," Grace said.

"You haven't met her."

The waiter reappeared like a ghost beside them, with a pot of hot tea. "Warm that up for you, sir?"

"Oh—excellent sense of timing," Pinkerton complimented, and extended his teacup.

The waiter poured, nodded, and disappeared again.

Glancing around for the pillar-thin figure of Abraham Lincoln, Grace asked, "Where is he?"

"Who?"

"The President."

"He must be occupied in another room in the White House," Pinkerton said, "else Seward wouldn't be promulgating so."

"Hm," Grace huffed. "So he keeps quiet when the President's around?"

"In this issue."

Grace eyed the door as though hoping Lincoln would walk in. She wanted to see for herself what a man like Seward would do. Choke? Keep talking? Stumble? Shout? Confront?

"Hmm," she uttered again. "Wonder if he keeps quiet because Lincoln disagrees with him, or to keep European diplomats nervous about the disagreement?"

Pinkerton turned, gawking at her sudden grasp of issues. Or was it really so sudden . . . ?

The waiter returned with an oblong fish platter. "Salmon rosettes, miss? Sir?"

Pinkerton blinked and came out of his trance. "No," he said. "Fish disagrees with me."

But Grace plucked a salmon rosette off the platter. The waiter nodded and drifted into the crowd. Grace surveyed the rosette briefly, tasted it, then looked around for somewhere to throw it away.

Secretary of State Seward's voice suddenly turned loud and caught her attention.

"They haven't forgotten the War of 1812," Seward ranted. And Pinkerton was right . . . there was a chilling steadiness under that tone. "Yankee privateers nearly destroyed the British merchant fleet then, and we'll do it again if they force us to. They can blockade our ports, but who cares? The United States depends on Europe for absolutely nothing! Let England covet Southern cotton! Let Emperor Napoleon's wife covet Mexico! We are unbeatable on our own continent, gentlemen! On ten fronts if necessary, I will wrap the world in fire to preserve the Union!"

Grace watched a collective shiver go through the reception hall. Even people engaged in other conversation turned to look at Seward, but no one wanted to challenge him. She glanced at the doorway again, hoping the President would walk in. If only he would.

Seward's loud voice rang through the hall, picking the terrible wound of tension over the United States and Europe. In separate corners of the reception hall, Lord Lyons and Ambassador Mercier were, for all practical purposes, cowering. Lord Lyons was actually *trying* to keep a conversation going with the President's wife—which not many people cared to do for very long—just to give him an excuse to pretend not to be hearing Seward.

"If Lord Russell so much as wipes his nose with a handkerchief made out of Southern cotton," Seward proclaimed, "we shall consider it an act of war."

Then he laughed spontaneously—but he wasn't being funny.

"By God, I'll annex Canada! Let the British bear the expense of trying to defend it from way other there!"

If he'd had a saber, he would have rattled it.

"He's out of his head," Grace grumbled. She lowered her voice even more. "He's crazy!"

"Crazy like a fox," Pinkerton said, keeping his own voice down. "He thinks our divided nation will reunite against a common enemy before we'll let France and Britain get a hold on our continent again. At least he intends to convince the British that Americans think that way."

"He won't actually go to war—"

"Oh, yes he would," Pinkerton said. "And the Europeans know it. Remember, Mrs. Craig, *I'm* British. I know how the British think about you Americans. Why would Great Britain, the most powerful naval force in the world, fear the little United States? The image of the wild Americans, unpredictable, uncontrollable, quick . . . let's face it," he said with a flicker, "we think you're buggy."

She skewered him with a look. "And, of course, you Scots are the sanest monkeys in the cage."

He frowned, but after a moment he chuckled.

"On that note," he said, "speaking of buggy, I should introduce you to your contact."

Grace looked at him sidelong, wondering how much he would tell her—if Clyde Clyman's name would come up.

"I thought *you* were my contact," she said.

"I am in charge of the Secret Service. Besides, can you be dashing yon and back from Richmond to Washington without arousing a glance? Nor can I abandon General McClellan's intelligence network. Southern spies are getting better than I like at interception and decoding. Messages to and from our informants in the South must be more covert from now on. First I'll introduce you to one of my finest undercover men. John Scobell."

He stopped walking. They were standing in front of a truffle table.

Just the two of them.

Grace looked around.

"So," she began, "where is he?"

"Another salmon rosette?" a voice asked from behind.

She spun around.

The black waiter was standing right beside her, holding the plate of smelly rosettes. Suddenly a broad white smile broke out over his chocolate features—a teasing, impetuous smile, over eyes that were lighter brown than his skin.

"Christ and curst!" Grace bellowed. "You?"

Half of the reception room dropped to silence. The Secretary of State and his substantial audience turned to look.

Grace clamped her lips shut. She stared back at them.

Beside her Pinkerton nodded uncomfortably at the gaggle of eyes, took Grace's elbow, and maneuvered her behind one of the two Christmas trees that decorated the room.

It took a few seconds for things to return to normal and Seward's voice to take over attention again, as it had for the past hour.

Grace twisted around in Pinkerton's grip and said, "You—"

But the waiter hadn't come with them to this side of the tree.

"Where is he?" she demanded.

"He'll be here in a moment," Pinkerton told her. "He couldn't follow us. . . . How would that look?"

"What'd you say his name was?"

A brown hand poked out at her from the tree, right through the evergreen boughs.

"John Scobell, at your service, ma'am." Then Scobell saun- tered around the tree, grinning like a mischievous elf.

Pinkerton turned to Grace. "John is one of the cleverest agents in my Secret Service."

"Are you a freed man or an escaped slave?" Grace asked. "Or were you born in the North, or what are you?"

Scobell and Pinkerton exchanged a look, as though they'd known they should expect a strong reaction from her, but didn't know what that reaction would be. Scobell's bright, tricky eyes caught Grace again, and he spoke with an amused grin.

"I was a slave," Scobell said, "and now I am not. Anything else you'd like to know, ma'am?"

Not one to take a reprimand smoothly, Grace lifted one rus- set eyebrow and said, "Reckon that'll do for now."

Pinkerton watched them with the satisfaction of a proud stablemaster. "He's a former slave and can put on negro man- ner of speech at will, which makes him of great value on un- dercover missions in the South. But he can also read and write good English." The Scot turned to Scobell and said, "Thank you, John. We'll be in contact. Better slip back in."

Without another sound Scobell dipped his dark head, dropped any expression save that of a perfect butler, and flowed away into the crowd, pausing to serve salmon rosettes.

Watching the black spy at his art, Grace mumbled, "Mud puppy on the riverbank . . ."

"Pardon?"

"He slips in pretty good."

"He does, yes. Now there's one thing more. I brought you here tonight to let you see what the South is up against." He nodded toward the volatile Secretary of State. "But also to offer you an out."

"An out? Why would I want an out?"

He gazed at her so cannily that Grace was inclined to move back a step. His gift of insight showed keenly on his face.

"I sense," he said, "your heart is not completely in this."

There was nothing flippant or casual about what he said or the tone he used. He had studied her and come to a conclusion based on facts and tempered with skilled intuition.

Suddenly horn-mad, Grace growled out her response.

"Never you mind my heart. I'm in this."

Pinkerton paused. He wouldn't back down. He was indeed giving her a chance to back out of her involvement, and he was making certain the chance was long and opportune, so she could never say he hadn't offered. No matter what happened to her, from this moment onward he was cleared of responsibility for what happened to her or because of her.

Very well. That's how it would be.

"I'm offering you a chance to get out," Pinkerton said, "because I already have an informant at the mill."

Simmering, Grace controlled her tone, but not the counterblow in her eyes. "You're talking about that idiot Clyman."

Pinkerton's eyes widened in surprise.

"I know all about him," Grace said. "Found him hiding in a closet. He let himself get caught. Good thing it was me that did the catching. That's how good your alternative is at the Craig Powderworks. You've got a brass ball up your behind if you think you can get the better of me on my own grounds. Things are going to start changing. Your mud puppy over there is your operative, and Clyman's going to be mine. They're going to do the running between here and Richmond. From now on I don't work for you anymore. I've got my own operation. Take it or leave it."

His stubby brows popped up. "What if I leave it?"

"I'll kill Clyman," she said bluntly. "Then you'll have nobody at the mill."

The shock took a few seconds to wear off, but when it did, he was glinting at her with those quick little eyes and nodded in appreciation. After a moment he chuckled. "You're a very interesting woman, Mrs. Craig."

"Got that right."

She was about to say more when a voice cut through the entire hall and made several ladies gasp.

"I'll be damned to hell!"

All three turned, and so did everyone else in the ballroom. It was Secretary of State Seward again.

"They can call us Yankees," the center of attention was booming, "they can call us impetuous, they can call us insignificant in the scheme of world affairs . . . but I'll be damned if we shall be called cowards, ladies and gentlemen!"

Women gasped again at the vulgarity, but Seward was

doing that on purpose. Men cleared their throats, self-conscious. No one dared to argue, or to encourage.

Seward paused and waited until he thought everyone was sweating just a little under their fancy clothes. Then his voice lowered, just enough to give a blade of threat to his tone.

"If Britain officially recognizes the Confederacy, we from that hour shall cease to be friends and become once more, as we have twice before been, enemies of Great Britain. Domestic convulsions will pale, and North and South alike will rally under a common flag! That flag!"

He pointed grandly at the giant Old Glory draped across an entire wall behind the holiday table.

"We may not win," Seward said, "but the world will know there has been a war!"

★

———— ★ ————

PART FIVE

THE BONFIRE OF
WHITE GOLD

CHAPTER TWENTY-THREE

——————— ★ ———————

A sixty-some-year-old man with white hair and a build like a locomotive came lumbering across the grounds between the composition house and the roll mills. His rubber soles left packed tracks in a quarter-inch coat of snow that had fallen in the night. The boss was waiting for him, and Henry Brecker didn't like to keep folks waiting.

There, standing between two of the ten roll-mill blockhouses, was Wyatt Craig. Henry stopped walking when he saw the boss and paused just to watch.

Wyatt was facing the river, basking in the shimmering morning light reflecting off the water onto his sawdust-colored hair, which was being brushed by a motherly winter breeze between the two roll-mill blockhouses. The rock wall of one blockhouse caught the morning slant of sunlight, while the next blockhouse put a sharp wedged shadow down across the ground and the bottom of Wyatt's legs. The young man wore no uniform today, as usual at the mill. He didn't care for that uniform, Henry knew, and neither did most of the workers, though many had come to enjoy wearing their butternut Confederate Artillery jackets with the new red cuffs and collars. In such duds they felt more important than mill workers.

Today, as most, Wyatt looked like any of the millwrights or machinists or powder monkeys. He didn't even have a coat on, despite the chilly December air. He must have dashed out of the office in a hurry this morning. His blue-and-white-checkered cotton shirt was rolled up at the wrists, its pleated back caught by the crisscrossed suspenders in back, and blooming out at the sides from the river breeze that blew through the undone collar. Henry wouldn't have spotted Wyatt for the boss in a crowd of drummer boys, except maybe for his height.

From the road skirting the roll mills, Henry saw the weight of responsibility curving Wyatt's shoulders as though someone had laid it there like a cloak. Those shoulders now raised and lowered beneath the checked cotton as Wyatt inhaled a deep breath of the river air, but not a long second one, because along with the air came the constant aroma of the willow wood burning endlessly and turning into charcoal, and the stink of the pulverized charcoal being incorporated with refined sulfur in those ten brick mills.

Yet there were soothing elements to the mill yard. Henry understood. He took a moment to watch Wyatt standing there in his moment of peace, and to let Wyatt have that moment.

The endless grumble of the roll mills inside the blockhouses, which went on day after day, milling charcoal, flowers of sulfur, and crystals of pure potassium nitrate—Henry always got a picture in his mind of the colors, white niter, yellow sulfur, black charcoal whenever he thought of the big cylindrical mills blending the grains wet for safety's sake. As he paused, he heard what Wyatt heard—the reassuring *kussssh* of the half-dozen waterwheels . . . the river's hum. The rattle of wagons going across the covered bridges, people clacking up and down the boardwalks by the stores, children playing among the houses, the three churches, the clubs, the barns, or the music building where the brass band practiced. . . . The powdermill was its own world, a town community unto itself, really quite separate from the city of Richmond down the river. Maybe that's why the workers liked those uniforms tying them to the outside world with what seemed a noble string.

Henry sighed, shook his head, and started forward, nursing a crick in his lower back. Over the growl of the mills he called, "Morning, son. Ain't you chilly?"

Wyatt noticeably flinched, then turned.

"Henry," he said. "Morning. I'm enjoying the air today. I just came from the furnaces. You wanted to talk to me?"

"Went looking for you in your office, but you wasn't there. How's the wife?"

"Pardon? Oh . . . she's fine, I guess she's fine, Henry."

"Got trouble in the furnaces?"

Wyatt nodded. "Bad duct."

"That's trouble."

"We're losing half the heat before it gets from the furnaces to the drying house. It's getting *very* dangerous over there. I've cleared the area until the ducts are mended. The drying process still makes me nervous. I'm sorry to make you meet me out here, Henry. I was just so darned warm."

"No, son, you're the boss."

"You wanted to talk about something?"

"Well, I hate to hand you another problem, but we got one with the coopers," Henry said. "They're complaining the last order was too big to fill."

"It was a military order, Henry. Regimental quantities. That's why it was so big."

"Right. Trouble is, our keg factory can't make production on them big orders. Can't ship powder if you ain't got enough properly constructed kegs."

"No," Wyatt sighed, "sure can't. Can we order barrels from off sight?"

Henry rubbed a forefinger under his nose and sniffed hard. "Last time we tried that, we got kegs with metal hoops, put together with nails. Them city coopers just don't understand you can't ship any kind of black powder in kegs with hoops and nails. One spark and *kafoooom*. A godrotten mess. Hell, they don't even think about why we wear rubber soles and don't allow—"

"Henry," Wyatt interrupted, drumming his fingers on the old man's shoulder by way of apology, "isn't it funny how a problem can seem like a blessing at the same time?"

"Whatcha mean, son?"

"Here we've got complaints about orders being too big, and before long I'm going to wish I was still hearing it. We're having trouble importing saltpeter. I can barely meet demand now, and it won't hold. The Union's trying to corner the market, and Europe's afraid to send any to the Confederacy because of Union threats. Getting to where my whole day is wrapped up in trying to locate saltpeter sources. If we don't get it from someplace, there's just no war."

"Judas priest," Henry groused.

Even through his preoccupation, Wyatt was flattered that his men were picking up on his expressions. Did they pay that much attention to him?

"Well," Henry went on, "there's a couple of ways to distill the stuff . . . urine, I mean."

Wyatt sighed. "Mighty unpleasant commodity to store, and we're talking about some massive quantities."

"We might have to resort to it."

"Right . . . but where do I go for machine parts that're coming up short? Can't ask the men to pee out cleaning fluids, or machine oil, or mechanical parts I can't get anymore. . . . Half the workers haven't had a new pair of shoes in a year now—"

"And a powder factory can't have yer ordinary hobnails clacking around," Henry finished.

"Nope . . . up till now the government's been wringing funds out of those fancy planters who've been raising regiments and promoting themselves to generalships—"

"And majorships, Major?" Henry screwed his white brows up and snickered.

"Yes," Wyatt laughed. "I'm a good example. Never had a lick of soldiering experience, can't shoot a hole in a bag, carrying a star I don't merit—"

"Now, I didn't mean nothing by that, son."

Wyatt sighed and nodded. "Oh, I know you didn't. It's just that the government can't squeeze saltpeter out of those aristocrats the way it squeezes donations out of them. I can't run a factory this way, and if I can't run this factory, and others can't run theirs, then the South isn't going to get any gunpowder. Without gunpowder there isn't going to be a snowflake's chance in hell of winning this war. Winning . . . we can't even *fight* it. Gonna look mighty silly starting up a war we can't even fight."

"Can say that again," the Kentuckian grumbled. "You know, son, I didn't realize the blockade was causing you so much headache."

"Not just the blockade, Henry," Wyatt said, much more

darkly than was his usual way. "The Confederacy's got bigger problems than the North can cause us all by itself."

Henry helped him mourn for a few moments, then snapped him a salute, though snapping to attention made his paunch stick out and his knees crack. "Permission to go off'n figger out something to do about them kegs, *sir!*"

Returning a miserable excuse for a salute, Wyatt chuckled, "Granted, Sergeant Brecker. Figure away."

Henry turned on a heel and paraded back down the road like a very proud duck.

A shaft of cold wind flew off the river and hit Wyatt in the back—and with it came a voice.

"That has a ring of benevolent despotism about it, Major Craig."

Wyatt spun around—searched for the voice—

—spotted a form sequestered in the shadow of the next blockhouse, between the wall and the river.

An ankle-length Inverness cape, a black silk opera hat, a walking stick poised like a sword, a field of gray and grass with captain's bars on the collar—

"Well, I'll be!" Wyatt exclaimed. "Look what the wind blew in!"

He glanced around to be sure there was no one nearby and hurried along the blockhouse to the solitary figure. The frosty grass crunched beneath his feet.

"Dorian—or whoever you are this week!" He grabbed for Dorian's hand even though it hadn't been offered. "I thought you'd fallen off the continent or something. I was starting to worry again!"

Dorian pulled off his elegant hat. "You know I'm a bit of a derelict."

"Here, back this way."

Wyatt glanced again at the powder yard and ushered Dorian behind the blockhouse, keeping close to the wooden riverside wall. If there was a spark inside this mill, the ensuing explosion would take out the wooden wall, and the three heavy rock walls would funnel the blast over the water—and right on top of the two of them. A nice safe haven, these shadows.

He took Dorian's elbow, pushed him into a band of sunlight, looked squarely at him as though searching for bruises beneath the surface, and dropped to a tone that asked gently for straight answers. "You all right?"

Shadowed and exotic even in daylight, Dorian's black eyes never flinched, but the cocky edge of harshness did leave them. His voice took on a gravelly weight. A mystery narrating itself . . .

"You mean, has the bounty hunter caught up with me and put me through damnation again? No. I've been out in the world buying false trails for that beefhead to follow."

His soft Virginia accent suggested secrets under his words. A touch of candid warmth came into those unimpressable eyes. The sable bat-wing brows lost some of their angle.

"Thank you, Wyatt," he went on. "Something about me makes very few men ask . . . how I am."

Wyatt softened, but the concern didn't leave his face, and he couldn't smile.

"That bastard Quist," Wyatt said, "scares me. He's the only man I've ever seen who wasn't afraid of you."

Dorian laughed. His bright teeth flashed. "*You're* not afraid of me."

"Want a bet?" Wyatt hooked a hand around Dorian's collar, relishing the protection the gray wool cape offered his friend, then tightened the space between them down to nothing as though he could protect him too. "Let's go inside the mill. I don't want you out in the broad daylight."

"Necessity's made a vampire of me. Some would happily see my coffin chained shut."

"Oh, don't talk like that. Come on, here's the door."

"I know where the door is, Wyatt. I commissioned the architect."

"That's right, you did. Watch the frost here . . . don't want you swimming the old James with that heavy cape on. Here we go, inside."

The cool interior air of the blockhouse coiled around them, and so did the noise. There was something animalistic about the breathing, crunching, and hissing of industrial noise. The two enormous iron cylinders, as wide across as Wyatt was tall, slowly turned around a common axle, rolling over the concrete bed on which a ton of charcoal, niter, and sulfur were being milled into gunpowder. The millwrights looked up and squinted against the daylight pouring in the open riverside-access door—nobody ever came in that door—then they nodded when they saw it was the boss and Mr. Trözen.

They stared a few seconds, hadn't seen Mr. Trözen in months, didn't know what was going on any more than bits of gossip around the mill community and a few detached whispers from Richmond that didn't make any sense to anybody who knew the man. Ties evidently hadn't been completely severed between the mysterious administrator and the mill boss. And the man who brought them all out of the hopeless pioneer squalor of Bloody Kansas back to this chance at new life was entitled to his privacy and their discretion.

It was an unspoken code at the mill . . . *take care of our own.* Check all whispers at the gate.

They turned quickly back to their work and gave the two men polite quarter.

Wyatt closed the door and noticed it was warping. He forced it shut. He was comforted by the noise of the mill and the clatter of waterwheels outside, constantly providing power and pouring water onto the dangerous graining process. The sound covered their conversation from the other men.

"Come away from the draft," he invited. But when he caught Dorian's elbow again, the other man pulled back.

"No, my boots have cobbler's nails. I'll move no more than absolutely necessary." And he was holding his silver-footed walking stick tight against his torso, tucking it inside his Inverness cape.

"You know," Wyatt began, "you dropped off the earth after only being back a day. I kept expecting somebody to come back with your corpse in a box—didn't get ten minutes sleep in a week. Couldn't you have left a note?"

"Notes are clues," Dorian said, but Wyatt's paragraph caused him to frown at himself. "I'm sorry for all that. I haven't been accustomed to being searched for by people who mean me well."

"I know, I know. Where are you staying? Not between those warehouses in Shockoe Creek again—"

"No, I never haunt the same hole twice. I've taken a room in Goddin's Tavern. Temporarily, of course."

"Mmm, of course . . . under the name Parthens?"

"Of course," Dorian echoed. A grin tightening his cheeks as he made fun of Wyatt's worry. "The Vice President needs to be able to reach me, you know."

Wyatt hung his knuckles on his hips. "Him . . . but not me, uh?"

The grin dissolved from Dorian's classical jawline and sculpted mouth. What seemed too much like a statue's face at times suddenly changed. He wavered.

He would never have let anyone else see it.

"You're right, of course," he finally said to Wyatt.

"Of course."

Punishing him with a glare, Wyatt ticked off five seconds, then let him off the hook with a grin. He was genuinely relieved to see Dorian here again, safe.

Dorian shifted under the glare and the grin. His composure was sanded down and milled as completely as that stinking compound under the grinding wheels over there.

"By Zeus," he said, "you can be a juggernaut. Highly contrapuntal to your raw nature."

Wyatt scowled. "Who's Zoos?"

"A Boston lawyer. Now listen to me. I want you to get your tunic and your driving gloves."

"My tunic? Why?"

"Because you and I have been called to a little town meeting. On the Fulton Street cotton docks."

Wyatt brought Dorian up from the mills to his office, keeping him close to the buildings and trying to draw no attention. Most of the people bustling around the mill yard were huddled inside their collars against the winter breeze, going about their day's business, and didn't notice the returned prodigal at all. Just as well.

Until they nearly ran into Grace at the door of the office. She was coming out, as she had several times a week since she started keeping his office papers in order.

She stopped and backed up a step when she saw them.

"Ah," Dorian said, in that tone he reserved for Grace.

"Oh," Wyatt said at the same time. He'd forgotten all about—

He let go of Dorian and moved between him and Grace.

"I've got some . . . well, some news," he said. He took Grace by the elbow, but looked at Dorian. "We . . . uh . . ."

Grace eyed them both with her lips clamped tight. Dorian tilted his head and waited.

"We got married," Wyatt blurted.

Dorian laughed. "Of course you did. Notify me when you're up to commedia del l'arte."

"Dorian?"

"Yes, yes."

"We really are married."

The smug grin dropped from Dorian's face. He studied both of them, one at a time, searching for a smirk that would tell him he was being put on. But Grace offered only a terse expression, and Wyatt looked like a boy confronting a parent after burning down the henhouse.

All at once it hit him.

"What?" he gasped.

Wyatt wagged a hand helplessly between them. "I didn't know how to contact you. I wanted you to stand up with me. . . ." He shrugged guiltily. "I couldn't find you."

But Dorian was glaring at Grace. Every hint of humanity had left his eyes, the set of his mouth, and suddenly his very skin seemed tight. It was an expression of pure shock they had seldom seen on his face. Grace stared back. They both knew.

Only Wyatt was in the dark. He stood there, eyes hopeful, holding Grace's elbow and looking back and forth at them, expectantly.

There was nothing on Dorian's face that let hope be part of the picture. There were only questions. *How could you? Why would you? Why her?*

Whatever passive suspicions he had harbored toward her in the past suddenly hardened into ugly disdain before their very eyes.

"Well—" Wyatt stepped to one side and gestured emptily. "I'll fetch my coat and be right back out."

He disappeared—escaped—into his office building.

Grace never took her eyes off Dorian.

It was Dorian who finally moved. He started to go around her as widely as the narrow entranceway would allow. She didn't turn. When he paused at her side, they were shoulder to shoulder, he facing one direction, and she the opposite. He lowered his voice, but spoke very clearly. His voice was absolutely cold.

"Lost your broomstick?" he said. "So you have married yourself another?"

★

CHAPTER TWENTY-FOUR

——————— ★ ———————

"What's wrong?"

Wyatt tightened his hands on the reins as the carriage clattered toward Fulton Street, but he was watching the unusually quiet form of Dorian beside him.

"What could be wrong?" Dorian kept his eyes facing forward, as though he couldn't bear to see him.

"Well, you've been kind of quiet."

They rode on in this crawling silence a few more blocks.

Then Wyatt said, "Oh . . . is it Grace?"

Dorian fixed a sidelong glare on him. "Wyatt," he said, "what were you thinking?"

The way he said it, there was no right answer. Luckily for Wyatt, there wasn't time either.

"Oh—here we are," he said.

Clouds had blown in over the coast of the eastern Confederacy and turned a sunny morning into a glowering afternoon. There was even a haze of light snow coming down in the distant hills.

Wyatt drew his carriage to a stop on the dock. A busy place, the dock was always invigorated with the comings and goings of humanity and industry, goods in, goods out, raw materials in, out, ships in and out and waiting. Steamers, schooners, barks, paddle wheelers, sloops, and even one lonely little canoe skulling between two anchored square-riggers. And along the dock and at anchor was a constant hairline of masts up and down this entire side of Richmond.

Beside Wyatt, Dorian sat back against the tufted carriage seat, his knees apart, his walking stick between them, and both hands poised on the ivory handle. He scanned the docks.

"Let's walk."

He was out of the carriage before Wyatt realized what he had said. The Inverness cape moved elegantly in the sea breeze, the long and short layers moving together.

Wyatt tethered the horse to a piling and caught up with Dorian two floating docks down. Dorian was standing with both feet evenly apart, gazing not at the docks, not at the ships, but east and south down the James River, the long thread that linked Richmond to Chesapeake Bay and the outer world. The Atlantic. Europe. South America.

Drawing up beside him, Wyatt was suddenly caught by the somberness in Dorian's face, by the . . . was it sentiment?

"Look at it," Dorian said. "The river does what railroads can only dream of doing."

The dark eyes in shadows of their own making, the lashes that lined them like kohl in some Egyptian drawing, were now pinched in a squint. His peach complexion was sallow with unspoken memories drawn out by that river. Its horizon, its relentlessness, its gray waters moving east . . . they meant something to Dorian.

Wyatt paused. He didn't want to ask him again if he was all right. They both knew he wasn't, deep down where the pain lurked. Something down that river, something about Dorian's fermenting past, his missing mother, her missing negro child, and the thousand sins he assigned to himself as some kind of twisted birthright . . . if Dorian was sensitive to the river, Wyatt couldn't help but be sensitive to Dorian, to whom life had been such a steeplechase.

So he simply pressed his hand flat against Dorian's back and said with his nearness what he would not speak outright.

After a few moments Dorian shifted, raised his chin a fraction. But his eyes stayed on the river.

"Flows to Hopewell," he murmured, "to Jamestown, Newport News, Portsmouth, Norfolk . . . to Tidewater . . . where I was first sentenced to life. 'Still as I hail thee, thou gloomy December, still shall I hail thee wi' sorrow and care. For sad was the parting thou makes me remember—'"

He drew in a breath and couldn't stop a small wince. He pushed out a whisper.

"I miss my family."

The river whispered back. Ships brushed past the two men standing at dockside, great triangular headsails breathing as they skirted past other ships. Their booms were canted to starboard to catch the breeze from aft, bowsprits pointing downriver, toward Tidewater.

Acute sympathy almost melted Wyatt where he stood. So did his helplessness to change things, past or present, and the knowledge that Dorian would never show anyone else this soft underside. Wyatt felt his heart thud with responsibility.

Without waiting for help or even a response, Dorian forced himself out of it. He turned, slammed Wyatt between the shoulder blades, and blurted, "God alone knows why he lets me keep *you,* eh? Let's clog."

He struck off down the dock, his great wool cape wagging. His mood had changed completely, and he baffled Wyatt by waving at the passing ships and tipping his hat to sailors who waved back. In fact, he was even laughing in a sudden delight, as though the sad man was someone else entirely.

Wyatt shook his head and followed, wary of these wild mood swings. In anybody, never mind Dorian.

Dorian Parthens, Dorian Parthens. Wyatt tried to get the name into his head. Last thing he wanted was to endanger Dorian by spitting out the wrong name at the wrong time. And there were certainly wrong people about to hear it.

He hurried to catch up with Dorian. His uniform tunic's upright collar was chafing his neck again. He reminded himself again to get it laid down. Had his wife said she knew how to sew or she *didn't* know how? Or she knew, but didn't like it?

Down the long lateral dock he clattered after Dorian. The dock timbers shook under him with a sense of extension into the water—not exactly land, not exactly sea—a reach beyond the continent toward something very distant.

"Prince Albert of Britain died a few days ago," Dorian was saying.

Wyatt jogged up beside him and fell into the stride. "Are you talking to me?"

"No, I thought that barge out there should know. His Royal Highness possessed very poor timing."

"Is that all you can say?"

"What should I say?"

"A nation loses its father, and you talk about timing."

"Considering the war," Dorian said, "it is poor timing. In May, Victoria issued a proclamation of neutrality in the

American situation. Since then the Confederacy has been trying to change England's cautious little mind. The only exception so far is British recognition of the Confederacy's claim to
'belligerent rights.' Do you know what belligerent rights are?"

"Pretty much describes you, I'd say."

"Rights to stop and search on the high seas, sanctuary in
certain ports, neutrality of foreign powers, and recognition that
there's a genuine dispute," Dorian said, holding his hat's brim
against a stiff offshore bluster. "The South wants more. In
September the Confederate ambassador to England got fed up
and fired himself. So President Davis put two new men on a
blockade runner and started them running. Their goal is to talk
to England about recognizing the Confederacy and supporting
it. They were to approach Britain's foreign whip, a man by the
name of John Russell. However, the Union's secretary of state,
a god of thunder named Seward, is pounding Washington tables, threatening trouble with Europe if the South is so much
as glanced upon by the nations of the world. The U.S. Navy
failed to intercept the blockade runner before it got to Cuba—"

"But a Navy man put his thirteen-gun sloop between the
packet and England," Wyatt interrupted, "took the two ambas-
sadors and stuffed them into Fort Warren, and the stock market took a plunge and Secretary of State Seward is raging
again. Right?"

Dorian drew up and gawked at him. The greatcape twisted
around his calves. "By God! You *do* read the papers!"

"I read the stock market," Wyatt corrected. "I also run a
factory. And the Confederacy's got an empty treasury right
now. No printed money, no engravers—we even hired a
Northern bank to print our money, but Lincoln seized that. We
asked for credit in Europe and got laughed at—"

"Oh, good man!" Dorian took Wyatt's arm and pulled him
along.

"Wait." Wyatt forced him to stop. "I'm all in the dark.
What's been going on with Stephens? I haven't heard a thing.
I need to talk to him, but I waited because I kept expecting you
to come back."

"I did come back."

"I mean sooner. Dorian, the war's barely started, and the
Confederate government's already crying poor. How can they
be out of money so soon? And don't start talking about the

Southern Du Ponts. I know they've got money, but they can't supply a whole war by themselves."

"No, but they *are* supporting your mill as much as is possible under the current conditions."

"Well, conditions are getting less and less possible. Last week I couldn't even get a shipment of baking flour in. How long do you suppose before I can't get sulfur anymore? I already can't get—"

"Yes, yes," Dorian broke in. "This is all why I've brought you here tonight. You're going to find all this financial warfare almost as interesting as the movement of armies, I predict."

"I find it a little nauseating," Wyatt confided.

"Of course you do," Dorian tossed back. "That's the way you are. Keep in mind, my friend, that war has always been good to the Du Ponts, no matter who wins. In 1812 a Du Pont had the only powder factory in America. His grandsons are the adult Du Ponts today, and nothing will change to usurp their influence. These inside traders have been polishing their stones since long before either of us were squeezed out. But you are quite right," he added, lowering his voice. "The *finances* of the Confederacy, not the guns or the battles or generals, will win or lose this war. And the king of the Confederacy's finances . . . is *that*."

He stopped and pointed.

Far over and down, to a broad lower area, a flat expanse of bricked pier, adjoined by tiers of dockage to where they were standing.

It was a loading pier, low to the water and very wide, broad enough to accommodate enormous flatbed wagons and teams of draft horses. On the flatbeds, piled five men high, were square bale after square bale of stock wrapped in burlap and lengths of hemp.

"You brought me here to see cotton being shipped?" Wyatt asked.

"No, I brought you here to see cotton *not* being shipped."

Wyatt's brow knotted. "What?"

He frowned down at the loading dock and realized that indeed there was no loading going on whatsoever. The cotton was being stockpiled, and that was all.

"What's it doing here?" he asked. "Richmond isn't a major

cotton export town . . . is it? I confess not knowing much about agriculture."

"Agriculture is the South's blood and bones," Dorian said. "Our vast tracts of cotton, tobacco, rice . . . speculation in cotton is going up and up as the cotton sits here and on docks up and down the thousand-mile coast. That's why you have so much of the Confederacy's black powder business. Can't buy it from the enemy anymore."

Wyatt shuddered at the idea of the Northern states as "the enemy." He shook his head, bit his lip, and watched the strange goings-on below.

"Let's go down there," Dorian invited. He dropped off their level to a lower tier of dockage, the short top layer of the Inverness cape rising like wings, and thus gave Wyatt no choice. A minute later they were walking across brick, inches from the water.

The cotton bales were piled higher than had seemed from where the two men had stood before. Wyatt realized he had misjudged just how much cotton was sitting here. The mound was nearly the size of a two-storied house now, and more was being added to it from those flatbeds.

Dorian stood beside him in silence. Wyatt felt like the brunt of something that hadn't been revealed to him.

Before them men were moving the cotton, but not onto ships. The bales were being piled tightly and pushed together in columns that left less than a foot between—and this was being done carefully, and the spaces between the columns were apparently something special.

A screw of foresight twisted up Wyatt's spine. None of the sensation was good or emboldening, and it didn't fade.

Dorian eyed him. "Are you cold? Would you like to borrow my cape?"

"Oh . . . no . . . just nervous for some reason."

"That is the whisper of your business sense, Wyatt," Dorian sighed. He gazed at the bales of cotton. "It is a mountain of white gold. King Cotton. The Union has put several ships of its Navy along Virginia and the Carolinas to embargo Southern exports. The cotton barons and Jefferson Davis's administration are all delighted."

"Delighted? With the North's blockade?"

"It's that British element again, Wyatt." Dorian planted the point of his walking stick on the dock and cupped both hands over the handle. "Twenty percent of Britain is dependent upon spinning cotton into textiles. The Confederacy is even patrolling its own harbors to make double sure no cotton gets out. They're not even planting any more. They want to create a cotton famine and blackmail Britain into supporting the Confederacy. We cut off their cotton, their textile workers starve."

Wyatt shifted his weight thoughtfully. "Might work."

"In theory. Unfortunately, war rarely entertains theory. The South's cotton men perceive themselves as the great New World whip. A ubiquitous view through the South, I'm afraid."

Smiling, Wyatt asked, "Do you really know what 'ubiquitous' means?"

Dorian looked at him. "Don't you?"

Wyatt was rescued when something started happening around the cotton bales. Men were hauling small kegs of liquid and pouring it between the stacks. It streamed along the brick pier around the pile of cotton.

"What are they doing?" he asked.

"Watch."

There weren't only dockworkers maneuvering between the stacked bales now, but well-dressed society businessmen as well, several with slaves hovering about them or holding their horses. Some had brought their wives with them to observe whatever was happening. Wyatt couldn't help but think of the battle of Manassas back a few months, when spectators gathered with picnic baskets and monoculars to watch what they thought would be a news- and gossip-worthy skirmish. Turned out they'd been witnesses to a bloody rout, and they'd stumbled over several limbs to get off the battleground before they too were cut down.

That sensation tightened Wyatt's shoulders. While Dorian stood beside him without so much as a shift of his shoulders, Wyatt twitched, shivered, and went from foot to foot.

This wasn't normal. All the people here seemed too aware of everyone else. At one corner of the pier, near a row of fishing shacks, a fire brigade was operating some kind of drill. Some people were watching them, but most were also watching the white and brown bales of cotton being stacked. Why?

Now, suddenly, Wyatt stopped fidgeting. It was as though an unseen hand had taken him by the throat and would squeeze if he moved or breathed—he sensed something.

One of the businessmen, a big man in a blue cape like Dorian's, with very short silver hair and a pinched red face, was raising an unlit torch. There was a woman beside him, her gloved hands clasped and resolution on her face. She wore dark clothing, almost as though attending a funeral. The pink-faced man stepped away from her in a manner that suggested he was doing it for her safety.

Immediately a slave stepped forward and put a lit match to the torch. Fire began to twist through it and win out against the stiff river breeze. The pink-faced man held it at arm's length. Then he and a half-dozen other men walked toward the mountain of baled cotton as though processing through some solemn mass.

The dockworkers backed away. The women were waved to a safe distance. The horses stomped and pulled sideways.

The man with the torch held the flame downwind, waved it once like a great sword, and swung it toward the cotton bales.

"Oh!" Wyatt gasped. "My God!"

He bolted forward, at an instant dead run. His rubber soles dug effectively against the moist dock planks.

Behind him Dorian sucked in a breath, snatched at empty air, and cried, "Wyatt, no!"

★

CHAPTER TWENTY-FIVE

———————— ★ ————————

Good God, what's got into you all? What do you mean by deserting now the great principles of our fathers, by returning to the vomit of that dog Great Britain?

> —Henry Adams, son of the American minister to Britain,
> after U.S. seizure of the *Trent* diplomats in international
> waters, a maritime habit of Britain that caused the War of 1812

"Wyatt!"

The sudden sprint put fifty feet between them before Dorian could throw down his hat and walking stick, shrug out of his cape, and plunge after him.

By then it was too late.

The mineral spirits that had been poured between the stacks fed the fire violently. The flames flashed, and suddenly that part of the dock seemed to explode with a great *fooom!*

Wyatt skidded, trying to stop, and threw his hands up.

The man with the pink puffy face and squinty eyes raised his flashing torch and caught Wyatt hard across the midsection with the handle, driving him backward. Wyatt's balance went with his breath, which gushed out all at once and left him gasping and staggering.

Right into the bonfire!

A blast of heat knocked him sideways. Something hit him again—the torch handle across his shoulder. His eyes blurred and he lost equilibrium. He rolled against a rough wall of burlap and the give of baled cotton. All he saw was a wall of yellow and white. Sulfur . . . saltpeter? And the black of rising smoke and burlap curling back as it cooked—Dorian?

A woman's voice cried, "Barry—stop!"

Wyatt would have struck out to defend himself, but that voice made him pull his punch. He couldn't see and didn't want to hit a woman by mistake—and he was on fire—

Two slaves nearly lost their own hands in the flames to yank him back at the last second, just before his hair and clothing would have caught fire. Sparks fanned around him, stinging his hands and cheeks. His head rang, and he realized what he had nearly stumbled into.

"Wyatt! Good lord!"

Dorian's Olympian stateliness had hit the dock only a tick after the cape and hat. He fiercely slammed the two slaves aside and took possession of Wyatt. He caught him with one arm and raised the other arm in clear threat to the pink-faced businessman just as the man's torch came up between them for a second attack.

The man stopped, torch poised in the air.

Oblivious, Wyatt staggered sideways, choking on the billowing smoke, and leaned gratefully into Dorian. He blinked his eyes in time to see Dorian warn off the slaves and the pink-faced man with a demonic glare.

"Mr. Swanborough!" Dorian bellowed, "that blow was not necessary!"

"But this fire is, Captain Parthens." He lowered the torch. "That officer has no call to interfere in private business."

"You mean here on your *private* dock at your *private* bonfire?"

"Captain?" a voice interrupted.

A figure moved between them. The smoke coiled.

Dorian stopped short, one arm around Wyatt's waist, suddenly not aware of Wyatt anymore. A woman was standing between him and Swanborough. Her small eyes were the steadiest things on the dock. Shaped like arrowheads and set in a plain face with small lips and large cheekbones, under honey-blond hair parted severely and capped with a nominal gray bonnet, the unflinching eyes were suddenly all Dorian saw.

Womanhood in the midst of inferno—she rose before him as Greece in his dreams.

"Captain," she said, "forgive us our transgressions."

Her voice was so soft, he barely heard it . . . but he heard it as clearly as if she had whispered in his ear. Her Deep South accent drew the words out and put his mild Virginia to shame. She never blinked, but only begged with her eyes, as though she had spoken what she truly wanted him to do.

The fire blazed beside her, but Dorian no longer saw it. He saw only what it did to her mellow form. Yellow light made the creases in her skirt seem large and alive, and the shadows seem bottomless. A piece of fire glow made a round burning ball of one large cheekbone. She was completely out of place, out of purpose, but she was here, not floating back there with the other women.

Forgetting Wyatt, who was stumbling against him, he choked one word out of his stupor.

"Madam . . ."

He reached up to tip his hat, but it wasn't there.

"Orienta," Barry Swanborough said from behind her. "Come away from those men."

Swanborough seemed completely unaffected, seemed to have no temper whatsoever. His voice had no snap or snarl to it, but only a disparaging judicial coolness. He took the woman's arm and drew her away, but she continued to look into Dorian's eyes no matter how he turned her.

"I shall harvest my cotton, Captain," Swanborough said, "sell it, wear it, or burn it. This is freedom."

Dorian shook out of his trance and blinked.

"Sir, *this* is assault!" he countered, holding Wyatt like a rag doll, who was rubbing his smoke-filled eyes and wobbling.

The other man nodded once. There was no malice in his pouchy face; in fact, there was nothing in it at all. No guilt, no worry, no concern. Only arrogant detachment.

Blandly he said, "Arrest me."

He pivoted away and took the woman with him. He suddenly paid all his attention to her, ushering her over obstacles and rough places in the brick pier, back across the breadth to where his coach, his aide, and his slaves were waiting.

"Hosanna," Dorian muttered. "Have them tie you in."

He would have preferred malice.

Turning his attention where it did some good, he drew Wyatt away. The bonfire licked the air after them.

The fire began to climb, spread, and turn colors. Down the wharf the fire brigade stood by in case sparks flew where a

spark might not be wanted. They made no movement to interfere in the altercation. Dorian balanced Wyatt forward over a
piling and held on to him, but watched the fire.

"He—hit me," Wyatt choked. He leaned on the wood and
ropes, holding his bruised ribs and blinking his eyes clear.
"Why would he h—"

A fit of coughing doubled him over the piling. Only
Dorian's firm grip kept him from tumbling sideways into the
water.

But Dorian was watching the Swanborough carriage,
watching the small-eyed woman being ushered up into the
seat, and watching with strange resentment as Swanborough
sat beside her.

"Odd," he murmured. "Didn't know he was married . . ."

"What—?"

"Such a . . . true shame."

Across the distance, across the brick pier, the crowd, the
fire, Dorian felt the woman's eyes still on him. She nodded at
him behind Swanborough's shoulder.

Dorian held his breath and forced his neck to remain stiff.
Tragedy, to nod back.

The bonfire did not roar or race or flash as flames climbed
high onto the mountain of cotton, but crawled like some awakening beast just turning over to show its yellow underbelly.

And it made very little sound. No roar or hiss. Instead, as
any thousand candles would be, it was silent. The burlap covering peeled back like a corpse's lips, and beneath it white cotton was slowly eaten to black.

Holding firmly on to Wyatt, Dorian said, "It is the sickest,
most ill-judged stew ever cooked." He looked at Swanborough
sitting in his carriage, and the other people watching. "And
there stands the chefs."

"I was only going to tell him—"

"What he already knows, I assure you."

"Who—who—?"

"Barry Swanborough. Cotton baron. Alabama man, I
think."

"That's quite a scowl he's got. . . ."

"Yes, his face long ago made a pact of mutual support with
his personality. We should kick him in the pebbles, render him

down into soap, and be done with him." He stooped to one knee, cupped his hand into the James River, and wiped Wyatt's stinging eyes with the water. "Steady. How are you?"

Wyatt waved him off. "All right now." He dabbed at his eyes with his sleeves, then turned to the fire and blinked until he could see. "Pity's sake, look at that! Dorian, we've got to stop it!"

"I didn't bring you here to stop it, lily-white. I brought you here to *see* it. You must stay as close to me as ten-cent drawers," he warned, "or those good men of business will take your head off and toss it in."

"But don't they understand?" Wyatt choked. "I heard rumors and threats about burning the cotton—but there's been talk like that for months—I never thought they'd actually do it! Don't they realize what they're burning?"

He pushed himself off the piling suddenly, but this time his hands filled with the dove-gray wool and gold piping of Dorian's frock coat.

"You brought me here to see this because we can do something about it, didn't you? Didn't you!" His grip tightened. "Tell me what we can do!"

Dorian gazed into the desperate blue eyes, the fire-ruddied face, the tousled gravel-colored hair of the only person on earth he hadn't been born near and still trusted. Indeed, large-hearted Wyatt Craig was his only friend, the only one he had ever had in his life. Everyone else he cared about was a member of his family, joined to him by blood. Wyatt was the only human being joined to Dorian by caring what happened to him.

Difficult to ignore, to set aside.

And Dorian was clearly right now what he already knew—that he wasn't the only thing Wyatt had room in his heart to care about.

Dorian cleared his own throat and hung both hands over the knotted wrists at his collar.

"Over the coals, Wyatt."

★

They retrieved the cape and topper, headed back to the carriage, and there they found—

"Mr. Stephens!" exclaimed Wyatt, blinking his burning eyes.

The Vice President's wild stringy hair, wide-set dark eyes, narrow nose, and pinched mouth just barely poked over a coil of scarves, shawls, sweaters, and an overcoat. His chin was buried altogether, but those eyes—

Wyatt desperately wanted to be on the favorable side of those terrible eyes. For one who looked like a cadaver, Alexander Stephens had the life of ten men in his eyes.

"Are you all right, Major Craig?" the tiny man asked. "I witnessed your little altercation with Barry Swanborough."

"I'm over it, sir."

"Are you shocked at what you've seen?"

A bitter chuckle, not the least bit funny, coughed out of Wyatt. "Shocked right through, Mr. Stephens."

"Good. Hello, Dorian."

"Aleck."

"How was your voyage?"

"Pleasant and profitable. Glad I could serve."

"Posterity will laud your risk."

Dorian snickered and responded, "Posterity will blame somebody else."

Poking between them, Wyatt suspiciously asked, "Voyage?"

He received nothing but silent looks from the two others and unwillingly put an end to the conversation.

"Let's go, gentlemen," Stephens said abruptly, waving a spidery hand toward the carriage.

Stephens's carriage was parked behind theirs, with one slave at the reins and another acting as footman, but the Vice President got into their carriage, not his own, and took a seat opposite Dorian. Wyatt started to climb into the driver's seat, but Stephens's footman appeared beside him, tipped his cap, and took the reins from him.

"I'll do the driving tonight, Major," the footman said, and Wyatt was back in the passenger seat beside Dorian before he knew it. A snap, and they were clicking over the gaslit Richmond cobblestones through a cool, moist riverside night.

Even facing away from the docks, Wyatt couldn't avoid the glittering reflection of the bonfire in Richmond's glazed windows.

After three or four blocks of silence, he found himself slumped against tufted buffalo leather, staring at his knees. His stinging face and acrid-smelling clothes prevented the clear night air from making him complacent about what he had seen.

"Up in smoke," Stephens said, watching him.

Without saying anything Wyatt met the Vice President's rodentlike glowing eyes.

Stephens huddled tightly in his own seat, keeping out of the breeze. "They mean to claim the burning is to prevent the Union from confiscating the cotton, but that's a lie. What they really want is to cause cotton starvation in Europe and force Britain and France to break the Union blockade of our ports."

More silence.

Stephens asked him, "What would *you* do, Mr. Craig?"

Wyatt licked his dry lips and answered immediately. "I'd establish credit in Europe with the cash crop they're torching back there."

"That's right. After all, no one will give the Confederacy unsecured credit. That's where our cotton barons are going wrong. They mean to destroy the cotton crop and starve Europe into dependence upon Southern trade. They hope it'll force recognition."

"It'll force resentment, is what it'll force."

"The Du Ponts are in England even now, using their tremendous influence to corner the market on saltpeter for the Union Army. You will now attempt to get saltpeter, and you won't be able to."

Wyatt sat up a little straighter. "Yes, I'm already having some trouble getting the pure Chilean niter. Commodities futures must be tied up already."

"We'll make sure you get it from somewhere, don't worry."

"He never worries," Dorian tossed in lightly.

"Money is power, Mr. Craig," Stephens said. "I need a businessman of your stature to go before the Confederate powers and make a scene that without money, without credit in Europe, you cannot get supplies for gunpowder, and without gunpowder there is no war. You're the perfect man for this.

You're in Richmond, everyone knows you're supplying the powder, you've accepted a commission from the Confederate Army and funded an artillery-supply company. Your voice is strong here. I need you to make a plea before this cotton embargo foolishness gets out of hand."

His stomach roiling, Wyatt sat forward. "Sir . . . why can't you do this? You're the Vice President. Your influence is—"

"Worthless," Stephens said. "No one listens to me. Look at me . . . I'm a mouse in a world of lions. I'm struggling through the bog of life in my pathetic casing, crawling through thorns. What good is my quivering voice when champions like Bob Toombs and Judah Benjamin are talking?"

"Aleck," Dorian scolded.

"No, no, my friend, I'm a bewildered nothing at best. I am already estranged from the real power in the Confederate government. I was a compromise candidate. President Davis and I are oil and water." Stephens crossed his slender legs and shivered. "I simply despise the man."

Background noises ground in Wyatt's mind. Horses clopping in front and behind him, the hoot of ships' horns on the river, birds in the gutters, even the tinkle of a doorbell down a narrow side street. A pawn in someone else's game now . . . a thousand wrong turns, another thousand that might be right— how could he know? Complications left no room for plain integrity. He could add things up in his mind, but there were smarter and trickier men in the world than he, and chances were he was sitting with two of them right here in this carriage.

"No man has ever been more devoted to the religious and civil liberties embodied in the Constitution than I am. That's where I get all the strength my pathetic body lacks. I can only hope to master evil and leave no foe standing to my rear. My greatest courage is drawn from my greatest despair. The only thing I do really well is my patriotism."

Dorian chuckled and shifted his legs. "Such self-torture, Aleck. *Ene skotino.*

"*Yiati yelateh? Ti mas sistenete? Borete na mu doseteh mia sindahyi yia afto?*"

"Oh, *ti semehni ekino? Grapsteh toh.*"

They launched into a Greek argument, during most of which Dorian was either laughing or raving, and Stephens was shaking his scrawny head. Wyatt slumped deep into his seat and tried not to pout through the next half block.

"I didn't ask to be born," Stephens said in English finally, "but if I must be committed here in this mediocre frame, I shall at least do my best to affect the asylum. I've had no say in the making of the cabinet, and I have little purpose other than to be a dissenting voice, but no one in the South wants to hear a dissenting voice right now. If a businessman of repute comes to the Southern power lords and speaks of deep trouble . . . they just may listen." He bent his narrow body forward and fixed his eyes on Wyatt. "Will you do this, Major? Will you help me rescue a continent?"

There was something in his voice. A signal. Warning—anticipation. At the same moment Wyatt realized the carriage was passing Governor Street.

And heading for Court End.

He groaned. "You mean *now*?" he asked hoarsely.

"Now."

Dorian added, "The Witches' Sabbath."

Without speaking Wyatt made his question clear with just a lift of his brows.

"A few textile industrialists," Dorian said, "Swanborough and a handful of cotton belters, the Secretaries of War, State, the Treasury . . . Aleck and yourself . . . and the devil will want his say; therefore I shall be there also."

Wyatt caught Dorian's shoulder in the one hand he had cast over the back of the buggy seat—but both he *and* Stephens spoke at the same time:

"Stop talking like that!" they chimed.

Dorian smiled and shook his head as though he had just made the match of the century. He and the Vice President broke out laughing.

Wyatt hunched deeper into the leather, feeling as if an iron weight were sitting on his stomach.

"Sakes," he mumbled.

The two carriages pulled up tandem in front of the Confederate White House. The footmen tethered up, bounced to the brick sidewalk, and took Stephens's hand to help him down.

Wyatt stood up in the carriage, preparing to step down after Dorian. He noticed a row of carriages and buggies clustered on the street, each with a slave or two in attendance. Suddenly he was stricken by how different all the slaves seemed from each other as they clustered near the middle of the row and exchanged gossip over tea that White House slaves were just now bringing out. There was no one kind of negro, any more than there was one kind of white. Even in the dark of evening he saw the variance of skin color among the slaves, and knew that some of them must be like Dorian . . . half, quarter, or eighth something else.

But none of them looked even remotely like Dorian. No one would ever look at Dorian and see a hint of the negro, or even a hint of the white. Dorian looked Mediterranean, just as he *felt* Mediterranean. It was as though his outer physical nature and the nature of his heart were in perfect concord.

If only the Confederacy could find that kind of concord within itself—

Stephens's footman took Wyatt's arm as he jumped down. Stephens was already halfway up the front walk, but Dorian waited intuitively as Wyatt smoothed his tunic and stalled, hoping his stomach would settle.

Dorian asked, "Don't feel well?"

"Sure don't."

"You knew this was a possibility when you agreed to take the factory, Wyatt. The Du Ponts are no one's fools."

"Guess we know who the fool is," Wyatt sighed.

"Now, now, don't go coldcock in the middle of the humping."

Wyatt started to respond, but stumbled on the curb. His arms flew out in front of him, grabbing for balance and the vain hope of not falling flat on his face. Dorian caught one arm, but it wasn't enough. Wyatt felt himself teetering—

Then something caught his other arm, and he stumbled against what he thought was a horse.

It wasn't a horse.

An enormous form veered out of the night in front of them—a slave so big that he blocked out their view of the Confederate White House. A very big coffee-skinned young man dressed in a fancy coachman's tailed coat and bow tie. *Very big*.

As Wyatt nodded gratefully and stared up at the human

mountain, he realized where he'd seen those shoulders and those clothes before. At the docks.

This was Swanborough's coachman.

The coachman pulled Wyatt up onto the brick sidewalk with one hand, as easily as setting straight a toppled whiskey bottle. But the square face, boned like a statue and decorated with pitch eyes and long, curled eyelashes, was glaring unashamedly—at Dorian.

"Thanks," Wyatt muttered.

Dorian pulled him away from the big slave and at the same moment pushed a dollar into the slave's hand. "Good job," he commented, and waved the coachman away. "Go on. I've got him now. Back, back."

The coachman did move back, but only a few steps. He continued to glare at Dorian, his arms stiff at the sides of his fancy coat, his throat visibly pulsing against the bow tie.

"Get your feet under you," Dorian murmured to Wyatt. "We have to make a good impression."

"Still shaky, is all." Wyatt glanced back at the big black coachman, who was glaring at them and clenching both fists. He took Dorian's arm. "Move along. I don't like the way that massive slave is looking at you."

In his usual flameproof manner, Dorian fluidly kept from looking back. "Swanborough's coachman. He's probably been instructed to hate me in advance."

"Or just saw you yelling at his master."

"And saw his master backhanding my companion," Dorian said defensively.

"Let's move on anyway."

There was little outward sign if Dorian was worried at all, but after a moment Wyatt did notice that Dorian's hand was now resting on the hook of his watch chain. Suddenly Wyatt was sweating even in the cool December air, and he hurried his mysterious friend along toward the building.

"Yes," Dorian drawled, "I pity any animal owned by that gasbag."

"Do you see the shoulders on that boy?" Wyatt commented.

"How can you tell how old he is? Or are you using 'boy' in another way?"

"Well, he's young. Something about the way he's standing there staring right at us and twitching."

"Don't look back. He'll stick to his knitting if we ignore him."

They walked together down the sidewalk toward the White House, where Stephens was already inside the main entrance.

"Lammot Du Pont is after the English saltpeter," Dorian said. "His influence is very strong and will hit the sky if he succeeds." Those black eyes glowed under a gaslight and grinned conspiratorially. "Either way, we win."

"We who?" Wyatt persisted. "We the powdermill, or we the Confederacy?"

"We the mill. As for the Confederacy . . ."

Gazing at the looming White House of the Confederacy, Wyatt saw the three-story double pillars sharpen to dreamlike crystal before his eyes.

He hovered and held his breath.

"Who's in there, Dorian?" he asked. "Who am I going to have to face?"

"You won't remember if I tell you now. I'll point them out to you inside. These are the explosions, Wyatt, burning from fuses set weeks ago—"

"Now that's enough!" Wyatt snapped, and faced him sharply. "I want to know what's going on. What've you gotten me into this time? And exactly where were you on that 'voyage'? Tell me now, or I'm not going one more step, and I mean it."

Dorian hesitated, but couldn't buck the sudden determination in Wyatt's face. Wyatt was clearly not going inside until he got at least part of an answer.

Dorian glanced about the dark night as though to be sure they were genuinely alone on the sidewalk.

Finally he said, "I've been to Cuba."

The rocky set of Wyatt's jaw and an abrupt hardness in his eye belied suspicion. He wanted more.

Dorian lowered his voice impatiently. "I'm the one who told Captain Wilkes of the *San Jacinto* that Mason and Slidell were aboard the *Trent*—"

"*What?*" Wyatt clutched at Dorian's cape and drove him furiously against a lamppost.

"Keep your voice down, man!" Dorian snapped. He raised

a defensive hand, and only by the greatest of restraint kept from striking back at Wyatt as the iron lamppost dug into his shoulder.

"What've you done!" Wyatt choked.

"The business of politics, that's what. It'll win this war and win it right. We can't have Jefferson Davis's emissaries succeed! He *must* be undermined. How often must you hear it? How much do we have to beg to get you to act upon what you say you believe? Get a backbone, Wyatt! And let go of me before I take you personally."

Quaking in his coat, Wyatt gave one last push before he untangled his fingers from the wool shoulder cape. Dorian brushed the rumples out of the cape and scolded him with a glare.

"Now that we've arranged for Britain to swallow enough of Seward's thunderation," he said, "we'll go inside and help the South make some thunder of its own."

They were ushered to the end of the hallway, past a stone pedestal with an oversized vase sprawling with lilies, to the same receiving room where Wyatt had been shocked out of his brass buttons once before. Except now the room, stinking of cigar smoke, was occupied by no more than fifteen men, statesmen, businessmen, cotton men, in various descriptions of proper evening suit. Wyatt was unaccustomed to the smoke, since so little smoking was allowed on the mill grounds, and his eyes, already sensitive from the fire, were watering profusely by the time they reached the other end of the room.

Wyatt dabbed at his eyes with a handkerchief, then blinked around and tried to estimate who was who. He didn't want to turn and ask Dorian.

Stephens wasn't here in the room yet, though Wyatt peeked behind all the normal-sized men to see if the Vice President was tucked in some shadow.

Perched on the chesterfield, ignoring Wyatt's presence, was Barry Swanborough, his pinched red face nodding through a conversation with a mammoth man whose bulk weighed down one end of the couch. The stranger's big round head was crowned with a swept-back brown mane and he possessed a booming voice that punctuated the buzz in the crowded room. Wyatt instantly pegged this roaring giant as Robert Toombs. Confederate secretary of state. Proslave. Son of a cotton planter. Known for his prowess in the face of injustice, and for his entertaining, offhand speeches, and genial tavern-type conversation. Everybody knew who he was. His grumbles would make the newspapers, and he could fill up a theater on the mere chance that he might come and lend his splendid power of oratory to the public.

A fiery advocate of Stephens—until lately. There'd been articles about disagreements between the two of them during public addresses since the secession. Toombs was speaking to Swanborough now, pointing a stubby finger at the other man's chest, and the rumble of his voice created an underpinning for the general talk going on in the room. Wyatt had read about that finger—Tombs was known for keeping half of Congress silent with that finger, while he debated them down.

There were so few men here that Wyatt began to get an idea. It might be a secret meeting, or at least an unofficial one. Limited attendance, probably by invitation. No President Davis here tonight.

"This way," Dorian muttered, and led the way deep into the room. He spoke to hardly anyone, but went straight to the fireplace where a short stocky man in a black suit was standing, reading a letter. The man was round as St. Nicholas, except that he was darkish, with a beard but no mustache. He was just throwing the paper into the fire and watching it burn when Dorian startled him with a greeting.

"Judah, *qu'est-ce que tu fabriques?*"

"Ah, my friend! Oh, *c'est la paperasserie seulement,*" the man responded, gripping Dorian's arm in a friendly manner and watching the paper dissolve in the fire. Then he looked up. "*Aleck ne vient pas?*"

"*Oui, il est ici,*" Dorian said. "How's everything going?"

"*Tu tombes bien.*" The roundish man leaned closer and muttered, "*Il n'y a rien a en tiere.*"

"Well, we have a wild card here." He turned, gripped Wyatt by the arm, and hauled him closer to the fire he was avoiding. "Wyatt," Dorian said, "Judah Benjamin. Secretary of War."

Wyatt stuck out a hand. "Heard of you, Mr. Benjamin. All good things."

"So kind, Mr. Craig," the secretary responded in his sweet, delicate tones. He had a high-pitched voice that children would like, and that adults never really outgrew liking if they heard it early.

"*Il est carré en affaires,*" Dorian went on. "*Autrement dit, il est un homme bien pensant.*"

"Well, good, good," Benjamin murmured, beaming at Wyatt suddenly, but he seemed troubled and kept glancing at the burning paper in the fireplace.

"*Qu'est-ce qui vous travaille?*" Dorian asked him.

Benjamin sighed, smiled ruefully, and lowered his voice even though they were speaking French. "*Je ne sais plus a quoi m'en tenir. Toute cette histoire me retourne.*"

"Oh, Judah, I don't believe anything upsets you," Dorian said. "You're too buoyant."

Benjamin laughed and patted both Dorian's and Wyatt's shoulders. He spoke in a broad New Orleans accent. "Mr. Craig, I'm impressed that you troubled to come here. Aleck and I deeply need your kind of support in the business sector. We're just politicians, after all."

"Do what I can, sir," Wyatt offered, mopping a wing of bangs out of his face.

"Gentlemen, good evening."

Alexander Stephens came into the center of the room and was immediately gestured into a chair by one of the other men. All the scarves and shawls were gone now, and Stephens's skin-and-bones body could barely fill the ordinary jacket, waistcoat, and trousers that draped valiantly over his skeleton.

Dorian leaned toward Wyatt. "*Prenez une siege.*"

Wyatt scowled. "What?"

Judah Benjamin laughed. Dorian clapped his hand to his forehead and said, "An idiot attack! Sit down, Wyatt, is what I was stumbling over."

Dorian steered him to a tufted side chair beside a Chippendale table and pushed him down, then perched on the broad window box behind Wyatt's left shoulder, crossed his legs, and melted into the decor. Judah Benjamin stayed between Dorian and the fireplace, hands in his pockets, and they whispered a bit more in French.

"My friends," Robert Toombs said, standing up and waving toward Stephens, "you all know Vice President Stephens. . . . Aleck and I are at odds about secession—you know that too. I say the sword of freedom has hacked us apart from the Union, and that is how it must stay. But this man is one of the brightest minds to walk the earth since the Founding Fathers, and I'm inclined toward his wisdom now that secession has happened. This man begged that we not secede until there was actual aggression by the North. But when the North backed us up into firing the first shots, Aleck Stephens went with our beloved Georgia, for he's a true patriot and a man who believes in the power of the sovereign state." He turned his enormous bulk toward the Vice President and added, "My deepest admiration, Aleck, whatever our differences."

Stephens smiled and cleared his scrawny throat. "Thank you, Bob." He sat forward a little. "Gentlemen, you all know what we're here to discuss. You are our cotton barons, and the future is suddenly in your hands. It'll be a short war. Britain is the world's greatest tyranny, and we Americans are the greatest democracy. The Confederacy can be friends with them only briefly, before all friendship falls apart. Our bond must be swift, efficient, and carefully exploited. We must *use* Britain, but not depend upon them."

"We'll drive them prostrate," Swanborough spoke up. He spoke calmly, almost with a tone of disinterest. "Fear of war with the North has kept Britain neutral; therefore, we should give them something worse to fear. They're tied to our cotton. A fifth of Great Britain depends upon the textile industry. We cut it off, their spinning and clothing workers starve."

He sipped his brandy as though that were the end of the conversation.

Wyatt glowered at the man and wondered where all his passion was. Southerners were known for their passion, and Swanborough was apparently here to voice the concerns and intents of the cotton powers, yet he had no thrill or venom in his voice at all. It was frightening. Perhaps that was his method.

Stephens said, "Fear has kept them neutral, and now this *Trent* business has come up. Secretary of State Seward in the North is rattling his saber to pick a fight with Britain. He's threatening to seize Canada, which Britain would have to defend at great expense."

"Great expense for the Union too," one of the other cotton barons said. Wyatt knew he was a cotton man because Swanborough was nodding as the man talked. "We would be thrilled with war between the Union and Britain."

"Wouldn't that be something to see," Dorian muttered from behind him.

"This whole decade's going to be something to see," Wyatt whispered back over his shoulder.

"Every British coin going to war in Canada would be a coin less support for the Confederacy, Mr. Brown," Stephens said. "Seward's a bastard, but a shrewd one. He knows Parliament will hesitate to spread their own resources too thinly. Lord Lyons wrote from Washington and warned the British Foreign Office that Seward will be a dangerous man to deal with. The Union's own minister in London, Charles Adams, called Seward a beast."

"Called him 'an ogre resolved to eat all Englishmen raw,'" Robert Toombs thundered, chuckling. "His 'go to war with the world' policy is capitalizing upon the reputation of us Americans as spontaneous, quick, and crazy like foxes. The British think we're bad boys, liable to do anything as long as it's rash and naughty." He chuckled again and added, "It's exactly what I would do were I a Yankee."

A few of the men chuckled with him, but many remained stern and on edge. Including Wyatt.

"Tell us your plan, Aleck," Toombs said, virtually interrupting himself.

"My plan," Stephens began, "is this. Two million bales of last year's cotton crop and two of this year's crop, paid for with government bonds. A fleet of steamers will carry it to England and France and store it there until the price swells. Then we'll sell it and net a profit of seventy or eighty million for the Confederate Treasury."

"Why, we could arm hundreds of thousands of soldiers in time for the next major battle!" Toombs said supportively.

A third man was sitting on the chesterfield with Swanborough and Toombs, a squinty-eyed fellow with wild white hair and a wide thin mouth, which now opened up.

"No, Robert, we couldn't! Aleck, I'm sorry, but this plot of yours is unconstitutional and financially unsound. We'll find ourselves with a heap of credits, a burden of crop for which there's no market, and planters who have been bought off. It's soup-house legislation to keep the cotton planters comfortable, and these fine men won't have it!"

Brown, obviously another strong cotton restrictionist, added, "And it's downright unpatriotic to be comfortable in time of war."

He was all but applauded openly by the rumbling response of the other cotton men.

"Thank you for helping me think, Mr. Memminger," Stephens said to the man sitting with Swanborough and Toombs. He managed to get a few good chuckles out of the other side of the argument.

Memminger, Wyatt thought. *Christopher Memminger. Secretary of . . .*

"Treasury," Dorian whispered near his ear. Reading his mind, as always.

He nodded a little thanks.

Swanborough killed even the enthusiasm on his own side with that damp, cool tone of his. "We cotton planters don't need government relief, Mr. Stephens."

"Pardon me, Mr. Swanborough, Mr. Memminger?" Stephens responded very strongly. "Relief? You carry the greatest cash crop of this century, and you think I'm offering you 'relief'?"

"I'm not giving up my stock cotton for Confederate bonds," Swanborough said.

"There's loyalty," Dorian mumbled.

Swanborough ignored him, but everybody heard. Suddenly everyone was sitting on eggs.

"There's not as much cotton available as you see in your fantasy, Mr. Stephens," Brown said. "We have no two million bales left of 1860 cotton."

Secretary Toombs roared, "How much *do* you have?"

"A few hundred thousand bales. And we have decided not to plant more." His glance took in the other cotton men, some of whom nodded, and others of whom waited to see what the reaction would be.

"Not plant any!" Wyatt blurted, instantly regretting his outburst. "Sorry . . . ," he muttered.

"Not at all, Major," Stephens said. He paused as his eyes caught Wyatt's.

Wyatt waited for the Vice President to continue, but that's not what happened. Stephens sat still, intrigued by something in Wyatt's face. The clock on the mantel ticked audibly, in spite of the roomful of fifteen men.

Had he said something wrong?

Everyone was looking at Wyatt now, except for Swanborough, who was sitting back on the couch, wagging a crossed leg and sipping a brandy.

Wyatt wanted to proclaim his innocence—but he couldn't look away from the bright, magnetic chestnut eyes of the Vice President.

Thoughtfully Stephens said, "You're actually listening to us, aren't you, Major?"

Wyatt's own eyes widened and he grew even more uncomfortable. "Of . . . of course I am, sir—"

"No, no, I mean, you are truly *listening*."

Knowing how helpless he must appear, and how confused, Wyatt didn't know what Stephens was getting after or what he wanted him to do.

"All these other gentlemen," Stephens went on, waving at his peers, "they hear me, but they're busy thinking of what they'll say when I finally shut up. You aren't doing that. You're *listening*. There's someone else I know who does that. Do you know who that is?"

"Uh . . . no, sir . . ."

"Abraham Lincoln," Stephens said. "He does that."

Under any other circumstances, Wyatt could have taken the compliment as it was intended. But today he sat with some of the most powerful moguls of the Confederacy, to whom Abraham Lincoln was the enemy. For the first time since meeting Aleck Stephens, he saw a flash in the Vice President's eyes that said Stephens realized he might have just made a mistake. A compliment, but ill-timed.

Stephens shook it off and plowed ahead. They all knew how he felt about Davis and how much he admired Lincoln, and any harm was done already.

"Gentlemen," he said, "you're all familiar with the Craig Powderworks, the largest mill of black powder in the Richmond area, currently a main supplier of the Confederate

Army for gun, cannon, rifle, and blasting powder. May I introduce Major Wyatt Craig, owner and general manager of the
mill. Major, why don't you let us hear your analysis of this
subject now?"

Wyatt thought about talking sitting down, but he couldn't.
He shuddered to his feet and felt Dorian's push of encourage-
ment on his elbow just before he straightened. It helped a little,
but not much.

He cleared his throat. Twice.

"Thank you," he said, nodding at Stephens. "Gentlemen,
closest I've ever been to cotton before tonight is this shirt I'm
wearing . . . but I just came from the docks, and I saw something there that put the fear of God and hell into me all over
again—"

"You're welcome," Swanborough popped off, without
doing Wyatt the courtesy of even looking up at him. The
sound was muffled inside the brandy snifter.

Wyatt paused, but refused to be thrown off. "I saw good
bales of your cotton being put to the torch. Mr. Stephens says
you plan to tell England that you can't get the cotton out because of the Northern blockade, in hopes of making them hostile to the Union as cotton starvation sets in."

"Correct," somebody offered.

Wyatt glanced in that direction and forced himself to continue. They didn't seem to be getting his point.

"How long can you keep them believing that? It's not as
though letters and newspapers don't traffic the Atlantic. The
blockade is silly. The North can't blockade three and a half
thousand miles of Southern coastline with their skimpy armada, and the whole economic world knows it. You're going
to tell England that we can't get past the one or two little ships
in the blockade—but you're *not* telling them you're *burning*
the cotton!"

"We're patrolling our own harbors to make sure the cotton
isn't shipped," Brown said.

"Well, why on earth would you do that?" Wyatt wrenched
toward him and ended up spinning all the way around. "I'm
sorry, sir, we haven't been introduced, and I don't mean to insult you, but you're putting a gun to your own heads and saying 'Don't move or we'll blow out our brains.' We can't
possibly hope to blackmail recognition out of Europe."

"How do you *know* we can't?" Stephens asked him, obviously planting the question on purpose. His arms were folded and his legs crossed at the ankles, and he was giving Wyatt a fatherly little smile.

The coaching caught Wyatt off balance, but after a second he realized Stephens was trying to help him and managed to force out a completely honest answer.

"Because you can't blackmail it out of *me*," he said. "I can't imagine Parliament ducking under. How could Britain, of all places, justify that in front of the world? It can't work!"

"It is working," Swanborough interrupted again, still not looking at him. "The mills of Lancashire are already dying of starvation."

"Sir," Dorian spoke up from behind Wyatt, "at least be honest."

His clipped enunciation sliced through the discussion.

Swanborough straightened on the couch and twisted around to level a look right at him, so abruptly that the man sitting next to him grabbed the couch's arm for support.

"Am I lying, Captain?" he demanded.

"Isn't it a lie to fail mentioning that the cotton embargo can't have taken hold this early?" Dorian said. "Stocks of raw cotton in England and France are higher now than last year. The cloth market is saturated, and *that* is why the weavers have no work."

"Bushwah," the other man snorted, mostly through his nose.

Dorian's black brows shot up. "Oh, spell that for me, *Barry*."

Toombs's voice cut through them and brought attention back to where Stephens wanted it. "What *should* we be doing, Major?"

Wyatt shifted uneasily and wished he had a hat to twist. "Well . . . we *should* be stockpiling our cotton in Europe—it won't be considered safe if we stockpile it over here—and we should spend this whole year establishing credit. If you want to do your cotton embargo next year, fine. But let's ship all we have now to Europe, hold it in warehouses, keep it off the market so the price drives up. It'll force the recognition you want, and at the same time it'll be white gold sitting in its warehouses. We can borrow on the collateral and not have to release it until we're ready to turn a sharp profit." He raised a hand and gestured toward the southeast end of town. His voice broke. "Instead, you're dragging it down to the river and burning our national credit foundation!"

His words throbbed. They all noticed his face, still red from the heat of the burning docks, and his scorched uniform. He saw doubt flicker in many faces and wondered if he was having the kind of effect Stephens hoped for.

"You're trying to starve the wrong people," he went on. "You can't extort support out of Europe—you'll just make them hate us. There are so many alternatives! If you don't want to warehouse the cotton, you should *still* be sending it to Europe as fast as you can and let them produce textiles. The textile mills and clothing factories in the Union'll go crazy watching a flurry of economic activity between the Confederacy and Europe, while the *Northern* textile people starve. Starve the *North*!"

Silence fell. Doubt and second thoughts began to flicker in the faces of some of the cotton barons. Toombs and Stephens had the brains to let the stew simmer without adding anything more.

They just let Wyatt's words operate.

Wiping his hands nervously on his trousers, Wyatt tried not to shift back and forth on his tingling feet.

"Mr. Craig," Swanborough began, "how old are you?"

"I'm . . . twenty-eight."

"It shows."

Wyatt would have responded, but he didn't have any idea what the bejesus Swanborough was getting after.

"Where are you from?" the cotton baron asked. "What is that accent?"

"I'm . . . from Kansas—"

"No one your young age is from Kansas. Where were you born? Raised? Educated?"

"Oh . . . born in Massachusetts. Raised there and in Connecticut . . . educated in Delaware—"

"A Northerner."

Wyatt fell silent, taken aback. He'd never thought of himself as the one with the accent.

The roomful of men almost visibly flinched at the cold,

rude treatment. The other men glanced uncomfortably at him and fidgeted in empathy—but also in sudden distrust. Suddenly they heard the Northern ring to his words.

Then, before all their eyes, Swanborough performed a feat of pure stout nerve: he ignored Wyatt completely, ignored all those words, ignored the sentiment and the predictions, and played perfectly on the anti-Northern bigotry that he knew he could stoke perfectly in this room tonight.

He shifted on the couch, crossed his legs in the other direction from Wyatt, dismissing him by turning his back, and addressed Stephens. "How do you propose to pay for a fleet of ships?"

Stephens glanced at Wyatt, but after a few seconds he simply answered the question. "We have loyal Southern shipping magnates," he said, "who will donate their carriers' time, I'm sure."

"Have you *asked*?"

From his tone they inferred Swanborough knew something of the nature of business that they were forgetting. Men who had spent their lives building businesses might wave the Confederate flag, but they would vote their nationless pocketbooks.

"A ship can carry roughly a thousand bales," Memminger said to Stephens. "Where are you dreaming to find three or four thousand ships to transport a new crop to England?"

From beside the fireplace, Judah Benjamin spoke up now. "We needn't send four million bales. A hundred thousand stored bales will net nearly fifty million in early revenue. In fact, we can ship five hundred thousand bales right away. Cotton finance is war finance."

"Britain will come and get the shipments," Dorian added. "We can send the cotton to Cuba in several short trips as quickly as possible and hold it there. England can send large vessels and ship it at leisure."

Memminger shook his head. "European ships are afraid of the blockade—"

"Insurance rates have gone to the skies," Swanborough interrupted.

"It's war, gentlemen!" Dorian roared. Frustration wore on his tone. All eyes turned to him, except Swanborough's.

"Perhaps the Confederate government should take control of all cotton exports and act firmly on the resource, as a unified force."

Swanborough answered, but he looked not at Dorian, but at Stephens. "You do, and you'll see a secession from the secession."

Brown added, "That's why we left the Union in the first place. Perhaps the Confederate government should buy all the cotton and burn it all in one gigantic holocaust!"

There was a touch of laughter, though Brown was serious, but it was approving laughter, and it was accompanied by applause from the cotton men. Swanborough didn't look at Brown either, but he raised his snifter in a toast.

"You're ignoring the important fact," Brown went on. "We don't *want* to export our cotton. The Federal blockade is a godsend! Not one bale is going to those monarchial pigs in Europe until they come forward and formally recognize the Confederate States of America!"

The cotton barons applauded.

Under cover of the ripple, Dorian leaned forward to Wyatt's ear again and whispered, "Albert Gallatin Brown. Senator, Mississippi."

"Thanks," Wyatt murmured back.

The applause dropped off as suddenly as it started, probably in sensitivity to the Vice President. But no one's expression changed.

"We're independent now," Swanborough punctuated.

Then Dorian did something that surprised Wyatt—and everyone. He got up from the windowsill and paced into the middle of the room, where he generally did not like to be at all. Uneasy silence gripped the whole room.

He glared right down at Swanborough, and by his posture forced the other man to look up.

A moment ticked by. Then another. Long enough to make everybody damned nervous.

Finally he spoke.

"We're fighting for the *ideal* of independence," he said. "But we have to get there first. We don't have independence simply because you say we do. We need the North in our economic structure as much as we need slavery. Once our point is made, we'll reunite, and together North and South will be a firm force among world powers. British aristocracy having fear of the South is *your* fantasy, Mr. Swanborough."

"Guess I'm dreaming then," the other man said without inflection. "Britain will loan the Confederacy money out of need for our crop when they see that we're going to win. It's benign coercion, and it's going to work."

Dorian laughed through Swanborough's last sentence. No one could figure out what was funny.

"'Loan,'" he said finally, "is a noun."

Suddenly the whole room was disarmed. The men exchanged puzzled glances, everyone nervous.

This time Swanborough did look up. "What did you say?"

Dorian rocked on his heels and rattled some change in his pocket. He wasn't laughing anymore.

"The verb is 'lend.' You *lend* a loan."

"Really, Captain," Swanborough droned, and sipped his brandy. "This isn't the time."

"Isn't it!"

The sudden fury in Dorian's voice made everyone flinch. He leaned down at Swanborough, his eyes full of warning.

"And when we go before the British Cabinet and ask them to *loan* us money because they need us so badly, they won't hear because they'll be laughing too hard at the Southern hillbillies." Without taking his hands out of his pockets, he pivoted halfway around and said, "This panther piss is filling my bilge. Major Craig, I'll meet you outside whenever you tire of licking this marmalade. Aleck . . . *efkaristo yiatin vradia. Kratisteh ta rehsta.*"

Stephens nodded conspiratorially and raised his brandy in silent salute.

But Dorian was already out the door.

All the men stared at the doorway—with fear he wouldn't come back in, fear that he would.

Wyatt gaped at the empty door frame in empathy, knowing Dorian's inner motivations, and thought about following—

"No self-control," Swanborough muttered, and sipped his drink.

"Even sovereign states must act in a unified manner," Stephens commented. "He knows—"

Suddenly, from the hallway, the oversized lily vase smashed into the door frame, and exploded into a hundred pieces.

The roomful of men stared in astonished silence, afraid to move or speak, as a dozen lilies died on the wooden floor.

Water drained down the wall like blood.

He was halfway down the hall by the time the vase struck the floor and the flowers sank into the spilled water. Blind rage melted against that wall and kept anyone from following him. Even Wyatt didn't come out of that room.

All respect for the walls and rugs, painted molding and wallpaper, dissolved before him. He cared nothing for the trappings of mankind, the dressings, and ruffles and accoutrements. He yanked his steel watch from its quiet rest on his waistcoat, coiled the end of the chain around his hand, instinctively judged the weight of the watch, and began smashing whatever he saw. Pictures in frames on the tables. Flowers in little pots. A chair. Another big vase. A small cherry sideboard, and the flow-blue china teacups set on it to decorate the hall—he smashed them all.

He smashed them. Humanity. He should spit.

He left a wake as ugly as he felt tonight.

Then he swung the watch against his own leg so hard that he staggered.

The accidental blow from his own hand knocked a touch of sense back into him. He leaned against the wall, his thigh throbbing, and let the watch dangle. It bobbed against his ankle at the end of its chain, waiting for him to recover from his fit.

But there was someone else waiting . . .

A voice softened his name until there were only ripples in it.

"Captain Pawthens?"

Dorian gazed in that direction for a blurred second or two and held his breath while his leg's pain subsided. He straightened slowly, retrieved his watch, and carefully piled it and the chain into a pocket, avoiding its razor edges—difficult to do when he was staring at the woman before him.

He steadied himself with a long breath, squared his shoulders, and began moving forward.

"Good evening," he began, "Orienta Swanborough . . ."

CHAPTER TWENTY-SIX

———— ★ ————

"Orienta Swanborough . . ."

He moved toward her, his eyes wide and his brows at their most devilish. He paused and dropped her a bow. When he raised his head, she was blushing and offering him a consummately Southern, genteel smile.

"Captain Pawthens," she murmured, "how kind of you to remember me."

She spoke very slowly, one word at a time, as though to give herself time to think of the next word. And she nearly whispered. If the letters weren't smooth enough by their own nature, she smoothed them out as she spoke them. Her plain looks brought out her unaffected smile.

All he could do was hover before her. She was all circles and globes—round cheekbones, round hair, a round skirt, round breasts caught up in a corset under a shirred cotton blouse. Her hands were white balls at the ends of long dark sleeves. Her shoulders were round too. So were the tip of her chin and her earlobes.

But her eyes were arrowheads. The only pointy things about her, and they smiled all the time. Remarkable.

No one smiles *all* the time.

Dorian's corrosive mood blew away. Her presence kicked his prudence in the groin and knocked it breathless.

"Your name belongs on an opera bill, madam. And I'll bet you carry a fan big enough to cool Congress," he said as he met her beneath the archway. "Are you *Mrs.* Swanborough?"

In that broad Deep South accent that put his mellow Virginia to such a test, she murmured, "Yes . . . I am."

A hundred nasty retorts popped into Dorian's mind and

would have come out had he been talking to anyone else. But she was so unvulgar that he simply couldn't contaminate her with a vulgarity.

"I hope you can forgive Barry," she said faintly, "for striking your friend, sir. . . . Oh, I hope your friend is all right."

"A bit scorched, but rallying," Dorian managed, struggling only slightly to remember what friend she was talking about and who the hell Barry was . . . and what city he was in. . . .

Her restraint made her elegant. Her appearance wasn't severe, but only essential, and behind those eyes Dorian saw a subdued civility. She was looking into his eyes too, and truly seeing him, with great sympathy for him, as though she knew what he had been feeling a moment ago. He was entranced by her simplicity, by the lack of effort that made her face so soft. A hundred memories of childhood flooded back at him, of a time when a slave boy was also the son of the plantation owner and moved in both worlds. There was something about her that brought back those stirring times of security, when his whole world was only a few acres wide and covered with shimmering leaves.

Without realizing he was speaking aloud, Dorian uttered, "Solace in crinoline . . ."

Orienta Swanborough blinked up at him. "I beg pardon?"

Dorian shook himself.

"Pardon," he began. "I regret your witnessing my lack of—" He waved a hand weakly toward the mess in the hallway, but couldn't finish his sentence.

"Oh, no, Captain Pawthens," the woman said softly. "I understand your frustration . . . I have felt it myself these occasions."

"Yes," he moaned. Then he had to clear his throat. He paced away from her a few steps and grumbled at the walls. "Pietistical mummery, some of these occasions," he added with a sign. "A dozen men, each trying to hold his throne with theatrical—"

He turned around, and the sight of the woman once again chopped his words right off his tongue. She was simply standing there, her elbows bent and her hands clasped as though in prayer, radiating tact, and she was genuinely *listening* to him. Suddenly he had no idea what he had been about to say.

Her skirt brushed this way and that as she took two steps toward him, then paused and held out one of her delicate hands. Her gaze took on a concern.

"Captain," she began, "may I invite you to my cottage for tea . . . by way of repairing Barry's treatment of your friend?"

Dorian screwed his brows as though he didn't understand. "Mmm—me?" he stammered.

Her angular eyes twinkled beneath the sand-colored hair. Her round cheeks pinked up, and she glanced at the floor. "Your friend is most welcome as well . . . of course."

"Does your—" Dorian began, then stopped and started again. "Do you live . . . are you and your husband . . . in Richmond?"

"Oh," she murmured, almost as a prelude to apology, "I've been unclear to you. Barry is my husband's brother. I am a widow. If my husband were still among the living, it would be improper for me to speak to you under such circumstances."

Somehow avoiding chortling with relief that this woman wasn't married to that stuck pig Barry, Dorian bottled his sarcasm and wondered, "Circumstances?"

"Oh, yes. You're from Virginia," she breathed, "and I am from Alabama."

He shrugged with his expression, but she offered no further explanation, as if that was enough.

"Yes?" he prodded.

She struggled to be clear. "I am a homebred woman . . . my utter fidelity is to Alabama. But we have purchased a cottage for these occasional visits when my brother-in-law is here to further the War against Northern Aggression."

Her breath seemed to run out, and the sentence ended on a whisper. Her face paled.

In modest discomfort, Orienta Swanborough slipped past Dorian to the middle of the hallway. He was knocked off his perch when she got down on her knees in spite of her hoops and corset, and one by one began picking up pieces of the china set he had broken in his tirade. She glanced up at him forgivingly as she gathered his humiliation off the floor before anyone else saw it.

He took a faltering step forward. "Madam," he mumbled, "you needn't tidy my errors. . . ."

But she beamed up at him. "Oh, Captain, it is my pleasure to serve . . . even in the smallest way."

She turned back to picking up his mess.

Dorian stood in the archway, rendered powerless, his wings utterly clipped. He melted into her pleasantness and found himself speechless, weakened by her company. The feeling bewildered him. He'd been many things before, but speechless wasn't one of them. Normally so ascetic and removed, he struggled to be cold again, but couldn't find it. Suddenly he was in the presence of someone he couldn't be cynical about.

He stooped beside her and also began picking up broken china. Reproachfully he said, "I lost control of myself."

Orienta paused in gathering the bits of flow-blue as if to concentrate on one thing at a time, sat back on her heels, and gazed at him.

"Oh, no, no," she responded. "I respect your depth of conviction, that you dare release your anger. . . . I regret being so dreary and Spartan that I forever buckle to decorum. Not like *you*," she murmured. She beamed at him gratefully. "You are the strength I lack . . . the strength of the Confederacy."

She gazed at him with purer forgiveness and adoration than any he had been offered since he was a child.

Humiliation rammed through Dorian, chased by sudden guilt at misleading her. What could he say? *I'm keeping the South together only long enough to track down my negro slave mother. After that, I don't care what happens. I'm legally a slave myself, you see—*

He nearly choked just on the idea of telling her, of destroying that gracious, prosaic gaze. She was so happy to be picking up broken china. . . .

They heard the other men still arguing down the hallway, none of whom had possessed the nerve to come out of that room yet. The noise shook Dorian out of his trance. He took Orienta's elbow and lifted her to her feet again, and urged her silently to deposit the pieces on the cherry sideboard.

He continued to hold her elbow and turned her. Her massive skirts and underskirts rustled.

"Let us retire into the drawing room," he said, "while the idoloclasts finish their mouth honors."

She said nothing, or at least he *heard* nothing. Her lips

moved in some barely whispered agreement, and she let him usher her away.

"You're very brave, Captain," she uttered. She spoke so breathlessly, he had to strain to hear her. "You wondrous men who keep the Confederacy on its footing. . . . Southern superiority is preordained. . . . The world will collapse with no South to give it a moral foundation. Judgment Day will come if the South should fall."

"You rhapsodize the South, madam," he said as he settled her onto the couch. "Your probity is heartening."

She blushed and hunched her shoulders in a silent giggle. "My brother-in-law says I give to the South what most women give only to Christ Jesus. He says it is a flaw."

Dorian poured himself into her eyes whenever he could get her to look up from her shy downward glances. "Well, your brother-in-law would know all about flaws," he drawled.

She smiled briefly, as though she disapproved, but understood. "Do you enjoy music, Captain?"

"Do you, madam?"

"Oh, my, yes. I believe it is the voice of angels on earth. And our privilege to hear it."

"Do you sing, madam?"

"Oh—pitifully, sir. . . . I play my harp and my clavichord . . . it's nearly one hundred fifty years old. . . . I try to bring some joy into this world in my small way. . . . I sometimes commit to notes the songs of my slaves. Music is the great gift of the negro. Indeed it is their music that made me love them, Captain Pawthens."

"My God, madam, I adore how you say my name. . . ."

Her smile was an opiate. Dorian was drowning in it when a figure moved in the doorway. They both looked up. It was Swanborough. He didn't given Dorian so much as a glance, nor did he react at all to their being together. He acted as though his sister-in-law were the only presence in the room.

"Orienta," he simply said, "we're leaving now. I have your wrap."

He utterly ignored Dorian as the two came to their feet.

Wyatt slipped past Swanborough at the door, taking care not to brush him so they wouldn't have to exchange any false politeness, and hurried to Dorian's side and only noticed at the last moment that Dorian was conversing with a woman. Bottling any comments to Dorian about the evening's goings-on, Wyatt nodded at the woman and received only the shyest of glances back. She was sour-milk homely compared to the women who were Dorian's usual "company," a mere button-hole of a woman. Wyatt was about to interrupt their conversation, but he caught the magnetism on Dorian's face and saw how it was firmly directed to this scarecrowish woman.

The woman was gazing at Dorian through this last moment. She placed her hand over his and murmured, "A visit on the weekend will be most welcome, Captain Pawthens. . . . Perhaps I can entertain you with a melody."

Dorian managed a weak nod. "I . . . I would . . ."

"Orienta," Swanborough snapped. "Now."

Others were also coming down the hallway toward the door, and suddenly the hall was full of slaves offering over-coats, fetching hats, opening doors, and calling for carriages. Some of the guests glanced into the drawing room at Dorian, but only Judah Benjamin had the grace to offer an encouraging nod and a wave good-bye.

Wyatt looked at Dorian to see if he would respond, but Dorian was busy watching Barry Swanborough putting a shoulder cape over the plain-faced lady. This was an expression Wyatt had never seen in his partner's face. So he waved at Secretary Benjamin on Dorian's behalf and hoped the gentleman wouldn't be insulted. Benjamin smiled within his Amish-style beard and nodded his understanding at Dorian's ignoring him.

The guests continued flocking out the big front door, and Swanborough wasted no time pushing his sister-in-law out.

Dorian continued staring at the archway where she had been standing.

"The surfeiting breath," he whispered.

Barry Swanborough handed Orienta's elbow over to his big black coachman and gestured for her to be deposited in his landau. Then he moved toward the horses and nodded good-byes to the other cotton barons, who were likewise dispersing to their carriages. He busied himself adjusting the silk scarf at his throat.

"Sir," his footman said, approaching him with a courteous bow.

"Yes?"

"Here you are, sir." The footman handed him a dollar note, as Swanborough's slaves were required to do with all tips.

Swanborough took the dollar and almost stuffed it into his pocket, but then looked more closely at it and asked, "Where did you get this?"

"That other man, he give it to Buckie."

"Which man?"

"The man he came in with Mr. Stephens."

"Dark hair? Dark eyes? Opera hat? Cape?"

"Yes, sir."

"Interesting. Thank you. See to the lady."

"Yes, sir."

The footman left him alone, but Swanborough didn't get into the landau yet. He stood near the horses and drew in a few gulps of fresh air.

Within a few moments he was joined by a longtime family retainee named Felix Carter. Carter was a lawyer, average in every possible description, and had kept resolutely silent during the meeting inside, and pointedly had kept away from Swanborough. The better to keep their relationship inconspicuous.

They chatted idly about the Southern moguls' willingness to sacrifice their profits for the Confederate cause and getting so little appreciation. Finally the carriages bearing the last few guests were clicking rein and heading down the street, and Swanborough and his lawyer were more or less alone. They kept their voices down.

"Instructions?" Carter asked.

"A problem," Swanborough said. "Who is this Parthens intruder? Do we have any information about him? Where's he from? What's his background?"

"I have no idea."

"Well, I don't like him."

"You don't like him siding with Stephens," Carter corrected.

Swanborough dug for a cigar, leaned forward out of the breeze, and made a great show of lighting it. They both paused to nod good-byes to Christopher Memminger as his carriage clattered past.

Through a puff of smoke and his own gritted teeth, Swanborough said, "Parthens doesn't respect any of us. That's dangerous. He and Craig both have the stink of the North about them."

Carter clasped his hands and nodded, waiting.

"I don't like not knowing the men in my way or where they come from," Swanborough went on. "I want you to look into Parthens. Sniff out his past. I want an advantage over him. See if perhaps you can find one for me."

"Any suggestions about where I should start?"

"Follow his money." Swanborough paused and searched through the pocket of his overcoat to pull out a one-dollar note. "Here. Look what he gave my coachman."

"A dollar."

"A dollar note drawn on a Delaware bank."

"So?" Carter shrugged. "I still have some Northern notes. It hasn't been that long."

"*Lōok* at it, man." His pink face and silver brows glowed as he held the note up into the light of a gaslamp and turned it in front of Carter's face. "It's *new*."

"New . . ."

Suddenly fascinated by the clean-edged, once-folded bank note, Carter took it in two fingers as though it were poison.

"Trace it," Swanborough instructed. "Find out where he does his banking, and you'll find out all about him. Talk to the bankers. Tell them whoever gives us the best information will get our account. Tell them we have one hundred thousand dollars now in New York currency and expect to have a million within a year." He buttoned his coat and drew in a lungful of night air, suddenly self-satisfied. "We'll pull the floor out from under Captain Parthens and his Northern friend."

"You daren't let them stop the cotton hoarding," Carter said.

"I won't let them," Swanborough drawled. "I shall continue to strongly encourage my colleagues in cotton to stick to the embargo." He inhaled deeply and no longer met Carter's eyes. "I'm going to get rich on it."

"Dorian?"

There was no reaction at all.

Wyatt shook his head and muttered, "Well, I expected a lot of things, but not this."

Instinct brought a nervous grin to his lips, seeing his friend so completely disarmed. He pushed a hand into the fold of Dorian's elbow, jostled him, and tried again.

"Say—are you okay?"

Dorian roused a bit, but still stared at the archway. "Have you ever witnessed such . . . such . . . de—de—"

In empathy and relief, Wyatt chuckled. "Cripes, listen to you."

"Decency—" Dorian shoved out. "An Everywoman! She makes me snow-blind . . . did you see her?"

"I think I better help you walk."

"No . . . I'm . . . I'm . . ." Suddenly he laughed at himself, clapped a hand to his forehead, and blurted, "Does this room still *have* a door?"

"You're staring at it," Wyatt reminded. "What say I help you, eh?"

"Pathetic behavior . . . I'm disgusted with myself. Did you witness that? If I lean over, will you kick me soundly? I behaved like a sponge! I may never swagger in self-content again—where are we going?"

"The Vice President wants to see you again."

"I should get myself starched. . . ."

"Somebody else might starch you," Wyatt commented. "I don't think you made a friend of Swanborough by aligning yourself with Stephens."

"What a shame . . . she made not one single demand on me, did you notice that?"

"Well, I wasn't in there, but she seems real nice."

"I find her tasteful. She reminds me of someone . . ."

"Nobody I've ever seen you with. Here we are."

Wyatt pulled him by that arm into the same room where

minutes ago the fate of the South had faltered. Aleck Stephens was alone here now, and looked up from ruminating into the fireplace when Wyatt pulled Dorian in and closed the door.

"Well, I found him," he said. "Not sure what state he's in, though."

"Dorian! I'm profoundly sorry," Stephens said immediately. "I never planned to subject you to that."

Tugging out a handkerchief, Dorian dabbed at his brow and muttered, "My kind of torture . . ."

Trying to muster his apathy, he wandered away. He felt Wyatt's eyes following him with silent concern until the Vice President interrupted.

"You see what we're up against, Major Craig," Stephens said. "We're all frustrated."

"Seems to me you're frustrated because none of you are doing jobs you're right for," Wyatt responded.

"How do you mean?"

"*You* ought to be President, for one."

"Oh, Major, you're too kind."

Wyatt swung toward him and waved off the mutual compliments. "Sir, no offense, but I'm not saying this to be kind. Jeff Davis should've been Secretary of War, since he's pretty much doing that job. And Mr. Benjamin ought to be secretary of state instead of Secretary of War, and Toombs should be secretary of the treasury instead of secretary of state." He shook his head and paced out his confusions. "I've never seen such a muddle of misplaced titles."

"True," was all the Vice President said.

"And this cotton embargo is going to bankrupt the Confederacy for sure," Wyatt added. "With enough money the South can hold out forever, and these men are burning the money."

Stephens nodded silently, went to a serving cart, fastidiously arranged three small glasses, and began pouring wine into them.

"Well, gentlemen," he said, "things are still cooking in Britain, and now we know which way the tide of Confederate business will want to flow. Therefore, it's up to the three of us to do whatever we can, covertly or otherwise, as conscience and duty dictate to rescue the nation from itself."

He delivered wine to Wyatt, and Dorian came to the middle

of the room to get his own. Then Stephens placed a hand over his heart and raised his glass.

"May this Christmas find us resolute, and the new year of 1862 see the right kind of victory to save the United States of America as the whole she should be. If our hopes are to be blasted, if the Republic is to go down . . . let us be found on the deck with the Constitution waving over our heads!"

THE BURNING FUSE

24 DECEMBER 1861

Lonely soldiers and their families spend Christmas apart. In inactive camps the young men of the Federal and Confederate armies stand guard over a stalled war that has yet to really get started, bloodied only by pointless skirmishes in Kentucky, Missouri, and other isolated places.

25 DECEMBER 1861—CHRISTMAS DAY

More skirmishes and scouting movements . . . Virginia, Maryland, Missouri, and the coast of North Carolina.

The United States of America and the Confederate States of America spend Christmas as two separate nations. Lord Lyons has met with U.S. Secretary of State Seward and demanded the release of Mason and Slidell into British hands. President Lincoln says he will decide about Mason and Slidell tomorrow.

26 DECEMBER 1861

The U.S. Cabinet decides that the Trent *affair has been humiliating, troublesome, and far more dangerous than if Mason and Slidell had gone to Europe unhindered. Dividing itself between two wars cannot possibly further the stability of the United States. Ambassador Mason may continue on his voyage to Britain, and Ambassador Slidell may continue on to France, where they will respectively attempt to minister the advancement of the Confederacy in the eyes of Europe.*

The United States is embarrassed, the Confederacy appears gallant, yet the Davis administration cannot honorably take credit for the diplomatic audacity of a U.S. Navy captain.

The Confederacy has survived the year, but remains wanting of the recognition it desperately needs to become a nation.

———————— ★ ————————

CHAPTER TWENTY-SEVEN

— ★ —

One war at a time.

—Abraham Lincoln

SOMEWHERE IN NORTHERN VIRGINIA, NEAR THE MARYLAND
BORDER, THE MIDDLE OF THE NIGHT

"This way! Down to the creek! Hurry along . . . this isn't the
time to dawdle."

The countryside was rolling and forgiving. Exhaustion running up a long slope, relief running down the next. Over and
over, slope after slope. Grazing country. The very description
of America for which immigrants came yearning. The fulfill-
ment of foreign visions. Just ahead . . . Maryland.

Maryland. Where a thousand dreams waited.

Crystallized over the long northern winter, washed in
spring with fresh rains, veined with rivers that never grew too
warm, cooked beneath a summer sun that coaxed brilliant
plumage from long grasses, flowers, and harvests, licked by
the endless ocean on one side, girded by bulbous green-and-vi-
olet mountains on the other, the meat of dreams and the step-
ping-stone of travelers from all directions, heading
everywhere.

This time the travelers were from the South. The boiling indecision of Maryland, pocked with violence and venting fears,
long known as a swing state and even now holding only tenuously to the Union, would later tonight provide a kind of
shield for the travelers. If they got there safely.

Before them was the border between two states that were at war. Ahead, Maryland wasn't proslave country, but it wasn't exactly freedom country either. It was the land of the incoming. Into the great port at Baltimore the world's hungry and disenchanted came seeking a drink from Fountain America. Very few of them had ever seen a negro face before. To them, a negro face meant only one thing—threat to a job for which the newcomer had abandoned family and home and traveled hundreds of sea-tossed, disease-infested miles at unthinkable risk.

Maryland. The boiling state.

Tonight the travelers ran as much as possible, carrying the smallest children and pulling the others. They had passed the broken fence with the two apple trees. Instructions had been for each of them to eat an apple, for strength. Now they had to find the creek. They would go along the creek until they came to a bridge, which was the road into town. Continue along the creek to the row of houses. Somebody will be there with a candle.

After traveling the civilized world himself, Alexander Wallace had come to the conclusion that there were no children in the world as well behaved as black American children. These children knew from their first breath that they must behave, or there would be payment either from them or from their families. Constantly in fear of separation, just as white children were taught to fear hell, negro children were quiet and observant. Family was the negro's only possession, therefore greatest pride. A man who could make a family and keep it together was honored among his kind.

Usually Alex did not come quite this far up the state himself. Usually he passed along the instructions of how to judge distance, how far to go, where to head, and how to go by the stars and the moon. Get to within sight of the glowing lights of the town, go to the creek, walk in the water so the dogs can't follow, then go five houses into town on the first street. Often he had to explain to them what "five" was. Same as the fingers on a hand.

Tonight Alex had come to deliver the cargo himself, because there were many more children traveling than adults, and one of the adults was a very old woman. Two slave families followed Alex tonight. One family—made up of a man,

his mother, and his two grown daughters and their babies—
had come to Alex by way of several handwritten notes with
the right signals drawn in the corners, one station to a corner,
funneled from Arkansas. The second family—a man, woman,
a twelve-year-old boy, three children under ten, and two toddlers given to them by negroes who couldn't get away but
wanted their children free—Alex had picked up from a face-
less voice in a boat. The voice had spoken with a strong southern Georgia accent. The slaves weren't talking about where
they had come from, and in the four days together Alex hadn't
asked, nor would he. They were all thin and had probably been
traveling for weeks, giving their only food to the youngest
children. He shuddered every time he looked at the smallest
ones; there had probably been severe punishment for the mothers once the babies were discovered missing. Such was the
Deep South.

Yet Alex knew what mothers would do for their children,
and he clung to that whenever his motivations began to trem-
ble.

There was little satisfaction in this work for any white man
or woman. No reports of success ever came back along the
chain. There would be no sighs of relief that lasted, no com-
panionship in times of danger, no tales of victory or adventure
over secret coffee. Certainly he gained no friends in whom to
take solace, or even to trust.

There was only the torchless corridor leading toward New
York or Canada into which he had no choice but to funnel his
charges, never to know what became of them. He rarely had a
hint of routes beyond the next twenty-five miles. Messages
were relayed in discarded bottles, tucked under piles of manure, where no one would ever think to look. He had to endure
the terrorized white-ringed eyes of the people he led, the danger he meant to them, which was always greater than the
hope—for they were leaving lives of confinement, yes, but rel-
atively safe and secure confinement. All slaves had heard
about freedom, and some talked about it. Some dreamed about
it. But only when a slave was already on the tracks, unable to
turn back, did he get that awful realization of what true risk
was all about. That was life on the Railroad, for blacks and
whites.

Now there was this new complication . . . war.

Since the armies began moving, stations had winked out all along the Maryland–Virginia border with no explanations. Very few remained. Risks had lengthened considerably.

Alex stomped through his own anger toward himself. He should have done this years ago. Think how many slaves he could have saved if he'd only started five or six years ago, when the borders were open!

But no. He'd let Dorian talk him out of it. Dorian had been protecting him, but Alex knew now he should have stood up to Dorian and insisted upon taking action against the brutality of slavery. Instead he had sacrificed Dorian, Yula, their mother's happiness, his own sense of honor . . . all to remain safe and quiet. How many other white men were there like himself, who had stalled to take action because they couldn't think of what action to take? Free the negroes? And put them where?

Dorian, why did I listen to you? Why didn't you stand with me and prove that negroes could learn and excel? If there had to be slavery for the South to survive, we could have stood up for humane treatment of slaves throughout the South. We could have passed laws and exacted punishment for failure to meet standards. Instead, we let slavery reach this breaking point, where I must put these people into a boat with many holes and hope they make it to shore before they sink—

"Dogs!"

Everyone stopped, held their breath—listened—

The baying of bloodhounds in the distance!

Well named, for they would rip their prey to pieces.

The smallest children began to whimper, then to cry. They had heard what those dogs would do to them. No slave child in the South went without hearing the hideous and utterly true stories about dogs. Very few blacks liked or trusted dogs—for good reason.

Alex swung around toward the sound, tried to gauge its distance. Then he hurried forward, scavenging in the dark for his charges. He found his little band of escapees huddled like quails in the grass, except for the twelve-year-old boy, who was pulling on his father and begging for action.

"Go!" Alex shouted. "Don't stop now! Run! Run for the creek!" He drew his pistol and waved it high. *"Run!"*

The slaves saw the pistol. They scooped up the littlest children and ran.

Alex almost called that the gun was for the dogs, but the negroes were already running, and if it got them going, then fine. Maybe if he fired a shot or two, they would learn to fly.

If there were dogs, the slave hunters wouldn't be more than two or three miles back. If they were on foot, Alex calculated twenty minutes of leeway. If they were on horseback—

"Hurry!" Alex called to his charges. "This is no time to stop! I'll hold the dogs at—"

Too late.

Black forms broke out of the trees into the moonlight, plunging through the overgrowth so fast and low to the ground that the landscape hissed. Hounds! Trained slave-hunting dogs. Three . . . four . . . five of them!

Alex immediately took a rough instinctive aim and fired. A form stumbled, rolled, and fell. He squinted into the vagueness of night movements, aimed, fired again—but it took a third shot to bring down the second dog, and two more shots to bring down the third. The third dog shrieked and lay in the grass, yowling horribly, and Alex had only one bullet left. He aimed at a form streaking toward him, but he missed. The damnation of night!

That was all the time he was allowed. The other two dogs were on him! White teeth flashed in the light, lips peeled back and glossy with saliva—

—but they charged right past him, brushing his legs, and headed directly for the escaping slaves!

Alex spun full about and called, "Here! Here! Come here, boys, come here!"

But the dogs knew better. They were trained to seek out *dark* faces, to sniff out slave scents. Easy enough—they smelled of the field and the cooking hearth, not of the manor house and the fireplace. If they were allowed to bathe at all, they didn't bath with the same soap, or even the same water, as wealthy whites.

"Go ahead!" Alex called to the negroes. "Keep going!"

The two dogs charged toward the slaves, who were holding the smallest children over their heads and up on their shoulders. The children shrieked their high-pitched horror, the dogs growled and snapped, then attacked.

God, what sounds! What an awful gaggle of noises! The only one fighting was the twelve-year-old black boy. He kicked at the two dogs' faces until one of them got him by the foot and wouldn't let go. Apparently that was what the boy had in mind, for he fell to the ground and let the dog have his foot, while waving and shouting, "Ge' gawn!" to the others.

"Do what he says!" Alex called as he ran toward them. "Run!"

As he shouted out his anger, he reached the boy and began beating at the animal with his empty pistol until the dog turned loose of the boy's foot, recovered, and turned on Alex.

Alex felt the creature get a grip on his arm and forced himself to think clearly—his arm was padded with his thick woolen overcoat. The pressure of those jaws was agonizing, but the teeth might not penetrate—

"Go! Go!" he called to the boy.

The boy got up on a mangled foot and hobbled toward the creek. The older girls clutched their babies to their bosoms and went in leaps through the high creek-side grass, right down into the water. Then they splashed foward, following the middle of the creek toward the glowing lights of the town. They had the sense to stop screaming as soon as they hit the water, and put all their breath into struggling upstream.

On the slope the last hound tore at the two grown men and their children. The men were each holding children over their heads as the other dog snarled and tore chunks of skin from their legs, coveting the tender young limbs held just high of jumping range. The men shouted at each other, argued, then one of them started running while the other kicked at the dog and annoyed it enough to keep it from chasing the others. The children screamed, the dog snapped and tore out a chunk of the remaining man's thigh—

Until the man's old mother—the one everybody had forgotten about—came out of a shadow with a broken branch.

Without uttering a sound she plunged the ragged point of the branch into the back of one hound's neck.

The dog made a strange supernatural sound—and collapsed.

Only half-aware of all this, Alex was a hundred feet away, fighting for balance against the enormous hound that had him by the arm and was nearly pulling it out of the sleeve. The natural human terror of being eaten nearly drove him insane, and he battled against his own fears to remember that he was doing this for a reason.

"You need help, mistuh?" the negro man called. He handed the child to his mother and clutched at his bleeding thigh.

"No!" Alex choked. "Go, please!"

In seconds the awful sounds of the children's crying and the splashing of creek water began to fade northward. The fading would be his only reward.

Suddenly he wanted to hear it. *Really* hear it.

Without a dog snarling in his ear and wrenching at his arm!

He drew a deep breath, forced himself to think clearly, took a wild swing with his other arm, and caught the dog in the side of the skull with a crushing blow of the pistol.

The dog's jaw clamped tighter on his arm—then the hind legs went limp, and Alex found himself dragging a dead hound with a locked jaw. The sudden weight almost yanked him over.

He bent forward to let the ground take some of the animal's weight, and pried the twitching, slobbering jaws from his arm. His hand was nearly numb, but he was free.

The hounds were all dead.

Alex staggered back a step and surveyed his strange victory. He kicked the dead dog away. It flopped over. The last lungful of breath heaved out of it.

"Oh . . . oh, my Lord . . . my Lord," he gulped. His arm felt as though it had been twisted off at the elbow. To his astonishment he found his woolen sleeve nearly shredded. Another few seconds, the dog would've been through to his flesh.

"Whoever said," he gasped, "a firearm had to be loaded!"

The terrorized group of slaves splashed down the creek without remembering to stay quiet. Anyone nearby would hear the splashing—but they didn't care. Panic had set in, and they no longer heard themselves. The children were bawling. The older girls were gasping out high-pitched yelps with every step, the men were shouting at them, and the only one with any common sense was the hobbling twelve-year-old. He kept hissing at the others to "Shet up! Shet up!"

Then—there was a candle. The tiny light was amazing in the darkness. A candle in the light of a half-moon . . .

And a spirit carrying it . . . a young ghost in a white night-dress, with a white face and huge eyes the color of water—piles and piles of white-blond ringlets—

The slaves fell silent. Was this *the* candle?

"This way," the pile of ringlets called. "This way quickly, please!"

As his family and the others gaped like empty skulls, the twelve-year-old looked around frantically and started adding up houses. Had they passed the right finger of house? Thumb . . . pointing finger . . . middle finger . . . finger on the almost-end . . . little finger on the end—

"Papa, it the right finger!" he called to his father. "I mean it the right house! Do what she say!"

He grabbed one of the exhausted toddlers, hung the child on his hip, and hobbled toward the girl.

"You can call me Flo," the girl said. She reached to help the old grandmother up out of the creek. "This way, ma'am."

And out of the night came three more spirits in satin night-clothes, bobbing curls catching the moonlight so brightly they didn't need torches. They carried blankets and without being asked started wrapping the soaked refugees. They took the babies and led the way without formality up toward the house.

At a cellar door a white child of five or six years with glittering amber curls was watching the way the slaves had come. Extremely well trained, the little boy allowed his curiosity only a glance or two at the incoming negroes. Primarily he paid attention to the countryside with his giant doe-eyes. He knew he was a big boy, big enough to let out a yip if he saw anybody coming.

The twelve-year-old black boy looked around. He was beginning to get the idea of all this. He made a bet with himself—

And sure enough, in a second-story window there was another face—about the same age as this little boy, or maybe a little older. That face also wasn't looking down at the slaves, but was watching the street that led up from the south end of town.

The boy had to stop suddenly when the old grandmother pulled at Flo's bulbous satin sleeve.

"This baby here, she gotta have goat's milk," the old woman said, pointing at one of the infants. "She throw up when she get cow's milk."

"Yes, ma'am," Flo said. "We got that message, and we have a nanny goat waiting out back to feed the baby. Come this way, ma'am."

The old negro woman hesitated and peered curiously at the girl.

"Is something wrong, ma'am?" Flo asked her.

A little croak of disbelief came up from the grandmother's throat. "I'm sevenny-fo yee'ode . . . an' I ain' nevvuh bin cawed ma'am befo'!"

Flo patted the old woman's hand, then took her elbow and said, "Then I shall call you ma'am for as long as you are with us. So shall my brothers and sisters, every one."

The old woman shook her head and muttered all the way into the cellar.

Flo led the odd queue into the specially designed cellar.

Designed to be used as a safe haven, then put back quickly to appear to be just a cellar—in case one of the parents decided to come down here on one of their rare visits to their own home.

Luckily that didn't happen very often. Colonel Richard and his wife were off being uppity in Philadelphia, going about their fancy-pants ballerina business almost as if there wasn't a war going on.

Funny how things worked out. The Richards were gone lots anyway, and now that the war was on, they had trouble traveling back and forth over the state border, so they stayed gone even longer.

So the cellar could stay nice and cozy, and runaway slaves could go in and out just like a real-live railroad station.

As she straightened from fixing beds for the babies she knew were coming, Yula beamed at her beautiful white children. Flo, Charlotte, Ernest, and Abigail were busying themselves in the care of the new negroes with the enthusiasm that struck other white children only at Christmastime. She never saw her children happier than when there were runaway slaves under the Richard house.

She knew Malcolm was in the kitchen, stirring the broth that would warm these people, and that David was keeping an eye on that road. Her pride made her shiver.

She'd loved a white baby before, but that one had come out of her own body. Never had she imagined she could find it inside herself to love children quite *this* white. She knew who the *real* family was in this house—the Richard children, the cook, the footman, and herself. The actual parents had nothing to do with family in this household.

It was the bain of wealthy whites all over the modern South—their children were raised by negro mammies, and if the parents failed to instill class supremacy into their children, they grew up caring for negroes. Thus were born the confused second and third generations of wealthy slave-owning whites—their parents were saddled either with insensitive snobs or guilt-ridden abolitionists for children. An astonishing number of Railroad conductors were the sons of the Southern self-made.

Yula would never have guessed it might be so. She hadn't liked white people all that much before she opened her Underground Railroad station. She had always thought she was opening her station *because* of white folks. She'd even avoided white people who tried to contact her on the U.G.R.R. She hadn't trusted them.

They'd chipped away at her distrust, however. She had too often seen the white folks push and nudge and cajole reluctant negroes up the line, shoving the negroes onward beyond their own second thoughts. Never give up, never stop to rest, never lose hope. Bottle up that fear. Hush up that child. Don't lose the chance. Freedom's good. You'll make it. Don't quit. Get them feet moving.

She had also come to realize that the white folks were the ones who took the ugliest risks. If slaves were caught running on the Underground Railroad, including former slaves like herself who were participating, they would be sold back into slavery or delivered back to their owners. Perhaps they would have to start over.

But the whites . . . they'd be put up against walls and shot.

The blacks put their well-being on the line for their own

freedom; the whites put their own blood and breath on the line for someone else's freedom.

Yula looked out the cellar door and saw the flicker of the Virginia conductor's blond hair and white face in the very distant moonlight, on the opposite side of the creek.

She knew she would never think about white folks the same way again.

Alex Wallace leaned forward and dragged for breath. There was no hurry now. The winking out of the distant candle told him the cargo had been delivered and were being tucked away. He coughed a few times and rubbed his aching arm. Damn these hunting breeds of dog back to England or Norway or wherever they started . . . hounds and retrievers and all the kinds that sniff for a living—

He forced himself to move along, back southward. Now he himself was the only evidence, and there were no dogs left to lead their masters to him. In the darkness he could hide anywhere. Tomorrow he could go into town, board a train, and be back in Tidewater in a few days.

He looked up at the single squinted eye of the half-moon.

"I'm twenty-seven," he gasped, "and I'm already too old for this sort of work."

He jumped sideways when a sound flew up at him from the grass. He drew his pistol out of his belt—ready, aim . . . empty.

That's right. Come out or I'll threaten you to death.

He shook his head.

"I'm losing my mind," he muttered.

He picked his way forward, toward the sound. One of the dogs he'd shot, still alive and whimpering, scratching at the grass.

It was a black dog with brown markings. Alex had seen drawings in British books in his father's library. A Gordon setter. Pretty dog, except for the circumstances of its training. Not as heavy-boned as most slave-hunting dogs. In other parts of the world, this dog would be hunting birds, not negroes.

Of course, in others parts of the world, dogs hunted anything *but* negroes.

The dog whined, raised its pointy head, and looked pleadingly up at Alex, pawing at him. Not quite the hellhound it had seemed minutes ago. Much like the negroes, it had learned to look to the nearest white man to make a decision.

Alex tried to hate the dog, but couldn't. So he knelt down into the moist grass on his aching leg and showed the animal that though death flies out of the night after a loud boom, there could also be one last tender touch.

"Sorry, old man," he said. "I have no bullet left with which to finish you off. But I'll wait here until you go."

★

———— ★ ————

PART SIX

CRY "DEFIANCE!"
1862

★ ★ ★

THE BURNING FUSE

1 JANUARY 1862

Commissioners Mason and Slidell board the British sloop Rinaldo. The Trent *affair is over, but leaves a stain over international relations for both the United States and the Confederate States which will affect foreign considerations of the American war.*

Stonewall Jackson's forces are moving toward the hot spot of western Virginia. Skirmishes and bombardments pepper the area, and parts of lower Maryland.

The first week of January, in Pensacola, Florida . . . Coosaw River, South Carolina . . . Dayton, Missouri . . . Big Bethel, Virginia . . . Hunnewell and Columbus, Missouri . . . Bath, Huntersville, Slane's Cross Roads, Sir John's Run, Great Cacapon Bridge, Alpine Depot, all in western Virginia: skirmishes, skirmishes, skirmishes. A war of skirmishes.

General McClellan is flat on his back, ill, so President Lincoln confers with other generals in attempts to get the Union armies actually moving for a change. He requires of Generals Halleck and Buell to specify a day when they will begin to move.

★

CHAPTER TWENTY-EIGHT

———— ★ ————

5 JANUARY 1862
THE CRAIG HOUSE, GOVERNOR STREET, RICHMOND

As she turned into the imperial gloom of the grand house's brick-and-iron fence and started up the marble steps, Grace found herself face-to-face with a plain woman in half-mourning dress—a blue jacket, blue-and-pink bonnet with a pink ribbon, but a completely black skirt, and black lace gloves. The woman was puritanically unadorned—no jewelry, very little lace, hair in a simple roll—but she was obviously a lady of some means and carried with her a concentrated Southernness that Grace could have seen in the dark with a stick. There were two female slaves with the woman, each carrying a big wicker basket loaded with what looked like rags, old clothes, or both.

Grace took a little start at the woman's face between those two black slaves, because the white woman's cheeks were almost celery green in the early daylight. Whalebone corsets that nearly cut women's waists in half tended to make them pale and breathless, and this one was a good example.

A tickle ran up Grace's arms when she saw that face—recalling her upbringing in the Kansas netherlands with nothing to wear under her rag but another rag, and a mother who couldn't tell a corset from a dead cat. What some women would wear . . .

She hunched inside her coat, pushed her bonnet back a little, and mounted the steps. "Can I help you?"

The celery woman had been about to pull the doorbell when they all saw Grace coming home and turned to meet her.

"Oh—" the white woman began. "Are you the mistress of the household? Mrs. Craig?"

Grace pushed back a stray lock of hair from her forehead and said, "Yes, I'm Grace Craig. Something I can do for you?"

"I met your husband ever so briefly in town, and I have discovered that he is a prominent man of business in Richmond. I'm calling upon the wives of such gentlemen, collecting old clothing, towels, and rags . . ."

She didn't finish the sentence, but fanned a hand at the slaves and their baskets.

"What are you doing with rags?" Grace asked as she came up to an even step with the breathless socialite. They all huddled against a chilly morning wind.

"Oh, some other ladies in town and I are making uniforms for our gallant soldiers—"

"With rags?" Grace blurted.

The woman smiled shyly. "Oh, my goodness, no . . . but the uniforms are taking nearly all the new cotton and wool. All the gold and silver, of course, is being sent to buy armaments in Europe. But we must not forget that the average citizen will still need clothing . . . farmers and laborers are generously abandoning their very families to defend the honor of the Confederacy. So we are gathering donations of dry goods, to make clothing for the children of the soldiers, and for the little negro children whose masters have turned their funds to the cause of the war. Mrs. Craig, they won't have clothing this year . . . is there anything in your household which you can spare?"

It had been a snake of a morning so far. Grace had been at the mill for four days straight and was just coming back here to keep up the wife look and to see if there was anything in Wyatt's office here that would be of any use to Pinkerton, to take to McClellan, to get this stupid war going and done with. She stood in front of this woman, looking into those sharp, hopeful eyes, and sighed. All of a sudden it didn't seem quite so bad a day. There was something about this woman that was so utterly selfless—and when she talked about the children . . .

They were nobody. Destitute settlers upon whom the political onus had fallen. They were just poor whites, for whom there was no escape once they had found a trickle of sustenance. These people were slaves in their way too, slaves to the

*tannery down below and the paltry wage their son could
scratch out as an errand boy. Scrawny, happy Patrick . . .*

"Well," she sighed, "reckon there's got to be a thread or
two in there for you. Do you want rugs too? Blankets? Come
on inside and I'll rustle you up a bundle."

The woman actually got tears in her eyes. "Oh, Mrs.
Craig—I would be so grateful!"

Feeling somewhat untrimmed next to this woman, Grace
pushed open the wide front door, and both their skirts swished
through at the same time. The slave women stayed on the
porch until Grace waved at them and ordered, "Inside. Nobody
should be standing on marble in the middle of winter."

"Yes'm," they chimed, as though practiced to that response.

Grace pushed the heavy door closed only seconds before
Edmund arrived to capture her coat as she shook it off and
offer to take the lady's and apologize for not opening the door
for her.

"Don't be a wart, Edmund," Grace said. "That's the day
when I can't push my own door open in front of me. Give
these people a hot drink while I go rumble around in some
closets."

"Yes, Mrs. Craig." Edmund made a little bow. "You two,
come with me," he said to the two females slaves. After a nod
from their mistress, they followed Edmund through the servants' kitchen entrance in the depths of the hallway.

Grace peeled off her bonnet and handed it to the lady.
"Here. You can start with this."

"The very hat from your head!" the woman gasped, and
grew paler. "You're too kind, Mrs. Craig."

"No, I'm not really."

"And your husband—" The woman caught Grace's wrist as
she tried to turn.

Grace paused. "You know my husband?"

The woman retracted her hand and clutched the silk drawstring bag she carried. "We have not been formally introduced . . . but Major Craig is a fine young man."

"Is he?"

"Oh, I can see it in his eyes. . . ."

"Can you?"

"He's got a good, good heart."

"Wouldn't say that. You want to come with me through the house and tell me what's usable and what's best left?"

"Oh, Mrs. Craig, your judgment will suffice for us, to be sure."

Grace shrugged, started up the carpeted stairway, then turned back at the last moment and asked, "Did you say what your name was and did I miss it?"

The woman never got a chance to speak for herself.

Movement and conversation at the top of the three-story staircase drew their attention and made them look up.

"Benjamin cracked right down on speculation across the whole Confederacy, yesterday. Mostly on saltpeter. Now it's a crime to withhold almost anything from the market. Saltpeter prices may not be stable, but at least they won't be held artificially high because of the war."

"Judah Benjamin is a gentle giant in the world of international finance—gentle until he comes upon a giant. However, I refuse to be impressed with market stability considering the pot we're in."

"Niter's not easy to find these days at any price, that's my big worry. I can get flowers of sulfur from Sicily and sublime it right here on site, but everybody's afraid to sell us their niter because it's so rare, and selling it to us signifies support for the Confederacy. It's the explosive item in more ways than one now."

The voices and footsteps came down to the second-story level as the women were held silent by the conversation of men—and Grace was listening now, very carefully.

"Perhaps we can procure our own."

"How? You mean buy a ship and bring saltpeter around the Horn ourselves?"

"No. Procure it for ourselves in Chile, ship it up to Panama, and mule-train it overland to the Gulf of Mex—"

"Through that vomit of jungle? Dorian, it'll cost a year's pay to the month to bribe men to go through that!"

"Paleface, when have you had to worry about money since you took my claw? Money is fluid, my friend. There's always more to be made. One can start with nothing, and believe me I started with nothing—"

At the top of the second-floor landing, Dorian stopped as though caught on a thorn. Words, body.

Because he saw *her* at the bottom of the stairway.

And it wasn't Grace he was seeing. It was her antithesis.

His lips parted, but there was no more sound. He simply paused on the third step from the top and left Wyatt to wander on down alone, glancing back at him until finally approaching the woman in the black skirt.

Wyatt also had stopped, saw the visitor and the slaves, but the woman he ended up staring at was his own wife.

He looked down at Grace's hard and stoic expression that cooled even more when she saw him, her look reminding him yet again of the condition of their marriage. To this day she was as distant as the day they'd met—not in body, but in heart. She tended his business as if it were her own, she tended his household, she kept up her own cottage at the mill, and she had continued teaching the mill's children even though she was now a married woman. She insisted that wartime made things different. Married women, all women, would find things demanded of them that would never be acceptable in peacetime. She even came to his bed at night.

But there was nothing else.

He came down the stairs first, questioning her with his eyes to see if today would be the day she would accept him in her heart.

In moments he saw there was no hope yet.

He simply touched her arm in silent communication as was his habit with his workers, or anybody. He focused on the visitor.

"Miss Swanborough?" he began.

Gazing up the stairs, Orienta Swanborough blinked and gave Wyatt spare attention. "Oh . . . I'm . . . a widow, sir. . . ."

She continued looking upward, past Wyatt.

On the third step from the top, Dorian, the unapproachable pariah, almost forgot to put his foot out when his hand started slipping down the madeira rail. Gradually, though, he made his way down the stairs toward them.

"Sorry," Wyatt muttered. "*Mrs.* Swanborough." He studied the woman for a moment, trying to see whatever it was that Dorian saw. But he sure couldn't see it. "Where's Edmund? Haven't we got tea or something in the house?"

"Brewing," Grace stuck in.

The two of them stood awkwardly while Dorian and

Orienta stared through them at each other. Dorian was his usual aloof self, except that he was uncharacteristically quiet. His lips were curved in a wry grin, which most people would take as arrogance, but which Orienta Swanborough took as a compliment. They could all see that in her eyes.

"What . . ." Wyatt began.

"They're here collecting old clothes and fabric," Grace explained, "to make clothing for needy children."

"Oh, isn't that nice—"

"A balsam for our ills," Dorian murmured.

Normally such a remote baronet, Dorian had fixed on Orienta Swanborough's smiling reception. And she appeared grateful even for his smallest attention.

Within seconds Grace and Wyatt were both itching to escape. This stageless play unfolding before them was so unlike their own relationship that they were suddenly too aware of each other.

Grace met her husband's eyes, but felt herself submerge at the same instant. As always, she shielded the storm of frustrations and refused to let him see the swirl.

Damn, it was hard to hate him. She had to work constantly to remain committed to her own purpose. She had to avoid him, keep away from that accommodating manner of his and the sad confusion in his face when he looked at her and wondered what he had done or what he was failing to do. She knew he was confused. She didn't dare start explaining, or it would all begin to sound like the machinations of a frivolous, vengeful white-trash yokel.

Maybe that's all it was—but they were *her* frivolous, vengeful doings. She had obligations. What could she do? Cast away what the fates had put on her? Her parents and Patrick would rise up from the cold night ground and drag her to hell if she failed to see this through. There were obligations in a family. That's why animals were born from other animals instead of popping out of flashes of light. So there'd be family. Somebody to stick with. Somebody to beat off an attack. Or punish one so that the future would be warned.

But right over there, not ten feet away, the dangerous Dorian stood completely bowled over by a woman. He and Orienta were staring at each other without even conversing, as if that were enough between a man and a woman. Their light cast back upon Grace and her husband and made them both feel inadequate.

Hell if it wasn't just like playing Milton Bradley's *Checkered Game of Life,* trying to reach Happy Old Age while using her own bedamned buttons as game pieces!

To her relief Edmund reappeared with an enormous tray of tea and cakes.

The slave nodded for Orienta to follow him. "This way, madam, into the parlor?"

The woman's small eyes fluttered as Edmund walked around her into the parlor archway.

"Oh—thank you," she whispered. With a last glance at Dorian, she followed Edmund into the parlor.

"I'll just do the upstairs," Grace said, hauled her skirts up, and took the steps at a run.

"I'll round up a few things from the basement," Wyatt called up.

Dorian came out of his trance and blurted, "And I'll help you—"

He twisted at the waist, but a hand caught the back of his collar, thrust him into an about-face, shoved him into the receiving parlor archway so hard it made him gasp. There was an extra push for good measure. Then Wyatt was gone and Dorian was gritting his teeth in frustration—while Edmund poured *two* cups of tea.

"Here's yours, Cap'm," the mulatto said, "right next to the lady's."

"Edmund . . . thank you," Dorian growled. He came stiffly forward and accepted the hot cup with obvious reluctance. "God *will* reward you, along with Mr. Wyatt."

Edmund chuckled. "Praise the Lord, sir," he responded under his breath, and slipped out of the room.

Orienta Swanborough arranged her voluminous skirts on a love seat, the significance of which was not lost on Dorian at this particular moment. Never mind that he also did not want to sit that close to her.

But in a moment he was sitting beside her. A most comfortable place, despite internal warnings. What was it about her that was so different from any hundred other women on any hundred streets? So different from the women who had thrown themselves at him for his company, his money, his attention, or what they imagined was his status?

There was something in her eyes that he hadn't seen since—

The awareness rushed away, like a bat in the night. Was it a memory? Or something he had only wished for too long ago to recall clearly? What was this magnet she held for him?

Though he knew all his own dangers, Dorian succumbed to curiosity. Perhaps the bat would fly back in, and he could tag it.

She handed him his teacup, then sipped her own, but her eyes never left him.

"How long," Dorian began, "have you been in mourning, madam?"

"Seven months . . . since my husband passed on to his reward. He was a few years my senior, but a robust man," she said. She spoke very slowly. "It will always be my suspicion that the doctor failed to diagnose my husband's ailment correctly."

"Doctors," Dorian agreed. "I often wonder how much medical science kills us. Look what they did to Robert Burns. A man with a chronic heart condition, and the doctor had him bathing up to his neck in the cold briny sea."

"A friend of yours?" she asked.

He blinked. "Madam, it was the year 1796."

"Oh!" she exclaimed, and chuckled at herself. "The poet Robert Burns . . . that's whom you mean."

With a touch of relief, Dorian sighed, "Of course."

He smiled at her, and suddenly she seemed to think of something different. Her attitude changed completely, and she gave this new thought her entire attention.

"You have such a striking coloration, Captain," she uttered, openly looking at individual parts of his face and hair. "Those ebony curls . . . your eyes, so large, with those dark lashes and brushed brows. A woman would die to possess natural lines around her eyes such as yours. But the lids are pale . . . and do you know your eyes curve just the slightest downward at the outsides . . ."

She raised her hands toward his eyes, outlined the shapes with her fingertips, but never actually touched him.

"They're rented," Dorian said.

A wider smile broke on the woman's face. She seemed to admire him for that far more than the joke deserved.

"There's a bit of the swarthy about you," she said, "but it's . . . it's not the dirty kind—if you understand me. Your lips are arched and so well defined . . . like a painting. You are clearly of strong ethnic descent. Are you Spanish, Captain?"

Dorian's stomach quivered as she analyzed his features, which before this moment had never frightened him. He knew she was seeing the strong pencil-drawn lines and colors of his negro birth mother. He knew everyone could see those lines, but muted like faded watercolor in his father's peach skin and clearly European bone structure.

He cleared his throat. "My mother is Greek."

"Bless me, how unusual! Do you speak the Greek?"

"I do. Also a smatter of French and Italian."

"A classical education, sir?" she asked.

"I was raised by my mother and her Greek family and servants. They're quite cosmopolitan. Madam, you speak like a painter. Do you dabble?"

She recoiled both hands into her lap, dropped her eyes, and blushed. "Oh . . . I have attempted the odd ink portrait, and a little chalk drawing, but I do no more than commit feeble memories to paper for my own revisitation."

"I would kill to view them."

She looked up again, and he expected her to fervently refuse, but instead she drew what little breath her corset allowed and asked, "Would you . . . would you do me the honor of dining at my cottage in Mechanicsville?"

He leaned foward slightly, but he hesitated.

Orienta seemed to note that, if he was reading her accurately. With a flicker of intuition in her eyes, she added, "Barry is in Florida . . . on business."

So she wasn't as innocent as her demeanor implied, Dorian realized. Yet inside he had known that.

"I . . . should not put it upon you to entertain me alone when your brother is away."

"Oh, Captain," she said, "I have no real concerns about my reputation. I am . . . not a maiden, after all. I have been married . . . but most of all, this is a time of war. You are one of our gallant soldiers. War changes things, Captain Pawthens, and nothing is too much a sacrifice for the Confederacy. I shall think it my honor to . . . entertain you."

For all her innocent behavior, for all that was still pure in her heart—which Dorian could almost see as a bright beacon in front of him—she knew the facts of war and society. Innocence, yes, but innocence in moderation. Somehow she had found the golden mean.

"I would be a fool," he uttered. Then, against his will, he added, "To decline."

Her tiny hands cupped both of his. "Oh, I'm so happy! I shall cook the dinner myself. Do you have any preferences of the palate? Anything you . . . like? Or something you haven't tasted in a while . . . that you might miss and wish to taste again?"

Deny her. Resist her. Tell her no.

He begged himself to do these things. To turn her down. Tell her he had made a mistake—that he was leaving Richmond for the west, the north, the moon.

She was stable, patient, as he obviously vacillated before her. She was willing to wait.

And that was enough to make Dorian forget all the back matter he carried with him in his life that kept him unaligned. His neutrality went to hell, overridden by a deep call in his chest, arousing something he had long committed only to memory—something so distant he couldn't find it now, but he could still feel it. The comfort of being with Orienta Swanborough besieged him and crowded out all his creeping apprehensions. It killed his foresight. He had to be near her. Conversation, company. *Near.*

"Anything," he murmured, finally. "As long as it does not involve rice."

"Dorian?"

"Are they gone?"

"Yup, they're gone. What's the matter. You look a little— pardon the expression—white."

Wyatt finished his observation by waggling his fingers at Dorian's vague stare.

"Did I hear the dingdong of little bells in here a while ago?"

With a self-deprecating sigh, Dorian croaked, "She is the single note against which I tune my lyre. . . ."

"Oh, for cripe sake."

"Wyatt, take me to the horse trough. Drown me."

"What's wrong now?"

"I've agreed to take dinner at the Swanborough cottage."

"You're having dinner with Barry Swanborough?"

"That dull thud should be so privileged. Sadly, he took his veneer of honor for a walk out of the city. The smell has faded, so I suspect he even left the state."

"Oh—so it's dinner with . . ."

Dorian cranked around and pressed a hand into the hollow of Wyatt's shoulder, pushing him back into the bookcase.

"You've *got* to come with me. You can even bring your bone-breakingly charming wife, but I've got to have you there. Remember that I know how to use a gun."

"What do you need me there for?"

"Propriety."

Wyatt jabbed at him playfully. "Oh, holy Moses! You don't give a shake about propriety, and I know it. So let's have the truth. You're really fond of this one, aren't you?"

Dorian straightened his clothing tensely and tried to gather his remoteness.

"Don't be pedestrian," he said. "I'm fond of all womankind. This one . . . corralled me with that rotten tactic of hers."

"What—you mean that she's so nice to you?"

Dorian leveled a finger at Wyatt's thoughtful, amused grin. "You do the same evil on me, and you owe me this. Your presence will undergird me."

"Well, that's flattering," Wyatt laughed, "but whatever that is, I'm not doing it to you. *I'm* a married man." Then he glanced at the empty corridor and muttered, "I guess."

"Technically, yes," Dorian flipped uncomfortingly.

Wyatt paused. His teasing dropped away. "Judas priest, Dorian. Why is one dinner so serious? If you don't want to go, then don't go."

Even as he asked, he read in his friend's posture, in the lack of light in those black eyes, that whatever it was to anyone else, to Dorian it *was* serious.

"I intend to go."

"Why?"

"There's something about her that stirs a . . . curiosity in me. I don't know what it is. Once I discover it, I'll be able to dispel it. Until then . . ."

He was staring into the rug when he spoke. Disturbing, for this was not a man to stare into rugs.

"I dare not be alone with her," he said.

CHAPTER TWENTY-NINE

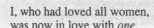

I, who had loved all women,
was now in love with *one*.

—Robert Burns

Grace Craig, her husband Wyatt, and his uncharacteristically submerged business partner were admitted by a female house slave to the Swanborough cottage in Mechanicsville, not one of them free of doubts about the wisdom of this.

For a rented cottage, Grace noticed, the place was very well furnished, obviously with personal and family items. She got an instant sense that the residence was a semipermanent one for the Swanboroughs. There were gloomy Gothic revival chairs with backs like church spires, a finger-cut walnut recamier with scrolled ends and claw feet, and two rococo revival love seats in the living room, one of which had what was probably an incomplete cross-stitched pillow cover cast across an arm. Everything was all consummately Southern, down to a gaudily framed painting of the Alabama state seal, which dominated the wall over the fireplace. There was also a very plain but well-preserved four-foot-long antique clavichord whose natural keys were black and the sharps and flats white, a 1700s' reversal of the more popular modern style. It provided the room a deep taproot into the colonial.

Next to it sat an enormous, ugly steamer trunk that had absolutely nothing to do with the rest of the decor. In fact, it was quite hideous and scratched up, and served to remind them that this residence was a mere convenience for the Swanboroughs, probably to be used when this man Barry Swanborough that

Wyatt had told her about wanted to come to Richmond to wield his influence as a Southern planter.

She hadn't wanted to come at all, but married was married. She knew, had admitted to herself weeks ago, that having the advantage of being married to him also meant keeping up the image of marriage socially. That meant going visiting.

Grace shuddered and sneered at the upcoming evening—*visiting*. Uch.

The slave gestured them through the living room into the dining area, then disappeared. A rich, heavy aroma of cooked cabbage leaves and vegetables smothered in spices struck them at the dining-room entrance like a tidal wave.

Dorian suddenly paused and lagged behind them.

While she slogged off her coat, Grace heard Wyatt ask under his breath, "What's wrong?"

"Bombardment by the Frigate *Nostalgia* abaft my beam," Dorian uttered, waving a hand under his nose at the heavy cooking smells. He drew in a long breath that obviously wasn't long enough for him. He let it out reluctantly and sucked in another one. "Oh! Pardon while I drop dead!"

"Please sit down," a soft but distinct voice called from the kitchen. "I shall be in promptly!"

Grace looked at the two men, neither of which wanted to move first. Finally she said, "Well? Let's sit down like she wants."

Gesturing her and Dorian to the fruit-loaded dining table, Wyatt said, "This is all real nice. Where'd she get these big fat grapes this time of year?"

"She whispered to the vines and they bloomed," Dorian supplied. There was a touch of sarcasm in his tone, but only a touch.

Wyatt wordlessly steered him to the table, sat down beside Grace, and watched them both cautiously.

Dorian lowered into his chair as though not really putting his weight on it. He seemed ready to spring up and make escape any moment. He scanned the table, with its bowls of fruit and goblets of wine, lips slightly parted as though he were about to say something more but couldn't quite think of it.

The kitchen's swinging door bumped open, and a huge black bustle poked into the dining area. Orienta backed into the room, tugging a cart loaded with platters and covered bowls. She had on a small apron, which only pretended to cover the front of her skirt, yet lent a homey appearance as she turned to them.

"Here we are," she cooed. She bobbed a curtsey to them, then deposited a large silver platter at the table's center. Arranged upon it were skewered chunks of meat that smelled of heavy spices and olive oil. She continued transferring platters and dishes from the serving cart to the table.

Dorian watched each dish come before him as though each were dripping molten gold.

"Souvlakia in lemon sauce," Orienta said, "dolma with dill, beets and sesame seeds inside . . . baklava . . . prokola . . . koulouria . . . wild pigeon stuffed with raisins and pine nuts, covered with avgolemono broth . . ." She struggled endearingly with the pronunciations, but now paused, bent to peek at Dorian around his shoulder, and smiled. "With *no* pilaf."

Her cheeks were pink from the heat of the kitchen and rounded from her tight little smile. She beamed at him.

Speechless, Dorian stared at her, then at the food materializing before him.

"What is this?" Grace asked, since the funny food seemed to have a significance.

"It's all Greek," Orienta told her. "And such a pleasure. Since my husband passed on, I've little chance to explore the kitchen. Barry has very plain taste in food . . . meat well done, potatoes baked, but rare else." Then she nodded to Dorian. "I can't thank you enough, Captain, for inspiring me."

"Oh?" Grace said, leering playfully at Dorian. "There's something Greek in your past *too*?"

She was pleased with herself when both the men tensed up and stared at her, not having the foggiest idea why she was peering at them with this knowing glint in her eyes. They didn't know . . . that she knew. That she had seen the poster about the half-breed. That she knew its subject sat here tonight. That was the name of the spy's game—know more about the enemy, and the enemy's friends, than the enemy realizes.

She knew what he was. She had turned him in once for it, and for the twist it gave to Wyatt Craig's heart. Yet here they both were, none the worse for wear, and Grace had taken another tack.

Where the wind would blow her on this heading, she couldn't tell yet. All she knew was that she would be in position to take advantage when that destination showed itself on the horizon.

She felt eyes on her and looked up. Wyatt was looking at her with that touch of confused apprehension she could almost always get out of him. She enjoyed it while she dished some whatever-this-was onto her plate.

Dorian had only flicked an eyebrow at her, unlike Wyatt, who was confused and worried now, and plunged with ravenous delight into the food. His reaction to every bite was plenty to thrill Orienta. She kept piling more and more onto his plate, offering this or that sauce or spice, apologizing for not getting the recipes just right on her first attempt at Greek cuisine.

At the other side of the table, Grace almost laughed aloud the third time Orienta apologized. From the look on Dorian's face, she could be putting decayed fish in front of him and pouring ouzo on it, and he would have drowned in the pure joy of her efforts on his behalf.

"Captain," Orienta purled, "I admire you for volunteering to stand before the oppression of the Union. . . . I begged my brother-in-law to found a brigade and stand on the side of the great right." She nodded to Wyatt. "And Major . . . your wonderful mill supplying cannon powder and gunpowder to our soldiers . . . you had such foresight to set up that mill when the war was only a whiff on the wind. I wish I could be a man and go to stand in the War to End Northern Arrogance."

Trying to smother a grin of mockery, Grace buried her voice inside a wine goblet. "You seem mighty enchanted by the whole idea of slaughtering Northerners."

The two men stiffened.

But Orienta nodded graciously, not embarrassed at all by what was clearly meant to sting her.

"They would be happy to kill us," she said. "We must die if necessary. I am certainly willing to die for this cause. We must preserve the Confederacy for the sake of the entire world."

"The world?" Wyatt asked.

"Oh, yes, the whole world." She seemed surprised that he hadn't understood.

Grace prodded, "The South, no matter wrong or right, give or take?"

Orienta turned to her. "Mrs. Craig, the South can only *be* right." She leaned forward primly, and an acute innocent faith emerged upon her face. "Without the South as a bastion, who will there be to show the world what decency is?"

She looked at them, one by one.

Through the ensuing silence, Dorian's murmur broke.

" 'O heavy loss, thy country ill could bear! A loss these evil days can ne'er repair—Justice, the high vicegerent of her God, Her doubtful balanced eye, and sway'd her rod'—"

" 'Hearing the tidings of fatal blow, She sank, abandon'd to the wildest foe,' " Grace finished.

Unlike Dorian, though, she even got the Scottish accent in there, and got it so authentic that the poem rang even when she finished.

The others all stared at her, for she had not only finished the poem, she had broken Dorian's mythic control of the moment. She looked back at them with a vixenish glow in her eyes.

"It's Robert Burns. Patron saint of Scottish plowboys," she remarked. "Which doesn't describe you very well, Mr. Tr— Parthens. I forget the name of the poem. Address to the death of somebody, Esquire."

She gave him a shrug and stuffed a cabbage leaf into her mouth.

"How," Wyatt began tentatively, "how do you know?"

"Me?" she responded. "By spending my teenage years as companion to a Scottish battle-ax."

"Taught you everything you know, hm?" Dorian cut.

Grace snickered at him and said, "We won't talk about who taught you everything *you* know."

With an annoyed, even perplexed, scowl, Dorian pressed his lips tight and smirked at her. Suspicion ran very deep.

"I think it's lovely that you have such things in common," Orienta interrupted. "Do you enjoy Scottish folk songs, Captain? Mrs. Craig? I can play some for you upon my clavichord . . . shall we?"

She obviously picked up on the repartee and meant to quell it by simply overfeeding it. She got up and flowed into the front parlor, glancing back to be sure they were all following. Instantly three black servants appeared out of the walls and gathered up the dinner dishes. In seconds the dining room was virtually clean.

Even Grace couldn't help a submissive grin at Orienta's smooth handling of the underlying tension. For all her prim Southern-bred surface, the woman had a way of handling people so that all three of them responded like schoolchildren.

"Somebody should put her in charge of the war," Grace muttered as she followed the men, both of whom were following Orienta in undisguised respect. Her exaggerated skirt turned on her tiny corseted waist like a bobbin on a spindle and caught on one of the big iron hinges of the steamer trunk next to the clavichord, nearly pulling her off balance. She threw both arms into the air to steady herself, but it was Dorian who caught her by that little waist—as if to satisfy a fate. While she gazed up at him gratefully, Wyatt stooped past them both and tried to detach the hem of the skirt from the hinge.

He worked at it for several seconds before declaring, "It's not going to come off without ripping."

"Open the lid," Grace suggested flatly. "She's snagged in the hinge."

The trunk was situated so that the front was facing the wall and hinges faced outward. Wyatt leaned over the arched top and flipped the locking mechanism open, then pulled the lid up. Orienta's skirt was immediately released, but Wyatt's attention had gone to something else—

"A trunkload of dirt?" He looked at Orienta. "Topsoil for planting flowers?"

Dorian set Orienta gently back on her own two feet. He gave Wyatt a warning expression. "Wyatt, it's private."

"Oh, no," Orienta countered. "I'm not ashamed, Captain, not at all." She swished to the trunk reached down, and smoothed the clunky clayish soil. "This is Alabama," she uttered. "I take it wherever I travel. It sustains me. Whenever I feel unsure . . . when my heart pounds with fear as I feel the days passing too quickly, the war moving at this earthshaking

pace . . . I come and touch a bit of Alabama." The dirt took on
a pattern of finger strokes, as though it enjoyed her touch.

But then she straightened.

"And it comforts me," she went on, "when the suddenness
of death makes me afraid, when I waken expecting my husband to be beside me and realize how abruptly I lost him . . . I
know Alabama is nearby, in case I die suddenly too."

Wyatt's brows went down. "In case you *die*?"

"That I might be buried beneath my native soil," she finished.

Grace smothered any further reaction Wyatt might have
had by blustering, "Holy clapping smoke! You *are* a Southerner!"

"Oh, yes," Orienta said, very casually. "Alabama is my life,
my reason to continue."

"Now I've heard it all," Grace chortled. She swung around
and dropped onto the farther love seat, shaking her head. "The
dirt has nationality."

But Orienta smiled at her and practically beamed with generosity. "Georgia has its red clay, Michigan has its pure white
sand, Florida has it palms, and Alabama has its rich soil. . . .
This bit of Alabama is a buoy for my being. A silly indul-
gence, of course . . . but not very costly for what I receive."
She turned to Grace and smiled again. "If I were strong like
you, Grace, perhaps I would not need such buoy."

Holding a retort on her tongue that she had been ready to
spit out for a few sentences, Grace suddenly felt herself swal-
lowing a lump. Strange. Grace had always figured aristocratic
Southern women for brainless biddies smothered in lace and
propriety. People who spoke their mind and possessed courage
had to wear burlap. Those were the rules. Burlap, leather, and
no shoes. That was the only way to grow smarts. It took years
to get to know people well enough to size them up, so how had
Orienta sized up every last one of her guests between the souvlakia and the stuffed pigeon?

The women let Grace off the hook and shocked her with a
very personal touch on the cheek—only admiration could pro-
voke such a gesture. Grace was knocked silent.

Orienta glanced at Wyatt and finally turned to Dorian.

"Let me play a tune for you," she said. She didn't take her eyes from him.

They sat together on the bench. Out of what Grace thought was plain discretion, Wyatt sidled over to the fireplace and seemed to try to be invisible, but Grace noticed him and he noticed her, and neither could shake the awareness.

The clavichord sounded beneath Orienta's fingers, a twangy old-fashioned sound, much quieter than its triangular case suggested.

"My clavichord is nearly one hundred fifty years old," Orienta said. She placed her hands on the black keys and began to play. The sound was tinny and unsustained, as though the strings were being plucked.

Unable to take a complete breath because of her corset, Orienta sang in nearly a whisper, without holding a single note. Her voice was curiously like a tinny whimper of the clavichord, short, unsustained notes, instantly damped.

" 'Ye banks and braes o' Bonnie Doon . . . how can ye bloom sae fresh and fair . . . how can ye chant, ye little birds . . . and I sae weary . . . fu' o' care? . . . Thou'd break my heart . . . thou warbling bird . . . that wan-tons through the flower-ing thorn . . . thou 'minds me o' departed joys . . . departed never . . . to-o return.' "

The clavichord's harp rang briefly on a chord.

She smiled at him, he smiled back, and they were alone in the world. The dangerous world was gone.

Grace could feel herself and Wyatt slipping into nonexistence. Instinctively she stayed quiet. She felt Wyatt looking at her, stealing a private moment to see if there was a hint of sentiment on her face, warmth for the magic of falling in love that was so potent in the room tonight.

Hope flared—he noticed a softness on her lips and in her eyes as she watched a man and a woman she didn't like fall in love with each other. Perhaps it was only sympathy for Dorian and Orienta in their wartime oasis, or perhaps it was even less than that. Only common courtesy.

Grace hadn't had much to say all night. All through dinner she'd let Orienta do most of the talking, plying Wyatt with questions about running the powdermill while she basked in Dorian's passion for the Greek food. She had valiantly tried to converse with Grace on a woman-type level—sewing and teaching and the Southern woman's role in the war effort—but Grace hadn't felt like letting the conversation develop into much more than dinner survival.

Now Orienta was fully involved with the only person she genuinely wanted to talk to tonight, and Wyatt and Grace were relegated to silent, uncomfortable glances between themselves.

"Would you allow me to sketch you, Captain?" Orienta asked, turning on the piano bench to face Dorian almost squarely.

"I beg your pardon?" he asked.

She bent over and foraged beside the clavichord and came up with a folder of artist's paper and what appeared to be a box of well-worn drawing chalk in blacks, whites, and grays. Dorian's colors. She showed them to him and smiled. Her cheeks turned into little pink bubbles.

"A picture of me?" Dorian murmured. "I don't believe I've ever seen a picture of myself. . . ."

"Oh," she whispered. She slid from the bench, fetched an easel from the corner of the room, and returned to the piano bench. She set up the easel, placed the papers upon it, and sat on the bench again, this time facing outward from the clavichord.

Dorian stood up, hesitated, backed away.

Grace watched very carefully for his reaction. This was probably a dilemma he'd never faced before.

A picture of himself. A recording of his features. Interesting problem for a wanted man.

But Orienta was already making strokes on the paper.

The three of them couldn't see what she was doing, though Grace saw in her mind the curves and angles of Dorian's face evolving from every movement of her arm and hand.

Dorian slowly sat down on the edge of a velvet love seat.

The negroes brought fresh tea and finger cakes to them in the living room, and for several minutes the sketching went on in virtual silence.

Then, gradually, Orienta began to hesitate over her work. Her brow puckered and her mouth pursed with effort. A few more lines, some blending, and she frowned more deeply.

"There's something missing . . . in the eyes . . . even my

black chalk is not black enough. . . . And the structure of the orbs . . . I somehow cannot capture it—"

She looked at her sketch, looked at Dorian, at his eyes, their lines, then her sketch again. His eyes, his lips. The sketch.

Her smooth brow bore a crease now. "There's something I'm failing to find. . . . It will not traverse from my eye to my hand, yet I'm sure I see it. . . ."

Her voice trailed off. She pressed the chalk again to the paper and put all her attention into attempting a few more lines.

Grace noticed Dorian meeting Wyatt's eyes across the room. They both fidgeted. Then, even more eerie, he caught her own sly glare. She knew he was nervous about her, even though he didn't realize she knew why he should be nervous. There had always been this odd, instinctive recognition between them, even before she had discovered his secrets. A dog with a past could always spot the same kind of dog, and they had spotted each other early. She had sensed his mystery from the first time she saw him standing at the warehouse door with his cape and walking stick.

The crackle of paper jolted through him and made him flinch. He blinked. Met Wyatt's eyes again. Wyatt hadn't stopped watching him with that clear empathy he carried in his pocket.

"Let me try again," Orienta was saying. She shuffled for a fresh piece of paper, pressed it flat, and began to sketch him all over again.

Up, down, curve, in long streaks and short wisps the chalk scratched across the paper. The clock noisily marked off each minute, the only sound in the room. Occasionally she would pause and use her finger to smooth a line, then take to the chalk again when the line failed to satisfy. Her eyes flicked to Dorian, caught a nuance, then rushed back to the paper to commit it before it flew.

The clock sounded the quarter hour.

Orienta pressed her rounded lips into a line and shook her head.

"Failing," she murmured, as though to herself. "There's an

elemental key. . . . I am missing it. . . . Perhaps two dimensions will never do you justice—"

Dorian flashed to his feet. He snatched up the discarded papers and the one Orienta was still working on, tore them from the easel, knotted them into a ball.

"No, don't!" Wyatt plunged forward, fingers spread, reaching.

But Dorian was a shade faster. He ripped the papers, crumpled them, and cast them into the fireplace in front of all their astonished faces. The torn edges glowed red, blackened, and began to curl.

He turned to the others, his arms flared at his sides.

"Nothing can do me justice," he snarled.

Their stares shamed him. But worst of them . . . hers.

Horrified, Orienta was pressed back against the clavichord, both hands to her heart as though to shield it, the chalk in her hand making a black mark on her blouse.

A black mark across her heart . . .

Before his eyes he swore he saw it begin to bleed. Worst of all, behind the horror and shock, Dorian saw sympathy for him in her expression. Understanding. Tolerance—sympathy!

He couldn't bear it.

"Do yourself a favor, madam," he chaffed. "Cancel the search."

His exit, however petulant, retained a certain panache that left the women and Wyatt tense and clearly warned them not to follow.

Wyatt moved to the foyer, but the front door was sighing shut already.

"How 'bout that," Grace muttered. "Scared of that shadow he hauls around."

Wyatt hit her with a look, but it was Orienta who took hold of their unease and caressed it.

"No, it was I," she said softly. "I have insulted him somehow . . . in trying to put on paper what he carries in his soul. No man should be forced to have his image made. Never so proud a man as the Captain . . ."

She stood up, shook out her big skirt somehow without even touching it, and rustled to the garden window.

From her posture, from the way she scanned the dark garden, Grace knew she couldn't see Dorian out there. The phantom had retreated. Lamplight left the room's corners dim, and the window at which Orienta stood with her fingers touching the glass was dominated much more by the moonlight clearing two willows whose skirts brushed the ground across the entire back of the cottage. She seemed ghostly in that haze as she looked out. A spirit looking for a phantom.

"I am privileged to see what I cannot describe . . . the South embodied in the figure of Captain Pawthens. . . . God will not allow such men to endure a loss in this war. . . . I am proud that he reproached me, for I have no right to peer into his elegant, turbulent soul."

"Oh, for my uncle's stuck duck!" Grace blurted, and rolled her eyes.

At the doorway Wyatt spun around, his own face filled with apprehension that she might say the rest of whatever rhymed with that. Both hands were out to beg her not to.

"Don't worry," she said. She pushed to her feet, and she interpreted his gesture perfectly. "Maybe you can stay around to witness this corn opera, but I don't have to. I'm taking the carriage and going back to Richmond before I turn goose-turd green from all this. Have your funny friend drive you back in his own buggy after he drains his bilge." She headed for the halltree on which the servants had hung her coat and bonnet. At the last minute she tossed back, "Have a nice rest of the war, Mrs. Swanborough. You seem to be enjoying it better than a weekend at the follies."

"Grace!" Wyatt tried to follow her. "Please—"

"No," she said, and stopped him with a gesture. "I've had enough."

A swirl, and she was out the door.

Outside in the crystal air of night, Grace shook her head at herself and wished she could pretend the role of wife with more fluidity. She waved for Edmund to drive their carriage up.

As she climbed in, she grumbled, "Maybe it's just not in me to be on the stage."

★

There was only the sound of footsteps crunching outside, then the clack of the carriage.

Wyatt stared at empty air.

When he mustered what social anchorage he had left, he stepped back into the parlor, offered a pathetic shrug to Orienta, and shook his head. His mouth hung open, but several seconds passed before he could choke anything out. "Oh, lord-amighty, I'm so sorry."

But the tolerant Alabama woman was smiling back at him.

"Major," she said, "your wife is so strong. . . . I don't know her well, I don't know her beliefs, but you will find that she'll act upon them more powerfully than either of us dares imagine. Someday you will come to cherish that in her."

"I sure hope so, ma'am," was all Wyatt could manage. "If you'll excuse me, I'll . . ."

He waved toward the back garden.

Orienta nodded. The message in her eyes and her smile was clear: *Thank you for comforting him.*

Wyatt tilted his head in doubt.

"I'll do my best," he said.

Six years since he had smelled it, tasted it. Food from the hands of his mother, his aunts, the Greek servants. The repast of Macedon, the aroma, the laughter, the sneaking of affection, the naughty attention from Alex, Nick, Lydia, and Rose Dimitra, the glares of threat from Lucas. A house filled to the rafters with this thick, spicy aroma, enough to make a man dizzy—the adoring, protective touch of Iphigenia . . . in the shield of her love he had flourished.

All came rushing back to him. All these things he had steeled himself to forget, or ignore. These memories that were dangerous.

Dorian grasped with both hands a wall of ivy vines that nearly covered a six-foot-tall brick fence and let his head hang. He closed his eyes and battled for rationality. His heart thudded against his breastbone hard enough to leave a bruise. Nausea twisted through him.

He had tried to go away. To run from Richmond, from

Wyatt, from Grace MacHutcheon—Craig—before his past tore them all down.

Since leaving Plentiful Dorian had never allowed anyone to get to know him. Wyatt was the first, the only gift of friendship he had given himself in his life. Now he was rediscovering that he could not have only Wyatt. There would be others who would get to know him, for better or worse, mostly worse, if he stayed in one place too long. But Orienta and Grace could sense the depths of his soul, and in the past he would only have dashed away to another section of his life.

But here he was, back. An indistinguishable bond had drawn him here again.

Self-reproach chewed at him. He could have left Wyatt out of involvement with Stephens. He could have come back to Richmond with his new name and new contacts and stayed away from the powder yard, a stranger with everyone, forever.

Orienta Swanborough was the embodied South, and Dorian was its embodied terror. He was fighting to preserve a system in which this primitive attraction between himself and this woman could never make a home. She was courting disaster and did not realize it. Her presence made him incautious, turned him into a babbling clod who couldn't bring himself to pull away from her as he knew he should.

Whores were easy to leave behind. That's why he had always gone to them.

Yet it wasn't only his loins and his taste for drama that wanted Orienta Swanborough. Something inside him that had been lying dormant, a coloration he never knew he had, a latent meaningfulness he saw only when he looked at *her*—

It wanted her. Suddenly he was only a vehicle for an arcane need deep inside him.

He pressed one arm across his stomach and fought to keep his dinner down. If only they would leave him alone . . . if only the world would leave him alone—

"Where are you?"

The voice wasn't nearby. But it was in the garden area, at the gates. A moment later came inevitable footsteps, crunching over the ivy carpet and the path of stones. Briskly at first, they slowed as they grew nearer, louder.

Dorian felt Wyatt's calm presence acutely. Hated being caught weak—physically ill and emotionally tilted.

"God rot you," he croaked, "why can't you mind your own affairs? Devil knows they need minding."

A hand touched the back of his arm in spite of that tone. He pulled away from it, not looking. His arm tingled.

Retrieving his fingers as though burned, Wyatt gave Dorian a few steps breathing room. "Thought I'd better check on you."

"No doubt your exit was subtle."

"Mmm, 'bout as subtle as yours," Wyatt said. "That was quite a scene. My ears still hurt from the air crackling between you two."

Dorian refused to meet his eyes. "Go peddle your papers somewhere else tonight."

"Aw, come on. Listen to yourself," Wyatt uttered. "She cooked you Greek food. How'd she even figure out how to make Greek food? Went plenty out of her way, is my guess. She sees something when she looks at you."

"She sees this uniform. She sees the unblighted Southern knight, champion of the cause clouding her eyes, something she can't effect but through someone else. She sees a way to feed the War against Northern Aggression when she cooks for me. She sees her idea of all Southern men. Self-confident, independent, and in uniform. She sees all this only because I am such a practiced liar. When she plays Robert Burns's tunes for me, she's singing "Dixie' in her mind and heart—and that . . . is *all*." He hesitated, too aware of himself. "She's not seeing me."

Moonlight turned Wyatt's straight brown-sugar hair into two ashy gray wings framing a tolerant face.

"Come on, now," he said, very softly. "You never give yourself credit. You're a good man, a good friend. Some people can't see it in you. She sees it, that's all." He closed the space between them, shrugged one shoulder and added, "Maybe it's just God's will and you shouldn't fight it."

"Then he and I have a score to settle before I descend into hell." With a little growl deep in his throat, Dorian shook his head and said, "God must have no sexual organs, for he seems to live vicariously through the sexual activities of humans, with which he is endlessly preoccupied."

Wyatt watched his friend intuitively, waiting for the rest of the sentence. None came.

"And?" he prodded.

Dorian looked up again, and there was a flash of apprehension at having his silence read—but then he remembered for the hundredth time that Wyatt knew his secret.

"And . . . I cannot help myself," he croaked. "She is clover . . . she is prose . . . a peripeteia which I can't correct. She makes me seem vulgar. Until I set eyes on her, the future and all its dangers was only an aroma from afar. Never since I left my family's plantation have I known such . . . peace."

The last word fell away.

"Good Lord, I hate it," Dorian added on a breath.

Wyatt slowly realized how long it must have been since anyone tended to Dorian's feelings instead of the other way around. Not like the women he paid for, but tending him out of affection for *him,* out of caring about what *he* needed. Not for money or reputation or the stylish company he offered, but for *him.* Unlike the world's wayward bitter waifs who had never known love, Dorian was a young man who had been adored— whom people had risked everything to adore—and who had been torn away from that adoration. He was a man who knew the comforts of nearness with a family to whom he was a central joy, a force of life, and a symbol of their unity. Separation from them had embittered him, and he had been further hardened by the realities of the outside world. He missed those people desperately in spite of the callous outer performance he'd perfected.

For several seconds Dorian tried to regain control over his expression. He gripped the vines so hard that the leaves tore between his fingers.

"I don't like this feeling. It hurts."

A sad smile was Wyatt's only response to that. Dorian seemed not to have had a feeling like that before, as though he somehow had been sheltered from these bruises most people experience early in life and get used to.

Finally Wyatt asked him, "The way things are in the world now, why would you turn away a chance at happiness?"

The black eyes struck hard even in evening's dim moon-light.

"Must I spell it out for you?" Dorian asked. "She is a *white* woman. Not just her skin, but her whole being. Her past. Her heritage. Her hopes. Her future. Whatever this war does for you, me, the blacks, the mulattos, the immigrants—no matter what it does to anyone else, when it's all over Orienta Swanborough will still be white. She probably bleeds pink blood. Lord knows she probably imagines someone like me would bleed black."

"Nothing's that clear-cut," Wyatt said. "You don't know how lucky you are." He gazed back toward the house. "I'd give my left foot to hear a little of that crackle, myself."

Suddenly he realized he'd made a mistake. The one subject he shouldn't have brought up had popped out on its own.

Sure enough, now Dorian turned a cold eye on him. His voice turned particularly bitter and cryptic. "We've yet to ford that issue . . . haven't we?"

Suddenly nervous, Wyatt rubbed his thighs with the palms of his hands.

"Not much to ford," he sighed. "Wish there were some-thing." He shifted his weight. "All I know is, I haven't seen in my whole life what happened between you and Mrs. Swanborough in there, and if you take my advice, you'll give in to a good thing."

Dorian ironed him with a glower. "How long shall I prowl around her heart, towing falsehoods? There can be no future for such a woman as she with such a man as I. She didn't fin-ish the song. Do you know how the song ends, Wyatt? No, of course, you don't." He paced away, crunching a few steps into the ivy ground cover. " 'Wi' lichtsome heart I pu'd a rose, fu' sweet upon its thorny tree . . . and my false lover stole my rose . . . but ah—he left the thorn with me.' "

"Oh, now, cut it out," Wyatt droned. "You know, God's heaped so much on you, sometimes I think I'm gonna have a few questions for him myself."

"Yes. She is worse for me than you are." Glaring into the ivy, he muttered, "Suddenly my mind is independent of my will."

Wyatt looked up. "Not your mind, Dorian . . . your heart."

He barely got the last word out.

A massive piece of shadow on top of the garden wall, crouched there like a panther, suddenly unfolded above them, trees rustling and twigs snapping with the fury of the jump. The thick black form shouted something at them—it sounded like a distortion of Dorian's name or a shriek on the attack— there was no way to tell in the instant before it crashed on top of them. Yanked off balance, Wyatt threw his arm up to defend them both and was propelled backward by a blow to the chest. He tumbled into a spiderweb of ivy that went along the ground and up the stone wall. In seconds he was tangled.

There was one breath left in his body, and with it he shouted, "Dorian, look out!"

Through eyes blurred with pain, he saw Dorian go down beneath a shrieking piece of the night.

★

CHAPTER THIRTY

———————— ★ ————————

Even in the dimness Wyatt witnessed the color drain from Dorian's face and felt it drain from his own. He propelled himself off the wall, willing his feet to pull out of the entangling ivy, which snapped with great protest and tripped him twice, giving a precious second for the attacker to drop onto Dorian and slam him down on his back. Desperately Wyatt leveled his body and lunged onto the back of the assailant. He got one arm around a brawny left shoulder and one under a tree branch that was probably another arm before realizing that his own feet were leaving the ground!

The dance on the assailant's back was disorienting. Wyatt lost equilibrium, lost control of where the ground was in comparison to the sky, and a blinding wave of pain through his wrist sent him reeling. His hand was being twisted—

He gritted his teeth and squeezed out a long howl of pain. He was turning, rolling off the field of black—for an instant his entire weight was borne by his right shoulder blade. That instant was agony. He felt the muscles and tendons wrench, stretch too far, felt something give—then he was released and struck the ground on his side. He rolled over, then over again onto his back. His right hand seemed wrapped in layers of gauze, his elbow numb, his shoulder full of needles.

He tried to scramble up, failed twice, agonized with awareness of Dorian ten feet away beneath a shrieking, bellowing clump of bone and muscle—Swanborough's big slave.

That much Wyatt knew, that much he recognized in the midst of his confusion and pain. He scraped on all fours toward the struggling pair, betrayed by the bad hand, and was tossed off a second time.

His throbbing shoulder struck a tree. This time the shock of impact sent him sinking to his knees. Madly he tried to remember if either he or Dorian was carrying a gun.

On his knees, propped with one hand in the ivy ground cover, gasping, Wyatt was forced to listen helplessly to what was going on ten feet away from him.

Dorian was indeed on the ground under more than two hundred pounds of black flesh—but he wasn't fighting anymore. He was poised, listening, staring.

His head was raised, his knees bent, his hand clutching the slave's velvet jacket. He too was breathing hard, in short, deep gasps.

"The Lord brung me to you!" the slave was shrieking. "I'm bully! I'm bully!"

Wyatt tried to comprehend, but his ears were ringing. He did realize, though, that the whining noise wasn't a shriek on the attack—it was the noise of sobbing. The slave was *crying*.

Dorian's voice cut through the ringing in Wyatt's head.

"Get up immediately. Back away."

Wyatt struggled to one knee before realizing the slave was standing up, backing off. The darkness shuffled, and the ghostly shape of Dorian rose against the moon-washed ivy.

Dorian stood a few seconds, drawing long breaths, staring through the dim night at the slave. The slave stood also, no longer threatening in spite of his size, but sniffing and quaking with emotion, his big hands balled at his sides.

Pacing laterally a few feet, without drawing any closer to the quivering monster, Dorian moved with his arms straight and his shoulders at attention. The seconds seemed elongated, ticking by too slowly, distorted. Each detail was swollen out of proportion—Dorian's boots moving in the ivy, heel first, toe last, crunching, rustling—the tortured gasping of all three of them, none of it in unison, but a terrible chorus of heaving chests.

"When were you born?" Dorian rasped.

Prosecution.

Without allowing a heartbeat to pass untampered, the slave panted, "Eighteen forty-eight."

"Where?"

"Third brick shack over from the well."

The slave was shaking so hard that the ivy and nightshade beneath him crackled. He sucked air through flaring nostrils, his lips were pressed shut before and after every utterance and quivered noticeably.

Moving across a narrow bricked path toward the slave, Dorian leaned this way, then that way, studying the slave's features in various angles of moon- and starlight. The slave didn't move, didn't turn his head. Obviously he had been scrutinized before. On the block, probably. Probably by Barry Swanborough.

Tonight was very different, however. Though he knew the stance and the attitude, the slave was holding a volcano of emotion within his body. This was clearly the most important scrutiny he had ever undergone.

Fourteen years old? This human pier buttress was a young boy?

Wyatt huddled on the ground, one knee skewered into the ground cover, his injured arm cradled deeply against the curve of his body, and tried to see what Dorian was seeing. Skin of dark chocolate. Eyes the same color, set in opal, ringed with long tightly curled black lashes, lines as unblended as an Egyptian ink drawing.

As Dorian circled behind him, the black boy still didn't move, still kept his head facing forward, though his chestnut eyes followed Dorian as far around as possible until periphery ended. The movement squeezed tears from his eyes, to drain down the set of rock formations beneath his glossy skin.

Shaking inside the velvet jacket, the slave asked, "You know where Mama is?"

Dorian stopped. Raised his head slightly. Held his breath.

The question brushed over the garden foliage with the bristles of its thousand implications.

Stiff as a palace guard, Dorian answered, "I know she is alive."

The boy's only reaction was to close his eyes in a wince of relief, then open them again.

Working against a vague memory of a devoted little boy, a weight on his knee as he sat in his office, surrounded by books about alternative planting, crop rotation, and efficient smoke-housing, a voice in his ear reading from the classics, Dorian tried to swallow, but his throat was stone dry. He walked around the boy once, then continued around a second time.

"Can you still read?" he asked.

"Yes, sir, I read everything," the boy said, still without turning his head. "Mama talked about you all the time. She made me read. Signs on the town stores. Signs on the roads. Billboards. Newspapers people had thrown away. Said I had to keep you proud. Said I had to keep ready. Said the world was getting little and we'd find each other . . . said Dohrian would find me."

At the sound of his name spoken in a manner he hadn't heard in years, Dorian suddenly caught himself on the rim of the wall and bent over as though punched in the diaphragm. Several seconds went by as he steadied himself.

"How old—" he began. "How old were you the last time—"

The words closed up in his throat.

Wyatt watched him, not daring to interfere, piecing together the facts and stitching in other things he knew. Clearly, Yula—the slave woman bright enough to make a deal with immigrants to save her child, smart enough to work around the animosity of the plantation's boss, the father of her half-breed baby, the man who mated her to a traveling slave breeder— hadn't raised any dullwit children. The boy anticipated the part of the question Dorian couldn't manage, did an instant calculation, and choked out an answer.

"I was eight last time I saw you. They came in the night. Took us right out of the cabin. Boss had two niggers with guns behind him. Even Jeff was scared to move on 'em. Me and Mama got sold off to a candle-and-lamp factory, but Mama wouldn't behave. They punished her by selling me off. I got sold three more times, 'cuz the folks who bought me saw how big I was getting, and they was afraid I'd turn into trouble. Then I got bought by Mr. Swanborough when I was twelve and I'm still there." He paused, and his trembling drowned his voice. Tears began flowing freely down his face. "I gotta see your arm. . . . I gotta see it."

With a huff that might have been a hundred different feelings, Dorian unbuttoned his uniform coat and shed it in a single gesture. It puffed to the ground and sighed flat. With a series of little jerky movements, he unbuttoned his right cuff and began to roll it up, gradually exposing his forearm.

He turned it in the moonlight. An onionskin pattern glittered in the chalky light.

Ordinarily Wyatt shuddered even to think of that mark. Tonight was different, though. Dorian had nearly ripped the sleeve in half to show his arm to the boy.

The enormous slave boy held out both arms as though to catch a star.

"It's you. . . . I told myself I was lying t'me . . . but I wasn't. I knew it was you. . . ."

He collapsed onto both knees, his arms coiled around Dorian's legs so hard that they both wavered for balance.

Dorian held his arms outward, not touching the enormity that clung to the lower half of his body. He looked down at the glittering black curls and the handsome face pressed against his thigh, the eyelashes curled so tightly they nearly came back around like ringlets, the emotions of childhood quaking against him, not a monster's drool but the tears of a child soaking into his trousers—

From the sidelines Wyatt's astonishment finally croaked out. "I—I don't believe it!"

Dorian didn't look at him. He continued gazing downward.

"Don't you? Then I'll say it." He waved a limp hand toward the black boy clinging to him. "We have the same mother, he and I. You know what a mother is?" Now he lowered a hand and made the commitment of touch. "The baby was fairly small," he murmured. "In fact, we wondered if he would live. We thought Boss might have wasted his money . . . that too much of Yula had gone into the baby. There were three others born that month on Plentiful . . . the children of the Breeder . . . but this particular colossus is my baby brother."

The phrase came out on an insufficient gust.

Wyatt's brow furrowed. Was that it? Was that all the reaction Dorian could choke out after all this time, all this trouble?

The black boy clutched at Dorian's legs and sobbed in abject happiness.

"The big world wasn't big enough to keep us apart," the boy smothered into Dorian's trouser hem. "You and me and

Mama . . . we'll be together again! And we'll prance back to Plentiful and show boss he can't take us apart never again!"

Dorian patted the boy's head and nodded, even though the boy wasn't looking up. After a moment Dorian looked across the garden path and commented, "He speaks very well, doesn't he? I taught him that, Wyatt—oh, Wyatt!"

He tried to move, but the boy had him in a hammerlock. His arms flew wild, and he caught himself on the boy's shoulders.

"Burlie, my elemental force of nature, uncrank the vise."

The boy looked up, but didn't understand.

"Turn me loose," Dorian said plainly, his brows raised.

"Oh!" The boy let go of him and staggered to his feet—taller than Dorian even at this age—and stood aside, sniffing with joy. Who could guess how long he had harbored fears of not being recognized through the changes over time?

Dorian didn't wait for the blood to flow back into his legs. He forced himself across the path to Wyatt.

On the ground, holding his right wrist, Wyatt could feel the lack of blood in his cheeks and lips. What had been a numb throb was quickly turning to real pain. His fingers simply wouldn't respond anymore, no matter how he tried to make them go.

"Witch piss, look at you," Dorian said, dropped beside him and took him by the good arm. "Can you stand? Are you all right?"

"I—I—" Wyatt attempted, "don't believe it—"

The wall of young negro knelt before him now, still sniffing and wiping his eyes, shaking his head sorrowfully.

"I'm sorry I hurt you, Boss. I didn't think what my hands were up to."

"Wyatt," Dorian said sharply, taking him by both shoulders. "Are you all right? Can you get to your feet?"

"It's your little brother—?"

"Yes. Absorb it before you faint. I'm the one who's supposed to be fainting. I don't appreciate being upstaged."

"But he's . . ."

"Yes, he's on the large side. Were you looking for an eight-year-old boy all this time?"

There was something in that question—as though he were

asking himself. Wyatt gaped from the boy to Dorian and perceived that Dorian was babbling. It was intelligent babbling, of course, unrecognizable to anyone who didn't know him, but he was definitely burying his own shock.

He took Wyatt's injured wrist and probed it—until Wyatt stiffened, choked out a gasp, and shuddered. Dorian had to keep him from falling forward.

"Is there pain in your shoulder, or only the wrist?"

"Mostly the wrist . . . shoulder hurts too. . . ."

"Damn the skies. I think you've got a good sprain going for you. It's swollen twice normal." He surveyed Wyatt's face and added, "Yes, you're four shades whiter than usual too. Might have a broken bone in the shoulder. Let's put you inside and have a look."

He took Wyatt by one arm and Burlie took him by the belt, and they lifted him to unsteady feet.

"Wait—wait," Wyatt protested, wobbling. "We can't talk in front of Orienta. . . . What are we going to do? We can't leave him in Swanborough's hands. . . . If Swanborough ever finds out, he'll take it out on the . . . on the boy."

His phrases were broken by gasps of pain, but his message was crystal clear—and dead true.

Still holding onto Wyatt, Dorian looked at Burlie. "How does God the Second treat you?"

The boy sniffed away a few more tears. If there was any further proof needed as to his identity, this quick answer was enough. He didn't bat so much as an eyelash at Dorian's reference, but knew exactly what he meant—because he evidently had never forgotten how Dorian said things.

"He treats us all right. He doesn't muster enough emotion to get mad or whip us. Got kind of a cold heart in him."

The two other men stared at him in admiration. He *did* speak well. No formal schooling, little chance in a world against him, born with the traits of size and color that would prevent him from blending in even among negroes, the boy had never forgotten some very simple advice and the values of a big brother he adored. *"Learn to read. Speak clearly. Pronounce all the letters in a word. With those weapons at your belt, there will be no bounds set upon you by mankind that you cannot break."*

"I'll," Wyatt managed, wincing, "I'll buy him—any cost, Dorian—offer anything."

Dorian's only answer was a squeeze of gratitude on Wyatt's arm, and a pat on the bad wrist. Very gentle, much gentler than Dorian's usual contact. Usually it was Wyatt who did the patting and the squeezing and the reassuring. The bolt of intimacy spoke for itself.

"I refuse to pay that canker—or anyone else—for my own brother." He gazed at the black boy in sudden poignant anger. "My family is *mine!*"

He stalked off a few paces as though the concept were an insult. Wyatt was simply shocked—or was it the confusion of his pain? Was this Dorian, who would buy and sell anything, anyone, to accomplish his purposes? To whom the world was a giant cash box?

But the boy shook his head to Wyatt. "Mr. Swan won't sell me to you, Boss. He likes having me, and he's looking forward to when I'm even bigger."

"And when that voice changes, no doubt," Dorian pilloried. The boy lowered his head self-consciously, and tears flowed again from the dark painted eyes.

The two of them were interrupted when they had to catch Wyatt as he sagged under the pain running from his fingers to his neck.

"Lordamighty," he choked, cradling the arm. "Feels like he tore it off—"

"Sorry, Boss," the boy said again.

"No, no, I'll be fine . . . worth it, worth it . . ."

"Come along, my friend," Dorian said, catching him around the waist. "If the world changes half as much in the next few weeks as it has tonight, you and I shall have a piping-hot year on our hands."

As he walked his injured friend toward the house, Dorian battled to control the funnel cloud of emotions spinning in his brain. On one side was a man who had given him devotion he hadn't deserved, and on the other he had regained his mother's precious black baby, a responsibility that had haunted him perhaps more than his need to find his mother. All these years he had buried his thoughts about Burlie, for the horror was too much to live and sleep with day after day.

He shuddered and tightened his grip on Wyatt as though clinging to a floating log. He had been many things in his life, but lucky was not one of them. Never. Through his repressed joy, he began to worry. He felt the nearness of Burlie mere inches from his sleeve, and he wondered.

Could he keep from infecting the boy with a scratch of the devil's fingernail?

★

CHAPTER THIRTY-ONE

———— ★ ————

"Major Craig!"

Orienta Swanborough came to her feet and dropped her cross–stitch when she saw the tousled trio who had minutes ago been two fine Confederate officers and a very proper slave boy. Now they were rumpled, had ivy leaves clinging to them, and Major Craig was the color of paste and could barely walk. The two others were holding him between them.

"Oh, my goodness, what happened?" she asked, hovering before them as they entered from the garden door. "Oh, Major—"

"I'm all right, ma'am," Wyatt choked, lying through his gritted teeth.

"What happened to you?"

"Oh, I slipped."

"Let's place him on the couch," Dorian said, bearing most of Wyatt's weight now.

Orienta ran before them to one of the love seats and arranged two throw pillows and a large sitting stool to accommodate Wyatt's legs, which were too long for the little couch.

"Slowly," Dorian said. "Coat off first."

Easily said, like "pull the tooth." It took all three of them to get Wyatt's frock coat unbuttoned and worked off the shoulder. He turned a few more colors and nearly passed out.

"Down," Dorian said.

He turned Wyatt onto the couch and supported him until he was reclining keeping the bad arm immobile and without pressure, then unbuttoned the cuff of Wyatt's checkered shirt and pushed it up to keep pressure off the sprain.

Wyatt lay back, but couldn't relax. He might as well have been clinging to a tree branch. His muscles quaked from head to toe and his legs were kinked, heels digging into the big tufted stool. His neck was corded with effort.

Dorian straightened and surveyed him critically.

"The pain's not fading, I take it."

"I'll be fine . . . fine."

"Valiant," Dorian murmured, with a strange, warm grin. "But you're hurt, Lancelot."

"I'll fetch the doctor!" Burlie shouted. Everyone flinched at the power in his voice. "He's only ten doors down! I'll fetch him!"

Before anyone could suggest otherwise, he thundered across the house to the front door and slammed out.

Even the Alabama coat of arms rattled over the fireplace.

"I'll make a hot compress," Orienta said before the echo fell, and she too dashed out of the room.

Dorian watched her go, then for several seconds watched the empty space where she had been.

Soon he turned his attention back to Wyatt—and found the paper-white face beaming up at him right through the pain, and even managing a smile.

Wyatt made a feeble reach with his good left hand and caught Dorian's hand, squeezed it.

"By God . . . I'm so . . . damned . . . happy for you!"

His voice was weak, choked to a high note by the noose of discomfort, but his blue eyes were crimped with genuine joy.

Dorian couldn't help a smile at his friend's expense.

"Shhh," he warned, partly because they might be overheard, and partly because he could see what the expression was costing Wyatt.

He took a seat on a small wrought-iron footstool beside the couch and grew thoughtfully silent. He watched Wyatt quake and beam at him and was gripped in the chest by Wyatt's generosity in the midst of discomfort, to be thinking not of himself, while half his body was twisted nearly off, but of Dorian and the little brother.

"What's wrong?" Wyatt choked. "Aren't you glad?"

At this moment Dorian realized how thoroughly he had been adopted by Wyatt Craig. So much so that his problems had been adopted also by this easygoing, generous fellow who gave such fresh meaning to the term *humanity*.

For the first time he began to muse over those months he

had dropped out of Wyatt's reach without a word. All those months he'd never given Wyatt a thought—unlike his family. After all, he'd known where Wyatt was. Safe and sound in the powdermill. Rarely had Dorian given any attention to the thoughts of those who cared for him, who might wonder what became of him, who might blame themselves for what happened to him. Always he had been too busy blaming himself for what became of *them*. Until now he had never considered the other face on the card, for he had never looked it in the eyes as he was doing tonight.

"Here." He plucked another pillow from the recamier and gingerly touched it under Wyatt's numb right arm, trying not to hurt him further. "Don't move, and stop thinking about that conversation I see in your face. I really have no desire to hear anything a self-absorbed lone wolf like you has to say, so hush up."

Wyatt managed a smile. His breath was coming in chunks. Before him, propped on the pillow, his right hand was so white that the blue veins showed.

"He really dismantled you, didn't he?" Dorian observed.

"No, no, don't make—don't make him feel bad, hm? He's big, but—he's just a boy."

"Hush. Warned you once."

"Gentlemen?" Orienta flowed back into the room with a tray, a set of towels, and a steaming copper teapot. "Major, I have heat for your arm here. Shall we attempt to comfort you?"

"We're awaiting the professional," Dorian said to her, "to see if heat would be beneficial, or a cool damp dressing. I've heard conflicting old wives' and witches' medicine for such swellings." He faltered then and said, "Madam, I meant no reference to you—"

Orienta waved him off with a suddenly wise laugh. She might pretend to be a belle at supper, but she evidently had the constitution of a seasoned pioneer and couldn't be insulted by the improper or imperfect. Most women forgot to leave such petty sensitivity behind when they left girlhood.

For the first time, through the gauze of pain blurring his eyes, Wyatt began to see past the plain features, pale coloring, and pointy eyes, to what Dorian saw when *he* looked at Orienta Swanborough.

"Doctor's here!" The front door banged open, and in came Burlie, hauling a terrified white man with a banana-sized mustache and a pair of trousers hauled over the bottom of a nightshirt.

Dorian vaulted sharply to his feet.

"God's clanking corpse, boy, turn loose of that man! Two wrenched bodies in one night is unthinkable!"

Burlie let go of the doctor so suddenly that the man came spinning into the parlor.

Dorian caught him by the sleeve and pulled him upright. "Pardon the inconvenience, Doctor."

"Is that your slave, sir?" the doctor bellowed. "Doesn't he mind common manners?"

"I never teach my slaves manners," Dorian popped back, waving an aristocratic hand. "Why waste politeness on the underwits a slave would speak to? There is an injured man stretched from this couch to that tuffet. Would you care to get paid for helping him, Doctor, or shall I have my slave deposit you in some nice wet spot?"

"Dorian," Wyatt scolded. "Don't."

The doctor shook off the situation and bent over Wyatt single-mindedly.

"Well, let's see what we've got here." He took Wyatt's hand first and worked his way up to the wrist, then muttered, "Sprained."

The upper arm was next, but other than purpling with a bruise, it was still intact. The shoulder, however, was a different prognosis. After poking and prodding until Wyatt's eyes teared and everyone else was wincing in empathy, the doctor straightened and sighed.

"Got a textbook-looking dislocation of the shoulder socket here." He straightened and began rolling up his sleeves. While he did so, he nodded to Dorian and Orienta. "If you and the lady would like to wait outside, Captain, I'll take care of it."

Stepping forward protectively, Dorian said, "I prefer to stay with him."

The doctor was unintimidated. He'd already survived being hauled ten houses by a six-foot monster, and Dorian wasn't succeeding in impressing him away from his work. "I'd rather you take the lady outside briefly. I'm going to have this negra stay here and provide leverage."

Feeling like a piece of sausage being argued over at the breakfast table, Wyatt squinted up at the doctor and dared ask, "What're you gonna . . . do?"

The doctor looked down at him from way, way up there, and said, "I'm gonna put it back in, son."

As the door clicked shut behind them, Dorian flinched. He knew Orienta saw it.

"He'll be all right, Captain," she murmured. "Such a gentle young man . . . your friend."

"He is a good friend, Mrs. Swanborough. I am as privileged as he is cursed."

She came around to face him. "Oh, Captain . . . such a way to speak about yourself."

Dorian adopted a chill and spoke as though making both warning and prophecy. "You don't know me, madam."

She smiled and just that simply contradicted him right into the porch floor. She did know him, and there was nothing he could do about it.

"Madam," he sighed, "pray do not look at me that way."

"Which way is that?" she asked.

"As though you're still drawing me in your mind. I no longer care to be etched."

She folded her arms around about her body against a chilly wind. "I believe that may be the only thing you have in common with Barry. He also does not care for me to draw him. I drew him once sitting in the garden. . . . He paid me for it, then destroyed it."

"Paid you? Mmm," Dorian grunted. "I'm afraid your sultan-in-law and I find each other disagreeable."

Orienta swished to the other side of him, a move that shortened the space between them, and she touched the porch rail. "It's very generous of you, Captain," she said, "to call him only disagreeable."

Dorian squeezed his eyes shut and tried not to smile, but ended up chuckling at her disarming honesty.

Only a sudden sharp bellow of agony from inside the house cut him off. He spun around, facing the closed window, unable to see inside through the drawn curtains.

Orienta's face came between him and the window. "Captain," she implored, "please don't worry. Dr. Braden is most competent."

"It's not the competence, madam," Dorian said tightly. "It's the pain."

"I know," she responded. "You're so concerned for the wellbeing of others . . . it shows in your face."

"I told you to cease exploring my face."

She was unintimidated. She continued gazing at him. "We must enjoy each other's faces while we can," she said, very softly. "There is a war here now. . . . We shall be looking into a great many faces, and many of them will be lifeless when we see them."

He tried to strike her with a retort, but he was watching her eyes, and she was watching the sky beyond him. Suddenly Dorian couldn't be rude to her anymore. All defense flowed out of him.

"You say that," he began, "as though you know."

Her eyes welled almost instantly, and her lips quivered. "I awakened to find my husband beside me. His eyes were open . . . he was turned toward me. I had slept through his passing. Never again shall I be afraid to waken beside a man."

Dorian ceased prodding for details. He suffered enough loss in his life never to wish that someone else should relive a loss on his account.

A haunting guilt pulled at him. The boy . . . Burlie . . . inside, doing a man's job—

"So many will sacrifice their lives," Orienta went on, twisting her hands to warm them. "I see so much nobility, so much character . . . like yours." She looked at him. "The Yankees don't understand our way of life. They're like the negroes and the Chinese . . . not the same race as you and I. Our victory is preordained, but God means us to pay a price, I fear. He wants us to appreciate our slaves more than we have done . . . and appreciate our fine young men like you."

"Please stop," Dorian rasped. "Stop speaking of me in that—that *way*. I have yet to raise a hand for any other cause but my own."

She moved very close to him. Her eyes, simple and unadorned, glowed at him in utter generosity.

"Someday," she whispered, "you may share with me . . . your cause."

Her breath wreathed his face. He felt himself weakening. That which he had controlled in spite of a hundred whores of every shape and size over the past six years overwhelmed him and for the first time took utter control of him. Never, never had he given every bit of himself—body, yes, but never the inside, never the beat of his heart or the joy of his mind. He had reveled in the company of every description of womankind, for he adored them all in some way, or he would find something in the twist of a curl or the flicker of a lash to adore. There was *something* in every woman on earth to appreciate.

They all plunged back at him now—a hundred women of the satin bed, or the tattered tassel, or the perfumed corset—swam around him until he felt dizzy, until breath fogged his eyes and he could see only the past, only the anointed Greek garden on the front lawn of Plentiful, the statues draped in morning glories, stone faces ever turned upward to the gods—

He would ten days ago, even two days ago, have laughed in the face of anyone who suggested he dare to go forward, to go anywhere, with this relationship.

When had this turned into a relationship? At which moment, which breath, inhale or exhale, which blink, which instant had this touch stopped being the touch of a stranger? When had this become a lover's touch?

Fairy tales alone possessed this love that ignited so quickly, and Dorian knew his life, his destiny, had never been and wasn't now a fairy tale. Life had saddled him with harsh reality every step of the way. Since conception, in fact. Fortune was spitting in his face again, trying to fool him now, toy with him, make him stumble.

He dipped his head toward her, but could not make contact—so she did it for him. She reached upward on her toes. Her hand slid to the hot back of his neck, drew him downward to her lips. Cool, gentle lips, a forgiving touch.

A lover's touch. A thing of trembles and quivers. A thing of intimacy. A burning touch heavy with promise, with what only lovers could deliver . . . but more, weighted with a promise of two hearts beating as one.

He felt himself breathing against her cheek. Inside his mind he chided himself for his lack of moral courage, unable to do what he knew he should.

Orienta's lips, swollen now and moist, moved before him.

"What is," she began, "Iphegen-ya?"

Startled, Dorian felt his shoulders knot. He realized his arms were cupping her back. "I—beg your pardon?"

She gazed up at him, unblinking. "You uttered that name just now . . . while you kissed me. Is it the title of a poem?"

"God!" He choked.

Bushwhacked by a hidden demon! He tried to push her away physically, but simply couldn't do it.

"Please go inside!"

"You can tell me," she said.

Dorian shuddered. That was it! That was the attraction! Her looks—her manner—*yes*.

He squinted and analyzed her face, her simply done hair, the muted colors and shades of Orienta, the way she saw through his protective barriers and nurtured the soft tissue beneath—and suddenly she was a thousand times more dangerous to him if he failed to resist her now, tonight—this minute.

But now he knew! Now he could defend himself! The bars could come up between them, and he could keep them up. He knew what his weakness was, and he would flail her with it. If he couldn't push her body away, he would push her mind away!

"Iphigenia," he said, pressing backward from her, "is another woman."

He managed to let go of her and slide along the porch rail. He gave her his sharpest, most arrogant glare.

"There have been many women. More than you can guess. Most have been paid. Women have been kind to me all my life. I've been left with a fondness for them, in any form, any clothing or want of it. You find me victimized by that debilitation, and I caution there have been plenty more before you. That's *all*."

Was she disgusted yet? Was she running inside?

"I have been with another man," she said. "We are not youngsters, Captain. . . . We know what we are."

Damn her!

He gripped the porch rail until his hand hurt. He raised both brows and hardened his eyes. He skewered her eyes with his, for most people would buckle to such a direct glare. He knew all the tricks. He could back her down.

"I'm not a decent man," he began. His voice was cold. "I've purchased life like a commodity. My own and others. I'm a manipulator and an extortionist. I'm known by a dozen names in a hundred whore pens. I take out each tenderloin once and only once. She gets the finest supper in the finest establishment. Price is no consideration. She gets a corsage and champagne. We attend opera or a play or concert. People stare at us because they know what she is and they see what I am, and I parade like a fiend through the streets with the cat of that night suspended on the point of my pitchfork. She gets one night and only one. I am never—*never*—with the same woman twice."

He waited for a reaction. A hint of fear, of self-defense.

Nothing. She was fascinated, patient, forgiving, and she understood.

Damn, if he could just cut that word from the language! Nothing shocked her. She continued forgiving him with her expression. She saw more in him than he saw in himself, no matter how he tried to blind her, no matter how he blasphemed and vilified himself.

Desperate, he drew a breath to reveal the second-most-vile thing about himself. He steeled himself to tell her what he had never told anyone. The one thing that caused him disgust in himself. The worst thing about himself, shoved out in order to save her. The ultimate peccadillo. It never mattered if the whores heard.

"Iphigenia is my mother."

It stabbed out toward her. Quick. A shock, a nip, needles. He felt blood rush to his face, and at the same time felt his lips drain. His voice guttered, but he forced it out.

"I've varnished my cane with a hundred whores," he said, "and I bite my mother's name into every one of them."

There.

Humiliation ripped at his lungs until he could barely breathe. He turned slowly away just as he would turn if he were wearing his Inverness cape—to make the hem flare and to make a point. To brush an end to a conversation.

He didn't look at her. The last thing he wanted to see was the face of tolerance dissolving into horror. If he wanted kindness and understanding he could sit and listen to Wyatt snore. Then in the morning Wyatt would tell him that everything was all right and they would go home and never set foot in Mechanicsville or anywhere remotely near a Swanborough ever again for the rest of their lives. That would have to be it. Yes.

He waited to hear her spin around in disgust and run away. He had whispered his mother's name in the heat of passion. Orienta would be sickened, and he would have saved her.

Her hand touched his arm.

She pressed close against his spine. Her hand moved down his back and caressed his thigh.

Her tone said a hundred things. Said he was here for the night and she would be here too. Said his loneliness was an aberration. Said it knew what her hand was doing.

And it said other things. Then there were the words.

"Shall I pretend . . . to be your mother for you?"

When the doctor opened the door and gestured them back inside, Dorian didn't remember crossing the porch or any part of the room. He dashed in as quickly as possible, contemplating crazy ways to avoid spending the night here.

All he knew was that he was abruptly at Wyatt's side, and that he was gazing down at a rag of a man.

No longer digging his heels into the satin tuffet, no longer curling upward in strung-up tension, Wyatt now lay collapsed. His eyes were hollow, and his face was the ashy color of his hair. His shirt was cast over a chair, and he was bare from the waist up. His right arm was strapped to his chest by a sling and a figure-eight bandage around his neck and shoulder, and some color was returning to his lips, but he seemed as though he had been beaten into submission. His breath still came in bolts, but more deeply.

"Oh, my," Dorian groaned. He leaned over him, tilted his head sympathetically. "How are you now?"

"I think it's worse than it was before," Wyatt croaked.

"But now," the doctor said, rolling his sleeves down, "it'll improve. The pain will go in eight or ten days. Before, it wouldn't have gone in ten years."

Wyatt found it within himself to cast the doctor a thankful smile and a little nod. "Good job, fine . . . feels much better."

The doctor chuckled. "The shoulder is actually more serious than the wrist and will take longer to heal. There is likely some tearing of the joint capsule and tendons. Keep him quite warm tonight, because he is exhibiting symptoms of shock."

Wyatt grinned and graveled out, "I think all my blood's down in one of my feet."

"I'm going to give you a shot of morphine. It will blur the pain somewhat," the doctor said.

The hypodermic syringe looked to Wyatt about the size of a pine tree. No one said anything as the needle went into Wyatt's good arm.

"After it takes effect, you'll be able to sleep."

"Stout and sturdy in no time," Dorian agreed, defying an urge to glance at Orienta.

"He will be if you *don't* move him out of the house tonight. Any mishandling may cause further damage to blood vessels or another displacement of the bone from the joint."

Orienta leaned past Dorian, who drew in a quick breath as she came too close, and said to Wyatt, "The cottage is large enough to accommodate you both."

She said it very firmly, as though issuing an order.

"Thank you, ma'am." Self-consciously Wyatt moved his good arm to try to cover his bare chest. Orienta, rather than acting embarrassed, offered an amused and sympathetic smile, as though she were tending a shy little boy with a scratch on his backside.

She interpreted his gesture perfectly, gathering up a knitted blanket and covering him right up to the neck.

Dorian was clearly deeply disturbed by the prospect of spending the night, of not escaping Orienta.

Wyatt immediately sensed Dorian's distress. Dorian couldn't even muster a thank you, couldn't even look at Orienta. He silently paid the doctor, muttered his thanks, and ushered the man out.

When he came back, Orienta was pulling Wyatt's boots off.

"I shall place you in my room, Major," she said.

"Oh, ma'am, I wouldn't put you out. I'll be fine right here on the couch."

"Major, you cannot gain any real rest with your body suspended between a couch and a tuffet," she insisted, "and I'm certain you would gain no respite from sleeping in Barry's room." She pivoted to Dorian and exchanged a playful gaze. "Captain Pawthens will no doubt bask in that irony."

A surprise to everyone, most of all himself, Dorian laughed right out loud. Then he shook his head as he couldn't help chuckling nervously, rubbed raw by all this . . . and all that out there on the porch. No woman had ever made him laugh out loud—at least not on purpose. He had laughed at the expense of many women, but few were smart enough or open enough to say what was on their minds. Other than Grace, whose clever comments were always tinged with bitterness and venom, no woman had ever affected him like this prosaic puritan to whom even Virginia was a foreign land—but *he* wasn't.

With a rumbling sigh he admitted, "You know me dangerously well. Excuse me."

Get out. Go back to Richmond. Take a sharp right turn. Go to the western frontier. Get away.

He abandoned the parlor and began glancing into the hallway and out the windows. He even bumped the kitchen door open and peeked in there.

Finally he returned to Wyatt. "Let's haul you upstairs before you take root."

"I'll prepare the bed," Orienta said, and floated out the room and up the narrow stairs.

Dorian glanced in that direction only once, long enough to see her slip up the stairs. The back hem of her skirt licked at the edge of the parlor doorway, as though to beckon him.

Dorian gingerly lifted Wyatt to a sitting position without bothering the shoulder, but he was broodingly silent and preoccupied.

Wyatt resisted getting to his feet long enough to whisper, "Everything's all right?"

"Everything's peachy. Save your breath."

"You look a little . . . uh . . . ."

"The drug is making you hallucinate."

"Where's the boy? Where could somebody that size hide?"

"I don't know. Did he help the doctor?"

"Sure did. He had hold of my rib cage and he held me right down."

"How did he feel about it?"

"Tell you the truth, Dorian, the doctor was tearing my arm clean off. I didn't notice much else."

"I'll find him. Let's get you settled first."

A slow management of the stairs, many groans and winces, and eventually Wyatt was settled.

Dorian slipped out of the bedroom while Orienta puttered around Wyatt, assuring herself that he was warm enough to throw off the shock, and that the comforters in her bed were long enough to cover his feet.

The lower level of the cottage seemed a haunted place as Dorian came to the bottom of the stairs. Burlie was here somewhere . . . or had he dreamed it all? Maybe this cottage didn't even have a garden or a porch.

He remembered what it had been like to have a little brother. Burlie was the first person who had treated him like an adult.

He nudged the kitchen door partly open to take another glance, but only the house slaves were in there, cleaning up dinner plates. They glanced at him, but he wasn't *their* guest, so they made no politeness at all, but simply turned back to the work. A strange place, this Swanborough household. Dorian found himself wondering how different this place was when Barry was home.

He bumped the garden door open and slipped out, realizing again how self-centered the past six years had been for him. At least he had spent his childhood in his mother's arms, had the blessing of two mothers, and had been sold away as an adult. Not so for Burlie. Yula had been a grown woman and knew the world. Burlie had been a child of eight, sold away into that world, to fend for himself.

Taken. Right out of his mother's arms. Slavery had many faces, rules and allowances, some better than what poor whites endured, some more hideous than the lot of animals in line for slaughter, but this was the only one which was the same across the board—the right of some strangers to take a child from its mother's arms. There was no way to forgive it, to ease the terror of those first few months among strangers, or to bring back a lost childhood.

Mother, mother, mother, mother—

He shook himself and moved forward. A worm of melancholy burrowed deep into him. Burlie was so *changed*.

How long six years really was. . . . What else had changed? How much had he sacrificed to his fear that if he buried himself in the bosom of his Greek family, he would eventually give up his search for Yula?

Maybe there was a back way out of the garden. There had to be. A way to avoid spending the night here. Wyatt would be all right. . . .

Orienta, Orienta.

Was Grandpa Dimitrios still alive? And Iphigenia—had she returned to Plentiful with his sisters? Or were his sisters married now—living in Europe, so far from him? If Burlie was grown, then Lydia and Rose Dimitra were women now. Had Alex finished college in Athens? Married? Was Dorian missing nephews and nieces? Was he sacrificing family for family?

Or had they returned to Tidewater? Perhaps they were only a hundred miles away, convinced he was dead. Where was Nick? How much had Dorian's disappearance affected them? What story had Lucas Wallace told them about it to keep his precarious hold on them?

Mother? Where are you? I can't see you in the darkness.

Had any of them contracted one of the hundred illnesses that could strike in the night . . . and had they died? Rose Dimitra had been coughing the last time he saw her . . . water in Europe wasn't always safe to drink—

Had he failed to be there in the last hours of one of his beloved sisters? Alex, Nick?

Mother?

Six years . . . longer than it had seemed going by.

He crunched through the ivy toward the brick walk. Then he heard the sound. He trod slowly into the moonlit garden, moving toward what he heard.

When he reached the source of the noise, he looked into a deep, shadowy corner, and there was the boy.

Huddled with his knees to his chest, sobbing until he could barely breathe. Tears put a sheen on his chocolate face, his lips glossy, and the crimp of misery was destroying the beauty of his eyes.

"I know you dint wanna find me," Burlie sobbed. "I'm too big and too black. . . . I dint mean to hurt him . . . I'm just too big."

He turned his face up to Dorian. No longer an intimidating

chunk of the night, the massive form seemed very small right now. Only a boy. A little boy, disappointed by his idol's restraint. His voice turned high, like a child's.

. "You're . . . shamed . . . of me."

The words rang and rang through Dorian's guilty heart. His throat knotted up for the first time—how long?—at the sound of Burlie's sobs. The boy wept to be forgiven for hurting Wyatt, for being too big, for being different, for somehow failing to meet standards his adored older brother must have been holding him to all these years. Too much to take . . . the whole evening had been too much to take.

Before him Dorian saw his own handiwork. A boy who had clung to the hope of finding him, only to be pushed away.

Orienta, Orienta . . .

A groan of regret pushed out of his throat. He knelt beside the boy. Belatedly he gathered to his chest a bulk that once had squirmed against that very spot—he had been the first to hold Yula's black newborn boy, birthed into the white arms of his brother.

Into those arms the baby now returned. Years withered and blew away. Without taking a step toward Tidewater, two lost boys found their way a little closer to home.

CHAPTER THIRTY-TWO

———————— ★ ————————

"Just didn't like it, that's all. I just didn't like what I saw. The way she looked at me and how she talked. She implied I'm not a good wife."

"You're in bed with me, and I ain't your husband. How good a wife can you be?"

"None of your business what goes on between me and my husband, and don't you forget it. I just didn't like the way she talked."

"Well, what'd she say?"

"It's not what she *said*. It's the way she moved and the way she served the food and the way she treated both of them, like some kind of a biddy servant or something. I haven't seen such upsucking since the well come in at Eli Suggins's pig farm on the Kaw River's smelly side. I'm a damned ·good wife, and I'd be a damned better one if my husband hadn't blown a hole in my little brother's chest. Can I help it if he killed my brother? Is it my fault? Was it my finger on the trigger? I sew up his rips, I keep his house in order, I clean his office, and I grill his cockles. I'm no white slave! I do this because it's the right thing for me to do, godsuckit!"

"Girl, you got a tongue."

"My tongue's none of your business either. And get your hand off me. You got enough tonight, Clyman."

Clyde Clyman's head went down in a scowl, and his eyes got those white rings under them. Grace had seen it before, often enough to ignore it. His voice took on that gravel she'd also heard before.

"I don't want to hear no more," he grumbled, "about your husband."

She waggled her fingers at him dismissively. "Who cares what you want? You're getting more than your share. I got a husband, and that's how it is. I'll talk about him if I flapping well please to."

"Y'know," he said, "you had me settin' out by the riverside in town for nigh on four hours waiting for that nigger Scobell to pick up a note. I was cold out there. Damn near froze. And then we got chased by some sailors who didn't like us being on their dock. Don't know what they thought we was doing out there—"

"Oh, quit whining," Grace mourned. "Damned if you don't whine like a wet dog."

"I hear down at the south end of town they caught a spy and the soldiers beat him to death, no trial, no nothin'. I coulda got killed!"

"Oh, so what? I'll beat you to death myself if you don't quit jawing your baby fat off. And *get* that dad-gasted hand out of there!"

Grace threw the quilt from her bed and strode naked across the cabin to the window. She looked out over the dark powder yard and listened to the *kssshhh* of the waterwheels. The James River didn't care that it was night, that powdermilling couldn't be done in these lost hours, because there was no manner of lighting safe enough to be used near gunpowder.

"Day after day I see wagons leave those gates," she sighed. "Shipments going out of this mill just as if you and I and Pinkerton were still sitting in our mama's outhouses with our thumbs up our backsides. Everybody talks about the South winning, and that crybaby McClellan sits on his butt out there, doing more of his nothing. The North talks about giving up. About how the war's not worth fighting. They don't want to send their boys down here to fight for the niggers. They want to just throw up their hands and let the South go its own way. Then what! Then what'll I have? I'll have to just kill the Craigs, and that's all I'll get to do. What kind of revenge is that?"

Pinkerton had been right. Her whole heart wasn't in this. She wasn't a spy by nature, but by necessity. Because of a decision. Decisions she'd made for herself had been the only forces in her life that had moved her forward, and she had learned to depend upon them and stick to them. But the past was retreating at the same clip as the future was thundering down upon the nation. War could do that, she guessed. She had to pull from a deeper and deeper place the memory of her parents' bodies hanging from the ceiling of their Kansas cabin, disemboweled and dripping, because of slave trouble at the Craig Tannery. Even the image of Wyatt Craig with his pistol against Patrick's chest no longer carried the sharpness that had prodded her this far. Lately temptation to discard the past altogether hit her more than once, and only her stubborn nature held her to the course set.

She flung her arms in frustration and paced back toward the bed.

"Day after day I give you numbers from the office, and you get numbers from the grounds and take it to Pinkerton, and day after day nothing happens. I stay Craig's wife, and what's changed? How come I'm the only person who wants to get this war moving?"

Clyman lit up a cigar and drew a long puff. "You always talk big. Pinkerton's happy about the numbers, so what're you cackling about? You're just plain a dirt-road traitor, same as me."

Rage flared as Grace reached over the breadth of the bed, snatched the cigar out of his mouth, and left him spitting the torn shank. The cigar flew into the opposite wall and exploded in a flurry of sparks.

"You're a traitor for money, *Clyde*," she reminded, drawing his name into an insult. "And don't smoke in here. My husband doesn't smoke, and he'll smell it."

"He runs a powdermill, and he used to run a leather tannery!" Clyman rasped. "Probably hasn't smelled nothing in years. Besides, he ain't on the grounds. You said so when I asked if he might walk in on us. 'Member?"

"Don't take stupid chances. Smoke in your own place."

She paced up and down the side of the bed, scratching her thighs and glaring at the floor.

"Yes, Pinkerton's happy with the numbers," she mocked. "Every number that comes out of this mill gets tripled by the time it leaves his mouth. McClellan looks at it and sees double again. Maybe he's drinking behind everybody's back, I don't know. But something's got to start changing around here."

"Around the mill?"

"No, you pickle-assed mouse! Around the *South*."

He leered at her, his eyes half-closed, but not in fatigue. "Don't talk to me that way. . . . I don't like it."

Grace wasn't listening. "Gunpowder and cannon shot leaves this mill every day, heading out to make Wyatt Craig's reputation nice and solid. Somehow I'm going to crack it up. There's got to be more happening here than useless information flowing out to a general who hasn't got the nuggets to use it. We're going to take some action, you and I."

She folded her arms so tight that the skin ached, and fell onto the bed.

The mattress and old springs bellowed.

"I'm going to do something," she grumbled. "Cripple the mill somehow . . . do some damage. That's right . . . I'm going to do it. I'm going to get this war started."

The tall lilacs struggling through Richmond's mild winter put a scent in Barry Swanborough's bedchamber.

Dorian lay with Orienta as a boy lies beside his first love. The man who had explored every bird cage in Richmond and five states in every direction was suddenly a teenager again. He even kept the sheet twisted between his legs.

He still wore his ascot and shirt, but nothing else. The flannel sheet stayed up as he talked about himself, lawyer for the prosecution.

She accepted him. No matter what he told her, no matter which obscene details he plucked from his dark past, she nodded in understanding. She had even played the role for him, as she promised. She was a quiet, shy lover, not like the whores. Not like anything he had ever experienced. She had let him do almost everything. So different . . .

Over the past year or so there had been fewer and fewer visits to the brothels. He was tired of purchased passion. Orienta couldn't offer passion. Hadn't even tried. Perhaps she knew that no one could outpassion a whore. She was nearly silent after the game of roles, and sank into a peaceful completion without the theatrics that rattled a whorehouse's window like advertisement.

This was something else, completely strange to Dorian.

Never had he lay with anyone who cared whether he lived, died, or suffered after he left the bed.

Affection. She *cared* about him. It was new.

He wasn't even sure whether or not she respected him. The whores were always in a little awe. He didn't feel that tonight. He had never experienced Orienta's brand of balance.

He must find something she couldn't accept.

I'm half-negro. I'm half-negro.

"I'm—"

"I know what you are," she said. "I had eleven good years with my husband before fate stole him away. I'm thirty-four years old . . . older than you, Captain, I know . . . and there are parcels of truth that have made themselves known to me. I have discovered there is not time in life to sift for sin. God judges us soon enough . . . shall we also judge each other?"

He gazed at her, unable to defend himself with a response.

She touched his cool face and whispered, "No."

"I'm half—"

"Teach me, she murmured, "a poem in the Greek . . . my son."

★

CHAPTER THIRTY-THREE

———— ★ ————

Lammot Du Pont shoved his stovepipe hat into the hands of Lord Palmerston's aide, Briggs or Braggs or whatever his name was, and followed the man's balding head through the elegant halls of 10 Downing Street. He forced himself not to admire the graceful architecture or handsome furnishings. To look, to be in awe, to be too much the appreciator, would be inappropriate at a time when he wished to establish an upper hand with the upper crust.

But the corner of his eye couldn't help catching the intricate moldings framing every doorway, the curtains made of brocade and Westminster lace, the velvety banister on the stairs he was led up, or the brass keyhole covers on every door, to ensure absolute privacy. This place made the White House seem almost pedestrian.

He'd seen all this before, four times since arriving again in England, and without exception he had been asked to sit, to wait, only to be then refused an audience with the Prime Minister.

Lord Palmerston's chargé d'affaires, a Mr. Thorsby, met Du Pont as he had the last three times . . . just outside the Prime Minister's office. Close enough to make Du Pont feel accepted, yet without ever quite accepting him.

"Mr. Du Pont, welcome back to England. I'd heard you left the country."

"Thank you. I did, but I'm back," Du Pont barked. "I would like to see Lord Palmerston now."

"His Lordship is—"

"Detained, busy, ill, involved, indisposed, meeting with someone else?"

"He does have a government to run, Mr. Du Pont," Thorsby said unflappably.

"And Mr. Lincoln has a hemisphere to preserve."

"Perhaps if you can wait a few minutes—"

"Yes, I'll *wait*."

"This way, then."

The same scenario. Each time a request, each time a rebuff.

But not this time.

This time, when they approached the waiting room to the prime minister's office, Du Pont suddenly plunged forward, knocked Briggs and Thorsby aside, pushed the door open before him, and plunged into the office.

There behind a resplendent mahogany desk, beside carved and glazed bookshelves and a fireplace with an Indian spark screen, sat the astonished Prime Minister Viscount Palmerston.

The old man instantly pierced him with a beady-eyed glare.

"Your Lordship," Du Pont said carefully, hoping to prove with courtesy if not with posture that he was no assassin, but merely a disgruntled visitor. He did not bow.

Palmerston replaced his quill in its brass ink stand.

"You are . . ."

Du Pont parted his lips, but Briggs stepped in front of him, determined that British tradition not be slaughtered during his duty hours.

Through his teeth Briggs said, "Mr. Lammot Du Pont, of Delaware, America."

Du Pont added firmly, "And I beg an audience immediately."

Beg, but what he meant was demand.

Many seconds beat by, slowly. Palmerston gazed at the impertinent American distant cousin until he was sure the young man was sweating at least a little under that black coat.

Then His Lordship dismissed Thorsby with a wave, motioning for Briggs to remain. The aide reluctantly offered Du Pont a seat in a chair beside a chess set whose pieces were turbaned and veiled figures from India, and all the pawns were elephants.

"Brandy, Mr. Du Pont?" Briggs asked. "Or tea?"

"Tea," Du Pont accepted with a little snap. Maybe this was a test.

A pause gnawed at them all until Briggs poured the tea, then went to stand beside the door, his hands folded behind his back. He would not leave. That remained clear in his face. Americans were not to be trusted. He was quite certain that beneath the black suit, Du Pont was wearing loincloth and feathers.

"As you know, Mr. Prime Minister," Du Pont said, "the United States' civil disturbance between the North and the South is over the subject of states' rights, partly concerning state-to-state economic dependence upon chattel slavery or free industry. We of the North believe that a nation under God can not only survive, but prosper, only without the shame of slavery. England feels about slavery as we do, I know, and wouldn't wish any obstruction to its end."

Palmerston's tiny eyes widened. "Slavery is the last remaining bane of civilization," he agreed. "It has existed since the beginning of time, yet we, you and I and Mr. Lincoln, find ourselves on the brink of finally ending it. While in the Foreign Office, I took it upon myself to send the British fleet into territorial waters off Brazil to suppress trade of slaves. That was some time ago, of course. In 1847, I believe, when I was Foreign Secretary. . . . You know, Lord Russell and I trade off positions from time to time—"

Du Pont nodded, gratified to have done his homework on Palmerston's view of slavery.

Palmerston went on without noticing his guest's approving silence.

"—I appealed to the United States government to adjust their laws about Negro British citizens on British ships. But . . . they wouldn't do it."

Du Pont frowned and asked, "What was the issue of contention?"

Palmerston huffed. "Well, sir, our negro sailors were being seized by some port authorities in the South. They were being mistreated, imprisoned, some even impressed into the slave system. They were British citizens, by God, these negroes!"

"Unforgivable," Du Pont agreed, careful not to be too cheerful about already having Palmerston on his side.

"Those incidents proved to me," Palmerston said, "that the

advocation of slavery involved no legal or moral consideration, nor any measure of a negro person's abilities, but only the color of skin. It was the sole ground of seizure and detainment. That was a revelation, and I charged myself never to forget it."

"The United States agree, Your Lordship, let me assure you. This motivates many Northerners to support the war effort who otherwise would never raise a stick against his fellow countrymen."

"I suppose," Palmerston said in a noncommittal tone. "I keep a most friendly attitude toward the United States, but I really haven't paid undue attention to this new problem of yours."

Du Pont faltered. "You have *not*?"

"I find myself compelled to keep my eyes eastward, Mr. Du Pont. To the European continent. I remain suspicious of . . . changing alliances."

Palmerston drew in a sigh that forced him back somewhat in the chair, and prudently kept the next thought to himself. He wanted to say "suspicious of France"—but he was speaking to a man with a French name. Did Napoleon III have a hand in the Du Pont's activities? Was he engineering embarrassment for Britain? Trying to drive a wedge between Britain and the Confederacy? Palmerston had always dreamed of expanding British influence into Central America, but as time passed he had come to realize that the United States and the United States alone, with its mob rule, would say what happened in the entire Western Hemisphere. Now that mob rule was ripping the North American continent into pieces, only a fortuneteller or a madman dared claim to know what was coming. In his long life he had seen British influence wane on that continent, and he was determined not to let it wane further in the world. Therefore, he must watch the world very carefully. America was cooperating nicely by destroying itself without European intervention.

"President Lincoln sent me a steamship with five hundred thousand dollars in gold bullion in the hold for me to spend on the commodities market, with which we purchased saltpeter for gunpowder. I had arranged for four million pounds of it to be loaded aboard five ships bound for America, only to find that you, sir, have ordered my ships docked indefinitely."

Lord Palmerston was introspective for several moments. He quickly translated the dollars into pounds in his head. Ten times a king's ransom. Lincoln had given the Du Ponts an incredible powder contract, and Lammot Du Pont was here to usher it through personally. Palmerston had, of course, heard of the Du Ponts of Delaware; one should have to be encased in ice for a thousand years to have missed them on the international market.

"Your purpose is to corner the niter market, Mr. Du Pont, isn't it?"

Du Pont's face pinked slightly, but he showed no other sign of his rather obvious collusion.

"This niter purchase was meant not only to supply the North, but to deprive the South," Palmerston added. "Yes?"

Lammot Du Pont was a young man, full of a young man's spirit and a young man's doubts. He felt the doubts creeping up through the pit of his stomach, making him feel insecure in this place and clouding the concepts of right, of wrong, and of the channels to reach them.

He stood up abruptly and let his doubts be buried by the spirit within himself, which he trusted, and by the anger that gave him strength.

"Mr. Prime Minister," he began, "you have been in this tangled world much longer than I. Perhaps you've lost interest in it, I don't know. Perhaps America is nothing but a temporary aberration to you in the world. Perhaps I am unsung in the rules of proper social threats, but here's one from myself to you, from the United States to England. It's going to be saltpeter for my nation, Mr. Palmerston," he said. "Saltpeter or war."

★

CHAPTER THIRTY-FOUR

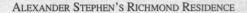

"There are four possible outcomes to the war. One, the North wins and the Constitution is forfeit. Rights will be little more than spice on the burned cake. We may as well live under the Czar. Two, the South wins, and we lose half our nation and live at each other's throats as Europe does. Three, both sides fight to exhaustion and finally make a compromise, at cost of thousands upon thousands of lives and the spirit of the nation. Four, the three of us and a few chosen compatriots engineer a Southern victory at the right time, under the right circumstances, to guarantee reunification with the North, with the best possible interpretation of the Constitution."

Vice President Stephens punctuated his analysis of the situation with waves of his tiny hands and the clink of china as he made tea in the corner. Ordinarily his slaves would have stayed to make the tea, but this was a very private conversation. "During times of war," he had told Wyatt and Dorian a few minutes before, "nobles make their own tea."

Wyatt was still on his feet, despite being gestured toward any of the drawing room's three chairs or the muscular mahogany sofa, but he was anxious to sit. The British-red walls made him tense, and the green doors made him nauseous, on top of the fact that these clandestine meetings with Stephens always came bundled with surprises, and Wyatt couldn't bend his legs very well when he scented surprises coming.

Dorian, on the other hand, was his usual flameproof self, lounging on a sofa among blue-and-burgundy paisley pillows, flippantly picking at a loose string on his waistcoat. Wyatt simply glared at him in annoyance for not getting any help being nervous.

A clink in the corner drew his attention back.

Stephens had picked up the teapot in both hands and was swirling it. He looked at Dorian and asked, "You have a honey-and-milk fetish for tea, if I recall?"

With a tilt of his head Dorian answered, "Yessuh, Massa Flyspeck, I does."

At the same time that a chill ran up Wyatt's spine and he held the breath he'd just drawn, Vice President Stephens reeled back and laughed. He cuddled the hot teapot to the four scarves around his neck, pointed at Dorian, caught a gasp, and spoke to Wyatt.

"Isn't he marvelous? Oh, Major, such a companion you have here. We took on the subject of slavery the other day, and Dorian is simply remarkable at it. He fell into the negro dialect to argue their points of view—and by the word of God if he didn't sound just like one of them! You should have heard, I swear it, you should have heard."

He shook his head and chortled as he remembered.

Wyatt tried to avoid reaction and nearly choked trying. Dorian just sat there like a naughty priest, with both eyebrows up and his lips pressed mischievously.

"Gentlemen, on to business," Stephens said. "I summoned the two of you here for a very specific reason, which I'll get to shortly. It is now time to act upon our resolutions. And I have decided *how* we will act."

He brought the teapot and several cups on a tray to a table in the center of the room. He straightened and looked at Wyatt.

"Don't you want to sit down, Major? Your injury—"

"All it's doing is making me itch, sir," Wyatt said, rubbing the sling on his right arm. "I'm fine standing here for now. Little stiff."

"Then I shall stand also," Stephens said. Before Wyatt had a chance to argue with him, he strode around behind the sofa and palmed the cameled mahogany strip that lined the back. "We are on the edge of a new chapter in foreign affairs. The *Trent* affair is officially closed. Mason and Slidell are now free to ambassadorialize England and France until the Gulf Stream changes direction, and yet the Davis emissaries will both be as impotent as mules. We have made sure of that. Now we move on to the next step. As you may recall, in early 1861 everyone was dancing around the slavery issue. No one wanted to make it *the* issue of secession."

"It *wasn't* the only issue," Wyatt pointed out.

"No, it wasn't, but the cards of public opinion can always be reshuffled. Everyone assumed back then that European recognition would be automatic because the benefits of our breakup were so great for Europe, and because people like Barry Swanborough thought Europe needed Southern raw materials too much to rile us. I confess to those beliefs myself. None of us thought the North had the will to fight, and the South assumed the border states would join us. So far, not one of those things has come true, but mind you, we all thought they would. I did too. I was mistaken and desperate that the South should not win too quick nor too complete a victory. In order to bring events under control, I got up in March of that year, in Savannah, and made what is now being called my 'Cornerstone Speech.' I described slavery as the cornerstone of the Confederacy and said the Confederacy was founded on the truth that the white man is superior to the negro. You both remember, I'm sure."

Wyatt only nodded uneasily, but Dorian flipped, "You made international news, and that's right where Wyatt and I both live."

"Yes, the thing rumbled for months. It did exactly what I planned . . . it sent a shiver through Europe."

Without turning to look at him, Dorian added, "You were blamed far and wide for damaging relations with Europe, because no one in Europe wanted to be involved in a proslavery fight."

Stephens nodded, then gestured at Wyatt. "Do you remember that speech, Major?"

Wyatt went back and forth on his two feet. Very touchy subject. What was Stephens getting after? Finally he uttered a noncommittal, "Yes, I do, sir."

"Do you know why I did that? Why I sabotaged British recognition of the Confederacy then? Was I an idiot?"

"Well, I—uh—I—"

Stephens nodded briskly in his quick way. "I was willing to

appear an idiot for the nation's sake. Recognition from Britain at that early time—"

"Would've meant sacrificing the nation," Wyatt finished for him. "Now I've got it." He narrowed his eyes and looked squarely at the beetle-browed little man. "You did that to your own reputation just to stall recognition?"

"Yes, I did. I made my Cornerstone speech knowing it would enflame the antislave British into *not* recognizing the Confederacy too early. The Davis government would have gotten all the credit, the Confederacy would have won without firing a shot, and there would be no hope of reunification with the Union. The United States was in danger of becoming a thing of the past. I had to do something quickly to distance Britain from the early Confederacy."

"That's amazing, sir."

"Not at all. In fact, I miscalculated. I thought things would move much faster and with much more deadliness to the continent. Now those who look beyond the surface can see the tide turning from a Southern advantage to a Northern one. Despite the fact that the war is going well, I can see the deprivation already."

"Bet you can," Wyatt blurted. "We just lost the battle at Roanoke because I can't get—"

"Niter. I know." The Vice President came around the sofa and poured three cups of well-steeped tea. "We're still playing the balancing act. Neither side must prevail yet. The North is gaining military advantage, and we must even the score."

"What do you mean, they're gaining advantage?" Wyatt asked. "General Lee's been winning skirmishes all over the eastern theater—"

"And even so, the North is still strangling us. They're moving slowly down the Mississippi, New Orleans is gone, Chattanooga is gone—a major railroad hub—and one by one our ports are slipping away. No, Major, now is the time to act. We must even the scales, give the South more fighting power. The war *must* drag out. Of course, I want a Southern victory, but the South must win a *humble* victory and end up aware that there is no future in being a separate nation. Now, gentlemen, now is the right time to angle ourselves back toward whatever courts British recognition. We haven't the money to fight an extended war. The trick is to get Britain to recognize the Confederacy when *we* want it to, and in such a way that Jefferson Davis gets no credit."

"Could you explain that part to me a little more, sir?" Wyatt asked. "I can't figure how it matters who gets credit."

"Don't go into the whole *discursus*, Aleck," Dorian popped in. "Just hit the high spots."

Stephens smiled, nodded, and scolded himself with a shake of his head for talking too much.

"I'll try. It matters, Major, because those who get credit will have power in forging the conditions of reunification . . . or of the way the war ends, in any case. I've always questioned Jefferson Davis's judgment, and he has done nothing as President to make me cease questioning. Look at this man Mason. Davis has chosen the worst possible man to go to Britain. For one thing, Mason has been vocal in criticisms of the British over the years. On top of that, he is so proslavery as to embarrass the most consummate Southerner. He was even the author of the Fugitive Slave Law! What a man to pick to go talk to England! Why, it's an insult to England."

While Stephens handed Dorian a small tray with honey and milk for his tea, a thought formed in Wyatt's mind that turned his stomach sour.

"Did you ever think," he began tentatively, "maybe Davis chose Mason for the same kind of reason that you made your Cornerstone speech? Maybe he sent the wrong man on purpose? You know . . . ulterior motives?"

Stephens stared at him, then turned and stared at Dorian. Plainly that thought hadn't occurred to either of them—a little note that flattered and frightened Wyatt at the same time. The idea that there were pockets of collusion other than their own.

Frightening. Who would really be in control when the war ended?

Dorian applauded him with a widening of his eyes and a few seconds of wordless analysis. Suddenly all three of them were a touch more uneasy that they had been at the beginning of this meeting.

"The Europeans aren't stupid, sir," Wyatt said, as long as he had the moment. "They don't like being blackmailed. They know the South could send cotton if it wanted to."

"And they will credit that blackmail to the Davis government," Stephens said. He had been ready for that. He tabled their doubts and continued. "Bismarck is doing anything he can to weaken England and France, because their power weakens his. Prussia is headed for a war with France and probably with Austria. Britain and France are both too busy with Bismarck to worry about the Americans."

"We can use that," Dorian offered.

"I intend to. It is my plan to send a man to Europe with a private message from me and my faction, technically unofficial but diplomatically binding. We'll tacitly tell Lord Russell that in the event of hostile actions by the continental powers, the Confederacy will come in on behalf of Great Britain."

The weight of the promise stirred tension in the room.

Dorian commented, "Interesting fable, Aleck."

"You think it's interesting?" the Vice President said. "Here's the interesting part. I'm going to promise France the same thing."

"My God!" Wyatt suddenly got a hot flash that set him sweating, and he dropped into the nearest chair. What had he gotten himself into?

"Of course!" Stephens said. "Lie to them! Promise them anything they want to hear. Why not? What can they do? Go to war with us over secret negotiations? Hardly."

He crossed the rug and looked Dorian squarely in the eyes.

"Dorian," he said, "I want you to be that man."

In the middle of a sip of tea he had hoped would calm him, Wyatt sputtered, "What?"

"Me?" Dorian choked at the same time. The sudden subject of attention gasped a few times, then just sat there chuckling at the whole idea. "Oh, I can see that. 'Hello, m'lord, Devil J. Advocate calling on behalf of the rebels—' "

"You're the perfect man," Stephens said. "Very continental."

Dorian uncrossed his legs, then crossed them in the other direction. "Just like Benjamin Franklin, that's me. Do you know that the French expected him to appear in buckskins and moccasins, but he stumped them by appearing in velvet? I could do something like that, show up at Buckingham Palace in a silk Kimono with a sprig of mint in my lapel, and when I corner these animals, I'll tell them what I'm going to do for them. Aleck, really."

"Dorian, you must go."

"Why must I?"

"Because of your connection with the Du Ponts and the powder trade. You know the details and the dangers, the names and nuances—"

"Lovely. Recite it again. What rhymes with 'nuance'?"

"You can make Du Pont money work for the Confederacy."

"It already does," Wyatt drawled from his chair.

The Vice President turned to him. "Yes, and you're already feeling the pinch of the niter shortage. Your mills are shutting down at a rate of one per week, correct?"

Reluctantly Wyatt fell silent and nodded.

Stephens went on, "That is because Lammot Du Pont is over there cornering the market of British saltpeter. We can take advantage of that and get some of the saltpeter for ourselves. There is a worldwide network of industrialists and aristocrats who will sympathize with the South when Du Pont money tells it to, and who will get Russell and Palmerston's ear unofficially for Dorian, when Mason and Slidell will not be able to get it at all, officially or otherwise. And Major Craig," he added, turning, "I want you to go with him."

Gaping like a kicked dog, Wyatt gulped, "Me?"

"Me! Me!" Stephens mimicked. "This room is beginning to sound like a South American aviary! Gentlemen, where is the mystery here? I ask a scholar and a prominent businessman to travel in representation of me on foreign soil. Dorian has the clandestine power but is somewhat abrasive—"

"I beg your pardon?"

"And you, Major, are the symbol and function of American business. You, speaking personally, are also very much a velvet glove to ease the scratches of this one over here."

Seeing himself indicated again like a bag of salt being delivered to a kitchen, Dorian waved a hand cantankerously. "Don't rattle the windows, Aleck. I'm not going to England. Wyatt can go be a glove if he wishes, but the sandpaper shall cling to the land."

"Please change your mind."

Dorian stood up.

"Nothing," he ground out, "will drive me off this continent until all my purposes here are fulfilled."

He stepped past the Vice President and put some distance between the two of them.

"Then tell me what they are," Stephens begged, "and I shall do everything in my power to help you fulfill them."

After a pause that suggested the wild thought was actually batting about the corners of Dorian's better judgment, he simply said, "Thank you. No."

And he continued walking away.

Stephens paused, contemplated the carpet, paced this way, paced back, stopped to think, paced in another direction, and back again.

Ultimately his harsh dark eyes fell on Wyatt.

"And what about you, Major?"

Wyatt shifted, cleared his throat, scratched at his sling—at least gave the Vice President the idea that he might be vacillating, thinking about the options.

"Sir," he began, "I'm just not sure your calculations now will play out any better than they did in March sixty-one. Antiwar sentiment is growing in the North every day. And I can't help wonder . . . how many men have to die in this 'dragging out'?"

Even Dorian looked up and held very still as that question rang.

"Oh, Major," Stephens uttered. He shook his head as though disapproving of himself, held his hands out, and begged forgiveness with his expression. "You may very well be right. If you feel this is a mistake, you may leave with no ill words from me. I am certainly no god, as no one knows better than I. Oh, no, no. We're taking some tremendous gambles, and I rarely sleep nights through anymore. We may succeed . . . we may not. We may all be hanged as traitors. Or we may go down in the annals of history as the second set of Founding Fathers. Who can tell the fortunes of such times?"

A silence fell around his words like a frame.

It was neither of the two great talkers who broke that silence, but Wyatt himself. He stood up and put down the teacup from which he had taken not a single complete sip.

"I'll have to think about all this for a couple days, Mr. Vice President," he said. "I'm sorry. I think you and I are both willing to die for our principles . . . I just don't know if I'm up to making other men die for my principles. Not when I haven't told them the reasons."

"Take your few days, Major," the Vice President said. "I am no different from you. I shoot blind into the foggy future, as must we all. But remember . . . time is howling at our ears, and it bites in the dark."

CHAPTER THIRTY-FIVE

PLENTIFUL

It was almost nightfall when the wagon pulled in. A second-hand rig, rented from the railroad yard in Norfolk. When he heard it rattle into the curved carriage drive, Jeff lumbered out of the big brick mansion's front door, over the wide veranda, and out to meet the wagon.

"Mr. Alex! Lord, if I wasn't getting plenty worried about you! You been gone nigh onto ten days!"

"Ten and a half, Jeff," Alex called. He snapped the old horse to a halt, fully realizing his voice was missing its usual upbeat lilt.

He was tired. He'd been five extra days in Leesburg, trying to get out of Leesburg. Movement of the armies, or at least talk about anticipated movements, had tied up travel, trains, coaches—the North could probably win the war just by gagging the South's day-to-day getting along. Right now Alex would have surrendered.

Instead, he settled for climbing out of the wagon and straightening his spine.

"Oh, my goodness," he grunted. "I'm bent permanently, Jeff—what's the matter?"

Jeff was staring at the wagon's bed, at a bulk covered with burlap.

"Oh, sir," the big negro moaned, "don't tell me that one of them pretty little children—"

"No! No, Jeff, not at all. I'm so sorry—they all got away

clean. At least they got to the Leesburg station. Beyond that, I can't say."

"Then . . . what's in the back?"

"Well, go have yourself a look."

Jeff eyed him suspiciously, then strode to the wagon's bed and lifted up the burlap sheet.

"Aw, Mr. Alex . . . I don't think you got a huntin' dog back here you're gonna try to feed . . . do you, now, sir?"

Alex grinning. "No. *You're* going to feed him." He joined Jeff and looked down into the soggy-eyed, pathetic face of the scruffy setter that had looked much more grand in a moonlit field than he did here. The dog whined a little and tried to stand in spite of the thick bandage wrapped around its middle and one hind leg. "Stay there," Alex cooed, patting the pointy nose. "Jeff will take care of you."

"Aw!" Jeff howled. "This is a nigger-killin' dog, Mr. Alex! Which niggers on this farm you gonna tell to stick their hand by this dog?"

"You and your family, and anyone else who calls Plentiful home. I want him tended solely by negroes. I want him tended, petted, fed, and talked to by negroes. I intend to change his extremely small mind. I've been with this dog for several days now, and I can tell you that while he has a good heart, he is in desperate straights for a brain."

"Aw . . ."

"What's the trouble, Jeff? After all, if we can change the world's mind, we can change a dog's mind. As for the negroes . . . they'll have to bend a little too."

Alex trudged inside and went straight upstairs. The enormous house was too quiet. It carried only the echoes of all the children raised here, Alex and his brother Dorian and their sisters, the laughter and quarreling of the Greek servants, visits from the aunts and their husbands and children . . .

Seemed so empty now. The only vestige of those days was

the mural of Iphigenia in her wedding dress on the library wall.

The library . . . where Lucas Wallace now spent most of his time. With a picture of his wife, memories of his dead political aspirations, and a bottle.

Alex couldn't even bring himself to peek into the library tonight, just to make sure his father was still alive.

Tonight he couldn't bring himself to care. If Lucas was alive, he was alive. If not, the war would go on and so would the Underground Railroad. Nothing would change.

Alex shuddered as he slipped into his own bedchamber and peeled off his torn overcoat and began to undress. He hadn't intended to spend ten days in the same clothes, and the clothes came off with protest. Gratefully he slipped into one of his satin smoking jackets and knotted the belt. He thought about asking one of the slaves to make him a meal, then thought again. They knew he was back . . . someone would be up here with hot food before too long, whether he asked or not. Better to let them do something nice for him without diminishing the gesture by asking.

As he flopped onto his reading chair and let his eyes go out of focus, someone pounded on his chamber door. Before he answered, Alex already knew who it was. He could smell who it was.

"Come in, Father," he called drearily.

The door groaned open. In came Luke Wallace, preceded and followed by the cloudy stink of whiskey that was always with him these days. His beard was silver-streaked and wild, hadn't been clipped in a month. His clothing was rich but sloppy, his shirt untucked. At least he had bothered to button it, probably in an effort to make a good impression on his son.

"Alex—"

"Yes, Father."

"I wanna talk to you."

"I'm very tired at the moment, Father, if you don't mind."

"Won't take long."

"Fine," Alex acceded. "Unless it deals with putting you back in control of the plantation. That I will not consider. The slaves are doing a fine job of processing the yield, and they have become competent managers and laborers. If I ever doubted that American negroes could be self-motivating and self-managing, I no longer doubt it. Everything that happens on Plentiful now convinces me that the Southern idea of right and wrong has been twisted up for a hundred years. No—don't make a comment. Plentiful is perfectly all right. Until, or if, the war comes to Tidewater, you needn't worry that I'm letting your life's work go up in the smokehouses, all right?"

Lucas held onto the bedpost for stability, digested what he had just heard, and nodded as though he agreed with everything Alex was doing.

Clearly there was something else on his mind.

He straightened and tried to stand without wobbling. "I want you to write a letter to your mother again."

"Father . . . I did write to her. You saw the response. She refuses to come back."

His father looked suddenly like a scruffy little boy who hadn't been able to reach the plum on the tree. "You know, son . . . I got my regrets. Maybe you got yours. Mine, mostly they seem to come from doing things I shouldn't have done and not doing things I should have done, I know all that. You know, about two weeks ago I took a gun off my library wall and I sat there all night trying like a fiend to blow my brains out, but I ain't got the guts, Alex." He sniffed through his swollen nose and nodded in sad agreement with himself. "Guess I ain't got the guts to write to my own wife. I need you to write to her again, son . . . won't you do that for your old pa?"

"The last time I wrote to my mother," Alex said, battling his fatigue, "I had to endure telling her that I had given up trying to find Dorian . . . that Dorian is either dead or wants nothing to do with us. What am I to tell her now that would cast light upon the dirge of that last letter?" He stood up and stretched his aching legs. "I cannot mend your marriage for you, Father. I cannot erase your mistakes. . . . Jesus Christ knows, I've my own to deal with."

The smell of whiskey was making him nauseous, and it

changed his mind about wandering down to the kitchen. He tightened the velvet belt on his smoking jacket and went to the doorway.

There he paused and looked back at his father.

"If you have a message for Mother," he said, "I suggest you let yourself go sober enough to hold a pen in your hand . . . and write it yourself."

★

CHAPTER THIRTY-SIX

---------- ★ ----------

"Captain Parthens. Turn around."

Dorian turned first. Beside him Wyatt also turned. Here in the last hour of business at an outdoor market in the center of Richmond was the last place they expected any confrontation. The crowd of citizens sought to fill their pantries and squeeze out a sense of normalcy while armies moved in the mountains and on the coasts. The crowd had provided the two men a kind of shield. Not thick enough, however, to keep them from being sought out and now confronted by Barry Swanborough.

It was Wyatt's first public outing with the bad shoulder, still in a sling, and he had gotten lots of attention and sympathy for his "wound" from passersby, to whom he wasted many long minutes explaining that it wasn't a battle injury in spite of his uniform. Dorian had encouraged him just to take the compliments because it made people feel good to be touching a battle veteran, but Wyatt couldn't manage the facade or take credit that belonged to real soldiers. He'd gladly have gone out into a battle to avoid a confrontation with Swanborough, much less one that was a surprise on a wide-open public thoroughfare.

Swanborough stood before them in the middle of the street wearing a heavy burgundy overcoat, a gray muffler and day hat, looking like a clipping for New England menswear. He had two slaves behind him, neither of them Burlie.

Squared off before him was Dorian in that Inverness cape, with his opera hat and ascot and no uniform today, but instead wearing a daycoat and waistcoat, making the street a very fashionable arena.

"Ah, the prime impeder," Dorian said, damning Swanborough with a smile. "If it isn't Plato Socrates, with Thunder and his brother, Rumble."

"You've tampered with my political concerns for no apparent reason that anyone can discover," Swanborough said, "and now you have taken to tampering in my household affairs."

Without missing a beat, Dorian said, "Groan you, master doctor?"

"Over the two weeks of my absence, you've maneuvered into a position of interference. You have convinced my sister-in-law to take possession of my coachman. She has insisted that he be her personal attendant."

Dorian firmly placed his walking stick's silver foot onto the street and struck a pose of cold fascination. "A wise woman's choice in these martial times."

"It wouldn't have been her choice had it not been your suggestion," Swanborough said. "I ordered the slave back to the stable, but my sister-in-law countered the order. She has never done that before. She refuses to allow me to make the decision, though I have always protected her and decided which of my slaves does which duty. This is new. I resent your influence."

Dorian tossed Wyatt a glance and said, "A *benevolent* despot. They always mean well."

"Captain," Swanborough said, loudly enough to get their attention back and the attention of about half the street. "What do you want with my sister-in-law?"

"What do I *want*?" Dorian echoed. "I comprehend that we're both speaking English, but what is your point?"

"You've been keeping my sister-in-law's company. Let's be honest. She is lacking in appearance and carries with her little social influence. I don't know what a man like you can want with a plain woman who is obviously too well-bred to be your usual fare, but I suspect there are questionable motivations."

Untouchable and unimpressed, Dorian actually chuckled and shifted his feet.

Wyatt stepped in front of Dorian, a forefinger raised.

"Look, you," he said. "You're . . . you can't . . . you're an arrogant hammerhead if you think I'm going to let you talk to my friend that way!"

"Two points," Dorian added benignly.

Swanborough looked right through him. He declined Wyatt even the minor courtesy of meeting his eyes. Instead he stepped sideways to get a clear view of Dorian. "Excuse me," he said.

It was a clean insult that left Wyatt sidelined, floundering, brow screwed up in anger. He tried to move between them again.

"No, no." Not wanting protection at his friend's risk, Dorian muted the tension somewhat with a rare pat on Wyatt's good arm, then gripped the same arm and drew him back out of the reach of Swanborough's two slaves. "Down, Rosinante."

Impatiently Swanborough continued, "I have plans for my sister-in-law. When the proper period of mourning is completed, I intend to court her myself. I also intend that nothing will stand in my way."

" 'Come,' " Dorian recited, " 'let's devise how we may add more shame to the black scandal of his hated name . . .' " He leaned toward Wyatt and said, "Faustus. Ever read it? Chilling."

Wyatt glanced nervously between the two men, wondering which one was closer to exploding. Or was Dorian actually enjoying this confrontation? Or was that classic stance a nobleman's prepare-for-blood pose?

Dorian thought half the world was scum and the other half epic. Which was in him now?

"That includes any interest you've convinced her to have in you," Swanborough said. "I don't know what you've told her or done to her, but your attention is indecent, and you will leave her alone from this moment forward."

Standing to Dorian's side, Wyatt suddenly bristled. A line had just been crossed that even his unspurious nature couldn't rub out. He stared at Swanborough, but spoke to the side.

"I've heard enough," he murmured. "Go ahead. I'll support you."

Without taking his eyes off his adversary, Dorian said, "I know you will."

Solid as a rock while Wyatt agitated beside him, Dorian eyed the other man.

"Mr. Swaggerborough," he said incombustibly, "I have naught against you personally, give or take that face, but I'm sure I could come up with a thing or two if you insist." His eyes widened, and he leaned forward on that walking stick just enough to show he wasn't intimidated. "Are you . . . insisting?"

Suddenly Dorian's flippancy was gone. He became so dead serious, so dead threatening, that even the people crowding on the street fell still in anticipation of trouble. Even Swanborough shifted his weight, and his two slaves tightened their shoulders.

"Whatever it is with you," Swanborough said, "it cannot possibly be in Orienta's best interest."

Wyatt, and indeed the entire late-day shopping crowd, stood paralyzed, aware of the daggers drawn in Dorian's eyes and the ill blood between these men. Dorian's hand casually rested upon the business end of that pocket-watch chain.

Yet a muted change came into Dorian's expression—or came beneath it. To double everyone's astonishment, the sizzling gentleman in the gray Inverness paused, then shuffled backward a step.

"*Arbiter elegantarium,*" he said. " 'I will renounce this magic and repent.' Thank you for coming between us. I shall never see her again."

With a complaisant tip of his hat to Swanborough, he dropped a bow toward the baffled crowd, turned on his heel, and simply strode away.

Swanborough and his two slaves stood watching as the captain and the confused major disappeared into the general public. A few moments passed, and the crowd, learning they would find no entertainment here after all, also drifted apart.

"Back to the coach," Swanborough said without looking at his slaves. He felt them move away.

Before he himself could let go of the unrequited challenge and head back, Felix Carter appeared at his side.

"Barry."

"Good evening, Felix."

"Thank you for meeting me in public."

"Quite all right."

"Speaking with the subject of our business, I see," Carter commented, watching Dorian and Wyatt disappear.

"I was suggesting to him that he keep away from my sister-in-law, Felix. Anything else you'd like to know?"

"Mmm." Carter nodded. "What reason did you give him?"

"You know I plan to marry her myself."

"And lay claim to that fifty-four percent of your plantation she inherited from your brother, yes? Marry the controlling interest. Sound decision, Barry, very sound."

Swanborough turned to him. "I earned it. My brother and I built the plantation. She had nothing to do with it, but to marry it. You have something for me, Felix?"

Carter drew him to the middle of the street, where the clack of carriage wheels and horse hooves curtained their conversation.

"I have something for you," Carter echoed, "which is worth your year's yield in blackmail value."

He parted his coat and drew out a large envelope, from which he extracted a battered handbill, obviously aged and passed through many hands. As he handed it to Swanborough, he grinned. "You owe me a long holiday abroad."

"Do I," Swanborough muttered, not making a question.

He read the faded, dusty lettering. The paper was almost completely yellow, bearing only faint print, but after several moments he began to pluck out the words and form them into sentences, names, numbers—and add them up.

"Oh, no, no," he mumbled. "No, no . . ."

Carter pursed his lips deviously. "Yes, yes."

"Oh . . . oh . . ." Swanborough shook his head in joy. His face cracked into a smile. "*This* . . . is *he*?"

"He is the end element of the theory. We traced the money and the Wilmington connection, then expanded through rumor to several bawdy houses . . . Well, no need fatiguing you with the details."

Swanborough didn't look up. He knew and understood that Carter was keeping his contacts private and his own value high.

"This is too much to ask. . . . Is there proof of the connection?"

"Easily enough acquired," Carter said. "It says there he bears a slave's brand on his right forearm. When you're ready, I'll have him assaulted in an alley. We'll strip the arm and have a little look."

"Unthinkable," Swanborough uttered. "Amazing . . . *amazing*."

He strode off a few paces, periodically chuckling and shaking his head at the phenomenal luck with which he had been blessed.

"Oh, Felix!" he gulped. Then he laughed, nearly choked on his own delight, and gasped, "Oh, this must be *saved*!"

Carter simply stood in the middle of the street, nodding.

Swanborough held the paper close to his chest and closed the space between them quickly. "Does anyone else know?"

"No one," Carter said. "One Richmond messenger made the connection, but I had him disposed of."

"Take care no one else finds out. Not yet . . . not until the right time."

"I shall take that care."

Swanborough read the handbill again and again, shaking his head and chuckling.

Two weeks.

That was Dorian's allotment of happiness. Actually, thirteen days.

A nice odd number.

He stalked into the Governor Street house, loathing himself for accepting Wyatt's invitation to take up residence here instead of in some politely unidentifiable boarding house somewhere on the dirty side of Richmond. He slammed the big front door hard enough to scare all the slaves into the back of the house. A left turn, and he was in the library.

Frightening—so much like Lucas Wallace's library at Plentiful. Rows and rows of classic literature, all put there for decoration and the smell of dignity.

Rows and rows of lies.

No matter how he tried to stay detached, he hadn't been able to stay out of events. He ruined his youth by defending his black mother on Plentiful. He'd stuck his neck out for a slave woman at Chapel Mount, told off Noah Sutton in front of his workers, and got himself hunted for the rest of his life. He couldn't have left well enough alone, let matters take their natural course. He had been a slave. He should have stayed one. Safe and cared for, nestled in the slave community of Plentiful, where he belonged and where he was loved.

No . . . not good enough for heroes. He had burst into the big world and tickled it until it rolled over on him. He had tried to buy off a duel that nearly killed Wyatt, and botched that too, caused yet-to-be-harvested trouble for Wyatt, and now he was tampering with a war he'd sworn to remain callous about. Dorian had read heroic literature, nurtured himself with it in his cloistered youth; as a disillusioned adult he had cast it off, but apparently not thoroughly enough, for he had acted upon that heroic ideal in every circumstance.

That damned ideal had brought him to this. That lie.

Dorian pulled out one of the dozens of books. *Morte d'Arthur*. Yes, that was a good one to start with.

He yanked the book open, tore pages from it, then more pages, and cast them into the fireplace. The little fire guttering there suddenly caught the fuel and flared. Two more books came out, were torn and cast into the flame. He yanked and tore and tossed volume after volume, until he was gulping— then he pulled his Inverness from his shoulders, flung it to the floor, yanked off his uniform and threw it down also, and continued ravaging literature in his shirtsleeves.

Book after book. He no longer consulted the titles. All literature was to blame. All history. All philosophy. Two Bibles.

The fire snarled and chewed, glowing redder, yellower, like the sulfur in the mill—began to smell of burning leather and burning dust. For a few minutes it was satisfied, but soon began to struggle and fight, overwhelmed by the mountain of torn paper and bindings. Overwhelmed by what literature expected of it.

By the time Dorian was gasping and weakened enough to grab the back of a chair and cling to it with his lungs heaving, the fire had begun to rally again.

But there was one more.

Gritting his teeth, he shoved a hand down into his boot and drew out the tiny volume of poetry that had for the past half-dozen years been his only continuous possession, the only thing he would not relinquish or replace. The gift from Alex when they were only eighteen years old.

O, were my love yon lilac fair, with purple blossoms to the spring, and I a bird to shelter there . . . when wearied on my little wing. . . . O, if my love were yon red rose that grows upon the castle wall . . . and I myself a drop of dew, into her bonnie breast to fall.

Dorian crushed the little volume to his forehead in misery and listened to the fire churn.

With a heave that nearly twisted his arm off, he sent the tiny book rattling into the flames. He clung to the high back of the chair to keep from dropping to his knees. The grief was tantalizing, as if he were caught in the seduction of looking at someone else's grave. Happiness, he knew now, was an emotion so raw that it would never be more than a tease before disappointment.

" 'Who made the heart, 'tis He alone decidedly can try us. . . . He knows each chord, its various tone, each spring, its various bias. . . . Then at the balance—"

" 'At the balance let's be mute, we never can adjust it; what's done we partly may compute, but know not what's resisted.' "

Dorian's heart jumped in his chest. He straightened, fought for composure, and looked across the room.

Grace was standing at the doorway.

He straightened a little more and recovered. "Ah, Medusa," he uttered. "Beautifully done. Scottish accent and all."

She came into the room, watching him cannily, and glanced at the mess he'd made. "What are you doing to my husband's home?"

"The same thing you're doing to it," he said. "Turning it bricks over boards."

"Where's Wyatt?"

"He's gone to the mill to save the South's powder supply. I think he's planning to organize a peeing party."

As the fire burned and the books shifted in their smoldering pile, Grace made no attempt to correct the mess he'd made, but simply asked, "Something's wrong?"

"Pardon? Oh, no, no. I always destroy libraries. Keeps mankind on its toes, having to come up with new literature every few thousand years. Doesn't it make a pretty fire?"

Maneuvering closer, Grace saw the dark Inverness flared over a tea table and Dorian's Confederate coat tumbled onto the floor with its arms spread and its lining showing, and noticed that he was gasping every third breath or so.

She circled the tea table without touching the Inverness and approached him, no longer paying attention to the fire or the room or books, but only to him.

"You all right?" she ventured.

He held his breath a moment. "I felt strapping an hour ago. Must have ingested something foul."

He sighed and laid a hand against his chest. The words were cocky, as usual, but the sigh was real.

Grace tilted her head. "Orienta Swanborough?"

His onyx eyes struck her like buckshot. His pencil-edged lips parted.

It was answer enough.

"Tripping over your latest identity?" she said. "Why don't you tell her the truth?"

"Good idea!" Dorian righted himself, managed to walk without holding on to the chair, and wandered toward the fire. "Vast, Orienta, my dear, hold onto your Hepplewhites and part the sheets. Your knight is shedding his armor to show you his naked sins." With a cold hand he gripped the mantel and faced Grace. "You're the only person on earth living a bigger lie than I am. If I told your husband that, he would beat the messenger. All the heroes burning in this fire—they're all Wyatt. He would insist I've misjudged you and blame himself for the bitter antepast of a marriage into which you've somehow locked him. We're involved with the wrong people, you and I, Grace. Wyatt deserves Orienta, and I'm quite certain you deserve me. Spirit-charging, yes?"

"Pretty jarring," Grace admitted, "but don't have a spell. We all have things to hide." She stepped past him and knelt before the fire. The books smoked before her. "We all make promises to ourselves. They don't always sound so right later, do they?"

"Mmm," he grumbled. "Later they turn into a welter of ruts."

"Sounds like something that makes you itch."

He fell silent. She was frightening in her lack of fear of him, or of anything else. Looking at her was like looking into a cracked mirror. She had secrets, as did he. Dangerous ones. A hard edge. Dorian knew he would do whatever necessary to meet his ends—and knew Grace would too. This they had in common. It frightened him. What would she do to Wyatt in order to meet her own ends?

She was reaching into the flames, digging through the top of the smoking books, picking at the hot leather and curling pages.

Roused suddenly, Dorian stooped down to grab her shoulder and pull her back. "What are you doing!"

As she came backward in his grasp and slipped to one knee, she held up the tiny volume of Burns poetry. Its thin vellum pages fanned toward him, and a column of smoke threaded up from one corner of the burned tartan cover.

Confused, and even humbled, Dorian stared at it. Suddenly he felt remorse at his thoughts about her and had to fight to keep them straight.

Grace licked two fingers and snuffed out the glowing corner.

"You threw this in by mistake," she said. She put it in his hand, then brushed ashes from her fingers. "Better stick that back in your boot."

The sudden honesty flowing between them was so strong a tide as to leave Dorian stripped of any quick answers. As he glared into her eyes, he knew he couldn't throw her off. Very well. He too would retreat into candor.

"Thank you," he said. "Perhaps I lost control."

He offered a hand to lift her to her feet, but she ignored him and got up without his help.

"Lost it whole hog," she agreed. As she stood, she scooped up his coat and Inverness. "I'll have these hung up in your room. Don't forget to stir the fire. Might as well get a night's heat out of it, right?"

She gave him a peppery glance of—what was it? Warning? Compliance?

And she headed for the hallway.

At the last moment Dorian called, "Grace—"

She turned. "What?"

Dorian surveyed her standing there in her blue dress, her waist uncorseted so that her natural figure showed, her dark volcanic hair loosely rolled with the firelight fingering it, and candor continued to push at him.

"I don't know what you want with Wyatt," he said, "but

when the moment of execution comes, I intend to protect him from it."

Grace simply gazed at him, guarding her expression, and raised an eyebrow as her only answer. She thought how funny it was that he should pick that word.

CHAPTER THIRTY-SEVEN

———— ★ ————

"Major Craig? May I . . . disturb you?"

Wyatt looked up from the group of men with whom he was surveying the last load of available Chilean saltpeter. The very last.

"Mrs. Swanborough," Wyatt exclaimed. "What are you doing way over here?"

He shook from his mind the numbers of just how much powder they'd be able to glean from this one last load of critical ingredients, stepped away from the other men, and crossed the mill yard to where the woman was standing very prim and alone, very out of place.

He caught her elbow gently. "Did you come here all by yourself?"

She shook her head and murmured, "Buckie drove me in."

"Who did?" Wyatt looked across the yard toward the powder town and saw the Swanborough carriage with Burlie standing beside it. "Oh, 'Buckie.' Right."

The big boy nodded discreetly at Wyatt, but made no other attempt to communicate with his brother's friend, who was still wearing the sling on that damaged shoulder.

"May I speak with you, Major?" the woman asked. "Privately?"

"Oh, of course, ma'am. My office?"

"I'm very grateful."

"Right this way."

He gestured toward the brick building at the riverside. As she stepped passed him, he waved at Burlie, patted his right arm, and mouthed "I'm fine," so the boy shouldn't fret over the little accident. Even over the distance between them, he saw the boy swallow a lump, then nod unconvincingly.

Before Orienta Swanborough was even seated on the leather fireplace bench in his office, Wyatt sensed she was upset, that this wasn't business or charity, and surely not a casual visit.

Which meant it was probably Dorian.

He dropped into a brass-studded buffalo hide chair and leaned forward on his knees in his best listening position.

"Am I disturbing you, Major?" she asked.

"Oh, no, ma'am. I was just about to send a little note to Vice President Stephens to tell him I'm not going to do something he wanted me to do, and truth is I'm grateful to you for giving me a good excuse to put if off another half hour. Go right ahead."

She fidgeted, wiped her nose with a lace-trimmed hanky, and had great trouble meeting his eyes.

"You care for Captain Pawthens very much, don't you, Major?" she muttered eventually.

Yup. Dorian. It figured.

"Yes, ma'am," Wyatt said. "I sure do."

"As do I . . ."

"I know you do, ma'am."

She looked up at him now, puzzled and somewhat surprised.

Wyatt shrugged, smiled, and plainly said, "I'd have to be in a fever to miss it."

Her pale face flushed. "I am so embarrassed. . . ."

He caught one of her hands and patted it. "Oh, don't be, ma'am. We get precious little affection in this life. Shouldn't be embarrassed when we find some."

"You're so kind, Major. And I am so selfish—"

This time Wyatt actually laughed. When she blinked at him, he squeezed her hand again and said, "Mrs. Swanborough, I don't think you fall into the selfish category as folks go."

She offered a small smile. "Please . . . call me Orienta."

"I will, thanks. You call me Wyatt."

She made no response to that, but Wyatt sensed she couldn't manage that one. In fact, he had yet to hear her use Dorian's first name.

He was in the middle of this revelation when suddenly the woman broke out in sobs. Wyatt was left stammering and flew around the office digging up one of his big white handkerchiefs for her. That little lace thing wasn't going to sop up much. When she buried her face in his handkerchief and nearly went into convulsions, he went flying again, this time for a glass of water. Maybe he should get tea—

He clattered back to the fireplace with a jug of water and a cup, crouched in front of her, wondering if he should drink it himself. No—she was dabbing at her eyes and sniffing, fighting for control—he could almost see her eyes past the white cotton—yes, she was blinking and dabbing.

"Oh—" she croaked. She rubbed at her nose, then folded the handkerchief and saw the cup of water. "Oh—thank you."

"Ma'am, are you all right?" he asked.

His question broke her into sobs again. "I'm not worthy of him . . . but I adore him. . . ."

Wyatt settled into the chair again. "Dorian?"

"Oh, yes . . ."

"Well, isn't that nice," he sighed. "I mean that you . . . not the other—"

"You know more about him than anyone," she said. It was partly a question, partly not.

"I—well, I guess," he answered. How much had Dorian told her in his storm of attraction? How much could be admitted? And what the hell was she getting at?

She blinked up at him, her eyes reddened and pathetic.

"Do you know," she began, "where he is?"

"Well, I haven't seen him for a couple of days. . . . He tends to drop away now and then—"

"He was paying me visits almost every day for a fortnight," she said, "but then he suddenly stopped. . . . May I ask a favor of you?"

"I'll do anything I can, ma'am . . . Orienta."

She nodded gratefully. "I am doing something very, very wrong. I have made some terrible . . . untenable mistake. I need your help to correct what I have done."

He wanted to interrupt her, to insist that she couldn't have done anything all that bad, certainly nothing Dorian couldn't see over, considering how Dorian felt about himself most of the time, but he sensed he was on the edge of the point of this visit and managed to keep quiet.

After a difficult few moments, Orienta continued. She could no longer meet his eyes.

"I came to ask you whether you know something I am failing to do for him, or failing to *be* for him. . . ." She sniffed, trembled, and was forcing herself not to sob anymore. The effort blotched her face. "So that he will come to me . . . instead."

Her voice dropped away, and the last word came out as a squeak.

Wyatt parted his lips to say something—he had no idea what comforts he could offer or what was planning to come out of those lips—but at once he realized what she had said.

"Instead?" he asked. "Instead of what?"

A final sob broke out of her and shook the chair.

"Instead," she gasped, "of Evee Mapes."

Wyatt had been in whorehouses before. Well, twice before. His seventeen-year-old cousin had dragged him to both. What he remembered most was that they smelled of perfumes meant to cover other odors, and that he was nervous the whole time. They took care of him, but everything had been too expected and predictable, even for a boy of fourteen. Afterward all he had felt was guilty, dirty, and laden with a secret that everybody knew but nobody would talk about.

On his arm was a Chinese girl with long slick hair piled high on her head in a bad imitation of a theatrical hairstyle and secured with chopsticks. She spoke no English, so the walk up the stairs was uneasy to start with.

She walked him past several doors, some open, some not, depending on the eccentricities of the customer. Some men apparently liked the adventure of being spied on, and the women, obviously, didn't care. Customers' fetishes could also be convenient modes of advertisement.

The hall was very long and cluttered with furniture—velvet-covered chairs with tassels, chests of drawers, bookshelves heavy with collections of dishes, bottles of perfume, elixirs, herbs, and linens—

"Ah!" a familiar voice crooned. "Had enough of the vixen?

Come to get your club oiled by someone less indifferent to you?"

Wyatt turned, even though the girl was pulling on his left arm to get him into her own room.

There was Dorian, lying on the hallway runner, lounging up against an enormous highboy, with two women in under-things pressing against him. His legs were crossed, his waist-coat unbuttoned, his ascot hanging into columns down his chest.

"'She is not the fairest, altho' she is fair . . . O' nice educa-tion but small is her share, her parentage humble and humble can be, but I love the lassie because she loves—'"

"What," Wyatt interrupted, "are you doing here?"

Dorian blinked up at him. "Arranging for purchase of African niter in exchange for Grand Banks cod. Obviously."

One of the girls pulled on his ascot. "What's niter?"

"Saltpeter."

"What's saltpeter?"

"Bird droppings."

Wyatt leaned forward. "Do you know I had to pay just to walk up here? Get up on your feet, Dorian."

Shaking off the confused Chinese girl, Wyatt knotted his fists in Dorian's clothing and somehow hauled him up in one long heave in spite of his bad arm. Even Wyatt hadn't realized how angry he was until the pain in his shoulder came second to getting Dorian on his feet and out of here.

Dorian wobbled and pulled back hard, striking the tattered wallpaper. He glared bullets at Wyatt. "The last time someone handled me that way—"

"I don't want to hear it." He kept his left hand twisted into Dorian's collar, but he waved to all three women and said, "Leave us alone, please. Go on."

One of the women kept hold of Dorian's ascot and protested, "But we haven't—"

"You'll get paid anyway," Wyatt said. "Go, go."

The girls wandered around the two men for a few moments, doing whatever they could to make Wyatt change his mind, but he waved them on down the wide stairway and maneu-vered Dorian into the nearest unoccupied room.

"Take your paws off me before I pull out your other shoul-der," Dorian warned, and shook himself free. "Thank you.

There's a mirror over every bed in the cock-happy peghouse. You can look at yourself and see how you screwed your face on too tight this morning."

He crossed the overly draped and flowered room, nearly swallowed by grotesque red paisley wallpaper, and kept his back to the door as Wyatt closed it.

"What kind of a chowderhead are you?" Wyatt said. "I thought I'd seen it all from you. You've got a good woman who cares what becomes of you, more than you do, apparently, and this is what she gets. You owe her better. You've had your fun with her, and now it's time to do something right. You're always crowing about how múch you do wrong, so let's have some *real* dignity for a change."

"Such an entertaining friend," Dorian said, very coldly. "I never expected this from a perspicacious Gothamite like you. Certainly you haven't forgotten my little pigmentation problem. Or have you?"

Briefly Wyatt vacillated over that sore subject. Then he collected himself and flatly admitted, "If I cared about that, I wouldn't be here. Who your mother and your father were doesn't have as much to do with what you are as you think it does. We're in the middle of a war, Dorian. This continent's going to be nursing scars for decades. Who's going to notice anything about you one way or the other when it's all over?"

"Oh, yes," Dorian mocked an agreement. "No one will notice a half-breed roaming in the bed of an Alabama plantation widow after a war ignited by the issue of slavery's extension into the new states. Whatever was I thinking? Silly me."

"Maybe it's just God's will. Maybe it's all for the best. Maybe you've paid long enough and Orienta is your reward."

"Oh—*God*! Yes, him! Children around the world are starving, and God spends his nights worrying about how Jews slaughter their chickens. Of course—this is just his kind of joke! Notice I didn't fall in love with an Egyptian whore, or a Chinese widow, or an Indian woman who wouldn't care. Or a French woman, or even a *Northern* woman. No! Of all the women for me to be touched by, I fall in love with a Confederate torchbearer who carries Alabama dirt wherever she goes. A woman of the *upper crust* who carries Alabama dirt. A woman to whom Virginia is a foreign land! When I die, God and I are going to have a very long conversation with many, many questions before I descend to take charge in hell . . . I've rehearsed it many times, and I'm looking forward to it. Too bad you won't be there. Perhaps you could check your harp at the gate. 'Sensibility, how charming, Thou, my friend, canst truly tell; but distress, with horrors arming, Thou alas! hast known too—' "

"That's enough!" Wyatt roared. "Damn it all, is the world in your way, Dorian? What's the matter with you?"

"What's the *matter* with me? I'm filled with my mother's blood. Good wombs have borne bad sons, they say. Do you suggest I weld Orienta to an evil-starred marriage?"

"You're not evil-starred. I don't believe stars can be evil. Why do you talk like that?"

"I'll spell it for you. B-l-a-c-k b-a-b-y."

"We all take our chances in life," Wyatt said. "You could have a black baby. Or a white baby." He shook his head. "Are you going to wait until the world is perfect?"

"Perfect?" Dorian argued. "Do I ask for perfection? I came forth into the outside with hopes to gladden the country and make my mark. I found I couldn't do it by being proper, so I decided to do it by being improper better than anybody else. However, I think it would be asking too much to force a woman like her to have children who, white or black, will be legally slaves. A drop of negro blood, you know—"

"Unless the North wins."

"Oh! Then I'm working for the wrong side."

"I don't know what in hell you're working for!" Wyatt broke in. Then he lowered his voice deliberately and said, "Can't you figure out how I knew to come here looking for you?"

A sudden silence dropped over them. Neither of them wanted to hear the answer to that question spoken aloud.

Burying his fury enough to sound reasonable, Wyatt closed some of the space between them. The old, well-worn house creaked beneath him.

"You've *got* to talk to her. You can't just walk away from another person and leave her wondering for the rest of her life what happened. If you aren't man enough to grab up the facts and try to work things out and make a decent life for yourself, the least you can do is tell her why. Go to her, and do the honorable thing one way or the other. This . . . you know this isn't right. Don't make her wonder every morning for the rest of her life if today's the day you'll come back."

Somewhere in that speech—he wasn't sure where—Wyatt had pierced Dorian's iron heart. Dorian stared at the forest of perfume bottles and said nothing.

Nothing.

Wyatt paused and lowered his voice.

"Get off your wagonload of predictions and take your chances in life like a man," he said. "Marry her, Dorian. Marry her now. Or go and tell her why not."

Mechanicsville.

He was walking along the sidewalk from where Shockoe stood in front of the carriage, enjoying her feed bag. He moved along the iron fence in front of the cottage, yet an illusion washed over him that the building was moving toward *him,* pivoting on a giant pinwheel whose stem bored deep into the ground beneath the cellar.

He had rehearsed the words over and over again all the way from Richmond—words that would break it off, would change her way of thinking about him and finally excise him from her life. Blinded by need and confused by an emotion he had never experienced before, he had plunged himself and her into a terrible risk. A tragic surprise, this one emotion. He who had been the receiver of every brand of love and hate the world could offer had missed this one brand. The one kind of love a thousand poets had tried to describe to him all his life. He couldn't shake a premonition that he would eat dirt before the evening was over.

Orienta's round face brightened when she opened the door and saw it was him.

He blew past her in a swirl of iron gray and black on black. He did not remove his opera hat.

"Hello. Don't say a word. Not a word. Come over here and sit down and don't say anything."

She pushed the door closed. "May I at least take your hat—?"

"No, you cannot have my hat. Come in here and sit."

He kept his hat and Inverness on, intending not to stay. He would remain distant, button-down cool, and shine a harsh light on the facts.

Orienta followed him into the front parlor and did what he ordered. She sat on a tufted straight-backed chair, and indeed sat very straight, with her hands folded on her lap. Something about her posture made Dorian think she was enjoying this air of subservience to a man she—

No, don't think it!

"Wyatt made me come here," Dorian began. "You know, the fellow with the bunny-brown hair and the delicate touch of a jackscrew. He's ham-fisted for a knight, but he went after me with tinsnips, and when he was finished, I looked like free verse."

He indicated an imaginary pile on the floor, then paced around it. His tone was biting, eruptive, and warned her to keep silent.

"You know, I should have gone to Scotland when I had the chance," he said. "I should have gone to sit on the grass at Dumfries and tell Robert everything. He would have kept his mouth shut about it. Oh, he may have penned a little ballad about me and shoved it up through the slot in his gravestone, but no one would have made the connection. I come from a world glutted with legend. Where some of the people believed that ghosts and haints were the devil coming to get someone. There were small brick slave quarters built with lime mortar, doorways with corn-shuck floor mats, and coon-fat soup. The smokehouses that carried a constant aroma. There were cabins on the estate which were little factories for the plantation's needs—a weaving and spinning house, a smithy, a flour mill, and even a brewery. In those days the plantation was virtually a community unto itself. My father wasn't an absentee proprietor as so many are. Most masters let their overseers handle the actual planting business, and overseers tend, as you know, to be incompetent white trash, inclined to severity. My father had the physical background of dockwork and spent his time in the fields, with his slaves. A little too close to his slaves at times. And on the other side of the lawn was a circular carriage drive with a walking garden in the center. It was a world of mulberry fezzes with long silk tassels, lotus and bud friezes, desks of tiger maple, sizzling lamb, oyster-shell fireplaces and

symbolic exoduses." He paced away from her, staring at the
floor, muttering, "Exoduses . . . exoduses . . . I wonder if that's
the correct plural for that word. . . ."

He glanced up, to find Orienta gazing at him forgivingly,
which he hated. To avoid glancing at her pallid face again and
seeing that unconditional forgiveness, he continued pacing and
glowering at the furniture, touching it or running his fingers
around its edges.

"You see, I am the devil's trigger man," he went on, touching his chest to indicate the hollow place there. "Marc Antony
would call me honorable. No matter what good I attempt, it
turns out for the worse. No matter whom I touch, they wither.
Except Wyatt—he's made of rubber, I think. He keeps bounc-
ing along in spite of me and that clapper-tongued harridan he
married—" He waved his hand before his own face and shook
his head. "Never mind her."

He moved to the fireplace and took a pose. If he kept a
brash bearing, he knew he could distance her. That meant not
looking at her face any more than necessary. So he fixed on
the marqueted wall clock and talked to its face instead of hers.
He was starting to feel the heat of his outerwear still on his
shoulders, and his hat brim picking up sweat.

"I came into the world expecting a pageant, orchestrated by
director God, the Great Voyeur. Instead I found a devitalized
cinder-gray hare hunt. It stumbled and howled in all directions,
churning up storms. Panacea turned out to be a half tone off
the classic pitch. All literature revealed itself as faena, a tease
before the slaughter—"

"Oh, no," she murmured, "no . . . you musn't think—"

"Hold your jaw, damn you, woman, I'm not finished.
Where was I? Oh, yes, my first taste of the big world. The
winds of indignation blew very hard upon me in those first few
days. I discovered that information I took as commonplace
was unknown by the common American. Did you know that
Egyptian influence on Greek thought is evidenced by
Heliodores, a Syrian who read Homeric lore by way of the
pyramids? Did you also know Greece was conquered and re-
conquered and sewn back together a dozen times? You are
probably closer to Aristotle than my Greek mother. She has a
hundred races in her. Modern Greece is a polyglot. So is
America. So is history. No one really understands what hap-

pened more than five months ago. For instance, did you know that the Black Irish are really Spanish? Yes, their forefathers floated ashore after Elizabeth mangled the Armada. They married into the Red Irish, and there you have it. Dark-haired children with eyes like mine. Oh, yes! I see puzzlement in your face, madam. Good for you. Stay puzzled for a moment. These are common ethnic misconceptions that rattle my teeth when I hear them. The idea that our negroes are African. Hah! There hasn't been an African slave on the American continent since 1818. Not legally anyway. . . . What else? Oh—here's one. King Arthur was actually a Roman soldier named Arcturus. *Les Romances de Cretien De Troyes* gave Arthurian themes their first literary treatment about 1200-ish, A.D. And did you realize that the Irish patron saint, Patrick O'Shamrock, key word *sham,* was actually a French missionary? I doubt there ever were snakes in Ireland. Patrick simply had a very good campaign manager. Mmm . . . a campaign for sainthood . . . I'll have to remember that one. That's a good one."

He put a finger to his lips and chuckled unconvincingly. Was he making her nervous yet? He didn't dare look. He pushed off the mantel and started pacing again.

"Another of my favorites is Cleopatra, queen of Egypt. She was actually a Greek girl. Not a drop of Egyptian blood. It was all a fake. Cultural adoption. She wore Egyptian clothing only because she shopped in Cairo. You see, Alexander's empire cracked up because he died without an heir, so all his generals took a country each instead of cash. His general Ptolemy took Egypt. Also, did you realize that Henry the Eighth, who rattles down through history as the man who whopped off the heads of his wives with royal abandon, actually beheaded only two of those six wives, primarily due to political pressures? In fact, one of the other wives died after childbirth, and Henry was so devastated that he wore black for a full year. And his last wife outlived him. Ah, history! Such a patina! Too bad we missed it, eh?"

He stopped pacing, swung full about, and glared cruelly at her.

"The world is full of these falsehoods and men living lives of deception," he said. "You're looking at a dilly of one."

The woman's face was flushed with emotion, and probably

with fear. She knew whatever news was on the end of this sermon was not good news.

She simply uttered, "What are you saying?"

"I'm saying I can't have you committing suttee on my corpse. I'm wrong for you. I've been with women who would blind someone like you with a glance. I've drowned myself in West Indian rum and laid pipe in every Adam's arsenal from here to Botany Bay. You know what I mean? The naturalia that is womankind? I fear it's this cabbage field that led me to you and forced me to deny my lies. These lies are the reason I go to women quite other than you." Now he met her eyes, keeping his own as hard as practice had taught him. "And I'm here," he finished, "to cram them down your throat. Tell me when you're ready to hear something you cannot accept."

Orienta sat unmoving, framed by the hand-blocked wallpaper, flanked on one side by her five-octave clavichord and on the other by her trunk of Alabama dirt. She was trembling slightly. His eruptive glare cooked her as she sat there, her elbows twitching, her hopes sanded down by his tirade. She was no fool, he could see. She had picked up on his tone if not his roundabout meaning.

Her eyes were lowered, fixed to her toes, and tears were flowing down her cheeks in two constant streams.

These two little streams struck Dorian windless. Suddenly he couldn't say anything.

Without looking up Orienta swallowed several times and finally forced herself to speak. Her voice came out in shreds.

"I have already accepted it," she whispered.

Dorian scowled. He thought back on the past few minutes, reviewed his own prattling, and even he couldn't make much sense of it.

He leaned forward a bit. "You *have*?"

Her throat was tight and reddened as she nodded slowly. She dabbed at her nose with a handkerchief she had twisted beyond recognition. Then she hunched her narrow shoulders and drummed up the courage to speak.

"A man wants a woman he can be proud of," she murmured, "and I am . . . too homely."

The wall clock began to chime. One. Two. Three. Four.

A single sentence.

Six. Seven . . .

Dorian stood in the middle of the hooked rug, staring, speechless.

By the time the clock struck nine, he was three pounds lighter.

Because his heart had been ripped out.

CHAPTER THIRTY-EIGHT

———— ★ ————

She was the empress of his touch. He saw the full moon in her eyes. Her hair was undone and lay like plumage across his right sleeve. When he touched her, there was a sudden authority in the response, as though she had gotten a glimpse of life without him and meant to nurture every available moment.

No one had done that for him before. He had always been worked as a blacksmith works a horse. She had something utterly unique to give him—affection. He could not help but return it.

Before long, his staggering pangs of doubt began to fade, and she opened him like a leather-bound book. She pampered him with her adoration and a gratitude he couldn't fight. She rocked him and held him, sang to him and drew him in. He penetrated her longing for him, caressing and combing until he found his own longing for her.

She held him as though she knew this might be their last time together, and because of that he could never bring himself to tell her it was.

Possessed again, by devils . . . unable to keep up the ice barrier he had tried to put between himself and her . . .

Instead he heard other things coming out of his mouth, words meant for the woman who loved him so much she was willing to become a Virginian for him.

"Wear lilacs in your hair," he said, "and marry me in the morning."

The ceremony was small. The bride wore only her ordinary Sunday best, a rather simple salmon-colored dress with a lace neck that still bore tiny black ribbons of partial mourning on its hem, and there were lilacs tucked into the twisted buns over her ears. The purple flowers clashed with the not-quite-pink dress, and made Orienta look like a bottle of medicine.

Grace and Wyatt stood as witnesses, neither of them able to crack much of a smile or much of a congratulations. A Mechanicsville judge pronounced Orienta to be Dorian's wife, Dorian signed his current false name to the papers, and Orienta signed her dead husband's name between hers and "Parthens." The irony of "Orienta Swanborough Parthens" caught the eye of the groom and his witnesses. The bride was too delirious and teary-eyed joyful to take any note. Hers was an expression of disbelief at her phenomenal luck to have such a man at her side, much less vowing to stay there.

Such a man. Her vision of Southern knighthood. A man in whom she sensed and saw something she could not identify, whom she loved not in spite of his mysteries, but because of them.

Barry Swanborough was nowhere to be seen, traveling on business as he frequently did, and therefore was not present to give his sister-in-law away and represent the Swanborough name. Orienta seemed not to miss him one whit and was perfectly happy to accept Dorian's suggestion that the slave Burlie stand in to represent the Swanborough estate. Orienta was so open to anything the wind blew toward her today that she threw her hands up, wiped away her tears of happiness, and whispered that Dorian could have ten negroes and a dozen criminals stand today if he wished. She seemed passive until they saw her walk into the tiny courtroom alone. She was clearly and decisively giving *herself* away.

Grace watched all this with feelings churning inside her so strongly they nearly knocked her down. She was more aware of Wyatt than of Dorian and his bride. Wyatt was gazing at Orienta with unbridled generosity and warmth, and at Dorian with admiration and something like sympathy. He was patting arms and holding hands and guarding everyone's emotions with the attentiveness of a stablemaster. Didn't make any sense.

How could a downright murderer seem so tender-conscienced?

Just didn't fit.

There stood that undefinable Dorian, and in spite of the sins Grace knew were there, Wyatt forgave and forgave him.

She hovered in that courtroom in Mechanicsville, watching the unusually somber groom, the bride who was actually blushing, and her own husband, who gazed upon his friends with a good wish so genuine, demonstrative, and readable that no manner of hatred could tarnish it. Her husband, who treated people with such a natural protectiveness, it was almost story-book.

As Grace kept to one side, feeling like half a wife in Orienta's shadow, looking hard and deep into her husband's expressions while he wasn't looking at her, she bumped her shoulder against a wall, sighed, and muttered to herself.

"Slam and damn . . . if he doesn't make me wonder maybe I'm getting something wrong."

THE BURNING FUSE

15 JANUARY 1862

Edwin W. Stanton is appointed Secretary of War of the United States. He has a frequently hostile attitude toward Abraham Lincoln and often speaks in unflattering terms about the President. He is, however, a suddenly vigorous and driving leader for the War Department, which has until now slogged along under indecisive management.

17 JANUARY

Union gunboats move against Fort Henry on the Tennessee River.

19 JANUARY

The Battle of Logan's Cross Roads, Kentucky, on the Cumberland River. Union and Confederate troops fall forward and back alternately, but ultimately the Confederate line collapses. The battle results in few casualties, but the break in the rebel line is strategically damaging to Confederate purposes and inflates pro-Union attitudes in Kentucky and parts of Tennessee. The news of this loss, the shelling of Fort Henry, Union occupation of parts of Missouri and of Hatteras Inlet, North Carolina . . . all reach Richmond under a cloud of disillusionment for the South.

CHAPTER THIRTY-NINE

———— ★ ————

Gunshots rang over the powder yard. Instantly came the cries and shouts of the workers.

Grace ran down the incline toward the James River ahead of several of the mill wives who also ran, their faces drawn with fear at that sound. What was happening? Had Richmond been swarmed in the night? Had Federal troops sneaked by boat downriver and come into the powder yard? Was there a standoff at the grinding mills?

The Craig Powderworks was a legitimate target, everyone knew that. All of Richmond was a target, and to debilitate Richmond defenses, the powder yard was a strategic preliminary factor.

So the women ran toward the sound of gunshots in the Lower Yard. They hid their children under the beds, and they ran. Some of them were hiking their skirts up with one hand and carrying their own guns in the other. They clattered over the little wooden walking bridge over the man-made vein of water diverted for household purposes from the James, and dashed into the industrial section of their mill town. They came around the corner of the new keg factory and skidded into a cluster.

After digesting what they saw, they heaved a collective sigh of relief and shook their heads at the boyishness of their husbands and brothers and the boss of the mill.

There was Wyatt Craig, dressed as always in bare shirt-sleeves and a worker's vest, with his arm out of the sling for the first time since his injury, the sling dangling around his neck.

"Son," Henry Brecker was bellowing. "You are goldang hopeless with a firearm! You got one bad eye or what?"

All the men were laughing.

Wyatt was laughing too. He let his right arm hang with the weight of the pistol in it. His ruddy face grew ruddier as he stood at the center of a great half circle of his own workers. A hundred feet away, its back to the brick wall of the machine shop, was a straw man they'd built for him as a target.

The straw man had arms twice as long as they should be, legs about the same length, a head made out of a flour bag stuffed with straw, and the men had dressed it in a pinned-together jacket hacked out of an old United States flag that once had flown over the yard, and a Union slouch hat brought back from a skirmish by an enthusiastic delivery boy delivering notice of a powder shipment.

There were bullet marks in the brick wall, but not one in the straw man.

Wyatt pointed at his right shoulder and said, "It's the arm, it's the bad arm! See?"

"Sure! Sure it is," his men hooted, along with shouts and harangues.

Grace folded her arms and cocked a hip as she watched. Around her, some of the women dispersed and slogged back toward the town, but some stayed to watch, intending to get some entertainment out of nearly getting their hairpins scared out of their heads. She watched the crowd of men. From the cluster, she saw Clyde Clyman staring at her.

He always stared at her that way when he caught sight of her at a distance. With his red brows straight and his chin down, and the whites showing on the bottoms of his eyes.

She ignored him. No point flagging down trouble with unscheduled contact.

"Try it again, son," Henry encouraged. "You got three more bullets left. Keep your arm relaxed this time. Sight right down the barrel. Ain't no real trick to it. Just hold your breath."

"How 'bout if I hold my breath and you hold my wrist?" Wyatt called from the center of the horseshoe.

The men chortled, and he smiled and shook his head at

himself, perfectly content to provide them entertainment if not reassurance of his soldierly skills.

Grace squinted into the sunlight. Its midday brightness glinted off Wyatt's hair, surrounding him in a halo as if to enhance his good nature. She began to have those thoughts again. The ones that told her she had misjudged something, missed some critical detail, interpreted something just wrong enough to kick her in a completely mistaken direction.

Maybe I should just call an end to it. Quit right now. Leave him and head west or north. Maybe to Pennsylvania to one of those German settlements—call all promises done—

"You'll be a crack shot before you know it, Boss!" one of the blacksmiths called.

Wyatt let his arm fall from his attempt to aim, turned partly around, and called, "That's right. I crack anything standing next to what I'm aiming at!"

The mill women still standing near Grace shook their heads in relief, and some of them smiled as the men laughed and applauded their boss's good nature.

"Wanna do it with your left arm?" someone else suggested.

Wyatt looked into the bundle of workers, apparently recognizing the voice, and said, "My left arm's even worse than my right!"

"Can't be."

At that, the women standing at the keg factory laughed too.

Rubbing his sore shoulder briefly, Wyatt angled himself in firing stance and took aim again. He closed one eye and tried to sight down that barrel.

"If I miss this time, I'll just put this straw fellow in charge of the company, and I'll go take a good long nap. All right, everybody stay real quiet so I can concentrate."

One of the pipe fitters called, "Want for us to arrange some nice quiet battles for you?"

Wyatt laughed and nodded, "That'd be real accommodating, Sam. Here I go—"

The horseshoe of men fell silent and waited. He aimed very carefully, paused, aimed again, held his breath, and fired.

The bullet hit high. Real high.

Everybody laughed. Wyatt hung his head, and his whole body shook as he chuckled at himself. He turned and threw up a hand. "You know, if I ever get enough of you chowderheads and decide to kill myself, I'm gonna have to have somebody do it for me!"

"Two more bullets!" Henry called, also laughing so hard that his wide belly shook.

"I'm gonna get him this time," Wyatt said. "I've just been faking up till now. Here I go. I'm gonna get him."

Grace smirked as she watched him accepting his lousy prowess with a firearm in his typical sportsmanlike manner, and so openly providing entertainment for his workers. A grin pulled at her lips. She noted Clyman watching her instead of Wyatt, but she had no more for him than a casual glance.

The men cackled false encouragements at Wyatt, then settled down as he aimed again, very carefully . . . fired . . .

Boommmmm—crack.

The outbreak of laughter drowned out the echo of the gunshot.

Henry Brecker threw his hands in the air, shook his head in an exaggeration, and was laughing too hard to straighten up. "One m—one m—one more—"

Wyatt strode around his little arena, making eye contact with his workers, laughing and mourning his pathetic lack of talent. He said nothing, but only shrugged and helped them laugh at him, then continued striding across the open space. His pistol wagged at his side.

All at once he pivoted on a toe and strode toward the straw man, closer and closer. Grace presumed he would get close enough that he couldn't possibly miss—

But he kept walking. Past that point . . . closer still . . .

He put the pistol barrel flush against the chest of the straw man, pressed it deeply in—

Grace drew a breath, suddenly ice cold from the heart down.

Her husband pulled the trigger.

Emotion crashed through Grace as the bullet passed into the straw man's chest and out his back. The blast blew through the straw man and came out carrying a funnel of black smoke and straw bits, which puffed against the brick and continued to roll outward.

Grace's hands clapped over her mouth, pressing until they hurt. Memories inside her shattered, reassembled, then shattered again. Every shard cut her in a new place. Her doubts likewise shattered.

When she breathed again, it came in rags. She no longer saw a straw man tied to that stake.

The women around her were holding her arms and asking if she was ill, if she wanted water, if she should sit down—she couldn't move, that much was evident—

Not until some of the men also turned and looked, and one of them was Wyatt.

His smile dropped away, and he gaped with the same kind of growing concern she had seen him give Dorian or his own men. He started toward her.

The land between them expanded as Grace focused on him and the fact that he was stepping toward her . . . the men were parting for him to come through . . . the ground was swelling . . . it would explode—

"Fire!"

The call drew Wyatt's attention away from his wife and her sudden outburst. He swung around and was torn between Grace and the flames licking up from the back of the straw man. The Union slouch hat was on fire around the brim. The head of the straw man began to dissolve. Smoke piled and piled.

Wyatt started back toward the straw man, then turned around toward Grace, obviously torn.

So she took away his choice.

She shoved the women off, and she ran.

She ran until she was gulping. When she could no longer run, she had no idea where she was. Somewhere between the mill and Richmond. She fell against a small maple tree whose bare branches groped for the sky and begged for spring. She clung to the trunk. The trunk lacerated the side of her face. Visions of her parents hanging there in the ravaged cabin—hanged by the slavers—she had failed to protect them—failed to protect their boy—what had Patrick seen as he looked up into the eyes of his mentor, his friend—watched his friend take that pistol and put it to the devoted heart—what had he thought—?

Her choked gasps made the bare branches shiver.

"He came back! . . . He . . . came . . . back . . . from the grave to remind me. . . . He heard me forgetting . . . he heard my doubts . . . he sent me a message! He came . . . back. . . ."

GOVERNOR STREET, THE NEXT DAY.

"Dorian? You hiding in here?"

"Guilty," a voice sounded from the guest bedchamber's walk-in closet.

Wyatt came in, managing to carry a tray with two steaming cups of coffee with his one good hand. "What are you doing sneaking in so early without poking into the breakfast room for hello? I'm down there eating by myself . . . haven't seen Grace since yesterday. I'm kinda worried about her. Think she got a little scare at the Lower Yard."

"Leave her to her own devices. She's a pioneer. She'll rebound."

"That's what I figure. . . . She pretty much comes and goes as she pleases. . . . She likes her privacy. When I ask her if I can help with anything . . . well, anyway, I put a few men out looking for her, but nobody's found her yet. Edmund had to come and tell me you'd slipped in the back way."

"I asked him not to tell you anything. Gave him an extra-large tip. Seems he betrayed me."

"Why? Come on out. I brought you coffee."

"Ah, liquid beans."

"What are you doing in there?"

"Nailing my latest victim behind the wall panel. Almost finished. Did you know the Monroe Doctrine was actually a British concoction, but they let President Monroe announce it?"

"No, but I'll bet you did," Wyatt chuckled. He set the tray down on the trunk at the foot of the bed, braced a foot on the trunk, and sipped at his coffee.

From the closet Dorian kept talking. "The British accepted and supported American domination of this continent to keep France and Spain weak. The British rule the seas. They didn't want to colonize, but they *did* and still do want to prohibit others."

"Why don't you come out here and get your coffee?"

"Aleck Stephens has never liked Jefferson Davis. You've probably picked up on that. If Aleck's representative can bring about European recognition for the Confederacy and virtually assure our victory, Aleck will have sufficient power to remove Davis, who is moving the Confederacy away from a true constitutional interpretation of government."

"Aren't you hungry this early?" Wyatt asked, somewhat perplexed. He leaned his good arm on his knee as he stood with one foot on the trunk, and let his eyes blur as he thought about that.

"I turned into a bat last night and drank blood." Dorian came out of the closet, tugging a medium-sized carpetbag and holding three of his characteristically plush waistcoats, a few shirts, and his black daycoat—the one with little pearls sewn onto the cuffs.

"What's all this?" Wyatt asked. "Moving some things over to Mechanicsville? Are you going to live there once Barry Swanborough gets back from wherever he is? Can't see you two living in the same household, even with Orienta running between you. Since you moved in with us, I assumed you'd just bring Orienta here to live in this big house. Why don't you do that? There's plenty of room. It'll be real pleasant. I haven't heard you talk about that."

"I haven't talked about it."

He started pulling his collection of ascots—not really very many for a man with his taste in clothing—out of a drawer and deposited them in the carpetbag. Somewhat solemnly he said, "It would be a shame if the South were to win too soon. . . . Think of it. The United States and the Confederate States, forever separate. Like France and Italy. Germany and Prussia. Burma and India. Forever alienated. Such a great loss for the world, to be without Americans."

Hiding behind a sip of coffee, Wyatt flipped him a smile. "You're starting to sound like Stephens."

"Thank you."

"Don't know if I meant it nicely."

"Fear not—I'm sure you did. The emissary will be empowered to offer England anything it wants for its cooperation, and also to offer France toeholds in the West and Mexico. When this continent is reunited properly, Stephens means to throw their backends off Plymouth Rock. I've been communicating with my Du Pont contact, and he says Lammot Du Pont is stirring up trouble in England with Lord Palmerston. The name of Du Pont is carrying tremendous weight in the British financial circles. My contacts, the Southern branch of the family, have dropped a tacit note in the ear of Lord John Russell to meet with their confidante, even as Palmerston is making deals with Lammot for the North. In a way, while working for Lincoln, Lammot Du Pont is actually helping the South gain Britain's ear."

Wyatt disguised his curiosity by strolling to the bright morning window and peering out on the early activity of Governor Street.

"This Lammot," he prodded carefully. "He's your contact?"

"He has no idea I exist. Currently he lives only for British saltpeter. In any case, I rose this morning, kissed my wife while she was still asleep, gathered my essentials, came to Richmond, barged in on Aleck Stephens, and told him I changed my mind. I am going to England."

At the window Wyatt spun around so sharply, he nearly dislocated the shoulder again.

"What'd you say?" he gasped.

Dorian wouldn't look at him. He continued folding and packing. "I don't enjoy playing God, but he seems to have abdicated the task to me. Perhaps he too is disillusioned."

"How . . . how does Orienta feel about this?"

Several seconds pounded by. Long enough that it seemed there wasn't going to be a straight answer.

Then, also without looking up, Dorian said, "She doesn't know."

Wyatt's blood dropped to his ankles. "Oh, no . . . no! You're abandoning her?"

"That's right. And don't tell me to go talk to her. Look what happened the last time."

Thunderstruck, Wyatt gulped, "My God, man, you're married to her!"

A shrug. "To act is always easier than to live up to it afterward."

Wyatt slammed into the middle of the room so hard that his coffee sloshed over his left hand.

"I don't believe this is happening! What's the matter with you? You're white enough for everyone except yourself!"

"I'm abandoning her so she can find somebody better."

Halting suddenly, Wyatt drew a deep breath and forced himself to think clearly. "There is nobody better."

For the first time Dorian stopped packing. He paused, stared at his reflection in the dresser's oval mirror, leaned forward, and shuddered. Obviously struggling, he made a deep noise in his throat, shook his head, forced himself to recover, then turned to Wyatt and studied him as though he'd never laid eyes on him before.

When he held out a flat palm, there was a tinge of accusation in the gesture. "Is this what our friendship is based upon?"

Wyatt squinted at him. "What are you talking about?"

An encounter that had started out pleasantly abruptly went sour, and in the air there was now only paralysis. The most hideous of conflicts petrified them, the kind where two right things come up against each other and cannot both survive.

Dumbstruck, Wyatt felt his face go stiff. He paced across the room until the bed stopped him, then back again, never taking his eyes off Dorian.

"Damn, I'm sick of these requirements you put on your life," he said. "You're a man whose philosophy of life is 'Let them all kill each other after I get what I want'!"

He stopped pacing.

The strain between them was bone crushing.

"Some people fight and other people reap rewards," Dorian said. "Even you."

"That's not fair. I've never asked anyone to do my fighting."

"You will not need to ask at all," Dorian said sharply. "There's going to be a draft law soon. With it, complications. Have you heard yet of the law they're talking about passing? The one our legislators are already calling the Twenty Nigger Law? It exempts from conscription any man owning twenty negroes or more. Plantation owners and their sons may now legally avoid fighting. *You* may now avoid fighting."

Wyatt snapped, "Don't you put that on *me*. I didn't come to Richmond to hide behind my negroes, and you know it."

"The law will do more harm than good. Anyone with nineteen or fewer niggers will be pissing gravel."

"Don't change the subject! That's all you can think about, isn't it?" Wyatt leveled a finger at him. "How black and white adds up in the world? You of all people should see a few other colors! Maybe, just *maybe* somebody invented that twenty-nigger thing because any man who owns twenty slaves has a successful business going, and just maybe the business he runs is more valuable to the economy of the South than his two hands with a rifle in 'em!"

"The pen is mightier than the sword, eh?"

"It is when it's keeping a ledger!"

"Point taken. I hadn't thought that way."

"Know why?"

Dorian scraped him with a glance and mocked, "Oh, tell me why."

"Because there's still part of you that thinks like a slave!"

The words buzzed through them both.

Never had Wyatt said anything like that to Dorian in their years together. Tight horror engulfed them that they should be speaking this way to each other.

Burned, as so rarely happened, by his own words, Dorian briefly smoldered. His eyes were obsidian, his face pale as though in defiance of his point. For a moment it seemed he might have nothing with which to answer.

Then he tapped a cadence on the bedpost with his fingernails.

"Yes," he said acidly. "Half of me."

Some wagons clattered by in the street below before either of them spoke again, or even moved. The pleasant music of morning, which came every day over and over again, whether there was war or not, was suddenly a bitter reminder of how quickly time could pass.

Dorian drew a steadying breath and angled back toward his carpetbag. Then he stopped with his back turned and stared at Wyatt in the mirror. "Why did I let you speak to me? This is your fault. You forced me to make the latest, largest error of my life. In fact, I should've thrown you out of my jail cell last year and just let them come and hang me. Then I wouldn't be feeling what I'm feeling now. If you were any kind of friend, you'd take out a gun, stand very close, aim eight or nine times, and shoot me dead."

"Aren't you talking to the wrong person?" Wyatt asked. "Shouldn't you be talking to your wife?"

"The last time I talked to her, I ended up married."

"You're blaming me?" Wyatt responded. "Me, God, the devil—you can't just run over people and push off the blame when they get crushed. All right, you were handed some rough luck. So are plenty of other people—"

He cut himself off.

Behind Dorian the floor creaked. A hand caught his arm and wrenched him around.

Wyatt wrestled until Dorian was facing him. The wild indignation in Dorian's eyes was frightening, but Wyatt was unaffected.

"I've put up with your smart mouth and your scrap-iron wit," he said. "I've put up with your butchering of other people's feelings. I've put up with your mysteries and your vague explanations and your tampering with my business, never telling me who's behind the money that comes in and who gets the money that goes out. I've put up with your dropping out of sight for months on end and trying to make sense of things while you're gone. I stuck by you when the whole South wanted you taken out of that jail cell and hanged for that scar on your arm and the five-thousand-dollar reward . . . and I've *never* demanded anything of you."

He stopped, and the sudden quiet clawed at them both.

When Wyatt thought he saw Dorian begin to flicker with unease and the weight of this debt, he added, "But now, I'm demanding this. Don't go."

Dorian jolted away from him.

"I *am* going!" he insisted. "I shall board the fastest packet in Richmond Harbor, catch the Gulf Stream, be in England in ten days, and make sure the South does not lose. Meanwhile Aleck Stephens will stay here and make sure the South does not *win*."

Starched by a feigned indifference he couldn't maintain, he began throwing his clothing into the carpetbag without folding it.

"This is the only way," he said. "It's best for Orienta."

Wyatt stepped closer. "Why don't you let Orienta decide

what's best for her? Take her with you. Stay in Europe, where nobody'll care."

"God's back teeth! If it's so easy, why don't you go and ask her yourself? Be sure to tell her everything. Don't leave anything out." He plunged a spare pair of boots into the bag, then suddenly snapped around, glaring. "Oh! What's that on your face? Apprehension? You mean you'll have some difficulty explaining all this to her? Can't find the right words? After all, what do you think a woman like Orienta will say when she discovers what she has done . . . with a nigger?"

They stared at each other in boiling discomfort. Dorian ticked off five seconds, then seized the moment and continued to grill relentlessly. His voice turned fierce and ice cold—but beneath the ice there was a pain drilling so deep that it drove the life from his eyes and the steadiness from his voice.

"Is this the best I can get from you?" he rasped. "My friend telling me these things as I attempt to do the most difficult thing I have ever done? Aren't you supposed to provide comfort to me at a time like this?"

With effort Wyatt said, "I can't be friends with someone who could do what you're about to do to Orienta."

"Then how can we be friends!" Dorian roared. "How can we? If you will not accept *what . . . I . . . am . . .*?"

He scooped his top hat from the quilted bedspread with one hand and clapped shut the carpetbag with the other. He popped the hat on his head, grasped the handle of his carpetbag, and swung out the door.

The morning hadn't gone the way it should have. Earlier today, Wyatt had felt fit for the first time in weeks—felt that at least one of the world's myriad problems might work out all right . . . only to find that very problem festering under his own roof.

What could work with Dorian? Had he ever seen anything truly sway Dorian off his course? Dorian was a man who made a decision, then acted upon it instantly with the agility of a darting trout. He could disappear without a word, had done that to Wyatt, and now was doing it to Orienta. Wyatt tried to tell himself Dorian would reappear, but he couldn't shake the sensation that there was something very dark and different about this departure. This time there was a completely innocent woman being broken in two, and that had never happened before.

His heart and head both pounding, Wyatt bolted from the room and into the hallway and thudded toward the second floor landing, where he gripped the newel post and called down, "Dorian—"

At the bottom of the stairs, having his Inverness settled on his shoulders by Edmund, Dorian pivoted just enough to look up at him.

They communicated silently for a moment. There was hope, and there was ugliness.

Then Dorian probed. "Yes?"

Wyatt locked his knees and waited until the tension between them forced Edmund to lower his eyes and even to step back. The two masters passed their final moment in strange communication.

Then Wyatt forced himself to speak without clearing his throat first. His voice came out as gravel under a wheel.

"Don't come back."

———— ★ ————

PART SEVEN

DIPLOMATIC ESPIONAGE

The future of England demands that
American progress be put in check.

—Lord John Russell,
British Foreign Minister

CHAPTER FORTY

--------- ★ ---------

Renowned London fog obscured the otherwise tolerable morning air. The entire vicinity was speared with masts and draped with rigging.

An agreeable-faced man clattered up the gangplank of a Baltimore packet while the crew was still getting the sheets coiled and flemished down. He was not a tall man, but built like a stack of barrels, dressed impeccably in a brown houndstooth daysuit whose wide lapels, velvet collar, and two rows of horn buttons on the double-breast were meant to stir an illusion of slimness. His brown beard was skintight, his cheeks florid, eyes elvish, and his mustache Spanish. He carried a bone walking cane and a glint of dare in his eyes as he moved across the beam of the barely docked American packet.

His frequent, frivolous smile and habit of tapping the brim of his bowler in greeting disguised a talent for analyzing others as he moved through the crew and departing passengers. After he greeted each person, the smile would drop and a cold assessment would replace it, just for a necessary second. By the time he crossed midships to the starboard beam, he had categorized the value or risk of knowing every person who had passed him by.

He was looking for one man in particular. Looking for a greatcape of iron gray and a gentleman beneath it of moderate stature—a dark human cloud with dangerous eyes and skin as pale and peach as a woman's shoulder.

He found that man on the stern, where no one should be

while a ship is coming into port, staring back the way the ship had come.

"Mr. Trozen," the man in the houndstooth suit began. "Welcome to England, sir. I'm relieved to see you. I waited on the dock, but you weren't forthcoming."

With his hands coldly gripping the ship's taffrail and his oil-black stare still fixed on the seamless Thames, Dorian did not move at the sound of his former name.

"Cousin," he acknowledged. He guarded his expression. "How are you?"

"Uncommonly well."

That was all he knew of his associate's identity. A Du Pont, of course, but which Du Pont?—Dorian had no idea. The money had always been there. The power was obviously there, and Dorian had intuited from the beginning that the wise course was *not* to investigate. For years—was it already years?—this man had been "Cousin."

Since shortly before he approached Wyatt on their behalf, Dorian had entertained a tenuous relationship with the Southern-sympathizing Du Ponts, all through this one pouchy-faced man whose smile was only part truth. Dorian had actively avoided learning much about the Cousin.

Nor was he sure how much this Du Pont knew about *him*. The Cousin made no personal inquiries, never nudged nor fished, nor pursued the natural slips that pop out when people talk. Meetings were brief, polite, and colored with the clandestine. Dorian had forced himself to assume that while he judged it wise to avoid poking into the Cousin's identity, perhaps the Cousin and the other Du Ponts in question knew better than to investigate their mysterious agent. If any knew too much, a mutually beneficial relationship would be lost to all.

He was in a kind of numb daze—Europe! It was not just a story, not a legend! Like the outside world when he left the plantation for the first time in his life. He had read all of Shakespeare, all of Burns, all of any British literature he could acquire, yet Britain had always been a kind of Valhalla.

"Are you ill, Dorian?" the Cousin asked, pressing an elbow to the rail and gazing up at him. "The voyage?"

Dorian allowed only his eyes to move. "Do I look ill, sir?"

"You don't look yourself. You're brooding upon something."

"Deciding whether to commit *seppuku* and put an end to my closet drama. Or perhaps join the Royal Navy under an assumed lordship, standing yardarm to yardarm and giving broadsides to some French privateer—"

The Cousin interrupted with a chuckle and said, "I confess, I expected you to have maneuvered yourself into a position of power on this scow, given ten days on the Atlantic."

"Just so. I'm pressuring for an admiralty," Dorian said. "They're holding out."

"There is no title of admiral in the United States Navy."

Dorian turned his shoulders a little. "Indeed, is that so?"

"Despite repeated requests by the secretary of the Navy to establish grades of an admiralty. I believe it's coming, especially with the War for Constitutional Liberty."

"Odd . . ."

The Cousin surveyed him keenly. "That there's no admiralty or that you didn't know it?"

"That second thing. By rights I'm a repository of pointless points."

The Du Pont Cousin's cheeks pouched up with a smile. "Congress holds that an admiralty is too much an echo of royalty. Did you have any trouble slipping the blockade?"

"I did not slip it. I ghosted in the night from Richmond to Baltimore and boarded a ship flying United States colors, as you see there above us."

"Of course—yes. I was curious as to why your letter instructed me to meet a Baltimore packet."

"I'm surprised you received the letter at all. I anticipated having to seek you out and shock you with my presence."

"The letter preceded you by only two days, on that surly black-hulled steamer you hired to bring it to me. Mind, I was dismayed to find a sooty, glowering sailor at my chamber door. He had no teeth left in front except the two pointed ones that a vampire might use and he smelled of fish and tobacco. Thought I was being kidnapped, but then he handed me your announcement. Let's get brisk, now. Daresay you need some time on solid ground. Let me take you to a place I know. The publican was a sailing man himself years ago, and he specializes in food that squares away the stomach, as he puts it. What do you say to it?"

Dorian pulled against the man's grip. "May I request you simply drive me around London?"

He turned away and strode down the deck planks, one hand lingering on the taffrail, and communed with the fog-veiled old city.

"Show me sights I have read about, imagined, heard of," he said. "St. Paul's, Guildhall, Kensington Palace, the Houses of Parliament, the dirty East End, Blackfriars, Bloody Tower and its Yeoman Warders, the Tower Bridge, the oaken stalactites of Middle Temple . . . Show me Threadneedle Street, show me the scarlet and silver pikemen of the Honourable Artillery, show me the Roman Wall, the crypts of Nelson and Wellington and Wren, and let me stand where King Henry watched the *Mary Rose* turn over and sink. . . ."

He drew in a sharp breath and only by the strongest of self-demand was he able to keep from choking.

"Take me from these decks and show me all the ambergris and dragon's blood that make Britain *Britain* . . . and perhaps I shall hunger less for that which I have abandoned."

The Cousin laughed right out, so abruptly and loudly that Dorian actually flinched. He had the laugh of a gambling bartender.

"You're the only man I know who can make the city of London seem like a dowager codwife. Comfort yourself, Dorian . . . and come with me."

He brushed aside the short upper cape of the Iverness, found Dorian's elbow with his gloved hand, and turned him from the direction that looked down the Thames away from London. Wherever Dorian's mind was, they were both here now, with *this* day's business lurking.

"You shall have a tour that will leave you breathless," he said, "and you and I shall have a conversation of impending intrigue."

London's tight old Henry Tudor veins pulsed around the Du Pont's hired landau. The English people moved in the streets, well dressed, gloved and shawled, making decisions about Americans from this removed vantage.

The Du Pont Cousin had spoken privately to the driver of their landau before the reins snapped even once. Now the carriage was rolling down back streets and oldest alleys. They passed the fragmented Roman wall, relic from a settlement called Londinium. They rode not just past the spires of Westminster, St. James Palace, and Henry's Arch, but into the seamy London as well. The landau was swallowed by London's darkest corners, rich with the scent of opium and whiskey, serpentine alleys with no apparent ending, so close to the Thames that the air was constant with creaking of masts and docklines, grumbling with muffled voices making clandestine deals, exhausted sailors loading and unloading the never-ending shipments of wool, tea, rubber, ivory, and wine. It was a cold tour, stirring and haunted. They had to change horses twice.

Dorian realized he was being given exactly the tour *he* would have wished for.

The Cousin knew him disturbingly well.

Their talk was idle at first, as Cousin always encouraged when they first met after long periods. Nothing had been agreed upon; the conversation just always went that way.

They chatted about the horse-drawn omnibuses with people riding in seats on the roofs for a better view, the new tram service, and the proposed underground railway. They rode past Fortnum and Mason and watched the colonial figures of the founders on the clock turn and bow to each other on the hour.

And there were people everywhere. Unlike American cities, which were lightly populated and tended to sprawl into the countryside, London was old and crowded and cramped, built inland on a place where the Thames could be waded at low tide, so it wasn't even accessible from the ocean with any particular ease. People upon people, in narrow old streets with narrow old windows. A thousand eyes behind a thousand more.

Dorian could feel the decisions and judgments being made all around him, in every market and square, every shop and vendor's, and in the hand of every boy selling a newspaper.

It gave him an unanticipated distaste. Something fluttered in his stomach that had never fluttered before.

"Interesting to think," the Cousin murmured as they sat side by side and gazed out at the people on the cobbled streets. "A hundred years ago, *they* owned *us*. Fancy being owned."

Suddenly swept with a chill, Dorian somehow kept from looking at him, and somehow said nothing. He simply wasn't sure enough of the secrets, or of the Cousin. Anything could be a test. Anything. Suddenly he turned cautious. Stephens had given him reason to come here with authority in his pocket, Orienta provided personal cause for escape, the Du Pont element gave him a net to fall into—but whom could he really trust?

"In a week or so," the Cousin said, "I shall arrange for us to put our despicable fannies down on the leather couch in the library of the House of Lords. Would you like that?"

Dorian could only nod. Then, knowing his silence would give him away, he forced out, "I shall polish my unpeered fanny in anticipation."

"I will take you to the city of York ultimately. You'll like it. York will make you feel good."

Dorian sat back against the leather seat, and for the first time in weeks began to work his shoulders loose. Perhaps here he could think.

London had its own smell, the musty scent of a giant antique emporium from which the dust was never quite cleared nor the moisture ever quite dried away. Its sounds were old sounds—the scream of pigeons, the chatter of wheels over cobblestone and brick, the crackle of fountain water, the gong of Big Ben striking the hour, and the elusive buzzing report of military drummers practicing somewhere nearby.

It made Dorian feel tight in the chest to be so far away, in a place so obviously different and removed—

"Dorian," the Cousin began with a taint of warning in his voice, "there is something you should know. Someone is poking about in the North, looking for you."

As his stomach and shoulders knotted at the same time, Dorian kept a stiff face. "For me? Why should anyone? Can you be certain?"

The Cousin didn't bother to answer that question, for they both knew.

"But who?" Dorian asked. "Have you a name? A description? No hints for me at all?"

A big mountain man in buckskins?

"The questions are all financial," the Cousin said. "Tracing money and documents. Banks. The like."

Then it wasn't Orville Quist, Dorian concluded instantly.

"We are attempting to screen you off," the Cousin told him. "To block the questions, or at least the answers, until we trace the source of interest."

"I am grateful for that. Truly."

"And we to you." The Cousin clutched Dorian's wrist in open reassurance.

"You won't be shocked, considering all this, when I tell you I'm using a new *nom de guerre*."

"Not all all. What are you using?"

"Parthens."

"I'll use it," the Cousin said. "Don't worry—we shall protect you, *if* we can."

With an understanding nod Dorian forgave him for that *if*. "In the meantime I have a mission of great immediacy—of which I assume you are already aware?"

"The potassium nitrate, I know. My cousin Lammot has been given a massive contract by Lincoln, and is about to leave, tomorrow if he can, with five hundred thousand pounds of niter." He shifted on his seat to face Dorian and lowered his voice to be certain the landau driver couldn't overhear. "I have made sure that Lammot had to pay what he thought was an inflated price for his niter. In reality he was buying six hundred thousand pounds, not five."

"Mmm," Dorian uttered. He capped his surprise that things had gone so far and that the Cousin had such power, moved on such levels, and he dared not even ponder what the true cost, in money and blood, had been. "Does Lammot know you are in England?"

"He may. He has his own sources, you know. If we spent all our time fretting over that, we should get nothing done. The extra hundred thousand pounds of the stuff has been kept off the paperwork and is at this moment being diverted to storage at the London Docks, about a half mile from where your packet tied up. It will be all yours."

Dorian tipped his head. "My thanks. I always wanted a hundred thousand pounds of unsalted bird guano."

"*Bon appétit*. The entire operation is safely under the table so far. However, we still have the devil to pay out and only half a bucket of pitch."

"How do you mean?"

"We still have to get the niter back to the Confederacy. The Union blockade may be *nearly* impotent, but they're capturing one out of eight blockade runners, and I don't prefer to dare that twelve and a half percent risk of impoundment. We dare not lose this niter to the Union. How can we get the shipment back to your friend's powder yard without costing Victoria's ransom?"

Dorian gave the Cousin a savage little grin. It clearly reminded both of them that the Southern Du Ponts hadn't struck up a relationship with him because he was the tidiest boy in school, after all.

"Leave that," Dorian said, "to me."

The Bazaar, Baker Street, Portman Square, London

She breathed as she had for nearly a hundred years. Her breasts moved in the deep drumbeat of sleep, beneath a bodice of tapered pink satin bows, one arm cast upon the pillow over her head, the other resting upon her lavender satin gown.

"The revolutions she has slept through," Dorian murmured thoughtfully as he gazed down upon the mistress of all mistresses. "Think of it."

"She is the likeness of Madame du Barry," the Cousin said, "modeled ten years before the American Revolution. And here she still lies."

Dorian pondered the waxwork figure upon its canopied bed and thought of moving his mouth upon those tiny breasts. "What makes her breathe?"

"A clockwork," the Cousin said, moving to his side. "The Sleeping Beauty. Would I could sleep so well."

"Would I could at all," Dorian groaned. "I've heard Marie Antoinette's face or nose, or some part or other, is here along with her husband's."

"Her husband *and* the very blade that whopped off their heads. There's also an Egyptian mummy here three thousand years old, the shirt King Henry the Fourth was wearing when he was assassinated, and—"

Dorian turned. His expression caused the other man to fall silent. "The actual blade? The guillotine?"

The Cousin shifted his feet. "Madame Tussaud was most scrupulous in fashioning her tableaux. She seemed to have possessed a keen perception of what makes the public curious. The heads are the actual death masks of Antoinette and Louis. The original molds are kept safely below, in a basement. Poor woman, she was commanded to make death masks from the heads of dozens of decapitated victims of the French Revolution. Too bad France failed to improve any after that godforgotten mess, eh?"

"Is she still alive?"

"Passed on in 1850. Her own body—well, not her body, but her waxen figure—is here also. She did it herself."

"By my soul, I should fancy putting my hands upon that blade!" Dorian said distractedly, his eyes flashing with excitement.

"You won't be allowed to."

"Never underestimate me, Cousin. Deader men than you have tried."

He laughed, and the Cousin laughed also, as they turned away from the eternally breathing Sleeping Beauty.

There was something of the library about Madame Tussaud's and Sons Exhibition that kept voices down, even though there was no one else here at this early hour other than the proprietor, who had met them at the door and accepted the Cousin's "honorarium" for an early showing.

This something, this aura, impelled the two conspirators to keep quiet as they moved from display to display, past the various kings and queens, figures of Cromwell and Voltaire, Wellington and Napoleon, and the actual coronation robes of George IV hanging on his effigy, a little sign proclaiming that the robes had been purchased in 1840.

Each display was cleanly illuminated by a brightly burning camphine candelabram. The meticulously costumed wax figures were far more haunting than ghosts, for they were really here, visible, with faces, eyes, ears, staring across the decades at two men of the living time.

"Cousin, I need more from you than potassium nitrate," Dorian finally said as the two of them paused before the tableaux of Marie Antoinette, her king and children during happier times. "Oh, very nice," he commented, waving at the figures. "Little did they know. Back to this other thing, I need an audience with Lord Russell. Unofficially. You needn't even tell him my name, if he prefers not to know it."

The Cousin struck him with an amused glower. "Is that all you need? And which of your names shall I tell him if he asks?"

"Oh, Plato, Socrates, Duke Wellington—whatever you fancy. What can you tell me about him?"

The Cousin paused, turned serious, and surveyed him keenly. "What is your authority . . . other than me, that is."

Dorian faced him, then waited for the lower hem of the greatcape to settle around his calves.

"My authority is Alexander Stephens, Vice President of the Confederacy."

After a contemplative few seconds, the Cousin asked, "But not President Davis?"

Dorian leaned slightly toward him. "Not if *we* can help it."

"Ah . . . hmm, I see. My goodness, you run in interesting circles."

"While orbiting you," Dorian offered back with a nod. "About Russell . . ."

"Mmm. A tall order, my friend," the Cousin sighed. "Such things can't be arranged overnight. This will take weeks of delicate string pulling and manipulation."

"I have the weeks. Feel free to take them . . . all you want and more."

"Indeed? You're not in a hurry to return to the front?"

"No . . . no." Dorian shook off the subject poorly and knew he had given something away in his voice. "What do you know about Russell? What have the newspapers been saying?"

The Cousin paused, thought, then shrugged. "He may or

may not have Northern sympathies, but he clearly views the end of the United States as a done thing. Because of that, he's working on how England can best profit from it."

He strode a few more feet down the dim corridor of Madame Tussaud's bizarre establishment, looking at the floor instead of the displays.

"Here is the current condition of England on the subject of the American war. Lord Palmerston hates slavery, dislikes Americans and American problems. He doesn't want a war with the United States—well, you see, he has his eye constantly on Europe, and war with the U.S. would complicate things. Weaken England, he thinks. He's been watching the rise of French naval power—"

"And doesn't want to risk sending his fleet into a war in the west, I'll bet you."

"Exactly, exactly. The United States isn't a world power, and the experiment of democracy appears to be falling apart, so why waste the fleet over there? Britain means to stay in control of Europe. The English are very happy these days, Dorian. English interests revolve around profit and loss, and everyone's worried about long-term effects on England as Lord Maritime. After only seventy years the American experiment is a failure. The United States is now a thing of the past. Aristocrats all over Europe gleefully wallow in that kind of news. The American experiment in mob rule has come to this. Monarchies are exonerated."

Dorian, who had fallen silent, now felt a tense frown on his brow and his lips. Sitting in Richmond, discussing this with Aleck and Wyatt, all this had seemed like a board game.

"*The Times* is conservative in its opinions," the Cousin went on. "Generally it is favorable toward the South, while also being somewhat . . . oh, I don't know . . . what would you call it—'forgiving' toward the North. They're pretty set against going to war to avenge pirates running the blockade."

"I see. The blockade is illegal, but so are those who run it, yes?"

"Yes. *The Standard* is nasty on the subject, and openly smashes the North for what it calls 'terrorism against British shipping.' They've even let a fellow named Hotze publish articles in their paper from his propaganda piece, *The Index*. This

Hotze is rancorously pro-Confederate, to the tune of calling
the English all kinds of names. I don't think he's helping what
he intends to help."

"Some people never learn the velvet-glove advantage,"
Dorian agreed.

"Well, I know, but really! This *Index*—you'd swear they
were intent upon driving England off instead of encouraging
its help."

"Is that so? . . . Interesting. . . . I wonder if that's what
they're up to?"

"I don't think this Hotze fellow is that thoughtful. *The
Daily News* is pro-U.S., and calls names at Englishmen who
profit from our war, or anyone who *wants* England to profit
from the war. *The Spectator* and *The Army and Navy Gazette*
both preach observance of maritime law—"

"In other words, we should *politely* blow off each other's
genitalia."

"*The Morning Post* is Palmerston's personal megaphone. It
claims America has always been jealous of the British maritime superiority and is doing all these things on purpose, just
to snigger England."

Dorian tried to pop off a quick response, but ended up
chuckling and shaking his head.

The Cousin smiled and said, "*The Liverpool Courier* is
openly fanning the flames of war between England and us. In
fact, they claim that the U.S. is using the war to pirate British
vessels and as an excuse to get its hands on Canada, and they
call Lord Russell an imbecile for doing nothing from his
Foreign Office."

Dorian laughed and blustered, "Saints! I had no idea the
North and South were fighting each other for all these purposes involving England! We can't think independently at all,
can we?"

"Astounding, isn't it, what people will think?"

"It is."

"Then there's *The Manchester Guardian, The Sheffield and
Rotherham Independent, The Newcastle Daily Chronicle*—"

"Please—"

"*The Liverpool Mercury, Gore's General Advertiser, The
Southampton Times*—"

"Enough! You're making me tired. Suffice to have examples on my bed table this coming Sunday, and I shall read this palaver for myself! Does anyone actually pay attention to what these papers print?"

"They pay attention to each other. You'll have the time to become very familiar with all this if you truly intend to haul about England on the slim chance of seeing Russell," the Cousin said. Then the whole idea seemed to get more possible in his mind, and a little light came on in his eyes. "If you can deal directly with Russell," he said, "I shall manipulate Palmerston from afar."

"I approve of manipulation from afar," Dorian commented drably, still irritated. "How are the newspapers—oh! God!"

He jolted backward suddenly, his greatcape flaring and his heart whopping inside his chest after a terrible *snap*.

Before him—heads on pikes lined a dark stone wall. The bright camphine light was all gone suddenly, and the only illumination was a ghastly blue light designed to be obscure. Decapitated heads, bloodstained and blue-skinned, ghastly effigies with their mouths either gaping or frozen shut in death by the blade—

And *there* was the blade . . . dripping the juice of death.

"I'm sorry!" The Cousin caught Dorian by the shoulders from behind and kept him from stumbling backward any more. "I should have warned you we'd entered into the Chamber of Horrors."

"Roaring God!" Dorian crushed a fist to his clattering chest and sucked at the air. "What a thing to have in a civilized town!"

"Macabre," the Cousin said. "Sorry again."

"Eat your sorry and warn me next time! Go back in the main exhibit and get my heart, will you?—I've dropped it. What's around the next bend—a tableau of the plague? Is that a wax rat in the corner?"

The Cousin laughed and held on to Dorian's arm. "You're so funny."

"Indeed! Witch piss on it! Just look in that corner and see if it's not a wax rat! This place is more grotesque than I am, by God! You know, I pride myself on being very hard to shock, and here you've done it."

He gathered himself, held his breath a moment as two particular faces caught his attention—a narrow-nosed woman with a high, round forehead, and a square-faced corpulent man who seemed to be smiling in his sleep.

"So . . . Antoinette and Louis, I assume."

"Yes," the Cousin said, not without a touch of reverence, if not for the French monarchs, then at least for what they and their children were made to endure. "This is the rabble's version of toppling tyrants—to become more tyrannical." He stepped back, leaned upon his cane, and gazed at the heads. "The Revolution threw us Du Ponts out, you know . . . then the counterrevolution put the Napoleons in. We're hoping another strong aristocracy will be established and we'll be in on it. Now that you mention it—you know, this is uncanny!—I rather fancy the idea of putting the screws to Britain and letting France know I'm doing it!"

He grinned evilly and indulged in those thoughts.

"Uncanny," Dorian echoed, as though in a trance. He leaned forward over the display rope and scoured the haunting decapitated heads. "They could open their eyes and speak!"

"Their eyes were barely closed when Marie Tussaud took these death masks. Over there is Maximilien Robespierre, fresh off the guillotine. And here—Dorian? Here is the great deciding knife of Paris." He gestured at the triangular relic streaked with wax blood. "Tussaud's sons found it in 1846 and brought it here. Everything's in here from criminals' death masks to the terrorist Marat murdered in his bath, taken the night he was stabbed to death by some girl or other—who, by the way, stands in effigy not too far from him. The body snatchers Burke and Hare are here, murderers and assassins of every caliber, a hideous French Revolution journalist named Hebert . . . quite a few heads and personalities from the French Revolution, you see, because Marie Tussaud was at the Court in the thick of it and she knew all these people personally. 'Stounding how much the public will pay for a stiff shiver, isn't it? They have a great sense of history, these Tussauds. To come in here," he added, "is to feel that history is all finished."

He glanced around at the startling effigies, and his eyes lit upon the murderer James Greenacre, holding two pieces of his fiancée's hacked-up corpse, and on the rolled-up eyes of the dead French revolutionary Marat.

"By God, Dorian," he said suddenly, "I believe I *will* get you in to see Russell, if it takes all the season!"

But silent on the display platform, Dorian was only half-aware of his living companion. His mind, his eyes, and his attention were on the chopper that had done the deeds on so many French aristocrats, including Louis XVI and his wife.

He stooped to one knee before the guillotine knife.

The old metal was not shining at all. The only shine came from the wax blood glowing in muted light from a gffdfaselier behind them, its tinted bull's eye lens casting a blue light on the heads and the blade.

"It actually *happened*!" he intoned. His whisper betrayed deep-rooted awakening.

"Yes," the Cousin said. "All these people were involved in political intrigue . . . and they ended up here. I wanted you to see this, Dorian, before we set foot inside a British government establishment. . . . We must never think we shall become important enough to have our names taken off the list of expendables. We might be kings, or we might be a footnote."

Dorian didn't look up at him, but he clearly heard that sentiment and digested it. The Cousin watched his face for several seconds, just to make sure.

"I had always imagined," Dorian said, "the guillotine blade as being much larger. But look how small it is! It wasn't an ax at all . . . it was a *scalpel*."

The greatcape lay in a mound of wool around his knees as he crouched there. He raised one hand and drew off his hat, and lay it beside him without taking his eyes from the blade.

He uttered, "I wonder what the heads thought . . ."

"Beg pardon?" the Cousin blurted. "You mean, after—"

"Yes. There must have been some time of lag, some thoughts still percolating before the brains . . . blacked out. . . . I wonder if they thought about writing down their feelings—you know, expecting to recover the way we do when we're ill. . . ."

The Cousin was chilled to the marrow, his brows knotted tight as he stared at the oddest man he knew.

Barely audible, Dorian murmured, "I should like the chance to talk to a severed head. . . ."

These things had existed only in his mind for the first eighteen years of life, his cloistering on Plentiful. Stories. The world was nothing but stories, tales and legends, the myths seeming every bit as detailed and possible as the histories. Yet here he was, in England, having crossed the actual Atlantic, having toured the very streets, and now bending over the infamous knife, and suddenly he knew firsthand that these things were *real*. The French Revolution, the American Revolution, assassinations and overthrows, the kings and queens, their tumbling heads, Trafalgar—all the miscellanea he had grown up recreating in his mind—all had really happened. No more *stories*.

From behind him the Cousin spoke out. His voice coiled through the Chamber like a creeping reptile.

"What are you waiting for?" he asked. "Touch it."

★

THE BURNING FUSE

5 FEBRUARY 1862
LONDON

Lammot Du Pont leaves England with several ships loaded with five hundred thousand pounds of British saltpeter destined for Union powdermills.

13 FEBRUARY
WHEELING, IN WESTERN VIRGINIA

The West Virginia Constitutional Convention, seeking separate statehood from Virginia, decides to keep the area non-slave, but the method is to prohibit any person of color from coming into the area for permanent residence at all. There will be no slavery, and there will also be no colored people.

Fort Henry has surrendered. This major victory for Federal advancement allows passage down the Tennessee River. Grant's army now targets Fort Donelson. General Burnside's Federals have taken Roanoke Island, North Carolina, a defeat that strikes Richmond with fear. With control of Pamlico Sound, both Richmond and North Carolina are now in a direct line of threat.

After a day of fighting, the critical Fort Donelson surrenders. Reinforcements arrive too late. Unwilling to surrender, General Nathan Bedford Forrest and his cavalry escape; however, the number of Confederates who do surrender is estimated at twelve thousand. The loss of these two forts is disaster for the Confederacy. Kentucky and Tennessee, including two strategic rivers, now virtually belong to Ulysses Grant and the western limb of the Yankee army.

Ulysses Grant earns the nickname "Unconditional Surrender" Grant and is promoted to major general of Volunteers.

20 FEBRUARY
THE WHITE HOUSE, WASHINGTON, D.C.

President Lincoln and his wife Mary helplessly endure the slow death of their youngest son, Willie, at the age of twelve.

22 FEBRUARY
THE CONFEDERATE CAPITOL AT RICHMOND.

Jefferson Davis is inaugurated President of the Confederate States of America. "The tyranny of an unbridled majority, the most odious and least responsible form of despotism, has denied us both the right and the remedy. Therefore we are in arms to renew such sacrifices as our fathers made to the holy cause of constitutional liberty."

25 FEBRUARY

The Confederates evacuate Nashville. The Union occupies the strategic city. The next day Lincoln signs the Loan and Treasury Bill. A national currency is created, which can be financed by the sale of stocks, and is much more stable than anything printed in the South. There is now such a thing as the United States dollar.

27 FEBRUARY

Confederate Congress gives Jefferson Davis the power to suspend habeas corpus. When Lincoln did the same thing, it became one of the secessionists' reasons for leaving the Union in *the first place. He also orders martial law in Norfolk and Richmond. The differences of philosophy between North and South, which seemed so clear in speeches and in headlines, begins to blur in actual practice.*

———————————— ★ ————————————

CHAPTER FORTY-ONE

———— ★ ————

1 MARCH 1862
MECHANICSVILLE

"Christ cook a cake, it's raining out there! Took me half the day to get past those bedanged guards at the city line, and we were all soaked to the unders before they let me pass. Davis has declared martial law in Richmond. Think of that! He's just the same as Lincoln now. So much for the states running themselves. The government's becoming just another monolith, little bit farther south. Hardly any, on the continental scale, when you think about it. Lord knows how I'll get back into the city. I don't even have a Southern accent. You think somebody with a Kansas back-tongue like mine can get past Confederate guards? Maybe my name'll be enough. My husband's name on that big powdermill—everybody's heard of it. Maybe that'll be enough. If not, just have to slip in best as I—"

Grace shook the rain from her netted hair after handing her cloak and bonnet to the big slave called Buckie, who nodded tolerantly at her ranting. But now she stopped in the middle of her sentence, for she had come into the parlor and saw Orienta sitting at her clavichord.

But the round-faced woman wasn't playing the instrument. She was hugging it.

Her head was down on the music stand, one arm lying across the black keys, the other over her head on the wooden harp case, fingers clutching a newspaper she had apparently been reading.

Grace approached, somewhat stupefied at the woman's behavior. Orienta raised her head and looked up. Her face was bloodless and blotchy, tear glazed, eyes puffy, lips peeled back in misery she could not contain.

Grace groaned inwardly. *Jesus suck a pump! I'm not the comforting type. Damn that black-eyed wraith for leaving her to me. . . . Dump his poetry all over her like that and expect me to mop it up—just like him to fail cleaning up behind himself like some sick pig puking all over everybody and still wanting to be fed. . . .*

Orienta clutched the newspaper to her shirred bodice as she tried to straighten on the clavichord's velvet-covered bench.

Gawking down at her, Grace attempted, "Can I get you some . . . something?"

She didn't want to ask what was wrong. All she needed was to sit with a sobbing brokenhearted lovelorn dingdong like Orienta Swanborough and listen to the mourning and whining and the Captain Parthens this, Captain Parthens that. She wanted to slap the puffy cheeks and shout how they'd only known each other barely a month, and how much could a month mean in the whole scheme of things? And couldn't a woman who'd been through one husband already just throw off a second one and cast it up to experience? What was the matter with folks? He'd made a vow and broken it. What was there to talk about? Why sob over a vow-breaking man?

With fundamental disgust she glared at Orienta, who gazed back at her through eyes crescented in agony. She didn't really want to be unkind to the Alabama powder puff who thought she knew all about how to be a good wife, but neither was there any good reason to pamper such self-sorrow.

"Well," Grace began, "have you gone shopping lately? Do you like to do that sort of thing? Never saw much in it myself, but if if that's what you like, we'll do it, martial law or not. You know, there's an awful lot of charity work to be done, and all this war work. Women knitting socks for the soldiers and cooking food and sending it on, and . . . well, you know all that, because you were the one who told me about it in the first place. So we'll just have to keep you busy. 'Get over it,' that's my motto."

Sniffing and working hard at controlling herself, Orienta dabbed at her eyes. She nodded at Grace in unmistakable grati-tude—damn that bad habit of hers—and brushed at Grace's skirt in a sisterly gesture, smoothing the folds that had creased up during the carriage ride from Richmond.

The gesture was so pure that Grace couldn't disparage it. It carried some kind of valiant effort from the prim woman that even Grace's backwoods sensibilities understood.

But then Orienta sucked a gasp of air again and her eyes filled with tears. She blinked and looked up at Grace as though to explain.

"The President's little boy . . ."

She gazed up at Grace, as though pleading. As she broke into sobs, the newspaper fell from her hand.

Grace screwed her brows, bent over, and plucked the paper from the floor.

It was a week old. The headline callously discussed the death and funeral of William Wallace Lincoln, aged twelve years, at the White House in Washington, D.C., then went on to coldly calculate what effect this would have on the President's judgment regarding the war, and whether there would be any advantages for the Confederacy.

Grace looked up. "You mean all this . . . but I thought you hated Lincoln."

Orienta unfolded and refolded a handkerchief that had been knotted into a soggy ball in her other hand. She nodded slowly.

"That poor man . . . a war to run . . . a cloven nation—" Her mouth twisted into a bow of agony, closed in the center, open at both corners. "And his little boy is dead—"

Empathy overwhelmed her again, closed her throat, sent her shaking. Her eyes crushed shut, and she lost control again.

Knocked to senses she didn't know she possessed, Grace lowered herself onto the big tuffet near the clavichord and stared in notable shame through her own assumptions. Only now did she realize what she had been on the brink of saying out loud.

Solemnly she reached for human contact with a woman about whom she was suddenly changing her mind.

★

RICHMOND

"She married him! Can you believe it? She married him, and he abandoned her just that sharply. Just imagine this. I go away for a few weeks, and look what occurs. She off'n marries this flash-mouthed fancy."

"She has never obeyed you unconditionally, Barry."

"Obeyed me? This isn't even sound judgment."

"She doesn't know the truth about him. You haven't told her—"

"Hardly. I shouldn't have to tell her! Anyone who's around the man for more than ten seconds can sense something off center about him."

"Are you going to? Tell her, I mean?"

Barry Swanborough paced this way and that, up and down the standing bar in the gentlemen's club where he preferred to meet Felix Carter. Here, in veiled discretion and privacy, they could claim to be only two acquaintances having a pourparler over a brandy.

He paused at Carter's question, with his back to the other man.

Carter approached him from behind. "You been savoring the evidence, to use it at the right occasion . . . Is this the occasion you intend to fling it against Parthens?"

Swanborough took a sip of his drink and stared at the polished bar. "I don't give a hang about Parthens." Abruptly he laughed and turned to face the lawyer. "I don't have to. When that information comes out, he'll *be* hanged. I want to use it against Stephens."

"Then Orienta—"

"Can stay married to a nigger for all I care. She'll be soundly rapped in the mouth when this is revealed, and controlling interest in the plantation will be unquestionably back under my influence. She'll be so shattered, she won't even breathe right. She won't give a simpleton's damn over the plantation." He leaned the point of his elbow on the bar. "Probably be committed to an asylum."

Carter glanced about, stepped a little closer, and lowered his voice. "Parthens hasn't just 'abandoned' her Barry. That's what I came here to tell you. He's gone to England."

Swanborough's expression went to stone. "What? England? Why?"

His tone implied that he suspected why. He just wanted to hear it.

"To do Stephens's work in Parliament. To wheedle some kind of terms under which recognition will be acceptable to the English public and squeak under international law. That's, of course, any law agreed upon by Europe."

"Well, I can't have that, I can't have that at all," Swanborough muttered, stalking past Carter. "I'm just starting to see a real profit in the cotton underground. I've got thirty-five to forty-five percent of my crop stored all over the place, skimmed right off the stuff I'm burning just to keep the others burning theirs. Burning it is driving the price sky-high. I'm selling that thirty-five percent at a ridiculous profit. Ten times the peacetime worth of the stuff. If England recognizes the Confederacy too early, we'll be skunked. We must keep this situation at the status quo, Felix, and we'll be rich as royalty."

He paused, his eyes pinching, seeing in his mind Dorian Parthens getting off a ship in Britain and walking straight into the House of Lords.

"Is Davis involved?" he asked, turning.

"I do not have that information," Carter said.

"But it's definitely Stephens?"

"Absolutely. You saw how they were together."

"Have you a plan?"

"I have a connection," Carter corrected. "Henry Hotze, editor of a Confederate propaganda publication, *The Index*."

"Very good. This Hotze?"

"A wild-eyed maniac. Quite maneuverable."

"Excellent. We must spoil Stephens's plan, or at least set it back six months to a year. Felix, I want you to go to England."

"Pardon me? *I* am expected to go to that old-fashioned pesthole?"

"You'll be happy to lie with the pests when you get your stipend. Go in and rub this Hotze in his sensitive places. Maneuver yourself into de facto control over his publication and start printing inflammatory editorials. Do everything you can to damage the possibility of recognition too early by demanding it immediately. Paint their stalling as eccentric, dalliant, and spineless . . . something like that, then insist that they do whatever we demand. The English won't like that. Revile Palmerston and Russell in such a way as to make the English revile the Confederacy. Inflame their British arrogance, Carter. It's the only thing bigger than their Navy."

"And Parthens?"

Swanborough pondered coldly the man who came out of nowhere to lure his sister-in-law into an impossible marriage, who had tweaked him in public, who had been a thorn in his side for months, and who gave succor and mobility to Alexander Stephens's contrary plots.

"You have my unconditional permission," he said, "to expose his little secret at the moment of highest damage."

★★★

THE BURNING FUSE

Troops moving everywhere, with spotty skirmishes and considerable ground changing hands:

The Mississippi River is peppered with contentions; Columbus, Kentucky; Martinsburg, in western Virginia; Amelia Island, Florida; Cubero and Comanche Pass, New Mexico Territory; Pea Ridge, Arkansas; Bunker Hill; Murfreesboro, Tennessee; New Madrid, Point Pleasant, and Riddle's Point, Post Oak Creek, Little Santa Fe, and Island Number 10, Missouri; Big Creek Gap and Jacksborough on the Tennessee River; Middletown, Leesburg, and the Orange and Alexandria Railroad, Virginia. Fighting at Kernstown, Virginia, signals the beginning of what will come to be known as the Shenandoah Valley Campaign.

Few Southern localities go completely untouched by the sight, sound, or anticipation of troop movements or clashes.

Federal troops move up the Shenandoah toward Stonewall Jackson's command arena. More Federals advance up the Tennessee River. Confederate congressmen demand more guns to defend the Mississippi, but there simply are not enough armaments or powder.

The Federal iron ship *Monitor* leaves New York, heading for confrontation with the Confederate ironclad *Virginia*, made out of the refitted Federal frigate *Merrimack*.

In Richmond, General Robert E. Lee is summoned to consult President Davis on military maneuvers in Virginia.

The ironclad C.S.S. *Virginia* has one good day, damaging several Federal vessels at Hampton Roads, Virginia, near

Norfolk. The Monitor *and the* Virginia *come together and fight, but their iron construction is ahead of their armaments. Shells meant to damage wooden vessels bounce off the metal ships, and the battle comes to stalemate. The ironclads do far more damage simply by the fear they strike in the hearts of their enemy, rather than by their actual performance in battle.*

However, a new age of marine warfare has begun. From this day forward, the wooden fleets of the world, including that of the queen of the seas, Britain, are suddenly on notice: they are now obsolete.

Frustrated President Lincoln relieves Major General George McClellan of his command of the Federal Armies. McClellan still commands the Army of the Potomac, but is no longer general in chief. The post remains unfilled.

Lincoln also denies troops to McClellan, ordering a sizable division to guard Washington. Even though he has over one hundred thousand men on the Peninsula, McClellan grumbles that he has been left short of adequate troops for his advance.

While Lincoln is searching for a man who can replace McClellan and actually move armies, Jefferson Davis gives Robert E. Lee command of all Confederate military operations. In a major cabinet change, Judah P. Benjamin is appointed Secretary of State of the Confederacy. Davis puts George Randolph into Benjamin's former position as Secretary of War, citing Randolph's experience in the Army and the Navy, but at the real core of the move is Davis's desire to do the Secretary of War's job himself. Randolph will keep to duties of administration.

1–4 APRIL 1862

Tension and action accelerate on the Peninsula, putting pressure on Richmond. Everyone expects a major confrontation.

However, McClellan is still in charge.

Though his one-hundred-thousand-man army moves slowly toward Yorktown, on the Chickahominy Peninsula, he is stood off by an eleven-thousand-man contingent of Confederates under John Bankhead Magruder. Outnumbered nearly ten to one, Magruder has two advantages: a background in amateur theater, and George McClellan for an adversary.

Magruder orders his artillery to shoot randomly, at any-

thing, his musicians to play loudly, and he ingeniously marches a few hundred grays around and around one large stand of trees for hours on end. He knows McClellan's reconnaissance will report a huge Confederate contingent, and that McClellan will exaggerate that contingent further in his mind.

It works. Instead of attacking McClellan settles down to develop "lines of seige."

7 APRIL 1862

"The Warwick River grows worse the more you look at it. It seems clear that I shall have the whole force of the enemy on my hands, probably not less than 100,000 men, and possibly more."

—George McClellan to President Lincoln

Pittsburg Landing, Tennessee. Among the peach trees, florid with pink spring blossoms, the Confederates of Albert Sidney Johnston surprise the Federals of Ulysses Grant at Shiloh Church.

Though unprepared, the Yankees have an advantage in their commander, who is cool under pressure and at his most alert while being fired upon. The Federals fall back, but do not break.

Albert Sidney Johnston falls in battle and bleeds to death. During the stormy night Grant acquires reinforcements. The full-scale battle is bloody and horrifying to armies who had been used to skirmishes.

Grant holds the field. The Confederates retreat. The South still lacks even one noteable victory.

9 APRIL 1862

The Confederate Senate passes the Conscription Bill, and incorporates what came to be called the Twenty Nigger Law— anyone with less than twenty slaves must join the armed service. Southerners view this as yet another infringement upon the freedoms for which they had gone to war.

As news of the awful battle at Shiloh Church spreads across the continent, McClellan is still setting up seige lines.

This stalling gives General Joseph Johnston time to move his army from the Rappahannock to reinforce Magruder's tricky eleven thousand at Yorktown.

30 APRIL 1862

Joe Davis, five-year-old son of President Jefferson Davis, falls from the veranda on the Confederate White House and dies.

★

CHAPTER FORTY-TWO

---------- ★ ----------

But you must act.
—Lincoln to McClellan

WILLIAMSBURG, VIRGINIA, ON THE CHICKAHOMINY PENINSULA

Even in the heat of the battle, every one of the nine men on the artillery platoon knew his duty. This was the time when all the training came finally to a purpose. After hauling up a long, un-cooperative hill, they almost had their Napoleon twelve-pounder limber and caisson in position. Around them, hundreds of Confederates readied themselves for battle. In the near distance a brigade of Yankees were advancing, a thousand men in a raggedy line of mismatched uniforms and weaponry.

"Load!" the Chief of Piece shouted.

"Loading!"

The barrel was sponged while the round was brought from the limber. It was stuffed into the muzzle, the staff was reversed, and the round rammed home while one man covered the vent with his thumb to keep sparks from igniting.

"Train the gun!" the sergeant shouted, and simply pointed in the direction he wanted it trained. "Hold until my order. . . . I want them well within range! Calculate ratio of powder to shot for short range and elevate the gun for one hundred fifty yards."

"One fifty!"

The Gunner called, "Sergeant, that's mighty close, ain't it?"

Chief of Piece wheeled about and coughed out, "Well, can you see them any better than I can?"

Heavy clouds of artillery smoke crawled along the scruffy woodlands and provided the answer for him.

While another man showed the fuse to the Gunner for approval, the Chief stepped away from the Napoleon to a position where he could observe the fall of the canister shot.

Yankees poured out of the trees, barely a quarter mile across the open ground. They fired on the charge, in sections, then as their fellow soldiers charged, they paused to reload or drew out pistols and used those.

"They're charging!" the Confederate observer called.

"We've got to hold position," the Chief said loudly. "Richmond is only fifty miles away, men! If they take Williamsburg, they'll take Richmond! Step clear of recoil!"

"Clear!" the men called in straggled fashion as they jumped aside and covered their ears.

"Ready!"

The cartridge bag was pricked through the vent, the lanyard was hooked to the pull primer, the primer inserted into the vent, then a man again covered the vent with his hand to keep it from igniting early. The Gunner stepped to the side with the lanyard in his fist and waited for the Chief to decide when to start killing.

The Chief wedged his boot into the hollow of a broken tree for balance and leaned forward to watch the enemy advance. Lord in Heaven, but one hundred yards was practically in a man's trousers.

The Yankee swarm moved like migrating ants—no order, but all together.

Closer . . . closer . . .

"Fire!"

The Gunner yanked the lanyard.

PAAAAOOOOOOMMMMMMM—

The cannon erupted, lurched, roared, a great pounding boom preceded by a crack. It was the terrifying noise Napoleons were known for, something of a weapon in itself. A funnel of stinking smoke, sulfurous fumes—grapeshot splattered through the smoky air.

The nine men watched anxiously as the grape spewed toward their attackers—

And fell short! The rain of steel balls lost momentum and splattered into the open ground, to be pressed down into the earth by the onslaught of enemy soldiers.

Not a single Yankee went down, except maybe a couple who tripped on the run. But those got back up and kept charging.

"Good forty yards short!" someone shouted.

"Reload!" the Chief barked, choking. "Reload, for God's sake!"

The platoon scrambled frantically. Confidence fled out the soles of their feet.

But the enemy was moving. Hundreds of Yankees moving in a single horde, using up the time it took to reload the Napoleon.

"Damn it! Damn it!" Spitting tobacco onto the soggy ground, the Chief shook his head. "There's something wrong with our cussed gun today."

"Not the cussed gun," the Gunner responded, his voice gravelly. "The cussed powder! Not enough range!"

"Whose powder?"

"That'd be the Craig mill in Richmond, Sergeant."

They heard a Union commander fifty yards away shout, "Fix bayonets!"

Fifty yards and closing fast.

The order was as good as the knives to the Confederate gunners. Three of the nine men turned and ran for cover at the sight of those glittering bayonets. The chief grabbed his nearest man by the collar and yanked hard.

"Run!" he shouted. "Report to the captain about this Craig! He's got to be arrested. He is a traitor! He's a trai—"

Still in his grip, the man suddenly jerked to one side.

Blood began to pour out the Union side of the man's head. He was dead, even as the Chief held him on his feet.

The Chief pushed the corpse away, shocked. Smoke choked him, flushed him with rage about the cannon's shortened firepower, and he realized the cannon was hopeless against enemies closing in and that no one was listening to him anymore.

So he drew his sword and shouted, "Defend yourselves!"

His well-trained, organized artillery men who each knew

his task suddenly dissolved into disarray, and the enemy washed over them.

Unprepared, and outnumbered ten to one, the Confederate battery was in minutes reduced to slashed flesh.

The Yankees mowed them down, took possession of the twelve-pounder, turned it on the remainder of the Confederate forces, then continued to advance beyond the position.

Left bleeding in the weeds, the Confederate chief died uttering, "Traitor . . . traitor . . . traitor . . ."

CRAIG POWDERWORKS

PAAAAAOOOOOMMMMMM

Plugged or not, every ear for a half mile hurt.

This time the ladies in the powder town stayed home and tried to continue their day's work in spite of the shuddering walls and the shaking floors from the cannon shot. They'd been told well enough ahead of time to expect powder tests today.

In the powder yard itself, well clear of the dangerous zones, a regulation cannon stood smoking.

Three hundred yards downriver, a man yelled, "Short!"

Wyatt Craig cupped his hands around his mouth and shouted, "How short?"

"Forty yards!"

"Oh, my Lord—"

Henry Brecker shook his head. "That's what I thought. The priming powder looks funny."

"Funny?" Wyatt repeated. His stomach twisted.

"It's too . . . well, it ain't right, son." He gestured to the cannon squad. "Lemme see that priming powder."

"Looks okay, but that don't mean nothing. Ogelthorpe, stuff her agin and touch her off."

The cannon was loaded again, carefully, primed, and aimed.

The bell was rung again, to warn everyone. In the distance the men doing the range measuring took cover. All hands plugged their ears.

Ogelthorpe touched off the cannon.

PAAAAAAAOOOOOOOOM

The gun went off like Trafalgar. Painful.

This time Henry Brecker was watching the touch hole, pointing and shaking his finger.

"See that?" he shouted right through the echo. "Were you watching it? Warn't the right color."

"The flash?" Wyatt asked. He wanted clarity. He wanted exactness. If he had to retreat to grade school, he would do that.

"Right!" Henry shouted. "The flash. Too yellow. Too damn yellow."

"What's that mean? Salt in the mixture?"

"Salt in the mixture. Gotta be salt."

"That's impossible!" Wyatt complained, agonized. "Where? The master batch or where? And how?"

"The niter, that's my bet. Seventy-five percent niter, fifteen percent charcoal, ten percent sulfur, and if that's pitched off balance any, we got trouble. Half a percent off, trouble." Henry knew Wyatt understood all that. Wyatt was a good chemist, and his face had drawn tight at the mention of too much yellow in the flash. The creases stayed. "The original shipment's got to be contaminated," Henry went on. "Bet them natives got salt in their guano somehow. Made a bad batch of saltpeter."

Wyatt clamped his mouth shut and bit the end of his tongue. *Don't blurt out England, don't mention Dorian, keep shut up!*

He managed to keep a lid on his shock and skewered Henry. "It couldn't happen naturally—the natives would have to put salt in it on purpose. Why would they do that?"

"'Fore we figger how, let's go have a look at the shipment."

Sweating under his shirt, Wyatt strode after Henry on trembling legs like a confused puppy. A good two dozen powder workers hustled along behind them, grumbling, furious.

Dorian. The niter that had been funneled over the past weeks from Britain, shipped in small loads to Cuba, then manipulated to Richmond over a plethora of routes and channels, some land, some sea. Whatever Dorian's motivations, he was doing his job. Suddenly the spigot had opened again. The rolling mills were grinding, the evaporation retorts bubbling, the water turbines working, the bolting and graining and pressing and glazing going on—Craig workers were making black powder again, and just in time. McClellan was pressuring Richmond with his Yankee Army on the Peninsula. He was just sitting there, but he *was* there, and with a huge sprawling army. Richmond could almost smell him. Eventually even George McClellan would have to do *something* with all those men. A major battle in the east could come at any moment.

Now this.

"Where's this batch from, son?" Henry asked, squinting up at him in the springtime sunlight, one eye completely closed. "Chile or what? Calcutta, up through Bengal, or where?"

Where indeed? How many ports had this batch visited in order to lie here today? A dozen? How many nautical and coastal miles of poor security?

But Dorian wouldn't allow contamination! He'd use that watch chain on anyone who got in the way of getting unadulterated saltpeter to the mill. Wouldn't he?

"I can't tell you where it's from, Henry," Wyatt said. "it's kind of a military secret these days. . . . You know what I mean."

"Sure, son, sure. Don't tell me nothing. Too old to care anyhow."

Henry stuck his finger into the dirty-white guano. Potassium nitrate . . . niter . . . saltpeter . . . none of its names sounded very good as the finger then went into Henry's mouth.

Wyatt suppressed a burp of disgust and wiped his own mouth in empathy. Here it was, the prime ingredient, the oxidizer, the critical element, the rare substance . . .

"Nope," Henry said. "No salt." He creaked to his feet again. "Let's go check the master batch."

They crossed the mill yard to the refinery, where niter and crude sulfur were gurgling softly, being rendered down and purified, smelling so bad that the workers had long ago grown insensitive to smells. A few men were skimming the impurities off the tops of the bubbling niter.

Henry chose one of the niter pots, leaned over the brick retort's rim, and did that sickening thing again with his finger, this time pausing only to blow some of the heat off the stuff.

His mouth moved around and around, his eyes squinted, while everyone waited anxiously.

All at once his eyes popped open and wheeled toward Wyatt, wide and flickering under the bushy white brows.

"Lord," Wyatt blurted under his breath.

"Maybe two percent," Henry said. "Maybe more."

Wyatt stalked away a few steps. His workers parted to give him pacing room. He hung a hand on the back of his neck as though to hold in a fast-breaking headache. "Any percent . . . half a percent . . . throw off the ratio . . . oh, my Lord . . . contaminated oxidizer—and if it's contaminated, there's less force in the blast—"

"If any force," Henry said. "Might just lay there and fizzle."

Wyatt glowered at the ground and paced between his workers. First his hands were on his hips, then on his head, then covering his mouth, then back on the hips. Crazy thoughts clamored for attention beside thoughts of business and tragedy. Which soldier's gun would fizzle? Which canister or roundshot would fall short? Which gun on which Confederate ship would fail to go off? Which moment of history would go all wrong because of this?

And how much of the powder was contaminated? They'd gone weeks without testing—how much bad powder had already been shipped? How much of the powder sitting over there in the magazine was contaminated?

Quick answer—don't ship anymore.

Then how many Southern guns will go starved for powder when a skirmish breaks? Which Southern commanders would have to ration powder to this or that squadron—and which soldier would go without a means to defend his state, or even save his own life?

The mill itself . . . critical to the workers' survival, critical to the Confederacy, critical to defense of the capitol of Richmond . . . it could be bankrupt in an afternoon. They didn't dare ship any more powder until each barrel was tested—could take a week. A week of army movements, a week of skirmishes, standoffs, battles—if McClellan found out about this, even he might get up the gumption to advance upon Richmond.

Wyatt suddenly stopped pacing. He stared at the bubbling white substance in the kettle and tried to deal with the most fundamental horror of all.

"Henry, can I have a private minute with you? Fellows, 'scuse us, please."

He took Henry Brecker aside—far aside. The men behind them began to disperse slowly and talk among themselves.

"Henry," Wyatt said, very quietly, holding Henry by one knotty old arm, "there's bad news. The Federal army is getting close enough to spit on. There's been fighting in Williamsburg, and there are gunboats coming up the James. I don't know what we're going to do, Henry. They'll reach us first, and Richmond next. Now this—this adulterant in our powder . . . my God, how many men have we killed already? It's looking like things are all over with."

Henry shook his head. "Aw, son, I wisht you wouldn't talk like that."

"I have no choice. Can't ignore the truth. The Confederacy needs men and doesn't have them, and it needs powder and we can't supply it. It'll slow us down weeks to have to test every batch, and go in there and test every barrel . . . McClellan's army is there. Practically right *there*." He jabbed a finger at the nearest bend in the James, where the water rushed over rocks and ran swiftly toward the coastline. "Henry, listen. I want you to keep this very quiet, but I want you to do it today. Get five men you can trust—be *very* careful who they are. Rig charges and set them in key places all over the yard. A charge in every roll mill, in the graining mills, the magazines, the composition house, especially the new shipments. We can't leave any powder, but we also can't leave behind the means for making it."

"You talking about . . . uh . . ."

"Yes, I'm talking about evacuation. Set explosives all over the lower property and prepare them to be blown at a half hour's notice. Don't tell anybody about it except your team." He strode a few paces away, watching the workers disperse. "We can't take chances. It's happening right here, somewhere between the composition house and the press house," he choked. "There's a saboteur in the yard."

Watching from a distance, Clyde Clyman turned and strode away. He had seen and been satisfied with the face of frustration on Wyatt Craig just then. He could go back to his job at the chiproll machine and lay low for a while.

It would slow the shipment of powder down considerably to have to test every barrel, whether there was salt in every barrel or not. If salt was found, a hell of a lot of powder— which was, of course, a hell of a lot of rare ingredients— would have to be thrown away.

He paused before the footbridge and looked up the natural incline to the powdertown.

There she was. In the window of her cabin. She had hair the color of burnished leather, and her eyes were always angry. He liked that. Something about that made him do anything she wanted. He got sweaty just standing here. She made him steam.

He nodded. Bigger than a regular nod, so she could see it.

In response she pulled her window shades shut. Now they both knew their plan had taken effect. Salt in the saltpeter . . . it'd make a good camp-fire song someday.

Clyman turned and continued on his way to the press house. As he walked, he sucked the salt off his fingers.

★

THE BURNING FUSE

We are uncertain of anything except that a battle must be near at hand.

—May 1862: President Jefferson Davis to his wife, regarding Richmond.

5 MAY 1862

The Battle of Williamsburg forces the Confederates to retreat and leave the Union in control of the Peninsula. Invasion of Richmond seems inevitable. The city is in a panic. The South is going on borrowed time—borrowed from General McClellan.

8 MAY

Jackson's Valley Campaign is on the move and has the first battle victory in McDowell, Virginia. Jackson's troops do not hesitate over their win, but advance immediately.

9 MAY

The Confederates evacuate the valuable naval yard and military depot at Norfolk. Loss of the critical base means loss of southern Virginia and upper North Carolina. They burn the ironclad C.S.S. Virginia, otherwise known as the Merrimack, rather than leave her to be confiscated.

As for other activity, there is skirmishing everywhere.

Artillery fire echoes across Richmond as Confederates

meet the Federals, who are at times as near as three miles from the city. McClellan pauses to ask for more troops.

In the western theater, Farragut's fleet lays seige to Vicksburg on the Mississippi, but Confederate forces refuse to yield.

15 MAY

On the James River, just a few miles east of the powdermill, valiant outnumbered Confederates undertake the shelling of Federal gunboats. The shelling rattles the shingles in Richmond and shows just how close the Army of the Potomac has come. Federal positions are close enough to hear the bells of the city.

Somehow, miraculously, the shelling turns the Union gunboats back. This victory if darkly veiled by the shadow of McClellan's army, the bulk of which is less than twenty-two miles from Richmond.

Here McClellan stops again—to set up a giant supply depot, to wait for reinforcements, and to build eleven bridges across the Chickahominy River for "communication."

Richmond, and the powdermill, have miraculously acquired a few more days of leeway.

The month of May has seen troop movements, skirmishes, telegrams, battles, reconnaissance, refugees, and anticipation of invasion, but on the large scale nothing has changed. Miraculously the invasion of Richmond hasn't come yet.

The South's great showmen of the war are beginning to emerge from the confusion. Magruder's sideshow of deception is a masterpiece more than once—riding men around in circles to appear a bigger number, his musicians playing, his cannons firing at nothing, his officers shouting orders to empty thickets. The names of A. P. Hill, D. H. Hill, Longstreet, Magruder, Jackson, are becoming household talk both North and South. Stonewall Jackson's Shenandoah dance has confused the Union and kept reinforcements from McClellan, which keeps McClellan from moving. Jackson has also scooped up tons of supplies and munitions as he moved like a cloud across the valley. He has energized the Southern will to fight against the odds. No one can tell what he will do next, so

President Lincoln fears to give up troops guarding Washington.

Lincoln telegrams: "I think the time is near when you must either attack Richmond or give up the job and come to the defense of Washington. . . . Can you get near enough to throw shells into the city?"

EARLY JUNE

Skirmishes and battles everywhere. Each taxes the Confederacy's limited number of fighting men.

General Robert Edward Lee takes over the Army of Northern Virginia. Heavy rain plasters McClellan to the Peninsula, even though they are so close, they can hear the sounds of Richmond.

In less than fifty days, Jackson has marched a dazzling six-hundred-plus miles and utterly confused the Union. His reputation alone is enough to keep McClellan scared.

Brigadier General James Ewell Brown (Jeb) Stuart gains renown for himself and his twelve hundred cavaliers and artillery with a stirring ride all the way around McClellan's army to reinforce Richmond, and reports personally to General Lee.

Lincoln continually asks McClellan when, when, when will he attack Richmond?

McClellan's lack of movement gives General Lee and his dazzling generals time to plan an offensive near Richmond rather than a defensive. The long delay by a general who obviously has an advantage has shown them that McClellan can be beaten. They will push the Union general off his mushroom.

They plan their attack for June 26.

25 JUNE

Jackson's forces move toward Richmond. The plan is for him to shove Union General FitzJohn Porter's army backward. A. P. Hill will then cross the Chickahominy River and force the Union out of Mechanicsville. D. H. Hill and Longstreet will bring their men forward.

For unknown reasons Jackson's army fails to appear in

time. Unable to wait, A. P. Hill makes the planned attack at Mechanicsville. Porter is pushed back to Beaver Dam Creek, but there the Confederate charge is stopped cold.

It is the beginning of the Seven Days' Battles.

————————————— ★ —————————————

CHAPTER FORTY-THREE

———— ★ ————

"Evening, ma'am. I'm Brigadier General Andrew Humphreys, Third Division, Major General FitzJohn Porter's Fifth Army Corps, Army of the Potomac. This is Colonel Peter Allabach of my division and Lieutenant Colonel Robert Buchanan, First Brigade of Brigadier General George Sykes's Second Division. We deeply appreciate your cooperation thus far in our occupation of your cottage here as our headquarters. Your cottage is strategically located for quick communication with our encampment. If I have anything to do with it, we'll cause you as little trouble as possible. As you know, we had quite a tussle here in Mechanicsville today. Our bluecoats completely routed A. P. Hill's grays and killed upward of a thousand of them. I sincerely hope your husband wasn't among them."

Though he held his uniform hat in his hand, General Humphreys did not appear salutatory. He was much more schoolmasterlike as he looked down at the plain woman sitting with her hands folded on the front of her quilted dressing gown, and neither of them made any comment about her not being in proper garb for accepting visitors.

"There's going to be plenty of fighting in this area the next few days," the General went on, "but you can take heart in knowing that we guard our headquarters thoroughly. Your house, at least, will be safe."

The woman gazed at his Union belt buckle, not at his face. This vexed him a little, but he couldn't claim not to understand. Here they were, after all, on her clean floor with their

483

battle-muddied boots, having slaughtered the troops who were
her heroes. Like it or not, she and her kind would be forced to
become United States citizens again.

Still, if he could find a way to ease her mind, he would do
it.

"This house, according to records at the Town Hall,"
Humphreys went on, "is rented by a Barry Swanborough. Is
that your husband?"

The round-faced woman continued to stare at the belt
buckle and said nothing at all. Behind her an enormous slave
boy was held equally silent by two Union soldiers with their
pistols drawn. The loyalties of negroes were very hard to read,
so it behooved the Union soldiers to assume the slaves were
loyal to their owners until they demonstrated otherwise.

General Humphreys accepted the woman's silence as a
matter of course. He didn't expect enthusiasm; just compliance.

"Your slaves will cook for my officers," he said, "but beyond that little will be expected of you. If you like, you can retire to your room and rest. We'll have to confiscate all the
men's socks and trousers and shirts in the household for our
men. As you know, our lines here are less than six miles from
Richmond. You would do well for your own health to consider
the war over as of tonight."

Humphreys let his words fall upon the shoulders of the
woman, her slave, and his own men, and work the magic those
kinds of words could work. Having the upper hand was particularly invigorating. It gave him the prerogative of being polite
without obligation. Wallowing in the power of his advantage,
he paced across the room and gazed appreciatively at the
comely decor, the Alabama coat of arms over the fireplace,
and took particular notice of one piece of furnishing.

He leaned over it. "Is this here a piano, ma'am? It's a little
small. Dainty. Is it a harpsichord?"

"It is a clavichord," the woman said.

They all looked at her, surprised at the steadiness of her
voice. They had expected at least a shiver.

"How old is it?" Buchanan asked, taking Humphreys's
lead.

"One hundred fifty years."

"The keys are white on black instead of black on white,"

Humphreys said. "I saw one like this in a museum in Washington. They used to make them this way. Ma'am, would you play it for us just a bit? Just to hear what it sounds like? Maybe a tune or two?"

The woman didn't look at him, but she stood up, awkwardly and with some effort. For a moment they thought she might faint, as Southern women were known to do, and Colonel Buchanan stepped forward as though to catch her.

She put out a hand toward him in a policelike gesture, and he stopped in place. She didn't want to be caught, or even touched. She found her balance and for the first time met General Humphrey's eyes.

"Excuse me, Brigadier," she said. "I shall return in a moment."

She walked very slowly, with some difficulty, her arms straight down at her sides, and left the room. She headed back toward the kitchen.

"Can I go with her, Boss?" the big slave boy asked. "See that she's safe and all?"

"No, you sit down right there," Buchanan said. He gestured at the two Union men. "You two keep those pistols on this boy. Slaves are to be considered hostile until proved otherwise. When we pull out of Mechanicsville, we'll set the whole lot of them free and let them see to themselves."

The officers stood uncomfortably in the middle of the room, glancing at each other.

"Where do you think she went to?" Colonel Allabach wondered aloud.

"Probably gone to get tea or attend to herself," Buchanan suggested.

"Maybe the boy's right," Allabach said. "Shouldn't we keep a man on her? I mean—well, you know what I mean."

Humphreys shook his head. "She can't get past the guards outside. Where can she go? A woman like that. There . . . you see how it is, gentlemen? You saw her behavior. No resistance at all. The people of the South don't want to see the nation come to an end any more than we do. It's their leaders doing this and convincing the people to tag along. All will come to the surface in the end. We're doing the right thing."

"Good thinking, General," Buchanan said. "If she plays the

clavichord for a while, she'll loosen up a bit and take the occupation more easily."

"I am hoping so. I'm hoping things go much easier from here on. That was a son of a bitch of a battle today. We took a devil of a lot of lives. Once General McClellan moves on Richmond, all will be set."

Allabach made himself comfortable on a small couch, crossed his legs, and went about lighting his pipe. "That'll be a sung song before the week is out," he crowed happily. "A hundred thousand blues barely twenty miles from Richmond—a day's march? Our corps only six miles northeast of the capitol? The war's over, I'd say."

"We fell back more than I would like to talk about," Humphreys contradicted. "Where's the ordnance officer with my maps? I want to look at them."

Allabach kept quiet. He picked up a newspaper and discovered it was in fact two newspapers.

"Look at this," he said. "One's got the headline about President Lincoln's son dying, and the other one's got the headline about the death of the Davis boy."

"Well, I wouldn't wonder. Women get that way." Humphreys tossed his gold-corded hat onto a table. "After we secure the household, we'll notify General Porter and send messages to Barnes, Griffin, Stockton, Warren, and Lowell. We'll clear this room out and move this furniture into the— whatever that room is over across the hallway, and we'll bring that big table from the dining room into this parlor and spread our maps on it. Peter, I'll leave it to you to notify our brigade commanders and artillery that we have a headquarters on the edge of Mechanicsville. Our position at Beaver Dam Creek is strong. I don't think the grays will be able to push us back any farther. By morning General McClellan will be notified of the win today and that we're setting up lines. We've got Gaines's Mill to consider. We'll hold it at any cost. Well, gentlemen, are you proud of yourselves?"

He turned to smile at them, but what he saw wasn't two complaisant and victorious officers—but a small woman carrying a wood ax with a ten-inch blade!

The three officers stumbled away as the woman raised the enormous implement over her head. Allabach fell off the couch and crawled for safety. In the corner the two soldiers turned their guns on the woman, but neither could make himself shoot her.

Using those few seconds of shock to her advantage, Orienta Swanborough Parthens grunted and used every muscle in her body to lift the enormous glittering blade above her head. Then she heaved herself forward.

Like a great silver cloud, the ax blade swung high, back, then forward again, and plunged down of its own weight.

The two shocked corporals probably could have shot her easily enough, *if* she'd been tumbling toward any of the officers.

But when the ax blade came down, great-edged clapper that it was, it struck not someone's skull, but century-and-a-half-old mahogany.

The old clavichord dropped to its knees on the first blow, two legs broken. Inside, its harp rang with a scream too much like a cry for help, and rang and rang as she struck again and again, grunting and gasping with her effort, smashing what wouldn't cut and cutting what wouldn't crush. Black natural keys fell off like rotted teeth, white flats dropping among them—two black keys struck Humphreys in the face. Mahogany splinters flew from the ax blade and forced Allabach and the two soldiers to throw up their arms before their faces. Piano wire and taut string made a stormy din, snapping inside the case as the woman struck again and again. The men reached out to stop her several times, but no one knew exactly how or where to grab hold of her, and none could get their hands on the ax handle.

In seconds a precious relic of the New World was reduced to firewood, its ravaged shell bonging with each blow like an old clock tower in a storm.

At last the heavy ax blade struck the floor, and the woman had no more strength to lift it. She wobbled back and forth on her two feet, wishing she had four, grunting and gasping with spent effort. Her face was flushed, her arms like willow branches, but she was the only person in the room standing up straight. Her face was too calm.

She looked one by one at the officers, and even at the two men holding an astonished Buckie in the corner. She allowed herself a moment to catch back some of her breath and to brush away a lock of brown hair that had fallen across her forehead.

Beside her the destroyed clavichord was still vibrating.

"My clavichord has been one hundred fifty years in my family," she said faintly, "and I shall burn the splinters before it gives a Yankee one moment's pleasure. Thank you. I am going to rest now."

The clavichord lay there ringing for what seemed like an awfully long time . . . long after the woman handed the ax to Buchanan and shuffled out of the room.

The men glanced at each other while keeping one eye on the entranceway, half expecting her to find a second wind and come plunging back at them with a fireplace poker or a wagon whip.

"Good Lord," Buchanan choked.

Allabach crawled to his feet. "Should we have her arrested? Confiscate the household?"

Humphreys cleared his throat and said, "No . . . no. We will leave her to her house and find another house to use as a headquarters. Leave everything as it is. Tell the slaves they're best off staying right here. Put out that pipe. Get up, and let's get out."

Buchanan said, "Are you serious? We own the town. By week's end we'll own Richmond. Oughtn't we avoid backing off in any circumstance?"

The brigadier general scooped his hat from the floor, where it had fallen during the flurry.

"I've got seven children, Colonel," he said, "and I know how people are. All President Lincoln needs at this late juncture is Rebel newspapers crying to the nation about how the Yankees disturbed, dispossessed, and incarcerated a woman when she was fixing to have a baby."

London, late June

His hands were shaking. He didn't like the sensation.

He threw down *The Times* and grasped his teacup with both

hands, wishing there was something in there stronger than tea. News from the United States was enough to make a man learn to drink.

Even a former slave who had rarely had anything but a sip or two of ouzo on Greek holidays.

Battles. Stalemates. Offensive troop movement. Fifteen hundred Confederates killed or wounded near Mechanicsville . . .

Mechanicsville . . . Mechanicsville . . .

Union occupation near Mechanicsville . . . Confederates fall back from Mechanicsville—

Gunboats on the James River, barely five miles from a critical powdermill . . . McClellan near enough to shell Richmond . . . Jackson fails to support Hill . . . Confederates abandon Mechanicsville . . . the eyes of Europe are on Richmond . . .

"You take care of her, Burlie."

"I'll do it. Better than the Lord himself. Yankees show up here, I'll chuck'm out."

The rise of sick longing inside, pulling and pulling—it was enough to make a man choke.

Dorian kicked the London newspaper off the table with his heel and sent it flaring into separate sheets across the carpet. It landed among discarded editions of a dozen other British publications that had been his class work for the past several weeks. What was Burlie thinking of him? Had the worship turned to something sour?

He had turned sour himself.

England. The pulse of the Western World. A place he'd dreamed of visiting. Green roads and gray castles, roses and thatch and Thackeray, kings and commoners—

Quackery and strut.

In a few swift weeks Dorian had become utterly disenchanted with this realm, this England. Concern would have been tolerable. Interest, curiosity, even passive ignorance.

This . . . sniggering satisfaction . . .

He could barely stand to walk along an English street anymore. The ladder to Lord Russell was greased with dangling personalities up and down. Between private audiences with influentials, through the string-pulling power of the Du Pont name, chatter about the recognition question, people getting used to Dorian's presence as a nonofficial Southerner—between those meetings he had sought escape. York. The Lake District. Newcastle. Even Wales for a few days. Anywhere but the boiling streets of London—

There was no escape. Everywhere in England there was gloating. All the South had ever gotten from England was unofficial meetings and a declaration of neutrality, because accepting diplomats would be tacit admittance that the diplomats came from "another nation." Now the realm that was afraid to accept an ambassador was happy to rejoice at the collapse of America.

It was beginning to dig at him.

Easy job. Come to England, get meetings with Russell and Palmerston. Get England to help slap itself. Don't *claim* to be reconstructionist. Promise them the sun. Win the war, but don't break up the continent—but make the English *think* we want to break up the continent.

The Cousin had been working on that meeting for months now, getting people to use their social and political weight in Parliament, to provide Britain with a man who was completely unknown, nonpolitical, very intelligent, and of Southern blood. Dorian was the ambassador of complete deniability.

What good was it now? All was for nought. A few months ago the British had argued, Why should Britain get involved if the South was going to win anyway? That was the tightrope. Convincing the lords that *they* had something at stake in recognizing the Confederacy. If the North and South would tear each other apart, then this enormous economic rival would eliminate itself without Britain's raising a finger. Having the North and South run each other bankrupt was Britain's naughty dream.

Now the tightrope had broken and was swinging in the wrong direction.

Those headlines on the floor were more than a week out of date. The war might be over, and he wouldn't even know it yet. McClellan's crushing blow might have been dealt days ago. Wyatt in prison for treason, the mill confiscated, the Federal army inches from Orienta—

"Inches from Richmond," Dorian corrected aloud, and swallowed to clear his throat. He got up quickly, paced to the other side of the neat but somber rented flat.

There he rolled onto the bed and stared up at the draped linen canopy, and hated it because it was English.

All had come to this. Months of nothing. Months of Palmerston pretending the Union's blockade was legal, in spite of international law, allowing the U.S. to intercept British ships *before* they got to Cuba—how could Dorian even be sure his secret shipments of niter had been successfully disseminated through Cuba and into blockade runners, and up to Wyatt? Allowing the United States' claim that ships coming from Cuba were on a continuous voyage—shipments from Cuba were the same as shipments from Britain if they carried British matériel. The Union could interrupt the flow of war matériel anywhere on the high seas.

"Well, of course!" Dorian spat at the canopy. "If the North sets a maritime precedent for predatory cruising, then Britain can do what it likes should war come with France! Be off! Let the Yankees do our dirty work! Then we can say, 'Oh, but they did it first.' The North will be wrecked as an industrial competitor, the South will be shredded as an agricultural competitor, England will move right in on both those markets. Go ahead and breathe that sigh of relief! Aristocracy lives! Democracy has exhausted itself! It will not spread to Europe after all! The United States is falling apart! Jolly good procrastination, Pam. The epitome of statesmanship. Why thank you, John. Where's the Queen? Playing croquet on the green, I fancy. Who cares? Let's put her bum in a sling, long as we've got the Confederacy passing gas. Damned if all this isn't beginning to crack my eggs."

A knock at the door cracked the ice void inside him. Before Dorian could so much as raise his head, the door blasted open and in plunged the Cousin, frothing at the beard and waving his walking cane.

"Up!" he shouted.

Other than poising a hand upon his watch chain, Dorian scarcely moved. He didn't like to move before he knew what the move would get him—or what trouble it would put him in.

"On your feet! Tie that neck cloth! Chances like this come once a century, and ours is here! Precisely at half past noon, you and I have the ear of Lord John Russell for fifteen entire minutes!"

*Here's to the Confederates that grow
the cotton, the Yankees that keep the
price up, the Limeys that pay the price,
. . . and here's to a long war!*
                    —*Sailor's toast
                    during the Civil War*

Richmond was crowded, snarling, Nearly twice the forty thousand of the usual population swelled the streets. Even hours after dark there was no respite from the surge of refugees from the Peninsula and the confusion of people fleeing their homes in anticipation of Union invasion. To the east the camp fires of the enormous Army of the Potomac cast a faint lemony glow on the night horizon. The encampment was so vast, so crowded, and so dense with white canvas pup tents set in rows upon rows beside more rows, that there seemed to have been an overnight snowstorm blanketing the Peninsula in the midst of summer. The size of the encampment itself was enough to terrorize.

And Richmond was terrorized. Gunboats on the James fired salvos now and then, just to keep a city trembling. Rumors of burning the whole city had hours ago stopped sounding like just rumors.

The docks were no longer a place of business, but a place of panic. Ship owners loaded and overloaded their vessels, preparing to escape upriver, people tried to buy passages out of Richmond to almost anywhere, captains argued over which ships would set out in which order, who would get the best currents or the next port-clearance ticket. The Port Authority was threatening to close if people didn't keep their heads. Steamers were backing out and chugging upriver without consideration of the ships around them. There was no right of way considered tonight.

The atmosphere was uncomfortable, one of danger and distrust, one of humanity reduced to the basest tricks of survival. Women held their children particularly close tonight, men gathered their families tightly before them, placed guards over their shipments, and kept their wallets in deep pockets.

Into this nervous environment, Wyatt followed the huge slave boy who had turned out to be, of all things, Dorian's half brother. The boy had come to get him in the night, and Wyatt had assumed at first that something was wrong with Orienta.

Nothing was wrong. Nothing was right, but she wasn't ill or captured. Soldiers had come into the house, but they hadn't stayed. In fact, they'd moved north from Mechanicsville to Gaines's Mill. Burlie had taken a chance and left Orienta with the household servants, the two remaining who had refused to leave, even though the Northern soldiers had declared them free. The coachman, the stable hands, and the butler had gone, but Burlie and two women had stayed.

The boy had appeared at Wyatt's office, begged him to come with him, and refused to say why. Probably thought he wouldn't be believed. The boy curiously insisted Wyatt not wear his uniform tunic and had provided him with a black overcoat. In some discomfort, but not seeing any reason not to, Wyatt slipped into what was probably Barry Swanborough's spare coat.

So here they were, slipping along the lips of Richmond dockage, trying to stay out of trouble. And out of sight—Burlie kept trying to hide himself and keep Wyatt hidden. They went from shadow to shadow, pile of crates to pile of trunks and luggage, keeping to the sides of dockhouses and fishing shacks.

Not until the boy paused, squinted, and pointed at a secluded floating dock at the end of the wharf did Wyatt begin to understand the secrecy.

In the dim evening glow of the city's gaslights, Barry Swanborough was supervising the loading of a low-slung steam sailer.

When Wyatt realized what he was looking at, he became especially aware of the coat he was wearing. He put his hand out to Burlie's wide shoulder and asked in a schoolmasterly tone, "Son, what've you got me spying on your boss for?"

The boy—all six feet and something of him—turned about halfway around and gave Wyatt a truthful look no man would doubt. "You just watch, sir. Look at what they're loading on that there boat."

"Boxes. What's inside?"

"I broke one open the other night, just to be sure I wasn't mistaking." He dug into his own pocket, pulled out a white wad of fluff, and placed it in Wyatt's hand. "Raw unginned cotton."

Wyatt's assumption that most of the world had a sense of fair play flushed out his boot soles. He leaned against the fishing shack they were hiding behind and hoped it held. "Oh, Lord . . . How did you find out about this?"

"I read his mail after he leave it on his desk." Burlie smiled—and in the darkness of the docks it was a startling resemblance to one of Dorian's wicked smiles. "Mr. Swanborough doesn't know I can read. Mr. Wyatt, you know what kind of ship that is?"

Pulling his attention from the seedy fluff in his hands, Wyatt looked up. "No . . . it looks like a steamer."

"That there is a brig converted to a steamer," Burlie said. "Low, quiet, and real fast. You see how they got her painted black?"

"A blockade runner!"

"That's right, sir, and he got five hundred bales going in the belly of that boat tonight."

"You mean *he's* running cotton? But he stirred up the embargo!"

"Sure," Burlie said. "He want all the other cotton men to burn their stock up, while he gets rich on—what d'you call it—profiting?"

"Profiteering," Wyatt supplied sadly. "War profiteering. Where's the boat going? Do you know?"

"Oh, yes, sir, it's off to Cuba."

"Well, that's it," Wyatt sighed. "It goes to Cuba, gets broken up into a couple other ships, probably reflagged ships, and off it goes to England, where he'll sell it for pounds. With the other cotton barons holding their stock back, the price of Swanborough's cotton goes sky-high. Then he sells it for gold on the European market—Judas, what an unscrupulous bastard—he's probably got his cotton stockpiled all over the South!"

"Florida, mostly, near as I can tell. Cotton can fetch about three cent to the pound—"

"Cents. Three cents."

"And he can get forty cent—cents—up to a dollar in England for that pound."

"Dilly of a profit—he can make a hundred twenty-five thousand dollars on the five hundred bales going into that steamer! No wonder he didn't want it stored in Britain! Having a year's worth of cotton stored in Britain wouldn't do him a bit of good. As he makes more and more money, he'll buy more and more ships—that trickle of his will turn into a monopoly."

"I don't know much about that, sir," Burlie confessed, "but I do know that he sent away a boat last week that went up to Boston instead of Cuba. What d'you think that means?"

Wyatt grimaced as though a true pain had cut through him. "It means . . . it means he's smuggling cotton to the North for the new Union dollar, that's what it—oh, Lord, *Lord*."

"Bring a dooly of a price if he sell it up to the Yankees, even better than England. Right, sir?"

"Dilly," Wyatt moaned. "Dilly of a price. . . . This is the ugliest thing I've seen in a good long time. No matter how the war turns out, Swanborough'll be a rich man. Damned if it's not just what I'd do."

Burlie bothered to turn almost completely around and looked at him.

He said, "You wouldn't do this, sir."

The look was possessed of such humility, candor, and faith that Wyatt found himself honored and embarrassed for collecting the condensate from worship that was rightfully Dorian's. Perhaps it was that, or perhaps he was bad at hiding his real character, or the boy was particularly good at judging—as many negroes were, since their lot often involved silent observation of the white men floating through life a few levels over them. Like fish beneath the glimmering surface, many slaves developed a trait of keen perception about what was going on just above that surface.

With irony and grief he admitted, "Guess you got me there."

"And, sir," Burlie said, "I don't know if this will make a difference or not, but he got somebody working on a newspaper in England. Stirring up trouble over there. Man name of Carter. I saw a letter."

Wyatt met the boy's large dark eyes and with that meeting

confirmed that he believed him and understood the complications. In the set of his mouth he was sure his frustration and the danger of all this was quite evident to the young slave.

"You're gonna write a letter to Dorian and warn him, aren't you, Mr. Wyatt?" Burlie asked.

As his throat tightened and his gut turned hollow, Wyatt drew back a few steps. His eyes lost their focus, and his brows drew tight. He pushed a sweaty hand into his hair and let it fall through his fingers.

"I sure would do that . . . if I only knew where he was."

THE HALLS OF PARLIAMENT, LONDON

Foreign Minister Lord Russell bothered to get up from the leather couch in his subdued but very British-proper meeting room. A small man with a narrow head and sifted hair, he fiddled with his clothing constantly and seemed to be searching for somewhere to keep his hands.

"Mr. Du Pont," he greeted, "good afternoon."

"Your Lordship," the Cousin began, "may I present Mr. Parthens, lately of the great state of Virginia."

Russell paused in the middle of an Oriental carpet and squinted briefly at Dorian. While a red-haired attendant took Dorian's statement-making Inverness cape and the Cousin's more understated daycoat, the Foreign Minister studied his guest.

"Are you . . . Arabian, sir?"

Dorian raised an eyebrow. "One of my mothers is Greek," he offered cannily. "Will that do?"

Russell seemed at first not to get the joke, then chuckled. "Greek. I should have guessed by the name. And what do your fathers do, Mr. Parthens?"

"They are in the tobacco-planting spectrum of Southern agriculture, my lord."

"Yes," Russell said. "High breeding makes itself evident."

He stepped closer and accepted the hand of the son of a dockworker and a slave.

"What part of Greece?" Russell asked as he gestured the

two men into the center of the office, where the couch and two studded leather chairs made a sophisticated covey, plainly less official than a desk might have been.

"A little back alley called Macedon," Dorian quipped.

"Very nice," was all the British lord said. There were other things on his mind.

Lack of officiality was the order of the moment. A towering grandfather clock staidly reported the half hour with its single gong as the three men sat down together.

Fidgeting, and sitting on the edge of the couch with his knees tightly together, Lord Russell scooped up a newspaper from the top of a batch of unrelated newspapers on the table between them.

"Look at this," he said, his eyes wide with amusement. "Oh—look what your *Index* is saying about me now."

"Our *Index*?" the Du Pont Cousin immediately responded, making a strong show of disenfranchisement from the Confederate propaganda paper. "I confess, I haven't even read it in quite a while, sir."

"Then look her at this. 'Knock-kneed British cowardice' . . . 'skirting the inevitable' . . . 'whining behind coats-of-arms' . . . 'Russell possessed no muscle'. . .'stuffing English roses up his nose and those of all the peerage'—I wager they wanted to say something more execrable and reined in at the last instant, wouldn't you?"

"Your Lordship," the Cousin attempted. He glanced at Dorian for support.

But Dorian remained silent. His face was utterly forbearant, his eyes examining every flinch or blink from the foreign minister—of which there were plenty from this birdlike little man. He found himself thinking of Aleck Stephens. Russell was much like the tiny, twitching Vice President, his nerves all aflicker, his brain in a constant rush.

Such a man, twitching at all times, mind clicking, could be influenced by a saturnine approach, Dorian knew. He had measured many people in his life. He did that now.

He knew the Cousin was eying him, worried about the face of that big clock, which made an audible *clack* as the long hand moved from one minute to the next.

"Let us hope," Russell said, tossing the paper down, "that

The Times and *The Post* still cause more ruffle than *The Index*. What do you think of *The Index,* Mr. Parthens?"

Clearly a test. No sane man would take a middle course, having already heard Russell's opinion.

Dorian weighed his options, the evidence, his chances, and took a very big one.

"I must beg your pardon, my lord," Dorian said, "if you conclude the rattletongues at that cowflap are anything but surface readers. They fail to see through the shellac of nationalism and deduce that you have been working day and night for the Confederacy since the firing of the first gun."

A rocky silence crunched down.

The Du Pont Cousin frowned. Behind his thigh, where Russell couldn't see it, he dug a fist into the chair's leather and searched Dorian's face to see if this was a guess, a bluff, a dare? Suicide?

The clock ticked. Another minute gone.

Lord Russell poised one elbow on the other wrist and put his knuckles to his lips, evaluating what he had just heard and the man who had said it.

For what seemed a long time he simply studied Dorian. Dorian simply studied him back.

The Cousin was the only real casualty of this duel of patience. He was obviously beginning to feel warm. He was, however, also willing to wait, to let things play out—things and personalities. He had brought these two extraordinary men together, and which sparks would fly and how high—he couldn't guess.

"The American aberration is dead in the water," Dorian finally said. "Extinct. Your job is to calculate how Britain can best profit from the division. If you can tell me what Lord Palmerston is thinking . . . perhaps we can work at common purposes to blister up a better taste out of this international rotgut."

Russell began to speak again, rather quietly and in a reserved and thoughtful fashion, as though chiseling each phrase independently of the phrases around it.

"Lord Palmerston," he said, "is fixated upon Europe. France and Austria are foremost in his mind. . . . Bismarck is puffing his plumage. . . . There is much more going on in the world than your tussle over the water. Pray do understand that, gentlemen. Palmerston is an old-style conservative who believes in Britain's right to carve up the world as we see fit. After all, there sit the huge Americas, fully a third of the world, being ruled by Europe's poor relations! Think of it."

He waved a hand, then slapped it to his bony thigh. Dignity laced his tone.

"Her Majesty," he went on, "wishes to remain neutral in the question of you people. We have France to consider. Remember that in two wars with Britain in the past one hundred years, France has come in for the U.S. against Britain. We dare not turn our attention too much away from our own riviera. There are grounds to suspect an enormous international scheme engineered by France to deflect British attention and cause us to commit our Navy to a transatlantic altercation, during which the French fleet will promptly invade England."

The Cousin looked up sharply. "Oh, Your Lordship—"

Dorian remained taciturn and chuckled. "Would be interesting to see," he commented.

"Yes, it would," Russell said. "But we intend that it should not be seen. Palmerston wants to break the historical Franco-American tradition."

"It could be broken," the Cousin said, "with an Anglo-Confederate alliance."

"It could . . . but we can barely evaluate the United States' veridicality or that of the Confederate States with any accuracy. Look what's happened." He fanned the stack of newspapers. "In the North, Secretary of State Seward is bullying us, threatening war, threatening Canada . . . and the Confederacy," he added, gesturing toward Dorian as though Dorian were a legitimate representative, "speaking about us in epithets, hectoring us for what it labels indecision, and during all the malediction has attempted nothing short of extortion. Recognition for cotton! It's blackmail. Nothing less."

"I agree," Dorian said instantly. He punctuated his words with a nod, then measured silence.

Russell paused. "You do?"

"Oh, yes. I personally scatolized the Southern cotton barons for their want of foresight. I encouraged them to trade with Britain at all cost, to make a big show of running the blockade to get cotton to Britain. Think of the international sympathy, the partiotism—the profit. This is not the doings of the Confederate government, Your Lordship," Dorian finished. "It is the work of puffed-up cotton snobs."

Russell fell into one of his thoughtful silences. He seemed to be unconcerned by blocks of utter quiet while he distilled what he had just heard, no matter now itchy it made his company.

"What a shame we didn't meet six months ago," he pondered finally.

The Cousin leaned forward. "My lord?"

"Six months ago we may have done some engineering to our mutual ends. Now . . ." Russell shook his head. "Have you seen today's news from the American front? The Union army is at your doorstep. The Confederacy is about to collapse. I shall never be able to convince Palmerston to recognize you now. Why should Britain involve itself in a finished enterprise? And just in time to share in the blame? My God, this shock that the North might actually *win*—" He shook his head again, staring at the pile of daily papers. "Now I appear the fool. I must quickly retract advocacy of recognition and tolerate having my nose rubbed in a Confederate defeat."

The notification seemed grindingly final. His mind was made up. There were the facts, printed in so many words, with newspaper clarity, piled upon the burnished wooden table. Russell was about to turn them down, withdraw his advocacy in the House of Lords. Time to take a gamble.

So Dorian leaned forward. He gave Lord Russell his darkest, dirtiest, most conspiratorial glare, and the pause that made it potent. This glare was poison. It had caused riders to steer around him, thieves to pull back their hands, foremen to put him in charge, senators to vote his way, and slave drivers to belt their whips. Women enjoyed it because it was dangerous. Men wanted to stand behind it for power and protection. A horse had even turned away from him once rather than deal with that glare.

He lowered his voice until the even ticking of the clock was louder.

"Lord Russell," he began, "military tides can turn on a dime. George McClellan is playing into our hands. We know more about his mind and his ways than we know about the shape of our mother's breasts. He will be stopped in his tracks within ten miles of Richmond. The Union will be humiliated.

Let your detractors cajole. Let them laugh and scratch. Hold off denouncement of the Confederacy, Your Lordship. Give me one week. One week in this century. You shall cauterize your wounds on the greatest turnaround in history. You shall be proved right and be seen as one of the great visionaries of our age . . . instead of one of the sheep."

The clock made its haunting *tock* again.

It was the only thing moving in the room. Britain was still around them. They could nearly hear each other's minds working.

Tentatively Lord Russell murmured, "What is it you're intending?"

He was thinking aloud. That was evidenced when he seemed completely satisfied with Dorian's response of only the eyebrows—hints, but no commitments.

Timing even his breathing, Dorian leaned back in his chair, a careful but tactical retreat.

"Do you have someone to assassinate McClellan?" the Foreign Minister went on, enjoying the art of guesswork. "Or Lincoln? Or is McClellan a traitor? We have often conjectured so, given his recalcitrance in the face of obvious advantage. . . ."

Dorian remained resolutely silent, knowing his silence would imply that he had something up his sleeve besides an implicating brand. He allowed a very small suggestive grin to spray kerosene on Russell's spark.

"By George, if you're not somewhat clever," Russell said, "or somewhat devious, Mr. Parthens. If indeed you . . ." He paused for a long time, deciding perhaps what to say, or how to say it. "If you would like support from this body . . . Parliament, I mean to say . . . you must put a muffler upon this denunciatory *Index* of yours. The editors are using imprecatory language toward me and the House of Lords scurrilously, indeed the entire concept of peerage, and that does not wash well. It is becoming a matter of honor to ignore the Confederacy—"

"We'll see to that, Your Lordship," the Cousin said. His voice was not as steady as usual, but his tone implied a firm promise.

Russell nodded doubtfully. He plainly wasn't convinced. He now watched Dorian as though to peel away any facade and get to the grain of genuine abilities or covert plots, as though to see if his guest could take the brunt of a good scrubbing stare.

In that pool of heat, Dorian stood up.

He measured his stance carefully, artistically, but with just a touch of the scoundrel that reposed not far beneath the surface. He was staring down upon the powerful, small gentleman. He turned slightly and looked at Russell past the point of his own shoulder.

"Hold off, my lord. That is my advice. Good afternoon."

To the astonishment of the other men, he turned without a pause and strolled to the door, opened it without looking back, went out, and shut it behind him.

And there were still two minutes on the clock.

"Have you lost your eccentric mind?"

The Cousin kept both his arms flat to his sides to avoid attracting attention, though holding his voice down in the middle of Downing Street was a notable strain for him now. He came to Dorian's side near their landau and glared with eyes blazing.

"What have you implied?" he demanded. "How dare you take this upon yourself! You've promised the House of Lords that the South will win! How could you make such a claim? What were you thinking? You have ruined us both."

Dorian sniffed at him and made a long show of drawing on a pair of lambskin gloves some earl had given him as a gift. "I've ruined nothing. I've extended the Confederacy's life by a week. He reminds me of Aleck Stephens in many w—"

"The Confederacy is done for!" the Cousin growled. "You saw the headlines. Richmond is in Union hands."

"Go ahead," Dorian said. "Surrender. I, on the other hand, shall snatch at the wind for the one red leaf. If there is one in a hundred chances, I want it. We do not yet know what the outcome will be outside of Richmond."

"Or has been already," the Cousin said. "When this turns bad, you will have destroyed my influence in Europe—I want you to know that. Destroyed! Your risk was unconscionable. If

I drop a rock, there's a chance it will fall up, but I won't bet my life on it."

Dorian tossed his walking stick into the landau and stepped up onto the footboard.

There he paused. "Oh, I would," he said.

★

★★★

THE BURNING FUSE

1 JULY 1862
THE BATTLE OF MALVERN HILL

General McClellan draws his huge army back eastward from Richmond. General Lee follows, intending to end the war here and now. At Malvern Hill the Union stops and takes a stand. They give the energetic defense that should have been an attack on Richmond. With that energy, they repel Lee's Confederates, who are crippled by lack of communication and poor unity of effort. Though the battle is costly to the Confederates (as are all battles because of limits on manpower and gunpowder), the Union army continues eastward. In spite of having the upper hand, the Union moves back to Harrison's Landing, in full retreat.

★

CHAPTER FORTY-FOUR

——————— ★ ———————

A RAINY 2 JULY 1862
THE GRAIN SHELVES OF A DRY-GOODS STORE IN MECHANICSVILLE

"Is there something in his food? Has he been eating slugs?"

"Woman, hush your voice. We're in a public place."

"We're in a public place that's back in Confederate hands," Grace growled, leaning toward Allan Pinkerton as they both pretended to be sorting through sacks of corn and wheat.

The sacks had already been picked through. In fact, the entire store was down on its stock. Grace assumed most of the stock had been confiscated for the Union troops while they flapped back and forth across this part of the state.

"Well, what's he doing in that headquarters of his? Counting chicken eggs for reveille? That polesitter's got the Rebs outnumbered three and four to one!"

"That is not our information."

"It's the information *I've* been sending, God hang you by your beard! I not only sent sizes of shipments, but I sent word that my husband was having to hold back on powder shipments because of tainted niter, and you Northern maggots still didn't take advantage! Can you read, Mr. Pinkerton? That means the Rebs didn't have enough gunpowder or cannon powder. What kind of idiot wouldn't take that for a military advantage? McClellan's men were setting their watches by Richmond church bells, half the town was packing to leave and the other half was refugeeing in, and McClellan puts his butt in the mud building eleven bridges over the Chickahominy and ten or twenty miles of corduroy road! Have

505

I got to go back to Kansas and bark squirrels to find an animal with a backbone?"

Clearly uncomfortable, Pinkerton swallowed several times before responding. When he did speak, he was obviously holding his temper at close rein.

"You sent your man," he said, "to my man with a message that you had to see me personally. I'm here. What information do you wish to convey?"

"I want information *from* you," she said.

"Like what, precisely?"

"Like why you haven't gotten this war over with, that's like what!"

"Madam, keep your head."

"Horseshit, Allan."

"Good Lord, madam . . ."

Grace abandoned the grain sacks and turned to him. "What is it about Union reconnaissance? Why can't you keep from ballooning the troops numbers I give you to pass on to McClellan? Or is it his imagination all by itself that's preventing an attack that would finally end this war? Just what is it, Mr. Pinkerton? Where is the swelling, and why can't it be lanced? I'm here to find out why your whole army's still crawling around out there like some goddamned Madagascar cockroach."

Pinkerton's lips tightened. Grace sensed that even he couldn't find a justification for McClellan's hesitations.

He covered his embarrassment in a simple terse sentence. "It's not your business, Mrs. Craig."

Wrath bubbled up in Grace's eyes so hot that the man backed away a step.

"Not my business?" she repeated through gritted teeth. "I've damn near shut down the powdermill for you! I hear my husband talk about Rebel divisions standing around putting up a show, but without enough gunpowder to take target practice. We've had no less than a brigadier general and two colonels out to the yard, begging for shipments, testing or no testing, and I've about had it with you Unionists! Why don't you end this war? Get it over with and let us get along with our lives! If McClellan doesn't have the will to fight or he doesn't want the President to get the credit for a victory, why doesn't he resign? He built a whole army practically all by himself, and now he's scared to use it! In my opinion President Lincoln should come out of his tree, ride down here to the river, and have George McClellan's little mustache arrested for treason!"

THE COTTAGE IN MECHANICSVILLE

"Orienta!"

"I am here, Mr. Swanborough. You need not holler."

"What have you done with my clothing?"

Barry Swanborough pivoted to see his sister-in-law standing in all her disgusting female corpulence at the doorway of his bedchamber.

"I have been unable to come back here for weeks because of the Union occupation of this area, and now that I come back, I find my closet empty of every shirt, sock, and undergarment. Do you have an explanation?"

Orienta maneuvered with some difficulty into the room. Pregnancy had taken over her entire being. She was even rounder than before, her face fuller, her eyes glowing, her fingernails firm and shiny, and even her hair had a gloss that it had never before possessed.

However, she could barely walk.

"When the Yankee cowards skedaddled," she said, "the brillant Confederate heroes came through this part of the town, and they needed your . . . your linens and unders. I also donated all the blankets in the household and all the food."

Barry glared at her with unconcealed venom.

Suddenly something occurred to him, and he dived back into the closet and foraged like an animal. When he came out, his face was burgundy and his hands empty.

"Where is the strongbox?" he growled. "It was in this closet. Where is my box?"

"I discovered a box of gold," Orienta said, with her hands folded beneath her enlarged front. "I know why you are storing gold in your closet rather than depositing it in banks. You have no faith in Confederate banks, Barry. You have no faith of any kind. No faith in any principle or person. No faith that God will see the Confederacy to its victory for state's rights in this, the greatest war ever fought on the earth, the war which will be someday known as the Second American Revolution."

"Orienta, control yourself," Barry snarled, "and tell me what in the devil's name you have done . . . with . . . my . . . gold? You haven't sent it to your—that mockery of a *husband*—"

Standing with her two feet far apart for balance under her enormous skirt and hoops, Orienta gave him a stern twist of her mouth that cut off his sentence and implied she would tell him if he would cease talking.

"I have given it to the Confederacy," she said.

This time Barry didn't respond. He simply stood there, quaking and boiling.

Orienta saw plainly that he misunderstood. He thought she had donated the gold. That the gold was gone.

"I traded it for bonds," she explained. "Your gold is safe, while serving the great cause of freedom."

Not a breath, not a hair, not an eyelash changed on Barry's large form as he stood there, broiling—except that his eyes blistered her and seemed to have some kind of larval plague eating at them from behind. Some of the color left his face, leaving his skin corpselike.

Barry felt as though he were having a stroke. The bonds weren't worthless yet, but who would liquidate fifty thousand dollars in Confederate bonds for him? And for what? Confederate currency? Bonds which would be worth nothing if the Confederacy lost this war, which he could trade only for Confederate currency, with which he couldn't buy anything, and which would also be worth nothing. Such a transaction would not only be foolish and foresightless, but conspicuous. The woman might as well have dropped the gold into the James.

This was a man who did not like to be inconvenienced in life. Now he had not only been inconvenienced, but he had been compromised by a woman's patriotic obsession.

"Get out of this house," he said. "Get out. Don't dare take a single thing with you. There's nothing in here that you own any longer. You own only Confederate bonds now. Dress yourself in them and eat them."

She seemed not to have heard him. His words were so outlandish that she found herself virtually waiting for him to say what he really meant.

Within a few seconds, however, she realized she had heard right.

Scouring up her courage, she said, "You are my first husband's brother. You are not my husband."

He didn't answer this time at all. His conversation was terminated.

Without apology he took her by one arm and hauled her skidding and twisting out of the bedroom, virtually carried her exaggerated bulk down the stairway, holding her impossibly at arm's length while her hooped skirts caught on the rail and coiled around and around her.

Cupping her in one arm like a sack of refuse about to be thrown out, Barry scooped her toward the front door, hauled the door open, and pitched the woman out.

With the little breath left to her by pregnancy, Orienta cried out only once during all this, as her skirts uncoiled and sent her reeling across the porch. She nearly went crashing down the front steps, but caught herself on the chain of the porch swing, lacerating her fingers, but managing to bring herself to a stop against the porch rail. The spray of cold rain caught her full in the face immediately and left her confused as Barry slammed the door, leaving her locked outside. The porch swing percussed against the porch rail again and again.

She reeled like a feather caught on the bark of a tree, her hand scraped raw as it clung to the chain of the swing, for she knew that letting go would send her rolling, probably down those stairs. She had an obligation, a child to protect, Dorian's child, and she would not let go.

The porch roof creaked, the chain groaned, the swing crashed and hammered against the rail, but she clung for dear life and her child's life.

Two hands took hold of her. They steadied her and set her straight, and held her while she tried to find which way was up. Even as the hands took hold of her, so did a tremendous shudder, which left her weak and shivering. She clutched at her dress almost as though concerned about some lost moment of propriety.

"He hurt you, ma'am?"

"Buckie?" she gasped. "Buckie, is that you?"

"It's me, ma'am. What's goin' on?"

"He has . . . he has . . . put me out. . . . I must . . . I must go to . . . to Richmond now. . . . I must walk to Richmond. . . . Oh, oh—it's cold. . . . I'm so cold. . . . the rain—"

With one hand Burlie held onto the wobbling woman. With the other he steadied the porch swing and somehow maneuvered her into it, trying not to touch her in the wrong way— but those skirts had to be managed, and the backside of the woman inside had to end up on the seat and not in front of it, or down she would go.

"You wait here, ma'am. Don't you stand up."

Burlie rose thus to his full height, and even in his reclusive fourteen-year-old mind there erupted such a sense of right and wrong that he had no quandary about that front door. His foot struck it against the lock—and the whole side of the door cracked. The door fell open before him so sharply that it struck the wall behind.

He plunged inside, straight toward the astounded man of the house, and gave Barry Swanborough a punch square in the center of his chest. The man's air rushed out in a single *huff*, and he went staggering. As he wheezed, staggered, and gasped, Burlie veered toward the hall tree, collected Mrs. Orienta's knitted wrap, and managed to grab a parasol before the realization came back that a big black boy who looked like a big grown-up nigger could legally be killed for what he had just done.

He rushed out on the run, past Swanborough, who was on his knees and sucking like a boated pike.

The boy even closed the busted door behind him.

To his amazement Mrs. Parthens had made it all the way down the front steps and was standing in the rain, waiting for him, shivering uncontrollably. Burlie arranged the knitted shawl around her as quickly as his big hands could manage the tassles and satin ties.

"Come on, ma'am. Here's your wrap. There you go. I'll watch over you. Never let you out of my sight again, just like I promised Mr. Dorian."

She paused and looked up at him. "Did you promise him that?"

Pausing as he opened the parasol over her, Burlie realized

he might have erred. But a little truth now and then couldn't hurt.

"I did that, ma'am," he said.

"Did he ask you," she murmured weakly, "to watch over me?"

"Um . . . yes'm, I guess he did."

With a moment's hesitation, perhaps a prayer or search for her inner resolve, Orienta scooped the front of her skirts out of the mud and stepped foward. Burlie kept close behind her.

She would get to Richmond somehow, and she would protect and bear Dorian's child. She would simply walk all the way upon the firm road of the love she knew was still alive.

Inside the house Barry dragged himself to his feet and grasped a chair for support. His chest felt cracked. He sucked air only with horrible effort and wondered if his breastbone had been cracked by the nigger's blow. A nigger striking a white man— even to think of it . . .

Forget them. They were nothing. He now had an excuse to shoot the boy down if ever they crossed paths. One of his stashes of gold was sacrificed, but he could garner good worth out of this turn if he played it right.

His chest pounding and lungs struggling, he forced himself to the dining room and sat down at the table and began to write.

My brother's widow, Mrs. Bernard Swanborough, has summarily vacated the household and therefore the holdings developed through the efforts of my brother, Bernard Emmanuel Swanborough, and myself. I take her abandonment of the household to be a severing of any attachment to the plantation my brother and I built with our hands. Owing to the encumberance of war, I will no longer be able to notify her of any business decisions and take upon myself those decisions.

Barry Arnold Swanborough

Dated 2 July 1862

──────────── ★ ────────────

The rain was crushing. Grace huddled inside the surrey, glad the summer rain was plunging straight down rather than blowing in from the sides. The ride back toward Richmond from the store and the unsatisfying meeting north of Mechanicsville was slow going. This horse didn't like mud, and that's all there was between here and the city. Mud. Mud or brown water.

Mud, brown water . . . and a woman walking on the side of the road? With a slave holding something over her head? A few more yards showed the thing to be a parasol draped with the slave's coat, leaving his bare shirt plastered to his shoulders.

Grace clacked her horse to a trot, sending pasty mud splattering at every step, and realized as she drew closer—

The woman was—

"Hog shit! Look at you!" Grace drew the horse to a walk before the hooves splattered more mud onto Orienta and that black boy. She drew to a stop as the two pathetic, sopping creatures turned to her, and she jumped down into the rain she had so far avoided.

"Grace?" Orienta uttered through chattering teeth and swollen lips. "Is that . . . you?"

"What in blue hell are you doing walking on a day like this? And you fixing to hatch in a matter of weeks! Did you leave your brains in that trunk of Alabama dirt?"

She cursed and harangued as she and the slave boy hoisted the exhausted woman into the carriage and drew a riding·blanket over her mud-soaked shirts.

Spasms of effort and exhaustion wracked Orienta, but couldn't prevent a tiny grin of gratitude as Grace peeled off her own jacket and replaced Orienta's soaked shawl.

"He went and tossed us out, miss," Burlie told Grace. "That Mr. Swanborough, he tossed this good woman right out onto the porch without a wrap."

"Doesn't surprise me," Grace said. "You couldn't get her a carriage or a buggy or a damn thing?"

"No, ma'am, he didn't allow it. So I just took her."

"He ought to be gutted with a dull knife. Never mind. You did right. Get in the surrey."

"Oh, no, ma'am, there's no room in there. I'll just run alongside."

"What's this world full of? Arguments? I'm going to huddle with her and keep her warm. You get your skinny black butt in here and drive for Richmond."

MECHANICSVILLE, THREE DAYS LATER

Barry Swanborough made a point of sitting at the dining-room table, which he had confiscated as a desk now that there was no woman in the house. He continued scouring paperwork even though he had just received notice from his footman that he had a visitor and that the visitor was a Confederate officer.

He didn't deign to look up as Major Craig strode into the dining room and motioned that the two uniformed men with him wait outside on the porch.

Wyatt didn't take off his gold-corded gray-and-scarlet uniform tunic or even remove his wide-brimmed hat, because he wasn't here on a social call and he wasn't salutatory. He did, however, sit down.

Only then did Swanborough look up from his two handfuls of paperwork. "Craig, isn't it?"

"That's right," Wyatt said pointlessly. "I don't know if it matters any to you, but your sister-in-law is at my home in Richmond, and that's where she's going to stay. My wife is taking care of her. I'd advise you to stay away."

"I perfectly intend to stay away," Swanborough said emotionlessly. "You needn't have sat down for that."

"No, there's something else. I just told you that out of common courtesy and assuming any gentleman would have a concern or two about a lady out on her own in her condition, or any condition." Wyatt sighed shallowly, trying not to give away the fact that he took on this role awkwardly, but out of pure duty. "No reason to beat around the bush when I know where the bird is, Mr. Swanborough. I've been a businessman a long time, and I still don't know what it is in some businessmen's nature that makes them cross the line between success and excess. I'm not one to put a ceiling on how high a man can go, but there does come a point where you're digging a bigger pit than you're building a mountain."

Swanborough didn't react except to say, "Your point?"

"I've been to the docks at the right time," Wyatt said. He quit waffling and met the big man's steel demeanor. "I know your secret with the cotton shipments, most of it anyway. The rest will come out with investigation, and that's not for me to do, but you're doing a wrong thing, and I can't sleep knowing. I've got guards outside to arrest you. At first I didn't know who to report to, then I remembered that somehow I got myself into an officer's commission and I could report it to myself. I thought I'd come in here and cuss like a sailor, but now that I'm here, well . . . that's about it."

Swanborough said nothing for several moments. He seemed unconcerned, but seemed to be calculating a game plan. Or battle plan. He did not blink or give away his thoughts in any way.

Wyatt couldn't discern whether this impassiveness came from knowing the well couldn't stay full forever and being resigned to eventually facing the law, or from Swanborough's cold-blooded nature.

Swanborough sniffed, took a moment to wipe his nose with an initialed handkerchief, then said, "Have you ever seen a photograph, Major? Do you know what one is?"

Wyatt's brows drew in. He didn't know why, but he got the feeling that he was being talked down to. "Of course I know what it is."

"I have one here," Swanborough said, and dug deeply into a drawer in the china closet behind him. "I think you'll recognize the subject."

He handed a large envelope to Wyatt across the dining-room table.

Unceremoniously Wyatt opened it and withdrew a stiffly mounted photograph.

Which he instantly recognized.

Suddenly cold, he was glad he had his hat on so he could hide behind the brim.

"The original document was procured at great pains," Swanborough said. "This photograph is for my records, but the original is in the possession of my agent. I've had it for quite some time, in anticipation of just such an occasion as today. I suppose I needn't elaborate."

Wyatt didn't look up. He knew the photograph by heart.

"Who will be more reviled," Swanborough asked, "when I reveal this to the authorities, and to the public? I? Or you, for harboring this unseemly man in the white community? He will hang, certainly. You'll probably be shot. That leaves your wife to live you down and Orienta to birth a part-negro baby. We are both scoundrels, Major. You're a Northerner in gray, I'm a Southerner availing of an opportunity. If this is revealed, I will be in jail, and you and this man will be shot. The arrangement is this. I shall leave you alone, and you shall leave me alone. Your rapist half-breed slave friend can even have my sister-in-law. We'll go our separate ways and let the world adjudicate our fates."

The implacable man then fell silent to see how his pithy shock tactic would root. Everything was right on the table. Everything.

Heavily Wyatt cleared his throat. His shoulders had the set of a victim even under the stiff woolen tunic. He tried consciously not to let his countenance fall too low.

He handed Swanborough the photograph of the *WANTED* poster, stood up, and squared his hat upon his head.

"It's a deal," he said.

When the Major and the two soldiers were gone, and the sound of their horse's hoofbeats faded, Barry Swanborough put the envelope down upon the table and made a note in his head to place the valuable contents in a safer location. Even Wyatt Craig could have a place broken into, if he had the brains to think of it.

Then he took a piece of plain stationery that had no marks upon it. He addressed it to the associate editor of *The Index*, London, England.

He wrote:

The time has come to exercise our option regarding the Chameleon. Expose him for what he is, and as a false envoy. Embarrass the sources of power that have endorsed him and accuse the House of Lords of entertaining his approaches and conspiring with illegitimates. Inform me the moment it is done.

He did not sign the letter, but applied only the initials of the name of his Alabama plantation.

Then he folded the paper, put it immediately in an envelope, and sealed it with the wax of the candle that had burned itself to a stub on the buffet.

"The moment it's done," he muttered, "Wyatt Craig is dead."

CHAPTER FORTY-FIVE

———— ★ ————

"Look!" the Cousin said. "They're coming out of the office. Keep back, and for God's sake keep a sharp eye."

At the end of the block from the editorial offices of *The Index,* the two men stood behind the edge of a building and watched as the employees of the scandalous Confederate newspaper filed out at the end of the day.

"Tell me if there's anyone you recog—there!" The Cousin clutched Dorian's arm and pointed. "That's Henry Hotze! Does he look familiar to you?"

"Not at all," Dorian said immediately, knowing a total stranger when he saw one.

"Very well," the Cousin responded, disappointed. "Coming out now . . . yes—there's the most recent member of the staff. Associate editor. His name is Felix Carter. Does that set any bells ringing?"

Dorian's eyes narrowed as he carefully scrutinized the man. Had Carter come out of the building with his hat on instead of in his hand, Dorian might never have noticed anything odd. But there was something about the balding head and the way the eyes fit into it—he let his memory roll.

"Yes," he said. "I have seen him somewhere . . . though I can't readily place where."

"Are you certain?"

"Not certain . . . yet. . . . I have seen him . . . or have I been *watched* by him?"

"Can you think where? Here? Or America?"

Dorian paused. He scoured his memory, left to its own now as Carter disappeared into a cab.

"Back, quickly!"

The Cousin grasped his arm again and drew him into an alley as the cab rattled toward them, turned their corner, and passed within ten feet. The Cousin generously pushed Dorian behind him and took the chance of being seen upon himself.

"Thank you," Dorian said. "You needn't protect me."

"You're welcome, but I shall protect you. My family has a great deal pinned upon you, for which I'm responsible."

Settling back a bit, Dorian muttered a less enthusiastic, more ironic, "Thank you again," and found himself missing Wyatt.

Together they stepped out onto the street in time to watch the cab wobble around another corner.

"No idea of the identity?" the Cousin asked.

"Not as yet," Dorian said. His brows drew tight as he thought and thought. "But I associate his face with . . . anger. Frustration . . . argument. Around the emotion there's only fog. I don't believe I ever actually talked *to* him."

"Dorian, I want you to go away for a few days. The Lake District, or Scotland," the Cousin said. He ushered Dorian to turn, and they walked slowly toward their landau. "In that time I shall have this man looked into."

Dorian allowed his eyes to blur at the street as the cobblestones filed away one by one beneath his boots.

"Scotland . . ."

DUMFRIES, SCOTLAND

" 'Dare injured nations form the great design, to make detested tyrants bleed? Thy England execrates the glorious deed! Beneath her hostile banners waving, every pang of honor braving, England in thunder calls, the tyrant's cause is mine!' "

Like the thunder of the words, the voice echoed. Almost instantly it failed, absorbed by the moist earth.

"No. I haven't been drinking. I come by this mood naturally, thank you. For days I have avoided the newspapers. . . . I am as cut off from the world as you are, here. How irresponsible of me! I *should* stare at statistics about troops movements around Mechanicsville . . . around her . . . and anything I read is more than eight days old by the fastest clipper. I've made my outlandish statement to Lord Russell, and I shall never have the chance to recant. I may as well sit here, with you, sink into the Scottish rocks, divorce the world, and let the chips fall. They will land on top of me in any case, and I shall be cut. I am already bleeding from the gash of separation. I have pressed English moss upon it, I have stitched it with the thorns of English roses . . . and yet I bleed."

The response was nothing but stone, and the whistle of lowland wind across the churchyard. Stone beneath him, stone overhead.

Yet he clung to the sensation that someone was listening.

He reached down from where he sat and touched a name cut into a slab.

"'I joyless view the rays adorn the faintly marked distant hill,'" he murmured, "'I joyless view thy trembling horn, reflected in the gurgling rill. . . . My fondly fluttering heart, be still!—Thou busy power, remembrance, cease! Ah . . . must the agonizing thrill forever bar returning peace. . . . Encircled in her clasping arms, how have the raptured moments flown. . . . How have I wished for fortune's charms, for her dear sake, and hers alone. . . . And I must think it . . . is she gone?'"

A shoulder against the plow blade at his side, and he couldn't finish the verse. His throat closed up and left his mouth dry, his eyes moist with effort.

Why was this such a trial? Had he not walked away from Plentiful and never gone back? Hadn't he resisted contacting Iphigenia, Alex, Nick? Hadn't he hopped a dozen trains and coaches at a moment's notice, abandoning anything he had built during one of those pauses in his life as a hunted man, an escaped slave?

For Dorian there had never been anything but the future. He had not been born to a legacy, nor was he entitled to a past. He had read about the pasts of thousands of other human beings without ever really allowing himself to build one.

Now the foundation he had been reluctant to build upon was surging beneath him, dragging him back to its cornerstone and demanding that he stake a claim.

A claim. A wife. Friends.

But that had been days ago, perhaps weeks now. Days of disheartenment, and the cloying, blurring agony of a scorched soul.

Alone. Everything Dorian had known and cared for in his life, he had eventually been forced to leave behind. Perhaps that was his existence. Forward only.

His mood grafted him to the stone upon which he sat. Perhaps he should just stay indoors for the rest of his life. Then he wouldn't have to listen to any more scurrilous English opinionizing about Americans. How the American experiment in democracy was finished. Failed. Crumbled. Cracked. War proved it. Americans didn't even know the difference between a palace and a castle. Long live the queen.

He should stay in Scotland, wrap a tartan around himself, get lost in the western islands, and live on herring.

"Don't like eating fish," he mumbled, "or strong drink. I'm like you, Robin . . . ratin', rovin' Robin . . . the reputation of a drunken scoundrel follows me, yet fails to define me. I drink only in my misery, and seldom even then. I was a slave, and slaves do not have the opportunity to indulge. . . . It was in a lumber camp that I first tasted whiskey. Even now I can't stomach much of it, yet the reputation can serve purposes. . . . I know about the time you were ill, collapsed on a step, and women passed by you, spurning you for the drunken laureate. I would have stopped to aid you, Robin. I know it was all a myth for the sake of poetry. I know what myths are . . . I am a myth."

He shivered suddenly and coiled his arms deeply against his body as though the pain were real and biting. Sitting on granite could take the warmth out of anything.

Warmth . . . he began to envy the stone. It had no warmth and needed none. He needed it, but had none.

He turned his eyes up to the carved face of Robert Burns. Rendered in bas-relief, Burns was looking upward at an angel fluttering above them both, waving her stone gown. The poet's large, strong left hand held the handle of a plow, his other hand clutched his hat against his breast as he gazed upward at the visitation. Death, no doubt, coming for a visit, early.

"Do you realize," Dorian said through a raw throat, "that you died *before* I had the chance to talk to you? In fact, you died before I was born. That was indelicate of you. I can't even go talk to Sir Walter Scott about the time he met you. He's also incourteously deceased. No one thinks ahead anymore."

He shifted his feet and his aching backside on the edge of the bas-relief's base. Inches from his thigh the tomb announced BURNS in big block letters.

In Memory of ROBERT BURNS . . . And Maxwell Burns aged 2 years and 9 months . . . And Francis Wallace Burns aged 14 years, His Sons . . . And the remains of Jean Armour, and Robert Burns, his eldest son.

"Robin," Dorian sighed, "I've attempted in my life to emulate you, yet the formula fails to be a tonic for me as it was for you. Friends came to you like flowers to the fertile meadow, but not to me. Humane and human, heart and heartless . . . generally I boast to have no heart, but something in here hurts, and I'm sure it's not a lung. By my soul, I'm tired of aristocratic snickers, titled sneers, and English rejoicing at the end of popular rule, politics swinging away from suffrage and democracy, this prancing and crowing that the influence of the common clod is over with—I'm sick of people who are anxious that the United States break apart! Fancy . . . I, who am loyal to nothing—what's that you say?"

He looked up again, up to that time-polished relief, the chalk-stroke brows, rolling eyes and unruly thatch, immortalizing a face that could wash from rage to compassion at a moment's shift, then record it with the slash of a pen—a caprice that he had made a plowman poetic, and a poet famous.

Dorian gazed at that face and wished it would look down at him.

"What do you mean, 'to step aside is human'?" he groaned. "Is there no more sententious advice from the laureate of Man? 'Go back to America'? You witnessed the American Revolution—you were invigorated by it. How can you tell me to go back and watch it all wither? The Constitution is a dead letter, and I'm a traitor now. I've made Wyatt a traitor with me. And Orienta . . . I don't believe in sin, but she does. That is the poison of Dorian . . . to carry the disease, but never die."

His eyes fell upon the image of the plow blade Burns had made famous, quite a different kind of blade than he had touched at Tussaud's, this one rendered in stone as smoothly and artistically as though it were the bow of an archer or the harp of a saint.

Dorian lay his cool hand upon the cooler stone blade.

"I saw a man mutilated beneath a plow once, Robert," he

murmured. "Ghastly sight, but somehow . . . maturing. You were always sensitive to what your plow turned up, weren't you? Flowers, mice—little wonder you never got any farming done." He turned toward the vault again and pressed a shoulder to the bas-relief. "Perhaps I should stay here with you. Even I cannot malefact a stone poet."

Then gently scan your brother Man, still gentler sister woman. Though they may gang a kennin wrang, to step aside is human.

"I did not ask you, thank you very much," Dorian snapped. He pulled the battered little volume of Burns poetry from his boot, where it had lived for many years, and he tossed it across the tomb floor. It skidded off the stone and onto the wet grass of St. Michael's Churchyard. The well-read vellum pages instantly fanned, and it lay there, open.

The fear o' hell's a hangman's whip, to haud the wretch in order; but where ye feel your honour grip, let that aye be your border; its slightest touches, instant pause—

He stood up, paced around the vault and across the tomb, away from the book to the other side. He gazed out over the graves, and more graves.

"My honor," he whispered. "Instant pause . . ."

Something occurred to him that never had before. Never in his unsymphonic life had he realized one small thing.

In the end, all are dead. The soldiers, the poets, the slaves—and all a human being would have forever was memory of others, the resonance of whatever he leaves behind. No one running away, or even sitting in passive resistance, ever left anything worth remembering.

Only the shell of a man could be ruled, not the core. Even slavery hadn't kept him from developing his mind, his visions. Why was he letting it stop him now? Why shouldn't Dorian Wallace, Dorian Trozen, Dorian Parthens—have a life of his own?

The thing on his arm was only a scar upon the shell. Would it rule him?

On impulse he stripped off his coat and stood in the cold air in his shirt and waistcoat. The air instantly permeated his cotton sleeves and made the skin prickle on his arms.

He felt the skin tighten around the scar, the *S* that branded him by the standards of others.

No! No more!

The world was so large—and Wyatt was living proof that the modern world was not the limited, fenced field of the plantation and the slave barracks. Even through all he'd experienced, Dorian *hadn't* stopped thinking like a slave. He could go home, apologize to Wyatt for failing to win the war for him, get Orienta, take her to Europe—take her to the moon! Take her anywhere, and maybe in a hundred years after she loved him enough, he could tell her the truth, and it wouldn't matter. He could find some way to search for Yula from Europe!

"Yes," he murmured to the graveyard. "I shall go get my wife—my *wife*. I'm done giving things up . . . done!"

But as he turned in the wind of revelation, he brushed his arm on the granite wall of the tomb. The rock sent a chill through his shirt, to the scar. The scar—the mark of slavery.

It was still here, as though it had not heard the changes happening inside him. He had kept it hidden from all but Wyatt—even from Orienta. Sudden resentment flashed.

Why had he run from Richmond? Because of this scar on his arm. Because of the scar he had let the worst elements of mankind rule his life. His past had dominated his existence, though he kept telling himself he had no past. All his life he had let others say who and what he was, and what he could have . . . and what he couldn't.

It was only a scar upon the shell. Would it rule him?

Abruptly he turned to the edge of the tomb, stepped onto the grass, and retrieved the little volume of poetry that had so affected his life. He took it to the bas-relief and tucked it behind Robert Burn's sculpted hand upon the plow handle. Then he put his hand upon the poet's stone arm and noted that against all possibility it felt warm to his touch.

"The strong give up and move along," he murmured. "The weak give up and stay. Thank you, Robert. . . . I have found my time to move along."

Malodorous smoke was easily ignored by those who spent their lives around it, and that was the case in the blacksmith's shop at the end of a Dumfries street that night when a strange gentleman came walking aimlessly by.

Inside an open structure of rock and slate, the better to discourage fire, the blacksmith's forge belched and crackled and made a warm gathering place on a chilly Scottish night. A bellows heaved and kept the fire going, a fire that was never allowed to go completely out.

Here the poor tradesmen, farmers, some wives, and a few older children gathered for a last-minute brew before going home. The Scots were highly social people and did everything possible to stave off going home too early. Drawing their shawls and coats and scarves tightly about them against the cool night, they threw coins into an iron pot that had been cast on this very forge, and thus funded their weekly Saturday night at the smithy, where they shared a drop of barleycorn, stories about the week's work, and gossip about the rich.

Past this unassuming service, out of the dark night, came an eccentric upper-cruster in shirtsleeves, dragging his coat behind him on the ground. In his tan breeches, knee-high boots, black tie, and waistcoat, he looked like a laird or a banker—except for a diabolical flash in his eyes when he saw them.

It was enough to drop them all to sudden silence.

"Ah!" the gentleman gasped appreciatively. His smile flashed like a spark. "The Cotter's Saturday Night—at the smithy!"

The blacksmith and the farmers and wives heaved a collective sigh of relief and laughed as he came toward the slate-roofed smithy, his boots crunching on the dirty flagstone floor. Perhaps he wasn't a phantom after all.

He swaggered toward them, dragging his fine black coat heedlessly over the ground, so relaxed they wondered if he was drunk. He caught a hand on the supporting wall of the open-air furnace yard and swung like a child.

"Faith!" he crowed, " '—you and Applecross were right! To keep the Highland hounds in sight—I doubt na'! They wad bid nae better than let them ance out ower the water, then up among thae lakes and seas, they'll mak what rules and laws they please!' "

The people laughed again in delight with him. They recognized the poem, but had never heard it mangled in quite this manner. This man was a stranger, but stranger than most.

He reached into his waistcoat pocket with two fingers and drew out a twenty-pound note. Twenty pounds!

"Bread!" he called. "Bread and brew! Bed and breakfast! No, never mind the bed or breakfast. Just bread and something to wash it down with, that'll do! Who wants it? All of you, share it. There."

He stuffed it into the contribution pot as the people stared and gasped, then he patted the blacksmith's leather apron happily. Twenty pounds to share! He was no phantom. He was an archangel!

The weaver had the presence of mind to take the man's coat and slip a tin mug of brew into his hand, and two of the women ran off immediately to get bread and anything else they thought he might like.

Dorian waved after them theatrically.

"'Some daring Hancock, or a Franklin, may set their Highland bluid a-ranklin'!'" he called, and made all the people laugh with his antics. "Or some Washington again may head them, or some Montgomery, fearless, lead them, till (God knows what may be effected when by such heads and hearts directed!)—poor dunghill sons of dirt and mire may to Patrician rights aspire!"

He swung around on the pole, lost his grip, and nearly fell against the scorching-hot iron body of the forge, but the blacksmith's muscular teenaged apprentice reached out and somehow caught him.

"Mind, sir, that'll burn you!"

"Burn me?" Dorian howled, frantically clapping a hand to his head. "You mean Burns me? That's it! Robert Burns me! Brilliant! 'Satan, I fear thy sooty claws!'"

The apprentice set him on his feet again, and he stumbled between a farmer and the souter, hanging upon their shoulders as though they were the crew of his ship. The people laughed, unable to tell whether it was melancholy or euphoria that was on the man, but willing to bet to the good.

Dorian left those two and gathered up two others, a round old man and a round young woman, both of whom were thrilled at his attention.

"'They, an' be damn'd!—what right hae they to meat, or sleep, or light o' day? Far less to riches, pow'r, or freedom, but what Your Lordship like to gie'm? But hear, my lord!

Glengary, hear! Your hand's ower light on them, I fear'—oh, excuse me—"

He pushed away after accidentally brushing his hand upon the bosom of the woman, even though she seemed unoffended and simply made that experienced chortle of one who understood a man's type of mistake.

Dorian wandered closer to the forge. The warmth drew him in, closer, closer, until it blended to heat so heavy, it would suffocate him if he stayed so close. The folk were listening to his poem and not watching where he was standing, so he moved deeper into the invisible cloud of swelter around the furnace and felt sweat break on his face and shoulders. What had minutes ago been a cold evening turned suddenly tropical. What seemed random movements by a demented man were careful choreography, but only he knew it.

The people were enthralled, treated to a recitation none of them could afford, as he swirled among them, closer and closer to the heat. Dorian swung his arms like a jester on stage and went on.

"'An' if the wives an' dirty brats come thiggin at your doors an' yetts, flaffin' wi' duds, and grey wi' beas', frightin away your ducks an' geese, get out a horsewhip or a jowler, An' gar the tatter'd gypsies pack, wi' a' their bastards on their *back*—!'"

His arms swung wide, hard—

And his right arm hit the body of the furnace.

Pain bolted through Dorian as though he struck in the arm by lightning, but he thrust against it, pushing, pressing on the pain, his teeth grinding and his eyes draining—he felt the skin of his arm tighten, cooking, grilling to the cloth of his shirtsleeve. Still he pushed against it, harder, and even knocked away the blacksmith who plunged forward to pull him away.

Excruciation overtook him until sweat broke out on his entire body and he was suddenly soaked beneath his clothing. Near panic, the speechless people thrust off their shock and braved the torrid heat to reach him and pull him off—

They couldn't get him off!

He fought them! Delirious, Dorian pressed his arm back hard against the iron forge until his teeth grated and his knees began to buckle.

He sank into their arms, agony driving through his shoulders and into his heart, which he felt hammering as though he held it in his two hands . . . then blackness swam in to drown him.

The apprentice snatched up a bucket and spilled water back and forth over the gentleman's arm. The people held the strange man and gawked with horror at the sizzling fabric and the skin into which it was cauterized, and grimaced to think what torment the man would endure when he awakened.

"Oh—oh, what'll we dae now?" the woman asked, her breast tingling from where he had touched her. Somehow she felt guilty now. "It's sair burned him!"

"Look," the blacksmith said, kneeling and pointing. "There's a burn under the new burn."

"Hae can you tell?" the apprentice asked.

"I know burns, lad."

"They'll say we barnt him," a farmer said. "They'll say't was wutches!"

"Aye," the weaver agreed. "Let's poot him bae the roadside and let his ain folk find him."

"Muckle beasts, don't rant like dugs," the blacksmith scolded. "A burn's a burn, not a spell. It's my forge, and I'll tend him. Besides," he added, "he gied us twenty pounds for bread and whuskey—what'll be gie us tae nurse him back to health?"

The apprentice tossed away the bucket and fetched another, knelt down beside the odd visitor and used the man's own mug to pour dipper after dipper onto the bubbling wound.

"Poor man," he said, shuddering with empathy. "Gaein sae brawlie, too. Niver even got tae finish his poem . . ."

GRACE'S CABIN, ON THE POWDERMILL'S UPPER PROPERTY

"What do you even call him a husband for? Don't hardly ever see him, don't hardly talk to him."

"It's none of your business."

"I'm making it mine."

"Oh, shut your clap."

"I—I don't—like it when you tell me to shut up."

"Shut up, shut up, shut up. Like it any better now? Get used to it, or I'll take one of my buttons and sew your rod to your leg and you'll never thread my needle again."

Clyman got up on an elbow and showed the whites of his eyes. "What's grindin' you?"

"Nothing."

Grace ignored the tinder of threat under his tone and that ghastly mask he put on when he wanted to pretend he was a man. Lately he sickened her personally, and she was in serious doubt of his value professionally.

Professional. She had become a professional spy, for no pay, and a professional whore, for no pay.

No pay, no revenge, and no Union advance into Richmond. A whore and a spy for nothing. A spy for a cause that wasn't hers, to exact a vengeance that daily wavered.

Only the image of the pistol against the chest of the straw man—the bullet blew into a straw cavity, but when it came out, it carried a funnel of blood and splintered bone.

She winced and shut her eyes hard. "All right, all right," she growled. "Leave me to it, Paddy."

"Who? What? What're you saying?"

"Shut up. You had your catch tonight. Don't touch me anymore. I said *don't*."

Clyman sat up. "Look, missy, I risk my life to be your man on the road. Back and forth on the muddy old road, day in, day out, risking my life and limb. Don't you tell me what I can't git out of it. We got a deal."

"We got an arrangement," Grace snapped, "and any time I decide it's over, then that's it." She pressed her shoulder blade into her propped-up pillow and chewed on a fingernail. "Fuck a duck if I'm not thinking it's over. That lard-headed snake eater McClellan, general, my ass . . . took everything I did and everybody did and threw it down his latrine hole. . . . wasted my time, got married for nothing, risking getting storked by a dumb fuck like you, putting up with the whispering and getting ignored by those powdertown biddies who see you floating around me like some putrid smell, spending my time in this sulfurous industrial sinkhole, listening to those damned mills grind until I want to shriek—" She stopped rambling and screwed her brows together, thinking. "Something's wrong with all this, and I get the feeling I don't know what's up and what's down. All I do know is Paddy's dead, and I'm beginning to wonder if I'm not half or two-thirds wrong about that, too."

"Paddy," Clyman interrupted. Jealousy burned behind his eyes. "That your husband's name in the bed? That a game he plays between your legs? Paddy-cake?"

"Oh, shut up," Grace spat.

"I don't like another man on my ground," Clyman said, "If he lays a hand on you, I'll do away with him."

"You'll—" Grace vaulted from the bed, her breasts swinging freely as they had in her days as a dirty teenager dressed in a grain-sack dress, with no sense of undergarments and too much sense of men and women. "That's it!" she roared. "That's the end of it! Christ, you give me the gurks! I've had it up to my back teeth with you! You go near my husband, and I'll pull those red whiskers through your nose and out your poker, Clyman! He's got more right for his hands on me than you ever did, and if I want him dead, I'll kill him myself! Nobody'll rob me of my revenge, in my own time, in my own way! Get up! Get out of my bed! I'll communicate with Pinkerton myself from now on! I don't need you, you river-bottom slug! Here! Take your trousers! Get out! Forget about me! Forget about this powdermill, you snake shit. You just quit this job!"

"Hey! Hey!" he shouted as she whipped him with his own trousers. He stumbled out of the bed and backward toward the door as she pelted him with his own clothes. She was fiery and exciting, and he wanted her again, but she was hurting him, and she wasn't kidding, wasn't playing.

His last vision of Grace was a flesh-and-blood woman in the heat of rage, a naked mirror for brush strokes of silvery light from a single lantern hanging on the inside wall, doing the second-most provocative thing a woman could do to a man—fighting with him.

That last image burned into Clyman's mind as the cabin door banged shut on his nose. He stood on the porch, holding his clothes, and hungered to put his hands on that silvery flesh again. He would get it again. He would to anything to get it.

Still staring at the door and hearing her move around in the small rooms beyond, Clyman tugged his trousers on over his knees and his confused but enthusiastic anatomy, and took extra long to button up. He closed his eyes and thought of her body moving beyond the door, bending over to pick up the things she'd thrown at him, reaching across the bed to straighten the covers.

He would get her again. He would get her for good.

INN IN DUMFRIES

Torment cresting in waves, like boiling water washing over.

Burning . . . wave after wave of pounding, parching heat . . . was his arm welded to the forge? Was he hanging there by seared and melted flesh?

The throbbing began slowly to localize out to the right of his body. He felt the mattress beneath him and the distance between himself and the pain—his arm . . . lying away from his body . . . moisture . . . blisters rising and popping . . . cold and heat. He couldn't tell the two apart.

Instantly he yanked his arm up to protect his face but even that was its own kind of misfortune. The branding iron sizzled into the boy's forearm and burned in, cauterizing skin and sinew. He sagged back against the tree. His eyes glazed and rolled upward as agony overtook him. Air moved down his open throat and up again, but there was no scream—there was too much pain for screaming. The smell of scorched flesh filled the air. As the boy sank down the tree trunk, held there only by the ropes that tied him, a thin trail of smoke twisted from the muscle of his forearm.

He lay alone without a name or a past. The relentless pain had provided hours of welcome delirium. Perhaps he was in his grave. The cold was the grave . . . the heat was hell coming up to claim him.

Gradually, as though rising on well water as it filled, he came up in a single seizure out of his hole of darkness. He heard himself moaning, but the sound was detached. The pain was so cloying, so debilitating, that he could barely rouse his mind beyond it.

A pillow held his head, an eiderdown pillow. Not the feather pillows of his mother's quarters . . . *Yula . . . I promise . . .*

Consciousness flushed in suddenly, as though Dorian had been struck in the face by a bucket of water. His eyes pushed open and immediately began stinging. He moaned aloud and found he was panting with the effort of coming around.

"Don't strain," a voice said from his side.

Dorian shuddered, then grimaced and tried to get control. His lips cracked when he parted them. "Wyatt?"

A cool cup touched his mouth, and water flowed between his lips. He wanted to crawl into the cup, head, shoulders, and all.

"Don't push yourself. You'll come out of it."

Following the voice, Dorian turned his head slightly, blinked, and tried to focus.

The Du Pont Cousin sat beside the bed.

"Oh," Dorian uttered. Disappointment flushed through him. "Good morning . . ."

"Good afternoon. I won't ask you how you feel. I can see how you do."

Calling, calling, the hurt in his arm, triumph and agony, the scar beneath the scar . . .

"I did it," Dorian whispered. His voice was faint, too faint to seem more than a flick of the tongue on a breath, yet it carried a victory that even he in his exhaustion heard and clung to.

The evidence of sin. Gone. Seared beneath the bandage, the scar on his arm was no longer discernable as the S that had marked him since the age of fourteen.

Even that bit of identity was gone now.

He didn't know whether to miss the brand or not. Before, he had been a runaway slave, illegitimate bastard of the tobacconist. Now he was no one.

Reaching for his eyes, Dorian wiped them and found they were wet, straining. He let his hand drop to his chest.

"Consciousness," he moaned, "is grossly overrated."

The Cousin chuckled. "You're in an inn in Dumfries," he said. "No, no—don't move. You've been through bone-rattling chills and fever for six days, unable to keep any nourishment down. That's why you're weak. The arm has been tended by a local midwife. They had a bad time separating the scorched fabric from your skin. The blacksmith kept you at his house for two days while they tracked me down and wired me to come after you. There's some muscle damage, but the doctor here is only a patch man. I have a specialist arranged for you in London when we return. We must go back immediately, as soon as you can stand."

Fighting off a spasm, Dorian forced himself to think.

"Why?" he breathed. "Why go back?"

A wicked grin spread over the Cousin's lips, and his eyes flashed. "Because," he said, "you are the luckiest bastard on this earth."

He held a three-day-old edition of *The London Times* before Dorian's face.

Staring through his moist eyes, Dorian read the headline over and over and wondered if it would dissolve before him.

McCLELLAN HAS WITHDRAWN FROM RICHMOND!

★★★

THE BURNING FUSE

In June and July of 1862, the battles of the Orchard, Mechanicsville, Cold Harbor, Savage's Station, and Frayser's Farm—along with myriad skirmishes and activity in Vicksburg in the western theater, have changed the face of the immediate future. Porter's line north of Mechanicsville has broken. He has retreated across the river and merged with the Army of the Potomac, which was faced down by Magruder's much inferior forces.

Shaken by the Confederate drive, McClellan has drawn his great army back from Richmond in what is being called "The Great Skedaddle."

He telegrams President Lincoln, saying, "I have lost this battle because my force was too small."

★

---------- ★ ----------

PART EIGHT

SPOKESMAN FOR THE CROWN

THE BURNING FUSE

11 JULY 1862

The Peninsula is quiet. Richmond is briefly relieved, though the area remains under pressure. Major General Henry Halleck is named general in chief of Union land forces.

12–14 JULY

There are Confederate raids in several locations, and Federal expeditions and reconnaissance in Alabama and Virginia. Nathan Bedford Forrest's Confederates capture a Federal garrison at Murfreesboro, Tennessee, and reclaim the town. Lincoln continues badgering McClellan to move on Richmond, and McClellan continues dodging the topic.

    Lincoln also continues trying to deal with the slavery question. He says he would do anything he could regarding the slaves to ease the situation and bring the nation together again, whether that involved freeing all, none, or some. He is deeply disturbed by the idea of unconditional emancipation, because it represents a vast seizure of property by the government, and he cannot find constitutional or moral justification for that. His conscience makes him favor some form of compensated emancipation, in other words the slaves' freedom being bought from their owners to avoid economic strain.

    Unfortunately, that means the tax money of other citizens will be seized and used to pay the price. It is the same moral and legal dilemma of property rights either way: shall the hard-earned fruits of one group's freedom be appropriated by force of law and used to buy another group's freedom? Is this not simply slavery reversed?

16 JULY

Napoleon of France entertains the Confederate emissary John Slidell, lately of the Trent *affair.*

Major General Ulysses Grant takes command of the Union armies in Tennessee and Mississippi.

22 JULY

Lincoln reads a first draft of his Emancipation Proclamation to the Cabinet. It involves compensated emancipation in all loyal states, and unconditional emancipation in all states still in rebellion as of January 1 of the coming year.

———————————— ★ ————————————

CHAPTER FORTY-SIX

──────── ★ ────────

12 August 1862
London

"How is your arm? Still tender. And you're still weak. A sad accident. That's the Scots barbarian for you, still cooking over open fires."

"I appreciate your concern, but it was a forge, and I'm the barbarian. I decided to redraw the skin of my arm."

The Cousin shook his head at Dorian and chuckled. "Of course you did."

"How else will my mother recognize my corpse when I wash up on shore? The Scots have their tartans, the Irish have their knitting patterns, and I have my burn. What do you think their lordships' actions will be, given this vindication of my gypsy talents?"

"Haven't a clue. I have my people waiting at several locations, in case we should be summoned to Parliament again. I can almost assure you that will happen, but no idea when. I'm sorry."

"Not at all. If it's going to be a long while, perhaps I should change residences."

"Why on earth go to all that trouble?"

"My room is being searched."

The Cousin blinked at Dorian's announcement and swallowed his beer in one lump, but managed to make those his only outward reactions. Better, for they were in a public place, a small West End establishment called The Dragon, cooling their heels after their obvious win and dreaming of panicked communications from the lords.

They had adopted a plan of meeting or at least carrying their conversations onward in a series of pubs, but only once in each pub. By not being seen in the same place twice, they collected around themselves a certain manageable anonymity. This trick also gave them opportunity to notice anyone they saw more than once.

After a good long pause of digestion, the Cousin asked, "How can you know this?"

"Things are turned sideways. I have learned through experience that it's much easier to tell if a tousled room has been violated than a neat room. Violators are more careful in a neat atmosphere. Therefore I've learned to keep my atmosphere ruffled. I noticed when I came back from Scotland."

"Mmm . . . have we any idea *who* is ruffling it?"

"It's not you, is it?"

"No, it's not me."

"Then one may deduce it's either a daily paper or the government."

"Russell?"

"Likely. How many others could have uncovered the name under which my flat is rented? I would have had to be followed. Russell, Palmerston, or a newspaper are the only entities with an impetus to follow me."

The pub buzzed about them, its male patrons and female attendants making sufficient noise to cover any conversation more than a shoulder away. With its decor of rough wood, mounted spears, and pointed helmets upended for ashtrays, it possessed a heavy aura of the Viking. Dorian found himself wishing they hadn't agreed on the once-per-pub plan.

"I propose we use their curiosity to our own good," he said.

The Cousin raised a mug of dark beer to his lips. "Go on."

"Palmerston's only real weakness is his fear of France. We can use that." Dorian turned to face him. "You arrange for a forged document. Something on French paper that appears official. It should say that France is ready to break with England and recognize the Confederacy. It should also acknowledge that the Confederacy promises to recognize France's hold on Mexico, that we will defend that, and that we will form an alliance."

"Your . . . train of thought is . . . somewhat heartening. I like this idea. You're very devious. Yes . . . I shall get such a document for you as soon as I can do so."

Dorian rested his throbbing forearm upon the bar and held his breath for a moment. He was aware of the Cousin watching him with concern, and sensed that the concern wasn't the self-less kind, but the interruption kind—the kind that worried about completing the business they had come here to exact.

Before long Dorian had absorbed enough of that.

When he had control again, he put his Guinness back on the bar with a clunk of finality and added, "Make certain it looks official."

Three days later they came together in a booth at a restaurant all the way across the city from Dorian's flat. The Cousin had a devilishly self-approving expression inside his whiskers, and an accompanying flint in his eyes.

After they had been served their drinks and were assured of unbroken privacy for a few minutes, the Cousin tersely said, "If any of this is revealed in the wrong manner, many people I know will be shot or hanged. Quite probably ourselves included."

Dorian surveyed him a moment, but the Cousin was making no attempts at humor or satire.

"I understand," he answered.

The Cousin sighed and seemed resolved to follow through. He tugged an oversized envelope from his satchel, opened it, ushered an unfolded paper out, and holding it by the edges, placed it on the table and turned it so Dorian could read it.

"Is this official enough for you?" he asked.

Glad he was sitting down, Dorian found himself reading an agreement of conditional alliance between France and the Confederate States of America. Since that's what he had asked for, the words in themselves were no surprise.

The surprise was that the words were crafted in script upon a paper that bore nothing less than the watermark of the court of Marseilles and official royal seal of Napoleon III, emperor of France.

His uncharitable throughts toward the Cousin's cold efficiency and resentment that the Cousin wasn't Wyatt suddenly soaked back into the fabric of the moment. Dorian got a sharply renewed awareness of exactly what and who he was dealing with, and how far—how high—the Du Pont influence reached.

Keeping the emotion out of his face, including how impressed he was, Dorian buried the sensation of having been upstaged. He put the document back into the envelope.

"I'll see that it's . . . discoverable. Then we shall be able to trace who's searching my rooms, and if we're lucky, it will be Lord Russell and not that Carter of *The Index*."

"Oh," the Cousin said, "it won't be Carter."

Dorian looked up. "Why not?"

The Cousin took a moment to light his pipe. He appeared especially self-satisfied. "You recognized him," he said, "and that was enough for me."

"Enough for you?" Dorian puzzled. "Enough what?"

"Oh . . . just 'enough.'" The Cousin took a long draw on the pipe and watched the smoke curl. "I've already taken care of it. You see, he might have been too happy about McClellan's withdrawal. He might have had too much to drink. He might even have been lured into the arms of a woman in one of those East End opium dens. You know how a man can get, don't you?"

A chill of warning prickled Dorian's skin. Not even his eyes moved as he prodded, "What is your point?"

The Cousin sucked deeply upon his pipe again and rested back against the booth's old leather.

"I told you I don't like taking chances," he said with stylish callousness that Dorian actually envied. "Whatever problems Felix Carter may have caused us are non sequiturs now. Tomorrow morning, you see, Scotland Yard is going to discover him floating in the Thames."

And he didn't even lower his voice.

PARLIAMENT

"It's forged, John. What other explanation is there?"

"No, it's *not* forged." John Russell buzzed back and forth like an insect before Lord Palmerston's desk.

In Palmerston's hand was a rubbing of a document—not the document itself, for their agent had been ordered not to remove anything from the American's rooms. "Where did your people find this?"

Russell threw up both hands. "In the flat of that . . . that unofficial man from the Confederacy. I have an agent who slipped in, discovered that document, and took the moment to make a rubbing. It's not forged, Pam."

Palmerston's tiny eyes squinted at him, and his apish face took on an almost schoolboylike mischief. "You've been pushing for recognition. You didn't engineer this . . . did you?"

Anger flashed across Russell's face. He stopped pacing suddenly. "I should think you would know better!"

"All right, all right," Palmerston said immediately, backing off and realized what a tremendous insult he had implied.

Pointing at the rubbing, Russell said, "You see clearly that the rubbing came from a raised official stamp. It's the seal of France, by Saint George! They're communicating with Louis Napoleon and making agreements to support each other! It's everything you're feared from the start. France putting its toes into the situation and gaining advantage. Once the North gives up, the Confederacy can easily guarantee France's hold on Mexico. We must take this as evidence that Louis Napoleon is about to undermine Britain by recognizing the Confederacy. And all the bothersome lesser agreements—favorable trade between France and the Confederacy can undercut the flow of British textiles, the French can corner the market on materials needed to rebuild the South—why, Pam, it'll be as though the Confederacy were a French colony. We can't have it, I tell you. We can't."

Palmerston made a growling response in his throat and felt he owed his colleague something. "I never did trust those foppish fiends," he offered.

"Neither do I, and I also do not trust Secretary of State Seward. Do you know that he had the affront to order their minister—"

"That young Adams fellow," Palmerston muttered.

"—to refuse and refute any attempt by Great Britain to mediate in 'their' war? Think of it! Threats!"

"Their 'threats,'" Palmerston said calmly, "had better be a consideration for us. Like it or not, if the Americans move into

Canada, what can we do? If we tie up our fleet in a war over there, who will protect the Channel?"

Russell paced back and forth. "Our four grandmothers in a rowboat could dispatch the American Navy, and well you know it."

"Not if we run afoul of those ironclad contraptions. And you do remember 1812, I shall assume." Palmerston raised his thick snowy brows in proper British disapproval and sighed. "That entire continent has been populated for three hundred years with the world's malcontents, and it shows."

"Either way," Russell pressed on, "we will have problems with the United States. We must make sure this doesn't come through for them, Pam. We must keep Britain's foothold on favorable trade agreements on the American continent. They're going to fragment the continent in any case, and we cannot allow France to guarantee the existence of the Confederacy ahead of us and forge this bastard alliance. Strike me dumb, but the Confederacy is up to no good. Witness that their unofficial spokesman told me there would be a change in the tide, and there *was* an utterly remarkable change against vastly superior forces. Unofficial he may be, but my sources tell me he comes from none other than Alexander Stephens. This speaks of subterfuge in the Confederate White House itself, possibly an attempt to undermine President Davis. By God, they are craftier than we have given them credit for. Whatever's going on, we must make certain Britain is at the head of it, not at the tail of it. We *must* recognize the Confederacy as soon as possible!"

Even a prickly human being like Russell had learned long ago in the halls of Parliament the advantage of standing perfectly still at certain moments.

This was one of the moments.

Lord Palmerston's pear-shaped bewhiskered face and small eyes betrayed little emotion as he scanned the rubbing again. He appeared the quintessential English administrator and might as well have been be a banker or a barrister as prime minister of England.

Finally he drew in one long breath and let it out with his words.

"Oh, blind me," he wheezed. He stared down at the water-marked and sealed agreement between the two powers on the planet giving him the most trouble. "Contact your nonofficial man. I will meet with him. And for St. George's sake, hurry!"

THE CRAIG POWDERWORKS

"This location was chosen because the James River drops several feet in an expanse of six miles or so, and we needed the power of the water to make our hydraulic turbines work. I had the same thing in Kansas for the bark mills at my father's tannery, to make the tanning solution after the hides were limed. . . . Anyway, that was in fifty-six, and these are updated some. Up on the Brandywine River in Delaware, the Du Pont Company replaced their waterwheels in the 1840s with turbines. They're smaller and take less water energy for the same amount of power. Right over there you can see the iron retorts where the crude sulfur is turned from liquid to gas, then recondensed into a purified form—"

"How do you get it to do that, Major?"

"Oh, we just cool it, ma'am. The sulfur distillery removes all traces of acid and distills out the impurities. And over there just down this road you can see where the workers skim impurities off the hot niter—you know, the saltpeter. It has to be boiled, which causes fractional crystallization and makes the soluble impurities precipitate to the bottom, which gives us potassium nitrate crystals, which we mill."

"Oh, my goodness, so much to remember and understand! You must be quite an engineer."

"Well, thanks, but truth is most of this was figured out for me by others who came before. Down the river there is the pulverizing house where we mix the sulfur with charcoal, which we make ourselves out of willow in some big sealed kilns—ah, nope, you can't see those from here—but you can smell 'em."

"Yes, I do smell many things on these grounds."

"Anyhow, we mill those two ingredients into a substance we call dust, and right down there along the James are the incorporating mills, you know, the roll mills, where it's all combined with the niter. Niter's the oxidizing agent. That's what makes it all incendiary. You know, makes it blow up."

"How on earth do you combine it?"

"Mighty carefully, ma'am, that's how!"

Wyatt chuckled and slowed his pace down even more, though he'd already slowed down about three times so Orienta could keep up. She couldn't walk far, dominated as she was by her condition, but she'd been so quiet lately that Grace had started to worry and finally asked—ordered—Wyatt to run the lady about the mill for a tour. The distraction seemed to be working, for all that Wyatt could read a woman—and he had never pretended that he could.

He knew he was babbling to avoid the obvious subjects—in fact, he counted on his babble talent. He glanced behind them to where Burlie was walking about ten paces back, hands politely folded behind him, and took the boy's tentative smile as covert support.

Had to give the boy credit. He was looking after his half brother's wife to a point of obsession. He wouldn't even leave her alone with Wyatt.

Wyatt turned forward again and kept talking.

"Uniform size is crucial when you're talking about making black powder," he said, holding Orienta's arm as they walked down the incline toward the rushing river. "Basically we pulverize everything down to a common consistency under five-ton iron rollers on iron plates built for us by Tredegar Ironworks downtown. The roll mills are in those blockhouses right at the riverside."

Orienta held her skirts and did her valiant best to walk on the incline, though the days were long gone when she could see in front of her. "Oh, yes, Tredegar, yes."

"In the daylight I'll take you through the press house and show you the wheelcake. We press the mixture into a cake to increase its density, then send it on down to the graining mills, where it's reduced to grains."

"Then you send it out to our brave men in the field?"

"Oh, no, ma'am, we have to sort it and glaze it—cannon shot and blasting powder are the coarser grains. Finer grains make rifle and pistol shot. Priming powder is the finest grain of all. Then we send it to the drying house, where it's dried with hot air from steam-driven furnaces sent over through duct work from another building, the steam-engine house. The formula's never exposed to flame that way."

"It's a dangerous business, isn't it, Major?" Orienta said with laudatory admiration in her voice.

"Sure is, sure is," Wyatt said. "Just internal friction from jostling can set this stuff off. We even transport it on slings, and we try to buy or make packing kegs that have no nails or metal hoops, just pegs and rope or wood hoops. Between each process we go ahead and roll the product down this narrow-gauge railroad you can see down there. Handcars. That's about all there is to the whole sh'bang."

"I'd heard," she began, breathless. "I mean, Grace has told me there is some problem with procuring the saltpeter. Are you still having that problem, Major?"

Wyatt sighed, still uncomfortable with what he could tell and what he couldn't, what was a military secret and what was just normal industrial setback. "Well . . . I . . . we . . . prefer Chilean saltpeter because it's the purest, but Britain has a monopoly on that, and, well, you know there's a little problem with Britain these days . . ." He waffled over that, knowing they were both thinking of Dorian, and caught her tolerant glance. "Anyhow, after they pretty much froze the niter shipments, I've been trying to get some out of limestone caves in Georgia and Virginia, and even a little from Tennessee, but it's turned into a da—a darn—a doggone problem just moving across the countryside, what with the armies moving all over the place these days. We lost a lot to raiders. Cave niter's crude and hard to get at, and it costs a sight more than English saltpeter, but we do our best."

"Oh, and you're so valiant even to try."

Feeling his face warm up, Wyatt shuffled before her and tried to shake off Burlie's sideward grins. "Thanks very much, but don't give all the credit to me, ma'am, will you?"

Orienta nodded, knowing she was embarrassing him. She drew to a halt beside the nearest mill and paused for breath. Burlie came up beside them and took one of her arms to keep her steady, and she glanced at him but offered no particular politenesses. "My," she gasped, "such a trial to simply walk. . . . I never thought I would appreciate simply walking, Major."

"Why don't I take you back before it gets dark and you trip or something?"

"Fine, thank you. Goodness, I'm so warm now . . . and it's getting dark, isn't it? I've kept you from hearth and home. Oh, all the way back . . . it's uphill, isn't it?"

Wyatt hadn't even noticed the incline in quite this way before, but now noticed it would be a haul for a woman all filled out like Orienta was. He gestured to Burlie. "Son, why don't you dash up and get the surrey for the lady so she won't have to walk. Bring it right down over the footbridge. It'll hold all right."

"Yes, sir, Major!" Burlie sprinted off across the mill grounds at full tilt—and for a big boy, he could sure haul leather.

For several moments they both watched in admiration as the boy ran, until he was out of sight.

"There's only one thing more I want to know," Orienta said.

Wyatt faced her again. "What's that, ma'am?"

"Why, after all we have been through, do you insist upon calling me ma'am?"

Wyatt stopped short and wondered how to wiggle out of this, but Orienta's gaze was so frank, so open and honest and adult, that he couldn't fight her.

After a moment he smiled honestly too. "Reckon the same reason you still call me 'Major,'" he admitted.

She smiled, and the whole evening lit up a little.

"I generally do not address gentlemen by their given names," she said. "Even my husband . . . my . . . *first* husband, I mean."

"I sure wish you'd make an exception," Wyatt said, "after all we've been through? Hm?"

Her little mouth tightened, and her cheeks went round in a conceding expression. "I shall make one exception . . . Wyatt."

Silently he took her hand and pressed it.

"She loves you, Major . . . Wyatt. I can tell," Orienta said.

Wyatt felt his expression fizzle. "Pardon me?"

"Grace," she went on. "There is great tension between you, I know . . . but this estrangement is normal for a new marriage, believe me. Her emotions regarding you are very strong."

"They . . . they *are*?" He shook himself mentally and puz-zled over this. "You'd never know it. . . ."

"But I'm a woman and I can tell. Don't you give up hope."

She slipped her hand into the crook of his arm and some-how encouraged him to start walking. Slowly they strolled in the general direction that Burlie would come with the carriage.

"You're a good man, Wyatt," she said genuinely. "Your probity is enviable, and you want the best for people. That will show to her in due time. I'm sure she sees it already, in her hidden way."

Self-consciously Wyatt felt the tug of regret and doubt. "I'd sure like to think so. . . . I didn't mean to box her into a mar-riage that wasn't right—I'm sorry. I shouldn't even be talking about it."

"Nonsense," Orienta said softly. "You and I must talk to each other, because we no longer have Dorian . . . and we both need him."

Bowled over by her generosity, thinking of how he needed Dorian too in this time when she obviously needed Dorian more, Wyatt couldn't think of anything to say.

"Oh—" Orienta stopped suddenly.

He caught her arm firmly as she wobbled. "You all right? Did you turn your foot or—or anything?"

She blinked past his shoulder. "Was that a light in that building?"

He turned. "Which building?"

"That one, over there."

"The long one with the big doors? The pack house?"

"Yes. I thought I saw a light inside. Although it might have been a star reflecting in the window. . . ."

Squinting, Wyatt pondered, "Shouldn't be anybody in there—except maybe a guard."

"You don't run a shift at night? I know they do that in some factories nowadays."

"No ma'am—I mean, Orienta. We can't allow any lanterns in a powdermill. All natural light. Can't run a night shift." He continued staring at the pack house.

"Oh," she said. "Of course. I should have thought."

He shook off the eerie sensation and noticed that Burlie was driving the surrey toward them, coaxing the nervous pony to clop over the footbridge.

"Here you go," Wyatt said as the boy drew the reins and brought the surrey to a stop before them. "Thanks, son. You see her safely back to Governor Street, all right?"

"I'll do it, Major," was all Burlie said, and helped pull Orienta up while Wyatt boosted her judiciously from underneath. She made an awkward load, but somehow a precious one.

She settled into the seat, and between the three of them they got a blanket tucked into all the right places. "Wyatt," she said, "you have been so kind, and it was so very interesting to see your powdermill. I would certainly like to see it all in the daylight sometime, if a visit would not disturb your valiant efforts to defend Richmond."

He chuckled and blushed again. "Well, that's kind of you, but I'm not defending Richmond. I'm just supplying what powder I have the ingredients for. Better you keep your praise for those men out there putting their lives on the line to face the high odds. Get going now, and I'll have a look around the pack house, just to be sure—"

"That I was imagining things," she finished. Then she smiled. "He would be so proud of you. . . . Good night, Wyatt."

With a regretful nod Wyatt waved good-bye and was relieved when the surrey pulled away.

Strange . . . they either didn't talk about Dorian, or they talked about him as though he were dead.

Neither felt very good.

He shivered and wished he'd brought his jacket with him when Orienta arrived for their appointment. He'd been over at the composition house listening to the workers tossing ideas about gathering earth from stables and pig sties for niter to solve some of their troubles, and that's where his jacket was. The sun had been out then, and now it was dark and the night was chilly.

Knotting his fists against a breeze shooting off the river, he tucked his hands under his arms and made a note it was time to hand this shirt over to the house slaves to be washed. Wyatt wasn't one to fuss over clothing, but often grabbed the same duds from the day before, until Grace or one of the house women caught him and pointed out a few facts.

The pack house loomed before him, a split-level structure

built for function rather than style. Inside was the hope of Richmond—keg after keg of black powder in a variety of grains, all tested and marked for shipment to divisions of General Lee's army and anybody else who was authorized to get it. Order after order filed through here every day, in anticipation of a hundred skirmishes, some which ignited, and some which never occurred.

Where was the guard? Since they'd discovered sabotage, Wyatt had ordered guards posted at each building through the night, but this wasn't a military establishment at heart and rules were hard to cast in iron.

But as he cracked open the loading-dock door and stomped down the ramp to the storage area, Wyatt found himself utterly alone with a few hundred kegs of hope-and-pray. The pack house was a large, sprawling building with levels like stair steps down the incline of the river area, serviced by the narrow-gauge railroad running around the grounds, and at night, alone, it was like being inside a giant slumbering animal.

"Hello? Anybody in here?" he called. A shiver made him feel embarrassed. To himself he grumbled, "Just like Halloween, is all. Don't be silly."

He glanced around in the moonlight from the high, narrow windows, which provided only faint light, surveyed as best he could the stacked twenty-pound kegs of priming powder, light enough to be brought to the top level. Then he stepped down to the next level, crowded with kegs of rifle powder and handgun powder. He gazed down across two other levels, where the coarse cannon powder and then the heavy blasting powder were kegged in big barrels and stacked for shipping.

Nobody. Nothing. Dead silence.

Then he realized why it was dead.

"My God!"

He dashed down to the light-arms level and knelt beside the collapsed body of the man he'd put on guard tonight. It was Ogelthorpe.

"Ohhh, God, oh, no," Wyatt choked as he turned the man over.

Already stiffening.

He began touching the body to see if there was a head wound from a fall or what.

And he discovered blood. Murder. Murder, *here*.

The wound was ghastly and wide, a puncture in the man's chest cavity, slowly oozing shiny dark clots. There was no powder or sulfur smell, so it wasn't a gunshot—besides, the shot would have been heard.

A shudder rattled him. The mere thought of a gun on the grounds—no flintlock or percussion weapons were allowed, not even for the guards. That's why his target practice had been such a good side show. A firearm in a powder yard was suicide. . . . Poor Ogelthorpe . . .

Wildly Wyatt thought of who would be around to call to for help, and remembered that he and Orienta had strode past almost all the workers as the men walked back to their families at the company town up the grounds. He remembered saying good evening to them, one by one, until he was just about hoarse—

"Henry? That you?" He started, sure he'd heard a noise.

He was breathing heavily from sheer nerves as his hands began to feel cold on the corpse of his worker, and he realized that he could be alone in here with someone other than the corpse. Desperation made his arms and legs shake as he slowly rose. What was the best way out?

And how much damage could be done while he was off gathering help? What was here that he could fight with?

Arms out and tense, he started slowly toward the loading ramp . . . one step at a time . . . moving sideways, his head swiveling toward every breath of wind, every creak of the wooden floor, feeling his way like a cat.

He felt the edge of the loading ramp beneath his foot, felt the fresh night air—

A force struck him and sent him tumbling back across the floor. Turning over quickly, he found his balance and looked up into the open loading bay at the form of a thin man, half crouched in attack form. In one hand the man held a length of heavy-duty chain. In the other he held what appeared to be an ordinary sawtoothed brass poker from a household fireplace.

Wyatt recognized what he saw—and who he saw.

"Clyman?" he blurted. "Is that you?"

"It's me, boss. I wanted you to know it was me. Tell me what you like about it," the man said, "then I'll tell you what I like. And I'll tell you why I'm gonna kill your straitlaced ass."

The heat left Wyatt's body in one quick rush as he got to

his feet on thready legs. He held both hands out prohibitively. "Oh, now, come on—this is crazy. . . . Think what you're doing, will you? What *are* you doing, anyway?"

"I been thinking about her all day."

"What? Who? Oh, Lord, put the chain down, now. . . . One spark and we're dead—you—you understand that, don't you?"

Frantic, Wyatt gasped with frustration at being stuck in here with this yokel who obviously carried a demented grudge nobody had noticed before. There hadn't been a hint before tonight, and men in a powder yard are sensitive to hints. No one in a powder yard would work with an idiot or a joker or a man on any kind of mental edge—the risk was just too high. A lowlife belligerent who rarely talked to anyone and a coward who never volunteered for anything, even the safest of tasks, Clyman was a loner, and other than that sometimes spooky look in his eyes, he hadn't shown any signs of what Wyatt was seeing in the filtered moonlight tonight.

The fireplace poker caught a glint of moonlight, as though to snap him to reality by showing its four blunt teeth. Clyman held it not high like a javelin, but low like a blackjack.

Without warning Clyman thundered down the ramp toward Wyatt, howling like a dog, swinging the chain above his head. Only a quick drop to both knees on the rough wood floor saved Wyatt from having his head crushed by the chain, and as Clyman stumbled against a stack of kegs and the chain crashed against them, all Wyatt could see in his mind was a hail of sparks.

He covered his head, but no explosion came—miraculously. He scratched to his feet, unable to know if the sparks had been real or in his fears. If he didn't get that chain away from this maniac, the sparks would come—there would be no tilting the odds of that. Then the Craig powdermill would join a long list of powder-factory explosions throughout history. Mills went up all the time—now Wyatt had that fear chewing at him on top of fighting hand to hand with this insane scarecrow!

"Clyman, what are you doing?" he demanded. "Put that down. Think, now! You're gonna hurt somebody!"

"I'm gonna hurt you," Clyman said, and came at him again, lashing the chain. Pure loathing was undisguised in his voice and the set of his body.

"Why—why don't you tell me what you want?" Wyatt attempted, ducking a swipe of that chain. "Tell me who you're working for! Maybe we can come to some kind of—of—"

But Clyman dodged at him, striking out with both weapons.

Staggering backward, Wyatt tripped on the step up to the priming-powder level, and went down on his hips as Clyman rushed at him.

The next few seconds fell away slowly, nightmarishly. Wyatt, preoccupied with that chain and the threat of sparks, let his chemist's mind betray him. The chain was made of iron—it would spark to release energy of a sudden stop. He stumbled backward, got up on one knee, and reached for the chain. He caught it in mid-air, felt the flying end coil around his arm and thought about the pain as a kind of triumph—

And forgot all about the brass poker.

Brass was less conductive than iron, brass had a lower melting point, would leave a strike rather than make a spark. He was so busy thinking of iron as dangerous and brass as benign that he forgot to defend against the poker.

Until it rammed into him and punctured deep into his body.

The impact drove his breath out in a single concussive heave. At first he thought he'd been punched by a hard fist. The force of the short-arm blow transmitted down Clyman's shoulder, through his arm into Wyatt, and forced him right off the floor for an instant. Only when his knees cracked again to the wood and he couldn't straighten to fight back did Wyatt finally understand that he hadn't interrupted a saboteur . . . but that he was the target of an assassin. Something in the force of the blow communicated that very clearly.

Clyman whispered vulgarities at him as they sank together. The man's hard-featured face was goatish, satisfied in a way that was sinister, bizarre, even sensual, showing a demented pleasure in what he had done.

There was no punch quite like a hard blunt blow to the stomach, and this was not only punch, but puncture. The poker drove into Wyatt's body like the tusk of a charging elephant. It not only slammed the air out of his body, but continued through his shirt, his flesh, and sank in. He was denied even the mercy of a blade edge. It didn't cut in; it smashed itself a path.

He'd been punched before. He'd even been shot. This was different.

Dust and bits of black powder from the floor flew into his open mouth and eyes as he lay against Clyman. The attacker was laughing, holding the middle of the poker as though he meant to pull it out himself.

"All mine now," he said to his victim. "See y'later, boss."·

He let go of the poker and kicked Wyatt off like a grain bag.

Through astonishment and past short-winded panting and the pounding of his heartbeat in his ears, Wyatt assimilated the noise of Clyman's boots tramping up the loading ramp, then down the other side.

Horror swept through him at the prospect of being alone. Even the company of his assassin was better than to lie here, curled up, with the cold running up the brass poker and into his body.

"Oh, my God," he puffed, each breath a misfire.

Against every shred of common sense, he suddenly had to get the thing out of him. There was a foreign thing in him, and he had to get it out. He knew in his mind not to remove an embedded projectile . . . the thing might be inhibiting bleeding . . . but he had to get it out. It was in him, and he wanted it out.

He felt for the cool brass with both hands. Just gripping it made him choke and double up. Convulsions racked him and left him suffocating, lying on his side, swept with visions of walking.

"Do it . . . do it," he gasped, "One . . . two . . . okay, one . . . one . . ."

Gathering all the will he possessed, he put it into a single yank—and felt his insides rip. Agony sent his senses flying and his body constricting.

Blood ran down his arm. Lights flashed blue and yellow behind his eyes as they clamped shut. Air rolled up and down his gaping throat. Delirium claimed him—and he had no idea how long he lay there shaking.

Was it out? Was he bleeding to death now? He might bleed to death and not even realize he was going.

Wheezing and spent, he forced himself to roll over, astounded at what happened to him—and at the phenomenal pain. Even a bullet hadn't felt like this. The effort squeezed blood out the wound in such a gush that he thought his innards were pouring out—but he heard the poker clank to the wood floor. His small triumph was soon swallowed in the narcotic of pure pain screaming through his mind and body.

He lay still, on his side, completely inhibited for what seemed half the night. It might only have been a few minutes, or seconds, but as he forced himself to think again, he imagined that the moonlight had moved along the floor. How long had he been here? How much blood was pumping out through his fingers onto the floor?

"Good—" he panted. "Least I found . . . who was . . . salting the niter . . . right? Right, right . . . get up. God, I'm dead tired—no . . . nope, don't say dead. No dead talk—"

Sharp pain cut off his air again and sent him gasping. The sound of it was awful in the warehouse, each pant a bitter trumpet that he was in some deep, ugly trouble.

There was a desert of wooden planks between him and the outside. He'd walked that twenty feet a thousand times, but never handcuffed, hog-tied, and dragging iron.

"Don't bleed to death," he told himself. Suddenly he let out an enfeebled laugh. "That'd be stupid—bushwacked in a warehouse . . . middle of a war . . . Dorian'll never—let me—hear the end of it. . . . Christ, that's *all* I need . . ."

Each breath was a punishing blow all over again. He felt sedated, but scared, like trying futilely to swim in mud. Pressing his hand against the hot wet hole in his gut, he reached out with the other hand, brought one knee up to his side, and began the travail that would bring him to the loading ramp. He had to get out of here if there was any chance of being discovered before morning. He'd never be found if he didn't get to the top of that ramp.

The back of his mind was clogged with awareness that Clyman had the run of the yard. What would a desperate man do?

Wyatt saw once again the burning of his tannery in Kansas and felt again the helplessness of watching it go. He could already feel the powdermill blowing up around him, taking half the countryside with it and rattling Richmond with the concussion.

He had to get to that ramp.

Somehow he kept crawling, smearing the blood that had already spilled on the wood beneath him. He forced his legs to come up beneath him and pulled himself up on a stack of kegs. Getting to his feet was a victory that almost made him shout, but he collapsed forward over the kegs and did everything he could to hold on and not go down again. He pressed his hand tighter to the wound and weighed his need to survive against his need to rest. Right now they seemed about equal.

Moaning to keep aware that he was still alive, he lurched along the stacks from one to the next, trying not to think about how far he had to go. He was straitjacketed by increasing pain and could barely think. Just as well. And he was cold, trembling.

"Middle of summer," he groaned. "Can't freeze to death . . . be stupider than bleeding to death . . . think what people'd say—come here, door, will you? . . . aw, God . . ."

The ramp! There it was. The bottom inside half of the ramp.

Might as well have been the Blue Ridge foothills.

He stepped toward it—and took down a stack of kegs as he toppled and struck the floor on his side. The twenty-pound kegs of priming powder rolled around him like beans. He imagined their clatter, but never heard it in the midst of convulsions. When those played themselves out, he lay there ravaged, concentrating only on getting air.

Something was pressing into his cheek. Something hard and cold. The chain!

So it was the chain. So what?

At least it was something. An ingredient.

Wyatt put all his energy into a single heave that put him up on one elbow. "Think," he grunted, "think, think like an engineer—"

He managed to tuck the chain's end into his belt. With his head hanging, he gulped for air and gathered enough strength to toe one of the kegs over to a position between his feet. If he could just roll it up the inside ramp, and down the outside ramp—out onto the grounds . . . maybe he could ignite the one little keg and get somebody back down to the yard from the powdertown to keep him from dying here, like this. If he could just roll it up, and out—

With a sharp kick he sent the keg rolling awkwardly up the inside ramp. At the peak where the inside and outside ramps met, the barrel lost momentum. It rolled back to him and struck his feet.

"No, you gotto go *over*. Come on. Try again, huh?"

He placed his foot against the little keg, aimed as carefully as he could manage, and gave another heave.

The effort drained him. His mind turned black, lights went out before his eyes, and he fell over forward on the chain, robbed of any sensibility but the pain.

Consciousness swam back only slowly. When he could look up, he blinked—but he couldn't see the little keg. Was it outside?

On his hands and knees, with no idea how he'd gotten that way, he crawled up the inside ramp, inch by inch. Drops of blood fell onto the planks. It was the hardest uphill climb of his life.

When he got to a point where he could see over the top of the ramp, a thin ring of hope caught him. The little keg had rolled down the outer ramp, out onto the riverbank, and was lying there in a wagon rut.

Was it far enough away from the storehouse? If he ignited it somehow, it would surely signal for help, but would the vibration cause the powder in here to explode too? The storehouse would go up like a second hell. He tried to be an engineer for one minute longer and find the ratio of distance to explosive force of a ten-pound keg. For a moment he almost gave up. Better to die in here than to take the whole mill with him, just for one chance to live. How would all the workers find other jobs? What would happen to their families?

And Clyman—Clyman was still running free out there! He could do irreparable damage, kill somebody else as he'd killed Oglethorpe, as he'd killed—

"Me," Wyatt gasped.

He had to ignite that little keg. He had to hit it, just hit it, just cause enough vibration or enough spark . . .

He searched for the chain. It was still stuck in his belt. He gathered it up with his free hand, found the end of it, and somehow willed up the strength to hurl it up over his head. It spun once, and he let it go.

Whistling through the air wildly, the chain almost missed the keg—but didn't.

One end struck the wooden keg and the other flipped over.

The chain doubled up on itself, and true to every safety lecture Wyatt had ever given to his workers, it sparked.

The keg went up like the Fourth of July, making a kettle-drum bellow in the night.

On the pack-house ramp, Wyatt broke down. He lay choking, bleeding and played out, and waited to be blown sky-high.

CHAPTER FORTY-SEVEN

─────── ★ ───────

Splinters blew as though before a wind. The entire corridor rattled with successive crashes. The door was old and venerable and British, but couldn't hold against the blows of a determined boot.

Up and down the fifth floor of the old boardinghouse, other doors came open and residents dodged out to see what the racket was.

They found themselves facing the end of the hall and a black tunnel in the shape of a pistol barrel.

Behind the revolver, a man in black clothing was draped with an iron-gray cloak and took the shadows too well. His hat's brim cast a black blade across his face. They could see only one evil eye and the set of his mouth.

"Back," the enigmatic stranger said. His tone was undisguised, unmistakable. The revolver in his hand was so level and still that it disappeared in the wallpaper behind him.

A gun, though, has a way of telegraphing its presence, and the man holding it possessed a demonic steadiness, thus a demon's right to be here. He either didn't think he was doing anything wrong or didn't care. If he wasn't doing anything wrong, then they shouldn't interrupt him. If he *was* doing something wrong—he would clearly kill them to cover it.

They were in the eye of a storm. Better to huddle and wait for it to blow over.

One by one the residents slipped back into their own rooms. Up and down the corridor, all doors clicked shut.

Without lowering the revolver beyond waist level, Dorian turned his attention to the shattered doorway before him and stepped in through the destroyed frame.

Felix Carter's rented rooms. A studio and a sleeping area. Spartan, but functional. Obviously Carter's purpose in England required neither comfort nor permanence.

Had required. Dorian suppressed a shudder. The Thames was unforgiving to a struggling drunken man with a few bad blows to the head. The ruthlessness of this disposal surprised even Dorian, and more than once since his talk with the Cousin, he had scoured his brain to be sure he was remembering Carter right, or at all. A man had been disposed of on a maybe from him, and he wanted to know if his maybe was on the mark . . . or even in the ring.

Quickly and efficiently he began rifling the pockets of three suits in the closet, but turned up nothing. In the dresser, however, a little too available, in fact, was a leather case full of papers and a journal. Dorian flipped through the journal and encountered carefully noted dates and times of conversations—

With Barry Swanborough!

Carter had been using the journal to protect himself from Swanborough while also working with him. Foresight had done the man no good, though.

Dorian was chortling inwardly over the irony of it all when he pulled something from the case that backed his pleasure up in his throat. A paper, wind tattered and sun scorched. Clipped to it was a letter.

He held the paper in one hand and the letter in the other, and the key words of both washed over him along with a hideous chill.

*WANTED . . . SLAVE . . . HALF-BREED . . . REWARD . . .
The time has come to exercise our option regarding the
Chameleon . . . accuse the House of Lords . . .*

Dorian caught both hands on the edge of the dresser, crushing the papers, and fought to keep his supper down.

If Swanborough knew, then . . .

The toppling house of cards made an almost audible crackle in his head. Swanborough would delight in this, would use it against Dorian, against Aleck Stephens and the reconstructionist cause.

If Swanborough knew, then Orienta knew. And Wyatt—
back on the burning tightrope—

Pain and shock and all devotion's dizzy angers and hungers
and shrieks and stark staring panic blew through him all at
once as though he were the door being knocked in. Robert
Burns had made him realize he had gone from being the slave
of a landowner to being a slave of slavery. The world's biggest
tortoise, letting his shell weigh him down.

Now this! The moment he stepped back on American soil,
he would be met by a noose. His pulse pounded in his ears as
he felt his wife hanging him in effigy, felt his throat close up
until he couldn't choke the last proclamation of tainted but
honest love. He could never go back now, never. The law
would hang him, the South would disembowel the corpse,
Wyatt had disenfranchised him, Orienta was writing his name
only to scratch it out—they would all curse him to the dirt if
they could.

He could go to Europe. Disappear there. He could hide in
Athens, behind his fluent Greek, take a new name and never,
never contact anyone he knew again. Protect those he loved
from the poison—by hiding the poison—it was what he *should*
do—yet he felt America pulling on him, calling to him. . . .

Even footsteps in the hall failed to cut as deeply as the call,
or to ring as loud as the thunder of its ramifications.

Footsteps! Scotland Yard! Constables and detectives coming to seal off and search the murdered man's rooms—they
would find Dorian here and find the papers. They would add
two and two and come up with espionage. Word would get
back to Lord Russell that his unofficial Confederate emissary
was involved in murder and conspiracy, and all communication would crack like bad glass.

A dozen frantic possibilities flashed through his mind all at
once—the window, the back stairs, a fight in the hallway, a
fabricated excuse for being here—he'd come looking for
Carter and discovered the door broken in, he'd known the man
personally, been practically a brother, was devastated at the
condition of the rooms, did the Constables have any information—no time for that! He could surprise them, knock them

off, dash away before they saw his face clearly in the dimness. If he was caught here, the poison would spill.

He shoved both papers into a pocket and put one hand on the revolver and one upon his watch chain—

"Dorian!"

He froze in place. *That* certainly wasn't Scotland Yard!

In the dim hallway lamplight, stepping awkwardly through the shattered doorway, came the Du Pont.

"Look at all this—I knew I would find you here. Damn you! In spite of my warnings. You're exasperating as all hell, you know it? Scotland Yard is two minutes behind me, man! Do you want to be found here?"

"I want to be found on a fast boat," Dorian grumbled. He shed his fight-or-lie stance and forced cold fingers to release the gun and the watch. "Pray leave me alone."

The Cousin grabbed him by the wrist. "You and I have an appointment. Palmerston's offered to give you audience! Let's not miss him by being tossed in the Tower, eh?"

But Dorian shook off the grasp with such slow, icy elegance that the Cousin stepped back and stared.

The American enigma now turned to face his conspiratorial countryman, still as bronze, and suddenly looked very much a man fighting to survive in a world he didn't respect, a gardener regretting his neglected orchard, or an architect his roofless house.

"I'm not going to the Tower," he said. "I'm not going to Parliament. You're taking me to the London Docks." He scooped his hat from a dead man's bed and topped it on. "I'm going back to America."

AUGUST 1862
OFFICE OF LORD PALMERSTON, PRIME MINISTER OF BRITAIN

"It may be inferred that the Confederacy, unlike the Union, holds that the nations of Central and South America have the right to self-determination. That is, any fledgling government should not feel the grip of the American presence. The

Confederacy would, therefore, suspend the Monroe Doctrine in regard to foreign influence in the Western Hemisphere. You may also infer that, if all the mirrors are on the wall straight, the Confederacy can do that only if it is secure as a nation. It can become secure, gentlemen, only with foreign support."

Dorian finished his statement with a visible flare of his eyes and a vocal annotation that he had said "foreign" on purpose, and not "British." His message was clear, if he read the other three men in the room properly. They knew what he meant. The Confederacy would go to France for help if Britain did not commit that help, and soon.

He was playing no games. His voice was curiously without inflection. He wanted only to finish and get out of here, and out of England.

The faked document had done its job. Why else would he be sitting here, with the Cousin on one side and Lord Russell on the other, before the cherry blockhouse desk of the prime minister?

The Cousin was tense, but buoyed by relief that Dorian had finally agreed to come here instead of the docks. The price had been the Cousin's assurance that the fastest ship whose captain was willing to run the Union blockade would be at Dorian's call within an hour. Not a short order, to find such a ship and captain quickly.

Behind the big desk Lord Palmerston moved his bulk but barely. Yet his sluggish appearance, they all knew, hid great intelligence and a vault of experience. His voice was somewhat gravelly as he spoke.

"We might also infer," the big old man offered, "that recognition would be an easier pill to swallow if General Lee's army were within reach of Washington. Should that occur . . . I cannot imagine recognition being reasonably denied."

Somehow the Du Pont Cousin avoided leaping with joy, though Dorian did notice a particular sudden apprehension in his mysterious associate.

Dorian waited a few beats to be sure there would be no outcries or reactions to skid across the moment. He worked consciously to hold back his own expression. Ordinarily this was no difficulty for Dorian, but burns heal slowly, and his arm was still on fire. Summoning his deepest levels of self-control, he kept the pain out of his face.

"Your Lordship," he began, "am I to understand that you wish to see tangible evidence of the Confederacy's . . . resolve?"

"You must give us a victory," Palmerston said bluntly. "We cannot politically justify recognition without at least one major Confederate win."

Pausing, Dorian determined not to underestimate Palmerston again. The prime minister was much more direct than Dorian had expected. Sitting here in the presence of a man who had been around to witness the American Revolution, Dorian suddenly felt a little younger than he had ever felt before.

"My lord," he said cautiously, "the Confederacy has been invaded on a thousand fronts by superior forces, with a superior industrial and financial base, and has not fallen. That in itself is a victory."

"Granted," the imposing man said. "However, Lord Russell and I have the onus of political justification, and we are not asking for delivery of the moon to St. Paul's. Show us one victory, a strong victory, and we will get the votes in the House of Lords to recognize the Confederacy. Shortly thereafter we shall initiate something at sea, blame the Union, and legally break the blockade. Beyond that, if you claim any of this publicly, of course, I shall be forced to deny ever having heard of you."

Smiling, Dorian got back a little of his upper hand when he responded, "Nor I you, m'lord."

For the first time Lord Palmerston's saturnine face broke into a series of eyebrow bobs and something resembling a grin. The Cousin and Lord Russell also couldn't avoid some reaction, even if only to light a pipe or clear a throat.

With all things said that could today be said, Lord Russell stood up, still clearing his throat, and this signaled that the meeting was over and the matter shifting hands. Shifting—to Dorian.

As he stood, the Cousin and Dorian stood also and faced him.

The moment was uncomfortable, but charged with excitement and possibility, and four men calculating in their heads how many days needed for a fast ship to get from London to Richmond against the flow of the Gulf Stream.

"Go home, Mr. Parthens," Lord Russell said. "Go home and tell General Lee to invade the North."

★

———— ★ ————

PART NINE

MARCHING ORDERS

CHAPTER FORTY-EIGHT

8 September 1862

Alexander Stephens shivered his way into his private office in the Confederate White House, wishing he were home in Georgia, thinking about England, worrying about Richmond, and nursing an aching toe.

The lantern had been turned down to its dimmest. For a moment he simply glowered at it and wondered why the servants would turn it down so far, until only the desk was illuminated and the rest of the room was in a dark haze. Chilly, tired, and wishing he could be one of those men who can sweat on a warm summer night, Stephens bothered to cross the room and turn up the lantern's wick.

A bulbous light opened up slowly, spreading across the shadow, struggling to handle the entire room by itself.

Suddenly he jumped back, for the shadow before him had eyes.

"Oh! My God—you're back! My poor heart snapped like a stick!"

Dorian did not leave his shadow. Neither did he remove his Inverness. His opera hat hung from one finger.

"Very sorry," he said. "Aleck . . . we've done it."

"I'll inform General Lee at once! Invade! And he's not a man to dally, I can tell you that. What next, what next—I must announce to Toombs, Benjamin, those pigheaded cotton men . . .

569

I'll tell them that if they want to get in on this, they'll have to mount up against Davis! Davis will be in a complete bind! All the power brokers will know where the credit belongs. Davis will be impotent, and the power men will have no choice but to back me up. And the price?—when we win the war we re-unite with the Union under my conditions—Dorian, Dorian! This is prodigious! We've got it! We've done it! I can confront Davis that we've achieved what he could not! The ball will roll! We'll reunite with the North, but we will be the authority from now on. I've succeeded where they've failed! You and I, together—we'll sculpt a new future for the nation! This is wonderful! Why, Lee can undermine McClellan with both hands in his pockets and his sword in his tent!"

He paced the room, seeing history fly before his vision, without the slightest sense of toploftiness or self-congratula-tion in his voice, then swirled around as though he'd suddenly reminded himself of something. He waved a hand.

"Oh, you really should have seen it, my friend! They had us beaten! McClellan had half the North on our borders, close enough to sniff their cigars!" He turned away, then whirled back again in a dither, his mind clicking and whirring with possibilities. "Lee executed a few brilliant maneuvers, some theatrics, and the morale of the Union withered! That enor-mous armada *backed up*! The sea of tents collapsed like bub-bles, and back, back, back they went! Oh, *oh,* and now this! The United States will recoagulate and no longer be the tagtail of the world, satellite to Europe, but the new power!"

He slumped forward, clinging to a chair, gasping and shak-ing his head. Exhausted, he drew a few deep, trembling breaths, and during this pause he found the anchor of the mo-ment's significance.

As humility sank back into his marrow, Stephens turned to face that important shadow and the toreadorlike eyes peering from it. He spread his hands, as though words were failing him.

"Never in my life," he said, "have I witnessed such a fitting coda to a scheme. This changes the tenor of nothing less than the imminent century. The entire world, and all of history, shall recognize what you have done, my friend . . . what you have *done*. Thank *God* for you, Dorian!"

His laudatory tone was stirring, and there was even an emotional sob carried upon it, but it fell today upon too cool a surface.

Dorian remained uncelebratory, seemed even ashamed by the excess of Stephen's exaltation. He seemed particularly quiet tonight. If there was a blush, it was muted by the struggling lantern light.

Abruptly he put his hat on, drew the collar of his Inverness tight at his throat, and offered no gestures at all.

"No one will know," he said, "Take the credit for yourself, and welcome to it. Farewell, Aleck. Safe journey."

He was nearly at the door when the Vice President's voice, now soft, called to him.

"Dorian," Stephens began. "Wait . . . please."

His tone changed from the congratulatory to the personal. He came humbly forward, swathed in his four scarves and shawls.

"I know this has caused strain between you and your friend Craig. His responses to my letters are polite and kind, but he is uneasy and solemn when mentioning you . . . I never wanted this for either of you. I hope you can mend the rift. If I can assist in any way . . ."

His offer petered out. Neither of them knew what could possibly come on the end of that sentence.

Dorian hesitated.

"I won the war for Wyatt," he said, "That is all I can do. If he hates me, then he hates me."

"I don't think he has that in him." Aleck said.

There was a pause.

"No, I don't think so either," Dorian admitted. "But he is better off without me. I'm going to get my wife and go to Europe, and never be heard from again."

"Do you need anything?" Anything at all?"

"Not here, or now. After the war I will need a legion of detectives to work on my behalf. I shall have scattered family to find."

Aleck Stephens nodded compassionately and said, "Stay in touch with me."

The luciferous eyes, painted in their shadows, were devoid of their usual glare as they swept over and took on a chagrin Stephens had never seen before, even a solemnity, if Dorian Parthens was capable of that—and evidently he was. Stephens sensed Dorian had been knocked off a peg in England and had come home feeling more human than usual.

They communicated silently for many seconds, Dorian simply gazing with great pathos into the big childlike eyes of the Vice President. Between them all the world rolled.

"With my last whisper," he said.

CHAPTER FORTY-NINE

――――――― ★ ―――――――

11 SEPTEMBER 1862

"Ma'am? Sorry to disturb you at home. Are you Major Craig's wife?"

Grace opened the front door wider and gestured the Confederate soldier in. This was a corporal, and outside there were two enlisted men waiting on horseback.

The corporal pulled his kepi off by the brim. His course brownish hair came forward and made what looked like a second big brushy mustache to match the one under his nose. He was hot and smelly and had obviously been riding a long stretch. Even from here Grace could see that the horses were wet and foaming.

"Yes, I'm Mrs. Craig," Grace said. "Something I can do for you?"

"Ma'am, I'm Corporal Mike Steffers, courier for Colonel Chilton, adjutant to General Lee, delivering marching orders out to Major General D. H. Hill's Division of Major General Thomas J. Jackson's Corps—"

"Golly Moses," Grace groaned. "Keep all that in one head, do you?"

"Yes'm. I've been ordered to stop off at the powderworks and show these orders to Major Wyatt Craig of the Craig Artillery Supply, so as to deliver the right amount of powder to the right location to execute these orders . . ." He saw what he thought was total confusion on her face and gave up. "Well, anyhow, a man at the mill told me that the Major is sick and I should come on over here and show it to him, so as he could authorize the shipment and start delivering powder."

He pulled an envelope from his inside pocket and held it nervously, almost covetingly.

"Is it something special going on, Corporal?" Grace asked. "Have you seen these orders?"

"Oh, no, ma'am," his mustache said, "not allowed. Officers' eyes only. After the major sees them, I'm to take them directly to General Hill, then hightail it back to my own brigade. If you don't mind . . ."

He pointed at the stairway.

Grace held out her hand and took the envelope, knowing she was getting it only because most men didn't perceive a woman as a military element.

"I'll take it to the major at once," she said, and turned to the stairs.

"Ma'am—Mrs. Craig? I'm not supposed to *give* them to the Major. I'm just supposed to *show* them to the Major and keep them in my sight at all times. I believe I should accompany you on up there."

Grace hesitated. "If you like," she said in her best innocent Southern accent.

Something about a Southern accent delivered just right made a women sound severely lamebrained. She'd found it damned helpful at times like this.

The corporal seemed relieved and clunked along behind her up the stairs, his army riding boots making a heavy noise. Grace made sure to sway her skirts in front of his nose as he followed her up the stairs and down the narrow hall.

"I'll be just a few moments," she told him as she took hold of the doorknob.

The corporal held up a hand. "Ma'am—"

Grace swirled around and coyly asked, "Sergeant, you can't mean to enter a husband and wife's private bedroom. Can you?"

"Uh, well, it's Corporal, ma'am . . . and . . . I guess it'll do for me to just stand out here."

Grace smiled and waved the envelope between them. "I'll be out shortly, Colonel."

She slipped inside without opening the bedroom door any wider than necessary. She closed it completely until the mech-

anism clicked and she was sure the door wouldn't swing open
by mistake.

On the big bed her husband lay in the mercy of a morphine
sleep. She couldn't have awakened him with a cannon blast.
Nor did she intend to try.

With a foot up against the closed door, just in case that corporal got any more nervous, she opened the envelope and took
out the orders and read them.

*Headquarters, Army of Northern Virginia, Special Order
191, dated 9 September 1862 . . . to Major General D. J. Hill, by
command of General R. E. Lee . . . Jackson . . . Longstreet . . . Stuart . . . McLaws . . .*

The handwritten order went on to tersely describe in detail
what Stonewall Jackson was doing, what Longstreet and
McLaws and Walker and Anderson were doing and what each
was bound for, and why. Harper's Ferry, Loudoun Heights,
Maryland Heights, South Mountain, Hagerstown, Boonesboro.
The manner in which Lee's Army was segmented, the intentions for the coming movements—and which divisions were
isolated by which rivers—

And a timetable. A *timetable*!

"Awww," Grace murmured in gratitude. "Thank *you,*
Bobby Lee. I'll kiss your horse myself."

*Divide and conquer . . . three-pronged attack . . . on the su-
perior forces of McClellan's army . . . thus making best use of
a smaller contingent . . . element of surprise and confusion . . execute a thrust into Maryland—*

Grace leaned a shoulder against the door. "Maryland! Lord
hang me high," she whispered.

Signed, R. H. Chilton, Assis. Adj.-Gen.

"Slam and *damn*," she grumbled. "Three-pronged attack . . . damn, is that smart!"

The plan was nothing less than brilliant, typical of Robert
Lee's expert use of lesser forces, the fresh resilience and clev-
erness that had kept McClellan wallowing on his ass all these
weeks. The only thing 191 didn't say was how many men
there were in each division.

This was it. This was *it*!

She looked up as Wyatt groaned and swung his head from
one side to the other on the pillow, then settled back into his
groaning delirium. Jogged to action, she quickly rifled through

the papers on the dressing table which had been dropped off by Henry Brecker for Wyatt to look at when he was well enough. She found a confirmation of a power order to some Confederate corps or other—it didn't matter—and put the confirmation in the envelope instead of Order 191. After all, *something* had to be delivered by Corporal Steffers. By the time anybody figured out there was supposed to be something more important in the delivery—well, the whole war'd be over!

She tucked 191 into her apron pocket, composed her expression, and slipped back out the door.

"The major says your order should be delivered without much trouble," she told the soldier. "He'll get the numbers of troops from his sources at the capitol and deliver the right amount of gunpowder and cannon ammunition. I don't know how such wonderful things are done, but the major will take care of everything, Colonel."

"Corporal, if you please, ma'am. And thank you very much." He seemed very relieved at having the order envelope back in his own hand. He flipped his kepi back on, touched the brim, and nodded to her. "The major's services are duly appreciated. Afternoon, Mrs. Craig."

As he thumped down the stairs at an awkward trot, Grace leaned back and called, "Good afternoon, Colonel."

"You! Get over here, nigger! That's it, right over here. Get this wood piled up and out of the street so our soldiers can come through if they need to! What do you mean, standing around like a stump!"

"Ahz doin' it, miss, ahz cleanin' up, never you fear."

The quick black man rushed to where the white woman was pointing and began stacking remnants of wood that could only serve as kindling. The best wood had already been confiscated by one army or the other, collecting burnable fuel for their bivouacs.

The woman stood over him, glaring, her hands folded, and she began to hum, then to sing, rather badly, a folk song nobody in the vicinity had heard of.

"'His wig it was pouthered, and as gude as new, his waistcoat was white, his coat it was blue, he poot on a ring and a sword and cock'd hat, and wha could refuse a laird wi' a' that?' "

As the negro picked up the wood, after a moment he sang, too, much more quietly, but enjoying it more than she did.

" 'He took his gray mare and he rade cannily, an' rapp'd at the yetts of Clavers Ha' Lee', Gae tell Mistress Jean tae come speedily ben—she's wanted tae speak tae the Laird o' Cockpen! Mistress Jean she was makin' the elderflure wine, 'An what brings the laird at sic a like time—' "

"Scobell," Grace hissed when people in the street quit looking. "That's enough. I don't need ten verses to know it's you. Cripes, you needn't enjoy all this lurking about so much."

"Intrigue, Mrs. Craig," the black man drawled. "The juice of any war. What news have you for Mr. Pinkerton? You said in your note it was critical."

"I should say so. What the hell is that stupid Army of the Potomac doing? Encamping? Tell them for pity's sake to quit lighting so many camp fires. A blind man can count camp fires."

"Oh, I'll tell them," Scobell said.

Annoyed at being placated, Grace skewered him with a glower. "I've got something important. Get that Pinkerton to get that McClellan to start thinking about attacking."

"They are thinking about it, Mrs. Craig," Scobell kept his voice down. "They can't make an attack, because they don't know for certain where Lee's divisions are. Intelligence reports conflict. How many parts of the army are there? Four? Or five? Where is Stonewall Jackson? Is he trying to escape back into Virginia now? Is Longstreet at Boonsboro or not? Who are the Rebels at South Mountain? And who is the column around Harpers's Ferry and where are they going? How many divisions will meet us if we charge Turner's Gap? And what are the Reb numbers? We haven't a reliable clue. It's not as easy as you seem to think, Mrs. Craig."

"It's going to get easy if you do what I say!"

"Hush, ma'am, please," the skillful spy begged. "If you're caught, it's jail for you. If I'm caught, I'll be hanged and gutted by every law in the South."

"Those laws'll all change if you do exactly as I say." Grace insisted. "I don't want credit, I don't want anything, but today I'm putting victory inside McClellan's tent, since he never leaves it. But it's conditional."

"What's the condition?"

"That he moves, what else! If he fails to act on this, I'll be the one who kept this cursed war going, and I want a better legacy than that. You tell them. Understand? Do you understand?"

He continued stacking bits of wood and cast her an insulted sigh, but there was something in her tone that made him listen.

"Go ahead," he said.

She pulled a small stationery envelope from her button-covered silk bag and slipped it toward him behind her skirt. "Take it. Come on, take it, take it."

He did, and slipped it immediately into his shirt front, "What is it?"

"It's a receipt of orders. You make sure it gets couriered back to General Lee's adjutant, a man named Chilton."

"General *Lee*?"

"I said Lee, didn't I? It's a fake one. Supposed to be from Harvey Hill. If the general's adjutant doesn't get a receipt, they'll come checking with Harvey Hill to see if he got Order 191. Then they'll figure out that the Order was intercepted. So you *have* to deliver this back to Lee's headquarters. Then Lee won't be tipped off too soon to what we know."

"Really?" He looked up sidelong at her. "What do we know?"

"You got any troops around Frederick, Maryland?"

"The Twelfth Corps, I think, First or Second Division. I'm not certain. Why?"

"Because I was up there today," Grace said. "It was as far north as I could get before some of *your* smart-mouthed soldiers turned me back. I left something there. Tell Pinkerton to tell somebody to encamp along the snake-rail fence in the meadow just north of Frederick. Tell them they'll find a large envelope in the grass. It'll be worth three cigars to 'em."

THE NEXT MORNING—SEPTEMBER 12

"Oh, God . . . oh, somebody kill me."

"Don't talk crazy. Lie still and quit thrashing and maybe you'll live."

"Grace?"

"Yes, of course."

"Where . . . are we?"

"Governor Street."

"It . . . hurts something awful . . . can't breathe . . ."

"Don't wonder. Use yourself for a yuletide log, and what do you expect?"

"Am I burned? Was there . . . explosion?"

"No more than the one keg you set off. But you sure got pokered in the gut. Good thing we found you when we did. They'll never get all that blood out of that pack-house floor. Good thing the vibration didn't set off the whole stock."

"Will I . . . live?"

Grace looked at his pale cheeks and wondered how much revenge she could get out of making him afraid. With him stranded here in his bed, she could torture him with what she had done to his powder yard, and to the Confederacy.

Finally she decided against that and simply said, "Probably."

Wyatt tried to say something else, but sudden pain cut him off, and he rolled onto his side, knotted up, gasping and coughing, his knees drawing tight. The covers came with him and dumped over the side.

Other than keeping him from rolling off the bed, Grace waited for the spasm to pass, then mopped his sweating face with a dry cloth. He seemed innocent lying here like this. His face was like a boy's face.

"How long?" he managed.

"Long hell of a time," she told him. "You've been in a fever and chills. Thought we lost you a couple times. Orienta sat up with you most nights, and I sat up with you the others."

"She all right?"

"Asleep in the guest house. I think she likes it back there. Doesn't even want any slaves in the little house with her. She sits all by herself, talking to her baby and singing to it and telling it all about *him*," Grace said, then added, "as if she knows all about him."

Wyatt slipped partly onto his back again, his knees still tucked, and fought to assimilate everything. "Any word from him?"

"Not a twitter. He abandoned her. That's it."

"No . . . I don't believe that . . . I just don't believe it. He'll come . . . he'll come back—oh, my God—"

Grace pushed Wyatt's hand away from the wound in his stomach and checked to make sure he wasn't getting the bleeding to start again with all his effort.

"Quit talking," she said. "Then you'll be ahead."

"What's happening," he struggled, "in the war?"

Grace drew a deep breath. "Well, there's been orders for more powder every day, which Henry's been rationing out to the Rebels best he can, but there's been so much fighting all over the state that the railroads can barely move more than a mile at a time. Fighting all over the Rappahannock River, all kinds of big troop movements—hell, don't half of 'em know where the other half is anymore. Jeb Stuart's been assigned to run the whole Confederate Cavalry now. What else . . . oh, you missed a hallacious battle at Manassas Junction—"

"Another one?"

"Yeah, and they're calling it Second Manassas already, like every damn battle's got to have its own damn name."

"Bad? Who won?"

"Hard to say. I guess the Confederates did, because they're saying Richmond's relieved now. Nobody's calling it decisive, because the Union's still there, still strong. And the battle took a bad toll on Lee's numbers. Nine thousand casualties."

Trying to digest that number, Wyatt winced, "Oh, Jesus . . ."

"There were skirmishes and all kinds of nasty activity at Bristoe Run, Bull Run Bridge, the Junction, Buckland Bridge, Aquia Creek, Sulfur Springs, Gainesville—hell, I can't keep up. There seem to be nothing but conflicting reports all over the place. Scattered units, Jackson disappearing like a wraith with his whole division—" Suddenly she let out an ironic, bitter laugh. "That Union pomposity John Pope's been chasing Stonewall Jackson around as though it's a personal thing! But he can't find him. He keeps shuttling back and forth, looking. Using a whole army to go looking. Lee's been crossing the Potomac in fits and starts—there's been fighting everywhere . . . there's just blood everywhere. You're lucky you missed it."

"Lord," Wyatt whispered. "I should be out there with them."

"The way you shoot, you'd be dead already," Grace said. "There's just confusion, and you'd just contribute to it.

Frederick, Maryland's been occupied back and forth by both armies—they're all just washing back and forth like water in a wash tub. Fact is, nobody really knows what's going on in northern Virginia. Beats me blind where the Union gets its generals, really does, but I think they ought to let the wives take over or change catalogs or something. Halleck, Pope, Porter, McClellan—they showed what idiots they are at Manassas. I swear, if I was the wife of a Union man, I'd go into that big sprawling camp and roundhouse that Little Mac so hard, his back teeth would rattle."

"Are you," Wyatt grunted, "complaining? Their bad generals have been our . . . oh—"

A spasm struck him. He legs knotted and his arms trembled.

"Our blessing, yes, yes," Grace agreed, without enthusiasm. "That's all I hear anymore. 'Thank God for Union generals,' up and down every Southern street."

"I'd like—" He rolled onto his side again and lost his fight to a wave of delirium, clutching pain, and a struggle simply to breathe without stabbing himself in the belly every time he inhaled.

He had no clue how much time passed as he lay there, shuddering. His hair fell softly over his eyes and cut him off from the world. His thoughts were fogs, his words almost whispers. Pressed beneath his ribs, his arm trembled. A fireplace poker in the belly opened up a whole new plane of awareness—and revived an old pain that had almost healed, and memories he had almost managed to lay to rest.

"My God, I never felt anything like this," he moaned. "I had no idea . . . it hurt so much . . . to be stabbed. . . . Even getting shot wasn't this . . . *bad*. . . . Oh, Grace . . . I didn't know it would hurt like this. . . . Grace—"

"Yes?"

"I'm sorry."

She paused, looking at him, and sensing something that didn't involve armies.

Gathering all his strength of body and will, he met her eyes.

"I know this isn't what you wanted for yourself," he said weakly. "Reckon we don't get what we really want much, but I hoped . . . to give you . . . more."

Turning the cloth on his forehead over to the dry side, she flatly said, "You give me enough. Forget about it."

He managed to catch her cool hand and hold it against his chest. "When I think what Dorian and Orienta had between them . . . I wonder what's between us and why we're just polite to each other and no more."

"There's more," she said indignantly. "I do for you what a man's supposed to get from a wife, don't I?"

"I know, I know," he interrupted. "Not what I meant . . . please . . . things are clouding up for me. . . . I just want to be a better husband. . . . I want to be a better human being . . ."

His voice faltered again, and his mind flew into confusion. A hundred images of his wife Grace blew up before his knotted eyes—yet not the right ones. He knew so little about her, where she came from, whom she had loved, who had sat at her table, what she wanted in life—there was the confusion. She didn't seem to *want* anything. She was completely . . . *custodial,* just as she had said. Where would a woman get the kind of mouth Grace had? Certainly not from normal society, and she had alluded to a rough upbringing, but even now Wyatt realized he had failed to ask, and she had never confided in him, husband or not. Life was so short, could be cut off without a good-bye—he would give everything in his soul to have a few extra seconds with friends who'd died out of reach.

As he lay on his side, his face buried in the moist pillow, his body curled like a sick child's, his thoughts boiled to the top. Like a mill worker watching impurities leech out of niter in a vat, he began to skim them off.

"My powder is killing men, hundreds of men. . . . It's so blamed personal now . . . it's like I'm killing each of them with my own hand . . . and I know what that's like. I had a friend . . . got stabbed," he gasped. "He died in my hands. I tried to understand what he was going through. But I didn't. Not till now, not till I got stabbed myself. . . ."

"Well," Grace said uneasily, dabbing at his forehead, "forget about him. Dead's dead. Nothing you can do."

But Wyatt had slipped into empathy and let it become his anchor. It dragged him deeper down into the pool of painful memory, and he was too weak to stroke back up again. His eyes opened just a sliver, but they were looking into the past.

"Poor Patrick," he whispered. "God, it must've hurt—that

sword . . . stabbed right through the middle by his own leader just to get back at me. . . . All this time I haven't been able to forget his eyes—his voice when he begged me to shoot him—and I didn't want to. . . . I wanted to make him live with pain like this . . . worse than this . . . but, God, half his intestines were on my lap. . . . why Pat Ruhl, of all people? . . . Why'd it have to be him? . . . He begged me to shoot him, and I almost didn't do it. . . . I'll never forget the way . . . he lay there on me, begging, 'Shoot me' . . . 'Shoot me' . . . what could I do? Let him lie there, mutilated, till his guts finished spilling out on my shoes? God forgive me . . . I put my pistol to his heart, like I know where a man's heart is or something! Grace, I—I shot him. . . . I shot that sweet, innocent, kindhearted boy . . . swear I *felt* the bullet go down the barrel and into his chest. I took everything he had—I took his life. That was all he had, all any of us have . . . and I saw his eyes grateful for that! Grateful for what I did to him—oh, Grace . . . get down on your knees every day and thank God you don't know what it's like. . . . I might as well've been shooting my own . . . baby brother."

Misery twisted him, cut off his words, left him wracked, and brought the sensations of guilt and desperation surging back as though it had happened this morning. He lay insensible to anything but the pain in this stomach and the agony in his mind.

As such, he couldn't see Grace sitting beside the bed, her hands white as ice, her eyes wide as windows.

MECHANICSVILLE

Even for his mother, he wasn't going to lose Orienta. He wasn't going to be a slave anymore. Slavery had let him go, and finally he was going to let *it* go.

Where was she? Where was anyone? Why was the house empty?

With a familiarity that flushed back at him over the years, he plunged through two doors toward the back of the cottage.

Swanborough's slaves jumped and clutched at their children when Dorian invaded the kitchen. They panted, and one of the women nearly fainted but they digested quickly that it was Dorian and not the Union Army invading the house.

And he added the situation up instantly too. The children were hovering over bowls of watered broth. The shelves were bare. There was no smell of food lingering where before there always had been.

"Thank de Lawd!" the youngest of the women blurted, catching at her breast. "Mr. Dorian, thank Jesus it you and not them Yankee pigs in our house!"

"Daisy, the Yankees are nowhere near here anymore," he told her quickly. "Where's Miss Orienta? Where's Burlie— Buckie?"

"Oh, suh, you ain gonna bleeve it! He don sen'—"

"Daisy!" one of the older women shouted, and grabbed the young woman by the mouth from behind. "Shet up! It ain't yoh bidness!"

Daisy struggled and managed to free half of her mouth, out of which she spat, "He gotta know, he got—"

"Know what?" Dorian prodded, then roared, "Let her talk, damn you!"

The butler, wringing his hands at his concave chest, moved between the women and Dorian.

"What's gonna happen to us, sir?" he asked, his brown face dusky with fatigue and fear. "They be ten of us . . . two cooks, me, the butler, the footman, my granddaughter Daisy, Leola, and her four children over here. . . . The Yankees set us free, but we din have no place to go, so we come back. All we hear is talk about big battle comin', but Mr. Swanborough don't even talk to us anymore. He don't tell us nothin', don't give us enough food for these children, sir, he come and go and don't take care of us no more! Don't tell us what we s'pose to do, where we s'pose to go." The elder negro's brows drew to- gether, and he spoke with the force of frustrated anger. "We just need somebody to tell us what to do, dat's all! It ain't so much to ask, is it? For civilized folks?"

Already frustrated to the raw bones by nearly two days of trying to get through a maze of border guards, checkpoints, erupting skirmishes, and sniper's nests just to get from Richmond to Mechanicsville, Dorian controlled himself only with great effort. He dropped a hand on the negro's shoulder, but it was almost a claw.

"Calvin," he said, "there isn't enough food for anyone. I'll take care of all of you, I promise you that, I'll see you all safely away from here. But I must know what happened to Miss Orienta. Tell me, and I'll take care of you. Fail to tell me," he added, "I *vow* I shall murder you all and sell the children into foreign slavery."

They believed him both ways—that showed very clearly in their faces—but somehow their belief in him made them stronger in spite of the threat. They not only knew he *would* do either of those things, but they believed he *could*. He had power. They needed someone on their side who had power. What he had offered was plenty fair, and they all knew it.

"Sir," Calvin said, "You gotta know. The master, he done toss Miss Orienta out the door with nothin' but her dress on. Buckie, he went wiff 'er. We ain't seen hide nor hair of 'em since. We worried 'bout the lady, sir. We asked Mr. Swan where she go to, and he jus' got crazy. I think you better have a look at the rubbish heap. It tell you everything."

The rubbish heap was through the garden where Wyatt had been hurt and where Dorian had discovered the miracle of his half brother. By the back of the brick wall was a square cranny built into the original wall, cut off by a wooden gate, which Dorian threw open with such force that one of the hinges fell loose.

The gate shook as though it were afraid of him. Its brown wood reminded him of the shivering negroes inside the house and the vow he had made. Already his mind clicked with channels of possibility, what to do with those people when he appropriated them from Swanborough, and what to do with Swanborough.

He stared. In an instant he saw everything.

A pile of clothing, torn to shreds so it would be useless even as slave goods, fine satins and quilted cottons lying frayed, lace petticoats and graceful hoops lying twisted, useless. On top of the pile of clothing . . . .

A pepper of black and white piano keys, splintered wood, the discarded carved legs, the cracked harp, sprung strings lying across everything else like a giant cobweb.

On top of it all . . . Alabama dirt.

Dumped from the gaping trunk that had fallen to one side, the soil of Alabama had soaked days ago into the discarded fabric and stained the splintered wood. Rain had driven the dirt into every crease, and the pile had begun to smell, the fabric to decay, the trunk to rot, the dirt to seek its natural level.

Dorian felt his eyes begin to boil. Heat surged through him, carrying rage on its crest.

He plunged forward, grabbed the trunk, and heaved it backward through the gate. He scooped up handful after handful of Alabama dirt and slung each against the brick wall, his teeth gritted and his lungs heaving. He clutched the rags of his wife's clothing in his claws, swung it high, and sent it flying back into the garden.

Where was she? What had happened to her? Had Swanborough told her the truth? What would a woman like that do? Enter a convent? Run back to Alabama? Go west, alone, in shame?

The pieces of the smashed clavichord rang against the gate as he went through the rubbish heap like a storm striking.

Passing through the garden from the stable, Barry Swanborough stopped short when he saw his rubbish flying out of the gate where it had all been dumped. Yankees? Scavengers? Runaways?

Unarmed, he ducked behind a tree until he could see what he was up against.

He moved to another tree after a moment and looked past the gaping gate of the rubbish corner.

There he saw Dorian Parthens going through the rubbish heap with his comb of rage, as though he were expecting to find Orienta rotting underneath it all.

He's back. . . .

It made sense, he reluctantly knew. In his pocket was a notice from England that Felix Carter had been found bumping wharf piling at the London Docks. Probably Parthens had come on the same boat as this notice.

Swanborough stayed behind the tree and analyzed the movements of the man in the rubbish heap. He could learn a lot about a man by his movements.

What he saw was pure rage, unmistakable, raw and primitive. He knew better than to get anywhere near a man like that.

When most of the rubbish lay scattered in the garden, no longer identifiable as bits of clothing or a musical instrument, Parthens stalked through the mess, gave the gate a terrible heave that made it slam and rattle, then disappeared out the main backyard gate and out to the deserted main street of Mechanicsville, where most people feared to walk these days.

Swanborough stayed behind the tree until he was sure Parthens wasn't coming back.

Realization arose of how dangerous Parthens really was. Better not to play around anymore.

He went into the cottage, past a strangely mute band of niggers, who simply stared at him as though afraid to involve themselves in the intrigue between white men. He went to the dining room and retrieved from its hiding place the photograph that had changed everything.

WANTED . . . REWARD . . . DORIAN WALLACE, CALLED HINNY . . . CONTACT ORVILLE QUIST.

"Orville Quist," Swanborough muttered. "All right, then, 'Hinny.' I suppose I shall have to deal with this myself."

The large house was quiet.

In the master bedchamber the master himself lay once again insensible in a morphine sleep. The war became nothing more than a misty dream, its problems slipped under clouds.

Insensible, insensible . . .

Upon the stiff bandage that held life tenuously inside this noble and self-effacing young man, his treacherous wife lay her head with an ear to his violated body.

She listened to his heartbeat. And she stared and stared.

★

CHAPTER FIFTY

———— ★ ————

It was cricket-early. Still dark, except for a haze on the eastern horizon. There was the smell of coffee and the flicker of camp fires, and there were movements in the dark.

One of the movements was a woman.

Grace knew she was dangerously close to the encampment, and that soldiers in this part of the state had been nervous for a long time and were still nervous.

She was a superstitious Kansas backwoods girl, and she knew there was such a thing as luck, good and bad, and she had used up just about all her good. If she was caught, there would be no talking out of it. No woman would be wandering in this place, at this predawn hour, unless she was spying.

Wrong. She'd been wrong.

How could anyone be *that* wrong, for *that* long?

After driving all night at a hip-jarring clip to get here, she'd already been nearly two hours in the dark looking for the envelope she'd left in the grass near the snake-rail fence, and she was still wrestling with guilt. She'd entertained ideas about delivering the stolen orders to D. H. Hill herself, but then she'd have to be arrested when she couldn't explain how she got them. Or she could turn them over to Wyatt and confess everything—but then he'd not only arrest her, he'd probably feel so guilty, he'd arrest himself.

Somehow she'd always sensed that something was off-key about all this. Now she knew. *She* was the key that was off.

588

She hadn't imagined what she saw. Wyatt had certainly killed her brother. But she'd made up motives in her own mind from her days as the daughter of a tannery worker under the tyrant rule of Wyatt's father—not Wyatt. She'd never given him the benefit of a single doubt, or ever the chance to explain himself. The lowest criminal deserves a chance to explain, and she'd never afforded that to Wyatt, or let him know who she really was. She'd listed only to the withering of her own ungenerous soul.

Funny how things could turn out. Now she had to make up for things.

The simplest solution would be to get the orders back, then burn them. Then, at least, fate would take its natural course without her tampering.

That was it—it must be fate. Fate dictated that McClellan be a slug. Fate wanted her to get her fingers out of the pudding. Maybe the South was destined to win, even against the hundred thousand Yankees. The North could not win if it had no will to win, no matter its superior numbers or industries or resources. Sometimes victory or failure is that simple. The will.

She gulped and swallowed a yelp of triumph when she stumbled onto the envelope. It was moist with dew, but the three cigars and the orders were still inside.

Good! Now she would slip back into the fabric of the South and let the chips fall where they would.

She would retreat into her place as a wife, do whatever Wyatt said, do for him whatever he wanted and needed, and spend her life repaying Wyatt for the wrongs she'd done him, for the thousand ill thoughts, and for what he had done for Patrick.

A mercy killing. She had never thought.

Guess there's not enough mercy in my own soul—

"Hold it, breastworks."

The voice cut through her success, and a hand drove her up against the irregular rails of the fence. Instantly she knew the voice and the personal scent of the man who held her—with a fishing knife to her throat.

"Clyman," she snarled, feeling her pulse push against the blade, "turn loose of me, you bastard orangutang! I'm on business!"

"Yeah, Union business. Me too. Our union."

He took the envelope from her and kept the knife pressed under her jaw.

"What's this?" he demanded. "Message? How come you're pickin' it up instead of puttin' it down?"

"I changed my mind." Grace said. "What d'you care?"

He squirmed until he could get the envelope arranged in his hand while still holding her against the fence with the knife. He knew her well enough. Knew she'd kick him in the rocks if he gave her a chance.

So he never took his eyes off her face.

Holding her there, he aimed out of the corner of his eye and tossed the package back into the tall grass.

"Now General George is gonna get General Bobby's plans," he said with a truly ugly smile, almost as though he knew it was ugly and did that on purpose.

"How the fuck d'you know about that?" Grace demanded. A quiver ran down her spine.

"By following behind your back when you went off to meet that nigger Scobell, how the fuck else? Think I ain't got ears? I knowed I'd need something on you. You ain't tossing me out no more, racy Gracie. I went away and sat down and did some thinking, and here's what I come to. You're gonna go home to your dying husband. When he's dead and after this big battle everybody says is coming, I'm gonna come and get you. We're gonna go up North and live up there, and we're gonna tell 'em what we did, and we're gonna be heroes. What d'you think?"

Knife or not, Grace said, "I think you make me throw up."

His proprietorial eyes reflected the encroaching predawn light. Only then did Grace realize how obsessive a person could be—and all this time she thought she was the only one.

"I love you," Clyman said. His smile dropped away. There was a little sob of emotion in his voice. "I love you, you know? You do like I say from now on, or I'll kill you and him and everybody in your house, including that lady with the baby in her. And if you tell anybody about them papers before the big fight, I'll make sure the whole world knows just how General Lee's order got stole and who delivered them into Union hands. I see it in your eyes that I'm right. Goddamn!"

He suddenly laughed in true thrilled delight.

"Goddamn, I always wanted a woman like you," he went

on, waffling from thought to thought. "You done gave your flesh to me—now I got your soul—nah! No funny moves . . . I love you, but I'll kill you 'fore I'll let you put them sharp toes on my clappers. You hold still. There, now. Easy. I ain't gonna have my woman live with another man. I'll kill you first. Now, I'm gonna back away slow. Just keep feeling the point here— good. You go ahead and get going. I'm gonna watch to make sure you leave Maryland all the way. Then I'm gonna make sure somebody from that camp picks up that envelope. As soon as I can get back through the lines, I'll be there for you."

"You come near my house," Grace said, "I'll blow your face off."

"Can't be on guard all the time, Grace." he said. "Not even you. We'll see which one of us gets back to Richmond first, you in that carriage or me on my army horse."

He stepped back from her, keeping his legs and his private parts out of range of her feet. The blade stayed at her throat until the last second, then it too backed off.

Grainy morning light buttered his orange hair and his thready beard, and created a strange and eerie halo around Clyman's bony shoulders. Slowly he raised both arms and stood before her with his hands spread like a crucifix.

"Don't forget I love you."

General George McClellan was at his proud best as he entertained several civilian guests who wanted to discuss the details of the occupation of Frederick, Maryland. He enjoyed talking to civilians. They were always impressed with his burly, king-like frame, his rounded chest, his uniform, his youth, and his responsibility. He could always point out the beautiful army he'd whipped into shape with drill after drill, and how pretty it looked spread across the countryside. Their thousands of white tents, lined like folded paper notes from horizon to horizon, should be enough to dominate any landscape and send a thrill into any civilian. A model of military presence, the Army of the Potomac.

Into his moment of glory came a hot and babbling private from General Alpheus Williams of the Twelfth Corps, waving an envelope at him.

McClellan paused and apologized to his visitors, then paused to read the cover letter from Williams.

I enclose a Special Order of Gen. Lee commanding Rebel forces which was found on the field where my corps is encamped. It is a document of interest and is thought genuine. The Document was found by a corporal of the 27 Ind. Rgt, Col. Colgrove, Gordon's Brigade. Col. Pittman has deemed the handwriting to be that of Gen. Lee's adjutant Chilton, with whom he was stationed when we were all one army.

Brig. Gen. A. Williams

12th Corps

McClellan flipped the papers and found himself staring at what appeared to be a completely authentic detailing of the operational plan of the Confederate Army of Northern Virginia, including the location of every unit by name of the commanders.

The dispatch blurred before his eyes, and he jumped to his feet, both hands up, turning like a windmill.

"Now I know what to do!"

★

CHAPTER FIFTY-ONE

★

"But I'm just visiting, I tell you! I've got to get back to Richmond! You're not listening, are you? I'm Mrs. Wyatt Craig, of the Craig Powderworks, or the Craig Artillery, or whatever you want to call it to let me get past this motherfarting checkpoint!"

"Ma'am, if you'd just keep your head screwed onto your neck . . . after all, you've got no papers of identification with you, and I can't just let you go flying back and forth, what with armies moving all over this part of the country and shots being fired and all. I've got a responsibility for civilians."

"But I've got to get back to Richmond! My husband's life is in danger."

Her words fell in thumps on the wet ground. Rain pattered on the tent over them, and drained down the canvas sides to puddle, and ran through the grass. There was no getting away from it.

The senior officer of the checkpoint, a lieutenant with two big fuzzy whiskers running down the sides of his face, leaned back on his folding chair and frowned at her. "Suppose you just explain that to me. What kind of danger, and how could you possible know about it if you're returning from Maryland?"

Frustration grinding inside her, Grace clenched her teeth and both fists and weighed the back-and-forths about just admitting she was a spy—but then there would be no hope of getting out of here fast enough to help Wyatt. Clyman would still get through.

"I just know! Can't you indulge a woman's whims?"

"Not in the middle of a war, I can't. Are you carrying military information, ma'am?"

"Why don't you search me, you coward, and find out!"

"I can't do that," he admitted, gazing suspiciously at her big skirt and noting that she didn't wear a corset. "I'll have to delay you here long enough to get a woman down here from Mechanicsville to search you."

"That'll take hours!"

"You'll be fine here in the meantime."

"Why don't I just strip down right here and get it over with!"

In a rage Grace cranked her arms behind her and began unhooking the back of her dress.

The lieutenant stood up sharply. "Cut that out, ma'am!"

Then, out of nowhere, a dusky voice issued from the open end of the tent—the last voice Grace expected to hear ever again.

"Is there a problem, Lieutenant?"

Grace wheeled around at the sound and found herself staring at the least likely person on the planet who should be here, now.

Dorian!

Familiarity rushed through Grace. She drew in a sharp breath and let it out like a high storm wind.

"Oh, my God, I've never been so glad to see anybody in my *whole fucking life*!"

GOVERNOR STREET

Wyatt was downstairs and dressed. Stabbed or not, he couldn't stand slugging around the house with nothing on but a nightshirt and robe. Never had, never would. Luckily he hadn't thrown away his tie-waist trousers in favor of the button-fly uniform stripers. In his condition those would've been torture.

In his cotton shirt, with those tie trousers loosely on, he felt almost human again.

Couldn't loll around for the whole war. Already lolled a month of it. Up in his bed he'd heard his stack of paperwork whimpering at him and finally had gotten up like a new father going to coddle an infant in the middle of the night.

Downstairs in his office life seemed almost normal. He sat slumped in discomfort on the small leather couch, unable to find a position that didn't hurt, rifling through supply orders for the army and trying to separate them from blasting-powder orders from railroads. Which were military and which weren't? Which would get priority? Which would save or lose lives? Which would end the war faster? Making powder decisions was one thing; making life-and-death decisions was something else.

Funny. . . . all the high principles were coming down to that. End the war faster. If the Confederacy could win, fine—but Wyatt hadn't seen a manifestation of the Confederate principles for secession. The central government had grown stronger, not weaker. States' rights were daily succumbing to martial law. The haggling of the cotton men proved that sooner or later, somebody, somewhere, had to step in and make a decision. Maybe Alexander Stephens was right. Maybe the Confederacy would be better making a point, then remerging and trying to work out an economic plan. That was the whole problem—economics. Not slavery. Hell, Lee was against slavery and McClellan was for it. Everybody knew that. Slavery was part and parcel of Southern economic problems. If the slaves were all suddenly freed, they'd just go to the North and become part of Northern economic problems. Who could predict how the West would go?

The house was sure quiet . . . and dark. A cloudy, rainy day outside. Dark as evening inside. He'd had to light two lamps just to look at his paperwork. Through the open doorway to his right he listened even for shuffling in the kitchen, but it was a well-built house, and he couldn't even hear his slaves moving around in back. And he'd sent Burlie to sit on the covered porch outside Orienta's guest house . . . just in case.

Still, Wyatt sighed, shifted his feet, and wished he had someone to talk to.

"Hey, Major."

He looked up abruptly, thinking how timely this interruption was and how much he was wishing for some company. But it wasn't company.

It was Clyde Clyman.

Wyatt lurched to his feet, grasping the couch for support. "Wha— oh, no . . ."

Clyman came in the open doorway, holding a military-issue pistol.

"Hi, boss. Wife home?"

"Clyman," Wyatt said, "take it easy, now. . . . We can talk, all right?"

"Sure. Where's the wife?"

Working his way behind the couch, hand over hand, while Clyman sauntered into the middle of the room, holding the pistol trained on him.

"What do you want my wife for?" Wyatt demanded.

Clyman grinned. "Funny you should put it that way. Hey, I beat her!" he trumpeted. "I got through and she got stopped. She didn't get back yet from Maryland, did she?"

"What are you talking about?"

"Your wife. She was in Maryland this morning. You just didn't know about it. Just like you don't know what's going on at the yard half the time."

Kinked over the back of the couch, aware of the gun, Wyatt nearly choked. "My *wife*? What's she doing in Maryland? Clyman, are you lying for some reason?"

"Don't have to lie. I'm the one with the gun. I gotta finish killing you, Major."

What little color had come back to Wyatt's face suddenly dropped.

"Why?" he asked. "I don't understand why! What's this thing you've got about me? What've I done to you?"

"You're in my way. 'Cause I love Grace. And she loves me."

Gripping the back of the couch with all his fingernails, Wyatt choked, "What?"

"We're gonna go up North and be heroes. She's in Maryland to deliver General Lee's marching orders to General McClellan. Yeah! Hey, now you got it. She's a spy. Goddamn, ain't she a pretty spy too. Bet there'll be stories wrote about her when the war's over. I can prove it. You got orders to supply General Harvey Hill, and Grace headed 'em off. Ol' Harvey Hill's heading for the big fight with no gunpowder. I'm a spy too. You figgered that out, probably, at the pack house. I started out working for her, but now she's working for me. She's stuck at a checkpoint up there to give me time to come back here and kill you off. I just walked on past with this Reb uniform on. It's a good ticket. Grace and me, we work good together."

"I don't believe it," Wyatt gulped. He shook his shaggy, uncombed head. His legs began to rattle under him, and he leaned harder on the couch. "You've always been a pathetic deadneck, Clyman. Now you're a liar too."

"Yeah, I'm lying. Maybe I'm lying about the little scar on the inside of Grace's leg. On the upper part, inside. She got it when she was a kid, shimmying up a tree to bark squirrels with her brother. It's shaped like a bent spoon. I see it everytime we blow off the loose corns, if you know what I mean. That's what she calls it. She's got lots of funny names for it. You know, fuckin'. I like to lick that scar—"

"Oh, my God!" Wyatt gagged. His eyes clamped shut, and he bent forward in two kinds of agony. His fingers dug into the studded leather. "God—what kind of man talks like that—"

Clyman raised the pistol. "A winner."

He leveled the gun toward Wyatt. His finger curled around the trigger.

"Funny," he added, "the powder in this pistol's from your own yard."

Why Clyman felt he had to say that, Wyatt had no idea. All he knew was that it gave him a precious extra second to dive to one side, grab a stand of fireplace implements, and hurl the whole thing at Clyman.

Almost all of Wyatt's gathered strength went with it, but the stand and the brass grabbers and pokers struck Clyman's shoulder, turned upside down, and dumped all over him. The noise of it confused them both. Clyman stumbled sideways, trying to duck, and though he managed to stay on his feet, the pistol flew from his fingers and skidded along the edge of the rug.

They dived for it at the same time, and reached it at the same time, with Wyatt just an inch closer.

He almost yelled with victory as his hand closed around

the gun handle, but Clyman's sharp elbow drove into his stomach right over the poker wound, and crushed the air from him.

Only with his last bit of willpower could Wyatt react. He swung the pistol across the floor, then upward, and caught Clyman a ringing blow in the side of the head. The man fell away, and Wyatt forced himself on all fours in the other direction, back behind the couch. Somehow he made it.

His middle was pounding, his head pounding, his chest throbbing, and his legs like thread, but he had the gun, he had the gun! And he had the edge of the couch in his hand. One foot at a time he struggled to a standing—bending—position behind the couch, with the pistol leveled at Clyman as the other man got up, rubbing a bad bruise on the side of his face.

"All right!" Wyatt gulped, "That's it . . . back off. . . . "

He had one hand crushed to his knotted stomach, that elbow creased hard and painfully into the back of the couch, and the other hand holding the ten-ton pistol. Ten tons, and getting heavier. His arm quivered visibly with the strain. The barrel of the pistol wobbled as though to mock him.

"Go on—" he began, but couldn't continue. He felt as though his body were strapped by barbed wire being drawn tighter and tighter around the middle. Now he was hanging over the back of the small couch, unable to stand up on his own, wasting breath and energy for a pointless conversation. Heat flushed his face, neck, and shoulders. He had to get help, but the door was ten paces away, the main entrance ten paces beyond that, and he was entirely alone in this half of what now seemed to be a very big mansion. Maybe he could move along the wall while still keeping the gun on Clyman.

Maybe not. Already his legs were draining.

"Arm's shaking," Clyman said, eying him with weird satisfaction. "You gonna shoot me point-blank, Major? It ain't in you."

Sweat broke across Wyatt's brow and squished up from his grip on the pistol's handle. His body grew hollow, his breathing choppy. The gun trembled like a leaf in his hand.

"Go ahead," Clyman dared. He put his hand to his chest. "Shoot me right through the heart. That's where I was gonna shoot you. Right in the heart. Let's see if you got it in you. Let's see which of us is a better man for a woman like Grace."

Wyatt knew he would have to try to go along the wall. That

meant letting go of the couch and going those few steps.
Clyman's elbow blow had driven the wind from and left him
tortured for air, the barbed wire tightening, and the arm he
needed for the wall clamped hard at his middle.

He attempted to straighten, just enough to pretend that he
could make it to the wall. A stream of sweat ran down the side
of his face. He took a step back, and to the side, toward the
doorway. And another.

Clyman stepped toward him in a lurching move—but
Wyatt stopped in the middle and pushed the pistol out between
then, and Clyman halted there, poised.

Now Wyatt was in no-man's-land, without anything to lean
on, couch or wall. In his battered condition, holding the gun
was like holding an anchor at arm's length.

"You're too weak for this, Major," his tormentor said, "I
see it in your face."

"Don't worry," Wyatt told him. "I'll kill you before I fall
over."

The pistol quivered. He stood with his feet braced, one arm
clamped to his wound, the other beginning to feel like molten
iron.

Clyman grinned and said, "You really ain't gonna shoot,
are you? Christ, all that honor's got you by the neck. You're
almost down."

A sudden cutting pain and a shock of wet heat beneath his
shirt made Wyatt wince and tighten his hand to his midriff.
Exertion had taken its toll. Bleeding again!

He felt the slippery blood between his fingers. His vision
began to shrink behind a black curtain closing from the sides.
He was dead if it closed—dead. He had to be able to see, to
keep the gun up. To slip even a few inches . . .

Glaring at him, waiting for the kill, Clyman prodded, "Too
much honor, that's what you got."

The curtain was almost closed when a sudden warm support stole up at Wyatt's side. A hand swept under the weight
of the pistol and kept the weapon level with Clyman's astonished eyes.

Wyatt felt an arm around his waist. Amazed but exhausted,
he sagged against the structure that hadn't been there a second
ago. Finally he could use both hands to hold his guts in and try
to get his wind back.

"He may have too much honor," Dorian's welcome voice announced, "but I will put lead in your teeth. Keep your place and raise both hands. Gentlemen! This way, please."

Confederate artillery guards piled in the front door and into the room and took possession of the astounded assassin.

Only when the uniformed men whisked Clyman from the room did Dorian toss the pistol onto the desk and give all his attention to Wyatt, who was losing an inch to every breath that shattered through him.

Dorian supported him across what had seemed moments ago to be a desert of carpet and rolled him onto the couch on his side and held him there.

"Safe," Dorian said. "You're still struggling. Try to lie still. Breathe evenly."

Curled and gasping, Wyatt let himself indulge in the relief of the moment. He tried to relax, but his muscles screamed.

"Almost . . . didn't make it," he managed.

"You, or me?"

"Both. Oh, Lord, too close."

He lay back and groaned out the clutching pain and dizziness, drew breaths as complete as he could manage, until after several minutes the curtain began to peel back, the lights behind it stopped exploding, and he thought maybe he could talk in whole sentences.

When he opened his eyes, Dorian was bending over him.

"You're bleeding," the prodigal said. "What on earth did that polecat do to you?"

"Stabbed me a month ago with a—poker—then came back to finish the job. Got me with a pointy elbow that time—I'll be—all right—just a minute or two—"

Any sarcasm that might have been lurking in the wings suddenly dropped away from Dorian's face, replaced instantly by a wince of empathy. He pressed his hanky to the spreading maroon stain beneath Wyatt's cramping hand.

"I think it's stopping," he said critically, "Turn my back for a few weeks and look what happens. Next time you want to cut yourself in half, let me wire Tussaud's and get you a professional blade."

"Be all right," Wyatt responded, sniffing and wiping the sweat out of his eyes. "Listen—we don't have much time. You've got to do something."

"Do I?"

"Get through to one of the Confederate generals with a warning. Any one of 'em. Hill, Jackson, anybody. You've got to go right away—tonight. Say it's from me, on good source—good whatever-you-call-it . . ."

"Authority?"

"McClellan's got a copy of Lee's marching plan! It's been Grace all this time. . . . She's been shuttling information. My own wife."

Dorian lowered his voice. "Yes, I know."

Forcing his eyes to focus, Wyatt asked, "You do?"

"Yes. I discovered her at a checkpoint just south of Mechanicsville. She's being detained there for ten hours while her identity is checked. My commission papers got me through, despite my civilian duds, but they wouldn't take my word carte blanche for her bona fides."

"What?"

"They didn't trust me."

"Gosh, wonder why."

"Did she . . . tell you anything?"

"She told me many interesting things. Mostly she told me to get over here at a quickstep," Dorian said, and paused, "for your sake, Wyatt."

Leaning back, still wincing and unable to relax, Wyatt didn't attempt to hide the fact that half his pain was about Grace.

"I'll send Burlie up there with verification. If anybody's going to arrest my wife," he said introspectively, "it's going to be me." Deep regret creased his face. He groaned, "Lord, it's all my fault. I drove her to this."

"Wyatt, really."

"What other explanation is there?"

"She has many explanations," Dorian said. "Believe me, it's quite a story."

"Don't tell me—don't! I don't want to hear it. We've got real troubles. You've got to—"

The effort of turning over bound Wyatt's midsection in a vise. He curled like a leaf and gasped through it, trying to get up on an elbow. Dorian bent over him again, providing support and more than a little guilty empathy, but they were both aware of the remaining barrier between them.

Wyatt thought only of the words he was trying to push out. "You've gotta—warn—General Lee."

But Dorian suddenly turned statuesque and proclaimed, "Leave me out of it. This is not my fight anymore. I'm taking my wife and I'm going to Europe. If I don't take her *tonight*, I may get no other chance. Fate does not enjoy giving me chances in increments bigger than one."

"You've got to," Wyatt persisted, "warn Lee for me. You've got to. You've given the South its chance to win this war. If Lee loses, it'll be my fault. I'll have to live with this for the rest of my life."

Above, stormy black brows drew inward. "Won't it be . . . Grace's fault?"

"No . . . no, mine. I've done something wrong to make her do this," Wyatt said. "Somehow it's all because of me." Fancy arguments might have fit another day, another situation, but he had neither the mental nor physical wherewithal to summon them up. He simply stared up and said, "I *need* you, Dorian. Please do it."

The monolith might have withstood a barrage. This one tiny stab, however—

Dorian shook his head and sighed. "I suppose I haven't gone through all this only to let the Confederacy lose at this point. I'll warn Lee for you. But you must do something for me."

"What?" The question was touchy, as if Wyatt already felt pushed.

"Don't judge Grace too harshly yet," Dorian said. "I'm afraid . . . the devil has made puppets of us all this time." He hesitated, waffled, then finally forced himself to ask the question of the day. "Do you know where my wife is?"

Wyatt looked up at him wryly. If there was any private reading between them at all, Dorian seemed ashamed to be asking.

"Sure I know, '' he said. "Help me up."

Dorian offered a humble hand as though paying a toll.

Accepting the hand without ceremony, Wyatt used it to lever himself to a sitting position, then let go and pumped a thumb toward the back of the mansion.

"She's in the guest house. You'll be surprised when you see her."

His face lacking its usual hauteur, Dorian simply uttered, "Thank you," and headed for the back way. Only a glance as he was leaving the office stopped him.

Stiff as a midshipman's knot, Wyatt was trying to get up from the couch.

Dorian paused and asked, "What are you doing?"

"I gotta go—make sure a shipment of powder gets delivered to D. H. Hill. I'm going to see it through myself. Least I can do. Maybe there's a—a railroad connection—get it up there before something breaks—"

Every word was more gasp than talk. He got across the room, supporting himself on the furniture, and coaxed his uniform tunic from the halltree. The effort of getting it around behind him and onto his shoulders nearly made him pass out. He had to rest by sitting on the edge of his desk, sucking deep, tight breaths.

Though twitching with empathy, Dorian watched without attempting to help him. "That's absurd. Look at you."

Now Wyatt's eyes shot up, and he leveled a finger at him. "You left a decent loving woman when she needed you most. Don't talk to me about absurd, damn ya, buster."

A flash of indignation came back into Dorian's eyes, but his voice was mild, subdued, even regretful.

"Too late, Wyatt," he said sadly. "I was born groin-deep in damnation."

For the first time in their relationship, Wyatt felt something he never had before. At least, not like this.

Pity. Pity for this person, who defied pity.

Lately he had let himself forget that Dorian had feelings to hurt. Usually, they both knew, Wyatt was the only one who remembered.

With a sigh he closed the double breast over his wounded body, wincing with each brass button—and the buttons made him think of Grace.

Holding himself together somehow, he pushed himself up from the desk and moved toward the doorway. Catching Dorian by the shoulder, he leaned on him and steered them both toward the front entrance.

"Get going," Wyatt said. "Go see your wife, and send Burlie out here to me. He'll go fetch Grace, I'll take the powder, and you'll warn Lee. As for everything else . . . we'll have plenty of time to work it out later."

"Orienta! Orienta, I'm—"

Dorian stumbled into the archway of the guest house and stopped short, his lips hanging open in astonishment, his eyes like a child's eyes—poetically appropriate, considering what he was seeing.

For there she was, turning toward him from her quilting stand, where she was fashioning in pastel colors a blanket for a child's bed. She wore one of Grace's bed jackets, a cinnamon-colored thing made for a thinner woman. Its satin ties couldn't close over the swollen front.

Dorian took in the shape of her, the reality of her, of everything, and swallowed it all in a single hard lump. With his hands out to his sides like a bird about to take off, he blurted out what he had planned to say, what he had practiced saying across an entire ocean, and more.

"I love you . . . *both*."

Glorious in this moment, his wife sailed toward him, graceful in her way, her cheeks glowing, eyes wedged and glistening with tears. She pressed her fruitful, teardrop-shaped body against him as he caught her in his arms and buried his face beneath her ear.

Then she raised his chin, took his cheeks in her small swollen hands, and caressed his face.

Softly she whispered, "I know."

★

———— ★ ————

PART TEN

HELL DAY

They go with souls undaunted to their doom.

—An Irish patriotic song

★★★

THE EXPLOSION

11-16 SEPTEMBER 1862

Scattered fighting all over lower Maryland—Hagerstown, Frederick, Birkensfield, Harpers Ferry, and the Gaps of South Mountain.

As specified in Order 191, General Lee had broken his army into four parts, sending three prongs of attack to the vulnerable Federal garrison at Harpers Ferry. Because of Order 191, McClellan knows Lee's army is divided and has the perfect opportunity to cut each section off from the others. True to his own form, his only actions are to crow about how glorious his victory would be and telegram the President, promising trophies.

An anonymous civilian gets through to General Jeb Stuart, informing the Confederate high command that General McClellan is in possession of damaging details. Stuart immediately contacts Lee with the warning.

Rather than cancel the Harpers Ferry offensive, Lee bets on McClellan's personality and continues the operation, but he orders action to crack much faster, and the Army of Northern Virginia to reunite as quickly as possible.

The increased speed of Confederate movements causes George McClellan to pause. He delays acting upon his chance to cut the enemy into quarters for more than eighteen hours— until Order 191 is obsolete.

On the fourteenth at South Mountain, there are battles for the Gaps, the three passages through the fifty-mile wall of the mountain. General D. H. Hill's men, reinforced by James Longstreet's, maintain a stubborn, costly hold on Turner's

Gap that keeps two Union corps at bay until nightfall. Gradually the Union takes all three gaps, and the Confederates fall back, but Lee has been given an extra day.

On the fifteenth Harpers Ferry falls to Stonewall Jackson. Soon after, General Lafayette McLaws draws his forces to join Jackson's and General Longstreet comes south from Hagerstown, all converging upon the town of Sharpsburg, Maryland.

Here General Lee establishes a line of audacious defense.

16 SEPTEMBER

Now reinforced by his returning generals, General Lee takes up an unlikely defiance against the Army of the Potomac. With his back to the Potomac River, he positions his army in the V made by the Potomac and its heavily treed tributary, Antietam Creek. He then faces east and stands firm. The stand is in mockery of any textbook maneuver, but Lee knows McClellan has read the textbook.

He's right. Because the stand is contrary to any military precedent, it completely confuses McClellan, who deduces the Confederate forces must be numbering at the ridiculously inflated figure of 120,000.

The actual number is about 50,000. Lee had lost 15,000 before ever entering Maryland. Some of the dropouts were sick, weak, starving, but a considerable number dropped out because they could not justify becoming an invasion force. They had enlisted to defend their home states, not to invade someone else's state. The sense of state-by-state territorial isolationism that had caused the American Civil War would now risk the Confederacy's chances of winning it.

The 50,000 remaining are also dirty, starving, shoeless— but they are those who really want to fight and are ready to do exactly that.

The Army of Northern Virginia occupies the inside of a C-shaped attack line. The Army of the Potomac is a great arch across the eastern horizon that could, if used wisely, close like a maw.

The Confederates are hopeful, however, because they have learned not to use the words wisely *and* McClellan *in the same sentence. Rebel morale is as high as the odds against them.*

The northernmost wings of the Union and Confederate armies stand each other off across a cornfield just east of the road to Hagerstown.

Rather than closing like a single maw and overwhelming the Confederate smaller force all at once, McClellan's army attacks in fits and starts. His hesitation is contagious and spreads to his unit leaders. Ultimately Confederate survivors of each encounter along the Antietam will surge southward to fight again, later in the day.

In the two woods and the cornfield between, just north of a white-box building used as a chapel by the German Dunker sect, the conflict that has until now been a fishnet of skirmishes with an occasional bloody surprise suddenly changes character. What had been called "war" suddenly becomes truly . . . war. The burning fuse has finally and fully ignited.

The Union sweeps south along Hagerstown Pike. The Confederates meet them head-on. A maniacal fury takes over. Men laugh as they load and fire. The cornfield, poor protection even from rain, is no protection at all from lead balls. The corn is sliced down from harvest height along with hundreds upon hundreds of soldiers running in it. Over three hours it changes hands several times, punch and counterpunch, but eventually the Union wave flushes through.

In its wake are more than 8,000 dead or dying men, nearly equal casualties for North and South.

From now on, West Woods, East Woods, and the Cornfield will possess capital letters and an ignominious place in history.

The Confederates fall back a half mile south, take up positions at the Rebel center, and plan for the next surge.

It's not even ten o'clock in the morning yet.

---★---

CHAPTER FIFTY-TWO

———— ★ ————

"General Hill?"

"Take this to Ripley . . . this one to MacRae. . . . See if you can reach Lawton. Hurry it up! Move your fannies! Quicker! This one goes to General Longstreet—"

"Excuse me . . ."

"What is it? Who in blazes are you? And what are you doing on my command line?"

Daniel Harvey Hill looked up with eyes so rough as to knock back the men standing around him. They had been crowded at a stump upon which were spread several hand-drawn pictures and makeshift maps provided, probably, by scouts. Hill was a battle-toughened man with a bad morning behind him, and intolerance in his glare for the newcomer who tapped at his shoulder.

Wyatt tried not to step back too far from those harsh eyes and the intimidation of talking to a major general. He had always tried not to be too impressed with the men who ran the Confederate theater, knowing that he would have to deal with them in a businesslike way, but these were the real heroes, the leaders who gave their ranks reasons to act like heroes, the men who went up against the Yankee monolith and shook it again and again.

Hill's appearance startled him somewhat, for the general was absolutely filthy. He didn't straighten up. There seemed to be something wrong with his back. His gray uniform, and those of the men all around them, were so crusted with mud and cakey black smudges as to be indistinguishable from the butternut version. Even the general's gold braiding was invisible. These men were battle ravaged. They'd been fighting for days.

Unable to ignore the constant drum of battle still coming from the east, the Confederate left, Wyatt felt a little ashamed that his uniform was so clean.

He'd hauled his little supply line from Richmond, as fast as the touchy powder kegs could handle on special wagons and slings—and black powder was always a risky commodity to transport. He now stood on the crest of one of Maryland's rolling tree-lined hills, with his small force of uniformed powder workers and wagons, all nervous from the encroaching vibrations in the ground and the not-distant-enough boom of cannons.

"I'm Craig, out the Powderworks in Richmond," he said, trying not to breathe too heavily from the uphill climb.

"Harvey Hill. Be right with you." The general stuck out a hand for Wyatt to take, but kept an eye on the maps and drawings, still analyzing the landscape with part of his attention. Then he started firing off dispatches again and barking names.

With Hill shouting, "Hurry it up! Faster!" couriers broke away from the dozen soldiers crowded around the stump until that number was cut in half. Then Hill paused, looked over his eye-level drawings of the landscape, compared them to what he could see with his naked eye, and started shooting off orders again. Men saluted and took off at the quickstep, and it was down to the two of them before Hill turned to Wyatt.

Hill's broad-browed face was set in a constant analytical mask whose lines were crusted into place with black charcoal soot. His eyes were red and squinting from the sting of sulfur dust, which even now drifted south on a breeze from that noise of battle. His beard appeared black, but that might only have been from the soot, for his hair and eyes were lighter.

"You're Craig himself?" he asked. "Or his son?"

"No, sir—I mean, yes, sir, I'm Wyatt Craig. I run the mill, if that's what you mean."

"Aren't you a shade young to have built up an enterprise of such consequence?"

Wyatt hesitated, then shuffled his feet. "Well, I turn thirty in a couple months, and part of the mill I inherited and had the other part given to me. I just run it, really."

General Hill shrugged. "Twenty-nine. Jeb Stuart's twenty-nine. Guess that clean-shaven face makes you appear younger."

Embarrassed, Wyatt hoped he wasn't blushing. He wiped a dry hand across his face and muttered, "Well, I, uh . . ."

Hill peered past him down the hill at the powder wagons. "Can't say you're not the welcomest sight we've seen since the trees of the Potomac. Maryland was pretty when we crossed in, but there hasn't been the rally of support we hoped for. Cautious apathy is about all we've been handed. Bob Lee's been plenty worried about running out of ammunition."

"I know," Wyatt said, his voice low. "While we passed through Sharpsburg, I was ordered to leave three quarters of our shipment at General Lee's headquarters, to be distributed to the battle line, I'm sorry, sir, because it was all meant to fill your order from more than a week ago."

"That's all right. We'll take what we can get."

"Sir," Wyatt began, "there's one thing I'm worried about—"

"Only one thing? You're a happy man then."

"About your marching orders—"

"Which orders?" Hill looked up sharply.

"The orders General Lee dispatched about the Harper's Ferry offensive."

"Gracious Christ, that's days ago! Where's your head?"

But Wyatt persisted. "Did you . . . get your copy?"

"Of course I got my copy!" Hill roared.

"Where from?"

"From my division commander, Tom Jackson! Stonewall. He's my brother-in-law. Think he'd leave me without marching orders? Screw your head on, man, and get with the show! I've had three horses blown out from under me since dawn, and I'm 'bout ready to claw those bluejackets' eyes out with my fingernails! I've no time to discuss the doings of a day ago." Hill turned back to the stump and its maps. "Your men up to fighting snuff?"

Wyatt paused and bit his lip. "They're powdermen, sir, skimmers and grinders, lift-and-haul men, not trained soldiers. Don't know how much good they'd do you."

"Can they tell a trigger from a trouser button?"

"Well, sure, but—"

"You can fall in with us. Look here. Sharply!" He snapped his fingers to make Wyatt bend over the drawings and pointed to a roughly penciled map. "Our battle line is the four miles running north to south from the woods on Hagerstown Pike to below this slash mark, which is the Rohrbach Bridge. Right now we're here, almost directly south of this little chapel. I'm in charge of the Confederate center. You can see there's a defensible position six hundred yards southeast of the chapel, which is just about directly east of you and me right now. It's a farm road. Branches off Hagerstown Turnpike, goes east, turns southeast, then jags south to Boonsboro Pike, here, here, and here." With one finger on the map, he straightened, looked eastward into the midmorning sun, and pointed. "It's right down . . . there."

"What's defensible about a road?" Wyatt interrupted. "If you don't mind my asking?"

"It's an old road, Major, old and worn from loaded farm wagons over decades. It's been eroded to several feet below ground level and will make a formidable rifle trench. We've built a breastworks of fence rails all along it, from here to here. Can your men handle rifles?"

"Oh, yes, sir. We test powder regularly, and we've trained all our workers to understand how the chemical reaction—"

"Forget about that, Craig. You're not a chemist here."

"Sorry . . . ."

"Our supply lines are overextended where they exist at all," Hill plowed on. He scratched his beard and allowed himself a sigh. "My men are barefoot, vermin infested, famished, sluggish, and they can look over Antietam Creek and see a wartime spectacle of bluecoats parading on the horizon. My God, I've seen nothing like it in my entire career. Rifles bristling, rolling up and down like a lady's shawl fringe in a breeze—David against Goliath, that's all it is. David against Goliath. Took Harper's Ferry, though, did you hear that?"

"Yes, I did," Wyatt said. He offered the general a smile and one of those fundamental human tones that hinted they had a bond, even though they had never met. "Everybody's heard, General Hill."

Hill threw him a look of gratitude and team spirit.

"Thirteen thousand Union prisoners, seventy-three artillery

pieces, and a hell of a demoralizing sting on the Yanks across from us. Even so, we were in retreat." He shook his head, partly in bafflement and partly in awe as he said, "Then all of a sudden, General Lee decided to take a stand. I'd never have predicted it."

Wyatt clamped his lips tight. He didn't want to let anything slip out that he knew there was intrigue on high planes in the Confederate government that might have influenced Lee's decision. Whatever Dorian had done in England was having repercussions, that was obvious, and all this day needed was more entanglement from rumors spouted by some powder boss.

"They're still fighting at that cornfield up there," Hill murmured, straightening. He gazed into the distance, over the rolling Maryland countryside of tilled fields, grass, stubble, and rock outcroppings, to the sound of battle, where he had left part of his heart. "Bitter harvest, I'd say. We had to pull back from there . . . left those men to hold it. They're still trying. God's hand is in this either everywhere or nowhere today, and he is playing us for pawns."

He gazed for a few seconds, then shook out of his philosophical pause.

"We have many advantages even yet," he said. "I don't want you to forget that, Major Craig. For instance, McClellan won't know anything close-range about us or this terrain. He's got a fixation on holding his cavalry in check for a glorious military charge instead of using them and their horses for reconnoitering. Consequentially, all he knows is what he sees at great distance through field glasses. He's an idiot. He thinks they call him Young Napoleon because he puts his hand in his breast flap and runs a pretty parade. I say it's because he's stuck in the 1700s."

With a nod Wyatt stayed carefully silent. This general was on a hair trigger, he could tell.

Hill put a finger on the sketched line that represented the sunken road. "On this lane are brigade remnants and strays which we gathered up from the brigades of Garland, who died this morning, and Colquitt's, both of whom were routed this morning in those woods up that way. I've got no more than twenty five hundred men to face down more than twice that

number, and I'll take all I can get. There's also Rodes's
brigade, or what's left of it, God save them. I have complete
faith in him after what I saw the Alabama boys do at Turner's
Gap, couple days ago. Some of our men in that trench have already been through a morning of battle. They're in need of
support—" He stopped. "Major? What's wrong?"

Wincing hard, Wyatt had caught a tight breath and was
leaning on the ragged edge of the stump, gasping for air that
suddenly abandoned him in the clouds of sulfur stench—
stench a powderman should be used to.

"Major, you wounded?" the general asked again.

Cursing inwardly that he hadn't been able to keep it hidden,
Wyatt struggled against his knotted innards. All he needed was
to appear infirm while men were falling with *fresh* wounds all
around him!

"A brush with a Union infiltrator at the mill," he mentioned
with a dismissing wave. "Be just fine."

"You all right? Want to sit down?"

"Oh, General, *please,*" Wyatt insisted. "I don't want even
the *horses* to see me sitting down!"

Hill slapped him approvingly in the shoulder, said, "Good
man," and damn near knocked him over.

Apparently thinking Wyatt wanted his problem ignored for
sound command reasons, the general turned back to the reconnaissance maps. While Wyatt sucked short breaths and fought
for control, Hill continued jabbing his finger at points on the
drawings.

"I want you to take your people and some of their rifle
powder and go down there and report to Tige Anderson." He
looked up. "Now, that's George *B.* Anderson, not George *T.*
Anderson. There's also R. H. Anderson. Don't ask somebody
where 'Anderson' is and get confused and go off with the
wrong Anderson."

"I'll mind that," Wyatt said tightly. "I'll get it right."

"Tell Tige I've ordered you to fall in with his brigade and
hold that sunken lane. It's our center, and if it collapses, even a
turnip like Little Mac will not be able to resist surging
through. One of my colonels told General Lee not thirty minutes ago that we were going to hold that spot until the sun sets,
and that's what I want your help in doing. I expect to keep that

promise. I'll be down there myself before much more smoke rises. Any questions?"

Fighting to digest all this after so many hours of travel, Wyatt simply said, "No, sir."

He felt vague, like a game piece. The booms and clouds of rising smoke on the near horizons were distracting. Distracting, hell! It was damning! He found it hard to think through the constant haunting groan of a battle—real battle, happening now, happening right over there. . . .

Shaking himself, he straightened and tried to appear fit, though he had to press an arm to his belt.

"We also brought some priming powder and cannon ammunition—I mean, other than the rifle powder I mentioned," he said. "What do you want done with it?"

"Leave that to me. We'll see that it's distributed."

"Then . . . no questions, I guess, General."

"Dismissed, Major. Gather your men, gather your courage, gather your breath, and report to the sunken road, double-quick."

"Approaching this sunken road, the Federal troops will have no cover in those meadows and plowed acres! I will *not* give the order to fire until the Yankees have crossed that ridge directly before you. I want you to hold your fire until you can see the *belts* of the Yankee cartridge boxes. I want you to aim at these! In this manner we shall bring down the enemy as grain falls before a reaper!"

Shouting, a colonel named Parker stood at ground level above his men and most of Wyatt's men as they took up positions in a crook of a zigzagging trench that was apparently a road. As he yelled his intentions, some men were taking rifle positions while others hurriedly pushed sharpened wooden rails into the fence that ran along the sunken lane. Still others were using their unfixed bayonets to hack spear points on more fence rails. The chest-high "breastworks" was temporary but effective. It could hamper a Union charge, but the Confederates could still shoot through it.

Perhaps two thousand Confederates were lined up in this

mile or so of the hook-shaped trench, as far to the right and left as Wyatt could peer. Their long rifle barrels poked through the breastworks, and the only noise here was those bayonets hacking at wood. A sense of urgency ran like a taut fishing line through all their spines.

As Colonel Parker hurried southeast on the sunken lane to yell that order to another quarter mile of men, Wyatt was still standing, but down inside the trench. Most of his powdermen, with Parker's and Rodes's on one side and G. B. Anderson's brigade stretching into the distance on the other, were leaning on their stomachs on the northeastern embankment of the sunken lane. Way in the distance to his left, which he could barely see from this crook, were Colquitt's brigade of Alabama and Georgia boys, and beyond them were more North Carolina boys led by a man named MacRae. Or so he'd been told. There was simply too much information to take in, and he was painfully aware that nobody knew or cared if "Craig's Richmond Light Artillery" was here at all. They weren't anybody's anything; they were just more dirty Rebs, itching to shoot.

Funny . . . the names of the commanders and the loftly echo of So-and-So's fourth Alabama or Such-and-Such's twelfth North Carolina lost meaning for Wyatt as he stood here now, gazing down at this endless line of man after man, lying pressed on the embankment so tight beside each other that their elbows knocked. The Confederates were indistinguishable from each other here. There was no unit flag flying every few hundred men, and the filth caking their uniforms and trim colors made it impossible to tell cavalry from infantry, artillery from any farm boy who decided to fall in with them. They were the same color and in the same condition as the dried curled-up early-autumn leaves littering the sunken road.

They were in tatters, the word *uniform* mocked by their mismatched clothing. Their feet, most of which were bare, pressed into the wheel ruts, and their rifles were loaded and poised on the brink of this convenient trench, and each man had his ramrod and his cartridges laid out beside a leg. They knew what their job was and how mechanically they would have to do it.

Their two thousand pairs of eyes were fixed through the spiny, spiky breastwork rails. Only their faces were uniform.

"What's burning way over there?" Wyatt asked, squinting at a column of black smoke that obviously wasn't coming from cannon fire.

"A farm," someone answered. "We burnt it down."

"Why?"

"So's the Yanks can't use it for cover or a sharpshoot station."

A drummer boy, of all things, piped up at him from way down the line. "The field in front of us is from that farm. Now they got no cover at all. See how that works?"

Feeling ignorant for asking, Wyatt fell silent and simply tried to absorb the spectacle at his sides. He nodded and tried to forget that a boy no more than eleven was twenty feet away at this moment, readying for battle.

"Major Craig, I wisht you'd get down," one of his men said, rising on an elbow. "Why don't you come on in between me and Rusty here, and we'll just take a nap and let the colonels and generals do the standing up."

Wyatt smiled, leaned on the rifle somebody had given him, and tried to appear casually confident.

"Oh, I'll be all right, Jimmy. This is a defensible position. I'd like to see the Union Army just once, before we start cutting them down. I've never even seen them, you know."

"You don't wanna see'm, Major!" one of Anderson's Georgians called. "They're a holy blue fright!"

A crackle of laughter ran as far as Wyatt could see in both directions.

He laughed too. Spirit was exceptionally high, he thought, considering how gaunt and caked these men were and that godawful pound of gunfire and cannon booms from the north.

"Come on Major Craig," Jimmy called, "right here." He patted the hard clay beside him. A puff of dust rose with each pat, but the ground was so hard that the pats also made a thudding noise.

Jimmy Gundersen was a jovial, chubby, heavily bearded chemical mixer who had come to Richmond with Wyatt after the Kansas tannery troubles. Prospects of a steady job at a powdermill run by a man he trusted had been more appealing than taking the compensation offered—by the Du Ponts, though Jimmy still didn't know that—and striking off for the wild west.

So here Jimmy was, along with two dozen of the loyal workers whom Wyatt had come to think of as his little family.

Strange, what circumstances arise through nothing but chance. They hadn't intended to participate in battle, but only to deliver powder and go back and keep making more. Their wives all expected them home.

"Time's it?" Wyatt asked to the line of men at his feet.

One of his own called, "Ten."

"Mmm . . . wish I'd had breakfast this morning."

More laughter erupted from down the line, but this laughter was of a very different timber. It crinkled his spine.

"We wish we'd had breakfast last week!" somebody mocked.

They laughed again, but not *with* Wyatt. He suddenly felt ashamed, pampered.

He squinted into the morning sunlight and tried to see who had called to him and offered, "I sure wish you had too."

The North Carolinians seemed to accept the sincerity in his voice, and the laughter tapered away to agreeable nods. Hungry or not, they were enthusiastic, and it showed. Their hands twitched on their rifles, for they were hot to fight. They were practicing aiming.

They *wanted* to see those Yankee cartridge belts.

"Come on, Wyatt," Rusty Dwyer said. "You're all loaded up. Even *you* should be able to hit *something* today!"

The powder workers engaged in private humor, laughing and smiling at him at the same time. They seemed proud to be here.

"I will in a minute, Russ," Wyatt said with a wink. "Save my place."

Everyone faced east and waited.

In the ensuing silence he realized how *much* silence had fallen. The sounds of battle from the north had faded. For the first time he figured out that what he was hearing wasn't the cracking of rifles anymore.

Drumming . . . military drumming. An incessant, crackling racket whose consistency gave it away. The Yankee lines!

From where he was standing, Wyatt saw an undulating
fringe shaped exactly like the rolling land. Bayonets!

He drew a breath and gasped.

"They're coming!"

CHAPTER FIFTY-THREE

———— ★ ————

Wyatt Craig forgot his uniform, forgot his purpose, forgot his name.

He only stood and stared.

Before him bobbed a spectacle he could barely comprehend. Never had his mind made a picture of what five thousand *men* could look like. He knew what the number meant, in kegs, in pounds, in dollars, in gallons.

But in manpower . . .

Five *thousand!*

Not only in front of him, but stretching into the visible distance all the way to the right, and all the way to the left, hundreds upon hundreds of yards, and into the trees. He lived in what was considered a big city, the capital of a nation, yet the shaggy battle line moving toward him equaled one eighth of Richmond, Virginia.

The scene staggered him.

Silhouetted against the morning sun, shoulder against shoulder, pikes swaying in rhythm with the drum crackle, the Army of the Potomac's infantry made a swaying, splendid blue-black pageant. Giant regimental banners flew and flapped over their heads, proclaiming home states. New York, Massachusetts, New Hampshire, Connecticut, Pennsylvania. Like a lizard crawling along the ruffle of a woman's dress, just as D. H. Hill had said, the Yankees with their faces black from powder soot and their musket barrels waving, fringed the skirt of Lady Maryland. The blue reptile's long tongue and tail fit the landscape perfectly, up and down, up and down, all the way to both horizons.

And they were coming right toward Wyatt. Coming to pound the Rebel center to pulp.

Paralyzed by what he saw, Wyatt could no more move than fly. This couldn't be real. Outrageous storytelling couldn't concoct such a sight. Wasn't he looking at phantoms after all?

Yes, because the men in the sunken road were shocked too.

No one was shooting—no one at all. Even the distant battle had fallen into a lull. A cat's meow could have sounded, and everyone from one end of the Confederate center to the other would have heard it. After another minute, he was sure no one was breathing anymore either.

Nothing! Only the rap of Union drums. *Crack-a-tack crack—crack-a-tack crack—*

Even the crunch of thousands of Union footfalls was somehow . . . muted.

Wyatt almost shouted, just to make a human noise. But he couldn't shout, or even blink. Sulfur on the wind stung his eyes until they watered. Even at the mill it was never this thick.

"Fix bayonets!"

That must have been a Union voice, for the Yankee dragon began shifting even as they marched, and when they breathed again, bayonets flashed high over their heads. Now the dragon had quills.

"Chaaaaarge!"

The dragon leaned on its thousand ribs. Its quills tipped, and it rolled toward him.

"God bless us," he whispered.

Was he passing out? Had his wound finally claimed him? He was hot again, dizzy. He would awaken with Grace sponging his brow and Dorian making wisecracks from a close dark corner. Dorian—Grace . . .

"Hold your fire! Do *not* fire!"

Wyatt flinched and tucked both shoulders. Through his shock he registered that it was an officer shouting behind him and not grapeshot tearing through him from some Union smoothbore.

Somehow he swung around and saw another Confederate colonel about the same age as he, scanning the infantry onslaught with a far steadier eye and more nerve than Wyatt could claim to possess.

"Ain't that a sight," somebody murmured, as calmly as if he were paying out a trout.

When Wyatt turned forward again, he almost choked. The banners were enormous! Flapping first to the left, then to the right—whap, whap—

How could they come so much closer in just two seconds?

The ponderous Union line marching down on them now loomed in terrifying detail—the eyes, the hats, the sun flickering on bayonets, the officers riding in front, discolored banners waving beautifully, the resolute pleasure at finally being allowed to come forward, each face a storm cloud—a majestic animation of courage that almost made the Confederates want to applaud first, shoot second.

"Can we, Colonel Gordon?" a disembodied voice called from somewhere to Wyatt's extreme left.

"Not yet," the colonel on top called back. "Wait for my order."

The Union monster was advancing in two double ranks, very *long* ranks, stretching from horizon to horizon, a great dragon and its exact shadow maybe twelve or fourteen yards behind. That was four long lines of humanity, and it was a vision to behold.

Especially since not a soul was shooting, or even talking.

Wyatt stood there with both legs locked, his hands closed on the musket barrel, mesmerized, Why had he insisted upon looking? He wasn't even aiming his weapon.

He noticed the brass buttons. Handsome, all the same, not mismatched like Reb uniforms . . . saw the creases of eyes, the set of lips—

Buttons . . . Grace . . . the drums . . . was thunder rattling the windows of his bedroom?

"Fire!"

The earth opened up in a flash of red and white.

The Confederate volley felled more than five hundred union men in one hideous roar! Wyatt stared—could he be seeing the impossible twice in one day? The only thing more astonishing than the sight of the Union creature was seeing half its skin fall off in one blow. Five hundred, down just like that!

Suddenly the meadow was carpeted with bluejackets. The second rank simply stepped over their brothers and kept coming.

"Fire!" Colonel Gordon shouted again. Then he amended it to, "Fire at will!"

It was like giving hogs the key to the corn shed.

The ponderous Union ranks shed scale after scale. The Confederates, shielded in their trench, sent slaughter's own thunder at the bluecoats, aiming point-blank at the soot-blackened faces as though they were shooting niggers in a pen. Somehow Wyatt knew that's what some of these men were thinking.

They don't mean it, Dorian—they're just tired and sick— they've been threatened—men are horrible when they've been pushed—

Maybe it was his own warped Northern mind working overtime after having lived too long in the South. Maybe it was the din of battle so near at hand, too much like the nightmare explosion all powdermen lived in fear of hearing and imagined constantly.

From the distance artillery fire started—gigantic *boom*s so different from the *yap* of muskets. Grapeshot began splattering the ground here and there, forcing Confederates to duck into the sunken road, or fall into it, bleeding and screaming. But that was arbitrary, and for the most part the sunken road was doing exactly what General Hill had said it would—it was protecting them as they unloosed lead vengeance on the Union.

Above, Colonel Gordon suddenly bellowed and fell to his knees. Wyatt spun around, struggled up the backside of the trench, and hurried to him. He discovered the young officer struggling to get up on a right leg that was gushing from a lead ball in the thigh. Wyatt caught his arms and tried to help him, but Gordon shook him off furiously.

"No, no! Don't abandon your post!"

"Hold on, now!" Wyatt pointed at the leg. He had to shout over the surge and roar of the guns. "Don't you think I ought to tie that off?"

"What?"

"Tie that off!"

The colonel slammed a fist into the wound to cut off the blood flow and shook his head. "I have no intent of turning over this place! Go to your own men! They need to see us both!"

Somehow he got up and limped past, gave Wyatt a thankless shove, and went on shouting encouragements to his Alabama men at the left.

"Fine," Wyatt grumbled, staring and wondering where some men got what they had.

Something struck him then—he was spinning, falling. He slammed to the clay floor of the sunken road. Dry leaves puffed up at his sides.

Before Wyatt realized what had happened, Rusty and Jimmy had pulled him flat against the embankment.

So he hadn't been shot—yet—just kidnapped.

"You shouldn't even be here today, Wyatt," Jimmy Gundersen said as he used his ramrod furiously. "You're not fit to fight, with that belly wound. You done your part."

Jimmy leveled his rifle, didn't even bother aiming because he couldn't help but hit somebody, and fired. The report was deafening.

Without a pause Wyatt shoved his own rifle into Jimmy's hand and grabbed Jimmy's expended weapon.

"Shoot!" he bellowed.

As Jimmy aimed and fired again, Wyatt bit off the end of the cartridge and wrestled with the ramrod in these close quarters to reload the spent gun. As bullets whistled overhead, the two of them fell into this rhythm, and before long other men were pairing up the same way. Whenever he could, Wyatt also grabbed Rusty's gun and reloaded it.

More and more Confederates adopted this pattern, and the thunder of musketfire became an almost constant bass drumroll. The firing turned into a fire storm.

Yankees fell in whole groups, whole lines. Just dropped over in the grass, felled by the consuming musket barrage from the sunken road. No glorious fists waved, no defiant last words, no songworthy beckoning. They just dropped. Another brigade came up the slope and walked, ran or tripped over the fallen.

"Fire!" Colonel Gordon was calling, and followed that with

a barrage of encouragements, waving his left arm—which from here Wyatt could see had taken another ball and was also bleeding. How could a man take such a pounding and keep on? "Keep it up! Hold this place at any cost! If we fall, Lee falls! By God, I won't have it! Keep it up, boys! Brilliant, all of you!"

Wyatt had seen heroism before, but not in this degree. The rebels, lined up in their trench, loading and shooting with hurricanic fury, unable to move fast enough to satisfy their own mania.

Soon he too was caught up in this blood rush. Suddenly he worked faster, his fingers tangling. With the bluecoated, black-faced men falling like shingles before him no longer a shock, something else took over. Beside him Jimmy Gundersen fired and fired again, on the other side Rusty doing the same, between them Wyatt loading musket after musket until he tasted only powder and wadding and saw only his hands at work.

Rip cartridge paper, pour powder in, insert minié ball, wad, ram it down, place percussion cap, hand the musket over, get another, teeth, cartridge, powder, minié ball, wad, ram, cap—

Balls screamed above him, but all went high, overhead, struck the rail fences, or whined on into the meadow behind Confederate lines.

"They're falling back!" someone shouted—one of his own men. "Into the corn!"

Wyatt didn't get up to look, but just kept grabbing, biting, pouring, loading, ramming.

"Look at that! We got 'em so shook, they're shooting at each other!"

"Schoolboys," somebody else called steadily. "Don't get a big head over it."

"Back, you black bastards!"

A case shot, with several hundred lead balls inside, struck and exploded a hundred yards from Wyatt. Though fired from too great a range to hit the sunken road, it splayed the men in the trench with chunks of clay and bits of lead. Some went down, but the trench was good protection, and they could instantly rise again to continue their fire. Each volley razed another section of Union men.

As the galled Union fell back, leaving behind a carpet of

human spoilage, the Confederates shouted obscenities at them, called them names, laughed, screamed song lyrics like battle cries, and yipped like savages on the attack, taken over by some madness, going like a machine running hot.

Some of the Confederates to Wyatt's right jumped up, dug their bare toes into the side of the trench, hurled themselves up and over the breastwork fence and rails, and ran toward the Union retreaters, howling and yipping, some waving detached bayonets.

"Wait!" Wyatt shouted in that direction. "Hold your ground, damn it! You can't survive up there! Down! Back down!"

A few men heard him and jumped back into the trench, but far more ignored him in their frenzy and plunged up and over. They were ghoulish and angry, teeth grinding, lips peeled back, fighting the battle they'd been deprived of outside Richmond and had expected for so long. All that frustration and fear now gurgled up and poisoned them.

Cannoneers in the distance learned quickly just how to load and aim their weapons to reach the breastworks. Now whole lengths of the fence along the sunken road began to blow apart or simply to dissolve. Their protection . . . splintering before his eyes . . .

Minutes whizzed by with volleys of lead balls, carried on artillery fire from the distance, and still the Rebels kept chewing away at their enemy. Union reserves as they came forward up the ridge again and again, new men filing in to replace the heavy losses. There seemed no end to them! Were they just coming up out of a hole in the ground, score after score, like water out of a well?

Laughter! What an insane sound to go with the hiss of balls and the splatter of grape! This wasn't battle! It was hell risen a foot above ground!

It had to stop . . . these people all had to get a breath and think, everyone, both sides, *think*.

"Hold on, everybody," Wyatt blurted. "Hey! Everybody slow down—slow down! Let's think a minute!"

No one heard him. He barely heard himself. They had changed from men to menace. They didn't care to slow down. It was pure chaos now, all dignity thrown to the sulfur-filled winds. Black clouds, red flashes, white funnels—the muskets kept on slamming into the giant punching bag of Union lines, but there was no taking them down, no flinging them back. They just kept coming.

They just kept on coming!

Then something happened that hadn't before. Beside Wyatt some of the men started lying down, letting their rifles drop to their sides. He looked this way and that, but it was true. Had they gotten tired? Were they as confused as he was in this hornet's nest?

Why was everyone lying down? Were they taking cover? Some were dropping their guns and burying their heads.

"What are you doing?" Wyatt asked them, turning from side to side. "What—"

Then he noticed Jimmy Gundersen looking at him funny.

"What's the matter?" Wyatt demanded. "Jimmy? Are you scared?"

There was no answer from the longtime Craig worker. He just kept staring at Wyatt without even blinking.

"Jimmy, get a hold of yourself!" Wyatt grabbed the man and shook him—

Jimmy fell forward without his eyes even going out of focus.

As Wyatt gasped and dropped back against the clay embankment, he found himself staring at a hole in the back of Jimmy's head—a hole big enough to put his fist through. Dark red blood poured from the rim of the wound, and in the middle of it was a yellowish-gray lump surging out of the hole.

Taking air in chunks, Wyatt scooted sideways until Jimmy slid off his lap and went face down in the dirt. The yellow-gray mass fell forward into his skull.

Suddenly there was nothing but blood.

"Jesus!" Wyatt gagged.

He pressed backward and struck another body, went sideways and hit another. They collapsed around him, on top of him, dropping deadweight, changed abruptly from living, self-animating images of God to sacks of water and grain sagging to the floor.

"Oh! Oh, Jimmy . . . no, no . . . no . . ."

He gasped and scrambled, confused. Slowly he realized what was happening.

Somebody had found a vantage point! Some Union brigade had found a hillock with the right rifle angle! A portcullis had opened for the Union. Somehow, somewhere, the Union had discovered a vantage point, a place from which to fire *down* into the sunken road.

All the protection suddenly went to hell. An evil star rose over the Confederate's perfect protection, their ideal musket trench.

Men were dropping two-thick around him until it was all Wyatt could do to keep from being buried and smothered to death by his own men. His own men! Men whose wives expected them home! Even as bodies fell on him, he felt the impact of balls hitting the unresponsive flesh. Rusty, then Ed, Sam, Vance, Cecil, Bob, John, Dawsey, the other John—all his men!

The dead were shielding him!

Lead balls struck the hard clay embankment opposite of the Confederate line and were ricocheting and hitting the men in the backs. The sound of it was hideous—*thok, thok*—and each time a man would collapse and crumble to the sunken road's floor.

"Oh, my God, oh, God," Wyatt kept saying over and over, shouting it until his throat was raw, yet barely able to hear his own voice through the tornado around him. He turned his head to one side, then the other, yelling up the embankment at the Union men. "Wait! Where are you? Give us a minute! Just let us get up! Oh—God—stop for a minute! Let us get a breath! Hold on a minute! We're not thinking! Let's stop and have a talk!"

The gunfire kettledrummed all around.

Confederate enthusiasm turned to mass panic. The men tried to scramble out of the trench, but the sunken haven had become a death trap. They tried to scramble up its crumbling sides, but like ants in the ant lion's funnel trap, they slipped and failed. The moment their heads rose above the embankment, led balls smashed into their skulls, and they'd hover, flail, and crash back into the sunken road, in heaps.

Thok . . . thok . . . thok thok thok thok—

Just as Wyatt managed to get to his knees, a force tore across the top of his shoulder. Impact knocked him spinning sideways, and he slammed over a pile of bodies and tumbled several feet—without ever touching the ground. There was no more ground. There was only a gaggle of bent elbows and knees, heaving chest, gushing wounds, torn wool. Instantly two more bodies fell on top of him—dead or not, he couldn't tell. The carpet of men sprawled out from his sides, some limp and heavy, some trying to turn over, gain some vestige of control, as he was. But it was impossible.

In the salient of the sunken road, to Wyatt's far left, the road itself wasn't so worn down and offered less protection than Wyatt was getting. He happened to have his eyes straining in that direction—and was watching as the Alabama line collapsed. General Hill had mentioned whose men they were, but Wyatt couldn't summon the name from his numb brain.

How many minutes went by—he couldn't guess. How badly was he hurt? He was so numb . . . brain, fingers, legs . . . was there a musket nearby that he could pick up and use? He reached for a brown rod standing up from the bodies next to him, but found it was only a split fence rail. Couldn't shoot that very well . . .

Gotta clear my head.

"Gotta get up . . . clear my head," he said, clinging to the sound of his own voice.

Other Confederates ran right over him, scrambling in panic, trying to escape south on the sunken road, since trying to climb out of it was instant death.

"Wait! Stand your ground! Don't panic!" Wyatt pushed a groaning man off his legs and somehow got to his knees.

Pain pounded in his shoulder, and his left arm fell numb. He struggled to look up. He could see Colonel Gordon running staggering up and down the battle line, waving a sword and calling encouragements, probably the same as Wyatt had just called, and just as futilely.

There was blood all over the young officer now. How many times had Gordon been hit? Who could stop to count wounds?

Then, as Wyatt watched, Gordon's face became a splatter of blood. Just like that. Just standing there.

Gordon paused, stopped walking, reeled, then fell forward and disappeared into the grass.

"Oh, *no,*" Wyatt moaned. He muttered something about God for the hundredth time in the two hours, but this time he realized God had abandoned them.

If God was here, it was only as a spectator. Maybe Dorian was right.

Suddenly he shot bolt upright.

"Dorian!" he choked. "I sent him here! He's here—oh, God, here somewhere! Oh, no, oh no, no—oh, *nuts!*"

He swiveled this way and that, trying to peer through the maelstrom, to find Dorian and send him home to safety.

"Oh, no, no," he kept moaning. Desperation, separation—

He'd come to deliver powder, and now he was about to be in a battle! And he'd sent Dorian to get word to the Confederate high command, so Dorian was caught here somewhere too! And all the men who'd come with them—all caught!

Wyatt nearly choked. He hadn't taken any of his chances to smooth things out with Grace . . . so much left undone . . .

There was activity northwest of him on the sunken road. An officer moving along the sunken road where the road wasn't deep enough to protect the men, near where Colonel Gordon had fallen. Hauling a wounded man at his side, the officer paused and incredibly shouted, "Sixth Alabama, about face! Forward march!"

Wyatt jolted to his knees, his mouth gaping. "No!" he bellowed. "That's not right! That can't be right! Stay down!"

He waved his one working arm, but to no avail. As he watched, horrified, the entire Alabama rank rose from the sunken road, turned their backs on the Yankee onslaught, and scrambled up the steep embankment in a mass retreat.

"No! No!" Wyatt kept calling. "Go along the road! Stay in the road! Stay down, damn you all!"

The Yankee barrage was a single continuous thunder roll. As Wyatt watched, helpless, the entire sixth Alabama fell victim to its own disorder.

Men fell in bunches of twenty and thirty. They never even got up to ground level.

Wyatt staggered to his feet, bent over, unable to see through the stinging sulfur fumes. He waved at the air and stumbled forward—right into a puddle. His foot got stuck. Wetness soaked into his trousers and boots. It was like trying to walk on wet sponges—

He waved the air vigorously and looked down, trying to see what he was standing in.

He did see it and would regret looking down for the rest of his life. It was blood. Floating in it was a disembodied eyeball.

The blood of Antietam was looking up at him.

He stumbled backward, disoriented, and fell on his right hip. Instantly two men fell on top of him, crushing the air from his lungs. He lay there with the weight of bodies pressing against him, his shoulder bleeding, his ravaged insides knotting, his trousers soaking up blood from the shattered bodies. He lay back, twisted onto his side under the drag of fully grown dead men all over him, and crawled out from under them, moving on his stomach like a goddamned slug.

Then, somewhere in the distance, an experienced gunner got his trajectory just right. The terrible demoralizing *poom* of a twelve-pounder slammed across the sky.

Solid roundshot crashed into the breastworks above him. It dissolved to splinters with an awful crackle.

Wyatt twisted to look up.

His skull rang suddenly, and he saw lights. His hands went numb, then went into spasms on the embankment. He felt clay under his fingernails. His legs quivered, turned to string, failed.

Blood poured into his eyes.

The last thing he saw was the breastwork fence rails dancing as they came down on top of him.

★

★★★

THE CANNON'S ROAR

10:30 TO NOON, THE SAME DAY

The sunken road became a death trap.

For three hours the Confederates fended off Union hammer blows, but ultimately broke. Reinforcements came up from the Confederate rear, but soon even they were driven back into the cornfield and orchard of the Piper Farm, where they took another stand. The sunken road had been overrun. Union soldiers whose comrades had been slaughtered now knelt upon the "ghastly flooring" of Confederate dead and dying in the trench, and upon this platform they continued their barrage. More and more Yankees poured out of the eastern horizon.

Lee's critical center had shredded. The infantry scattered, running back toward the Potomac.

In one mile of trench twenty-six hundred Confederates lay dead or dying. The breastworks and the fences were reduced to a flat jumble of firewood. Blood ran in rivulets and formed puddles. Entrails and disembodied limbs lay separated from men who had been hit at point-blank range.

As morning passed to afternoon, the sunken road was being called "Bloody Lane."

Harvey Hill came to the battle front and tried to rally his infantry in the Piper Farm orchard, gathering stragglers from other units and calling for the charge. The Confederates drew together as best they could in the storm of shell and canister raining into the field and orchard, but they came under fire from Union men kneeling on the dead in Bloody Lane.

The "Rebel yell" rippled spines for a full mile in either di-

rection and had an effect on both sides—the Union men were annoyed, and the Confederates were galvanized. The Union fell back briefly, but did not break. The Confederate counterattack was choppy and eventually did shatter.

There simply were not enough of them.

At one P.M. there was a lull. The heat of a Maryland September had become oppressive, virtual torture to men fighting in wool uniforms. Corpses began to bloat very quickly under the steamy summer sun.

The chain of command was saddled with what they called "friction"—things going wrong, things left unknown, subordinates were unsure if orders were from their own commander or not, if those orders were timely, or if that commander had any sense of on-the-field changes. Most had little idea where their soldiers were. Neither field glass nor semaphore could penetrate the hovering fog of cannon, rifle, and detonation smoke. Reports were patchy, incomplete, rare. Many came from punch-drunk survivors with only a worm's-eye view of the circumstances.

Defense and attack of Bloody Lane cost roughly six thousand casualties in all. North of there another thirteen thousand or so were dying in the Woods and the Cornfield. The day was only half over.

The Union had gained about two-thirds of a mile.

★

CHAPTER FIFTY-FOUR

—— ★ ——

All other battles in this country are
merely skirmishes compared to it.

—A GUARD IN THE MCCLELLAN CAMP,
17 September 1862

ROHRBACH BRIDGE, ON THE CONFEDERATE RIGHT FLANK,
1:00 P.M.

Antietam Creek appeared as an ocean in a terrible storm,
chopped by artillery fire and the constant barrage of lead balls
crashing into the fast current. To wade in would be to invite
death even more instant than to try rushing the bridge.

So the Union was rushing the bridge.

Dorian crawled with considerable trouble across the
Confederate high ground on the west bank, an almost vertical,
heavily treed slope. Gunfire from overhead told him there
were Confederates up there on the limestone bluff, firing down
on the bluecoated soldiers who were so determined to take that
bridge. Erupted powder floated down and stung his eyes until
stepping from branch to root to rock became painful and te-
dious, the work of a blinded man.

This was his reward for gallantry. Offer to carry a message
from Jeb Stuart to one of the right-flank commanders, and
what had he gotten? Trapped on the cheek of some bluff,
watching a logjam of blue uniforms surge over some bridge.

He paused, breathing with difficulty in the smoke and

clutching a couple of young trees to hold himself on this up-down ridge, and he looked out upon Rohrbach Bridge.

The stone bridge arched with undeniable beauty across an also beautiful creek. The five-foot-deep water rolled under it, appearing forest green beneath the trees of summer. The bridge's three arches and spreading feet joined the banks with functional, classic lines. Yes . . . yes, beautiful.

Yet hazed in cannon belch, with poles wagging upon it unsteadily and banners flapping, then falling—the otherwise timeless beauty was injected with immediacy that wasn't pretty at all.

Robin . . . can you see it? . . . 'And sic a night he taks the road in as ne' er poor sinner was abroad in. . . . The wind blew as 'twad blawn its last; the rattling showers rose on the blast; the speedy gleams the darkness swallow'd; loud, deep and lang the thunder bellow'd!'—

"Halloo! You stay clear of me!"

Dorian stopped and waved at the smoke, squinted through it. He saw a man, Confederate infantry private, with a beard to his belly and blood from there down. He also was crawling along the middle of the bluff, trying to survive.

"Are you injured?" Dorian called over the ten or so feet still separating them.

"Ankle's broke," the man said. "Third time in my life. Think of that!"

He laughed at some personal irony.

Musing at the conditions under which men could rally a spirit, Dorian had to rouse himself when the man shouted again. They were scarcely ten feet away, yet could barely hear each other.

"What're you doing up here, ah . . . Captain?"

"Soil analysis for planting peanuts. Why are they taking this bridge? I have heard their army is already across the creek north of here."

"Supply line. Can't wade a cannon through five foot a' rushing water."

The infantryman rearranged his rifle and used it to brace himself on the steep side of the ridge.

"Why aren't you firing upon them?" Dorian shouted.

"Pardon?"

"Firing! Why aren't you firing !"

"Out of powder," the Confederate called back. "Heaven help the boys trying to hold them back."

Dorian blinked out over the bridge, and the surging lines of bluecoated men.

*'Now, do thy speedy utmost, Meg, and win the key-stane o'
the Brig—There at them thou thy tail may toss, a running
stream they darena cross—'*

"Nothing can hold them back," he said. "They can only hold themselves back." He paused then and flipped, "Of course, with George McClellan, that is a genuine forecast. Are you injured, private? All that blood on you?"

"Belongs to somebody else, thank Christ," the man said. "Got it at the Bloody Lane."

Dorian struggled across the nearly vertical slope, bracing his feet on juts of rock or tree roots. What had he just heard?

"Ruddy Lane—I know no such place."

The man dabbed at a cut on his lip and corrected, "*Bloody* Lane. That's what they're calling it now. And you'll come to know it, Captain. Our boys, oh Lord . . . we held that ground till hell opened up." He shook his head in wonderment and emotion. "We'd do anything for that Bobby Lee . . . we think he hung the moon—"

Dorian glowered suddenly and demanded, "Explain yourself clearly, sir! This is no day for gaming!"

The man blinked at him through the smoke and roar. Together they ducked as a canister struck the slope over them and sent a rain of lead, shrapnel, and rocks slashing toward the riverbank. Dorian straightened almost instantly and demanded, "Speak up!"

A barrage of lead balls whined toward them from some accidental coordination, and they both ducked for cover. All around them the trees erupted and shuddered.

*'Before him Doon pours all his floods, the doubling storm
roars thro' the woods, the lightnings flash from pole to pole,
near and more near the thunders roll'—*

The infantryman coughed as a sulfur cloud enveloped them, then said, "The sunken wagon road back on that homestead land up thataway. I hope I never see a sight as that again in my remainin' days, may the Lord let me live more than today . . . nothing but bodies far as the eye could see. We had to retreat. I swung south, and here I am."

Something in Dorian rose like a cobra. "You abandoned a counterattack? Abandoned your fellow men? Is that what you're claiming?"

"I ran!" the infantryman shouted furiously, screaming over the din of gunfire. "I've no shame! There was nothing to defend but a thousand dead goners! The Yankees, they come on us in a horde right outta the ugliest part of the Bible, and I don't care if I ran! I don't care if I had to step on General Hill to get away! Don't you judge me till you stand on the Bloody Lane and see where I'd be had I stood ground!"

In spite of the cloying September heat, a chill shot up through Dorian such as he had never endured before in his life. His feet turned so cold, they actually ached in his boots. He plunged along the steep slope, fingers clawing before him until he caught the infantryman by the throat.

"Which Hill?" he demanded. "Ambrose Hill?"

Shocked, the man twisted back, his elbows digging into the overgrowth.

"Harvey!"

"Where are they?" Dorian cranked on the man's torn collar. "Where are they!"

"I told you—dead! Dead in the ditch!"

"The survivors! Where did they go!"

"Back to that farm! The orchard back there! How can I know? I'm here same as you!"

"But Hill's *division*!"

The man stared up at him as though he were crazy for not understanding. A few moments more, and he began to comprehend what was happening behind the captain's black storming eyes.

Finally he pushed up his voice. It came out scarcely a whisper. Even through the overwhelming artillery thunder, Dorian heard him.

Reading lips or reading minds, he heard. Some veil of protection fell away from the infantryman's eyes, leaving only a pure reflected horror and the fear of a messenger who had read the message.

"Slaughtered, Cap'm . . . they're plain slaughtered."

CHAPTER FIFTY-FIVE

———— ★ ————

"Please . . . don' make me beg . . . Mama? . . . please, water . . . Mama . . . please—"

The pleading man was indistinguishable from the dead, but somehow Dorian found him among the carpet of carnage. He *looked* dead, but his hand was moving instead of just twitching.

Here, unlike other places, there were dead of both sides. Most places possessed either mostly blue uniforms visible in the grass, or gray and butternut. Here there were all kinds of colors. This field, plowed but not planted, had apparently been Confederate territory, then defended, then overrun by Federals, then fired upon from a locality farther west by retreating Confederates. Confederates had been moved down here first, and a few minutes later, their Federal counterparts.

His legs aching from crossing ragged terrain, ravines, hollows, tangled mountain laurel, and heavy woods, then trying to run through soft plowed fields, Dorian picked his way toward the voice.

The wounded man was a Federal infantryman in his twenties—or fifties, it was impossible to tell—blond, green-eyed, his face coated with black powder dust and caked with sweat. Blood discolored his entire lower half, which was moving spasmodically.

Dorian picked his way over to the man, somehow kept his opinion to himself about the man's lower half, and handed over his canteen.

639

"There's little in it," he said. "I regret not thinking to fill it when I noticed the trouble starting this morning. I'm sorry, but you're welcome to what's here."

Trembling fingers reached toward him, somehow closing around the canteen. He fumbled and dropped it.

Impatient, his mind in another place, Dorian stooped and helped the man remove the top.

"Tell me, if you can," he said as the two of them worked, "can you direct me to this place everyone is calling Bloody Lane? I've heard that phrase a half-dozen times, yet I cannot find the thing."

"Up there," the man rasped. His voice was a gravelly scratch. "Quarter mile . . . we walked over it . . . Seventh Maine . . . I'm Prosser . . . Jack Prosser . . . tell my mother— please, I'm begging you—Rebel crossfire . . . Prosser, Third Brigade . . . Colonel Irwin—tell my mother!"

"I will," Dorian assured him, and made a mental note of the name and unit. "Mothers are the only angels."

Working together, they got the canteen open and put it to his lips. The man took a swig, regurgitated half that he swallowed, but seemed greatly relieved and closed his eyes.

"Thank God," the man murmured.

With a crook of his eyebrow and a resilience somehow protected by the fortress he had built around his heart, Dorian stood up and gazed at the man. He sought out his coldest shields.

"Dorian," he corrected.

The ground moved. Steamed under the relentless sun. Bodies bloated, shifted, settled. Even in death, some turned over as their internal functions ceased or their organs collapsed or gas built up swiftly in the heat. Occasionally an arm rose, beckoning, pleading, only to fall again, heavily. Telling living from dead would be nothing short of pure art today.

Corpsmen from both sides wandered the fields in pairs, with stretchers, scanning the ground as they walked in the distance, looking for wounded among the endless dead.

Dorian stood on the embankment. He saw the lane, and he saw the blood. As far as he could look into the distance, it was a trench of bodies. Elbows, knees, gaping mouths and shattered skulls, chests embedded with pieces of shrapnel. Remnants of humanity like chewed matter, marooned in their own sea. The battle slaughter spread from his feet to the horizon, a giant stew slowly gurgling, a criminal disassembling of nature's handiwork.

Thousands of them.

How could he even begin to search?

Somewhere . . . in this godforsaken carnage . . . take a step and walk upon the dead, the dying? How could he?

Never had Dorian felt so wretched. Helplessness was not a companion he was used to.

The breeze changed, and the smell almost knocked him over. The slaughterhouse stink of blood—it had its own smell, like none other—mingled with the ignoble identification of urine. Men reduced to the condition of newborns had, in their last seconds, released everything.

Exhausted, Dorian tired to kneel and rest on one knee between rails of the smashed breastworks, and ended up collapsed on both knees. Holding his plight in his two cramping hands, he gazed out through misting eyes over the spectacle of Bloody Lane. His eyes burned, then tried to put out their own fire.

Loneliness crawled in his stomach. Loneliness, among the thousands.

It picked holes in his wall. His shoulders drooped. His hands fell between his knees. Not meaning to speak at all, not meaning to think or wish, he felt a whisper brush from his throat. His voice cracked.

"Work it out later," he rasped. "Oh . . . Wyatt."

None of them, not Wyatt, not the powdermen, not himself, not even Aleck Stephens had foreseen a confrontation of such magnitude—such slaughter. Dorian had managed to get his message to General Jackson and planned to turn and go straight back to Orienta, yet here he was. Caught in battle, searching, searching, searching for Wyatt.

What he thought was cannon fire in the distance turned out to be not at all, but a new sound, and not in the distance. Its like had never before been heard on the American continent. It answered his whisper.

The moaning of Antietam battlefield.

★

PART ELEVEN

HELL NIGHT

CHAPTER FIFTY-SIX

———— ★ ————

The sun seemed almost to go backwards.

—A North Carolina soldier

We were praying for night to come.

—An Alabama soldier

I have heard and seen pictures of battles, they would all be in a line, all standing in a nice level field fighting, a number of ladies taking care of the wounded . . . but it isent so.

—A Michigan private, sixteen years old

RICHMOND

Orienta was singing to herself and to her baby when she noticed the darkening windows and went to light a few lamps. The sun was setting.

She was all alone, and somehow it was right, for she knew she had never been less alone in her life. Grace had gone on an errand of some kind, Buckie had been sent off to deliver some missive for the major, and Dorian . . . oh, Dorian . . . he was back from his adventures, had returned to her, and for now was doing the glorious duty of a Confederate captain by delivering precious information to the battlefront. He would deliver it, and he would come right back here to the guest house and get her, and together they would go to Europe.

All this hubbub. She would be gladdened when it was all over.

Europe! She thought of it with burgeoning excitement. He would take her to all the places he knew from his aristocratic travels and his classical education. He would show her all the schools he attended and introduce her to his teachers. He would show her the brilliance of the Old World, and he would speak Greek to her, and she would melt. Their baby would be born in the shadow of kings, of the bluest bloodlines, out of sight of any riffraff.

He had said it to her.

"I shall wrap you in the excellence of the haut monde, and leave this lumpen proletariat behind. *Profanum vulgus* shall weep in our wake. You are my duchess . . . I your chevalier."

She giggled as she thought of it. He had such a way.

A dozen trunks and cases were spread across the parlor couches, for she was packing. Her new clothing, purchased by Grace and Major Craig because Orienta had come here with nothing, and things she gathered or made for the baby.

Strange . . . there was nothing to pack of Dorian's. Nothing personal, at least. His few suits were already packed. His Inverness lay there, over a high-backed chair. In the summer heat there was no need for such a garment. In Europe, though, he would need it. Orienta had heard of those cold Scottish nights.

She was musing over which ancient city she would choose to give birth in when a knock came at the guest-house door.

Well, that was odd. Perhaps the major had come back. Or perhaps it was Grace.

"Oh, no," she chided herself. "Grace wouldn't have to knock. Grace? Is that you? You know you needn't knock. . . ."

She pulled the heavy door open and almost threw her pear-shaped body off balance.

"Oh—"

"Evenin', ma'am."

The man was enormous, frightening, bearded, very rough, and layered with leather, but he wasn't making any overt movements, and he did tip his . . . whatever that dead animal was on his head.

"Don't fret, missus," he said. "Just passing information and seeking the same."

Orienta nervously pulled the door halfway closed and partly hid behind it, hoping that he hadn't noticed her obvious inability to defend herself. Of course, that was ridiculous. She wasn't one of these women who could hide such a condition. Even her hair was pregnant.

"May I . . . help you, mister?"

"Looking for information regarding an escaped slave out of South Carolina, missus. I got some private word that he was in contact with this household, that he'd been seen in these parts past coupla days."

"I have no such information. Did not any of the servants at the big house take care of you?"

"Nobody answers at the big house," the man said.

"I have no information regarding any escaped slave, Mr.—"

"Quist, ma'am. Orville Quist. Professional bounty agent, loan collector or freight guard. This man, you won't have no trouble spotting. He speaks like a king's brother and looks like one too. Black curly hair, black eyes, real fine skin like a peach, dresses in the fancy slick clothes, speaks five or six languages. But don't be fooled. He's passin', ma'am. You know what that means, don't you? Passin'?

"Ma'am? Something wrong? Well, tell you what . . . I'll just leave you with this here 'Wanted' notice. It'll tell the story, but better you sit down till you read it, ma'am, in your, uh . . . anyhow, it ain't a very pretty story to digest. You have a pleasant evenin', ma'am, and contact me like it says there at the bottom if this man comes anywhere near you. I'll come with my chains and take him off you. Thanks and . . . night."

Lantern lights bobbed like a will-o'-the-wisps over the night swamp of casualties. Fog and bloody steam mingled until neither could be told from the other.

Individuals wandered the field in every direction. Some were wounded hobbling toward the haze of Sharpsburg, or the torches at the Dunker Chapel, where a hospital had been set up. Some were search parties picking through the shivering mess, trying to identify the dead. Even more pitiful than the plaintive cries for help were the trembling voices of men calling for their brothers, friends, sons. Seldom were they answered.

Burial details moved sluggishly, beginning to line up the dead for interment. From makeshift field hospitals rose an endless single groan, punctuated all too frequently with screams. The dead were the lucky ones here; the wounded were more dead than alive, but alive enough for a long drag through hell. In any other condition, grown men would be embarrassed to make such a noise, but there were no grown men left between the town of Sharpsburg and the creek called Antietam.

North, South—all differences that seemed so important under banners were forgotten, or at least suspended. Men came together to chat, offer water, surfeit the shock, or share a smoke—men who in daylight had been murdering each other. Some asked in muffled voices how to find a particular brigade and were directed to heaps of dead from a certain unit.

In Bloody Lane, soaked to the thighs in other people's blood and torn sinew, a one man endured his ninth hour of picking through corpses. Unlike other places on the battlefield, there were almost no men left alive in Bloody Lane. Most of the fallen had been struck two or more times, by various forms of intrusion. Minié balls, shrapnel, shell, canister shot, and a disturbing number had been struck in the back by ricochet, or as they tried to crawl out. Their faces were something to behold. Like wax.

He had found only two men alive in nine hours. Far worse than the begging of "Help me, help me," was the call of "Kill me, kill me." He had collected three canteens in his search and left them with these two men, but otherwise there was nothing he could offer. His hands were shaking, numb. A few others had died as he picked his way toward them—he had noted the rattling of final breaths—but most . . .

At the tenth hour Dorian had been reduced to the core of his humanity. He either felt all the pain or none of it, and alternated between those. His senses went as numb as his fingers. His uniform was more red than gray now, dark and ugly in the foggy haze. Clouds were moving in overhead, making the night even darker, the going slower.

Has anyone see Major Craig?

He didn't recognize any of these men. Sometimes he thought he might have stumbled on one of the workers from the mill, but their identities were lost, simply lost in the extermination. He might be crawling over people he'd known since the Kansas deal, and he wouldn't even realize it. He knew more than ever before the meaning of the word *bloodbath*.

Somehow he drove himself onward through the human soup, taunted by frustration. The saturated ground was the consistency of pudding. When he wasn't sinking to the ankles, he couldn't get two steps without losing a foot between some poor man's knee and another's shattered head. The search was drudgery in its purest form, but he couldn't stop. Once started, he couldn't give up. Bellows of agony from the so-called hospitals harassed him and made him wonder if he wanted to find Wyatt alive after all, or mercifully dead.

No—he couldn't think of that. Couldn't think of Wyatt dead.

"*No*," he growled. "You'll have to *prove* it to me—"

There was no answer. No more sinister whizz of bullets to comfort him and disguise the fact that here, in a blanket of humanity, he couldn't even hear breathing. It was unnatural and stressful to be among so many people and have it all be so *still*.

He somehow ignored any guilt at treading upon the dead. Never could he have imagined feeling such guilt, but he did feel it. The dead were dead, after all, weren't they? Yet he went over them as if walking a hot griddle, beating down his torments, until finally he saw what he feared most of all. More than all this.

A body in an officer's uniform. A body wearing shoes.

Dorian plunged headlong toward the form, afraid to lose his place. He crawled up the body from the shoes to the chest, and there he encountered carrion.

"Curse it," he spat. "Why can't you at least cooperate!"

The face was nearly gone. What could he test? How could he know? A stand-up collar . . . Wyatt had hated that collar. . . .

Short-winded and frantic, Dorian grabbed the dead man by the throat and rubbed the collar fiercely until drying blood flaked and smeared his hands and the rank insignia showed itself—

A star. A single brass star. A major.

But was it an artillery major?

In desperation he grabbed the corpse's arm and held it up, but the darkness damned his purpose. He couldn't tell if the blood-soaked piping and cuffs had been scarlet before the blood soaked them. He just couldn't tell. He let go of the arm. It stayed up.

He looked at the man's face. Most of it was missing, the entire right side and lower jaw imploded by some impact or other. The remaining hair was greased back from blood. Impossible to tell the color of that too.

But the face . . . nearly gone. Only a single closed eye and part of the right jaw hinge remained. There was only one thing left to try.

Furious, gasping, crawling on his knees, Dorian ripped through the pockets of the dead until he found a flint box. Another fit of ripping gave him one of the few pieces of dry cloth in Bloody Lane. Working in shudders, he made a spark and lit the cloth. It caught flame and cast a hideous light on the death around him. He staggered back toward the body of the major.

The flame wobbled sickeningly. Time stopped.

Dorian held the burning rag high with one hand, and with the other hand he reached for the dead man's eye. His thumb pressed the eyelid. He pushed it up.

Puffed and stiff, the lid resisted. The eyelashes were stuck together. His rag was burning toward his hand. He felt the heat on his wrist.

He pushed harder. The eyelid popped open.

Dorian sucked in a harsh breath and held it. Then another.

The flame licked at his palm and suddenly found fresh air and burst around his hand.

He flinched and dropped the makeshift torch. It flapped, landed in a rut full of burgundy lather, and guttered.

He slipped to his knees in disbelief. Raw disbelief.

"Brown," he gulped. "Brown eyes . . ."

It wasn't Wyatt. It wasn't.

He slid onto a thigh, then down all the way. He couldn't move anymore.

With his hand on the stranger's dead body, he slumped against the embankment. He pressed bloody fingers to his eyes and felt tears streaming.

Then, supremely alone, Dorian passed the unquiet night.

★

PART TWELVE

THE LAST SHRIEK ON THE RETREAT

When that grim foe of life below
  Comes in between to make us part,
The iron hand that breaks our band,
  It breaks my bliss—it breaks my heart!

—Robert Burns

THE CANNON'S ECHO

Fourteen hours of battle, over 100,000 men and 500 artillery pieces along a three-mile front, with the day's gain less than a total mile of ground.

Whole divisions lay dead. Whole towns wiped clean of all their menfolk. The aftermath was worse than the battle, for the task of sifting through the carpet of dead and collecting the wounded was almost as daunting as treating the wounded in such conditions as the Dunker Chapel, in which 150 men at a time were relieved of shattered limbs, and too often, their lives. The true casualty count wouldn't show itself for weeks. The battle was over, but the dying went on.

The South's chance for a quick, decisive victory was gone. General Ambrose P. Hill's Light Division came forward from the Confederate side at the last minute and stopped the Union from overwhelming the retreating battle-weary Rebels. Lee waited all day for the final blow to be dealt.

Faced down again, though, McClellan settled back on his success in stopping the invasion and failed to follow through and destroy the Army of Northern Virginia when he had the chance. Lee took the advantage and slipped his columns back across the Potomac, to lick their wounds and fight another day.

Instead of being decided one way or the other, once and for all, the Civil War would go on.

CHAPTER FIFTY-SEVEN

————— ★ —————

General George McClellan rocked back in his chair beneath the tent that shielded him from the hot summer sun.

Here on the east side of Antietam Creek, between the creek and the Boonsboro Road, he was secure and really quite satisfied. Occasionally the warm breeze would shift and carry the pungent stink of the battleground, but for the most part he was free of having to experience such discomfort personally. He was very proud of himself. He had gone up against impossible odds, an army a third bigger than his own, and he had pushed them back. Now he could rest and let his men rest.

At once there was a scramble outside his tent. Someone hollered, "Halt! Hold there! You can't go in there!"

The General and his two aides looked up—

—in time to see a well-dressed woman with chestnut hair darken the open end of the tent.

Without pausing, without introducing herself, without even stopping to take off her glove, the woman raged toward him, lips set, reeled an arm back, and hauled forward. The back of her hand rocked across his jaw and sent his entire head reeling.

And just as quick as that, she turned and stalked out of the tent, without even explaining her wrath.

Two of the General's aides dived toward her and tried to grab her, but they were awkward, and she easily shook them off.

One called out to the guards. "Stop her!"

"No!" George McClellan caught at the aide's sleeve.

He dabbed at his jaw and discovered at least one tooth had been loosened.

"Let her go," he said. His aides were twitching, wanting to

throw the woman in jail for something, but the general shook his pounding head again. "No point . . . dirtying a clear win with controversy. Obviously . . . just some irate citizen. No one of consequence. Someone give me a hanky. There's a terrible amount of blood in my mouth."

THE FIELD HOSPITAL AT DUNKER CHAPEL

Blasted by artillery fire, the boxy white building was more black today. The chapel had no steeple. Its sect was so pacifist, so reclusive, that steeples were considered vain. So folk had taken to calling them "dunkers"—the people who hid their heads.

Today the little building was clogged with wounded men. Outside, heaps of disembodied limbs were growing with alarming regularity. Hardly anybody was getting to keep all his arms and legs. The ones whose arms and legs were all right had probably been hit in the gut or head and were dead already.

Dorian had just passed his third hour of hauling wounded men to the exhausted, blood-drenched surgeons. Even among those lucky enough to have been gathered here, he would go back for a man and half the time find a corpse that had died waiting.

Uniforms meant absolutely nothing. A tacit truce was understood here. Blue, gray, butternut, infantry, cavalry, Zouaves, gunners, drummers, musicians—all lay together, shook hands, shared stories, and helped each other walk or limp. The war was for someone else today. The uniforms were just "on" them.

The landscape steamed. The air was very hot and thin. The chapel stood on a softly sloping hill in the rolling countryside. All around for miles, men hobbled slowly toward it and toward the screams coming from it.

All this seemed like an opium illusion now. Dorian went through motion after motion, trying to move the wounded with some sense of order or purpose, and concentrating on that.

Then he saw an apparition. An officer making his way up

the long sloping hill toward the building. Blood covered, ragged, with even a muddy footprint on his sleeve where someone had stepped on him.

"Wyatt?"

They saw each other over a distance. They couldn't hear each other's voices over the song of the wounded, but Dorian saw the ghost's lips move.

Dorian?

Their day had been the same—they saw that in each other's eyes. Scavenging among the dead and dying for that one dreaded face. Afraid to find it, afraid not to.

Dorian spoke again, and his friend's name crashed up through him on a wave of nauseated disbelief. His empty stomach rattled.

As much as exhaustion allowed, they stumbled toward each other with slow disbelief, through the gathered wounded and the shrouded corpses being lined up for burial.

Twenty feet . . . fifteen . . . ten . . . was it real?

They moved closer, neither accepting what he saw.

Not watching his step, Wyatt tripped on a dead man and staggered. He fell so hard that he ended up on all fours with the wind knocked from his lungs.

He struggled onto his knees, and Dorian was there to catch him.

Like lost boys in a storm they clung to each other, each afraid to let go lest the nightmare start up again. Each felt half-dead to the other, but also half-alive, and it was this to which they clung so fiercely.

The rest of the nightmare went on unaffected around then, the groaning and bellowing and dying. The two of them were the only flicker of hope in this hell, and though they didn't realize it, two hundred grown men watching were also reduced to boys.

Around them Union and Confederates alike were openly weeping, watching with pure joy and misery, glad at least one little thing had gone right for someone today, and wishing they could find, or get back, their own lost friends.

CHAPTER FIFTY-EIGHT

──────── ★ ────────

The ambulance wagon rattled down Governor Street as dozens of astonished citizens watched from their front gardens. No one had heard the official news, and the gossip was simply horrifying.

The wagon left a trickle of blood on the cobblestones. Some of the men inside had died since crossing the Potomac. Some were alive. They were part of a scattered mass movement under the Maryland rains, the retreat into Virginia of General Lee's army. Defeated, but not destroyed.

Two of the men still living motioned the driver to stop in front of the mansions at the top of Governor Street.

Dorian helped Wyatt get down from the long wagon, then motioned the driver onward. The clatter of hooves blended with the clatter of other hooves, and the household surrey thundered up the street toward them.

"Wait!"

They turned sluggishly.

The calling voice belonged to Grace.

She was just arriving, judging by the way she whipped the poor pony and the way Burlie was clinging to the seat beside her. She hadn't even let him drive.

"Whoa! Whoa!" Wyatt called, leaning on Dorian. "What's all this! Slow down before you hurt somebody!"

Grace hauled the reins, and the surrey scratched sideways, the pony yanking it like a great tail, then stopped.

"We just got back! After the battle started, they impounded

everything! Wouldn't let us go till they heard about Lee's retreat and that MacClellan hadn't started following to head'm off yet—"

She jumped down, threw the reins at Burlie, and faced her husband.

"Are you hurt! You got hurt, didn't you? I *knew* it. I could *feel* it in ten of my foot bones!"

"You're just now getting back from Maryland?" Wyatt pursued.

"Yes!"

"How is it," Dorian interrupted, "we missed you on the road?"

As Burlie too jumped down, he dared to inject his comment: "Ain't no road! She drove smack through the farm fields, smack through the alleys, and smack through six old ladies' flower gardens."

Dorian retreated. "Of course. Should have thought."

Burlie tied the reins to a hitching post and slipped his arm around Wyatt to take part of the effort from Dorian. They started toward the mansion's looming shadow, but Grace square off in front of them.

"I must talk to you," she said. "Please—I must!"

Even supported between Dorian and Burlie, Wyatt momentarily forgot there was anyone else in the world but himself and his wife.

He hesitated, pouring himself into her green eyes beneath the eerie gaslights.

"We'll talk in the house," he said wearily. "I want to be inside a house."

She backed off. Her sudden silence made her seem not unlike a schoolgirl chastised for gossiping.

They made it almost to the top step on the great wide-skirted front entrance.

But then they saw the notice.

It was tacked to the burnished wood of the giant front door. It flipped in a light breeze, like a woman's laugh. A sign, a threat. Evil survived.

WANTED REWARD WANTED REWARD WANTED . . .
DORIAN WALLACE—

Together, as though in a dream, they all stared at it for what seemed half a year.

Then Dorian choked. He staggered backward down the steps. All they heard was his bone-chilling cry.

"Orienta!"

He took off at a full run, nearly falling as he skidded around the corner of the mansion.

Grace and Burlie were two steps behind him all the way, and Wyatt scrambling after.

Somehow they caught up to Dorian, and all of them crushed through the guest-house door in a mob. Pure meanness got Grace in first.

They piled up at the inside archway, and all poised there for an ugly second.

Then Dorian shrieked his wife's name. This time, though, it was like paper tearing.

Wyatt twisted, crashed against him, and bodily held him back, shouting, "No! No! No!" while Grace thundered across the room. Burlie was right behind her.

Blood splattered under their feet.

Grace skidded to both knees and grabbed the butcher knife on the floor beside Orienta. Without pausing she slashed at her own skirts until she had two strips of cloth, and these she used in an frantic attempt to bind Orienta's dribbling wrists.

Hopeless. Burlie put a pressure grip on Orienta's right arm while Grace bound the left, but the right hand was almost entirely severed. It clung only by a few threads of sinew. There wasn't even enough blood to gush anymore. It simply trickled, with a small surge at each fading heartbeat. Very weak heartbeats.

"*Orienta—wait!*"

Dorian's scream rattled the roof. His hands clawed at the air over Wyatt's shoulders. In his depleted condition Wyatt could barely hold him back. Before long, he couldn't.

Plunging to his wife's inert bulbous form on the floor, Dorian fell so hard that his kneecaps almost shattered even through the paisley rug. Wyatt dropped beside him immediately and grabbed him again—but there was nothing to be done for the woman. A circling bird could have seen that from a cloud.

Her eyes were glassed over, her face, once round was hollowed now. The last two or three breaths crackled in her throat as they all listened—

Then there were no more.

Palsied with shock, Dorian trembled and begged her to live. Wyatt held him with both arms as tight as he could manage, knowing Dorian wanted to touch her, but knowing he would be touching death again. Neither of them needed any more of that. Wyatt kept trying to think of things to say, but he knew not even Robert Burns could come up with words for this. So he bit his lip and held Dorian's shattering life in his arms, hoping only to keep the pieces from blowing away.

He twisted slightly and looked at Burlie. The young slave simply shook his head.

Dorian must have seen it too, for he suddenly went limp and convulsive, wheezing his misery into Wyatt's wounded shoulder.

There they sat. Helpless.

Grace gave up trying to bind the severed hand. She simply moved it back into place so it didn't look so horrifying. Burlie slipped down onto his knees and covered his face with both big hands, but soon the sobs pushed out.

Sitting as though at a picnic, with only the sound of the clock and Dorian's gasps and Burlie's sobs, Grace fell into a dreamy fog and started comparing the blood-soaked rug with the color of the paisley design in dry places. Then, probably in poor taste, which was her calling card, she brushed Orienta's skirts smooth and picked at the oyster-shell buttons that held up five flounces on the front. With a what-the-hell motion, she pulled one of the buttons off for her collection. The snap of threads embarrassed her.

I'm a fiend, she thought.

She settled back, and let her eyes blur again. She was the only one in the room with dry eyes. She hated herself.

Movement?

Couldn't be. The woman was dead.

But Grace was staring at movement. Impossible!

Wasn't it—

Abruptly she flung herself sideways and snatched the butcher knife from where she had cast it on the edge of the rug. Then she began digging and pushing wildly at Orienta's voluminous skirts, each effort squeezing a high-pitched gasp from between her teeth. She turned into an animal, that backwoods insane girl she had once been, digging to uncover a precious buried bone.

Wyatt gasped out, "Grace, no!"

"Shut your mouth!" she shouted back. Her determination was appalling.

From where he knelt, Wyatt could see only the arch of tulle and skirt hoops providing a shield and Grace's russet hair over it. The outer skirts bunched toward Orienta's pear-shaped front, and she seemed to be floating in an ocean of fabric. There was a rustle as Grace pushed and dug at the undergarments.

Somehow Wyatt managed to turn Dorian to face the opposite direction. There was no fight. Dorian clung to him and would have let Wyatt walk him over a cliff.

Grace dug and dug. Orienta's body shook, but her eyes were like a fish's eyes, her lips parted.

Then suddenly Grace stopped digging and fell into a mysterious slower movement. An overwhelming pungent smell washed through the room.

Over the arching hoops, Wyatt saw her brows draw tight. She pushed with great deliberation at her task. Then all at once she tossed the blood-caked knife aside with fresh blood on it now, and moved more quickly, her shoulders twisting first one way, then the other.

A tiny noise flickered in the room. Grace continued to work, mumbling to herself. She suddenly made a yelp of victory and disappeared behind the tulle shield.

The tiny catlike noise came again, sputtered, then grew.

"I don't believe it," Wyatt whispered.

His whisper was drowned out. Never in his life had he heard so *strong* a sound.

Still working, Grace appeared again. Burlie came out of his personal flood, summoned a slave's own brand of survival, and scooted to her. He was too big for the hoops to hide him, but his arms disappeared as he worked with Grace.

Wyatt murmured, "Dorian . . . Dorian. Look . . ."

Burlie helped Grace get up on her knees, then onto her feet, and move from the pool of liquid in which she had lately been sitting. They came toward Wyatt and Dorian.

She knelt again.

There was an odor around her—but then, there had been nothing but odors for all of them for days and days.

In her arms, grabbing at her breasts with walnut-sized fists, little purple wormlike body rapidly filling with breath, was the baby.

Orienta's baby. The infant born of a dead woman was grabbing and scratching for life, oval mouth opening wider and scooping at the world. Even the little black eyes were wide open with an analytical glower, perfectly round head swiveling, fascinated by the room's single bright lantern. Black eyes—

Gently Wyatt turned Dorian more forward, held him firmly, and made sure he saw.

Their fears dissolved into consuming irony. All their conversations up to this point seemed imaginary.

With his hand trembling, the half slave who feared more than anything forcing his wife to birth a black child reached to touch the fingers of his baby.

His peach-pink baby.

CHAPTER FIFTY-NINE

——————— ★ ———————

"I should have you arrested. I was planning to. But I've seen considerable heartache in the past couple days, and I don't care to see anymore. So I've decided to just have you leave. Just go, and don't have me see you again."

Grace stood before her husband with her hands folded, fingers still sticky from the occurrences at the guest house. Slowly her eyes turned upward to meet him. She swallowed a lump and nodded. She turned and walked toward the door.

"That's all?" he asked suddenly.

She turned. "Pardon?"

He shrugged, perplexed. When he saw that she really did not understand, he got up and limped around his desk toward her. "You're not even going to defend yourself? You're just going to take banishment and go?"

Grace licked her lips and softly said, "It's better than I deserve."

She turned again toward the door.

"Well . . . hold on."

He closed the distance between them.

"I don't know how you can sleep at night," he said, "but I'm not going to be able to, unless I hear what can make a person do this. How 'bout you sit down . . . and tell me your story."

"My name is Grace Ruhl. My brother called me Liz, short for Lizard, 'cause I was so dirty. We were born in a makeshift shack in Kansas. My parents were German immigrants, and since they were also lazy pigs, they turned into white trash and never made better of themselves. All the other Germans made decent settlements and built fine farms. Not *my* family. The slaves say they got it bad, say they wear rags, get beaten, go hungry . . . they don't know what real rags are, and they don't know hungry. In order to keep my father out of jail, I made a deal with the local law that I'd go as a serving girl to a well-off Scottish widow in the tannery town, name of MacHutcheon. My family would have some money coming and wouldn't be destitute. My little brother was already working a child-labor job. I didn't want him to work . . . people get sick in tanneries.

"My father had tried to work in the tannery, but he was fat and he couldn't keep up. The place was run like a sweat house, two twelve-hour shifts working by candlelight. We'd moved to get the tannery job, and there wasn't anything else to be had for him. So I got myself spooned to a working boy my own age, and we planned to get married. Figured I could support my family with two of us working and get my baby brother out of that sweat house. Maybe get my parents a real door for the cabin.

"I never set sight on the men running the tannery. I only knew their name. A father and son by the name of Craig. When my brother was hurt real bad in a tannery accident, I put a torch to the place and burned the whole fucking factory to the ground.

"My brother moved from Kansas to Richmond when the Craigs got the deal to come to build a powdermill. Despite his accident, he was as loyal as I was hateful. When the war came, my brother couldn't find it in himself to fight, so he got involved with the antislavers. When they attacked a powder shipment, my brother was there. He was all confused. Not a very thick thinker, that boy . . . just a backwoods boy . . .

"When trouble broke out, his own leader used him for a shield. Put a sword through him . . . until you came up to my brother Patrick and caught him and held him while he died. I climbed the ridge and looked over it just in time to see you put a slug through my baby brother's chest.

"I buried my grief in my wrath. I married you for wrath. I

spied for wrath. I ticked the clock till I could find some final, elemental way to hurt you. Didn't even have the sense to repent after I got to know you better. I was dead wrong.

"Because of me Lee's invasion failed. Because of me the Sharpsburg battle was a stalemate instead of a clear win for either side. The war will go on who knows how long . . . and it'll all be because I built up a spitefulness for a man who didn't deserve my grudge. All I've had clogging up my mind for months is the picture of your pistol going off into my sweet brother's heart. I deserve whatever punishment you give me. I'm ready to swallow it whole. All I know is . . . it all happened because we both loved Patrick."

Silence dropped.

Wyatt had listened to the whole story without so much as a flinch. It soaked into him without his making a move or speaking a word, or even allowing himself a sigh.

But when Grace was finished and sat there like a criminal waiting for the gallows, her husband got up, shook his head, and heard all this rattling in it. Then he stuffed his hands into his pockets and paced.

After a moment he strode toward her and gazed down. He rocked on his heels introspectively.

"Just tell me one thing."

She remained still and looked at the carpet.

"Anything."

He paused, paced from one side of her to the other, then turned and faced her again.

"How'd you keep from strangling me in the night?" he asked.

In disbelief she turned up to him. He wasn't being flippant.

"Are you," she murmured, "forgiving me?"

There wasn't as much hope in his face as usual. There were lines in it that hadn't been there before the griddle of Antietam.

"I woke up under a collapsed breastworks, and I was the only man alive for hundreds of yards, near's I could tell. I just can't muster up any bad feelings today. . . . I don't know if I can forgive you," he admitted. "But so much has been against us . . . I'd like to try going forward without the luggage."

In pure disbelief at her good fortune, at encountering in life a man like Wyatt Craig, Grace shifted toward him and stared up at him. She had been a pauper, a betrothed, an unfaithful wife, a seductress, a harridan, a spy, and all descriptions of womanhood except the good ones. Plaintively she lifted her hand and wouldn't blame him if he knocked it away.

He didn't. He took one fist from his pocket and stiffly unfolded it. She slipped her fingers into his hand, and he accepted her.

For the first time she was truly a bride.

THE RICHMOND DOCKS

It was night again. It would be night for a long, long time.

The ship was low-slung and wraithlike. Her fore-and-aft rigged sails were tanbark, her hull painted black. Fast, low, silent, and dark. Her name was proclaimed in somewhat faded condition on her old bow, and since the war had come, no one had bothered to replenish the chipped letters. The ship was better off with no bright elements.

Still, those close enough could read the name. *Clytaemnestra.*

A man's voice crowed from the wharf.

"What is this! Kidnapping? Impressment? Turn loose of me and I'll triple your money! I'm an important man! I have influence in the government—damn your eyes, every last one of you—I'll have your shipping license revoked—I'll have you hanged—"

Barry Swanborough kicked and plunged against the foreign-looking men who dragged him up the gangplank and threw him to the deck of the old ship.

Cursing, he struggled to his knees, then to his feet, yanking and rattling the chains that held his wrists and ankles. He drew a ragged breath and bellowed.

"Who's in control of this bastard enterprise!"

A moment of quiet fell, then a shifting on the upper deck behind him caught his attention, and he whirled around. His eyes flew wide, his face purple.

"You!"

Dorian Wallace Trozen Parthens stood above him on the *Clytaemnestra*'s afterdeck. Beside him were the Macedonian captain and his Turkish first and second officers, and the Cypriot and Athenian crewmen.

"Obviously," he uttered.

"Son of a dirty barnyard bitch—" Swanborough said. "You're behind this, ignoble coward that you are. Is this how you solve your troubles? Shanghai? Murder? I should have guessed. It's your level. You're nothing but a nigger, and that's all you'll ever be. That's all you are. No matter who you murder or how you try to erase your truth, that is all you are. Let me out of this before you dig yourself into a criminal's grave. You'll pay for killing me!"

From the upper deck the dark man spoke from among his field of dark men.

"Don't panic," he said. "You're going to live."

Swanborough stopped fighting, hesitated, his eyes squinting in disbelief. "Liar," he said.

"Not at all. Let me fill you in. This is a Greek ship. No one speaks English. The captain will get half his money tonight and half when he brings me proof that you have survived the voyage. If you show any signs of refusing the cooperate, he has been given my approval to kill you and bring back only your head. If you do survive, however, he is to bring me proof that you have been delivered to your final destination. Take no false hopes—it is your *final* destination. You will make port in Morocco and be handed over to your owners. You are being sold into slavery. Yes, a ghastly prospect, but one you understand. You, who are completely detestable, will fit in well over there. While the lowliest of Americans have been giving up their lives, you have used our two nations' misfortune to enrich yourself. Now you will pay for that ill judgment. If you survive the two-month trek through the desert, you will spend your days in the tractless, mamba-crawling deserts of Sudan. You will pick nuts, gut calabashes, and haul jugs for the rest of your life. If you misbehave, you'll be sold to the quarries. Your white skin will be very popular over there. Here, however . . . no one will look for you."

Barry Swanborough stood with both legs braced so far

apart that the gyves linking them were cutting into his ankles. He no longer yanked the chains upon his wrists. He began to absorb the foolishness of having challenged a man more devious than himself.

"I'll . . . I'll get out of this somehow. . . ."

The river whispered its endless song below them. From the quarterdeck came a very solemn promise from a creature who had nothing more to lose.

"No," Dorian said, "you won't."

The ship whispered out of Richmond Harbor under power of heads'ls only. Almost instantly she melted into the dark night over the water. The Union blockade was nothing but a game to the seaworthy old schooner.

Dorian stood alone on the dock and watched until he could see nothing but fog and water.

When he turned toward the city, however, he was no longer alone, and never would be again.

From a state carriage in the distance, watching in wordless empathy, was Vice President Aleck Stephens. Swathed in dozens of scarves and two overcoats, the little man with the big eyes and the bigger heart offered only a nod of absolute commitment.

Nearby, also watching, was Grace. She stood with Swanborough's disenfranchised slaves, who had been left masterless and with no way to support themselves. There, in seven black faces, lay a promise he would keep at the cost of his own freedom, if necessary.

He was gloomy about it until he heard the one sound that didn't belong here. His baby's piccolo wail.

Grace was holding Dorian's newborn, a little wiggle with no first name and no legal surname. The child's strong, defiant cry gave life to the empty wharfside and fortified the man to whom she had come at so dear a cost. The child might have no name, but she had self-possession and proclaimed that with almost comic determination.

Dorian closed his eyes, clutched the hilt of his walking stick with both hands, and breathed that sound into his life.

He began to whisper to the rippling water.

" 'O, my bonnie sweet wee daughter . . . through you come a wee unsought for . . . I'll never rue my trouble wi' thee, the cost or shame o't, but be a loving father tae ye . . . and brag the name o't. . . .' "

An arm closed around his shoulders.

"Ship's gone," Wyatt said gently. "You all right?"

Dorian opened his eyes and dredged up something resembling a smile. "I am supreme. While God's justice is chancy and fleeting, I am secure knowing I may exact my own."

"Where'd you send him?"

"He's going to be head hoof-picker to the Duke of Cornwall."

"S'at so? Doesn't sound so bad . . ."

Careful to maintain the tactile bond, Wyatt turned him, and they walked along the pier toward Grace and the slaves.

After a few steps Wyatt blurted, "Naaah—you're pulling my leg, aren't you?"

"Yes. He's going to be the linen maid. Don't you think he'll appear fancy in one of those little lace hats?"

"Not going to tell me, are you?"

Dorian gazed sidelong at his kindhearted friend and took great solace from that arm around his shoulders. Protection, though, would go two ways.

"No," he said. "I'm not going to tell you."

As they walked, very slowly, they noticed Aleck Stephens give them an approving, punctuational nod. Dorian nodded back, and Stephens tapped his driver. The carriage turned in a cumbersome manner, then clacked away into the city.

"You are too good to me, Wyatt," Dorian said. "I fear some day you too shall pay for it."

"Now, *look*," his friend snapped. He stopped walking and pulled Dorian around to face him and held him there. "Orienta didn't 'pay' for loving you, Dorian. Scrape that well you live in, and tell me something better."

Dorian pressed his lips tight for a moment. He held very still before Wyatt's unremitting eyes.

"I could have taken her away," he said finally. "Instead I went to Sharpsburg to warn General Lee. She wanted me to go. She told me I had miraculously replaced Alabama in her heart. I was the South to her. For a short while she was married to the South, and she was happy. And I . . . was happy." Softly he added, "To me, my wife Orienta shall always be a casualty of the battle at Antietam Creek."

★

CHAPTER SIXTY

———— ★ ————

Iron bars do a prison make, and Clyde Clyman was sitting behind them, mumbling to himself about revenge and escape and how stupid the world was for not understanding his value. He would find some way to get famous and go up North and live good. Sooner or later some jackass jailer'd make a mistake and there's be an escape. Out he'd go, just like a bird. *Foooosh*.

When the rattle came at the window, he thought it was just a passing carriage.

Then he realized it was someone knocking. He looked up and heard a quiet voice.

"Clyman, you two-eyed wart, get over here."

He let out a bellow of victory and danced toward the window.

"I know'd you'd come!" he said. "Been telling myself that all along! Couldn't stay away, could you? I know'd you loved me! I got this warm feeling down in my parts about you!"

"Yeah, I love you," Grace grumbled. "Come up here closer."

"Goddy doggies!" He grabbed the cold iron bars and stuck his face between them and kissed the air. "What'd you got for me?"

"Brought your tooth back." She pushed it through the bars. The tooth dropped to the floor.

Clyman bent to retrieve it. When he straightened, Grace stuck the barrel of a Colt Pocket Model Paterson pistol up his nose.

Then she pulled the trigger and blew his face to the other side of the cell.

UNDERGROUND RAILROAD STATION, LEESBURG, VIRGINIA

Business had been slow. Both armies had been through this town and brought their skirmishing with them. For a while the Confederates had been here, then the Federals, then the Federals had pulled back and the Confederates had come through on their way to invade the North. Now they had flushed back through, filthy and ravaged. Business at the station went up and down, depending which army was poking around in the area.

And whether or not the owners were in the house. Luckily they weren't very often. The war seemed hardly to be disturbing their theater business. If anything, folks were more anxious for a bit of forgetfulness.

Yula was perfectly happy for the folks to be out of the house. That meant she and her beautiful yellow-haired children could do their own business.

Tonight there were seven escapees shuffling down the creek bed to the makeshift shelter in the cellar of the house. An old man, a couple of women, some children. An uneventful group, with no distinguishing characteristics. They muttered and prattled their story at Yula, but she had heard a thousand such stories and had learned a professional nurse's nod to deal with them.

"We had a turr'ble time," one of the women went on, as she had been going on since she realized they had made the right connection and were probably going to get to Canada alive. They were practically in Maryland already. "I swear! You never seed sech gore and guts as come back to Richmond last Sunday night! Ma Lawd—dem white folks blow'd each other nigh to Chicagga and back. It wuh jus' as ugly . . . bless be they dint want me to go and tend dem tore-up menfolk, mmmm!"

"I'da gone and done my fightin'," the old man said as he

changed into a dry coat. "Them boys, they are fine young men to go and fight."

"You talk big."

"Yeah, I do."

"I dint see you takin' us north till you got help doin' it, you dumb man. Not till Mr. Dohrian had the guts to take us his-self."

Yula stood bolt upright and stared at the wall. The two slaves went on talking as they changed clothes and changed the children's clothes.

"What is it, Mama?" Charlotte asked.

Yula blinked and pushed through the tiny area to the very dark-faced negro woman. "Say dat agin."

"Say what agin?" the woman asked.

"Dat name! Your Railroad conductor."

"Oh . . . Mr. Dohrian."

Yula had been a slave all her existence. She knew how slaves talked and knew how she was hearing that name. Mr. Dorian. A first name.

"He got a last name? Wallace?"

The woman ducked back at Yula's sudden fierceness. "Parthens! Cap'm Parthens in the Rebel army down Richmond way. Why you gotta know? I heard all yawl conductors keep yawl name out of it. Ain' dat right?"

"Yeah," Yula muttered, "dat right. . . . What this man looked like?"

The woman shrugged. "He a fine-lookin' man, fo' white folk. Got black hair, real dark eyes for a white man—he look like a paintin' in the right light . . . ain' nothing much else."

Yula clutched at her chest as it tightened. "Black eyes? Black like mine?"

"Course not! Why he gotta have black eyes like a nigger? I jus' tell you he a white gentleman officer in the Confederate Army. Das all I know!"

Forcing herself to think clearly, to examine the odds, and to remember that she had stood over a grave and its marker and she knew the truth, Yula battled down her impossible hopes.

"Jus' got de same name," she mumbled, "das all. Get dem clothes on dem children and let's get some food into dem bellies."

"Yes'm," her platinum-haired beauties responded, and everyone settled into the business at hand.

Then the old man sighed with great relief at no longer having to cross the country in fear of being dragged back and hanged.

"He took some fine care of us," he said. "Never mind that he swore he'd kill us if'n we dint do his way. He a fine man in the end, I say. Even took off his coat and rolled up dem sleeves and carry two of the children in his own arms up dat dirty crick bed."

"Yeah," the woman agreed. "He dint like us seein' dat arm at first, but den he get used to it."

"Arm?" Yula swung around. "His arm? What 'bout it?"

They both blinked at her as if she were crazy.

The man shrugged again. "Got a turr'ble hack in it, right about there. You know . . . like it been burned real bad a long time ago—"

She knocked him over to get to the door. All they heard after that was the sound of her feet smashing relentlessly into the soggy ground, and the cries of her voice.

"Dohrian! Dohrian! Dohrian!"

Far, far off, a single wagon lantern wobbled faintly, a mere pinprick in the dark overcast night.

She could barely see it, but it was as good as a beacon.

She ran and ran, first down the hillside, then right into the creek bed, splashing along through it, tracing into the woods the trail she had described a hundred times, maybe two hundred.

Her voice cracked through the stillness.

"Dohrian! Dohrian! Doh . . . ri . . . an!"

She wanted to scream other things—*I'm yoh mama! Get yoh backside over here! Don't you go talkin' back to me when I know you out there! I love you, boy! You my baby boy! You alive!*

Yet there was nothing coming out but, "Dohrian! Dohrian!"

The water soaked her clothing, so violently she ran. It laughed beneath her feet and caused her to trip several times on the slippery stone bottom, but she ran and ran after the pinprick of light wiggling farther away with every one of her steps.

Her screams were those of a banshee, and she knew she looked like that awful ghost story, with her shawl flying behind her and her turban untying and flapping from the top of her head, her wet skirts hammering upon her knees.

Then the rocks took her, and she fell.

She lay in the creek bed, cold water soaking up around her, embracing her with its fingers.

And she laughed and cried and choked for air, then laughed more. Delight and joy bubbled up through her and pushed away every semblance of hopelessness that once had consumed her.

Whether separated by land or sea, war or the devil's own plots, she knew the only thing any mother needed to know.

Her boy was alive. Her boy was alive.

★

EPILOGUE

———— ★ ————

Harpers Ferry, 2 October 1862
to Mrs. A. Lincoln

Gen. McClellan and myself are to be photographed to-morrow
A.M. by Mr. Gardner if we can be still long enough. I feel Gen.
M should have no problem on his end, but I may sway in the
breeze a bit.

—A. Lincoln

MONDAY, 22 SEPTEMBER 1862

". . . On the first day of January in the year of our Lord, one
thousand eight hundred and sixty-three, all persons held as
slaves, within any state, or designated part of a state, the people whereof shall they be in rebellion against the United States
shall be then, thenceforward, and forever free."

Abraham Lincoln, after much argument and deliberation, issues the Emancipation Proclamation for the purpose of invigorating the Union's reason to fight. Just as England had agreed
to await a Rebel victory to recognize the Confederacy, Lincoln
had agreed to await a Union victory to release the
Proclamation.

The battle east of Sharpsburg town at Antietam Creek resulted in twenty-six thousand men dead, wounded, or missing in one day. Less than a mile and a half of ground was taken by the Union, but the Confederate invasion had been halted and driven back.

Neither side can claim a clear victory. It was vague enough, however, that Lincoln can release his Proclamation. With a stroke of his pen, Lincoln transforms a war to preserve the Union into a war against slavery.

Ironically, the Emancipation Proclamation frees only the slaves in states *currently in rebellion,* meaning the Confederate States. No slaves still held in the Union border states, Kentucky, Missouri or Maryland, are freed. Also ironic is the fact that the Proclamation, being issued by the president of another country, has no legal effect in the Confederate States of America.

Lincoln knows this, but his shrewd move smashes any chance of antislave England or France's intervention on behalf of the Confederacy.

Essentially, while destined to become one of the most ringing documents of history, the Emancipation Proclamation does not free a single slave.

And the banners of war still fly.

★

ABOUT THE AUTHOR

For D. L. Carey and her researcher/story developer husband Gregory Brodeur, *Distant Drums, Rise Defiant*, and *Hail Nation* (coming soon from Bantam Books) are a chance to showcase little-known facts about the Civil War, and to present the politics and economics of the 1860's—issues as complicated as ours today.

"The Civil War was much more than a series of battles," Carey says. "It was the deciding factor in what kind of world we live in today. Had the South's brilliant second set of Founding Fathers like Alexander Stephens managed to pull together the plans presented in this book, this continent would be like Europe—a puzzle of separate countries, managed from distant thrones, in constant tension. There would have been no United States to turn events in the world wars or to go to Iraq. Imagine what the picture of the world would be. In 1861 we came precariously close to etching that picture."

Brodeur adds, "The Civil War was an inevitable war, because the original Founding Fathers could not agree on the issue of slavery. The two competing economic systems that arose due to their compromise could not coexist. This resulted in a war unlike any other—not an uprising of oppressed people but a battle of right versus right. The South was legally right, but the North was morally right. That's why there was so much commitment and bloodshed."

Rise Defiant is published during the 130th anniversary of the events in the novel.

The four men stared into the camp fire, their sole relief from the day-to-day grind that their valiant war had become. Somewhere else in camp the colonel's Irish orderly was twittering on his pennywhistle. Made a nice sound.

They watched in silence as the yellow-orange flames chewed at the twigs and whispered at the night sky. The men took the peace as it came, for as many minutes as they could get it, and hoped morning took its sweet time.

A fifth man crunched over the dry ground and asked, "Mind if I join you, boys?"

One gestured for him to sit, and another, a corporal, poured him coffee, thinking it was funny to hear someone so young refer to them as "boys." The newcomer was a bugler and couldn't have hit nineteen yet. Trying to fit in. They'd let him on in.

"Lost?" the corporal asked.

"Can't find my unit in the dark," the bugler said.

He crossed his legs, set his dented bugle and satchel of sheet music aside, nodded thanks for the coffee, and fell into the fire trance.

For a few moments it seemed there were only five men in the world, rather than the ranks of a cavalry unit spread throughout this small wooded valley. Even the tethered horses had learned to take rest when they could get it. There was no sound of shifting hooves at all—

The fire exploded beneath a gigantic black shape. All

five men rolled backward as though a shell had gone off in the center of their circle. The bugler fell off his own buttocks and ended up with his shoulder under another man's knee and his foot in a puddle. Sparks and splintered firewood danced all over them.

"Damn him!" somebody spat.

The bugler shook his head and sat up, blinking through images of what he thought he had seen—flashes of tan and silver, moist black velvet, feathers—a man on horseback crashing through fire.

"What was that?" he choked.

"I thought he was crazy when I first met him," the corporal said, brushing sparks off his thighs. "Now he's gone even crazier."

"Don't think crazy's the right word," somebody else muttered.

The bugler jolted to his feet and growled into the darkened trees. "We should report that!"

All at once six hands grabbed him and hauled him to the ground.

"How long have you been in this outfit, son?" the corporal mocked. "Do yourself a kindness. Never cross that man, or that horse."

The boy swiveled from face to face and asked, "Why? What's the story?"

"Don't know the story," the corporal said. He pushed the scattered firewood back into the center as he talked. "We thought we really had something when that lieutenant came to command our unit. I've been on horseback all my life, but I've never seen a man who could do with a horse what that one can do. And I've never seen a horse like that pepper and piss he rides. Stands eighteen hands if it's an inch. First time we headed into a battle with him in charge, we were slogging through a swamp, hip deep in mud, feeling filthy, and here he comes on that black devil, tiptoeing across the top of the swamp without even getting its fetlocks dirty."

The other men chuckled, but there was some nodding and shaking of heads in what was clearly awe, as though he had spoken a near truth instead of a joke.

"I swear," he added, "if needs be, Noah Sutton could make that horse *fly*."

Still baffled, the bugler shook his head and sighed.

The cartographer handed him a pair of long-range binoculars and said, "Don't never get no closer than this."

The boy took the binoculars and peered through them into the moonlit forest.

In circular increments he saw pieces of slick black shoulder, white-hot eyes covered with black shags, and enormous square white teeth—the horse. The devil.

"That's the wildest horse I've ever seen," the corporal said. "Hooves the size of cannonballs, fetlocks shaggy as a Clydesdale's, temper so violent no other man can touch it except its master and his groom. Can't even tether that monster near other horses, can't put a bit in its mouth . . . it even twitches when it sleeps. In battle Sutton never even touches the reins of that hackamore. Rides like liquid."

"Rides like an Indian," somebody corrected.

The corporal nodded. "Just uses his knees and touches the neck sometimes, and sometimes he talks to it. Something to behold—long as you never get in front of them."

"I did, once," another man said, a cartographer whose hands were permanently stained with ink. "Almost lost my left eyebrow to that whip. Lucky it wasn't his sword hand. You ever been close to him in battle? Lord! He's horn-mad in a fight! Takes no prisoners. He stays longer if he can kill more. Calls the Yankees 'niggerlovers' and yells at them while he's cutting them up. He just *loves* it. Scares me, plain and simple."

The bugler peered through the binoculars as they talked quietly around him, and he shivered. In the moonlight he made out high black riding boots, tight deerskin breeches, buff gauntlets, the golden swash of tassels, and a cummerbund, the brass buttons and coiled piping of an officer's riding jacket. Then a flash of bare cheekbone, tight curls under a dashy feathered cavalry hat, the brim—

He flinched suddenly, fumbled, and dropped the binoculars.

The other men glanced knowingly at each other. They all knew the lieutenant had spotted him.

"It's a close call which is more animal," the cartographer said. "Him, or that chaos he rides."

"Good thing there's a war," the corporal commented, "or Noah Sutton'd be in jail for murder."

The bugler blinked and asked. "Murdering who?"

The corporal shrugged. "Somebody."

He leaned back on an elbow and tried to drink his coffee without thinking about home.

"I don't know what drives him," he said, "but I swear on my mother's grave that I'd sooner be in a Yankee prison camp than trade place with the man Noah Sutton's looking for."

WILMINGTON, DELAWARE, ON THE BRANDYWINE RIVER

"Who is this man named Parthens?"

The plush, overdone office carried a permanent odor of cigar smoke and an aura of royal sanction, probably granted by the gifts from Queen Victoria.

Behind the enormous desk, a man with a flame-red beard spoke again.

"I shall ask you once more in a minute. Imagine, if you will, a state dinner. A United States banquet. Secretary of State Seward was there. Secretary of State Stanton was there. The President was there. *I* . . . was there."

The smoke of the latest cigar snaked from an ashtray. The man behind the desk ignored it as he sat with his spine straight as a needle and his cold blue eyes doing damage.

A stout fellow stood before him, holding his bowler against his chest, pinned in place by a permeating weight of judgment. Terrified, he remained silent by digging his fingernails into his hat brim until they hurt. Every small thing in this office drilled into him like a thorn, and he had come three thousand miles to be so impaled.

The man behind the desk ground his teeth and began speaking again.

"Secretary of War Stanton approached me during the final course. He put this in front of me."

A small leather drawstring bag plopped onto the blotter before him.

"He asked how it could be that a powdermill in

Richmond, the enemy capital, could be producing state-of-the-art black soda powder using the Du Pont formula. He asked *me*. Me! Henry Du Pont!"

Before him, the man's hands turned white and tightened on the bowler.

"I, Henry Algernon Du Pont, I who have graduated West Point without the slightest indignity, without a mark against me, I who am head of this cartel, head of this family, was made to endure Stanton's noxious glare! I pounded the table. I disrupted dinner. I engaged in a shouting match with the secretary of war of the United States of America! Then I snatched this little bag, I stalked out, I had the chemical compound analyzed. Seventy-two parts Peruvian nitrate, twelve parts sulfur, sixteen parts charcoal, glazed with sulfite. I looked into the source. And what did I find?"

Heartbeats. Perspiration. Could sweat make noise?

"What . . . did . . . I . . . find!"

"You found . . . that someone in the Du Pont family has . . . has been funding a black powdermill run by a Du Pont apprentice, Wyatt Craig . . . for the Confederacy."

The echo fell, rooted, and festered.

Every other sound in the room was suddenly enhanced by the silence. The doves rustling in their cage. The enormous ship's clock over the fireplace. The two men breathing.

"And," Henry Du Pont said, "this has been held strictly secretive by Southern-sympathizing Du Ponts. Why would you finance a competitive mill? Were you planning to go up against the family?"

"No . . . no . . . no."

"The family cannot and will not be operated in this fashion. North, South, all can be damned. We are Du Ponts first, before anything. What does this do for us? Hm?"

The Du Pont Cousin swallowed, sweated. "I thought you approved of . . . risk."

"I do approve of risk!" Henry Du Pont roared. "What I am referring to is your doing this without the consent or even the awareness of the table of partners. This should have been a *family* decision!"

It seemed a pure truth, somehow. Not a mere fact for the Du Pont family, but an unbreachable truth—above any loyalty, above any philosophy, above religion, above life.

"What was in your mind?" Henry went on. "Does this increase our profit one dime? Does it expand our empire? Does it give us influence in the future? How? Where? Are you one of these idiots who cares whether the negro is enslaved on a plantation or starving in a Northern sweat house? If so, be you notified that it is not incumbent upon the white man to free the chattel slave! It is certainly not incumbent upon a Du Pont to get between two conflicting economic systems, damn it all. We should be concentrating upon expansion into the western territories, not tampering in armed conflict!"

The window behind the closed drapery shivered and rattled.

Henry went on.

"The North is going to win. Why influence the Confederacy? We're vastly expanding the Du Pont empire by having a virtually exclusive contract for gunpowder to the Union, which is bigger and richer than the

South, and you've set us up as a traitor to the Union! You've set us at a precipice! We'll look like undecided idiots to the President. If Lincoln finds out, he can send troops into our factories and seize our assets! I don't care about playing both sides, but this should have been a *family* decision! You have put the *family* at risk! You're ruining the integrity of the *family*!"

His fist somehow rattled the massive oak desk.

"We blame you," he said, eyes drilling. "You're threatening to destroy us. If this leaks out, whether now or later, we'll be seen as untrustworthy, and in matters of war we must *not* be seen as untrustworthy. There will be wars in the future and the Du Ponts will be there. Despite you and the Southern branch who are responsible for this disharmony, we will be there. In spite of any and all skeletons we must excise from our closets," he concluded, "we *will* be there."

From outside the window a noise disturbed them. With his customary caution Henry stopped talking and glanced behind him, though the window was securely closed. He rose, crossed to the window, leaned awkwardly over the liquor cabinet, satisfied himself that the sound had been only a groundskeeper at work, then drew closed the heavy brocades.

He returned to his chair and rocked forward, and did lower his voice even though it was only a groundskeeper who might have heard.

"Is anyone outside the family," he framed very carefully, "involved?"

This was the key. This was the asking again that had been promised.

"Parthens," the dark-haired cousin cracked out. His

voice was tinny, inadequate. "Our intermediary with Craig. Captain Dorian Parthens."

Henry plowed over the name as though he had never asked.

"This mess has to be cleaned up," he said. He picked at a bundle of old and mismatched papers, transcripts, travel receipts, foreign shipping manifests, some of which his Cousin recognized. "We must deal with your exploits in England. Your skimming of my nephew Lammot's nitre shipment. Your financing of the Confederate mill. These strangers who assisted you in betraying the family. It will be done by exposing these men as having deceived and abused both nations' trust. We must erase or obscure all trails and claims of Du Pont involvement. Then, if this surfaces even after the war, we will not be in the hot soup. Craig will have to be financially ruined. This other man, this Parthens . . . his character and reputation will have to be utterly destroyed."

Henry Du Pont looked up from the informative papers that had come at dear cost and with not a little intrigue.

"And *you*," he said, "are going to do it."

From the creator of WAGONS WEST

The
HOLTS

An American
Dynasty

OREGON LEGACY
An epic adventure emblazoned with the courage and- passion of a legendary family—inheritors of a fighting spirit and an unconquerable dream.
❑ 28248-4 $4.50/$5.50 in Canada

OKLAHOMA PRIDE
America's passionate pioneer family heads for new adventure on the last western frontier.
❑ 28446-0 $4.50/$5.50 in Canada

CAROLINA COURAGE
The saga continues in a violence-torn land as hearts and minds catch fire with an indomitable spirit.
❑ 28756-7 $4.95/$5.95 in Canada

CALIFORNIA GLORY
Passion and pride sweep a great American family into danger from an enemy outside... and desires within.
❑ 28970-5 $4.99/$5.99 in Canada

HAWAII HERITAGE
The pioneer spirit lives on as an island is swept into bloody revolution.
❑ 29414-8 $4.99/$5.99 in Canada

SIERRA TRIUMPH
A battle that goes beyond that of the sexes challenges the ideals of a nation and one remarkable family.
❑ 29750-3 $4.99/$5.99 in Canada
